Wedding Magic

Patricia Coughlin

BERKLEY SENSATION, NEW YORK

THE BERKLEY PUBLISHING GROUP
Published by the Penguin Group
Penguin Group (USA) Inc.
375 Hudson Street, New York, New York 10014, USA
Penguin Group (Canada), 90 Eglinton Avenue East, Suite 700, Toronto, Ontario M4P 2Y3, Canada
(a division of Pearson Penguin Canada Inc.)
Penguin Books Ltd., 80 Strand, London WC2R 0RL, England
Penguin Group Ireland, 25 St. Stephen's Green, Dublin 2, Ireland (a division of Penguin Books Ltd.)
Penguin Group (Australia), 250 Camberwell Road, Camberwell, Victoria 3124, Australia
(a division of Pearson Australia Group Pty. Ltd.)
Penguin Books India Pvt. Ltd., 11 Community Centre, Panchsheel Park, New Delhi—110 017, India
Penguin Group (NZ), 67 Apollo Drive, Rosedale, Auckland 0632, New Zealand
(a division of Pearson New Zealand Ltd.)
Penguin Books (South Africa) (Pty.) Ltd., 24 Sturdee Avenue, Rosebank, Johannesburg 2196,
South Africa

Penguin Books Ltd., Registered Offices: 80 Strand, London WC2R 0RL, England

This book is an original publication of The Berkley Publishing Group.

This is a work of fiction. Names, characters, places, and incidents either are the product of the author's imagination or are used fictitiously, and any resemblance to actual persons, living or dead, business establishments, events, or locales is entirely coincidental. The publisher does not have any control over and does not assume any responsibility for author or third-party websites or their content.

For Eileen Fallon, BAE
Best. Agent. Ever.

One

Sophie rose early and dressed for battle in a sleeveless black linen dress with white piping and a matching cropped jacket. It was more tailored and less comfortable than what she usually wore to work; she just hoped it was worth the effort.

For luck, she added the single string of pearls that had been her mother's.

One corner of her mouth lifted in a rueful smile as she fastened the clasp, thinking it a particularly fitting gesture, reminiscent of the knights of old who carried a lady's favor onto the field with them. If anything could bring her luck today, it would be conjuring her mother's spirit, and she had a feeling she was going to need all the luck she could get.

Fashion tips would also be useful, she thought as she turned her attention to the age-old dilemma of what shoes to wear. Arms crossed, lips pursed, she reviewed the options lined up like good little soldiers on her closet shelf. Life would be so much simpler if her style sense were as well honed as her organizational skills. Her gaze moved quickly over her favorite sandals and the ridiculously high—and expensive—designer creations she'd allowed herself to be talked into on a rare shopping trip with her sisters. The never-worn stilettos were Exhibit A for why she did her best to avoid those outings. Tucked away at the very end of the shelf was a glossy black shoe box tied with pink ribbon. She never looked inside the box at the sparkly party shoes she'd worn exactly once, on the night of her thirtieth birthday. Part memento, part cautionary tale, they were a reminder that the past consists not only of what happened, but of what might have happened and didn't.

She finally settled on a pair of black, open-toed pumps with a moderate heel. It was the safe choice, and Sophie was a big fan of playing it safe.

As battle garb went, the finished outfit lacked the intimidation factor of, say, a Kevlar vest or chain-mail trench coat, but it was infinitely more practical given the forecast for sunny skies and temperatures climbing into the nineties, well above the norm for June in Rhode Island. If her upper arms were more toned or tanned, she might have thrown caution to the wind and ditched the jacket. But they weren't and she didn't.

Her outfit also wasn't terribly au courant . . . at least she didn't think it was. She was never quite sure since, try as she might, when it came to fashion she always seemed to be a season—or two—out of step with whatever was currently in vogue. Okay, so maybe saying "try as she might" was a bit misleading. It would be a lie to claim she *tried*, as in putting any actual effort into keeping abreast of style trends, but in her own defense, when stuck in the dentist's waiting room, she did choose *Elle* magazine over *Consumer Reports*. Most of the time.

To be honest, from her vantage point—which was now officially closer to forty than thirty—wearing what looked fabulous on Sarah Jessica Parker was less important than wearing something that looked good on her. SJP's wardrobe options and hers were a twain that would never, ever meet. Sarah's style was slinky and sexy and adventurous, and her own was mainly focused on drawing attention away from her flaws. This morning she was satisfied she'd done the best she could with what she had.

Her sisters, unfortunately, didn't share that assessment. And the unwritten bylaws of sisterly love—even stepsisterly love—decreed they had every right to say so. It was for her own good, of course, though Sophie had never quite figured out why most things family did for your own good just ended up making you feel bad about yourself. They wasted no time exercising their critiquing rights when she walked into the offices of Seasons, the wedding and event-planning business founded by her stepmother. Or rather, when *they* walked in, since by the time they showed up, Sophie had been in her office long enough to grab a cup of coffee, go over her notes for the day ahead, and check both e-mail and voice messages with an eye toward squelching any pending disasters that had reared their demanding little heads overnight. Among the many things identical twins share, Jill and Jenna had the same rule about setting foot in public before they were ready to be seen. They didn't do it, period. Never had, never would.

Having shared a bathroom with them for a big chunk of her formative years, Sophie could attest to their tireless dedication to the wonderful world of grooming. And hey, it worked. They were several years closer to the big four-O than she was, with husbands and kids and homes to care for, and still they appeared each day looking like they'd been peeled off a glossy magazine cover, and Sophie, well, didn't. It explained why they held court in highly visible showroom offices out front, meeting and greeting clients and projecting a properly glamorous and upscale image, while her office was next door to the supply room in the employees-only section.

Sophie had no complaints. It was a practical arrangement, especially now that her father was retired and he and her stepmother spent much of the year in Florida, leaving the day-to-day running of the business to the three of them. She was at her best working behind the scenes, averting crises, slaying dragons, and generally doing whatever was necessary to keep the train on the tracks and moving forward. She wasn't good at showmanship, and although she was too nice to say so, the Js weren't much good at anything else.

"Is that what you're wearing?" Jenna asked her. She was standing just inside Sophie's office, her head tilted slightly to the side.

It wasn't the first time she or Jill had asked Sophie that same question using that same vaguely perplexed tone and expression. Actually the first time had been twenty years earlier, on the night of Sophie's very first real date. The Js—two years and many, many dates ahead of her socially—had been on hand when she emerged from her room feeling, maybe not beautiful, but pretty damn close, in a miniskirt and knit top under a baggy blazer with the sleeves rolled up. It was the eighties and she was feeling very Madonna meets *Pretty in Pink* . . . until Jenna's offhand question zapped all the air from her little fantasy world. With no time to change, she'd answered the door with sweaty palms and her stomach in knots and spent the rest of the night yearning to be invisible.

Now older and supposedly wiser, and seated safely behind her desk, she wiped her damp palms on her skirt and fought the urge to blurt *Why? What's wrong with what I'm wearing?*

Instead she responded with what was intended to be an intimidating show of nonchalance. "That's the plan."

"Hmm," said Jenna.

Jill nodded thoughtfully. "Maybe you should stand up so we can get the full effect."

"There is no effect," Sophie retorted, wanting to stand for inspection only slightly less than she wanted to stab herself in the eye with a letter opener. "It's a dress, period, no big deal."

"I beg to differ," said Jill. "Everything about your meeting with Owen Winters is a huge deal for Seasons. Helen Archer has social clout out the ying-yang and handling her only daughter's wedding will bring us lots of new contacts, not to mention the kind of local buzz we'll get if by some miracle you convince Winters to cooperate. Think about it, Sophie, there's never before been a wedding held at Ange de la Mer. This would be monumental."

"Historical," Jenna added.

"Mind-boggling," said Jill.

"If you pull it off."

Jill nodded. "Yes. *If.* Helen Archer was very clear: if we can't deliver Ange de la Mer, she'll keep looking for a wedding planner who can. So yeah, I'd say this is a very big deal."

"A colossal deal," agreed Jenna. "And it's all up to you, Sophie."

God help us.

No one said it aloud, but it's what they were all thinking. Even Sophie. Especially Sophie. It's not that she was afraid of taking on a difficult task. When it came to her job, she'd been known to tackle the impossible and pull it off. Sweet-talking, arm-twisting, begging and bribing, it was all in a day's work. She couldn't count the number of times one of the *J*s had promised a client something outlandish that they knew nothing about and she'd had to step in to save the day—and Seasons' reputation—by finding a way to deliver on it.

This was different.

For this meeting she would be taking the lead, and along with that went taking center stage. Hardly her natural habitat. She was more like the Wizard of Oz, content to work her magic from behind the curtain. What if she messed up? It was entirely possible. Owen Winters was an unknown quantity, and when she tackled a problem she preferred to know the facts and have them sliced, diced, and lined up in neat rows ahead of time. The problem was there just weren't that many facts to be had about Winters . . . at least not on such short notice. She'd Googled, of course. And she'd shelled out $24.95 for a copy of his latest book only to find the inside cover had the same long-distance photo and paltry handful of details she'd found online: *Owen Winters has vast military experience and has traveled the known world in preparation for writing about worlds unknown.* Big help.

If only she had more time, she thought.

"If only Shelby Archer hadn't gotten lost coming back from the damn ladies' room," Jill said.

She was referring, of course, to the other night, when socialite Helen Archer and her daughter, Shelby, the bride-to-be, had come in to put forth their unorthodox request and a bit of serendipity led to Sophie being thrust front and center.

"If only you didn't have that damn picture hanging on the wall right where she could see it," grumbled Jenna, glaring at the damn picture in question.

It was a framed watercolor of a castle, the original artwork from the cover of a children's storybook that had been Sophie's favorite when she was a little girl. As luck would have it, the artist's inspiration had been the Newport estate known as Ange de la Mer, the very place where Shelby Archer had her heart set on being married. The book itself was old and not very well known, but Sophie remembered her mother reading it to her over and over; the framed cover was a way of keeping those memories close to her heart. Shelby recognized the artwork because she too loved the book and they were happily chatting away about their favorite parts of the story when Helen Archer came looking for her daughter and Shelby surprised everyone by announcing that losing her way and winding up in Sophie's office had been an omen, and that

Sophie and only Sophie was the one who should plead her case with Owen Winters.

Jill sighed. "Oh well, what's done is done. We just have to make the best of it. You know, play the lemons we've been dealt and all that."

"Jill's right," said Jenna. "What matters now is that we work together to put our best foot forward."

"Our best-*dressed* foot," Jill added.

Sophie immediately thought about her sensible black pumps hidden beneath the desk. She knew just enough about fashion to know they weren't even close to what Jill had in mind when she said "best dressed."

"So come on," Jenna urged with the kind of encouraging smile Sophie knew better than to trust, but was too polite to ignore. "Stand up and let us have a look so we can see what needs tweaking."

Reluctantly Sophie dragged herself to her feet and stepped a few inches away from the desk.

"Hmm," said Jenna, bringing them right back to square one. "Well. I like the pearls."

"Thanks," said Sophie.

Jenna folded her arms and a second later, without looking at her twin, Jill did the same. They were freaky that way. Tall and willowy, toned and tanned, they weren't identical to the point where Sophie couldn't tell them apart, but it had definitely made life easier when Jill had her pale blond hair cut in layers and Jenna left hers all one length.

"Tell me, Sophie, what do you see when you look at yourself in that outfit?"

Sophie shrugged. "I hadn't really thought about it. I guess I see someone who's sensible and who you can trust to be honest in doing business with you."

"That's interesting," Jenna countered. "Because what I see is someone dressed for a funeral."

"Or tea with the queen," added Jill.

"Or tea with the queen," Jenna quickly agreed.

Tugging on the hem of her jacket, Sophie shrugged again. "What's wrong with having tea with the queen?"

"Nothing. Nothing at all. It's just not exactly the image we're trying to project, is it? I mean Seasons is about glitz and glamour and big, splashy celebrations. Not about tuffets and crumpets . . . and those." She pointed at the black pumps.

Sophie managed not to shuffle her feet.

"But not to worry," exclaimed Jill, moving closer to give Sophie a reassuring pat on the shoulder. "We'll have you fixed up in no time. I keep extra clothes in my office for emergencies."

"I am not an emer—"

"So do I," said Jenna. "I'm sure that between us—"

Sophie held her hand up. "Whoa. Aren't you forgetting something? Like the fact that you're both about three inches taller and twenty pounds lighter than I am? Even if I wanted to change into something else, something . . . splashier—which, for the record, I don't—nothing that fits you would fit me. And no, we don't have time to go shopping."

That quieted them for a few seconds. Jill brightened first.

"Shoes," she exclaimed.

"Of course," agreed Jenna, already kicking off the strappy black stilettos she was wearing. "Here . . . these will work with that dress."

"I really—"

"Put them on," she ordered. And then, as an afterthought, "Please."

Knowing it would be futile to argue, Sophie sighed and put the shoes on, adjusting the narrow straps until they felt as comfortable as heels that high could feel.

"Much better," pronounced Jill.

"They pinch my toes," Sophie protested.

"They pinch mine too. You get used to it. Now, lose the pearls."

Sophie frowned, her fingers moving instinctively to the necklace. "But Jenna said—"

"I lied," said Jenna. "I do like the pearls. They're beautiful against your skin . . . they make it look even more creamy."

"Peaches and creamy," Jill added, tossing her a bone.

"And with the right jeans and a slinky little lace tee, they'd be fun and fabulous. But at the moment they're just screaming Grandma. Here . . . take my necklace." She reached for the clasp.

"No," said Sophie. "The pearls stay." She took a deep breath and added, "They belonged to my mother."

Jenna sighed. "Fine. But let's at least try to jazz things up with a little extra bling."

A few minutes later Sophie was wearing platinum earrings, a matching cuff bracelet, and Jill's diamond-studded Movada watch.

Jenna gave a nod of lukewarm approval. "I guess I can live with that. So what time is your appointment with Winters?"

"I don't have one," Sophie answered.

"What? How can you not—"

"I tried," she interrupted to head off the dozen questions she could see forming behind their matching expressions of confusion. "He didn't return any of my calls, and when I took a chance and stopped by after work last night, he wasn't home."

"Maybe you should try again. Like right now. There's a lot riding on this and—in case you've forgotten—not a heck of a lot of time."

"I haven't forgotten." She waved her arm—which thanks to the platinum cuff felt five pounds heavier—toward her desk with its neatly arranged piles of paper. "But I have too much work here to be making forty-minute runs to Newport for nothing. And in case you've forgotten who you're dealing with, let me remind you that contingency plans are my specialty. I don't even schlep to the post office without having an alternate route in mind in case I need it. And I figured out an alternate route for this situation. You might say it's a way to be in two places at once. So you can both relax." She pulled her cell phone from her jacket pocket and held it up. "Everything is under control."

The call she was waiting for came while she was checking on an order for sixteen dozen out-of-season white tulips being flown in from South America. She immediately put the wholesaler on hold and grabbed her cell.

"Hello."

"This is Ghostship calling Valene," replied a voice that sounded lower and huskier than the teenage male voice Sophie was expecting to hear.

Frowning, she checked the caller ID a second time and sighed. "Cut it out, Josh."

"I know not this Josh of whom you speak," said the voice. "This is Ghostship, calling to report that Osprey has landed."

"I have no idea what you're talking about; just tell me what's going on there."

There being a car parked on Bellevue Avenue, a discreet distance from the Ange de la Mer estate. At least that's where Josh Spencer, stock boy and all-around errand runner, was supposed to be. Josh was her contingency plan, sent to keep watch so she didn't make any more wasted trips.

"I just told you what's going on," Josh countered. "I said Osprey has landed."

"Who's Osprey? You were supposed to be watching for Owen

Winters. I showed you his picture on the book jacket, remember? I swear, Josh, if you're screwing around—"

"I'm not. Jeez, lighten up. I've been sitting here watching all morning, which, for the record, is boring to the max. Even my butt is numb. Sue me for trying to break the monotony. I called you as soon as Winters drove in, just like you said to do. He probably wasn't even inside yet when you picked up. I mean, I can't be sure of that because of, you know, the wall and all. But it was definitely him. The guy's got the sweetest bike ever."

"Winters rides a bike?"

His heavy sigh indicated just how lame he found her.

"Bike as in motorcycle," he explained. "His motorcycle is primo."

"Oh, right." Of course.

"And I was just being, like, metaphorical when I called him Osprey."

"Osprey? That's a metaphor? For what?"

"Osprey. You know, the birdman with the black eye patch and the silver talons and those wicked hidden wings?" When she didn't immediately say "Oh, *that* Osprey," he went on. "Heck, Sophie, didn't you even bother to read the guy's book?"

"He writes comic books, Josh. I don't read comic books. And if I did, I promise you it wouldn't be one about a birdman with an eye patch. Osprey," she muttered, rolling her eyes.

"Graphic novel. They don't call them comic books anymore, you know."

"So I've heard."

"And you shouldn't be so stuck-up; his stuff is pretty amazing. There's a spin-off video game in the works and *ParaWorld* maga-zine says Lucas is after the film rights."

"That would be very helpful information, Josh . . . if we were in the moviemaking business instead of the wedding-planning business. I'm leaving now. You stay where you are in case he takes off again. If he does, call me right away on my cell so I don't drive all the way there for nothing."

"What if he leaves and comes back again? Should I just stay here and keep watching?"

"Good question," she murmured.

"I could follow him," he offered, real excitement chasing all traces of boredom from his tone. "Then you could hunt him down and corner him wherever he is."

"No," Sophie told him firmly. "That's called stalking. And it's against the law." Not to mention that cornering him in public was not likely to put the man in a very receptive mood, and she definitely needed Winters in a receptive, open-minded mood to hear what she had to say. A sense of humor also wouldn't hurt.

"I could follow him without him knowing it . . . that's what Ghostship does. Covert ops."

"Still stalking," she countered, trying not to consider the possibility that in another couple of days she might have to resort to it. "Do not, under any circumstances, follow him, do you understand? Just call me if he leaves the house and . . . and we'll figure it out from there."

"Roger, Valene. Ghostship out."

She flipped her phone shut. Who the hell was Valene?

Two

The sound of the doorbell interrupted Owen Winters in the act of sitting in front of his computer and staring off into space. Staring into space was only slightly less tedious than staring at the monitor, but he'd take what he could get. The screen itself was blank, same as it had been for . . . well, a while. Blank, that is, except for the relentlessly blinking cursor, which on really bleak days seemed to be taunting him. *Loser, loser, loser.* One of these days he was going to have to get his ass in gear and prove the obnoxious little blinker wrong by actually writing a line or two. But not today.

He didn't need to get up and look to see who was ringing the doorbell to know that whoever it was, he didn't want to see them. There was no one he *did* want to see. At least no one who was going to show up on his doorstep today or any other day.

The bell rang again.

"Go away," he muttered, thinking he really ought to get an electrician out there to fix the switch for the damn gates. And maybe, while he was at it, a plumber to dig a moat. Twelve feet of piranha-infested water ought to put an end to unwanted visitors. He glanced at his watch, sighed, and reached for a cigarette in spite of the fact that he was allowing himself only one an hour and it had been not quite nineteen minutes since his last. Was it his fault the stupid doorbell had broken his concentration and punched a Marlboro Man–size hole in his willpower?

He shoved aside the blank drawing board and rummaged through the dozens of pages of scrawled notes strewn across his desk without finding the cigarettes he'd ventured out to buy just hours ago. Deciding he must have left them in the kitchen, he pushed away from the desk, gave his stiff right knee time to adjust to his weight, and went to check, trudging past room after empty room to reach the other side of the house.

There were times when he questioned his sanity for buying such an overpriced monstrosity to live in all by himself. It was exactly the kind of disgusting display of self-indulgence he despised, and at times he felt downright guilty for doing it, for having his choice of beds to sleep in when there were plenty of homeless people who'd be grateful for just one. A better man would do something to rectify the situation. Like turn the place into a homeless shelter, he mused with a flicker of perverse satisfaction. That would soothe his conscience and piss off all the snotty rich people living around him. Bonus. He hated snotty rich people almost as much as he hated himself these days. Also, any shelter worth its salt was bound to have folks coming and going at all hours, strangers setting up cots and raiding the kitchen and turning his study into a playroom for their kids. All that noise and commotion would give him a legitimate excuse for not being able to write, as opposed to the piss-poor one he had now. *Loser, loser, loser.*

When you came right down to it, he wasn't sure exactly why he'd bought the place. One day he was driving by—for the thousand-something time—and he noticed the discreet Realtor's sign on the gate and knew he had to have it. The shrink his agent set him up with had suggested he bought it because he was searching for something, and that he needed to figure out what it was and act on it before he could move on. That's when Owen had quit going to see him. He'd been poor most of his life, and just because he no longer was didn't mean he should shell out a couple of hundred bucks an hour to have someone tell him what he already knew . . . that there was something missing in his life.

There was one good thing about living there, he decided as he trudged on, limping less than he had six months ago, but still more than enough to piss off a man used to being in good shape. Make that great shape, as in finely tuned human machine shape. Not so long ago, it had been a matter of course that his own life and the lives of others depended on his physical strength and agility and the speed of his reflexes. Those days were over. Now the good news was that he could afford a house so ridiculously large he didn't have to worry about getting enough exercise. Especially not at the rate he was losing things and going around in circles trying to find them.

It was weird. He'd put a beer down somewhere, go back a few minutes later to the spot he was certain he'd left it, and it would be gone. The same thing happened with his cigarettes and with the golf clubs he liked to keep handy throughout the house. He didn't actually play golf—too passive and pointless a game for his taste— but sometimes when he got stuck for the right words, swinging a club helped him think. At least it used to. Lately that well of inspiration seemed to have dried up along with all the others.

He spotted the cigarettes as soon as he entered the kitchen, the red-and-white box floating in about four inches of water in the sink. Perplexed, he scanned the room. The window was open. Maybe he'd left them on the counter on his last beer run and the wind had blown them into the sink. Again. Ocean breezes could be erratic, calm one minute and gusting the next. Of course, the capricious wind didn't explain the disappearing beer bottles that sometimes turned up back in the kitchen, empty, or the golf clubs he found tossed by the side of the patio out back.

Weird, he thought for the umpteenth time since moving into the century-old mausoleum. Just weird. And that's as far as he was ready to take it. Just because he wrote about the supernatural didn't necessarily mean he believed in it. If there was more to what was going on around the place than his own absentmindedness, then . . . well, then he was going to need a lot better proof than an empty beer bottle or two. He was going to need something up close and personal.

"Got that?" he muttered, glancing around as if there really might be someone listening.

He fished the cigarettes from the sink and shook the water off, hoping to find one still dry enough to light. He didn't. Disgusted, he tossed the pack in the trash, thinking that if this kept up he might have to break down and start buying them by the carton instead of a pack at a time. It would be more convenient, of course, but it would also shatter the comforting delusion that having a smoke now and then was not the same as actually *being* a smoker. He wasn't ready to face the fact that ten years after going through hell to quit, he'd really been stupid enough to get hooked again.

The doorbell sounded a third time . . . or was it the fourth? Whatever, it was quickly followed by some very assertive knocking. Growing even more irritated, with himself and with the freaking wind and especially with whoever was out there banging, he headed in that direction, automatically grabbing a beer as he passed the fridge and positioning himself where he could see out the narrow window beside the door without being seen. He recognized both the black SUV parked in the drive and the woman standing on the steps from her last visit, when it had taken nearly fifteen minutes of ignoring her to get her to go away. Whatever she was after, she was persistent; he'd give her that.

He stood for a moment, watching her fidget and glance around as if pondering her next move. Out of habit, and boredom, he lingered to take a closer look. She was pretty enough, in a low-key, forgettable sort of way. Average height, average body, unremarkable brown hair pulled into some kind of twisted ball in back. She had the sort of pleasant, low-key, inoffensive look that led him to conclude she was there either to try to sell him something or to save his immortal soul. And he had no interest in either.

"Mr. Winters," she called out. "I know you're home."

Owen took a quick step back, worried she was nosy and determined enough to peer in through the window.

"Look, all I want is a few minutes of your time," she called. "Really. I'm not selling anything, if that's what you're thinking."

Okay. That left saving his soul. He backed up another step.

"In fact," she went on, "I think you may be very interested in hearing what I have to say. This could be a great opportunity for you."

Oh, yeah. Definitely after his soul. Probably had that briefcase of hers stuffed with fire-and-brimstone pamphlets. Well, she could just stand out there and bang her ass off; no way in hell was he opening the door and letting her in.

That ungracious thought had barely formed when he felt a chill, as if a giant temperature vac had sucked the warmth from the air around him, and then just as suddenly and inexplicably the front door swung open, coming at him so fast he had to lurch sideways to avoid getting whacked in the head.

What the hell . . . ?

Sophie, standing on the other side of the door, was just as startled to see the door fly open with such force it literally bounced off the inside wall. She jumped, with a little squeak of surprise, which immediately made her feel silly. After all, wasn't the whole point of standing out there, pounding on the door for all she was worth, so that someone would open it? Well, now someone had. And he didn't look happy.

On the plus side, he wasn't dripping wet, as he would be if she'd dragged him out of the shower. Of course, that still left sleeping, working, or being tied up with a matter-of-life-and-death phone call as possible reasons he hadn't come to the door sooner. She'd considered all those possibilities as she stood there pounding, just as she'd considered them on her last visit. The difference was that today she was feeling more desperate than polite.

Judging from the way he was glaring at her, *polite* wasn't at the top of Owen Winters's list at that moment either. She braced herself for an angry tirade about the evils of uninvited visitors. Instead, when he finally spoke, his deep voice was quiet and icy with control.

"Do you always go around letting yourself into other people's homes?"

"Letting myself . . . ?" Her eyes went wide as the meaning of the question became clear and she jabbed her index finger against her chest. "Me? You think I . . . ?"

"Didn't you?"

"No," she replied indignantly.

"Then who . . . ?"

"I assumed you . . ."

"I didn't," he said.

"Oh. Then, well . . ." She glanced around and shrugged. "I guess maybe the wind could have blown it open."

"Yeah. Maybe." He sounded unconvinced. And annoyed.

He stared at her with undisguised suspicion for a few seconds, not saying anything. Probably trying to think of a way to blame her for the wind, Sophie thought, using the time to regroup . . . and crossing her fingers that the man was merely rude and not bat-shit crazy. Or dangerous. Not that she had any choice but to forge ahead. Whether he was sane or certifiably batty was a secondary consideration. It was her job to win him over, and by God that's what she was going to do.

"Owen Winters?" she ventured, recovering enough to seize the opportunity the wind had blown into her path. Fortune favors the bold, after all. She waited for a response, eyeing him speculatively because, to be honest, she wasn't one hundred percent convinced he was Owen Winters. Granted the book-jacket photo had been taken at a distance and Winters had been half turned away, leaning on a tree, but the man in that photo had looked a little younger. And a lot better groomed. She tried to picture the guy in front of her without dark stubble and bloodshot eyes. Ditto the faded All-man Brothers T-shirt that had been washed so many times it was impossible to tell what color it had started out. The neck band was frayed—mauled by stubble—and it barely reached the waistband of his equally decrepit jeans with a hole in one knee that looked to be the result of wear rather than a fashion statement. Did authors use body doubles? she wondered.

He ignored her greeting. "Who are you?"

"Sophia Bennett," she replied, offering him the business card she had at the ready. "Everyone calls me Sophie."

He took it with the hand not holding the beer bottle and squinted, reading the words under his breath. " 'Seasons . . . for all the occasions of a lifetime. One-of-a-kind parties, weddings, and celebrations.' " When he looked up there was no mistaking the curl of his lip. "Weddings and celebrations. What are you? Some kind of wedding planner?"

He said it with such disdain you might think she'd introduced herself as a puppy slayer or the Grinch's assistant.

Sophie nodded and proudly lifted her chin. "That's right. It's a family business, founded by my mother . . . well, stepmother actually. She's mostly retired, though she still—"

"Cut to the chase, lady. What does this have to do with me?"

Sophie couldn't blame him for cutting her off. In fact she was grateful for it. She'd been rambling and she never rambled. She hated rambling. It was so . . . disorganized.

"Good question," she told him, smile firmly in place. She refused to be intimidated by his brusque tone and unfriendly expression. Failing that, she refused to show that she felt intimidated by him. "The answer is somewhat complicated. If you don't mind, I'd like to come in and explain it to you."

"I do mind. And there's no need to explain. Whatever it is, I'm not interested."

He shoved the card back at her and reached for the door handle. This was definitely not going as well as she'd hoped.

"How can you be sure you're not interested in what I have to say if you don't give me a chance to say it? Please, Mr. Win—"

A sudden movement behind him caught her attention, but when she automatically shifted her gaze in that direction, there was no one there.

"What is it?" Winters demanded, his attention sharpening as he turned his head to look behind him and then back at her. "What did you see?"

Sophie shook her head. "Nothing. I thought I did, but it must have been a trick of the light."

He didn't respond, just stood there studying her with the same probing glare that had been in his eyes when the door first blew open. Then he startled her by stepping aside with a grudging wave of his arm. "Maybe you should come in after all. It can't hurt to hear what you have to say."

"It won't, I promise. One hundred percent pain-free, that's me."

Sophie thought he might have snorted quietly as she passed him, but she ignored it, moving inside quickly, before he had a chance to change his mind. She'd known going in that this was a long shot, but she'd told herself that if she could just get him to hear her out, she might have a chance. She clung to that hope as he closed the door behind her. For several long seconds they stood in silence, him frowning, her still working her best "Isn't this fun?" smile. He glanced around awkwardly, as if not quite sure what to do with her now that he'd allowed her in.

Something told her the man didn't do a lot of entertaining and she felt a pang of sympathy for him, quickly followed by a bigger pang for herself as it occurred to her that his recluselike habits didn't bode well for her chances of convincing him to open his home to a hundred and fifty or so strangers . . . not counting sundry support personnel and waitstaff.

"This way," he said finally, and started down a long wide hallway to the other side of the house.

Sophie followed slowly, partly because that's how he was walking, slowly and favoring one leg a little, and partly because her toes hurt and she wasn't used to walking in heels that high and she didn't want to risk twisting her ankle or falling on her face. She was probably going to fall on her face when she made her request and that would be humiliation enough for one day. The slow pace worked to her advantage because it gave her the opportunity to look around and make mental notes just in case she got lucky and Winters said yes. And on a more personal and sentimental level, it gave her time to deal with the sudden lump in her throat resulting from the simple fact that she was really there. She, Sophia Beatrice Bennett, was actually inside the Princess House. It was the ultimate dream come true for the kid who had curled up with a beloved book and wished she could crawl inside and be part of that fascinating made-up world.

The house did not disappoint. The rambling Queen Anne–style villa, which did indeed resemble a fairy-tale castle, was as spectacular inside as out, with all the style and sophistication Sophie associated with the 1920s, the era in which it was built. The foyer was spacious, with a starburst of black-and-white marble on the floor and pale gold walls that wore a faint sheen from the sunlight pouring in through dozens of curved and beveled-glass windowpanes. True, there were no talking sculptures to welcome her and no magic carpet to whisk her from room to room, but she was very pleased with what was there, from simply framed watercolors to pale silk window dressings to the timeless furnishings with clean lines and rich tones. And the humongous split staircase just like the one in the book with the banister the backward princess could slide *up*.

She only wished her mother was there to see it all with her. And she hoped she would be able to pull this off so Shelby would have a chance to see it too. If anything, the house was an even more magnificent setting for a wedding than she'd imagined. The overall mood was elegant and warm and welcoming . . . everything the lord of the manor was not, she thought ruefully.

As they passed the staircase her gaze lifted to where it divided in two and continued upward on either side of the foyer. Professionalism edging sentimentality aside, her mind automatically began compiling a list of ways a clever photographer could use the delicate, curved banister to frame a shot when again, from the corner of her eye, she saw movement. This time the impression was stronger, as if there was something sheer and white floating in the air above the staircase, like . . . like a wide ribbon of snowflakes, but once again, by the time she blinked and refocused, there was nothing there.

Nerves. It had to be nerves. *Get a grip,* she chided herself silently, taking a couple of deep breaths to try to slow the racing of her heart.

The man she had concluded must be Owen Winters led her to an immense sitting room dominated by a wall of floor-to-ceiling windows overlooking a rose-stone patio and rolling expanse of green lawn. What she assumed was a guesthouse was some distance off to the side of the patio, and in the distance, just beyond the lawn's edge, was Cliff Walk, the public pathway that ran behind the mansions on the east side of Bellevue Avenue and was a well-known Newport landmark. On the other side of that narrow walkway, silvery cliffs formed a rough, steep, dangerous drop to the ocean.

Two words popped into Sophie's head the instant she stepped into the room: *cocktail hour*. It was the perfect setting for cocktails between the ceremony and a formal, sit-down dinner. She pictured a full-service bar stretching the length of the back wall, with appetizer stations at each end, and maybe a half-dozen simple white banquettes by the windows. If the weather cooperated, the French doors could be left open and on the patio outside there would be a mix of small tables with chairs for sitting, and taller tables for guests to gather around. And maybe a few more banquettes. Also, possibly, shade umbrellas. She cast an assessing gaze at the sun high in the clear blue sky; she'd have to wait until she got the ceremony time pinned down before she could determine what the angle of the sun would be in late August.

Of course, that was just one possibility. Her mission was only to get Owen Winters on board. After that either Jill or Jenna would take the helm to actually create the wedding of Shelby Archer's dreams and she, Sophie, would slip back into the more familiar role of making sure everything went according to plan. To even think about scheduling and seating arrangements was putting the cart before the horse. If she couldn't convince Winters to play nice, none of the rest mattered.

"Wow," she murmured, drawn closer to the windows. "That view is even more spectacular than I imagined. How often do you set your alarm so you can get down here in time to sit and watch the sun rise?"

Silence.

When Sophie turned her head to look at him, he shrugged.

"Never actually."

"Oh. Well. I guess living here, you must get used to seeing it. But that's what I would do, every morning, me and my coffee and the sunrise to start the day right."

"Is that what you came here to talk about?" he asked pointedly. "The view?"

"Of course not. Not exactly anyway, but the view certainly doesn't hurt." She glanced at one of the cream-and-pale-blue striped chairs. "May I?"

He nodded, though he didn't look happy about it.

She sat and opened her briefcase to remove the file containing a few carefully selected photos of past Seasons events along with the detailed formal proposal she'd put together especially for this meeting, her version of bringing out the big guns.

"Let me start by saying that your home is beyond beautiful. Whoever your decorator is did a wonderful job."

"Decorator?" he countered, giving the word the same sneer of disapproval he had *wedding planner*.

"I just assumed . . ." She trailed off with a small, chastised smile and circled her finger in the air to encompass their surroundings. "So you—"

"Bought it fully furnished," he informed her. "The old lady who owned the place died and—"

He was interrupted by a loud *thump* and they both turned abruptly to see that a book had toppled from the table behind him to the floor. Without commenting, he picked it up and returned it to the table, careful to place it close to the center this time. He turned back to Sophie.

"As I was saying, she died and left her estate to a nephew who was her only heir. He'd moved to the West Coast years earlier and had no interest in coming back east, so he let the place sit and gather dust for ten or so years before he finally decided to sell it as is."

"I see. Well, I'd say that was his loss and your good fortune. Ange de la Mer isn't only beautiful; it's unique, which brings me to my reason for being here. At Seasons, our top priority is making our clients' dreams come true. No detail is too small, no request too big. So, in keeping with one of our clients' wishes, I'm here to discuss the possibility of using your home for a wedding the last weekend of August."

He looked horrified.

"I know it sounds crazy," she went on before he had a chance to say anything. "I know because that's exactly how it sounded to me when the bride-to-be and her mother broached the idea. First, there's the time factor. Less than eight weeks to plan a formal wedding for a hundred and fifty guests? That alone is insane. Then they explained that the bride wants to be married here, at Ange de la Mer. At Seasons, we've planned hundreds of weddings, weddings at country clubs and hotel ballrooms, a few at the beach. Naturally we've also arranged weddings in private homes, but we never before worked with a couple who want to be married in a home belonging to a total stranger, someone they'd never even met, someone with no connection whatsoever to them or to their families."

"So we're in agreement," he said. "It's an insane idea."

"It would probably be more accurate to say we *were* in agreement," she countered. "I should have said my first reaction was that it was a crazy idea, but then Helen Archer— the mother of the bride—pointed out that this sort of thing is done all the time by movie producers. They send someone out to scout the perfect setting for their film and then negotiate with the owner for use of the property. That's why I'm here: to negotiate."

"Let me save you the trouble; there's nothing to negotiate."

As he spoke he crossed his arms in a way Sophie found very distracting. There was something to be said for the rumpled T-shirt look after all, she decided, something a lot more intriguing than that posed shot on his book jacket. Maybe the stubble was growing on her, or maybe it was simply that she'd moved past her first, instinctive impression of a grown man answering the door barefoot and swigging beer from a bottle, but it occurred to her that there was something about his physical presence that eluded the camera, that drew you in for a closer look.

Something about him? Who was she kidding? It was *everything* about him. Under the stubble and the rumple, the guy was dead-on fine: he was classic, all-American male eye candy, tall and lean and rough enough around the edges to be interesting. Not that she was interested. She didn't know much about the man, but she didn't need to know much to know he wasn't her type. And it was beyond a safe bet to say that she wasn't his. Omens aside, this mission might have been better left to one of her sisters. Or both. That whole twin mystique really did it for some guys.

"Lady, you got it straight the first time," he said, snapping her wayward thoughts back to the matter at hand. "It's a crazy idea. And it's out of the question. I'm sorry you wasted your time—"

She lifted her hand to stop him. "Please, won't you just sit down and hear me out before you make up your mind?"

"That would only be a waste of more time for both of us. Believe me, my mind is made up and there's nothing you can possibly say to change it."

"Five minutes. Please."

He made no effort to hide his displeasure as he ran his fingers through darkish brown hair that was not so much long as it was shaggy, the ends touched with gold. She'd bet anything those sub-tle streaks, like his tan, were one hundred percent natural. She could no more picture him sitting still for someone to paint high-lights on his hair than she could imagine him in a tanning salon. Both were the product of long hours in the sun, the same sun re-sponsible for the lines etched at the corners of his mouth and eyes. Laugh lines? Sophie had only known him a few minutes, but she thought not.

"I'm listening," he said finally, ignoring her invitation to sit. Instead he stood gazing down at her, his full mouth settled in a discouraging frown, his long-legged, lean-hipped slouch the most eloquent of body language: it screamed for her to hurry up and go away.

She held the proposal out to him. "I prepared some notes to make sure I covered everything. Maybe you could—"

"Tick. Tock."

She realized he wasn't even going to glance at the bullet points she'd labored over long into the night. Trying not to become flus-tered, she forced a smile and carefully placed the proposal on the table in front of her. "In case you haven't noticed, this isn't easy for me. Knocking on a complete stranger's door for a cold-call hard sell isn't exactly my style."

"And yet here you are."

"Yes. Here I am."

"I wonder why."

"I told you why: I have a client—correction, a *potential* client with her heart set on being married here at Ange de la Mer."

"And you have yours set on clinching the deal."

"Well . . . of course. I'm a businesswoman, Mr. Winters. This wedding will be both lucrative and high profile. And from my point of view, that's a win-win."

"In that case, my advice is to tell your potential client to check out Rosecliff just down the street. It's much more high profile and I understand weddings are a regular occurrence there. They've probably got the whole routine down to a science."

"Precisely . . . and that's the problem. Weddings aren't science. They're the exact opposite; they're . . . magic," she exclaimed, her passion creeping into her voice. "I've done weddings at Rosecliff; it's a beautiful site, but it won't do for this bride. It has to be Ange de la Mer. She claims there's something magical about this house and I have to agree. It's the way it sparkles in the sunlight as if someone sprinkled it with fairy dust, and the way the copper angels at the top of the spires spin around as if they're dancing in the wind, and those cozy little balconies where you'd swear Juliet or Rapunzel could appear any second."

Something that might have been amusement flickered briefly in his eyes. "Fairy dust?"

She smiled. "I may have gotten just a bit carried away. But the fact is that Shelby has been in love with this house since she was a little girl and sailed by here with her father."

He stiffened, that small trace of humor gone as his expression hardened into a scowl. "Then I'm afraid she's out of luck. There's a long list of reasons it's not going to happen, starting with the fact that I hate weddings."

"You hate weddings?" Her hushed tone reflected her shock. Who was the puppy-slaying Grinch's assistant now? "How can anyone hate weddings? Weddings are celebrations of love and commitment and new beginnings."

"Marked by a display of pomp and pretentiousness, signifying nothing . . . a legalized crapshoot all gussied up with champagne and white lace, and with about the same odds of success as a shady carnival game, something I happen to know more than a little about."

"Carnival games? Or marriage?"

"Both. For instance, I know both are for suckers."

"That's a pretty harsh generalization."

"Have you ever been married, Ms. Bennett?"

"Well . . . no. But I really don't see what that has to do—"

"I have. It lasted eighteen months. Six of which were happy. Most of the time."

"I see."

She did see, clearly. And somehow she had to find a way to prevent his obvious bitterness about his own failed marriage from preventing Shelby from having a shot at the wedding she'd always dreamed of.

"That must have been a very difficult time for you. And it's understandable that it had an influence on your attitude toward marriage, but perhaps you could try to think of this strictly as a business proposition. It will be as if we were shooting a movie here, but instead of taking weeks or months, we'll only need one weekend . . . obviously with some time on both ends for setup and cleanup." She thought it best not to get too specific about just how time-consuming and involved preparations for a wedding on this scale could be. That could all be explained later, in baby steps. "You could use that time to treat yourself to a wonderful vaca- tion . . . a sky's-the-limit vacation. Helen Archer is a woman who knows what she wants and is willing to pay for it; she's made it clear she'll spare no expense to make her only child's wedding perfect."

"I'll bet," he drawled with a grim smirk. "I know the type. And for her sake I hope it happens, but they haven't minted enough money to get me to let it happen here."

Three

There was a note of finality in his tone. The realization that he wasn't going to change his mind was closing in on Sophie. She quickly reviewed the arguments at her disposal—financial gain, favorable publicity, the sheer pleasure of doing something from the goodness of one's heart—and concluded that none of those alternate routes was likely to get her where she wanted to go. That left begging and blackmail, which both her pride and her conscience prohibited. Besides, there was nothing about Winters to suggest he'd be any more susceptible to those than to anything else she'd said.

Maybe it was time to shift gears and start thinking instead of an alternate wedding site, one that would appeal to Shelby and soften the blow of losing out on her first choice. She really liked Shelby and she hated disappointing her as much as she hated losing the business. She could think of a half-dozen lovely, little-known sites that were similar to Ange de la Mer. Similar, but without the emotional connection. And there would be Helen Archer to deal with. She'd only met the woman once, but that was enough to figure out that she was someone who knew what she wanted and was accustomed to getting it. Somehow she would have to be convinced that following through on her threat to keep searching until she found a wedding planner who could deliver Ange de la Mer was a waste of time . . . time she didn't have if the wedding was to take place in a matter of weeks. At this point Sophie didn't think any other planner, including the *J*s, would fare better with Winters than she had.

She looked up to find him watching her.

"Look, this has nothing to do with you," he told her. There was a new and unexpected hint of regret buried in his gruff tone. "You gave it your best shot. But even if I wanted to go along with it, I couldn't. I'm a writer, which means I work at home, and I have a September first deadline. I wouldn't get any work done with people coming and going all the time, prancing around here bedecking things and unfurling white carpets."

She smiled slightly, a faint flicker of hope reigniting inside. It was just enough to let her see the signpost reading *Alternate Route This Way*.

"You'd be surprised how quiet my crew can be when bedecking and unfurling. And I'm glad you mentioned your writing because I was hoping for an opportunity to tell you that I'm a big fan of your work. A . . . friend recently turned me on to it. In fact we were discussing one of your books just this morning. And I can't wait to read it," she added, taking a shot that he was more susceptible to flattery than to profit. When it came to little white lies, her pride and conscience had more wiggle room.

"Really?" He looked dubious. "Which one?"

"Which one what? Oh, you mean which book . . . the, uh . . . the one with Osprey. And the Ghostship. And Valene. It sounds great."

"Yeah, that's a classic all right." He put his beer down, leaned back against the pillar between two sets of French doors, and rubbed his knuckles against his jaw. "Funny, though, I wouldn't have pegged you as a fan of sushi westerns."

Sushi westerns? Why the hell hadn't she taken a closer look at that stupid comic book? Correction: *graphic novel*.

"Really? Well. That just goes to show that appearances can be misleading. I adore a good sushi western. Which is why I would never do anything to interfere with your deadline; we would totally work around your schedule, and if at some point we did have to be here during your work hours, we would be as quiet as church mice."

"Church mice?" he countered, raising one eyebrow.

Sophie nodded, her expression solemn. "Yes, it's a little-known fact that they're the quietest and most discreet of the mice family."

Owen couldn't help smiling. It felt . . . strange. Almost painful. Which he supposed just went to show how long it had been since he'd done it. Apparently the smile muscle could atrophy just like any other. Who knew? It was worth it, though, because Sophia Bennett smiled back and he discovered that he'd been hasty in his initial assessment. There was at least one thing about this woman that wasn't even close to being ordinary or nondescript: her smile. Her smile was . . . radiant, dazzling, disarming, drag out all the overworked clichés you could think of. Her smile was amazing; it made her eyes look amazing too, like sunlight on a blue-green sea. Her smile lit up her face and there was beauty there too. Hell, her smile lit up the room. And, most amazing of all, it lit up something inside him.

Because he was an idiot. He shook his head and began talking to distract himself from things he had no business thinking about. Distance. He needed distance from those thoughts, and detachment . . . and he needed her to go. "Lady, the cold-call hard sell may not be your style, but you're damn good at it. For what it's worth, if anyone could persuade me to let the spoiled little rich girl have her way, it would be you."

"But?"

"But the answer is still no."

Accepting defeat gracefully, she got to her feet and very un-gracefully knocked her notes to the floor in the process. In a quick, reflex action, Winters stepped forward and they both bent and grabbed them at the same time, straightening slowly so that they ended up standing face-to-face with just a few sheets of paper between them.

Their eyes met and Sophie felt a sudden flutter of shyness. That feeling of wanting to look away and not wanting to at the same time. Not wanting to won out. It was silly. Absurd really. And un-settling. He was just so . . . male. He was the poster child for fla-grant, uncompromising maleness. Everything about him . . . his size and the way he stood, the way he was looking at her. His eyes were dark blue, blue verging on midnight, and they held a faintly speculative edge, as if he were wondering all sorts of exciting and inappropriate things about her. Sophie didn't know how she knew that, she just did. Even his scent was male. And all of it was alien to her world, alien and enticing.

The world where she spent her days—and nights—was one of . . . how did the nursery rhyme go? Sugar and spice and everything nice. It was a polite and pretty world where romance reigned supreme and the men were all spit-shined, tuxedo-clad, and on their best be-havior. Winters was none of this. And that, Sophie told herself, ex-plained why he was having such a strong effect on her. He was a novelty. A primal novelty. It was probably something to do with pheromones and musk and . . . swagger. Big surprise the guy wrote sushi westerns. Not that she knew exactly what a sushi western was, but western meant cowboy and cowboys were always big and tough and . . . well, primal. Maybe she really would read his book.

"Thanks," she said, indicating the papers, the creaking of her voice due to her suddenly dry mouth. She really hoped her cheeks didn't look as flushed as they felt.

"No problem," he replied, still without letting go. "I really am sorry I can't help you out."

"Me too. I know it probably sounds as if Shelby is a typical rich spoiled brat, but honestly she's not. She and her fiancé are great kids. They just graduated from college and signed up for the Peace Corps together. That's the reason the wedding is a rush job; they decided they want to be married before leaving for Ecuador in September."

As she glanced at the papers in her hand, one of the reminders she'd scribbled for herself jumped out at her.

"She wanted their marriage to have its start here at the Princess House because she thought it would bring them luck."

He let go as if the papers had suddenly caught fire in his hand. "What did you say?"

"That she wanted to be married here for luck?"

He shook his head impatiently. "No. The house . . . what did you call the house?"

"Oh, that." She smiled. "We call it the Princess House. Shelby told me that when she was a little girl her father used to take her sailing near here because Ange de la Mer reminded her of the castle in her favorite storybook, and it just so happens it was my favorite too. My mother read it to me so many times I knew the words by heart; she used to brag that it was the one book I could 'read' even before I'd learned to read." She tipped her head to the side, her small smile becoming sheepish. "You have no idea what a thrill it is for me just to be standing here, in the Princess House."

"Could you just stop calling it that?" he snapped.

"Sorry. I'm sure that's the last thing a guy wants to hear his house called."

He waved that off, still frowning.

"When I love something I get a little carried away: I even have a copy of the book cover hanging on the wall of my office. Until we talked about it, Shelby hadn't realized that this house actually was the inspiration for the castle in the story; she'd fallen in love with it all on her own. Her dad died when she was in high school and I think losing him made the idea of having the wedding here even more special and more important to her. It's her way of feeling closer to him and including him in her big day. *The Princess House* is actually the title . . ."

"I know what it is."

Owen also knew his tone was much too harsh and that turning his back to her while she was still speaking was rude. He didn't care. He'd heard enough.

Confused and agitated, he stared out the window, honing in on a spot at the far right of the property, just off the Cliff Walk, where a cluster of hippo-size blue hydrangea bushes provided shelter on blustery days, the perfect spot for a peanut-butter-and-jelly picnic after a couple of hours of fishing at a small cove about a fifteen-minute hike from there.

How many times had he sat in that spot staring at this house?

Once upon a time a perfectly ordinary princess lived in a perfectly extraordinary house by the side of the sea.

At the time, he couldn't afford to own as much as a square foot of lawn at a place like this. It didn't matter. On the days he got to spend just hanging out with Allie he was as happy as he'd ever been. Now he was rich enough to lay claim to every stinking blade of grass out there and happiness seemed as impossible and as far away as the make-believe worlds he created for his readers.

The Princess House. Sophia Bennett wasn't the only one who knew that book by heart. There was a time when he knew every word, and he knew where every blue bird and firefly were on every page. All that seemed far away now too. As far away as Allie herself.

But maybe he had it wrong. Maybe impossible wasn't what it was cracked up to be. Not an hour ago he was standing in the kitchen challenging the universe and anyone else who might be listening to prove to him that there was something out of the ordinary going on there. Could this be the proof he'd asked for? Was her mention of *The Princess House* meant to be a sign of some kind? A message?

He could think of only one way to find out, and it didn't involve showing her to the door and locking it behind her as he'd intended to do until about sixty seconds ago.

His mind made up, he turned to face her. "All right."

"All right?" she echoed in a tone hovering somewhere between hopeful and guarded.

"Yeah. Go ahead and tell the bride and her doting mother to start their engines. They can have their damn wedding here."

Humph. That was Ivy Halliday's thought as she stood at the front window and watched the young woman, Sophia Bennett she believed she'd said her name was, climb into her big, clunky automobile and drive away.

A wedding planner.

Humph.

Had she known that, she never would have flung open the door on her behalf. The audacity of it, to even think of arranging a wedding there, at Ange de la Mer, considering its history. *Her* history. As always, the twinge in her heart came quickly. A blink of an eye and it was 1927 again and she was standing at this very window, watching and waiting. Now she waited for the memory of those long hours and the days that followed to wash over her and recede. It was entirely possible that Miss Sophia Bennett knew nothing about all that. Young people were so focused on the future they failed to consider that places, like people, have a past, and the past cannot be undone or wished away simply to make room for the new.

Was she one of the Barrington Bennetts? Ivy wondered. Likely not. Say what you would about the Bennett women; they did not traffic in commerce. Not that Ivy wasn't a firm believer that a woman had every right to live her life as she saw fit. She had after all.

Today wasn't the first time Sophia Bennett had come calling, or the first time the ill-mannered Mr. Winters had refused to see her. Ivy had intervened in the hope that Miss Bennett was the woman he was so obviously pining over and that with a little encouragement she would keep coming back and—most importantly as far as Ivy was concerned—she would have a civilizing effect on him.

It was her dearest wish that the woman would succeed where she had thus far failed, by getting the man to use coasters beneath his odious beer bottles and close windows when it rained and to refrain from dropping wet towels on her parquet floors. She also didn't care for his habit of playing loud music at all hours of the day or night, but at least music didn't leave marks on the mahogany sideboard or make the whole place reek of cigarette smoke. In short, Mr. Winters was treating the home she'd loved and tended all her life as if it were a cheap, run-down, flea-ridden motel, and she didn't like it one bit.

And then there was all the pitiful moping about that he did. There could only be a woman to blame for that. The fact that Ivy had never married didn't mean she'd lacked for suitors, or experience. Quite the contrary. And for all that men stomped around and called themselves the stronger sex, she recalled just how easily a man's heart, and his ego, could be bruised. A woman had to tread so carefully lest she seem to offer more than she was willing, or had left, to give.

Owen Winters was a handsome enough man . . . at least he would be if he ever troubled to clean himself up. He could easily find female companionship if he only tried. Of course, he was a writer and everyone knew that in and of itself accounted for a certain degree of self-absorption . . . not that the man actually produced any writing that she could see. She checked regularly and some doodles and nonsensical phrases were all he had to show for the hours spent slouched at his desk.

Sometimes she was tempted to try to snap him out of his gloom with a good old-fashioned scare. She could do it so easily. She didn't care how nonchalant he appeared to be about her little "reminders"; she'd wager that one good ghostly "OOOOOO" and a bookcase crashing down on his head in the middle of the night would do the trick. The problem was she didn't want to send him running scared; she simply wanted him to pick up his wet towels. If she spooked him into moving out and selling the property, she could well find herself sharing her home with a half-dozen cats, or children, and that would mean a whole new set of problems. No, the devil you knew and all that. She would tolerate Mr. Winters for as long as necessary.

What she would not tolerate was a wedding under her roof. She was the bride of Ange de la Mer and that was that. Just because her own wedding had never taken place was no reason someone else should be the first to marry there, in the house that had been built expressly for her as a wedding present from her father. In fact, as far as she was concerned, that was reason enough why no other wedding should take place there.

What a bother. She supposed she must assume some of the blame since it was she who had seen fit to open the door to Miss Bennett in the first place, but Mr. Winters could have resolved the matter by simply being himself. He could have refused the woman's request with his usual lack of graciousness and put a quick end to the entire business on the spot. Unfortunately he had failed to do either.

That meant it was up to her.

She did it! Sophie couldn't stop grinning as she headed back to Providence, crossing the bridge over Narragansett Bay with classic Bon Jovi blasting from her car speakers and the thrill of victory a live current running through her. The only thing that would make the moment more perfect was knowing *how* she did it.

The fact was she had no idea exactly what it was she had said or done to cause Owen Winters to change his mind so abruptly. If, indeed, he had changed his mind. Not to get lost in semantics, it seemed to her that it hadn't been a change of mind so much as a change of heart, and it had come right after she mentioned the deep emotional connection Shelby felt to the house. One moment he'd been scowling and ready to show her the door, the next he was scowling and agreeing to allow Shelby to be married at Ange de la Mer.

It would be helpful to know how she'd broken through his resistance so she could file it away in her bag of tricks for future use. And because she loved delving into a good mystery and Owen Winters definitely qualified as that. A wealthy, wildly successful, and—beneath the scruff—hunky-looking beast, holed up in his luxury man-cave, seething with suspicion, cynical about love, and curiously familiar with a little girls' storybook . . . what woman raised on fairy tales and happy endings could resist wanting to know more?

As curious as she was, however, she'd understood that it was not the time to hang around asking questions. As soon as he uttered the magic words, she'd whipped out the standard bare-bones agreement she'd brought along for him to sign and beat a hasty exit before he had time to think. Or ask himself what the hell he was doing. She decided it was also not the time to mention that someone from Seasons would soon be back to take measurements and do a complete inspection of the place so they would know exactly what they had to work with, or that Shelby was sure to want a pre-wedding-day look at the house she'd fallen in love with from afar. Maybe she could schedule the two visits together to minimize the inconvenience. And, she thought, her mouth curving into a smile, she would bring along a case of assorted local microbrews, as a "disturbing the peace" offering.

Her smile faded as it occurred to her that more than likely she would be sending the beer along with Jill or Jenna, not delivering it personally. Her assignment had been to secure the client's venue of choice; she'd done that. There had been no discussion about who would take the lead for the actual planning of the wedding—maybe because they hadn't wanted to jinx themselves, maybe because no one had really expected her to pull it off. Then again, what was there to discuss?

She and the Js worked as a team. Translation: Her sisters worked directly with the client and Sophie coordinated and calculated and kept track of things behind the scenes. It was Jill or Jenna who escorted clients to sample catering menus and to audition bands; they went to the cake tastings and helped the bride in her quest to find the perfect wedding dress. It was Sophie who checked and double-checked to make sure the cake tastings didn't overlap and that the band the client chose was available on the date they needed them and that the perfect dress arrived in plenty of time to allow for alterations. And when something went wrong she was more often than not the one called on to fix it. As an event took shape, all the relevant information was funneled back to Sophie and entered on the Big Board that took up a full wall in her office. At one glance she could see the up-to-the-minute status of every event Seasons had scheduled for the next twelve months.

Sometimes Sophie thought of her office as the hub of a busy airport. Each upcoming event on the board was like a huge jet circling on its assigned flight path, and she was the air traffic controller responsible for overseeing them all, for knowing who was on board and what cargo they were carrying, for knowing everything she needed to know to bring each one in for a safe landing when the time came. Her role might not be the most glamorous, but it was important just the same. No event had ever crashed and burned on her watch, and none ever would.

She really wanted to be there to see her sisters' faces when she told them she'd gotten Winters to sign the agreement, but suddenly she couldn't wait until she got back to the office to tell someone. She set her cell phone to speaker and punched in the Archers' home phone number.

"Hello, Shelby," she said, recognizing the young woman's voice as soon as she picked up. Her voice, like her overall demeanor, was smoother and more relaxed than her mother's. Helen Archer's crisp, to-the-point delivery made it clear you were but one minor blip on her busy schedule. "This is Sophie Bennett; I'm calling because I have good news . . . great news actually."

"About the Princess House?" Shelby countered, anticipation lifting her tone.

"That's right. I just left there and I have, tucked safely away in my briefcase, an agreement signed by the owner. It looks like you're going to be getting married at Ange de la Mer."

Shelby whooped with excitement. In the background Sophie heard Helen Archer's questioning tone; Shelby quickly relayed the good news to her mother.

"I don't believe it," she then said, speaking to Sophie once more. "I don't believe you actually pulled it off."

"O, ye of little faith," teased Sophie.

"Only because you said yourself it was a long shot and I shouldn't get my hopes up. I was the one who said it was an omen that you happened to have a painting of the house hanging in your office."

"And it looks like you were right. Whatever the reason, I'm really happy it worked out for you."

"Thank you. I can't believe it . . . this has been my dream for as long as I can remember, but I thought that's all it was . . . I never thought it would really happen. To be completely honest with you," she went on, her tone sheepish, "when my mother first suggested we look into it, I thought she was crazy . . . and I told her so. This is one time I'm glad she never listens to me."

Sophie was as thrilled by Shelby's joyful reaction as she was over clinching the deal in the first place. It was moments like this that reminded her why she loved her job and that made the tough days and the occasional impossible-to-please client worth the trouble.

"Well, that changes now. From here on we'll all be listening to you, to you and Matthew," she amended to include Shelby's fiancé, "and we're counting on you to tell us what we need to know to make your wedding day perfect for the two of you."

"No problem. We've talked about it a lot and we know exactly what we want."

"That's music to a wedding planner's ears; the more certain you are of what you like and what you don't, the easier our job is. It would also help to see any magazine clippings or color swatches you have, and any notes you may have jotted down."

"Oh, trust me, my mother has that covered. I think she's been secretly subscribing to bridal magazines and tearing out pictures for years."

Sophie laughed. "Well, of course she has. This will be a big day for her too, especially with you being her only daughter . . . her only *child*."

"So she tells me . . . several times a day."

"The next step is a second consultation to discuss an overall theme for the wedding—which can be very subtle or very dramatic, depending on your ideas—and we need to bang out a time schedule . . . which I don't have to tell you is going to be tight from the get-go. Once we draft a detailed proposal and get your final approval, we can start pulling it all together."

"Sounds good. When?"

"Let's see . . . can you come in tomorrow morning at eleven?"

"Eleven it is."

Four

Strictly speaking, Sophie didn't have to sit in on meetings with clients. And she suspected that most of the time neither the *Js* nor the clients even noticed that she was in the room. Blending into the background just sort of came naturally.

She went because she'd learned that being there to take her own notes—particularly during the initial planning session for an event—was preferable to depending on Jill or Jenna's listening skills. It helped stave off future misunderstandings and screwups, and since she was invariably the one called on to resolve misunderstandings and screwups, especially those of the last-minute, drop-everything-and-work-long-into-the-night variety, making time now ended up saving her time and aggravation in the end.

She especially tried to be on hand for wedding consultations. True, corporate events were at the top of Seasons' food chain in terms of profit; they also brought free publicity and resulted in the greatest number of new referrals, but in the end corporate events were . . . well, corporate. Weddings were personal and intimate; a wedding was literally a life-changing occasion for the people involved, and as far as Sophie was concerned, that mattered a hell of a lot more in the grand scheme of things than celebrating record-breaking profits or the glitzy launch of a new product line.

She felt a special affinity for the brides who entrusted Seasons with the most important day of their lives, and along with it an extra measure of dedication to making sure every detail was not merely right, but perfect. It didn't matter how many hours a day she had to work or how tired she was or how much concealer it took to hide the dark circles under her eyes, she would not permit so much as an engraved silver bubble wand or a blown-glass Cinderella's-coach cake topper to slip through the cracks and mar a happy couple's day, not if it was within her power to prevent it. First, because by the time the big day arrived, most brides were stressed to powder-keg level and even a teensy-tiny glitch could set them off and send months of careful preparations crashing like a string of dominoes. And second, because that's what she did; she made things perfect. She made dreams come true.

It was entirely possible that her soft spot for all things bridal was a genetic predisposition, or at the very least that it had rubbed off on her at an early age. Her mother had been an artist with a needle and thread and the one-of-a-kind wedding dresses she created were truly works of art. Sophie had happy childhood memories of spending time in her mother's small dressmaking shop, the sewing machine whirring away in the background as she turned the silk and lace scraps her mother set aside for her into wedding finery for her dolls. Sadly, she never developed anything close to her mother's skill . . . though she sometimes wondered whether she might have if things had turned out differently.

Instead she took satisfaction in knowing she shared her mother's passion for her work. Her mother had taken pride in making sure that every one of her brides walked down the aisle in a dress that not only made her look and feel beautiful, but that was hers and hers alone. Among the most important staples in her shop, right up there with the bolts of silk chiffon and the glass vials filled with seed pearls and crystals, had been a pretty china tea service and an always fresh assortment of fancy cookies. Madeleine Bennett believed there was no better way of getting to know someone than over a cup of tea and she insisted on getting to know a bride before she started to sew. Observing how a customer held herself and how she moved, how she laughed and even what she laughed at, had been a crucial part of her mother's creative process. As they sipped tea, she would listen to the bride-to-be talk about the man she loved and about her dreams for their future together. They also talked about The Dress, of course, as they pored over pattern books and magazine photos, debating whether it should be ivory or white, silk organza or dupioni silk, but her mother insisted it was the offhand remarks and the little things revealed between those crucial decisions that helped her to really understand the woman's vision of herself as a bride, perhaps better than the woman herself understood or could put into words.

That was another reason Sophie was always willing to rearrange her schedule to be available for a wedding consult; just as every woman had a vision of herself as a bride, every bride-to-be had a vision of her wedding day, and it was her, Sophie's, self-appointed duty to see to it that this vision became a reality. Even if it sometimes meant swimming against the mighty and well-armed tide that was the Seasons' wedding-planning machine.

Joyce Mainelli Bennett—her stepmother and the third *J*—was a sharp businesswoman and a virtuoso when it came to spotting a new trend and making it her own. One of the first local wedding planners to promote the concept of "theme weddings," over time she figured out which themes were the most popular and fine-tuned them until she had each one down to a science. When she "semiretired" she left behind what were referred to in-house as

"The White Books," a set of oversize, leather-bound albums containing dozens of professional photographs of weddings by Seasons, along with promotional photos and material from preferred vendors. Each book was dedicated to one of Seasons' *signature* themes, from Fairy-tale Princess to Romance by the Sea to Winter Wonderland. All you had to do was match the BTB—Bride-to-Be—with a theme and hand her the right book. The photographs had been strategically selected and arranged so that the client could easily see herself stepping into the prefab fantasy and living it, and before you could hum "Here Comes the Bride," she was trying to decide which of the Ice Palace floral arrangements or Sand Castle cake designs she preferred.

It was a no-brainer; weddings-by-number. Joyce understood her daughters' strengths and their shortcomings; she'd known they would be taking over the business one day and she'd planned accordingly. If the cookie-cutter approach didn't quite mesh with Sophie's philosophy, well, so be it. In theory, Jill, Jenna, and she were equals when it came to business, and to their credit neither they nor Joyce ever suggested otherwise. They didn't have to.

It had been the same when Joyce and her father married when Sophie was thirteen, the year after her mother was struck by a car and killed crossing the street in a blizzard. Joyce had known her mother slightly through business and she had been persistent and resourceful in her effort to fill the sudden hole in her father's life. Persistent, resourceful, and fast. Sophie still hadn't gotten used to her mother not being there when suddenly Joyce, Jill, and Jenna were. The *J*s moved in, bag and baggage, Calvin Klein jeans, and strawberry-scented styling mousse, and suddenly her home didn't feel like home anymore. It wasn't really their fault. Joyce was just so different from her mother, as different as Jill and Jenna were from her. They tried to make her feel like she was one of them the same way they tried to overhaul her sense of style and find her dates, and with the same lackluster results. Then, like now, the fact that they didn't go out of their way to make her feel like a square peg in their world of sleek and sexy round holes didn't mean she wasn't one.

Sophie wasn't entirely opposed to the White Books. There was no denying that they were a brilliant marketing tool and for some brides they enhanced the whole planning experience and introduced them to new ways to express themselves on their wedding day. For others, they were just plain overwhelming. A wedding was like a puzzle, with hundreds of pieces that had to fit together perfectly when the time came to assemble it, and she was a firm believer that the final piece of the puzzle should come from the hearts of the couple being wed, not from a book. *That's* what she was listening for when she sat quietly on the sidelines at meetings, that handful of words or offhand comment that would reveal the final piece of the puzzle. It was impossible to predict, but she knew it when she heard it.

One bride had casually joked about how her fiancé carried in his wallet a snapshot of her taken when she was five, playing dress-up bride in her backyard with a lace tablecloth for a veil and a bunch of wild violets for a bouquet. Sophie suggested she add violets to her white rose bouquet without telling the groom. In a church filled with people, the moment when she started down the aisle and he first saw the violets, and their eyes met, was theirs alone, and one they would carry with them forever.

Sophie was convinced that every couple in love shared something—a secret getaway, a private joke, a memory of a lost loved one—that could add personality and joy to their celebration in a way no seven-tier cake or vodka ice luge could. You just had to work harder to coax it from some of them. There were women who hadn't spent a lifetime fantasizing about their wedding day, and some who had envisioned it right down to the smallest detail but weren't good at putting their vision into words.

Shelby Archer was not one of them.

*   *   *

"Hemp."

Sophie immediately looked up from her notes. The *J*s said nothing and that was probably for the best. Helen Archer laughed, a high-pitched bubble of sound that had more to do with surprise than amusement.

"I'm sorry, sweetie," she said to her daughter. "I must have misheard; I could have sworn you just said 'hemp.'"

"That is what I said," replied Shelby.

"Oh. Well, then you must have misheard Jill's question; she asked what sort of wedding gown you have in mind."

"I heard her. Hemp; that's the kind of gown I want."

The five women were gathered around the conference table in the room reserved for meeting with Seasons' wedding clients. Elegant black-and-white photos of past weddings adorned the walls and a specially built glass shelf held the White Books . . . except for the Fairy-tale Princess edition. Either Jill or Jenna had—understandably perhaps—assumed that would be the theme Shelby would choose for her *Princess House* wedding and they pulled the book and had it waiting when the Archers arrived, nestled right there beside the crystal champagne flutes and the silver bowl filled with fresh strawberries.

At the moment it sat in front of Helen . . . open to the re-touched photograph of a beautiful bride wearing the quintessential Cinderella ball gown. Helen leaned back in the cushy white leather swivel chair, lips pursed, and looked quizzically at her daughter.

"Hemp? Isn't that some sort of grain? Like barley? You can't make a wedding gown out of barley, sweetheart."

"It's not a grain," Shelby told her, smiling and relaxed. "It's actually a fiber . . . from the cannabis plant."

"Cannabis?" Her mother's impeccably shaped brows arched. "But that's . . ."

Her blue eyes twinkling, Shelby said, "Same genus; different plant. You could say that the kind you smoke is a distant cousin of the kind used to make wedding dresses . . . and paper and all sorts of other useful stuff. It's a legitimate crop, and fully sustainable, which is important . . . even George Washington grew hemp."

Her mother huffed. "Maybe, but I doubt he made Martha wear it. Really, Shelby, I know you have some crazy ideas, and I do try to be understanding, but this is your wedding we're planning . . . not a Greenpeace rally." She glanced imploringly at Jill and Jenna. "You're the experts: a hemp dress . . . really, have you ever heard of anything so ridiculous?"

The Js exchanged a cautious look; they knew, as did Sophie, that you had to tread carefully when stepping onto a mother–daughter battlefield. It could be laden with land mines that had been buried for years. Decades even.

"I'm vaguely familiar with the concept of hemp dresses," said Jill.

Nice dodge, thought Sophie, not really surprised that no one looked to her for an opinion.

"I remember seeing a few hemp dresses among the samples at the fall bridal expo in Boston," added Jenna. She gave Shelby a look of regret. "I have to say that, as I recall, they were all pretty dreadful."

Undaunted, Shelby flipped her long brown hair behind her shoulder. "Then you weren't looking at the right dresses."

Sophie's mouth curved into a smile. The kid was spunky, she'd give her that. Twenty-two was so young to be getting married, but there was a quiet, steadiness about Shelby Archer that made Sophie think she was more mature than lots of older brides she'd worked with . . . and that she could hold her own with her mother.

Smiling with professional excitement, Jenna leaned forward and tapped the photo of the bride. "What do you think of this style dress, Shelby? Naturally there's no guarantee that exact dress is still available . . . but I'm wondering what you think of the look."

"I think it's probably a great look for some people. But not for me."

"Don't be silly," said Jenna, entirely missing the point. "That dress would be beyond gorgeous on you. Look at you . . . those long legs, that tiny little waist. Do you have any idea how many brides would die to have your body and be able to pull off a gown with all those ruffles and flounces?"

"Just look at that big satin bow," urged Jill.

"And all the little bows made out of pearls and crystals."

"That is truly a dress fit for a princess."

Shelby nodded agreeably. "Exactly."

"It epitomizes the fairy-princess theme."

"Yes, it does," said Shelby. "Which is exactly why it's all wrong for me."

The *J*s frowned.

"I don't understand," said Jill. "Wasn't that the whole point of being married at Ange de la Mer . . . or the Princess House, as you call it? So that you could be a princess on that day? We thought it was your lifelong dream."

"Your vision," added Jenna.

"Your one nonnegotiable. Why else would we have gone to so much trouble to make it happen?"

Sophie had to roll her eyes inwardly at Jill's haughty tone and her use of the word *we*, considering that their only contribution to the venture was responsible for the blisters on her feet.

"It *is* my dream to be married there," acknowledged Shelby. "I just don't want a fairy-princess wedding. I never said I did."

There was the collective sound of three jaws dropping.

"Maybe not in so many words," Jill murmured.

"You didn't have to spell it out. The Princess House . . . that says it all," declared Jenna.

"I have to agree," said Helen. "Princess House, princess wedding . . ." Pointing at the open book, she added, "Princess gown. It just makes sense . . . and it will be beautiful." She gave Shelby's shoulder a squeeze. "You'll see."

"Mom, I love you, but I'm not the princess type. I know you wish I was, but I'm just not, and I never have been and you know it. And I'm not having some lame, fancy, fussy, prissy princessy wedding. I want to be married at the Princess House because of Dad, and because of the book, not so I can wear a dress that looks like what Scarlett O'Hara would have whipped up if the living-room drapes had been white . . . and had little crystal bows all over them. No offense," she said, casting a disparaging eye at the open book, "but Cordy wouldn't be caught dead in that getup and neither will I."

"Cordy?" Jenna queried.

"Princess Cordelia is the main character in *The Princess House*," Sophie explained. "And the most un-princessy princess there ever was."

"In fact she's known as the backward princess," Shelby added. "And she wears the name like a badge of honor . . . that's what makes her so wonderful. The only way Princess Cordy would ever wear that dress is at the point of a sword."

"And even then she'd probably insist on wearing it inside out," Sophie added, drawing a grin from Shelby.

The others appeared unamused, and a little confused. The *J*s liked being in control, or at least giving the appearance they were, and they disliked discussing things they didn't understand. But like any well-trained salesperson, their recovery time was negligible.

With her best the-client-is-always-right expression firmly in place, Jenna flipped shut the White Book and slid it off to the side. "All right, then, Shelby. Was there a particular theme you did have in mind for your wedding? Besides hemp, that is."

"Yes, do tell," urged her mother. "I can't wait to hear what sort of theme calls for the bride to walk down the aisle in a burlap sack. Old McDonald Had a Farm, perhaps? I can see it now, red-and-white checkered tablecloths and some sort of woven straw headpieces." She made a circular motion in the direction of her head.

Shelby appeared more bemused than bothered by her mother's comments. "Relax, Mom, I promise you there'll be no red and white checks anywhere . . . and no burlap. Matthew and I have given this a lot of thought and we want our wedding to have the feel of *A Midsummer Night's Dream*. The play," she added when there was no immediate reaction. She looked from one woman to another. "Shakespeare? Fairies? A magical forest?"

The *J*s exchanged a vague look and then Jill glanced behind her at the bookshelf. "I don't think we have . . ."

Sophie caught her attention and shook her head. "We don't. Shelby, I think this is a first for Seasons, and speaking for myself, I think it's a terrific idea. Romantic and whimsical and, my God, so full of possibilities."

"I know," countered Shelby, excitement rising in her voice. "And it's the perfect theme for us because it's how Matthew and I met, when we were both volunteering to help with an inner-city school's production of the play."

The final piece of the puzzle, thought Sophie.

"It is perfect," she agreed. "And I can see why you're thinking of a hemp gown; the designs I've seen in hemp are usually very simple and that would be in keeping with the play's sense of youth and innocence."

"You know about these hemp gowns?" Helen asked.

"A little," Sophie replied. "My mother was a dressmaker who specialized in wedding dresses, so I've always had a special interest in them and I like to keep up with what's current. Over the past few years hemp fabrics have come a long way, to the point where some top designers are starting to use them, especially the hemp silk or hemp cotton blends. They say they're every bit as good as the original in how they look and drape."

"Then why not just use the original?" Helen asked.

"Because no silkworms have to give their lives to make a hemp silk dress," Shelby explained.

The *J*s and Helen exchanged baffled looks.

Sophie explained. "It's a common practice for silkworm farmers—especially on large corporate farms—to toss the cocoons into an oven or boiling water to speed up the cultivation process. But a small group of eco-friendly farmers now wait and allow the moth to complete its natural life cycle even though it requires more time and more effort to harvest the silk fibers."

Nodding earnestly, Shelby said, "That's right. Did you know that over two thousand silkworms have to die to make one pound of silk?" She swept the table with a resolute gaze. "Feel free to laugh, I'm used to it. Besides being die-hard romantics, Matthew and I are also die-hard environmentalists, and we want our wedding to be as green as possible. Don't panic," she added, raising a hand to forestall her mother's protest. "Nothing heavy-handed, I promise; no speeches, no lectures. We did our research and I know our wedding can be both beautiful *and* green. It's really just a matter of making choices."

"What sort of choices?" inquired her mother, clearly wary.

"Well, for starters we want to use only local foods and wines, and for favors we'll come up with something organic, like maybe little trees, instead of monogrammed shot glasses or coasters. It will be done very elegantly." She grinned and squeezed her mother's shoulder. "You'll see."

Helen sighed. "Is this another first for Seasons?"

Head tilted to one side, Jenna smoothed the notebook page on which she had yet to write a single word. "We have had brides who insisted on biodegradable invitations or who wanted rose petals tossed instead of confetti, but an entire green wedding? That's a first."

Helen leaned forward, her eyes narrowing. "Will that present a problem? Especially given the time constraints."

"Not at all," Sophie assured her. "It sounds like Shelby has already done her homework; we'll do ours and I guarantee the end result will be everything you've ever dreamed it would be."

"I'm so glad you'll be handling the plans," declared Shelby. "I'll be away for most of July and I'll feel a whole lot better knowing you're running things here. Don't get me wrong," she added hastily. "I like working with all of you, but it just seems so obvious that Sophie . . . gets me."

"I'm sure she does," said Jenna. "But yours isn't the only event we're currently working on, or even the only wedding, for that matter, and we do things a certain way here at Seasons. We have our own system."

"A routine," said Jill.

"What does that mean?" Shelby asked.

"Simply that we work as a team. There are some jobs Jill and I are better at and others that fall to Sophie."

Jill elaborated. "Jenna and I will work directly with the designs in the books and put together an overall plan for your wedding . . . flowers, music, menu, everything. Subject to your approval, of course."

"But my theme isn't in your books."

"True. Which is why we'll have to take time to do some research of our own and get up to speed before we can present you with a detailed proposal."

"But Sophie is already up to speed," Shelby pointed out.

"Yes, but the way we work is that Jill and I deal directly with clients, cake tastings, dress fittings, all of that, and Sophie basically holds everything together behind the scenes," explained Jenna. "If we need someone to check on something—"

"Or find something," Jill interjected.

"Or make sure something gets where it absolutely has to be, Sophie's right on it."

"We literally couldn't survive without our Sophie."

Well, *they* might, thought Sophie, but she wouldn't place bets on the business.

Seeing Shelby's concern, Sophie smiled reassuringly. "Don't worry. I'll pass whatever ideas I have on to Jenna and Jill, and you can call me anytime you have questions or want to run something by me."

"I guess that will work," Shelby returned without enthusiasm.

Jenna smoothed the sleeve of her blouse and smiled. "It does work. Trust me; you don't get to be one of the most successful event planners in New England without teamwork. Ask any of the vendors we work with and they'll tell you, we get the job done in style." She broke into a smile. "There's even this one DJ, very hot commodity, who refers to us as 'The Divas and the Drone.' You know, like we're a rock group or something."

Shelby glanced across the table at Sophie, her eyes brimming with laughter. "Go, team," she murmured.

It had been three days since he made his deal with the devil. And make no mistake, that's what it was, even if it was hard to reconcile the image of Satan with his recollection of the way Sophia

Bennett smiled, or the light that danced in her soft green eyes when she did.

Owen paused midswing with the golf club extended behind his right hip and frowned at the imaginary golf ball on the carpet at his feet. Soft green. Was that even a color? Yes, he decided, and released his swing, managing to barely miss a nearby porcelain lamp; it was almost as if the unseen hand of his guardian angel intervened at the last second to nudge the lamp a few centimeters to safety.

Strangely, although he was unable to focus his mind on the work he was being paid a ridiculous amount to do, he could recall the precise shade of the intriguing little wedding planner's eyes. They weren't pale or light or grayish or bluish green; they were soft green, a calm, true green that made him think of fields of grass that went on forever, the kind of field where you could stretch out and rest your head without a care in the world, the kind of field that he was convinced didn't really exist.

Three days.

And for those three days he'd volleyed between wondering when he would hear from her again and asking himself the same existentialist question over and over. *Have you lost your fucking mind?* The answer varied with his mood.

On the one hand, there was nothing he wanted less than to allow a parade of complete strangers to traipse through the house, fussing and sprucing and doing God knows what in preparation for an onslaught of even more strangers, the main difference as far as he was concerned being that the second horde would be dressed formally and standing around sipping champagne and nibbling rabbit food off silver serving trays.

On the other hand, and at the same time, there was nothing he wanted more than to figure out who—or what—was sharing his house. He refused to use the word *haunting* because of the ghostly connotations, though he supposed that was splitting hairs once you acknowledged there was something there you couldn't see or touch or smell. Which raised another question he couldn't answer and couldn't stop asking: Was it Allie's spirit that was keeping him company? Was it possible he'd hit pay dirt when he followed through on the impulse to buy this particular house—the Princess House—in hopes of feeling closer to her and recapturing whatever scraps he could of all that he'd lost when he lost his only child?

The only thing he knew for certain was that he wasn't alone there. Things moved around, things went missing, windows and doors slammed in the middle of the night. Some of it he could chalk up to his own distractedness, but not all. The other night he climbed into bed and found a wet towel waiting for him. He might be preoccupied enough to misplace a beer, but why the hell would he bury a wet towel beneath the bedcovers when he could simply drop it on the floor as he usually did? It made no sense to him and he was becoming increasingly desperate to have it make sense. The fact that he didn't believe in ghosts only complicated the situation. He had no answers, and neither did Wikipedia or any of the other online sites he tried. He hadn't told anyone else about it for the simple reason that he was used to solving his own problems and he liked it that way.

He sure as hell hadn't gone looking for Sophia Bennett. She'd shown up on his doorstep uninvited and unwanted, but he'd known even before she set foot inside the house that whatever *it* was that was hanging around, she saw or felt or sensed it too. It was the only reason he'd let her in. There had been others in the house, of course: his agent, his lawyer, the guy who cut the lawn, the merry maids who came around once a week to pick up after him. And then there were the assorted delivery people who came bearing groceries or pizza or beer. But as far as he could tell, not one of them had ever tuned into anything out of the ordinary. Sophia Bennett had. And then she mentioned the Princess House, invoking all kinds of memories and leaving him no choice but to put aside his dislike of wedding foolery and his need to be left alone and agree to a wedding on his turf.

He'd assumed she would begin pestering him right away. He expected her to show up and be underfoot on a regular basis, which is just exactly where he wanted her and needed her to be if she was going to be any help to him at all. He wasn't sure yet how up front he would be about the sort of help he needed from her; he'd just take it one step at a time and see how it played out. Step one was getting her back there so he could keep her under surveillance.

When the first day passed with no contact, he wondered if she'd called while he was out. He tried to remember if he'd given her his cell number. Probably not; he hated giving it out because he hated getting calls when he was away from home even more than he hated getting them when he was home. Then he wondered if maybe he'd been so absorbed in work, he hadn't heard the phone ringing. Seemed unlikely, but just the same he went out and bought an answering machine. He checked regularly, some might say compulsively, for messages. Another day passed, and another. He started to worry that his complete ignorance of weddings had caused him to miscalculate how much advance preparation a wedding planner actually did. For all he knew, he might not hear from her again for weeks. And he'd go crazy if he had to sit around spinning his wheels, chasing down AWOL beers, and sleeping with wet towels for weeks.

When on the fourth day he happened to look out the front window and see her black SUV coming down the drive, it was like the answer to a prayer. Except that he didn't pray. Not anymore.

The sense of relief was so strong he didn't even pause long enough to calculate whether he ought to play it cool by waiting until she rang the bell. Barefoot, dressed in faded black jeans and an old T-shirt, he headed outside to greet her. It didn't occur to him that she might not be alone until the passenger doors started to pop open. Ignoring them, he circled to the driver's door just as a leggy blonde in a short skirt slid from behind the wheel.

"Who are you?" he asked, annoyed that she wasn't Sophie. Sophie. She'd told him that's what everyone called her, but it was the first time he'd thought of her not as Sophia Bennett, but as *Sophie*.

The woman wasted a thousand-watt smile on him. "I'm Jenna . . . "

"And I'm Jill."

Owen swung his gaze from the driver to the woman who slipped from the backseat and then back again.

"You two are . . ."

"Twins," the women confirmed, nodding in unison. "And obviously we're from Seasons."

They each waved an arm toward the car door, like a pair of game-show models revealing what was behind curtain number two. Written on the door, in script and pearlized silver paint, were SEASONS and a telephone number. It was all very classy and understated, which told him the business was successful enough that it didn't need a heavy hand with promotion and could send employees tooling around in luxury SUVs. Company cars. That explained why he'd mistaken it for Sophie's.

"And you must be Owen Winters," the driver twin went on, extending her right hand for him to shake. "I'm so happy to meet you and I'm really looking forward to getting to know you in the coming weeks. I work hard, but my motto is that you should always make time to make new friends. I can't tell you how thrilled all of us at Seasons are—"

"Thrilled and privileged," interjected Passenger Twin.

"—to be planning the first wedding ever held here at Ange de la Mer. Now come over here and let me introduce you to the bride, and her mother."

Owen's back teeth had begun to ache even before Helen Archer told him she had some ideas to make the landscaping along the front drive absolutely divine and asked if he would mind if they dug a small pond somewhere on the back lawn.

"Mom, I don't think it will be necessary to actually dig a pond," said the young woman beside her. "I talked it over with Sophie and she has a couple of ideas for creating the illusion of a pond."

"Illusion," drawled her mother, shaking her head. "It already sounds tacky."

"It won't be. It's basically a shallow pool with plants and lighting that make it look real. Sophie wouldn't suggest anything tacky."

For the first time he glanced at the youngest of the four women. Sophie mentioned that she'd just graduated from college. Which he knew would make her about twenty-one. Twenty-one. It was a great age. So full of . . . possibilities. He looked at her for a few seconds, thinking of someone else, and felt his throat tighten.

When she'd finished reassuring her mother, the young woman turned to him. "I'm Shelby Archer, Mr. Winters . . . the bride who started all this trouble for you. I really hope we're not inconveniencing you too much."

He liked the steady way she looked him in the eye even as he scowled at her; he'd had men in his command who couldn't do it so calmly.

"Why are you here?" he asked, wary.

"For the grand tour, of course," said Helen Archer.

"We really can't go any further with our plans until we see exactly what we have to work with in terms of layout," said one of the twins. He'd already lost track of which one was which.

"And also any special features the property has," added the other. "Is there a fountain by any chance? Please say there's a fountain . . . even a little one."

"Let me get this straight," he said. "You want to know where the johns are and if there's a fountain and so you just show up here unannounced?"

"Not unannounced. I left messages . . . the last one telling you I would assume it was all right to stop by this morning if I didn't hear otherwise. I'd have preferred a set appointment, but I also remembered that Sophie had better luck stopping by than she did calling."

"I'm glad you brought that up. Where is Sophie?" His annoyance with them for being there expanded to include Sophie for *not* being there.

"She's working," replied a twin.

"Back at the office," explained the other. "She's swamped with orders and paperwork—you know how June is—so she couldn't join us."

"But not to worry: we know you have your own concerns and Sophie's filled us in on all that. That's her thing, remembering picayune little details. Trust me, it's not a problem."

"For you maybe. The fact that you're standing here and she's not is a big problem for me."

"I don't understand."

"Then I'll spell it out. I never wanted a wedding here . . . no offense," he added with a quick glance at the bride.

"None taken. I completely understand why you would turn down our request . . . I'm thrilled that you didn't, but I understand."

"It was Sophie who changed my mind and it's Sophie I assumed I would be dealing with going forward."

"That's a completely understandable mistake," declared twin one, wasting another of those high-wattage smiles on him.

"Totally," agreed Twin Two.

"Sophie was the first one to contact you and it makes perfect sense that you would assume she would be the one to take the lead."

"But she won't be?" he asked

It was Shelby who answered. "No. She won't. I made the same mistake you did. I assumed I'd be working directly with Sophie since she's so obviously the best person for the job. I mean, she got the whole *Princess House* thing right away and then she was the one who convinced you to say yes."

"But as we explained to Shelby," said a twin, her smile becoming strained around the edges, "at Seasons we have our own system for planning an event. We work as a team."

"That's true," Shelby confirmed. "There's even a team name . . . what was it? Oh, right, the Divas and the Drone."

A look passed between the young bride and Owen.

The twins looked uncomfortable.

"That's just a joke," said one of them.

"Well, this isn't," Owen countered. "I expected to work with Sophie and that's what I intend to do."

"Oh my," murmured Helen.

Shelby bit the corner of her lip and Owen suspected it was to keep from grinning.

Both twins were suddenly clutching cell phones.

"Why don't I just call Sophie and see if we can't work this out?" suggested one.

"Good idea," he said, making himself comfortable on the low wall that ran along the front flower beds. It was as clear a signal as he could think of that he wouldn't be inviting them in for tea. "Just remember: no Sophie, no deal."

Five

Sophie was elated. And apprehensive. Cautiously optimistic and just a tiny bit worried. Maybe a tiny bit more than a tiny bit.

She felt the way she imagined Cinderella would have if there had been no fairy godmother to work her magic on the mice and the pumpkin and the spiderwebs. If, say, she were to have been suddenly plucked from the hearth midsweep and sent off to the ball "as is," barefoot and in tatters, no push-up bra, no breath mints, no glass slippers. Surely Cinderella would have had mixed feelings about what lay ahead. And so did Sophie.

On the one hand, how often does a plain Jane get the chance to go to the ball? On the other, if she was going to fail miserably, better to do so in the privacy of her own servants' hovel rather than before the royal court, to be immortalized in the society pages for all to see, thus providing her glamorous and ambitious stepsisters and stepmother with a reason to sigh and exchange long-suffering glances and ask one another whose bright idea it had been to let her out of the kitchen in the first place.

Once a drone . . .

One minute Sophie was happily, well, more or less, toiling away at her hearth . . . er, in her office, searching for a linen supplier who could handle a rush order for two dozen round translucent silver table covers to replace the two dozen square covers that had been delivered by mistake for a twenty-fifth wedding anniversary celebration only two days away, and the next minute she was on the receiving end of an emergency phone call from the Js. By the time the short, tense call ended, they'd been relegated to the backseat in terms of planning for the lavish, one-of-a-kind wedding to be held at Ange de la Mer in a little over six weeks' time and Sophie was the one in charge.

Holy shit, holy shit, holy shit were the words that kept running through her mind.

Needless to say, the Js were not happy to be usurped in their starring roles in such a high-profile project. That sort of thing just didn't happen at Seasons. But neither they nor Sophie had any choice in the matter. Owen Winters made that as clear as the expensive champagne they kept on hand for toasting new clients. Since they were already on the premises, he finally permitted them to go ahead with their walk-through of the house and grounds, but only after it was understood by all concerned that henceforth he would deal only with Sophie. The twins went down swinging, but to Sophie's amazement, their tag-team charm and talk of teamwork failed to put even a tiny ding in his resolve. Apparently there was just no arguing with the prince once he got something in his shaggy, stubbly-jawed head, and the image of the Js giving it their all and striking out brought Sophie a small, wicked smile as she hung up the phone.

She couldn't help it. Sweaty palms and trepidations aside, this was the most exciting thing that had happened to her in . . . maybe ever. Certainly the most exciting thing that was work-related. It was sort of like a backhanded promotion, albeit one she would never have sought, or expected. A woman had to know her limitations and Sophie knew hers. It was still thrilling and she only wished she had someone to call and share the news with. The one other person who was unreservedly thrilled to have Sophie take charge already knew. This is what Shelby Archer had wanted and lobbied for all along and Sophie was determined not to let her down.

For the next few days she went all out practically around the clock to keep up with her usual workload while pulling together her vision of a *Midsummer Night's Dream* wedding. As soon as she had the essentials in place, she arranged another meeting, which both Jill and Jenna were suddenly too busy to attend. Undaunted, she presented her ideas to Shelby and her fiancé using color charts and fabric swatches and sample sketches of specific areas within the enchanted forest that she proposed creating on the grounds of the estate. One sketch showed the illusion pond surrounded by petal-strewn paths leading to private nooks with cushioned benches and with a full-service bar nestled beneath a grape arbor at one end; another was of a dance floor illuminated by starlight—God willing—and white linen lanterns hung on brass shepherds' hooks. The overall mood was lush and elegant, but still natural and whimsical enough to suit the bride. Helen Archer was at the meeting as well, and before Sophie was halfway through her presentation, she could tell that the mother of the bride was now squarely in her corner, happy—not to mention relieved—to have found someone who understood what she considered her daughter's quirky notions and who promised to deliver on them without making her a laughingstock in front of her friends.

As the meeting was ending, Shelby brought up the subject of her wedding dress, specifically the trouble she was having in finding what she wanted.

"All I have to do is close my eyes and I can see my dress," she told Sophie. "It's simple, but not boring. It's light and airy . . . the kind of dress that makes you feel like dancing all night. And it's sparkly, but not weighed down with tons of crystals and beads. The kind of sparkle I imagine is more subtle . . . like fireflies on a summer night . . ."

"Like fairy wings," Sophie interjected softly.

Shelby nodded excitedly. "Yes. Yes, that's it exactly." She sighed. "I get it, and you get it, but I must not do a very good job of describing it to the saleswomen at any of the dozen shops Mom and I have been to. Either that or it doesn't exist."

"We ran out of local bridal salons last week," Helen explained. "And I think we must have hit every one in Boston yesterday . . . in fact, my poor feet are sure of it. I have to say that at this point I concur with whoever said that these hemp gowns are all dreadful."

"Mom," Shelby said.

Helen shushed her. "I'm not suggesting we give up . . . just that perhaps you should broaden your parameters a bit. What do you think, Matthew?"

At the first hint of mother–daughter tension, Matthew, a quiet, lanky young man with sandy hair and honest eyes, had become instantly fascinated with the photographs on the wall. Smart kid, Sophie thought, but Helen wasn't having it.

"Matthew, you don't think there's anything wrong with being open-minded about these things, do you?"

"I think . . ." His naturally slow drawl became slower as he searched for a way to avoid the trap. "I think Shelby will look beautiful in whatever she decides to wear . . . just like she always does. And I think that if you all are going to talk dresses, maybe I ought to go get the car. I know your feet got a real workout yesterday," he said, standing and aiming a solicitous smile at his future mother-in-law. "This way I can save you a few steps. And I can get the a/c cranked; I know how you hate having the windows open and the fresh air blowing your hair around."

"That would be lovely," Helen agreed, either oblivious to the fact that she'd been outplayed or enjoying it.

"Suck-up," Shelby mouthed as she caught Matthew's eye on his way out.

And then they did what Sophie had observed other engaged couples do, lucky couples: they exchanged what she thought of as "that smile," the one that only has room for two.

With Matthew gone, the talk returned to wedding gowns. Not only had none of those she'd tried on come close to Shelby's vision, but the message at every bridal shop had been the same: the designers they worked with required a minimum of six months for custom designs. Wheels were starting to turn inside Sophie's head even as she urged Shelby and Helen not to become discouraged.

"Shopping for the perfect dress is supposed to be fun," she reminded them.

"It has been fun, sort of." Shelby slanted a sheepish look at her mother. "What can I say? I'm not really the shop-till-you-drop type. And I'm getting worried about the time crunch."

"There is that," agreed Sophie. "I know of a couple of small salons off the beaten path where you might have better luck. Here, let me write down the names and addresses for you."

Shelby reached for the piece of paper Sophie slid across the table to her. "Thanks, Sophie."

"If you do find one—or more—dresses that you like and you want another opinion, you have my cell number."

"I'd love your opinion, but I know you've already taken on so much extra work for us. I hate to bother you."

"It's what I'm here for . . . and I can always squeeze in a quick fashion show. Call me. I mean it."

"I will . . . *if* I ever find something worth showing you."

"And if you don't," Sophie said, "if it turns out the dress of your dreams really doesn't exist, well, I just might have a solution. I'll check into it; you keep shopping. And we'll talk."

Their enthusiasm, as well as their confidence in her, was contagious. Sophie had gone into the meeting apprehensive and sleep-deprived, but she left feeling energized and raring to go. She didn't care what it took; Shelby was going to have the wedding of her dreams. If the diva division of the Seasons team chose to remain in a snit and provide only minimal help along the way . . . well, so be it. She'd just have to manage without them. And why not? She had no shortage of her own creative ideas and it was exhilarating to finally be free to present them to the client as a total package rather than trying to sneak one in here and there. As for the business side of things . . . who had more experience than she did at managing details and putting out fires? She'd proven she could coordinate schedules and oversee expenses and she had a good rapport with both outside vendors and the in-house staff. In fact, the more she thought about it, the more she thought it just might be a blessing in disguise if the Js sat this one out.

And then there was Owen Winters. A challenge of a different sort altogether.

The man was ornery and stubborn and clearly used to getting his own way, and yet Sophie had to admit that something inside her perked up at the thought of seeing him. It was funny how things worked out. She'd driven away from their first meeting wondering if their paths would cross again; now it looked like they would be crossing on a regular basis . . . and at his insistence no less. Something that continued to baffle her as much as it did the Js.

Baffling or not, it had felt good to be singled out by him that way, like being moved up to the head of the class and given a gold star while all the other kids looked on, wishing, for once, that they were her. She wasn't naive enough to think this meant only smooth

sailing going forward. In fact she was braced for exactly the opposite, for the possibility that Winters had picked her because he
thought he could ride herd over her more easily than he could the
*J*s. Whatever his motive, he added another whole dimension of
anticipation and excitement to what lay ahead.

Excitement of a professional nature. She certainly didn't expect anything to come of it on a personal level. She was far too
self-aware and realistic to get swept up in impossible flights of
fancy, and that's exactly what it would be to imagine anything
happening between her and the brooding Mr. Winters. Not that
she was an expert on men or relationships. The kindest way to
describe her romance résumé was to say it was flimsy, consisting
of lots of forgettable evenings and exactly one serious long-term
affair that she had wholeheartedly believed would lead to white
lace and promises of forever, and instead had ended in heart-
break and public humiliation. For her. But while she was no expert, she was an aficionado of both men and all things romantic,
as well as a dedicated observer, on the job and off, and what
she'd observed was that successful, über-wealthy men sexy
enough to walk on water and blessed with a dark and enticing
aura of mystery are invariably attracted to a certain type of
woman. And she wasn't it.

The second time she made her way to Owen Winters's doorstep
she went armed with assorted measuring tools, a notebook, and
her camera. She planned to sketch the layout of the house and
property and take measurements she would need when she met
with landscape and lighting designers and with reps from the
rental firms that supplied everything from tents luxurious enough
to make royalty feel at home to floating dance floors to—should it
come to it—the finest in portable powder rooms. Not to be confused with the familiar blue boxes found at rock festivals and
county fairs. She was talking air-conditioned minitrailers complete

with porcelain fixtures, marble countertops, and hot and cold running water.

At least this time she didn't have to bang on the door to get his attention, which was a good thing since she needed both hands to hold the case of beer she'd also brought with her. She'd called ahead to say she was finishing up at the office and would be there by late morning, but he appeared so quickly after she used her elbow to ring the doorbell that if she didn't know better she'd think he'd been watching for her.

She smiled as the door opened.

"Good morning. It's nice to see you again, Mr. Winters."

The greeting was out before she realized it was a lie. *Nice* didn't come close to describing what she felt standing face-to-face with him after rehearsing the moment over and over in her mind during the ride to his house. *Startled* was more like it, and a little lightheaded. The unexpected heat and rush of her response to him threw her. And for absolutely no good reason, because he looked pretty much as he had the first time she saw him—bare feet, ancient jeans, and a black T-shirt with that trademark fresh-from-the-ragbag look. But his effect on her senses was magnified a dozen times. Maybe it was because she was less preoccupied with other matters and free to focus on subtleties. All she knew was that his jaw looked squarer than she remembered, his cheekbones more chiseled, his mouth more distracting.

"Owen," he said.

She stared blankly at him.

"I have a feeling we'll be seeing too much of each other for formalities," he added.

"Oh. Yes . . . agreed. Please, call me Sophie."

"What's this?" he asked, eyeing the case of beer topped with a big red bow.

"An assortment of New England's finest microbrews . . . hand-picked by yours truly, who doesn't know diddly from squat when it comes to beer, so I hope they pass muster. The standard Seasons' thank-you is a bottle of Cristal, but I thought you might prefer your beverages a little less formal too."

"You thought right." He seemed about to smile, but stopped short of it. "Though you should be warned that gifts of any kind might be premature. I'm still not thrilled with this whole wedding thing, and I've been told I can be difficult to get along with under the best of circumstances."

"I'll consider myself warned. Maybe instead of a gift we could consider it a bribe . . . and it might already be working. You almost smiled."

"Don't get your hopes up." He injected a note of gruffness into his already deep voice, but she noticed that hint of a crooked smile lingered a split second longer this time. "Thanks for the beer. Let me grab it from you."

Stepping outside, he took the case of beer and hoisted it onto his shoulder as effortlessly as he would a box of cotton candy, and then extended his free hand in a silent invitation for her to precede him back inside. Sophie took a step in that direction, but before her foot landed on the threshold, the door slammed shut in her face with the same sudden ferocity it had swung open the last time she was there. A full second later she heard the lock click.

She glanced over her shoulder to see Owen glaring at the door. "Damn," he said.

Curious, she tipped her head toward the house. "Is there someone . . ."

He shook his head. "Just the wind."

"The wind blew the door shut *and* locked it?"

He shrugged the shoulder not weighed down with beer. "Old houses can be quirky. C'mon," he said as she wondered how those quirks might impact her work. "The back door should be open. If not, I'll give you a leg up to the kitchen window."

All thoughts of potential quirk complications shot to the back burner.

"A leg up . . . me?" She hurried after him, not liking the sound of that. "Now it's you who should be warned: I'm not very good at things like that."

"Like what?"

"You know, athletic things. Like climbing in windows."

"There won't be any climbing," he tossed over his shoulder. "Just lifting. And I'll be doing that. All you'll have to do is relax and enjoy the ride."

Yeah, right, Sophie thought. Like that would ever happen. She was already panicking just thinking about where he might have to put his hands to lift her high enough to climb in a window. Thank God for Spanx. But what about her thighs? What if he touched her thighs and thought they were too . . . squishy? At least she was wearing slacks and wouldn't have to wrestle with a skirt. Assuming he could lift her in the first place. If only she'd lost those ten pounds she'd bonded with over pineapple pizza and pints of Chunky Monkey ice cream, she wouldn't have to worry about his dropping her or throwing out his back. How embarrassing would that be? Talk about getting off to a humiliating start. The poor man already favored one leg when he walked; what if trying to get her off the ground aggravated the problem? Damn that stupid front door.

Sophie was literally dragging her feet as he led her across the patio and up a few shallow stone steps to the back door, which opened into the room where they'd sat last time. He tried turning the handle as she held her breath. His expression grim, he glanced over his shoulder at her and shook his head. Altogether there were four sets of French doors leading into the long room; the fact that he didn't bother to try any of the others told her he already knew they were locked. That didn't stop Sophie from trying them her-self. When she finished, she turned to find he'd put down the case of beer and was staring up at the house with a look that could only be described as perplexed.

"What are you thinking?" she asked.

Immediately his expression went blank. He looked at her and shrugged. "I'm thinking that you're going for a ride."

Again he loped off, leaving her to trail behind. His longer legs and her lack of enthusiasm combined to give him a good head start, and by the time she caught up, he was staring up at what she deduced was the kitchen window. He no longer looked perplexed, only purposeful, his dark eyes narrowed in assessment, his mouth edged with determination.

"Okay, here's what we're going to do."

"Don't say 'we,'" she protested, doing her best to sound pleas-ant, but firm. "Because there is no 'we' here. I wasn't kidding when I said I'm not good at stuff like this."

"Don't sell yourself short."

"Trust me, I'm not. I'm not being modest. Or coy. I know my-self. I know my strengths . . . and there are plenty of them. Well, maybe not plenty, but enough. If you need someone to oversee the details of a Jewish wedding ceremony, or Hindu, or Zulu, and to be standing by with her homemade Disaster Prevention kit in case at the last minute a bridesmaid's hem needs fixing or the best man needs a hangover remedy, and then to make sure the gifts end up in the right cars at the end of the day, I'm right on it. But being hoisted off the ground and climbing in windows? Not my thing."

"How do you know?"

"I just do." She waved her hand in his direction. "Look, you're obviously in great shape and can probably lift a refrigerator with one hand and do a gazillion push-ups. My hat's off to you. Really. But I know me, and I know that people like you don't know anything about people like me and what we can and can't do and just because you insist that anyone with half a brain can take an intermediate spin class without hurting herself doesn't make it true."

As she gathered herself with a deep breath, he raised one dark brow. "Issues?"

"Maybe," she allowed, shrugging. "I guess you could say that when it comes to fitness I'm the thorn in a family of roses . . . when it comes to a lot of things actually. But at the moment we're talking about fitness, so, yeah. Issues."

"That's tough."

Self-conscious, she brushed off his seeming concern. "Don't worry about it. I shouldn't have even mentioned it; it just sort of popped out when I was trying to make you understand why I can't do this."

He shook his head. "No. I didn't mean that's tough as in poor you. I meant that's tough, but you'll just have to suck it up."

"Suck it up?"

"Yeah. You could say that's the Winters family motto."

"How . . . inspiring."

"Damn straight. The first time I remember hearing my father say it I was five and didn't want to sit next to the Alligator Man in the back of the truck even though it was the only seat left and we were already two hours late setting up in Albuquerque."

"Issues?" she ventured because she really wasn't sure what else to say. Alligator Man? Albuquerque?

"Could be," he allowed, his tone indifferent. "I heard it hundreds of times afterward and I hated it each and every time. But it turns out it's not a bad motto, not to mention being the only thing the old man ever gave me that was worth a damn. I added the second half myself somewhere along the way: get it done. Suck it up and get it done. You'd be surprised how many problems can be solved using that approach. Such as being locked out of your house," he added. "So let's suck it up and get it done, shall we?" He backed up a few steps. "I'm going to stand here and—"

"And I'm going to call a locksmith," she interrupted, fishing her phone from her tote bag.

"Don't be ridiculous."

"I'm not. I'm acting on my own personal motto, which is 'when in doubt, call a professional.' "

"I am a professional," he shot back, his tone hard and dry.

Sophie's brows lifted. "Oh, really? In between your military career and your writing career you found time to become a locksmith?"

"Don't be naive. Locksmiths aren't the only ones who know how to get in—and out of—places without a key."

She held the phone without dialing, mulling over what that might mean.

"Think about it, Sophie," he urged, further distracting her by saying her name in that quiet, slightly rough way he had. "We could wait hours for a locksmith to show up. I have work to do and so do you. My way will have us inside and toasting our success with a cold beer in less than five minutes."

She couldn't argue with that . . . the work part, not the beer part. She had a couple of hours of work to do there and piles more waiting on her desk back at the office.

She gazed up at the window that was a lot of feet off the ground.

"Couldn't you be the one to climb in?" she asked.

"Not unless you can hoist me off the ground and onto your shoulders. Even if I could still jump that high, there's nothing up there for me to grab hold of."

Sophie was curious about his use of the word *still* and the telltale tensing of his jaw, but she resisted asking.

"What if you stood on something?" she asked.

"Such as?"

Hopeful, she looked around for a birdbath or wheelbarrow or stray lawn chair. Who doesn't have an old lawn chair hanging around? There was nothing in sight but a half-dozen empty and forlorn-looking majolica pots lined up at the patio's edge.

"Don't you have a ladder?"

"There might be one in the basement. I never looked."

She gazed up at the window and swore it was at least a foot higher than last time she looked. "Maybe I should just come back another day."

"And leave me stranded here alone?" he shot back. "Way to build a healthy working relationship."

Sophie sighed. "Oh, all right. It's your broken back I'm thinking of. If you're willing, so am I. Just tell me what you want me to do."

He ran through it step-by-step. It sounded impossible, but Sophie was slightly relieved to note that if things went according to plan, there would be no actual hand-on-thigh contact.

"Oh, one last thing." He pulled a knife from his jeans pocket and flipped it open with disquieting proficiency. "You won't be able to raise the screen because it latches on the inside, so you'll have to cut it in order to climb through."

He flipped the knife shut and then showed her how to open it using the small hidden pressure point on the side of the handle. Actually he showed her three times. She refrained from saying so and giving him another excuse to invoke his family motto, but the truth is she wasn't very good with knives either. Or with weapons of any kind, for that matter.

"All set?" he asked after she'd practiced a few times, but not as many times as she would have liked.

Sighing, she tucked the knife into her Spanx for safekeeping. *Suck it up and get it done.*

"No," she said. "But let's do it anyway."

Once they started, he talked her through it with more patience than she'd have credited him with. Sophie expected to be nervous and she was. The surprise was that she expected to be very nervous—hands-shaking, knees-knocking nervous—and after the first minute or so she wasn't. It was as if Owen's calm certitude radiated outward, like a force field of confidence strong enough to support her too.

He hunkered down and didn't flinch even a little as she climbed onto his shoulders, using the house to support herself as she slowly went from squatting to standing. There was only one slightly awkward, slightly remarkable moment when he cupped her butt with both hands to steady her as she found her balance. As soon as he sensed her control, he shifted his hands lower. Sophie was still afraid she was going to do something to screw it up, but she no longer had any fear of falling. She just knew with everything in her that Owen wouldn't let that happen. He felt like a rock beneath her and his grip on her ankles was absolute. Once her footing was secure, he stood, slowly, letting her continue to brace herself with both palms against the house, moving them higher a few inches at a time until she was able to reach the window with ease.

Still taking it slow, she pulled out the knife and used it to slice through the screen, following Owen's instructions so that the flap she created opened down and out of her way. Finally she listened as he coached her in a sort of sideways tumble through the window. The maneuver, while not the least bit graceful, was relatively painless.

"You okay?" he called to her as she sat with her butt in the kitchen sink, a silly grin on her face.

"Fine," she called back, feeling more swagger than tension now. She'd done it. And hey, it may not have been as demanding as an hour-long spin class, but it was just as far outside her comfort zone, and a hell of a lot more exciting. And she got to check out Owen's very impressive biceps and shoulder muscles in the process. For which she should probably feel guilty since she hadn't wanted him doing the same to her, but she didn't, not even a little bit. The man's shoulders were well worth a small moral transgression.

"Uh, Sophie?"

"Yeah?"

"About the door . . ."

"On it," she called to him, clambering from the sink. "Grab my bag for me and I'll meet you there."

She unlocked the door and held it open for him as he angled his way inside with the case of beer. He handed her the tote bag in passing.

"Thanks," she said, following him to the kitchen, still on a talky, adrenaline high. "I can't believe we did it. I guess I should say I can't believe *you* did it, since you did most of the work. Not to mention coming up with a plan in the first place. A *great* plan. I expected you to just sort of hoist me up like a sack of potatoes and shove me through the window, but I had a real Mary Lou Retton moment there."

"Who?"

"Mary Lou Retton. Olympic gymnast, gold-medal winner, face on the Wheaties box."

"Oh."

"That was something the way you lifted me onto your shoulders and then stood up. I mean, who can do something like that? Well, obviously you can. But where did you learn how?"

"The Winters Traveling Carnival and Show of Wonders," he replied without breaking stride.

Six

S ophie wasn't sure what she'd expected his answer to be, but that wasn't it.

"A carnival?" she repeated. "Seriously?"

"Seriously."

His earlier reference to the Alligator Man suddenly made more sense. "You said it was called the Winters Traveling Carnival; was it a family business?"

"Family? Not by a long shot," he said, his sneer telling. "My father ran it. He was a magician."

"And you were an acrobat of some kind?"

"No."

"Trapeze artist?"

"I was nothing. But I did dedicate a good chunk of my formative years to hanging around and watching the female acrobats rehearse. I guess I picked up a few moves by osmosis." He swung the beer off his shoulder and placed it on the floor in front of the open refrigerator.

"Wow. A traveling carnival," she mused out loud as he jockeyed bottles to make room for the new arrivals. "That sounds so . . ." *Exciting. Wild. Sexy.* "Interesting."

His response—a cross between a snort and a grunt—discouraged her from asking any of the questions that were bubbling inside.

She refused his offer of a celebratory beer, wanting a clear head for working, but hung around figuring that the kitchen was as good a place as any to start. Flipping open her notebook, she jotted down a few quick impressions. The kitchen was large by any standard, with plenty of open space for maneuvering. It had obviously been designed for entertaining. A plus. Double sinks. Long, deep, L-shaped counters. No center island. She also noted the adjacent breakfast nook with a large round oak table and double doors that opened to a humongous dining room.

She glanced approvingly at the more than adequate overhead lighting, and then winced at the circa twentieth-century appliances. Regardless of the menu choices, a caterer would need to bring supplemental ovens and cooktops. And most likely a generator to power them. The house was lovely and well maintained, but at first glance not much modernizing or remodeling appeared to have been done. The black-and-white tile floor and glass-front cabinets looked to be original. And while they were charming, an electrical system of the same vintage would not be.

After making a rough sketch of the kitchen, she pulled a laser measuring device from her bag.

"Need a hand?" asked Owen, finished stowing the beer.

"Thanks, but I think I've got it. This extremely cool laser tool makes measuring hard-to-reach places a snap."

"Does it really matter how deep the counters are?"

"Not to me personally, but I guarantee it will matter to the caterer who gets the job and has to set up in here. Caterers, tent makers, the guys who handle the parking . . . they're all the same; the first things they want to know are . . . how much space am I working with and how big is the budget? My mission here today is to measure everything that doesn't move."

"I'll keep that in mind should I feel a nap coming on," he said drily. He folded his arms, his expression thoughtful. "You know I hadn't given any thought to parking. How do you plan to handle that many cars?"

"Not by turning your front lawn into a parking lot, I promise. Obviously parking will be off-site and we'll need a small army of valets and some kind of relay system to get it done. On-site we'll need space to set up a valet station and enough room for guests to drive up and get out without causing a bottleneck at the beginning of the drive and tying up traffic all along Bellevue Avenue. Having that long circular drive is going to help a lot."

He looked reluctantly impressed. "I'm beginning to see why people hire wedding planners."

"Exactly. So they don't have to wake up at three A.M. worrying about traffic tie-ups or whether they remembered to tell the videographer to go to the groom's house first and then the bride's. Which reminds me, would it be possible to set aside a place upstairs, maybe a bedroom . . . or two," she added with a beseeching smile, "where the bride and her attendants can get dressed and do their last-minute primping?"

He shrugged, his hips resting against the counter behind him. "Sure, why not? My room is the last one on the left. The others are up for grabs."

"Thank you. While I'm up there I'd like to take some photos of the grounds; it helps to see it from a different perspective."

"Knock yourself out," he said, bringing the beer bottle to his mouth for a long swig. "You know it's funny, that kid . . . the bride . . . Shelby?" Sophie nodded. "She didn't strike me as the primping type . . . just way too damn young to be getting married."

"Trust me; every woman is the primping type on her wedding day. I think it's chemical or chromosomal or something. At any rate, it's inescapable. As for Shelby being young . . ." Her expression grew thoughtful. "Ordinarily I'd agree with you wholeheartedly, and as a general rule I still think that twenty-one or twenty-two is way too young to decide what you want to do for the rest of your life and who you want to do it with. But there's something about Shelby, and Matthew too for that matter, which makes me think it will work. You've heard the term 'old souls'? Well, those two strike me as very old souls."

"I hope you're right," he said, his skepticism obvious.

"I am." The conviction in her tone was heartfelt. "When it comes to romance, I have a sort of sixth sense. Trust me; Shelby and Matthew are in it for the long haul, all the way from clocks and pottery to silver and gold."

"Is that supposed to make some kind of sense?"

"It makes perfect sense," she replied, moving around to get the actual dimensions of the room itself. "Paper is the traditional gift for a first wedding anniversary, but clocks are the modern option. Pottery is for nine years married, either pottery or leather goods. Silver is twenty-five years, of course, and gold is for fifty. Shelby and Matthew are going for gold."

"Let me get this straight: each year is assigned a different gift?"

She paused to write a measurement along the corresponding side of her sketch before she forgot it. "Well, not assigned exactly. It's more of a tradition, along the lines of 'something borrowed, something blue.'"

"And these yearly gifts, you know what all of them are?"

"Pretty much."

"What's the proper gift for a twenty-fourth anniversary?"

"Opals are traditional. Musical instruments are the modern alternative."

"Seventeen years?"

"Furniture across the board."

"Nineteen."

"Aquamarine. Or bronze."

He shook his head. "That's pretty . . . absurd."

"Oh, I beg to differ. I have clearly pushed past the boundaries of the merely absurd." She said it with mock solemnity. "I am a living, breathing font of information on all things romantic. I didn't set out to be; it just sort of happened along the way. I think it might even be an occupational hazard. One day I woke up and realized my brain was cluttered with all kinds of useless trivia on the subject."

He looked amused in spite of himself. "You mean more useless than which gift goes with which year?"

"Pfff," she pronounced with a careless wave of her hand. "That's child's play. I know far more useless stuff than that."

"I know I'm going to be sorry I asked, but . . . such as?"

"Well, did you know that two out of five people marry their first love, or that only one in five men proposes on bended knee, but six percent of them do it over the phone? Or that there are more than nine hundred varieties of red roses?"

"No. And yet—brace yourself because this may come as a shock to someone with your hopelessly romantic sensibilities—somehow I've managed to eke out a life of sorts for myself."

"Only because ignorance is bliss. But now that your romance gene has been awakened, there'll be no going back. You'll find yourself wondering about the record for the most kisses in a movie . . . a hundred and twenty-seven, *Don Juan*, 1927. Or how many calories a kiss burns . . . nine, assuming it's passionate and not some lazy peck on the cheek. Or about the scientific name for the study of kissing . . . philematology."

"You might be right . . . *if* I had a romance gene to be awakened. I don't."

"Oh, you have one all right. Everyone does. It's standard equipment, like your funny bone. And goose bumps. Think about it: a person could live years and years without knowing they have a funny bone until one day they whack their elbow just the right way and it's like a lightbulb coming on. Same thing with goose bumps: years of blissful ignorance and then they take a sudden chill . . . or someone kisses exactly the right spot on the side of their neck, and *bam!* Life is never the same again."

She'd continued to work as they bantered and now, when he didn't respond, her attention instinctively shifted from the wall she was measuring to him. He was watching her; his gaze, intrigued and unwavering, made her feel flustered in a way she was much too old and too smart to let herself be flustered in.

"Tell me," he ventured in a deep, quiet drawl, still watching her in that thoughtful, heavy-lidded way. "This spot on the neck you alluded to . . . the one with such life-altering potential . . . does that knowledge come from personal experience?"

"Not exactly completely from personal experience. But I've heard . . . well, read—" She stopped and shook her head. "What I've experienced personally is irrelevant. I was simply trying to make the point that everyone has a romance gene, no matter how recessive it is or how much baggage it's buried under, and someday, some way, probably when you least expect it, it comes to life and—"

"*Bam.* Life is never the same again." He said it in an unapologetically mocking tone that she chose to ignore.

"Exactly."

He shrugged. "Interesting theory. Unfortunately it doesn't account for the possibility that some romance genes get switched on too soon and burn themselves out."

"That's because it's my theory," retorted Sophie. "And I refuse to give credence to that possibility. It goes against everything I believe in. Doing what I do, seeing what I see every day, I need to believe that when it comes to true love, it's never too late for anyone."

"To each his own." He downed the rest of his beer. "I should get back to work." Leaving the empty bottle on the counter, he started toward the door and then stopped and pulled a paper from his back pocket. "I almost forgot," he said, unfolding it and holding it out to her. "I meant to give this to you as soon as you arrived, but we got sidetracked."

Sophie took the paper and glanced at it, and then looked up at him, puzzled. "What is this? A list of demands?"

He lifted one shoulder in an offhand shrug. "You're welcome to think of it as a list of requests if it makes you feel more comfortable."

"A demand and a request having the same amount of wiggle room?"

"Pretty much."

"Then let's just stick with demands; it's more honest. Let's see. No work-related noise between eight A.M. and two P.M.."

"Those are my prime work hours," he explained.

Sophie nodded. "Also no loud music between eight and two. No rap or whiny-chick rock at any time." Biting back a grin, she glanced up. "Could you please define 'whiny-chick rock'?"

"No. But trust me; I know it when I hear it."

She gave a quick nod. "No unnecessary phone calls. No lengthy voice-mail messages. Weekly schedule of activity—including names and brief background details of anyone working on the property—to be submitted by the preceding Friday, oh-four-hundred hours."

She looked up, eyes wide and innocent. "Eastern Standard Time?"

Owen nodded, his expression inscrutable as he watched her refold the paper.

"You know," she said, "I think I'll just take this with me and go over the rest item by item when I can give it my full attention. If I have any questions, I'll get back to you."

She tossed the list into her tote bag.

"All right. I think you'll find it pretty self-explanatory . . . except maybe for that chick-rock thing. And even that could be negotiated, I suppose. I came up with the list because I wanted to make the process as easy as possible going forward, with no mixed signals. It seemed only fair since I'm the one who insisted on working only with you."

"I see. Well, since you brought it up, I do have a question. Why did you?" When he responded with only a quizzical frown, she elaborated. "Why did you insist on working only with me?"

"Oh. That." Owen ran his hand through his hair, considering his answer. He didn't want to lie to her, but it was too soon for the truth. He had no way of knowing how susceptible to suggestion she was and he didn't want his experiences to influence her.

"I suppose it was a case of the devil you know," he said offhandedly. "Also, it was obvious you were sent here to do the grunt work by getting me to go along with this crazy idea and then once you'd done the heavy lifting the A-team showed up with their matching smiles and matching bullshit, all set to slide into home plate and claim the win. That pissed me off in about a hundred different ways."

She'd been eyeing him with suspicion; now her expression relaxed, the wary glitter fading from her eyes and her mouth softening into something gentle and, from where Owen was standing, distracting.

"I don't think it was as calculated as you make it sound," she said.

"Really?"

Was she too trusting, wondered Owen, or too loyal? He knew something about both trust and loyalty, and as certain as he was that hers were misplaced, his admiration for her ticked up a notch.

"That doesn't mean I don't appreciate your concern," she told him. "It sounds like you wanted me to be put in charge because you thought I'd earned it. That was really sweet of you."

Sweet? No one had ever called him sweet; it was as unexpected and jarring as having a nail dragged along his spine. And as unwelcome.

"Don't get carried away," he warned, irked that something as simple as the slow dawning of her smile could play with his concentration. "It would be a mistake to ascribe altruistic motives to anything I do. I always act to suit my own purpose."

"Is that why you made Shelby's dream come true by agreeing to let her have her wedding here in spite of the fact that you claim to hate weddings?"

"No, it was because her mother's willing to pay through the nose for the privilege. And I don't just *claim* to hate weddings."

"I don't believe you," she declared, her small, knowing smile holding steady. She was like some green sailor, he thought, boldly steering her starry-eyed little boat straight into a gale. "I think you said yes to Shelby for the same reason you went to bat for me: to be nice. It just goes against your Big Bad Wolf image to admit it."

"I am the Big Bad Wolf," he told her. She'd earned that much truth at least.

"Oh yeah? Then explain to me how it could possibly suit your purpose to insist on working with me and only me."

"Easy. I wanted to keep distractions to a bare minimum."

*   *   *

His parting remark stuck in her head, replaying on a loop until she was halfway up the stairs and she hit the stop button to silence it. Her hand caressed the smooth white banister: the very banister she once imagined herself sliding up to all sorts of exciting adventures. Just being there was a childhood dream come true and she wasn't about to let some stupid remark keep her from savoring the moment.

So Winters didn't find her as distracting as Jill and/or Jenna. Hardly a news flash. Neither did any other man she knew. She'd been dealing with that ego-bruising truth most of her life and she'd deal now. Frankly she was more concerned with finding a way to keep herself from being distracted by *him*. She would have to exercise self-control and a perfect opportunity to practice presented itself as she reached the top of the staircase on her way to checking out the second-floor bedrooms. He'd said his room was the last one on the left. She hesitated, looking both ways as if getting ready to cross a busy street, and turned left.

Obviously she needed more practice.

She wouldn't set foot in his room, she promised herself, no matter how oh-so-tempted she was to poke around and maybe shed a little light on the mystery he presented. That would be nosy and unprofessional, not to mention totally humiliating should she get caught. No, she would limit herself to a quick, slightly less nosy, and unprofessional glance from the open doorway. It was the in-plain-sight rule of snooping. Whatever is in plain sight is fair game.

What she saw left the mystery intact. A treadmill, an unmade bed, a Bose stereo, and lopsided piles of CDs on the bedside table. So, he wasn't an iPod man. Interesting. She resisted the urge to check out his taste in music, but as she turned away she noticed something else on the table, something harder to resist. Half hidden behind the CDs was a picture frame. She glanced back toward the stairs, then at the frame, and drew the inevitable conclusion: if the universe hadn't intended for her to see the photo, it would have done a better job of arranging the CDs in front of it. Acting on behalf of the universe, she did a tiptoe sprint across the room and leaned down to see what it was Owen saw last thing at night and first thing in the morning, also known as the slapdash-no-touching rule of snooping.

The frame was simple and expensive looking; the photo it held was a composite of two shots. On the left was a much younger—and happier looking—Owen with a laughing little girl perched atop his shoulders. On the right was the same little girl . . . same wavy blond hair, same blue eyes—Owen's eyes—same sunny, look-out-world-here-I-come smile. But in the second shot the little girl was all grown up. The handwritten inscription across the bottom read: *Loved the view, loved you. Still do! Happy Father's Day, Dad. Allie.* Beside the name was a small open heart with the date.

So. Owen Winters had a daughter. A daughter he hadn't mentioned. Not that he should have necessarily. After all, they weren't friends who'd exchanged life stories, and they hadn't even spent that much time together.

Still.

Something about it didn't feel right. After all, they had been talking about a young girl getting married, and judging by the dated photo he kept by his bed, she'd guess that his daughter, Allie, was about the same age as Shelby. Wouldn't it have been the most natural thing in the world for a father to say "there's no way in hell I'd want my twenty-two-year-old daughter getting married."

It would be, she decided, hurrying from the room before her luck ran out, not at all happy with the fact that she'd risked her pride only to raise more questions than she answered.

It took real self-control to turn her full attention to work. Choosing the right rooms for Shelby and her attendants provided the perfect excuse for her to explore all seven remaining bedrooms. It was like wandering through the pages of *Town & Country* magazine. In each room, the silk wall coverings, bed linens, and window dressings were varying shades of a single color . . . rich colors like lavender and sage and periwinkle. The furnishings were old and solid, befitting one of Newport's grand summer "cottages," and there were touches of whimsy that convinced Sophie the woman who'd lived there had been blessed with both style and wit.

After playing Goldilocks and testing a series of overstuffed chaises and padded vanity benches, she finally settled on the two rooms opposite the stairs; the rooms shared a large bath and a panoramic view of the Atlantic. From the window of one of the rooms, the one she already thought of as the "Old Gold Room," she snapped a dozen or so photos of the grounds below and then couldn't help standing there for several moments watching sailboats drift on the open waters to the east and waves roll to shore on the crowded public beach in the distance. She would have lingered longer, lulled by the multimillion-dollar view, but she was startled by a sudden drop in the temperature of the air around her.

She turned from the window, instinctively folding her arms and rubbing her upper arms with her hands to warm up as she looked around to see if she was standing near an air-conditioning vent. She wasn't, but the change in temperature was that dramatic. The wind couldn't be blamed this time since there wasn't even enough of a breeze to stir the lightweight curtains. What was it Owen had said? That old houses could be quirky? Count her in the ranks of the true believers. Again she found herself wondering if these various and sundry quirks might interfere with the wedding. And whether she ought to warn Shelby. No, she decided quickly. If she mentioned cold spots and doors with minds of their own, Shelby would be on the lookout for strange occurrences; mix a runaway imagination with normal wedding jitters and anything could happen . . . or seem to. And for all Sophie knew, her own imagination was working overtime here.

But she didn't think so.

There was something different about the room . . . something besides the chill in the air. Something she couldn't put her finger on. Hoping to figure it out, she ignored the part of her that wanted to get the hell out of there and stayed to look around, peeking in the closet, where she found only a row of gold padded hangers, picking up and admiring the enameled hand mirror on the dressing table and putting it back. It was as she turned away that she thought she caught movement from the corner of her eye and she turned back to see the mirror resting about six inches from where she'd just placed it. She would definitely have thought that was her imagination at work but for the fine layer of dust on the table's mirrored top; it clearly showed where the mirror had slid across the surface to its original position. *Cue* Twilight Zone *theme,* she thought as she grasped the glass knobs on the table's drawer and yanked it open in search of wires or magnets or . . . something.

Nothing.

Okay. Her mind was still racing and coming up with nothing helpful when her gaze fell on the chest of drawers across the room and for lack of a better idea she walked over to check inside those drawers as well. Nothing. Nothing. Nothing. She tried to open the fourth drawer but it slid a few inches and then stopped as if stuck. No quitter, Sophie grabbed the front of the drawer with both hands to see if she could rock it loose. Instead the drawer slammed shut with her fingers inside . . . slammed shut so tightly she couldn't yank them free.

She shouted with surprise—and pain—and then clamped her teeth together as tightly as the drawer. What was she thinking? Did she really want Owen to come running upstairs to see what she was screaming about? And then have to explain what she was doing rifling through drawers in one of his guest rooms? Of course, if pressed, she could always blame her lapse in manners on the sudden chill in the room and the moving mirror, thereby confirming that she was a total airhead.

Then again, she might not have a choice. Her fingers were really beginning to hurt and she wasn't making any progress working them free. How the hell could this happen? Having her fingertips amputated would definitely put a crimp in her work performance. Visions of relying on the *J*s to drive her around and take notes for her amplified the tears that were already filling her eyes because of the throbbing pain. She bent her head and rested her forehead on the dresser's edge as if that might help her think.

"Go away," said a woman's voice.

The voice was clear and emphatic and chillingly close to her ear. Sophie jerked her head up and looked first over one shoulder and then the other, but saw no one.

"Go now," the voice said. "You don't belong here."

A couple of pounding heartbeats later, the drawer released her just as suddenly as it had trapped her and Sophie jumped back, cradling her bruised fingers against her chest. Anger and fear were tugging her in different directions; what she saw when she turned around made fear the hands-down winner. And she ran.

Owen heard the shout just as he gave up on skulking around downstairs trying to figure out what Sophie was doing upstairs all that time and headed back to his office.

Skulking; there was no other word for it. As an extraction specialist for a U.S. military dark ops operation, Owen had done more than his share of skulking, but today's undertaking presented a problem no terrorist or kidnapped foreign ambassador or psychopathic drug lord ever faced. There was always a risk of getting caught in the act, lurking in the shadows or crawling around on your belly like a slug, but in the past he'd never cared if he ended up looking foolish in front of anyone else. Or creepy. The past hour hadn't produced a scrap of information of the sort he was hoping for, but it had made one startling fact very clear: he never wanted Sophie Bennett to think he was creepy.

The instant he heard her scream, he turned and hurried back to the front of the house. He reached the bottom of the stairs just as she came barreling down, breathing hard, her eyes wide, her face pale. She landed in his arms and it felt like the most natural thing in the world for him to gather her close to him, stroke the back of her head, and whisper "it's okay, it's okay" against the sweet, fresh scent of her hair.

"Shh. It's okay."

After only a minute her breathing steadied; she lifted her head from his chest and looked up at him. She appeared slightly calmer, but no less alarmed. Mostly he was concerned for her, but a small reptilian part of his brain could focus only on the fact that she didn't pull away, and was pleased.

"Owen, you have to listen to me. Something happened upstairs. I know this is going to sound crazy, but you have to listen because I swear every word is true." She swallowed hard and said, "I think there's a ghost in your house."

He exhaled. "I think we need to talk."

Seven

"Tell me again," he directed. "Everything that happened. Don't leave anything out."

"I told you everything. Twice," Sophie reminded him in an even and much calmer tone than when she'd come running down the stairs a few minutes earlier looking, quite rightly, as if she'd seen a ghost.

"I know, but sometimes during a debriefing a subject spontaneously recalls a detail in a later round of questioning that wasn't included in their first account. Or their second."

She tipped her head to the side and raised her brows quizzically. "Debriefing? I'm being debriefed now?"

"Sorry. It's a military term. Old habits die hard. This isn't an interrogation; I'm just trying to get a handle on what happened up there. Please, start at the beginning and take your time. Tell it any way you want to tell it."

They were sitting side by side at the kitchen table, which was actually located in an alcove off the main kitchen. He'd brought her straight there, took one look at her fingers, which were red and beginning to swell, and went in search of a remedy. He returned with ibuprofen, a bag of ice, a bowl of ice water for her to dangle her fingers in if the cubes were too rough, and the softest towel he could find. His military efficiency didn't surprise her, but his solicitousness did.

"Okay," she said. "The first really odd thing was the mirror moving—"

He broke in. "What about the temperature?"

"Oh. Right. I forgot . . . that came first. I was standing by the window and suddenly it was like someone had switched on a giant air conditioner. It wasn't the wind or an ocean breeze; the drop in temperature was too great for either. And it wasn't my imagination, although to be honest I wasn't one hundred percent sure of that until the rest happened."

"So the mirror was next?"

She nodded. "Once the cold set in, I got this funny feeling, like something in the room was different . . . something besides the cold, I mean."

"What was different?"

"I don't know. Nothing obvious. Nothing visible. It was just a sense I had . . . like a chill running up my spine, but it wasn't a chill exactly. Except for the chill from the cold, of course."

"More like a change in the energy in the room?"

"I guess."

"What happened next?"

"I just hung around for a few minutes. I wandered around the room, looked in the closet . . . and then I picked up the mirror. And when I put it back down, it moved. All by itself. I told you about the marks in the dust?"

"Yes. That's when you decided to examine the dresser."

"Right. I'm not sure why really. I think at that point I was equal parts spooked and curious. A big part of me was thinking I should just get the hell out of there, but I also wanted to see if something else might happen if I hung around. And boy, did it ever," she declared, grimacing as she lifted her fingers from the bowl and looked at them. "That is one strong ghost. Not to mention rude."

"Tell me about the ghost."

She tensed visibly. Without thinking, Owen reached over and stroked her arm. Her skin was warm and smooth, the smoothest thing he'd felt in a long time.

"Maybe I should make you a cup of tea or something," he said, at a loss as to what soothing measures were called for in this situation.

The corners of her mouth immediately lifted. "It's eighty-something in the shade," she pointed out. "Not my idea of teatime. But if that cold beer is still up for grabs, I wouldn't refuse."

"Cold beer coming right up." From the kitchen, he called, "Bottle okay or should I hunt for a clean glass?"

"Bottle's fine."

He came back with two beers, opened both, and handed one to her.

"Thanks." Sophie took a sip. "Mmm. That tastes so good, and the cold bottle feels even better on my fingers than the ice."

"Good. So. The ghost," he prompted.

"I heard her before I saw her."

"Her? You're sure it was a her?" He had to bank down hard on the urge to jump to conclusions. Not to mention the urge to bark questions at her.

"Positive. This whole thing is confusing and crazy, but that much I'm sure of. That and the outfit."

"Go on."

"The drawer slammed shut on my fingers and I yelled—because it really hurt—and I tried to get them out, but the way the drawer is designed they were sort of trapped under this ridge and . . . anyway, that's when I heard a woman's voice. It sounded really close, but I couldn't see anyone. She said, 'Go away. Go now. You don't belong here.' "

"That's it?"

"That's it. And then a second later the drawer opened and I got loose and turned around and . . ." She gestured with the hand not holding the beer, signaling amazement and disbelief. "And there was a bride standing right in front of me . . . gown, veil, jewelry, bouquet, the works. And it wasn't my imagination."

"You're sure?"

"Totally. She was as real as you and me." Her mouth quirked. "Except she wasn't. I mean, she was real and she wasn't . . . she was . . . different. I can't explain that part of it. I just sensed it."

"It wasn't an illusion? You couldn't see through her? And you weren't seeing her in the mirror?"

Sophie shook her head emphatically. "No. She was solid. Flesh and blood. Well, solid anyway. I'm not sure about the rest."

"And you said she was young?"

"Right. Young and pretty, beautiful really, but not happy. Not at all. There was no mistaking that. The phrase 'if looks could kill' would not be an overstatement."

"But young?"

"Yes." She pursed her lips. "Well, yes and no. She was youthful, but now that I think about it, she was . . . I guess dated is the best way to describe it. Her gown, her hairstyle, even her makeup . . . it was all very old-fashioned. I can't believe I missed telling you that before." She gave him a rueful smile. "I guess you military types know a little about debriefing after all."

"The bride . . . she didn't say anything else?"

"I didn't give her a chance. I bolted."

He stared at the floor, his forehead creasing as he tried to make sense of her story.

"What would you have done?" she asked.

The hint of defensiveness in her tone drew his attention from his own thoughts; he could tell from her expression that she'd interpreted his grim silence as disapproval.

"You did the right thing," he said to reassure her. "Retreat is always better than defeat. You had no idea what you were dealing with. We still don't."

"What would you have done?" she asked again.

Leaning back in his chair, he crossed his arms. "I'm not sure. I might have tried to communicate with her. But then I've had a lot more time to consider my options."

She looked puzzled. "What does that mean?"

There was no longer any question about telling her the truth about his own experiences since moving in, only about where to begin. And where to draw the line between what she had a right to know and things he didn't talk about.

"It means," he said, "that today's incident wasn't the first bizarre thing to happen in this house."

Again he saw her tense, and again he felt the urge to comfort her rise from somewhere deep inside him. He curled his fist around the bottle and took a swig to keep from touching her again. Touching her—or rather his response to touching her—was adding another layer of complication to an already confusing situation . . . one he didn't need or want.

"So this has happened before?" she asked.

Owen shook his head. "Not exactly. I never saw—or heard—any ghost. But there was other stuff."

He gave her a brief rundown of his experiences, telling of things being mysteriously moved from place to place, and things disappearing and reappearing, and of windows being slammed shut in the middle of the night. He told her about wet towels in his bed and coming downstairs in the morning to be greeted by the smell of Old English furniture polish.

"And with all this going on around you, it never occurred to you to call someone to look into it?"

"Who would I call?" he countered drily. "Ghostbusters?"

She made a face. "Very funny. There must be someone who deals with things like this."

"Sure. They're listed in the phone book under 'Quacks and Charlatans.'" He turned in his chair and stretched his legs out to ease the stiffness that came from sitting still too long. "There were a couple of times I came close to telling someone just to get a second opinion, but I was afraid they'd laugh in my face . . . or else think it was a cheap publicity stunt for my books. Then you came along."

Her green eyes lit with surprise. "Me?"

"That's right. I had no intention of opening that door no matter how long you stood out there banging on it and calling my name. It wasn't going to happen."

"Lucky for me the wind kicked up at just the right time."

He stared at her. "Did it?"

Even before he asked the question, understanding sharpened her expression. "Oh my God, she was the one who let me in that day. And today she slammed the door in my face and locked it to keep me out." Her brow furrowed. "I don't think she likes me."

She looked so dejected at the thought of being disliked by a ghost who slammed a drawer on her fingers that Owen had to smile.

"I wouldn't worry about it," he said, his smile disappearing as it occurred to him that this might not be the best advice. The truth was, they didn't know anything about this ghost or what she was likely to do. And in his experience, what you don't know about a situation is exactly what you need to worry about.

"I'm not worried . . . exactly. It's just that . . . I mean, what's wrong with me? I'm likable. I'm damn likable. And I like brides. No one is a better friend to brides than I am. It's in my blood, for heaven's sake. Sophie Bennett, friend of brides. That's me." She spoke emphatically, looking around as if hoping to be overheard. "Don't you think I'm likable?"

She looked so damned earnest that he probably would have lied if he had to, but he didn't have to.

"You're plenty likable," he said, his tone gruffer than he intended. "A little klutzy, and a total wimp when it comes to physical challenges, but likable."

"Gee, thanks." She sighed and sipped her beer before returning her fingers to the bowl of ice water. After wiggling them for a few seconds, she stopped and frowned. "So why did you invite me in?"

"As I recall, you invited yourself in."

"And you very rudely said no. But then you suddenly changed your mind. Why?"

"Because you saw something."

Her expression clouded.

"Behind me," he prompted.

She nodded her head, remembering. "Yes. Yes, that's right. I *thought* I saw something—or someone—behind you, and then it happened again a few minutes later, when I was following you through the foyer, but there was nothing there either time. Or so I thought." She met his gaze directly. "You don't think so."

"Of all the people who've been here since I bought the place, you were the only one who picked up on anything at all. I let you in because I wanted to see what else would happen."

"I get that," she said, nodding again. "Curiosity. It's the same reason I hung around upstairs to see what would happen next."

"For me it was a little more than curiosity. I thought . . . I thought that if there was a ghost or spirit behind the things that were happening here, that maybe . . ." He cupped his hands around his beer and stared into it. "I thought maybe it was someone I knew . . . and lost. I wanted to know for sure, and I hoped that maybe you would see something I didn't."

"It might be the person you're wondering about . . . I only got a quick look, but—"

She broke off as he pulled out his wallet and opened it to Allie's picture. "Is that her? Is that the girl . . . woman you saw?"

It felt like his heart was lodged in his throat and about to explode. For a second . . . two . . . he couldn't breathe. Then Sophie shook her head.

"No," she said softly. "That's definitely not who I saw. I am so sorry to disappoint you."

"You didn't," he said, looking away from the sight of her eyes welling up with tears. He didn't deal well with sympathy, or any other tender emotion for that matter. Black and white. Suck it up and get it done. That was his comfort zone.

"I'm not even sure 'disappointed' is the right word. I know she's gone. I've accepted that. I guess I wanted one more—"

He halted abruptly, uncomfortable. It wasn't like him to say even that much and he sure as hell wasn't going to blabber to this woman he didn't even know that what he wanted was the impossible: to turn back time.

"Yeah," she said quietly. "One more . . . one more moment, one more word. I know what you mean. I lost someone I loved and I've wanted that myself from time to time."

Owen didn't look at her. He couldn't. Instead he dragged his fingers through his hair, tilted his head back, and looked at the ceiling, then at the floor. "But all along there was something about it that didn't feet right. I mean, no matter how much I wanted it to be her, the energy, or whatever you want to call it, never felt like Allie."

He paused and she just sat. If she pressed him or comforted him or God forbid touched him, he could retreat back into his shell and batten down the hatches. But she didn't.

"The thing is," he heard himself say, "I couldn't figure out why she would be following me around playing housekeeper instead of . . . instead of saying . . ." He felt the corners of his mouth lift as memory collided with longing. "Instead of saying, 'Hey, dad, procrastinate much?' We had a kind of shorthand that came from doing most of our communicating through letters and e-mails. If it had been Allie, she wouldn't have wasted time picking up after me and polishing furniture; it would have been more her style to write her message in the dust . . . 'Deadline . . . Butt . . . Chair . . . Now.' "

"Well, if you ask me, that sounds like pretty good advice no matter how the message got through to you."

Meeting her gaze, Owen nodded. "You're right. It's probably just the kick in the ass I needed. Isn't there a song or a saying . . . something about not getting what you want, but getting what you need?"

"It's a Stones' song." She sang a couple of lines, very softly and off-key. *"But if you try sometimes . . . you just might find . . . you get what you need."*

Even off-key, her voice had the power to smooth some of the raw edges inside him.

After a minute she said, "I'm sorry about your daughter, Owen. She's a beautiful girl."

Her gaze moved to the picture he'd forgotten he was holding. He flipped his wallet shut and shoved it back into his pocket. "Yeah. She really was."

She didn't say anything and Owen understood that she was giving him time and space to talk if he wanted to.

He didn't want to. In spite of that, he heard himself say, "It's been three years, but sometimes it feels like it was just . . ."

"Yesterday," she said quietly when he faltered.

"Yeah. And other times it feels like she's been gone a lifetime. Like she was here one minute and gone the next."

"Was her death sudden?"

Owen nodded without looking up. "Car accident. The week before she left for college. Her freshman year. She was driving home from work and a drunk hit her head on. At the hospital they said she died instantly. From the impact. And so did he . . . the other driver. Which is just about the luckiest thing that could have happened to the son-of-a-bitch considering what I would have done to him." He heard the venom in his voice and it was nothing compared to what was in his heart. "If I sound bitter, it's because I am."

He flipped his wallet shut and shoved it back into his pocket.

"So," she said when it became clear he was done talking. "What happens now? It's obvious you only agreed to the wedding because you wanted information. Now you have it . . . more or less."

"And you want to know if I'm going to renege on our deal?"

"Yes, but first I'm going to remind you that you signed an agreement."

"Unwitnessed. Which I suspect makes it less than binding in the eyes of the law. And even if it is binding," he said over her attempt to protest, "I'm confident the right lawyer could keep the matter on a legal merry-go-round for years . . . long past the time when the happy couple should rightfully be either divorced or exchanging goat's heads or totem poles or whatever the proper gift is for doing that many years' time."

"Has anyone ever accused you of being a romantic?"

"No."

"I'm not surprised. Are you saying you're not going to honor the agreement?"

"No, I'm saying the agreement is crap. But I gave you my word and that's not crap. You can go ahead with the wedding as planned . . . assuming you still want to."

"That was going to be my next question; what do we do about . . ."

"The ghost bride?" he supplied.

Sophie nodded.

"Wrong question. The correct question is what are *you* going to do about her? I've got a book to write," he reminded her. "Until she slams a drawer on my fingers, I'm going to stick with the 'peaceful coexistence' approach that's worked so far."

"Thanks a lot." Shaking water from her fingers, she reached for the towel to dry them. "Unfortunately that doesn't seem to be an option for me."

"So what's your plan?"

"I have no idea. So," she said, sitting up a little straighter, "I'll just start there . . . with what I don't know. Which is just about everything. It seems logical that the ghost is connected to this house. So, working backward, what do you know about the old lady who lived here before you?"

"Next to nothing. No, make that nothing. Technically I bought the house from her great-nephew and all I know about him is that he lives on the West Coast and has no interest in anything back here."

"Okay, then forget him for now. I'm going to research the house itself, see who built it . . . who lived here . . . who died here . . . who might have gotten married here. The Newport Historical must have records on this place. I also have a friend who works in the reference department at the library," she said, thinking out loud. "I'm going to give her a call as soon as I get back to the office." She stood.

"Leave that," he ordered when she started to gather the towel and ice pack. "I'll get it later. Are you all right to drive?"

"Of course. Wimp though I am, half a beer is not enough to incapacitate me."

"I meant your fingers."

"They feel much better . . . thanks to you." She held them up and flexed them to demonstrate as she headed to the kitchen to collect her bag. "I'm okay to drive. And I can't wait to get back to the office and start Googling Ange de la Mer. There has to be something on record somewhere that will help us . . . help me figure out who the ghost bride is and what she wants."

"Or maybe," he said, reaching for the paper he'd just noticed stuck to the front of the refrigerator, "the answer is much closer to home."

After a quick glance at the paper, he handed it to Sophie. It was the list he'd given her earlier and that she'd tossed into her bag before going upstairs. There was now a thick black line drawn through what he'd written . . . no noise . . . no music . . . no long messages. And with the same heavy black touch, in letters large enough to cover the whole page, someone had written two words: NO WEDDING.

Ivy was not at all sorry to see Miss Sophia Bennett drive away; she only wished she was taking her leave permanently, but there was, unfortunately, still work to be done on that score.

It had been a long afternoon, with many interesting revelations, and she was exhausted. Not physically, obviously; that was one of the benefits of being dead. She was weary mentally and emotionally and glad to have her house to herself so she could relax and think. Owen Winters didn't count since she'd grown accustomed to him being underfoot all the time. In fact, in spite of his many faults and failings and his bad habits too numerous to count, she'd grown rather fond of the man. It saddened her deeply to learn that he'd lost a child . . . his only child, she was quite certain.

She'd seen the photo of his daughter, Allie, by his bed, and wondered about her. She'd thought perhaps they'd had a falling-out and didn't speak. Such things happened in the best of families; it had happened between her brother Archie and her after all, and lasted years. Or else, she'd thought, perhaps Allie lived nearby and he went to visit her on his infrequent forays out and that's why she never called or came there. She hadn't considered that the reason Allie never came around was that she was dead. To lose a child was a tragedy of the first order and it shed a new and very different light on Mr. Winters's brooding ways.

She had never lost a child and couldn't claim to know that particular pain. But she had lost the dream of having children, the children she and Joseph had wanted and planned for and had even chosen names for during long hours spent dreaming and talking about their future together; she'd lost the three girls and three boys who would have filled the bedrooms that instead became guest rooms, empty rooms. And, of course, she had also lost Joseph. So she understood loss and she understood how some losses cast a shadow across every minute of every day of the rest of your life, even the good days, even the happy times. Unlike a lump in your throat or a thorn in your side, some losses create only emptiness, a permanent, irreparable hole in your heart that you eventually learn to step around lest you fall in. She imagined that losing a child you'd actually held and nurtured and whose tiny fingers and toes you'd counted left a hole that was very deep and hard to avoid.

She would, she decided, go a little easier on Mr. Winters. For one thing, in the future, when she found a wet towel on the floor, she would put it in the bathroom instead of in his bed. The same latitude could not be applied to Miss Bennett. Stopping her was proving to be more of a challenge than Ivy anticipated. The young woman was plucky and as a rule she liked that. She liked that the wedding planner hadn't turned tail and run at the first hint of a ghost . . . even though that's exactly what Ivy hoped she would do. And she appreciated her kindness to Mr. Winters. The poor man could certainly use a friend. Ivy even admired the determined, no-nonsense way she went about doing her job; she simply wanted her to go do it somewhere else.

In another time and place, she might have liked Miss Bennett very much. Who knows? They might even have become friends. But this was not another time and place. It was the here and now, and her only interest was in putting a stop to the wedding Miss Bennett was planning.

Eight

Shelby and her fiancé were neither procrastinators nor ditherers, and for that Sophie was grateful. They understood that there was no time to waste choosing a caterer and deciding whether they wanted a harpist or a pianist to play during the ceremony and nailing down the multitude of smaller details that make up a wedding. It helped that they trusted her to narrow the field for them ahead of time so they weren't overwhelmed with choices.

Sophie counted herself lucky on the other end as well. No matter how diligent Shelby and Matthew were, if the vendors they selected were already booked solid for the date of their wedding, it would be back to square one. Incredibly that didn't happen. It turned out that the chance to be part of the first wedding ever held at Ange de la Mer was a temptation most local professionals couldn't resist . . . even if they were booked. For those on the fence, the fresh creative challenge of the *Midsummer Night's* theme was enough to push them over. So far, their first-choice vendors were all willing to juggle whatever was necessary to make room in their schedules.

The days flew by, and though it seemed as if Sophie always ended the day with a to-do list as long as when she started out, things were falling into place a lot more smoothly than she'd dared to hope. Except, of course, for that one pesky dark spot lurking on the horizon, gliding back and forth in her mind like the fin of a great white. The ghost of Ange de la Mer. Did it really matter if she got every detail of Shelby's wedding exactly right—the wine from local vineyards and table linens the perfect shade of lavender and the water lilies and beeswax candles floating in the illusion pond—did those extraneous details matter if the place itself was haunted by a ghost that was hell-bent on stopping the wedding from happening?

Sophie shook her head at what only a few weeks ago would have sounded like the most preposterous thing she'd ever heard. A few weeks ago she didn't believe in ghosts. Not really. Oh sure, like all teenagers, she and her friends had fooled around with a Ouija board and swore it worked, and she sometimes watched *Ghost Hunters* and wondered if the sounds and images captured with all that high-tech equipment could possibly be real. Well, now she didn't have to wonder. She knew they most definitely could be real and she had the scary firsthand knowledge to prove it. She just had no idea what she was going to do about it.

At one point she even considered appealing to Jill or Jenna for help. Fortunately she came to her senses in time. The *J*s meant well, usually, but one of the many things she'd learned about them through the years was that the safest way to handle any problem was to keep them out of it. It wasn't a major loss. If Sophie had to guess, she'd say their knowledge of the mystical and metaphysical was a muddle derived from urban legend and old *Bewitched* episodes. And she knew for a fact that their combined experience as wedding planners didn't include getting rid of a single ghost. If it had, she'd have heard about it. Several hundred times over. The *J*s weren't exactly poster girls for discretion. Another good reason not to confide in them. They might not mean to, but sooner or later one of them would let word of the ghost bride slip out and the local press would pounce on it and have a field day covering the wedding. And not in a way that either Helen Archer or Owen was likely to appreciate.

Solving the ghost problem was going to require serious, uninterrupted thought and at the moment that was a luxury Sophie couldn't squeeze into her schedule . . . at least not when she was still awake enough to think straight. Her days were filled with too many people and tasks clamoring for her attention right this very instant and so the problem-that-dare-not-speak-its-name kept getting shoved to the back burner. When she did have a few minutes to spare, she didn't have much to work with. Detailed information about the house's previous owner was proving to be as tough to come by as information about Owen himself. Her friend at the library promised to look into it and get back to her, but a call to the Historical Society had proven to be less than helpful. The place was understaffed and underfunded, and if she wanted to know what might be buried in their archives, she was going to have to make time to go there and dig for it herself. When she heard that, part of her wanted to immediately drop everything and go ghost hunting, but she resisted. She was an old hand at clamping down on her adventurous side in order to do what was right and responsible and expected of her.

In this case, the responsible thing was to focus on a problem she did know how to solve: Shelby's wedding dress. Specifically the fact that she still didn't have one. It's not that she was a prima donna or a picky fashionista; Shelby simply had a vision of herself on her wedding day and—to her mother's increasing frustration—she refused to give up on it. Sophie admired her determination, but the clock was ticking, and before she'd even rolled out of bed that morning, she'd decided her number one priority for the day was to make sure the bride didn't have to walk down the aisle naked.

Bella Bridal was among the area's leading bridal salons. In fact it was one of the first Shelby and her mother had visited on their hunt for Shelby's dream dress. She recalled Helen's exasperated recounting of how she had charged into the storeroom of the exclusive shop—an area strictly off-limits to customers—and personally gone through each and every dress, hoping to discover a designer whose work was similar to what Shelby described. She was certain she would be able to convince the designer to produce the wedding dress that existed only in her daughter's imagination. Sophie could have saved her the trouble. Even if Helen had found a designer whose work had the right "look," successful designers worked seasons ahead of time, always under pressure and always rushing to meet deadlines for the major industry shows. No matter how good Helen was at the art of persuasion—or bribery—no professional designer would be willing to drop everything and work like crazy to make one bride happy. But Sophie knew someone who might.

"My name is Sophie Bennett," she said to the tastefully dressed young woman seated at an ornate ivory-and-gold desk directly inside the entrance of Bella Bridal. "I'm here to see Lina Merchant." She spoke quietly because it was that kind of place. She also automatically threw her shoulders back and sucked in her stomach the way she found herself doing when her stepmother was watching.

"Is this your first fitting?" asked the young woman, her tone polite but businesslike as she slid the sales appointment book aside and opened the one marked *Fittings and Alterations*.

Sophie shook her head. "No. Actually I'm not here for a fitting at all. I just want to speak with Lina. I'm sure if you let her know I'm here, she'll squeeze me in."

We'll see about that, the pretty blonde's expression said as she closed the appointment book and reached for the phone. Clearly it was not routine for the head of alterations to see someone without an appointment.

While she waited, Sophie checked out the gowns elegantly displayed on dress forms in the shop's reception area. There were only a few, just enough to whet a bride's appetite. At Bella Bridal, all business was conducted by appointment only, in the plush private dressing rooms behind the tall paneled doors with brass fittings as shiny as sunlight on water.

It was through one of those imposing sets of doors that Lina appeared almost before the receptionist had time to relay the message that she was on her way. Angelina—Lina—Merchant had worked with Sophie's mother at Wedding Magic. "The magician's apprentice," she had jokingly called herself. Her mother had respected the sewing skills passed on to Lina from her Portuguese mother and grandmother, and had trusted her to share the work that was her pride and joy in a way she trusted no other living soul. After her mother's death, Lina had stayed on, working tirelessly and with a broken heart, to fulfill the shop's existing orders. Sophie knew that her father and Lina had discussed the possibility of her taking over the business, but as a single mother of two children who were under five at the time, her top priority had to be a regular paycheck.

They'd stayed in touch, however; Lina was the big sister Sophie wished she'd had. Lina would call just to chat and several times a year she would arrange for a babysitter and take Sophie to lunch, just the two of them. She would tell Sophie stories about working side by side with her mother, stories no one else knew, stories that nurtured Sophie's fascination with the world of weddings and all things bridal. And she would listen to whatever was on Sophie's mind at the time without telling her that if she would only slim down or wear a brighter shade of lip gloss or be more outgoing, all her problems would be solved.

Then came a new love and a new marriage for Lina and college for Sophie. As the years passed and their lives shifted and changed, the way lives do, their contact became more sporadic. Their professional paths sometimes crossed, but Lina's work hours were as long and as crazy as Sophie's; Sophie knew because they exchanged notes at Christmas and traded war stories when they ran into each other at some work-related event. It didn't matter. Turns out they had the kind of friendship that isn't about being inseparable, but about being separated and having nothing change.

When Lina appeared they hugged each other hard and then stepped back with big, matching grins. Sophie saw a soft, pretty woman about to turn fifty, with lively dark eyes that were even more striking with her salt-and-pepper hair cut in short, spiky layers.

"I love your hair," Sophie declared, still holding on to her.

"Yeah?" Lina shrugged, but looked pleased. "I got sick of running off to have it colored every time I turned around and finally decided, what the hell, let nature take its damned course."

"Well, it looks great. Very edgy." She ran her gaze over her old friend. "*You* look great, Lina."

"And you," Lina countered. She touched Sophie's cheek with one hand. "You have your mother's smile, and your mother's eyes. You're just as beautiful as she was."

The compliment had Sophie blinking back a sting of tears, happy tears. Nothing Lina said could have pleased her more.

"Enough of that," Lina pronounced, turning and linking arms with her. "Come on down to my office, where we can talk properly."

Her office was roomy and comfortable. Jars of beads lined one shelf and pretty snippets and swatches were scattered across the desk and worktable, creating an air of controlled clutter that reminded Sophie of her mother's shop and made her feel very much at home as they got caught up with each other's life and family.

Finally Lina threw up her hands, her expression eager. "All right, I can't take the suspense any longer. Spill it."

"Spill what?" countered Sophie.

"The beans . . . spill the beans," demanded Lina, the words rolling excitedly off her tongue with only the barest musical hint of the native language she'd spoken at home as a child. "I know you are far too busy to come to see me in the middle of the day unless there's a very good reason."

Sophie nodded, sheepish. "You're right. I'm here because I need your help, Lina."

"I knew it!" Lina exclaimed, clasping her hands together with delight. "It's happened . . . you've met someone special, someone wonderful, and you've come to me for the most beautiful, absolutely perfect dress in all the world."

"Well, as a matter of fact, yes," confirmed Sophie, laughing because she should have anticipated the conclusion Lina would jump to. "I *have* met someone special, and I do want your help coming up with the perfect wedding dress, but not quite the way you're thinking."

As concisely as she could, she explained to Lina about Shelby and Matthew and the Princess House, about how they would be leaving for Ecuador in September, and about Shelby's youthful idealism in opposing the senseless slaughter of silkworms.

"My goodness, the Peace Corps," Lina said when Sophie had finished. "Both of them?"

Sophie nodded.

"Sounds like those kids have good hearts."

"They really do. That's why I want Shelby to have the dress of her dreams. I've sent her and her mother to every bridal shop I could think of and we've come up empty. The dress just doesn't exist . . . not in the fabric she has her heart set on. Not yet, that is. That's why I came to you." She leaned forward. "Lina, this is the sort of work you and my mother did all the time . . . it was your bread and butter back then."

"Yes, but that's because your mother was a creative genius."

"She would say the same about you," Sophie argued. "I know she would. And I know that you've done custom work on your own from time to time, for family and friends. Amazing work."

"Mmm-hmm. And now you're thinking maybe in my spare time I can design and make a custom wedding dress for this girl in . . . what? Five weeks?"

"Give or take," Sophie acknowledged, her expression sheepish. "Yes, that's what I came here to ask you . . . but before you give me an answer, let me show you the sketches Shelby made of her dress. They're rough, but you can get an idea from them."

Lina took her time studying the sketches Sophie put in front of her. "Mmm. The lines are very good . . . clean and simple," she noted. "That's a plus. No complicated tucking or pleating. If she wanted poufs and flounces and ruffles, I'd say no, can't be done in so little time . . . it's not just the extra labor, it's the number of fittings required to get it just right. But this . . . ." She looked at the sketches again and shrugged. "This is doable."

"In hemp silk?"

Lina gave a careless wave of her hand. "Of course. The fabric is no problem."

"It might be," Sophie said, and relayed Shelby's ironclad requirement of fairy-wing sparkle without heavy-handed beading or crystals.

"I know just the thing," Lina responded without hesitation. Sophie was encouraged by the hint of excitement that had filtered into her tone. The seamstress tapped her finger on the sketch. "The bodice will be entirely lace, with only the teensiest, tiniest crystals and seed pearls accenting the design. If I agreed to this—and I'm not saying I will—I'd do all the beading myself to make sure it was nestled into the lace so all you see is that soft glimmer when she moves. Now the skirt—you wouldn't think so, but that's the tricky part. We want flow and draping, but we also want movement—"

"And fairy-wing sparkle," Sophie interjected. "Don't forget the fairy wings."

"I'm getting to the fairy sparkle . . . and it so happens I know the right fabric to create exactly the effect you're describing. We'll use it in layers as an overlay for the hemp silk."

She got up, moved a few piles on her worktable, and came back with a sample piece of sheer fabric with a subtle but unmistakable sparkle. She held it out to Sophie, who rubbed it between her thumb and fingertips.

"It's so light," she said.

"But it drapes beautifully, which a lot of lightweight fabrics don't. It could even be used alone for the veil. It's strictly special order, and I do mean special. I've only worked with it once."

She placed the sample on top of a length of soft white silk and the sparkle came alive . . . like flickering candlelight . . . like fairy wings.

"Now, just so you know, it's not hemp," Lina continued, "but it's also not silk. It's a synthetic blend especially designed to take the paint that gives it that luster."

Sophie's brows shot up as she touched the fabric again. "Paint? Are you kidding?"

"No. Crazy, huh? The supplier is a small company . . . very small. The paint is a special organic formulation created by two sisters who basically run the business single-handedly. Artsy, creative types, the pair of them. The painting is done by hand with tiny little brushes. Very labor-intensive. And thus very expensive," she added on a warning note.

"Trust me. Not a problem. But time might be. Can you order this fabric and have it in time?"

"Not a chance," Lina returned, sinking Sophie's hopes. "It would only be possible if we already had a goodly amount of it on hand. Which it so happens I do." At Sophie's incredulous smile, she shrugged. "I ordered it for my niece when the plan was for her to marry the boyfriend who turned out to be a dirtbag." She gave a careless wave. "A story for another day. The important thing is the fabric is tucked safely away in my workshop at home. And finding a fine grade of hemp silk to work with it won't be any problem at all. Hemp is not exactly in demand."

"Does that mean you'll do it?" Sophie asked.

"You mean will I stay up all night, pulling out the hair I have left, to make a one-of-a-kind dress for a special bride . . . like in the old days?" Lina smiled. "Try and stop me."

The last thing Sophie did before meeting with Lina was turn off her cell phone. The first thing she did once she was back in her car was check for missed calls. There were five. Three from Owen.

Only two words came to mind: *uh-oh.*

Three calls in less than an hour? Something was wrong. Never before had he made first contact and . . .

First contact? Sophie rolled her eyes. Sheesh. Stealth speak. That's what she got for staying up till all hours reading graphic novels about a tough and brooding super-being who—at least in her increasingly fertile imagination—bore a deep resemblance to his creator. Owen might not have an eye patch or a pair of magnificent black wings to unfurl, but to her he was every bit as fascinating a creature as the darkly mysterious Osprey. More fascinating, in fact, because he was real. Flesh-and-blood real. And gifted. His work was a surprise. She began

reading the first book out of curiosity and finished it in one sitting. The next day she was at the bookstore in search of the
earlier volumes in the series and she tore through those with
the same fervor. Josh was right; Owen was a damn good writer.
The graphic format had taken some getting used to, but it didn't
stop the novels from being exciting and complex and
intriguing . . . and the more she read about Osprey, the harder
it was to get Owen off her mind.

It was a sure bet he wasn't thinking about her that much, or at
all, for that matter. That's how she knew that his repeated attempts
to get in touch with her could only mean trouble. The landscape
designer was scheduled to send a crew to do some preliminary
work today, but she'd made it clear there was to be no noise and
absolutely no interrupting Owen during his work hours. At least
she thought she'd made it clear. Bracing herself to be chewed out,
she dialed Owen's number. It took only a few seconds for it to start
ringing and even less time for him to pick up.

"Hi, Owen, this is Sophie Bennett. I'm returning your call."

"About time."

He sounded irritable. Which wasn't so unusual, she reminded
herself, trying not to jump to dire conclusions. She flash-froze her
smile in place, having read somewhere that just smiling when you
speak on the phone can make you sound more upbeat and confident. The best defense is a good offense and all that. "Is there a
problem?"

"Several. Get here as fast as you can."

"Well, let's see," she replied, conjuring up her schedule for the
rest of the day as she tried to keep her sinking heart from dragging
her smile down with it. "I have an appointment at two and—"

"Cancel it," he snapped. "We need to talk. I'll expect you here
in thirty minutes."

"Thirty minutes? There's no way I can—"

"Where there's a will . . . you do want this wedding to happen, right?"

"Of course I do," she told him, upbeat giving way to feeling cornered, and then resigned. "Oh, all right. I'm not guaranteeing thirty minutes, but I'll be there as soon as I can."

Somewhere deep inside, Owen knew he probably ought to feel guilty for dragging Sophie away from her work in the middle of the day because of a problem he'd already solved. But that place was buried very deep inside, beneath a lifetime of identifying a target and going after it. In the world of dark ops, the end always justified the means. Guilt didn't enter into it and rules of etiquette didn't apply. So he was understandably a little rusty when it came to playing fair. True, there really was something besides the disastrous events of the morning that he wanted to discuss with her, but that easily could have waited until she was done with her two o'clock appointment or even until later that evening.

He grimaced, slouched deeper in his deck chair, and stared out at the ocean, impatient for her to arrive. He was the one who couldn't wait and he wasn't sure why.

Scratch that; he knew why. He knew exactly what was driving his persistent need to see her. He'd figured it out when he was around thirteen and one of the college kids who'd signed on as a carnival roadie for the summer showed him a magazine with photos of Madonna dressed in fishnet stockings and a skimpy black leather thing that laced from crotch to tits. To his hormone-addled brain, those laces were the gateway to heaven and he'd done extra duty for weeks, mucking out the Prancing Palominos' trailers, to scrape together the exorbitant price the college kid wanted for that dog-eared magazine. Yeah, he knew what those rapid-fire phone calls he made to Sophie were really about. What baffled and annoyed him was that he was having these feelings for Sophie Bennett of all people.

To say that she was not his type was to say the ocean was a little wet. He'd bet his next royalty check that the no-nonsense little wedding planner had never owned a pair of fishnet stockings or a black leather thingamajig. A damn shame really, because she ought to. He'd revised his original assessment of her once he had a chance to take a longer, closer look and saw that the woman had the kind of curves that begged for leather laces . . . among other things. He considered that a compliment, but he was pretty sure she wouldn't. That was the problem in a nutshell.

And, hey, it went both ways. He sure as hell didn't meet her specifications for Mr. Right. As soon as she'd opened her mouth about love and marriage and fiftieth-anniversary pottery, it was clear she was looking for a forever kind of guy, and he was only interested in one kind of woman . . . the kind who came with no strings attached. It was a match made in hell.

So why in God's name had he pounced on the first flimsy excuse that came his way to call her? Why did he wake up every morning wondering if she would be stopping by to check on something? And fall asleep wishing she had?

Boredom, he decided. Boredom and frustration. It had to be that. The writing wasn't going well—another world-class understatement—and he was ripe for a diversion . . . any diversion . . . even one as blatantly, laughably wrong as Sophie. He was an idiot. A lucky one. At least he'd come to his senses before any real damage was done. He never should have agreed to the wedding. The whole thing was becoming way too complicated and trying to scratch this sudden itch for Sophie would only add to the mess.

What's done was done, he thought. The only thing he could do now was to avoid her as much as possible and keep things strictly business between them when he couldn't. When she showed up he would make it clear to her that his end of their business deal didn't include ghost busting or family-tree research or emergency medical treatment of any kind. The meddling ghost bride and blown electrical system and bee-stung workmen too spooked to hang around and work were her problems and she was welcome to them. With any luck she'd soon see for herself that having the wedding at Ange de la Mer was more trouble than it was worth.

When the doorbell finally rang he went to answer it filled with righteous resolve. Through the sidelight he could see Sophie standing on his doorstep, looking worried. Her hair was caught up in a clip, revealing the line of her throat. He came to a stop a few feet from the door.

Not good.

Among other recent, unsettling signs of insanity, he seemed to have developed an inexplicable fascination with the side of Sophie Bennett's throat, specifically the spot where it curved into her shoulder. When she was around he had to force himself not to stare, and when she wasn't all he had to do was imagine himself putting his mouth to that spot and his thoughts disintegrated into a tangle of soft, honeyed skin and long, lazy kisses. And heat, waves of heat, around him and inside him, pulling him in deeper and deeper. The way they could pull him in now if he wasn't careful.

It was ridiculous. The black leather fantasy was something he understood and could deal with. But this . . . this was something else entirely. His first instinct was simply to shrug it off, but the soldier in him knew that it was often the seemingly small and innocuous threats that prove most deadly because they slip beneath your radar.

Not this time, he decided.

Knowing your enemy was half the battle. He knew what he

was up against here and he would deal with it. His mission was the same as always: get in and get out alive. He'd gotten himself into this and he was about to get himself out. He reached for the door-knob, his target in sight, his objective clear.

He would bring Sophie up to speed on the situation and then hand her the reins and walk away. Mission accomplished.

Nine

"I got here as fast as I could," she announced, stepping inside without waiting to be asked. Given their history with the front door, Owen thought that was probably a wise move.

"What happened?" she asked, glancing around in a slightly wary manner. "Did the Gentle Gardener crew show up? Did they interrupt your work? Because I swear I made it clear there was to be no intrusive activity or noise before two. Now that I think about it, I guess the term 'intrusive' was a little vague and could be open to interpretation. So if that's what you're upset about, I'll call them right now and be more . . ."

She talked nonstop all the way from the front door to the kitchen and didn't show any sign of slowing down. Finally Owen broke in.

"I'm not upset."

"You're not?" She stared closely at his expression and he tried not to do the same to the graceful curve of her throat.

The silvery-blue dress she was wearing made her eyes look greener and it had some kind of ruffle thing at the neck that was cut just low enough to show a hint of shadow between her breasts, and because it was merely a hint . . . a suggestion . . . a mystery . . . it was irresistible. Somehow he managed to resist staring there as well, though the effort made his mouth go dry. His mission to put distance between them had seemed a lot less daunting when she was on the other side of the door and the subtle, flowery scent of her didn't drift his way whenever she moved.

"Because you sounded pretty upset earlier," she pointed out matter-of-factly. "On the phone . . . when you insisted I be here in thirty minutes if I wanted to go ahead with the wedding plans."

"Yeah. Right. About that whole thirty-minute thing. I can be a little impatient at times."

She arched her brows.

"And other times I can be damn impatient . . . obnoxiously impatient, I've been told . . . and I'm sorry."

She nodded. "Okay. So if you're not upset about anything, why did you call me three times? Why did I cancel my two o'clock meeting? Why am I here?"

He thought about how best to answer. Obviously not with the truth. It would be counterproductive to admit that when you stripped all the bullshit away she was there because he wanted her there . . . because he wanted to see her badly enough to grasp at straws to get her there . . . and that now that she was there, he really wasn't at all sorry, but rather was perversely glad he'd done it. He was an idiot.

"What's a Gentle Gardener?" he asked. He'd first learned the art of misdirection from his father. It was a magician's stock and trade. It was later, while working special ops, that he discovered how useful it could be when trying to save his own ass.

Sophie blinked, shifting gears. "The Gentle Gardener is the name of the landscape design firm working on the wedding. They're ultra-earth-friendly, which makes the bride and groom happy, and their unobtrusive approach means there'll be less work to do after the fact to restore the property to its original condition . . . which should make you happy."

"Earth-friendly, huh?" He nodded and crossed his arms as he leaned back against the counter. "That probably explains why they didn't approve of my method of dealing with the bees. Pesticide and plenty of it, that's my strategy."

"So they did show up." Her relief was short-lived. "But there was a problem with bees? No one was stung, I hope. They were only supposed to check out the area I chose for the illusion pond to make sure it was suitable, and then to place markers so whoever does the actual digging will know where to dig. Did they do that?"

"They made a start," he told her. "Did you know the illusion pond is going to have underwater lights? Real, nonillusion lights. The kind that require real power. Which is why one of the Gentle Gardeners was on a ladder checking out the power lines running to the house when the beehive fell on his head."

Wincing, she clasped her hands over her mouth. "Oh no. How awful. Is he all right?"

"Pretty much. The EMTs said—"

"EMTs? You had to call for help?"

"Just to be on the safe side, since he wasn't sure if he was allergic to bee venom. They said that considering the size of the hive and the fact that he was standing on a ladder and couldn't run, it was a miracle he wasn't stung more than eight times."

"Eight bee stings? That poor man."

"Lucky man is more like it. If he had been allergic he might be dead now. They gave him a shot of adrenaline as a precaution, but they were more concerned about his buddy, Gentle Gardener number two. The one who fell down the cellar stairs."

Shuddering, she squared her shoulders and let her hands drop to her sides. "Tell me everything."

Owen obliged, relating how it was the bee-sting victim's bloodcurdling shouts that had drawn him from the guesthouse, where, as luck would have it, he had a can of insecticide handy. He explained how when the guy jumped from the ladder, it fell sideways and knocked the meter box from the house, breaking wires and setting off a shower of sparks that sent his coworker racing to the basement to throw the circuit breakers. Three steps from the bottom the guy tripped over a golf club that just happened to be lying there, stumbled, and slammed his head against the concrete wall. He concluded with his own contribution: rushing in with a giant can of Raid and fending off the disgruntled and marauding bees long enough to drag the guy from the ladder into the house.

"Afterward I was all set to hit what was left of the hive with gasoline and torch it, but they insisted on taking a"—he smirked—"gentler approach. They called a bee specialist they worked with before to come and cart it away for a proper burial or relocation or whatever the politically correct procedure is for dealing with displaced hives."

"What a nightmare. That's worse than anything I imagined as I was driving here and I thought I imagined the worst. Are both men all right? Did anyone end up in the hospital?"

"They're okay. The guy who hit his head is going to get checked out by his own doctor. Their boss told them to take tomorrow off too and I promised them both tickets to see the Red Sox play the Yankees next week."

"You did?" Her startled expression softened into one of wonder. "You didn't have to do that. I mean, this really isn't your problem and . . . well, thank you. That was really sweet."

Sweet?

He shrugged one shoulder, almost as uncomfortable being called sweet as he was with the look she was beaming his way. He was no Galahad and he didn't want her thinking he was. "No big deal. The law firm I use has a private box at Fenway. All I did was make a call. Cheaper than a lawsuit."

"Thank you," she said again. For a few seconds neither of them said anything. Then she shook her head wearily. "I still can't believe all this happened. A damn beehive. What are the odds? Where was it to begin with? I mean before it fell."

"It looks like it was wedged beneath the crown molding on a window right above where the ladder was braced."

"Of course, it would have to be the window directly above the ladder. He probably hit it with the ladder and knocked it loose."

"He insists he didn't. And I have to agree. If he had bumped it, those bees would have started buzzing around right away; no one in his right mind would climb a ladder with that going on overhead."

"Why else would it suddenly fall at that precise moment?"

"Why do you think?"

Sophie groaned. Dropping her voice, she asked, "Do you really think she had something to do with it?"

"I think she had everything to do with it. I know for a fact that the golf club the other guy tripped over was by the back door earlier this morning and that I didn't move it. Face it: that note we found stuck to the fridge was Ivy's official declaration of war."

"Ivy? You're on a first-name basis with her?"

He gave a philosophical shrug. "We have to call her something and that is her name."

"I can think of a few things I'd like to call her right about now," she grumbled.

As soon as she said it, the ceiling fan above her head started whirling faster than any fan he'd ever seen. If a fan could be said to be pissed, this one was. Owen shot forward and grabbed Sophie by her shoulders to move her aside.

"Considering everything that happened today, I don't think it's such a good idea for you to be standing under rapidly spinning blades," he explained. "In fact, I don't think it's a good idea for us to have this conversation here at all." He thought for a few seconds. "Come with me."

His hand was still resting on her shoulder; without thinking, he dropped it and took hers to tug her along with him as he headed out the back door. It was only as they reached the side of the house that he considered the fact that he was still holding her hand and she hadn't pulled it away. It felt . . . nice, he decided. And strange. Women came and went in his life, some faster than others, but he couldn't recall the last time he'd held hands with one of them.

"Where are we going?" she asked.

"Somewhere we can talk without being overheard. You have an important decision to make about whether or not it's practical— not to mention safe—to go ahead with this wedding, and I have information that might help you make it."

They reached the section of the drive that ran in front of the garages that had been added sometime after the original house was built. Parked there was a black Harley with enough heft and horsepower to satisfy Owen's inner caveman.

Sophie looked from the motorcycle to him and shook her head. "No way. In case you didn't notice, I'm wearing a dress."

"I noticed," he replied, swinging his leg over the bike. He turned his head and met her gaze. "Believe me, I noticed. That's how I know that skirt is loose enough for you to hike it up or do whatever you have to do in order to climb on." He held out the helmet the law required passengers to wear. "So climb on."

Sophie took the helmet and stood staring at the motorcycle, which he revved to life and which now sat roaring impatiently at her. This was ridiculous. Owen stared straight ahead, either oblivious to her dilemma or choosing to ignore it. He was right: her skirt was loose enough to scrunch up without risking a charge of indecent exposure. The real problem was that she'd never ridden a motorcycle before and wasn't exactly sure how to climb on gracefully and stay there. She had seen it done. In movies. And back in high school when some girl would run out and hop on a waiting motorcycle, riding off with the wind in her hair and her arms wrapped tightly around her boyfriend's waist while Sophie watched and wondered if that could possibly feel as exciting and liberating as it looked from her vantage point at the bus stop.

Here was her chance to find out. She could stand there shouting over the roar of the engine to suggest they be sensible and take her car instead or she could climb on.

She climbed on.

Her inner thighs were still vibrating.

It was not, she decided, an unpleasant sensation. Nothing about riding behind Owen on a motorcycle was unpleasant. Not the wind or the feel of his abs beneath her clenched fingers. The man had a serious six-pack. Not the soft brush of his hair against her face or the way the muscles in his back tensed and shifted as he leaned into a curve and then eased out of it, making Sophie press closer to him until she felt as if she was one with him and the bike. She liked all of it. A lot. She especially liked the fact that he took the long way to get where they were going. They raced the entire length of Ten Mile Drive, a winding road known for its spectacular ocean views, and wound up back at a small cove close to the end of Bellevue Avenue where his house was located.

So, thought Sophie, now she knew what she'd missed out on all those times she was left standing at the bus stop and on the sidelines, watching and wishing. Except, oddly enough, at that moment she didn't feel like she'd missed out on anything at all, not a single thing. Nothing else could possibly have measured up to this . . . to the excitement of leaping out of her comfort zone and being swept away . . . of tossing caution out the window and doing the very last thing she expected to be doing when she climbed out of bed that morning. And, let's face it: nothing she imagined could compete with the unfamiliar thrill of doing it with a man like Owen. There was also the edgy anticipation of what could happen next. From the moment his front door whipped open and she first stood face-to-face with Owen, nothing had gone quite as she expected. Without trying, he tilted her careful and orderly world off balance. And part of her liked that too.

The cove was tucked out of sight from the road above, but it was plain he knew exactly where he was going. Sophie kicked off her sandals and allowed him to take her hand for the climb down to a wide flat rock by the water's edge. When they came to a good-size gap between boulders, she hesitated, gathering herself to make the short leap, but before she could jump, he surprised her by placing his hands on her waist and lifting her, wordlessly, effortlessly, his casual gallantry and the rustle of her skirt in the wind making her feel like the wispy heroine of a Merchant-Ivory film. It took all of four seconds and left her slightly breathless and secretly giddy. The heady sense of stepping into another, slower and simpler age was enhanced by the quiet beauty of the setting. Seagulls swooped and drifted across the cloudless blue sky. The strong, midday sun warmed her bare legs and the occasional fine spray from the surf rolling and frothing against the rocks cooled her. Breathing deeply, she tasted the tang of the ocean air and was content. Schedules and stress and the long list of things she could be doing and should be doing seemed a thousand miles away.

"How did you find this place?" she asked once they were settled.

"I used to come here to fish."

"Catch much?"

"I seem to recall doing all right. But it was a long time ago."

She nodded. She'd never been fishing, but the peaceful, isolated spot seemed ideal for it. "Did you grow up around here?"

"No. I grew up in a trailer, driving from one place on the map to the next."

Like her, he was staring out at the horizon, where a sailboat was drifting south, but from his tone alone Sophie could tell that his jaw had tightened and his gaze had become narrow and un-readable, the way she'd noticed it did when the conversation turned too personal for his liking.

"Of course. You must have done a lot of traveling with the carnival. I just thought maybe your family stayed put around here during the school year."

"We didn't," he said simply. "We didn't stay put anywhere."

"I can't imagine what that life was like," she told him, saying the first thing that came to mind to fill the awkward moment. "The freedom from the same boring old routine and the excitement of waking up in a new place. I'm sure it had its drawbacks, but I have to confess that like lots of kids I dreamed of running away to join the circus." She paused. "Mostly after my mom died and my father remarried. Life with my new stepmother and stepsisters made walking on stilts and taming lions look like child's play."

He nodded without looking at her. "I can understand that. Not having your mother around . . . well, it changes things. And just to prove that it's true what they say about the grass always being greener somewhere else, running *away from* the circus is what I used to dream about."

"Any particular destination in mind?"

"I wasn't picky." He reached for a small piece of driftwood ly-ing on the rock beside him and turned it over in his hands. "Some-times when I saw a family walking down the midway, I'd follow along and I'd watch how they talked and laughed together. I'd watch the father play the rackets—that's what we called the games—sticking with it until he'd shelled out six times the price of whatever crap prize his kid wanted. But the fathers never seemed to care. They always looked happy, even proud, to be pissing their money away trying to land a ring on a bottle or sink a basketball.

"And the mothers, they were even . . . weirder. I'd watch a mother wipe the ice cream dripping down her kid's chin and then wrap the ice-cream cone in a napkin and hand it back to him. Smiling the whole time. Not mad that the kid was making a mess or getting in the way of something she'd rather be doing. I'd watch and I'd wonder what it was like to be a kid in a family like that. A real family." He tossed the driftwood aside and hunched forward, resting his forearms on his bent knees. "I guess that's what I dreamed of running to . . . someplace that felt real."

Someplace that felt real.

His tone was haunted, his words like a vise around Sophie's heart. Her mother's death had shattered her small family, but at least until then she'd had a family. A *real* family. And because of that, she had her memories, memories real and happy enough to get her through even the toughest days.

What if she'd hadn't? What if she'd never known a place in the world where she felt completely safe and completely loved, adored in fact, not for anything she had or anything she did, but simply for being her? What if she'd never had the chance to know what that felt like? If she had only glimpsed that kind of love from the outside looking in, could she even be certain it existed? That it was real?

It was a chilling thought, enough to make her feel a little desperate even at her age, and her heart broke for the lost little boy lurking inside Owen's words. She longed to comfort him, but didn't dare. Owen was no longer a little boy; he was a loner and a very private man. Something about being there, in that out-of-the-way place from his past, had lulled him into opening up just a little, but she was sure he'd clam up and get all prickly if he caught even a whiff of what he'd consider pity.

"I was eleven when my mother died," she revealed after a short pause, her tone casual. "How old were you?"

"Six. But she didn't die." He turned his head and met her gaze. "She just left."

She just left.

Owen felt every muscle in his body tighten at hearing the words said aloud and quickly turned away. They tore the scab off a chunk of the past he preferred not to think of and would rather rip his tongue out than talk about. Too late for the thinking part. Images popped up faster than he could block them. As fast as that, he was back in that tin can of a trailer, curled up under the table in the spot that had served as his makeshift bed, a blanket over his head, his heart pounding as he waited for his parents' shouting to reach its nightly crescendo.

He knew the routine. They'd argue and his father would stomp out, slamming the door behind him. His mother would light a cigarette and pour herself a glass of wine, and after a while his heart would stop hurting with every beat and he would be able to fall asleep. Except that night was different. A few minutes after his father left, his mother did the same. She'd never done that before and he scooted to the window and watched her cross the dusty parking lot to the phone booth.

He didn't know it then, but she was calling for a taxi. He didn't even know what a taxi was or that one could suddenly appear in the night and swallow up the person you loved most and take her away so that you never saw her again. He didn't know about any of that, but he did know something was different and wrong. He smelled it in the extra perfume his mother put on when she returned to the trailer and he heard it in the impatient *click-clack* of her high heels on the metal floor as she rushed around stuffing things into a suitcase.

"Please, Owen, not now," she said no matter what he asked her. He didn't ask much, nowhere near all the scary questions that filled his head watching her. He didn't dare. She'd said "not now, Owen" in the snappish, rushing voice he knew meant not to pester her too much or a slap would be coming his way.

When he saw lights and heard a car pull up outside, he looked out the window again; that's when he found out what a taxi was.

His mother didn't say anything when she went out the door, dragging the big suitcase behind her, but at least when he ran after her, barefoot, across the dirt and cracked asphalt, and asked her one last question, she didn't just brush him off with another "please, Owen, not now." She gave him a real answer, one that grew bigger and more complicated just like he did in the years that followed. The more he thought about them afterward, the more her words shed light on life and love and the way things fall apart when you least expect it.

Can I go with you? That was the last question he ever asked her.

"No," she said. She only half turned to look at him over her shoulder when she said it. Mostly he remembered her looking past him at the trailer with its crooked steps and dented chrome and the sign with a black top hat and white rabbit and THE AMAZ-ING WINTERS written on it. Her eyes were hard and bright as she said, "I've had all I can take of this freak show. I'm done with all of it."

He understood what *no* meant. It had taken him a while to figure out the rest and that the "all of it" she was done with included his father and him. He never did get a hundred percent clear on how a mother could just take off and leave her own kid and never come back; he just gave up and stopped thinking about it, like it was a mathematical equation he would never be able to solve because he didn't have the right formula. If one existed, she'd taken that with her too.

It was a while before Sophie spoke to him. If she thought silence would get him to open up and say more, she was wrong.

"Is that when you came to Rhode Island?" she asked eventually. "After your mother left?"

She touched his shoulder tentatively. He knew it was intended to be a friendly, reassuring pat, but instead it sent heat rushing through him. And this time, when he turned his head to look at her, her mouth curved into a smile as soft and gentle as her touch, and he was swept by the sudden, fierce, and totally inexplicable need to kiss her. Long and hard. He wanted to kiss her the way he had a nagging feeling Sophie Bennett, for all her romantic notions and bravado, had never been kissed, and should be.

Damn.

Still smiling at him, she tucked her hair behind one ear, baring the side of her throat. His fingers itched to touch her and he was no damn good at resisting that kind of temptation. Especially not when it came out of nowhere and went off like a Roman candle in his gut. The reason he was no good at resisting was simple: he never had to. Not because of any special appeal or talent or charm on his part. It was because he always made sure the women he crossed swords with were interested in the same outcome he was, and nothing more.

Sophie wasn't one of those women.

But somehow it suddenly didn't matter.

He was dangerously close to giving in to the craving to kiss her when he remembered there was a reason he'd brought her to this place and it wasn't to find out if she tasted as good as she looked at that moment.

"No," he said, barely managing to recall her question from a moment ago. "I ended up here later . . . after my father was shipped off to prison."

Her startled expression quickly turned questioning. Owen

didn't give her a chance to say anything. He had no intention of answering questions about his family history, about how dancing the fine line between what was legal and what was a scam to cheat people out of whatever was in their pockets had finally landed his old man a few years in jail, or about how his aunt had reluctantly taken in his surly, fourteen-year-old ass and arranged for him to attend the private school where she was assistant to the headmaster. It had been a turning point in his life, an important one. All the highs and lows of his life could be traced back to that.

"I didn't bring you here to talk about me," he said. "We're here to discuss Ivy, and how you plan to make sure we don't have a repeat of what happened today . . . or worse."

He was clearly intent on changing the subject and Sophie didn't blame him. God knows there were things in her past she'd rather not dredge up or dwell on. And besides, he was right: after today, it was clear she couldn't waste any time coming up with a way to stop Ivy from interfering with the wedding plans.

"That's a good question," she acknowledged. "Wish I had a good answer. Do you happen to have any suggestions?"

"As a matter of fact I do."

"Great. I'm listening. You said you had information about her that I'd find useful. Which means you've had better luck than I did. I have a friend looking into the history of the house, but I wouldn't describe anything we've come up with so far as being especially useful. I really appreciate your help."

He shrugged. "I had some free time the other day, so I dropped by the Historical Society to see what I could find out. I wasn't helping so much as I was curious."

"That's on my to-do list," she told him. "Currently somewhere around item one hundred and sixteen, if I'm not mistaken. And now that I have to juggle things around and reschedule the landscape design team, it will get bumped even lower. I did try checking with them by phone, but the woman I spoke with insisted I had to show up there and do the research personally."

"Yeah, she told me the same thing. I didn't have *that* much free time, so instead I just hung around until they took their break and treated the entire staff to Starbucks. I was hoping if I got them talking, someone might loosen up and drop something helpful about the property or the previous owners."

"And did they?"

"Sort of. The assistant director gave me the name of someone she thought had been a friend of Ivy's and who might be willing to answer a few questions. She even made a call to arrange for me to speak with the woman. Evidently Mrs. Theodora Todd Whitman was once a fixture on the Newport social scene and she still loves entertaining. She lives at an assisted living facility called Seaside Villa; we're talking five-star cuisine, health spa, indoor pool . . . the place is swankier than a lot of resorts I've seen. And lucky for me, the assistant director also remembered that she's a big fan of handmade chocolates with raspberry filling."

"Starbucks . . . chocolates . . . is bribery your go-to fix for everything?" she teased.

"Whatever works," he replied with a matter-of-fact shrug. "Lately I have more money than I do time . . . or patience. Mrs. Whitman got her chocolates and I got some useful information about our psycho ghost bride."

"Please tell me you didn't actually mention anything about a ghost."

"I didn't. Trust me; I don't want that getting out any more than you do. Less, in fact, since it's my doorbell every kook within a hundred miles will be knocking on in hopes of a sighting."

"Then we're agreed: we'll keep that strictly between the two of us. So," she continued as soon as he nodded agreement, "what did she tell you about Ivy?"

"It turns out Mrs. Whitman is quite a bit younger than Ivy Halliday was, at least twenty-five years. They met at a handful of charity functions through the years, but they only spoke in passing."

"I don't see how that helps."

He shot her a quelling look.

"Sorry."

"It was actually her mother who was friendly with Ivy Halliday at one time. Seems they were both debutantes and made the same rounds of balls and parties when they were in their teens and twenties. In fact, her mother was supposed to be a guest at Ivy's wedding."

"Supposed to be?"

"Right. Here's where it gets interesting. The wedding was planned for Ange de la Mer. And from Mrs. Whitman's description, it sounds like it was exactly the kind of fancy, overpriced, over-the-top affair you specialize in," he added with no effort to hide his disapproval.

"I prefer to think my specialty is making couples happy by giving them the kind of wedding they want, not the kind someone else thinks they should have . . . it is their big day after all. But do go on."

"So her mother was invited to be there on Ivy's *big day*, along with several hundred others. Evidently the guest list read like a Who's Who of Newport, circa 1920-something, which means it likely included more than its share of famous names and society heavyweights. That wasn't long after the Gilded Age. Must have been wall-to-wall Bentleys and Rolls out front . . . and all for nothing, as it turned out. The wedding never took place."

"Why not? Did she tell you what happened?"

"Oh, she told me all right." His mouth slanted in a long-suffering grimace. "In excruciating detail. Who wore what, who said what, what they almost ate. Like it happened yesterday. Nothing I enjoy more than the play-by-play of a wedding story. This one was the talk of the season and Mrs. Whitman's mother never got tired of retelling it. Every time the Halliday name came up, she was off and running at the mouth. She told the story so often and so well that Mrs. Whitman said she sometimes forgets she wasn't there herself and that she only knows what happened secondhand."

"So what did happen? You might have been bored by her story, but the suspense is killing me." She swung around so she was facing him, her legs curled to the side. "Why would a bride who went to all the trouble of planning a big splashy wedding call it off at the last minute . . . in front of hundreds of guests?"

"She didn't."

Sophie threw her hands up, impatient. "Then what—" She winced as the other obvious possibility occurred to her. "Oh no."

"Oh yeah, you guessed it. The bride was willing and able. The groom was the no-show."

"Poor Ivy. That has to be every bride's worst nightmare. I've only seen it happen once, but . . ." She shuddered and shook her head, remembering. "Once was more than enough. It's humiliation on top of heartache on top of betrayal . . . on top of more humiliation." She sighed. "So what was this jerk's excuse? A simple case of cold feet? Or did he suddenly fall head over heels for some bimbo he just met and decide he'd only *thought* he was in love with the woman he'd known and who he'd been professing to love for years and years and who had quite rightly assumed they would be spending the rest of their lives together, except that only now, *après* bimbo, did he understand what it meant to be truly in love?"

Not until she ran out of steam did she realize that Owen was watching and listening with greater-than-usual interest, his expression somewhere between amused and speculative.

She gave an awkward shrug. "Sorry. Pet peeve. You were saying . . . about the groom's reason for not showing up?"

"No one knows. The guy—Joseph something—just disappeared, never to be seen or heard from again."

"Never?"

"Never."

"Not by anyone? Not even his own family?"

"Didn't have one, according to Mrs. Whitman. She seems to recall that he came from somewhere down south and met Ivy while he was in the navy and stationed here in Newport. Ivy was your average, everyday society princess volunteering as a USO hostess and he was your classic kid from the wrong side of tracks, no family, raised in an orphanage, not even close to what the Hallidays had in mind for their beloved only daughter. But apparently what Ivy wanted Ivy got. Eventually her father came around and gave his permission for them to marry. He even offered the guy a position with the family shipbuilding business. And he had Ange de la Mer built to Ivy's specifications as a wedding present. So not only was it to be her wedding day, it was also the grand unveiling of her dream house."

He reached into his pocket. "I almost forgot . . . this is from Mrs. Whitman's late mother's collection." He handed Sophie a photograph. "It's a copy so you can hang on to it if you like."

She studied the black-and-white photo, tipping it to see more clearly in the bright sunlight. It was a formal pose, obviously taken by a professional. An engagement photo was Sophie's guess. It probably accompanied the official notice that appeared in the society pages. The young woman's sweater and jewelry appeared dated, but her beauty was timeless. She had high cheekbones, a confident, almost cocky smile, and sleek shoulder-length blond hair. Except for the haircolor, a young Lauren Bacall, thought Sophie.

"That's her all right," she said. "The ghost bride. That's the woman I saw."

"The woman who nearly broke your fingers," Owen reminded her.

"She was very beautiful, don't you think?"

She looked up in time to see him shrug.

"She was all right, I suppose. If you don't mind all the trouble and complications that go along with that stuck-up, spoiled-princess type."

Tilting her head to the side, she regarded him curiously. "Once burned? You sound like a man who speaks from experience."

He averted his gaze, his tone gruff. "Let's just say it's a mistake you don't make twice."

She nodded and took another look at the photo. "Okay. So a kid from nowhere, with nothing, scores a beautiful princess and a brand-new castle and then just walks away? That doesn't make sense."

"That's what Ivy said. She refused to believe he would leave her and insisted that something must have happened to him. Something bad. Her father agreed. He'd come around to thinking his future son-in-law was a decent guy, and he had enough clout to force a large-scale police investigation into his disappearance and to get the FBI—or the BOI, as it was known at the time—involved."

"BOI?"

"Bureau of Investigation. When the official search came up empty, he hired a team of private investigators. They didn't have any better luck. After that, Ivy took on the mantle herself. Local legend has it that she had a team of investigators on retainer to do her bidding right up until the day she died. She moved into the house on the day they would have been married, lived there alone, and never gave up hope."

"Maybe that's because Ivy knew something no one else did . . . or could. She knew that he—Joseph—was her soul mate . . . her forever love. That's how she knew he would never leave her . . . and that something had happened to keep him from coming to her."

"Well, regardless of what she knew or didn't know, at least

now we know why she's pissed at us. Me because she doesn't want me messing up Ivy's dream house with wet towels and beer bottles, and you because she doesn't want anyone else getting married there."

"I can't blame her on either score. It's only natural she has such strong feelings about that place. It's not just her home; it's a shrine to what might have been . . . to what *should* have been."

"A shrine? Maybe. Her home? No. She's dead, remember?"

"She's dead, but her love for Joseph isn't. For Ivy, those feelings are as alive and real today as they were on her wedding day. True love is very powerful . . . a force to be reckoned with."

"True love? Sounds more like true lunacy to me. But I'll bow to your expertise on the subject. The important thing is that we agree our headstrong ghost bride won't be giving up the fight anytime soon."

"Definitely not."

"It could get ugly," he warned. "Someone could get seriously hurt. She's shown she's willing to play rough. Who knows how far she'll go? A woman scorned and all that."

"It's a very delicate situation," agreed Sophie. "We obviously can't force her to behave. And it's not as if we can call the police or threaten her with legal action if she doesn't cooperate."

"Face it: we don't have a lot of options."

"She definitely has us at a disadvantage."

"A major disadvantage. So I think we know what we have to do."

Sophie nodded and they spoke at the same time.

"Back off."

"Reach out to her."

Ten

B ack off?"
   Owen nodded emphatically. "That's right. Back off. Walk away. Find someplace else to have the wedding."

"Why on earth would I back off?"

"Why in God's name would you reach out to her? So she can hand you a homemade Molotov cocktail?"

Sophie's mouth curved slightly. "Don't you think that's being a little overly dramatic?"

"No," he snapped, exasperation evident in the way he dragged his hand through his hair. "I think you're being overly naive if you have some touchy-feely notion that you can deal rationally with a whack-job ghost." He shook his head. "I can't believe I'm even sitting here having a conversation about a ghost."

"Ditto. To the last part," she hastened to add. "Not the rest. For your information, I am not naive . . . or touchy-feely. And I also don't think Ivy is a whack job. Exactly. I think she's a . . . a romantic." She lifted her chin as she said it, ignoring his muffled snort. "I admit that at first I was at a loss as to how to handle this whole thing, but I feel much better now. Thanks to you."

He went from looking annoyed to aghast. "Me? What did I do?"

"Exactly what you said you'd do: you gave me information that helped me decide what to do."

"Only because I assumed you'd make the right decision."

Frowning, Sophie drew back a little. "Is that the reason you told me about Ivy's background? Because you *wanted* me to give up . . . to back off?" Her surprise turned to suspicion. "Is that why you were so helpful and went to the trouble of looking into it in the first place?"

"I never claimed I was trying to be helpful. And I told you because I thought you were smart enough and levelheaded enough to know when you've run into a brick wall, and to realize that having this wedding somewhere else would be the best—not to mention the safest—thing for everyone involved."

"Not for Shelby," she retorted. "Being married at the Princess House means everything to her. And not for me; I keep my promises and I promised Shelby the wedding of her dreams."

"And you did your best to deliver. Sometimes things happen that are beyond your control."

"Sometimes," she allowed. "But not this time. There's no way I'm giving up now that I know the whole story. Ivy Halliday and I share common ground. We're—"

"Kindred spirits?" he interjected in a sardonic tone.

"Bad pun aside, yes. I understand what she went through and how she must have felt that day . . . and I understand why she doesn't want some stranger barging into her house and having the beautiful, happy wedding day that should have been hers."

"And exactly what are you planning to do that will change any of that? You can't turn back time. You can't wave a magic wand

and make her missing groom reappear. What can you possibly say or do to change feelings she's nursed for the better part of a century?"

She tilted her head to the side, her mouth quirking with indecision. "I'm not sure . . . yet. Truthfully, I'm not sure I *can* change the way she feels." Before his triumphant grin had a chance to form, she folded her arms in front of her with serious determination. "But I just might be able to change her mind about the best way to deal with those feelings."

"How?" he challenged.

"Like I said, I'm not sure yet." She hesitated, thinking. It wasn't easy to do in the face of his disgruntled glare. "For starters, I might try telling her about Shelby. You mentioned that Ivy was a USO volunteer; I think she'll admire Shelby and Matthew's decision to join the Peace Corps. And then there's the house itself. Ange de la Mer was a gift to Ivy from her father and Shelby's father took her sailing near there because he knew how much she loved it. There's a strong emotional link there. If I can get Ivy to feel a personal connection to Shelby, it may be easier to get her to listen and to convince her that ruining Shelby's wedding won't change what happened to her . . . it will only add to the negative karma of the house she loves."

He looked coolly unimpressed.

"Look, I understand your concern," she said, wanting him in her corner. "Believe me; I don't want anyone to get hurt any more than you do. And I promise you I won't let it come to that. Please, just give me a chance to try to bring Ivy around. I've talked dozens of brides through bouts of cold feet and last-minute jitters."

"Ivy doesn't have cold feet," he pointed out. "She has a raging case of 'get the hell out of my house or I'll hurt you and break your stuff.'"

"Well, yes. True. But she's still a bride . . . at least I think she thinks she is. And brides can be emotional and irrational, and that's where I come in. I'm good at what I do. When it comes to brides, I've learned to trust my instincts and my instincts are telling me I can get through to Ivy. Who knows? This might turn out to be the best thing for her too. She can't be happy rattling around all alone in that big house. Maybe I can help her work out whatever is holding her there so she can move on in peace."

He almost smiled. "Yeah, right, you're not at all the touchy-feely type. So that's your grand plan? Two happy brides for the price of one?"

"Go ahead and laugh. But I can do this. You'll see. As soon as we get back to the house, Operation Befriend a Ghost goes into full swing."

She made a move to stand and instantly he was on his feet to offer her a hand up. With him supplying the muscle, Sophie rose gracefully, but as she turned away, instead of letting her go, he tightened his grip on her hand.

She glanced back to find out why, half knowing already. Not in words. This wasn't about words. She knew from the telltale heat and sizzle where his palm was pressed to her own, and in that wordless place deep inside, that place where she had somehow always known it would come to this, where she'd yearned for it from the start and welcomed it even now as her pulse skipped and her breath went still as glass in her throat.

He gazed at her without smiling, his dark blue gaze turbulent as it moved unhurriedly from her eyes to her mouth and back.

"Is something wrong?"

"Yes," he said. The frown lines at the corners of his mouth deepened. "No." And then, muttering, "Oh, what the hell . . ."

The instant of indecision behind him, he took her shoulders and pulled her to him.

There was ample time for her to resist, to say no, to say they should be sensible and go back to the house and back to work, and not do anything reckless that her heart would almost certainly regret.

Instead, curious and impatient, she leaned closer to him, lifting her chin so that their gazes met and held and heated, and then his mouth was on hers in a searching, drugging kiss that made her senses spin and her knees buckle. He held her and she clung to him with both hands on his back, her fingers curling into the soft, sun-warmed cotton of his T-shirt. He tasted smoky and intoxicating. His flesh was hard, his touch urgent, and with her eyes closed, it was like hurtling through the blackest of nights, no lights, no caution, just heat and excitement.

Her lips parted under his as his possession of her mouth grew harder and deeper. It started something burning between them . . . and inside her. It was a flame licking at her core, rushing in her blood. As unfamiliar as it was to her, it didn't feel new; it felt . . . awakened. Unleashed. Like a part of her had always been waiting for this . . . and for him.

The kiss ended abruptly with a cold shower, courtesy of a rogue wave that crashed hard against the rocks and sent spray cascading twelve feet in the air. They broke apart, breathing hard.

"Looks like true love isn't the only force to be reckoned with," Owen said after a minute, in that low, rough tone that made her shiver.

At first Sophie thought he was referring to the incoming tide, but then he lifted his hand to her face, rubbing his thumb along her jaw and trailing his fingertips down the side of her throat.

"You seem to have become an irresistible impulse for me." He said it softly, with a faint undertone of amazement. "I'm going to have to work on that."

Work on it how? Sophie wondered. Work on resisting the impulse? Or on getting better at giving in to it? With her lips still throbbing, she really didn't think that was possible. She managed to say nothing, which was probably for the best. She felt a little dazed, like one of those cartoon characters that walk off a cliff and end up with a merry-go-round of stars and chirping birdies circling their heads. Her most eloquent comment would be along the lines of "Wow."

Owen either recovered more quickly or he hadn't been nearly as blindsided as she was. She didn't want to think about that right now. Strong and sure-footed in spite of whatever had happened to his leg, he led the way back to his bike, helping her over the rough spots. There might have been another Merchant-Ivory moment along the way, but she couldn't be sure. She was distracted, consumed with thoughts of The Kiss, amazed that she, die-hard romantic and starry-eyed champion of love and passion, could have lived her whole life without knowing that that feeling existed.

"I don't get it," Sophie said. "Now that I want to talk with Ivy, she's gone all MIA on us. When I wanted her to go away, she was all about making contact."

"Was she?" countered Owen. "I'm not so sure."

He was comfortably sprawled in a big cushy chair in the sunroom at the back of the house, where he'd waited while Sophie methodically made her way through each and every room in the place, doing and saying anything and everything she could think of to entice the spirit of Ivy Halliday to appear. Candles, soft music, polite requests, and impassioned pleas, thinly—and not so thinly—veiled threats: she'd tried them all. And she hadn't elicited so much as a glimpse or whisper from the house's resident ghost.

With a discouraged sigh she dropped into the chair facing him.

"Let's see, squashed fingers, spooky bride vision, hostile warning, beehive assault." She ticked them off on her fingers. "The way

I see it, all the above qualify as making contact, and that's not even counting what's been happening with you."

"I think 'assault' might be the key word there. Ivy's shown she's willing and capable of lashing out and attacking on her terms, but I wouldn't classify piling wet towels in my bed or planting a golf club for someone to trip over as efforts to make contact with the natives. The way I see it, she hasn't shown any interest in a two-way dialogue, much less playing nice."

"You're probably right. But I'm too damn tired to think about it. I give up."

His dark brows shot up.

"For today," she clarified. With a sigh, she rested her head back against the seat cushion. "There has to be a way to get her attention; I just need to figure out what it is."

"Maybe I can save you some time." He stood and headed out of the room. Reluctantly, Sophie scrambled from her comfy perch to follow.

"Where are we going?"

She got her answer when he stopped in the formal living room at the front of the house and stood looking around. It was a huge room, big enough for several furniture groupings, with a white marble fireplace at one end.

For no particular reason Sophie found herself wondering if this was where Ivy put up her tree at Christmastime. She was envisioning the room decked for the holidays, with twinkling white lights and handblown glass ornaments and a towering, fragrant pine tree at the center of it all, when it suddenly occurred to her to wonder if Ivy had even bothered with a Christmas tree. Or with a Thanksgiving turkey or Fourth of July fireworks and barbecues. Had she bravely gathered family and friends there to celebrate holidays, the way she must have dreamed of doing when the house was being built and her future looked so rosy? Or had she put all that on hold and allowed her life to dwindle down to simply waiting for Joseph to return? She wasn't sure if knowing the answer would help her in her quest, but she was curious just the same. She wanted to believe that in spite of everything, there had been Christmas carols and champagne toasts and laughter in that house . . . and in Ivy's life.

"This'll do for starters," Owen announced. He was standing in front of a tall, narrow, enamel curio cabinet. She watched, first puzzled and then alarmed as he yanked open the door and began grabbing pieces of crystal and blue-and-white Wedgwood off the glass shelves and tossing them onto a pale gold velvet chair a few feet away. There was the sound of breaking glass.

"What are you doing?" Sophie demanded, hurrying to his side.

"Getting this junk out of the way." He removed the last item from the bottom shelf, a slender crystal vase perfect for holding a single bloom.

Sophie snatched it from his hand before he could toss it. "Why? Out of the way of what?"

"Out of my way. So it won't be as heavy when I drag it outside." He swung the door shut and bent his knees slightly as he positioned his hands on the sides of the cabinet, preparing to lift it.

"Stop." She grabbed his forearm. "What the hell do you think you're doing?"

"What does it look like?"

"It looks like you've lost your mind," she blurted.

"Trust me, I haven't. You wanted to get the attention of your ghost pal? I promise you this will do the job. She gets in a snit when I put a glass down on one of her precious tables; what do you think she'll do when I start tossing her stuff out with the trash? One fancy-ass piece at a time."

"Stop," she said again. "I mean it, Owen. You are not going to toss anything anywhere."

He didn't let go of the cabinet, but she felt his muscles relax as he turned his head to look at her. "I'm telling you: this will work. Sometimes you have to get tough and fight fire with fire. Do you think she'd shy away from breaking something of yours in order to get her way?"

"I don't care. That's not how *I* work. It's cruel."

"So was slamming a drawer on your fingers. Maybe two wrongs don't make a right, but it can still be damn effective."

She shook her head. "No. Maybe Ivy felt she didn't have a choice, that she had no other way of dealing with what she perceived as a threat. But I don't feel that way. I don't want to hurt Ivy; I want to try to help her. I know this can be resolved so that everyone is happy . . . or at least content . . . and without causing any damage. I just need some time to think about my next move."

For a long moment he scowled at the cabinet without saying anything. He didn't need to; his frustration fairly crackled in the air between them. Finally he took his hands from the cabinet and straightened. "Fine. That's just fine. We'll play it your way. On one condition. You do your thinking here."

"I didn't mean I could come up with a solution tonight, on the spot," she clarified.

"I'm not talking about tonight. I'm talking about you being here twenty-four/seven from now until the wedding day. I'm talking about you being the one to deal with whatever crap she dishes out. Because I'm done with it."

She gave a feeble laugh, eyeing him in disbelief. "You can't be serious."

"I'm nothing but. This whole thing has turned into a giant pain in the ass . . . my ass. My vote is to throw in the towel and cut our losses. You're the one who wants to keep banging your head against the wall. So it's only fitting that you be the one standing by, ready to stick your finger in the dike whenever your kindred spirit feels like poking another hole in it."

"That's ridiculous. Not to mention impossible. I have other clients . . . and a life. I can't possibly be here around the clock."

"Then you can't go ahead with this wedding. It's as simple as that."

"This wasn't part of our original *signed* agreement."

"Lots of things weren't part of our original agreement. Do you really want to air them in a public courtroom?" He paused. "I didn't think so."

He went on, saying something about being sorry he had to play hardball with her and about his deadline and ghosts with bad attitudes. Sophie only half listened. What he was proposing was beyond ridiculous. It was outrageous and unfair and out of line. And she had no doubt he meant it and wouldn't be backing down. He had her cornered. She couldn't disappoint Shelby and she couldn't just take a hiatus from the rest of her life and camp out there for the next few weeks. Forget about the overall inconvenience and the havoc it would play with her work schedule, she would be living alone in a house—granted, a very big house—with a man she hardly knew. As for the fact that the prospect concerned her and excited her in about equal parts, well, she wasn't sure how to factor that into the mix.

"Look, if you're worried about what happened earlier, on the rocks," he said, immediately commanding her full attention. "You don't need to be."

"You mean the . . . our . . ." She gave a little wave of one hand.

"Kiss," he supplied.

For an instant, amusement lifted the corner of his mouth, and suddenly she couldn't seem to move her gaze from that spot. With that wicked glint in his eyes and the dark whiskers shadowing his jaw, he looked like an advertisement for whiskey, or sin. The feeling of being in his arms shivered through her, undermining her concentration.

"Like I told you," he continued, "that kiss was just a momentary impulse. What I'm proposing now is about business. Period. It has nothing to do with my little lapse in judgment earlier. You can trust me to see to it that it doesn't happen again."

"Well, good," she said, disappointment a small, hard knot in her chest at hearing that he considered kissing her to be a "lapse in judgment." "That's good. And reassuring. Very reassuring. It's certainly not a mistake I would want to repeat."

So there. He wasn't the only one who could plead a lapse in judgment.

"Good. Very good. So we're clear."

"Very clear."

"Then it's settled, and the ball's back in your court. So . . ." He folded his arms, watching her. "What's it going to be Sophie? Wedding or no wedding?"

It had been a most interesting day, reflected Ivy as she watched Sophia Bennett return the objects removed by Mr. Winters to their rightful place in the curio cabinet. Most interesting indeed.

She wasn't certain what she would have done if he'd actually hauled the cabinet outside and tossed it in the trash. But whatever she did would have made a few bee stings pale in comparison. If Mr. Winters thought she had been a "pain in his ass" thus far, he didn't know what real pain was. It was her belief that she had exercised remarkable restraint under the circumstances.

The obvious recourse would have been to retaliate by destroying something of equal value to him. Except she couldn't think of what that would be. As far as she could tell, his worldly belongings consisted of little more than the silver frame holding his daughter's picture—which she would never touch, the clothes on his back—which were not worth the effort, and that horrible, noisy motorcycle—tempting, but alas, out of the question. What sort of grown man rode around town looking like a common hoodlum and didn't have a stick of furniture to call his own?

There was, of course, the computer he used for his supposed writing. Surely it was of some value monetarily, but her sense—based on the many times she'd heard him cursing at it—was that it was merely a necessary evil in his life, not something he cared about, and certainly not something comparable to the curio cabinet that had stood in the corner of her mother's dressing room when she was a girl. Back then it held her mother's silk scarves and her hair ornaments adorned with jewels and silky feathers and exotic beads; she still recalled the hours she spent sorting and rearranging them and posing with them on in front of the dressing-table mirror.

Those memories came back to her strongly as she watched Sophia Bennett carefully arranging the Waterford crystal and Wedgwood pieces on the shelves, and she felt herself smiling. Which was silly, because at the moment she wasn't even really there. Not in a physical sense. It had been a long day and she was too weary to gather the energy required to appear. No physical presence, no smile, but she felt herself smiling nonetheless and she wondered at it. The feeling itself was strange to her. It had been so very long. So long that she couldn't recall the last time she'd smiled.

It suddenly occurred to her that it was taking the young Bennett woman an inordinate amount of time to return the items to the cabinet and she realized why: she was trying to return each one to its original position and, Ivy noted, she was doing an impressive job. The fact that she had intervened and stood up to Mr. Winters was impressive. But this, the extra care she was taking to make things right again, touched Ivy in a way that had become as unfamiliar to her as her own smile. The show of kindness made her feel a trifle sorry for the way she had ignored the young woman earlier, and it almost made her want to gather herself to make an appearance and listen to whatever Sophia wanted to say to her.

Almost.

As moved as she was, she had no patience for lost causes. Nor was she a proponent of suggesting there was hope where there was none. She didn't have to actually hear her say it to know what the young woman had to say. She knew very well what Sophia Bennett wanted from her . . . and why she would attempt to curry favor to get it. She wanted a truce of some sort; she wanted leave for her wedding plans to go forward without interference. She wanted Ivy to step aside and let another bride take her place.

And that, thought Ivy as she withdrew from the room, was never going to happen.

Sophie got lucky and found both Jill and Jenna still in their offices when she arrived back at Seasons shortly after seven. It meant she would only have to tell the tale once and not have to rely on either twin to get it straight in the retelling.

She waited until they finished their meeting with a new client, using the time to catch up on her own work and put her desk in order. She joined them in Jenna's office. Like the twins themselves, their newly redecorated offices were nearly identical: white textured wall coverings, black lacquer furnishings, and photographs of Seasons' events in brushed silver frames. A pop of color was provided by the carpeting and a few carefully chosen accent pieces: turquoise in Jenna's office and lime in Jill's.

"Hey, you two," she said with a quick rap on the open door. "Got a minute?"

From her seat behind the desk, Jenna waved her in. "Sure. Grab a chair."

"Thanks, but I have to get home. I just want to fill you in on a problem that's come up with the Archer wedding."

She gave them a quick, sanitized, strictly need-to-know run-down of the day's events that did not include any mention of Ivy.

When she finished there was a second of silence.

Jill, looking bewildered, spoke first. "You can't be serious."

Sophie almost laughed. It was the same thing she'd said when she heard Owen's ultimatum.

"Nothing but," she said, borrowing his reply.

Jill's eyes grew comically wide and for a second Sophie thought she might slip from her perch on the corner of the desk. "You're moving in with Owen Winters?"

"No," said Sophie. "I'm—"

Shaking her head as if to clear it, Jill chuckled and cut her off. "Of course you're not. I knew that couldn't be right. But it sounded like that's what you said." She glanced at Jenna. "Didn't it sound like that's what she said?"

"That is what she said," Jenna snapped. "Sophie, what's wrong with you? You can't just move in with a man you hardly know. Especially not a man like Owen Winters."

"What kind of man is that?"

"Wealthy," Jenna said without hesitation. "Good-looking . . . at least he could be if he made any effort at all. Successful, famous, charming . . . when he wants to be. And at times rude and self-absorbed. Need I go on? Unless I miss my guess, and I seldom do when it comes to men, he's the kind of man who prefers his women young and hot."

"Twentysomething eye candy," Jill added, nodding with conviction. "No doubt about it."

"I really wouldn't know," Sophie responded, managing to keep both her amusement and her annoyance from her voice. "But what does his taste in women—or lack thereof—have to do with this? I'm not moving in with Owen Winters. I'm simply doing what I have to do to make sure there is someone on-site at all times to supervise the wedding preparations."

"Of course. I understand that's all there is to it. I just want to make sure you're okay with that . . . that you're not, well, reading something more into his request."

"It wasn't a request; it was an ultimatum. And the only thing I'm reading into it is that he has a deadline and doesn't want to be dragged away from his work and forced to do damage control the way he was today . . . which he is entirely within his rights to de-mand. There's a lot of work to be done to get ready for this wed-ding, a lot of complicated setup, and not a lot of time to do it. I'm going to have crews working overtime and weekends. Problems are bound to arise and it will be to our advantage timewise if someone is on hand to deal with them as soon as they do. A lot of thought and time went into coordinating this job to run like clock-work. If one work team runs into trouble, it could have a domino effect, forcing others to wait around or reschedule in order to get their work done. I called in a lot of favors to get vendors to squeeze us in at the last minute, during their busiest time of year; resched-uling will be a nightmare."

Jill gave an impatient wave of her hand. "We get all that. We have planned a wedding or two ourselves, remember? All Jenna was trying to say is that we don't want to see you get your heart broken."

"Again," added Jenna.

Jill nodded, her delicate features forming a sympathetic frown. "Do you remember how horrible it was when Keith dumped you?"

Sophie drew a deep breath. "Yes. Yes, I do remember."

"You were devastated," Jill recalled.

"Crushed," said Jenna.

"A mess. For weeks. Maybe months. I don't remember exactly, but it seemed like you were moping around forever. And we just don't want to see you get taken again."

"I wouldn't say I was taken," Sophie protested. "Keith and I dated for over three years—"

"Nearly four."

"Yes, nearly four. And for most of that time things were fine."

"So it seemed." Jill's tone was lilting and skeptical.

"I was in love with Keith and I trusted him. People change. It happens."

"And it's nothing for you to be ashamed of," Jenna assured her. "You were in love with love and that's just so you. You have this whole fairy-tale thing going on and it's adorable, and it probably made you see things in the relationship that weren't there."

"That's not quite . . . you know what? It doesn't matter. I got over Keith ages ago.

"And, more importantly, the situation with Owen Winters is entirely different. It's business: period." Her fingers were curled so tightly the tips were numb. A reflex. She felt like punching something. Maybe herself, for being stupid enough to try to justify her past to the *J*s. She knew better, and yet every once in a while she suddenly found herself feeling fifteen again and trying to convince them—and herself—that she really wasn't a completely clueless dork who needed their endless advice and guidance.

"And you're okay with that?" inquired Jenna. She smiled indulgently. "You're not moving into the castle with stars in your eyes and visions of Prince Charming dancing in your head?"

"Not at all," Sophie replied, loosening her fists before she drew blood. "But it's really sweet of you both to be so concerned about *my* feelings." Even if it meant dredging up one of the most painful and humiliating events in her life and rubbing her nose in it. Of course the subtext was lost on them, as she'd known it would be.

Jenna beamed her most benevolent smile. "Hey, what are big sisters for?"

Lips pursed, Jill spoke with a hint of petulance. "You know, I understand why someone has to be there to keep an eye on things, but all this talk of castles and princes has me wondering why that someone has to be you. I wouldn't mind spending a few weeks in an oceanfront mansion. No kids. No housework." She glanced at Sophie. "He does have a housekeeper, right?"

Hmm, thought Sophie, *tricky question.* She settled for a shrug.

"He must," Jill decided. "And probably a cook, too. I could live with that for a while."

"Now that you mention it, so could I," said Jenna. "God, can you imagine? My friends would be green when they found out I was living in a mansion on Bellevue Avenue. Do you think Winters would let me have people over once in a while? Nothing fancy. Strictly drinks and hors d'oeuvres."

"Maybe he'd like to join in," suggested Jill.

Jenna nodded. "I'll bet he would. He seemed kind of recluse-y. He probably doesn't know too many people here." She glanced at Sophie. "He's not from around here, is he?"

Another shrug. "I don't know where he's from exactly."

"I think having a famous author in the mix would make for some interesting conversation," ventured Jenna.

"Absolutely," agreed Jill. "And if we hit it off he might even let us handle his next book launch."

"That would be a real coup."

"Maybe we should take a vote on who gets to play princess," suggested Jill.

"Great idea," said Sophie. "Except that the only vote that

counts has already been cast." She did her best not to sound smug as she said it.

For a second or two the *J*s appeared stumped. Then Jenna grimaced.

"Shelby," she said.

Jill heaved a sigh of disgust. "Oh, right. You know, she turned out to be a lot more trouble than we bargained for."

"First, none of our wedding ideas are good enough for her. Then she wants to pick and choose her planner. And now there's not a dress to be found anywhere that meets all her requirements."

"A *hemp* dress."

"Right . . . and she wonders why none of them are flattering."

"Actually, the dress problem is solved," Sophie told them. "So you can cross that off the list of things you have to lose sleep worrying about."

Jill scoffed.

"As if," muttered Jenna.

"You don't get off scot-free however." Stepping forward, Sophie slid the list she'd prepared across the desk.

"What's this?" asked Jenna.

Jill moved so she could read it over her twin's shoulder.

"That's a list of the things I ordinarily take care of, but won't be able to for the next few weeks. I downloaded the files I need and set it up so that I can access my office computer from my laptop. Most of my work I can take care of by phone or e-mail. I'll shoot you a status update of current jobs every morning, but someone will have to update the Big Board in my office so you can keep track of everything. And at the bottom of that list are appointments I won't be able to keep. One of you will have to either fill in for me or reschedule. Oh, you'll also have to reschedule the appointment with the flower wholesaler that I had to cancel this afternoon."

The *J*s exchanged a look.

"This is a lot of work," Jenna said. "And a lot of running around."

"And that's on top of all the work we already do," added Jill. "I'm not sure we can handle all this."

"Oh, don't sell yourselves short." Sophie's smile was wide and genuine. "After all, you've planned a wedding or two in your time."

"Yes, but we don't usually get involved with background stuff."

"Or all these picayune details."

"Or the Big Board."

"That's right. You don't do any of that. But look on the bright side: anything I can do, you can do better. Think of this as an opportunity to get in touch with your Inner Drone."

Eleven

It was late by the time she made it back to Newport and arrived on Owen's doorstep, bag and baggage. Or rather, bag and bag and bag and baggage. There are people in the world who travel light, content to wander from home with a wing and a prayer and a favorite pair of flip-flops. Sophie wasn't one of them.

As much as she loved to visit new places and meet new people, she was a homebody at heart, into cocooning long before it became trendy. There were things she just liked having around, familiar things that made her feel safe and happy. When her father remarried and her stepmother moved in and gradually put her stamp on the house, Sophie's room became her sanctuary. She decorated it with castoffs that had been relegated to a box in the garage and that she rescued before Goodwill came to haul them away. Relics of happier days, those favorite things went with her to college and then to her first apartment and to the condo where she lived now. A few small treasures, mostly photos, always found their way into her suitcase when she was away from home, but three bags full were a little much even for her.

It couldn't be helped. She had a gut feeling that between dealing with Ivy and dealing with the feelings Owen stirred up inside her, she was going to need as many stress busters and creature comforts as she could get. First she'd decided to bring along her own pillow, then her favorite mug and the ginger-peach tea she liked, and it just sort of snowballed from there.

Owen met her at the door.

"You look surprised to see me," she observed. "We did agree that I would be back tonight?"

"That was the plan," he confirmed, nodding. "But I wondered if you'd have second thoughts."

"About moving in? Oh, I've had second, third, and fourth. You have to admit, the situation is more than a little unorthodox. And awkward."

"And yet . . ."

She sighed. "And yet when you come right down to it, I'd rather deal with unorthodox and awkward than have to look Shelby in the eye and tell her the reason she can't have her Princess House wedding is because I'm a quitter."

He didn't comment, but since he'd already made clear his feelings about love and marriage and happy-ever-after, Sophie figured it had to be pure cynicism that she saw glitter in his eyes. Naturally he would think she was wasting her time.

"Here, let me take that for you," he said, reaching for the handle of the suitcase resting on its wheels beside her.

"I've got this one, but there's more in the car if you want to help."

She wheeled the suitcase into the hall and then followed him back outside. By the time she reached the car, he had one bag on his shoulder and one under his arm.

"How about handing me that duffel bag?" she said.

"I'm all set."

"Yeah, but I don't want you to hurt yourself."

He stopped and glanced at her over his shoulder. "You think I'm going to hurt myself carrying luggage?"

"I just meant that maybe with your leg you shouldn't—"

He cut her off sharply. "Let me worry about my leg."

"Oops," she murmured under her breath, trailing slowly.

He grabbed the suitcase in the hallway with his free hand and waited for her at the bottom of the stairs. She decided not to point out that he was being ridiculous. Carrying all the bags single-handedly had clearly taken on some sort of testosterone-laden significance she couldn't hope to understand. She knew just enough about the primal instincts of the male of the species to be certain that there was no reasoning with a man having an MSS—Macho Shithead Syndrome—moment. In hindsight, she could see that she obviously shouldn't have tried to help him with the bags, or implied that he might need help in the first place, and especially not because of a physical infirmity. She made a mental note not to avoid taking a sensible approach to such matters in the future, but for now all she could do was stand by, ready to call 911 if his leg gave out and he came tumbling down the stairs in an avalanche of tea bags and down feathers.

"Do you want to go on up ahead of me and choose a room?"

"I already have," she told him. "Last room on the right, over-looking the water. It's the one with—"

"Yeah, I know which one it is," he growled, already turning away. "Last room on the right. Your bags will be inside the door."

Something was different. Not necessarily wrong. He didn't have enough to go on to make that determination yet. But definitely different.

His senses had been honed to detect the slightest change in his environment because there was a time when it had meant the difference between survival and that other thing. Bad luck and bad intelligence could screw up a man's leg and end his military career, but once developed, his spider senses remained ever vigilant. They interacted with life on a fundamental level: scent, sound, motion, temperature. And right now they were telling him that something about this morning was different from other mornings.

For starters, he was fully awake and it was still dark. He lay still, staring at the ceiling above his bed and listening intently, and then it came to him . . . the realization that he wasn't alone in the house. Of course. It wasn't some*thing* that was different about this morning: it was some*one*.

Sophie.

Owen held his breath, listening to the sound of water running and then the whisper of slippered feet at the other end of the hall. All the way at the other end. In the room farthest from his own.

There was a message in her choice of rooms. *Keep your distance, Winters.* It was a message he wholeheartedly agreed with and intended to heed. For both their sakes, he would keep his distance.

That didn't mean he had to like it.

There was a light on over the kitchen sink, a cool breeze coming through the half-open window and the rousing aroma of coffee in the air. Which turned out to be a big tease since the coffeepot was as empty and dry as it was every other morning. There wasn't even a jar of instant coffee in sight, although he did notice a few jars of other stuff neatly arranged at the back of the counter. Honey. Apricot preserves. Some sort of grinder with raw sugar crystals and chunks of cinnamon inside.

Sophie was exactly where he recalled her telling him she would be the first time they met: out back waiting for the sun to rise.

She was sitting on the wide steps leading from the patio to the lawn, the lacy yellow shawl pulled around her shoulders a beacon in the darkness, an oversize coffee mug cradled in her hands.

She glanced up as he approached, her pleased smile too quick to be feigned.

"Good morning," she said.

"Private viewing?" he inquired, angling his head toward the ocean, where the sun was still only a soft orange streak on the horizon. "Or would you like some company?"

"I'd love company." Still smiling, she patted the step beside her.

The warmth of her welcome was something of a surprise considering that last night she couldn't get far enough away from him. And in light of his own less than gracious response.

"You're not a coffee drinker?" she ventured as he settled in beside her, leaning back on his elbows with his legs stretched out in front of him.

"I am. I'm just not a coffee maker . . . not coffee worth drinking at any rate. I usually take a ride out to a coffee shop downtown, but I didn't want to miss the show. And I'm not sure they'd even be open yet. I'm not usually up this early."

He yawned as he said it and she slanted him a guilty look. "I'm sorry. Did I wake you? I tried to be quiet."

"You were quiet. I'm a light sleeper."

"Let me make it up to you with a cup of coffee."

"Then you'll miss the show . . . the pot's empty. I checked."

"Oh, I didn't use that. I brought my own single-cup brewer. I'm kind of a creature of habit. I like having my stuff around." As evidence, she sheepishly raised her mug and tugged on the edge of her shawl.

"Well, that explains why you needed a dozen suitcases."

"It was only three . . . it probably just felt like there were a dozen because you were lugging them up the stairs all by yourself."

He shrugged, ignoring the undercurrent of amusement in her tone. "They got there."

"Yes, they did. And I appreciated it. Another reason I owe you a cup of coffee. It will only take a minute. Less than actually. That's the beauty of brewing one cup at a time: it's fast . . . and you can have whatever kind you like. I brought along a full array of flavors . . . caramel crème, island Kona, mocha java . . . what will it be?"

"Hot. Strong. Black."

"Midnight Magic coming right up," she said, getting to her feet and heading inside.

It was fast. It was also the best-tasting cup of coffee he'd had in a long time. Maybe the best ever. Then again, it was entirely possible his judgment was clouded by the foolish rush of pleasure he got from knowing that Sophie had gone to the trouble of making it and bringing it to him. He added that to the growing list of feelings and motives he was being careful not to explore too deeply.

At the very top of that list was his reason for insisting that Sophie move in with him. The explanation he gave her and continued to cling to was perfectly plausible. This powder keg of a wedding was her problem, and by rights, if it was going to blow up in someone's face, it ought to be hers. Ivy Halliday was also her problem. End of story. Whatever else he might have been thinking or feeling when he got the idea to issue that ultimatum didn't matter and didn't bear thinking about.

Keep your distance, Winters.

"Good coffee," he said after several minutes. "Thanks."

"My pleasure. I knew you'd be a Midnight Magic man."

They sat quietly, watching the sun inching its way higher in the sky. The sky itself went from black to gray to blue as night melted into day.

"It really is beautiful, isn't it?"

"It is," agreed Owen.

It *was* a beautiful sight. The stuff of poetry. And he felt suitably boorish over the fact that he was finding it nearly impossible to keep his gaze focused on the magnificent ball of fire rising from the ocean with Sophie sitting only inches away. When he'd first wandered out there to join her, all he could see well was her yellow shawl. As the darkness around them lifted, he gradually saw her more clearly. It was like watching a Polaroid snapshot develop. Or peeling the wrapping paper off a present. And the more clearly he saw her, the more difficult it was to look away.

She was barefoot, wearing a snug, pale gray ribbed tank top and gray knit pants, like sweatpants and yet not at all like sweatpants. Sweatpants were baggy: the top and pants she had on clung to the soft curves of her breasts and thighs and hips in a way he found more fascinating than a thousand sunrises. Her face was scrubbed free of makeup and her hair was haphazardly gathered in a clip on the top of her head. She looked guileless and fresh and vulnerable, and he wanted her more than he'd wanted any woman in a very long time.

Which was just one more crazy incongruity of the sort that had been sneaking up on him ever since Sophie Bennett steamrolled into his life. He shouldn't want her for the very reason he did . . . because she looked guileless and fresh and vulnerable. She was the antithesis of what he looked for in a woman. He looked for polish and sophistication. He looked for long legs and nice tits and a distinctive air of self-absorption that told him the woman was so into herself she'd never notice if he was into her or not. He counted on that high-priced, high-velocity glamour to provide emotional cover and keeps things uncomplicated. You could sleep with a woman like that a hundred times and never get truly close to her. And that's just the way he liked it. To be honest, Sophie's sisters, as annoying as they were, were more his usual type than she could ever be.

He hurriedly shifted his attention back to the horizon as she stretched her arms over her head and turned to him. That smile again. That quick, strange tug on his insides.

"I'm going to give this morning's performance a nine on a scale of one to ten," she announced. "Only so I'll have something to look forward to. It was definitely worth hauling myself out of bed for. And to think I nearly hit the snooze button and skipped it."

Owen paused before taking a gulp of coffee. "So you managed to get some sleep after all."

"Sure. After the day I had yesterday? Why wouldn't I sleep?"

"I just know you were a little uneasy." He sat up so they were shoulder to shoulder. "Last night, I mean."

She shrugged. "Like I said, it's an unusual situation. That's not enough to keep me awake. Especially not when I have my own pillow."

"I meant that you were uneasy around me." When she appeared puzzled, he added, "Why else would you choose the smallest room in the house just to put as much distance between us as possible?"

"Are you kidding? Is that really what you think? That I chose that room because it was the one farthest from yours?"

"Didn't you? I gave you my word that I wouldn't put my hands on you again, but that obviously wasn't enough to put your mind at ease."

"You're wrong. I wasn't uneasy. Trust me," she said, her mouth curving into a rueful smile, "I don't consider myself so irresistible that you'd be driven to jump my bones in the middle of the night.

Unless you were deranged. In which case I wouldn't have accepted your ultimatum in the first place."

"Then why choose a room that small? It seems an especially odd choice for a woman who drags everything she owns around with her."

She heaved a small sigh. "If you must know, I chose it because of the bed."

"All the bedrooms have beds . . . a lot bigger beds than that one."

"Not canopy beds. That's the only room with a canopy bed. A *white* canopy bed. With a white ruffled eyelet canopy and matching dust ruffle . . . and white eyelet-trimmed sheets. Although I didn't know about the sheets when I made my choice."

"I don't know what the hell eyelet is," he countered. "But you're telling me the reason you picked that room was because you wanted to sleep in a bed with a hood over it?"

"Yeah," she admitted, sheepish and defiant at once, something he wouldn't have thought possible. "I mean think about it, how often do you get a chance to sleep in a fancy canopy bed in the Princess House?"

Owen shook his head. He didn't get it.

"It's all because of that stupid Sears catalog," she said.

He shot her a look of confusion.

"When I was a kid, around seven or eight . . ." She gave a small, defensive shrug. "And nine and ten, and maybe eleven, one of the most exciting days of the year was in the fall when the new Sears catalog arrived. I'd commandeer it right away, take it to my room, and open it to—not the toys, although I eventually spent a lot of time on the Barbie doll and bride-dolls pages too—but to the furniture section. Specifically to the white canopy bed with the matching dresser and vanity table and a full-length, oval freestanding mirror. Just like the one in *Snow White*. And I cannot believe I'm admitting any of this out loud," she groaned, rolling her eyes and shaking her head.

"It was my fantasy dream bedroom," she explained. "My vision of the ultimate in luxury and style. When I wasn't dreaming of running away and joining the circus, I was dreaming of being a princess and sleeping in that bed. It never happened, of course, since I already had a perfectly good, sensible bedroom set. So when I saw that canopy bed upstairs, I figured what the hell and I went for it."

It was the damn bed, thought Owen. She hadn't been trying to get as far as possible away from him. Not that it mattered, he reminded himself. She could be sleeping in the room next door . . . hell, she could be sleeping in the same bed and she would still be off-limits to him.

"So tell me," he said, "did it live up to your expectations?"

She grinned with delight. "Pretty much. I guess you're never too old for some dreams."

"Or too young for them," he said without meaning to, and then felt obliged to explain. "I was . . . thinking about Allie. She was three the first time I read *The Princess House* to her and from that day on it was her favorite book. I read somewhere that this place had been the artist's inspiration for the house on the cover, so I brought her here to see it."

"She must have been thrilled to see it come to life . . . I know I was."

"She was," he said, remembering that day. "After that, we came here a lot. Her mother and I had split by that time and it became a weekly routine when the weather was good. She was my fishing buddy. We'd fish at that little cove I showed you and then hike along Cliff Walk to get here."

"You made her walk all that way?"

"Well, it's not like I could pull into the front drive and park.

Besides, I did the walking: Allie rode on my shoulders most of the way. I'd pack a lunch and we'd sit in the shade of those huge bushes and have a picnic." He pointed to a spot at the very edge of the property.

"You never ran into Ivy?"

Owen shook his head. "Technically we were trespassing, so I did my best not to get noticed." He smiled briefly. "Of course, Allie wasn't nearly as concerned about that as I was. She'd eat two bites of her peanut butter and jelly sandwich and then be off running in circles, picking daisies so I could make her a princess crown . . . which she then insisted on wearing until the next week when I made her a new one. I imagine if she could have seen that canopy bed, she'd have wanted to sleep in it too."

"I'm guessing that it's no accident that you ended up living here."

He hunched forward and stared at the bushes, seeing instead something that happened a long time ago. "No, not exactly an accident. More of an impulse buy. Now I own the whole damn place, enough daisies to make a thousand crowns, and Allie's gone."

"But you made her those daisy crowns when it counted, and you'll always have the memory. I know it's not enough, not nearly, but it's something. And sometimes that's all you get."

He nodded and felt her hand rest briefly on his arm.

"Okay," she said, her tone taking a no-nonsense turn. "I confessed a deep, dark, and totally humiliating secret from my past to you. Now it's your turn. Fair's fair," she added as if to forestall any argument.

He eyed her warily. "What kind of secret?"

"The juicier the better," she drawled.

"I just confessed to trespassing."

"Tch. That's not even close to being juicy enough." She laughed at his sudden frown and knocked her shoulder against his. "Don't panic; I'm teasing. I want you to tell me . . ." She chewed her bottom lip, thinking. Her eyes brightened. "I know: tell me how you hurt your leg."

"I wouldn't call that juicy," he said. "It's not even much of a secret."

"It doesn't have to be an actual secret secret." She slanted him a look of amused exasperation. "The whole concept of friendly bantering is lost on you, isn't it?"

"It's just that getting injured isn't something I usually talk about."

"You think I go around sharing my embarrassing canopy-bed fantasy with everyone I meet?"

He hunched forward, fingers laced, saying nothing.

Sophie touched his shoulder lightly. "Look, it's no big deal. If you really don't want to talk about it—"

"It's not that. I guess I'm just not used to talking about myself at all." He stretched his leg out and stared at it. "I got hurt in the military. While I was still on active duty. It's what put an end to active duty for me."

"Were you in the army?"

"I started out there. Worked up to being a Ranger and eventually I was assigned to a multiforces unit."

"Is that like special ops or something?" Sophie asked. "And I should probably warn you that everything I know on the subject I learned from action movies."

He smiled at that. "Special ops covers a lot of territory. My unit specialized in off-the-books extractions. Missions of Last Resort, we called them."

"Sounds dangerous."

"The military is a dangerous place. You know that going in and you're trained to deal with whatever they throw at you."

"So what exactly is an off-the-books extraction?"

"Off-the-books means we operated under the auspices of the JSMC—Joint Special Mission Command—and that there was a minimal paper trail for whatever we did. Extractions . . . well, bad guys have a nasty tendency to take things that don't belong to them . . . weapons, classified documents, the occasional diplomat. Sometimes they make demands in exchange for their return: sometimes they don't. It doesn't really matter since official policy is that we don't negotiate with scumbags of any kind. We also don't like losing weapons and documents and diplomats to them. That's where I come in. It's my job to get whatever—or whomever—they took back by whatever means necessary. *Was* my job," he amended.

"And that's what you were doing when you injured your leg?"

Owen nodded. "The military especially doesn't like losing its own. We got the call after a reconnaissance chopper went down in Afghanistan. It was a two-man crew: only one survived and we had good local intel that he was being held in a mountain cave on the Pakistan border. It's never easy, but this was a pretty standard extraction for us. We were air-dropped in and then it was a four-and-a-half-hour climb to the cave."

"My God, this really is like an action movie. A four-and-a-half-hour climb would kill me."

His mouth quirked. "It would be shorter, but you can't go all out at that altitude or you'll be spent. When we got close to the cave, we set up our ORP—that's objective rally point—and the two of us making the final approach to the target went into full assault mode. It was late and it was cold and there were only three captors on watch. We . . ." He hesitated, glancing sideways at her as she hung on every word as raptly as if she were watching a film. "We dealt with them, grabbed our guy, and got out. He was in real rough shape and it wasn't until we were on our way back to the pickup zone that he suddenly looked around and asked us where his partner was."

"I thought . . ."

"Yeah. So did we. But the local intel got it wrong. Or maybe they wanted to double-dip and get paid twice. Both guys survived the crash and one was still in that cave. There are two things you don't want to do on a mission: veer from the plan, and linger too long. I had to make the call on the spot."

"And?" she demanded.

"I went back. Those caves are like damn wormholes; they twist and turn and keep going deeper. I finally reached the second guy and he was in even rougher shape that his buddy. I got him out, but there was no way he was going to make it to the pickup zone under his own power. So we found a spot with enough clearance—barely—for a Chinook to come in and drop a line for him. Not an easy thing to do in the mountains. It takes time, and it's loud. Damn loud. Loud enough to attract exactly the kind of attention we didn't want.

"I strapped him into the harness and grabbed the line and we were about twenty feet in the air when we started taking fire."

Her eyes filled with concern. "They were shooting at you? You got shot?"

Owen shook his head. "No, but they hit the chopper and sent it reeling. We lucked out because the pilot really knew his stuff. He got it back under control, but not before we got slammed into a solid wall of rock. A couple of times, as I recall."

"That's how your leg got hurt."

He gave a short, humorless chuckle. "Believe me, everything hurt, every last bit of me, but my left leg and hip got the worst of it . . . shattered femur, torn everything. I've got pins holding to-gether parts I didn't know I had."

"You poor thing. I can't even imagine how much pain you must have been in. How long were you in the hospital?"

"Four months. Six operations. And then a whole lot of rehab to get me back on my feet . . . literally."

"That must have been a really tough time. I can understand why you don't like talking about it."

"It was tough," he admitted, "but it also had its bright spots. Allie, for one. For a couple of those months she was out of school and she came and stayed with me. It was the first time we'd lived together since she was two." He stared straight ahead. "Now I'm . . . well, I'm thankful I had that time with her, no matter the price."

"I'll bet she felt the same way. My God, she must have been so proud to have a hero for a dad. You saved that man's life . . . both men."

"I didn't do it alone."

"You went back alone!" she exclaimed. "You went up on that rope thing with people shooting at you alone. If you ask me they should have given you a huge bonus and the biggest medal they have."

He couldn't help chuckling at her vehemence. "No bonus. No medals. No paper trail: no fanfare. That's how the game is played."

"Well, that sucks. And it's not fair. If it were me, I'd want everyone to know how brave I was."

"I doubt that."

She folded her arms across her chest, looking torn between suspicion and indignation. "What's that supposed to mean?"

"It means you don't give yourself credit or demand credit for a lot of the things you accomplish. It means that since I've gotten to know you and watched you work I've broadened my definition of bravery and loyalty and honor."

"I'm not sure why. I've never climbed a single mountain," she reminded him. "Or rescued anyone from a cave."

"And I've never talked a single bride off a ledge."

She made a face. "That's not quite the same thing."

"I'm not saying it's the same. I'm saying I've seen the way you work. What you do isn't just a job to you: it's a mission . . . and it's an important one because of how much the outcome matters to the people involved. You do what it takes to get it done right for them. And I respect that."

"Well . . ." She shrugged, looking both pleased and flummoxed. Was she so unaccustomed to compliments? Owen wondered. Or simply surprised it came from him? "Thanks. I just hope you don't revise your opinion when this is done. I did some tossing and turning last night. I'm worried Ivy may be tougher to win over than I hoped. I have a tendency to tackle problems by looking on the bright side and running with it."

"No kidding. I've gotten mowed down trying to play defense against a couple of your looking-on-the-bright-side plays."

"If only it worked that well on Ivy. So far she seems a lot less susceptible to my approach. Hell, I can't even get her to come out of hiding and hear me out."

"I'm still available if you want to try the tough-love approach."

"You mean toss out the stuff she loves? Thanks, but I'm not desperate enough to declare all-out war. Yet."

"Then I'd say you've got your work cut out for you. As far as I know, there's no course in how to communicate with wayward ghosts."

She swung her head around to look at him, her eyes widening slightly. And then she laughed, an all-out whoop of excitement that had him smiling even as he braced himself for what might be coming next.

"You're a genius," she told him. "You just gave me a great idea."

"Again?" he countered. He really had to stop inspiring her to make his life more difficult.

"Yep. I can't believe I didn't think of it before now. It just so happens I know someone who could teach that course. And she's the perfect person to help me connect with Ivy."

"I'll bite. At the risk of knowing more than I want to, I have to ask. How?"

"Easy. One word. *Séance*."

Twelve

There was no guarantee the séance would work, but it was way ahead of Sophie's next-best idea simply because she had no other ideas. The Queen of the Backup Plan had hit a wall when it came to communicating with Ivy . . . as she now found herself thinking of her, rather than as "the ghost bride." Owen was right: she had a name . . . and a past. Complete with hopes and dreams and heartaches. And it was now Sophie's hope that the séance would remove some of the baggage from the past and pave the way for a happy ending for all of them.

As soon as she made up her mind to give the séance a shot, she was eager to get on with it. Unfortunately, Carla Bonnet, the one person she trusted to make it happen, wasn't available for a week. The delay translated to seven long days of small disasters and petty annoyances. Not to mention the ongoing challenge of explaining random weird noises, sudden temperature changes, and other various and sundry odd occurrences to whoever happened to be around at the time. Ivy took top honors in both persistence and innovation and every day brought a new challenge.

On Tuesday, the instructions for the landscapers that she'd left pinned to the back door mysteriously disappeared, replaced by alternative instructions that mentioned nothing about the wide stretch of daisies growing wild at the far edge of the lawn, the daisies that WERE NOT UNDER ANY CIRCUMSTANCES TO BE DISTURBED. The daisies were important to Owen: they were a link to the past, and to his daughter, Allie. Sophie understood and she was fine with leaving the daisies untouched. They added a whimsical touch that was in keeping with the enchanted forest of the wedding's *Midsummers Night* theme. Unfortunately the guys on the ride-on mowers weren't so tolerant; where Owen saw something worth protecting, they saw only blight on the green velvet turf they were being paid to maintain. A melee ensued. She rushed outside and managed to calm Owen's fury over the daisies that had already lost their heads, and then she stood on the lawn and supervised as the crew created a natural-looking line of demarcation to establish a no-mow zone going forward.

On Wednesday, she was catching up on paperwork when the window-washing crew went ballistic because they suddenly found themselves squeegeeing jet-black water from the windowpanes. It was as if, in the words of one man, someone had come along and squirted black ink into all their buckets. But who would do something like that . . . who *could* do something like that without being seen?

Who indeed?

Grumbling and unhappy, they emptied their pails and started over, but naturally the ink turned out to be oil-based, so that when it dripped from the glass onto the white window frames it had stained them, adding another job to the to-do list from hell.

Day after day her cell phone disappeared and reappeared minutes or hours later. It happened so many times—resulting in dozens of missed calls and messages as she searched for it—that she finally went MacGyver and jimmied a way to hang it on a cord around her neck. It wasn't pretty, but it worked . . . at least it worked when Ivy wasn't screwing around with the reception.

And then there was the ongoing, random cacophony of slamming doors, falling objects, and strange noises in the walls and ceiling. They spooked the work crews and they also finally drove Owen and his laptop out of his office to work in the guesthouse.

Sophie missed him.

She missed bumping into him here or there as they both went about their days. She missed that little tickle of anticipation she felt just knowing she might bump into him. She missed seeing him smirk and shake his head over Ivy's latest stunt. She missed that drift of fresh, sort-of-soap and sort-of-pine scent she smelled whenever he was close.

At least he continued to join her for coffee at sunrise. She secretly thought of that as "their time." Time to talk about how the wedding plans were progressing and about the day ahead. Time to laugh over yesterday's disasters, which never seemed at all funny at the time, but somehow became less nerve-racking and more amusing when she was sharing them with Owen. Time to become friends.

Sometimes they ended up in the same place at the end of the day too, sharing a sandwich or a bowl of popcorn in the small den with the humongous, man-cave-worthy TV that had been Owen's contribution to the decor. He was turning her into a fairly knowledgeable Red Sox fan and she'd introduced him to the wonderful world of cooking shows. Although he'd disparaged them at first, the shows must have been growing on him because he kept coming back to watch. Sophie had to laugh at his disgruntled announcement that not only did he now understood what ceviche was and how a pressure cooker worker, he could even name a few of the *Top Chef* contenders.

As much as possible he stayed out of Ivy's way and left all damage control to Sophie. That was his reason for wanting her there around the clock after all. It seemed to Sophie that the séance was an exception, however. He didn't talk about it. In fact, outwardly he maintained a bemused skepticism about the whole thing, but as the day of the event grew closer she could sense his anticipation mounting along with her own.

"She's late," he said, wandering into the kitchen at approximately four minutes after eight on Friday evening.

Sophie glanced up from the pitcher of iced tea she was making, not at all surprised that he'd remembered that tonight was the night or that he was also watching the clock. "She called to say she'd hit traffic and would be a few minutes late." She held up the glass pitcher. "Iced tea?"

"Sure."

"You said this woman is a friend of yours?"

"Not really a friend," she replied as she grabbed a tray of ice cubes from the freezer. "Seasons handled her sister's wedding last year, so we spent a lot of time together at dress fittings and the like, and I remembered that she did this kind of thing . . . séances, consultations. And I trust her to be discreet."

Shouldering the freezer door shut, she got a lemon from the fridge, where the wall-to-wall beer bottles had slowly but surely given way to real food: fresh fruits and veggies, Greek yogurt, sliced turkey and lobster salad from the great little deli she'd discovered not too far away. Prior to her moving in, Owen had lived on drive-through fare and whatever he could have delivered. He didn't seem to mind the change at all; in fact he even mentioned picking up a couple of steaks and firing up the grill on the weekend. Sophie repeatedly reminded herself not to read too much into the offer, or anything else he said or did. It would be so easy for her to get carried away with . . . possibilities. In spite of what she'd told the *J*s about knowing exactly what she was getting into, there were times when she wondered what the hell she'd gotten herself into. Handsome man, killer smile, two lonely people marooned together in a fairy-tale castle under precarious and emotionally charged conditions. She'd read enough romance novels to know how that story ended. But life wasn't a romance novel. At least hers wasn't: she had to remember that.

Owen ambled over to take the lemon from her. He tossed it in the air and caught it a few times and then stood beside her to slice it while she poured the tea. Instantly Sophie was engulfed by him. Not only by his familiar scent that made her want to inhale deeply, putting her in danger of hyperventilating; she felt swamped by *him* . . . his nearness . . . his *thereness.* Her brain might know better, but as far as her senses were concerned, when he was in the room . . . when he was that close, he was all there was.

He put down the knife.

She reached for a slice of lemon.

And their hands brushed.

Sophie's pulse jumped and her gaze shot to meet his.

His blue eyes were dark, his expression somber and guarded, but there was no hiding the feeling of explosive awareness that suddenly thickened the air between them. There were no words. Only the *tick, tick, tick* of the kitchen wall clock.

And then, the sudden trill of the doorbell.

Damn!

She pulled her hand back.

Owen cleared his throat. "Must be Clara."

"Carla," she corrected automatically. "Carla Bonnet. I'll go let her in."

She practically jogged to the front door. Hopefully Carla would assume it was because she was rushing that she was breathless, instead of guessing the embarrassing, adolescent truth . . . that she had gotten all flustered because a cute guy had touched her hand. Sheesh. *Snap out of it,* she told herself. Then she told herself she ought to be thankful and not annoyed that Carla had arrived when she did. For good measure she reminded herself that she was there to work, and that she didn't have time for distractions. No matter how good they smelled.

Her *self* listened to all of it without enthusiasm.

"That's her?" inquired Owen, frowning as he glanced through the sidelights at the woman standing on the front steps. "That's Clara the hotshot psychic?"

"Carla."

"Sorry. Clara just sounds like a more fitting name. Like Clara the zany sidekick. Or Clara the wacky neighbor."

"Be that as it may, her name is Carla. And yes. That's her. Why," she demanded when she saw his dubious expression. "What's wrong with her?"

He shrugged. "She's just not what I pictured. I expected her to show up wearing . . ." He gestured toward his head. "You know, big hoop earrings and some kind of red silk turban thing. Maybe a cape."

"I think you have her confused with Ali Baba . . . or Harry Potter."

"Let's just say I expected her to look more like a psychic and less like a lawyer."

"She's not a psychic. Not exactly."

"I just assumed . . . what is she exactly?"

"A college professor. She teaches Anthropology of the Occult at Brown, and she writes about all things paranormal. Séances and consultations are something she does for research purposes, and also because she's genuinely interested. She downplays having any special psychic gift, but she does describe herself as an empath. That means she's especially sensitive to—"

"I know what an empath is." He was still peering through the sidelight, looking unconvinced. "I thought she'd at least bring a Ouija board. No way is that bag big enough to hold a Ouija board."

"Maybe they've downsized them," Sophie retorted, shaking her head as she opened the door and welcomed Carla inside.

Slender, with short dark hair and pretty dark eyes, she did appear a little lawyerly in a simple black suit and heels, the look only slightly softened by a pale blue silk T-shirt under the jacket. But then she had said she'd been busy all week with curriculum planning sessions. That probably explained the suit.

"Thanks for coming, Carla," Sophie said. "I'm really in a jam here, and when the idea of a séance came up, you're the first person I thought to call."

"I'm so glad you did. Just from the little you told me, it sounds like a fascinating case." She gazed around. "Wow. This is quite a place."

"Isn't it amazing?" agreed Sophie. "And this is the man who owns it . . . and who has graciously agreed to let my client be married here. Owen Winters, this is Dr. Carla Bonnet. Carla, Owen Winters."

Carla's brows lifted as she offered her hand to shake. "*The* Owen Winters? Author of *The Fane Chronicles*?"

"Guilty as charged," he replied. "It's a pleasure to meet you, Dr. Bonnet."

"Please, just Carla. And it's a treat to meet you. I'm a big fan of your books."

He gave a small nod. "Well, it's flattering to know I have an Ivy League professor of the occult as a reader."

"Are you working on a new book now?" she asked.

"I am."

From her eager expression it was clear she would love to have him elaborate. And it was also clear—at least to Sophie—that he wasn't going to. He didn't talk about his work. At first she thought that was just more of the same since he wasn't comfortable talking about himself in general. Lately, however, she'd come to suspect it wasn't his work, but his work progress he didn't want to discuss . . . and that there might be more getting in his way than either Ivy or the wedding.

Silent, he regarded Carla with what looked to Sophie like interest bordering on speculation. She wasn't surprised. Even in drab business attire, Carla had a sultry, exotic look that turned heads. Men's heads in particular. And both being writers, they shared a common bond. It was only natural he'd be interested. Then he spoke and she realized it wasn't Carla's writing or her sultriness Owen was thinking about.

"So," he said, folding his arms across his chest. "No Ouija board?"

Smiling, Carla shook her head. "I'm afraid not. I've never had much luck with them. I did bring along a few crystals," she added, tapping the black leather bag slung over her shoulder. "Those and some candles are about as high tech as I get." She turned to Sophie. "The candles are because I prefer to work without overhead light and I never know what will be available where I'm going. The crystals I arrange on the table in front of me to help gather and focus the energy in the room."

Sophie nodded. "I'm all for doing whatever makes you comfortable . . . and whatever works. While we're on the subject of high tech, I wanted to ask if you have any objection to the séance being recorded." She quickly explained. "I just don't want to miss anything and I thought it might be good to have a record of everything that happens to review later."

"I have no objection at all, though in the past I've found it's usually better to have a third party do the recording. That way you can focus your energy on making a connection with whoever shows up."

"I thought of that, and I'm also not particularly tech savvy myself, so I had one of Seasons' assistants come out and set up the equipment ahead of time. Josh is a whiz with everything electronic and he fixed it so it's completely out of the way and all I have to do is hit one button and we're up and running."

"That sounds fine."

Noticing Carla's curious glance at the cell phone hanging on a cord around her neck, Sophie gave her a rueful smile and shrugged. "It's been a long week, filled with ghost tricks like the disappearing cell phone."

"You poor thing. I'm sorry I couldn't get here sooner."

"I'm just glad you're here now. You mentioned choosing a central location, so I had Josh set the camera up in the dining room. I can't wait to get started."

"We will," said Carla. "But first I'd like to do a walk-through so I can get a feeling for the house itself."

"All right. Let me show you around: it will give me a chance to fill you in on what we've found out about the woman who used to live here."

"Actually," Carla said as she fell into step beside her, "I'd rather get a clean impression of the house first. No preconceptions. Then you can share with me whatever background information you have. And *then* we'll see if we can persuade your elusive ghost to join us."

The walk-through didn't take long. Most often Carla stopped a few steps inside a room and glanced around. The only place she lingered was in the room at the top of the stairs where Sophie had first encountered Ivy. While Sophie waited at the door, she walked slowly around the room, pausing to rest the fingertips of both hands on the dressing table without saying anything and then moving to the bed and curling her hands around the rail at the foot of the bed, as if the old, polished wood had secrets to tell.

"This was her room," she announced finally, her tone matter-of-fact. She moved to the door connecting with the adjoining room and opened it. "And this was designed to be the nursery. It was never used."

She closed the door very gently and gazed around the room again.

"There's great heartache here," she told Sophie. "And great longing."

She spoke with quiet certitude and tears pricked the back of Sophie's eyelids. She bit her lip to hold them back.

Great heartache and great longing.

Since moving into the house, she'd been doing a lot of thinking about Ivy. In spite of all the aggravation she caused, Sophie found herself feeling a kinship with her. They had things in common. Not the made-to-order castle or the family fortune obviously, but both Ivy and she had had their hearts broken by men they'd loved and trusted and they had both survived and gone on to make satisfactory lives for themselves. At least on the surface.

Had Ivy been satisfied to live in that big, beautiful house alone? Carla's insights made her wonder. After being left at the altar, she had traveled extensively and dabbled in horticulture and photography, as well as being involved with several charities. But she had never married. Never had a family. Only a nephew who had been disinterested enough to dispose of her beloved home, part and parcel, from the other side of the country.

After standing by the window for a moment, Carla moved to the center of the room, took a deep breath, and closed her eyes. When she opened them she met Sophie's gaze and nodded.

"I'm ready," she said.

*   *   *

They were seated in the dining room. Carla sat at the head of the long table with Owen and Sophie on either side of her. She had listened intently and without comment while Sophie ran down the pertinent details of Ivy Halliday's life. Fairly certain that Ivy was in the vicinity and would not take kindly to either pity or amateur psychology, she chose her words carefully.

When Carla finished listening, her expression was somber and thoughtful. "It's easy to see how the idea of having a wedding here could be a sore point for her."

"I understand that, believe me. I don't blame her for being upset. That's exactly why I want to reach out to her and try to make her see that this isn't just any wedding. I want to explain to her what a great kid Shelby is and how much it means to her to be married here. To her this is *The Princess House* and she's loved it since she was a little girl. It's something she shared with her dad when he was alive. I think if I can appeal to Ivy's kindness and generosity—"

Somewhere upstairs a door slammed.

The three of them exchanged looks.

"Kindness and generosity," Owen repeated. "Good luck with that."

"It could have been the wind," Sophie insisted.

He snickered.

"I understand what you're hoping to do," Carla told her, "but as I explained when we spoke on the phone, this isn't a science. There's no guarantee it will work. And even if we do succeed in connecting with a spirit in this house, it could happen in a number of ways."

"Such as?" Owen prompted.

"I've conducted séances where the only response was the vibra-

tion of the table, or random noises. There could be a silent appari-
tion, or even some form of psychography . . . automatic writing.
That's why I always have a pen and paper handy." She indicated
the notebook in front of her. "What I'm saying is that I can't promise you there will be a dialogue, or that she'll even listen to anything you have to say."

"What can you promise?" inquired Owen.

"That I'll do my best."

"That's good enough for me," declared Sophie. "What's next?"

Carla took several items from her bag and arranged them on
the table in front of her. "This is my own interpretation of a traditional séance. Some of the elements date all the way back to Nos-
tradamus. Sandalwood oil," she explained, placing a small
earthenware bowl on the table and pouring a small amount of oil
into it. Next she placed three white candles around the bowl and
lit them.

"The oil and candles create a welcoming atmosphere of light
and warmth. The crystals help ward off negative energy and gather
the positive."

With the crystals in place, she turned to Owen. "I know that
your interest here is divided. There's someone else, another spirit,
someone close to you, someone you've lost, whom you're hoping
to make contact with." He started to shake his head, but she
stopped him. "There's nothing wrong with that, but I have such a
strong sense that what you're hoping for is not going to happen
that I felt I should say something. It will be better if you're not
distracted by other thoughts." She seemed to hesitate before adding, "When there's no unfinished business, a spirit moves on." She
smiled. "That's not a bad thing."

"I understand," he said quietly. "And . . . thanks."

Allie, thought Sophie. Of course Owen was thinking about the
daughter he'd lost. Thinking and hoping. She hoped he took com-

fort from Carla's insight that Allie could move on because she was at peace.

"So do you think unfinished business is what's keeping Ivy here?" she asked Carla.

"Pretty much. Or perhaps she just thinks there's unfinished business and she's keeping herself here. Whatever the cause, I'm as certain as I can be that she's tethered to this house . . . and that her energy is directly linked to her strong emotional connection to this place."

"Does that mean that if she was to go out into the yard or down the street, she wouldn't have the same power or ability or whatever you want to call it . . . that she couldn't move things around or—"

"Slam a drawer on someone's fingers," interjected Owen in a dry tone.

Carla nodded. "That's right. I think if she left this house, her energy would slowly dissipate, and she would most likely have to move on . . . ready or not. Be that as it may, within these walls, she's a power to be reckoned with. She has a strong and turbulent history here . . . it's like a tapestry of emotions that have built up over a lot of years. Lots of different colors and textures."

"And that's what she draws energy from?"

"Yes. Either consciously or not," Carla replied. "And the stronger the emotional connection, the more energy she'll pull. Usually a ghost uses gathered energy to either manifest or to manipulate their surroundings . . . slam a drawer shut, move a vase. One thing at a time. But you told me that Ivy has done both at the same time."

"Yes. That first day in the bedroom. I saw her and heard her *and* she moved things around. Since then I haven't actually seen her . . . although she's sure done plenty of manipulating," Sophie added, her mouth curving in a wry smile.

"She obviously has the power to materialize at will. Let's hope she sees fit to appear tonight. Shall we get on with it?"

While Carla lit the candles, Sophie started the recording equipment Josh had set up on the mahogany buffet. She and Owen followed Carla's example and placed their palms flat on the table, with the tips of their pinkie fingers just touching the person beside them. Carla gently guided them in taking a few deep breaths and relaxing their muscles. In a soft, soothing tone, she urged them to focus their thoughts on connecting with Ivy. After several quiet moments she began with a blessing.

"We invoke the Power of the Sword of Michael and the Angels of Protection to surround and protect us. We invoke the Power of the Light and we align ourselves with the Love of the Universe. We come together with open hearts and pure intentions, to learn and to better understand every stage and aspect of life. We seek harmony with all and harbor malice toward none. May our circle and our efforts be blessed."

She paused for a few seconds and then, in a warm and friendly tone, said, "Ivy Halliday, will you please honor us with your company and join our circle?" She spoke slowly and calmly, pausing between sentences to wait for a response. "Sophie and Owen and I have come together this evening especially to speak with you. We're eager to hear whatever you have to share with us about this beautiful house which was once yours."

Immediately the temperature in the room plummeted.

Sophie was pretty sure it was the "was once yours" that Ivy objected to. Something told her it was going to take more than a deed or a death certificate to change Ivy's view that the house was hers and always would be.

"Deep breaths," Carla reminded them. "Relax your shoulders. Focus."

Sophie tried to relax her muscles, but it wasn't easy to do while shivering. It was *that* cold.

"Ivy, are you here with us now?" Carla asked. "I sense another presence in the room, but we can't be sure it's you unless you communicate with us. Please share your thoughts with us."

Silence. Ivy wasn't biting. Sophie noticed that when she exhaled she could see her breath. She wished she'd worn something a little warmer, but of course, she'd had no idea when she chose a gauzy cotton skirt and tank top that she'd be risking frostbite. Was it possible to get frostbite indoors? she wondered. In August? And if she did, how would she explain it to the folks at the ER?

Carla tried again.

"Ivy, if you can, please give us a sign that you understand."

She'd barely uttered the last word when the candles sputtered out, leaving the room in near darkness. The only light came from a lamp in an adjoining room.

"All right, Ivy. Thank you for that sign. Now I have another request." Carla's tone was steady and unhurried. "Sophie would like to speak with you about the wedding that she's—"

That's as far as she got before the video camera came flying across the room, causing all three of them to duck. It whizzed past them and crashed hard against the opposite wall before landing in pieces on the floor. So much for reviewing the action later.

"Well, that was close," Sophie said, straightening cautiously.

"Too close," growled Owen, running a concerned gaze over Sophie. "That damn thing missed you by an inch. Who the hell does this woman think she—"

He broke off as the candles reignited on their own, the flames flaring high in the air and then cascading onto the table in a puddle of fire while the candles remained standing.

Immediately Owen was on his feet and using a linen place mat to smother the flames. As he did, a loud whooshing sound drew their attention to the white marble fireplace at the end of the room, where another blaze ignited. Both Sophie and Carla scrambled to their feet.

Owen swore as he headed in the direction of the kitchen, nearly tripping over a chair in the process. There was no longer any light coming from the other room. *Great,* thought Sophie. In addition to the pyrotechnics, Ivy was playing with the circuit breakers again. There was no moon in the sky and the house was set far back from the streetlights of Bellevue Avenue. She flipped open the cell phone hanging around her neck: the screen light was better than nothing, but not by much.

Owen was back quickly, bringing a small fire extinguisher from the kitchen. He sprayed the embers on the table in passing and then turned it full force on the fireplace, where the fire was roaring without benefit of firewood or any other fuel.

When the candles reignited a second time, Sophie grabbed the place mat and went to work.

"Oh no. This isn't good," muttered Carla. She no longer sounded relaxed or patient, but it was too dark for Sophie to see her expression clearly.

Sophie was still slapping at the flames—which were a lot more resistant to being squelched this time around—when Owen came over and grabbed the candles. "I'll take care of these."

Before she could ask just how he intended to do this, there was a loud crash in the hall as the front door flew open. It was quickly followed by the high-pitched wail of a car alarm. Correction: two car alarms.

"My car," Carla exclaimed as she bent down and began feeling around on the floor beside where she'd been sitting. "My bag . . . my bag. Where's my damn bag?"

Sophie moved through the darkness to find her own keys and she and Carla ended up on the front steps together, aiming and clicking their remotes to turn off the alarms. The sudden quiet was a relief, but her heart continued its frenzied pounding. The calm might simply be the eye of the hurricane.

Owen joined them and they waited, silent and stiff and edgy, like cats poised to pounce at the drop of a feather.

When a minute passed, and then two, and nothing happened, Carla heaved a deep sigh and turned to Sophie. "Well. That was . . . scary as all hell. God, Sophie, I'm so sorry for all this."

"Don't be. It wasn't your fault."

"Something I did—or said—provoked her."

"She was already provoked. And besides, the séance was my idea. You were only trying to help."

"I'm afraid I only made things worse. You really have your work cut out for you here. Have you considered moving the wedding somewhere else?"

Sophie shook her head, ignoring Owen's quiet snigger. "No." She crossed her arms in front of her. She didn't like conflict, but something about being bullied and threatened with fire and flying video equipment had brought out the stubborn in her. "Shelby has her heart set on being married here. And I have mine set on not seeing the time and effort I've already put in go to waste. The wedding is going to be here and that's that."

The front door slammed shut.

The lock clicked.

Séance over.

They had no trouble getting back into the house thanks to the keys Owen had hidden outside.

Fool me twice, shame on me.

The problem apppeared once they were back inside. The lights were still out and Ivy had been busy rearranging things so that making their way to the kitchen, where Sophie recalled seeing a flashlight, was like tackling an obstacle course blindfolded. Owen led the way: he whacked his shin a couple of times and singed the air with a string of suitably uncomplimentary observations about Ivy. Going second gave Sophie an advantage and she made it most of the way before being blindsided by an open door and ending up with an egg on the side of her head.

"You okay?" he asked when she cried out.

"Yeah. Stupid door. Stupid ghost."

"No argument here," he retorted. "I still say it's time to get tough."

"Maybe," she allowed. "My approach was certainly a spectacular failure. I mean, the séance literally crashed and burned."

"It was still worth a shot," he allowed in a gruff tone. "Now you can say you tried and you don't have to feel guilty when I haul a Dumpster out front and start chucking her crap into it."

Sophie listened for some reaction from Ivy . . . a slamming door, a rattling window, an explosion in the middle of the living room. Nothing. Maybe she'd worn herself out. Or maybe she was afraid she'd gone too far and that this time Sophie might not stop Owen from carrying out his threats. Sophie rubbed her head where it hurt. She was right to worry: at that moment not only would she not stop him, she just might join in. Hurling china and crystal would at least burn off some tension.

She was tired and stressed and time was running out. She'd tried to reason with Ivy and failed. Owen was right: the time for diplomacy was over.

It was time to get tough.

Thirteen

"Y ou're sure the flashlight was in this cupboard?"

Owen's question pulled her from her thoughts. She heard the clink of china and glass as he felt around in the cupboard next to the refrigerator.

"I think it was that one." She thought more and added, "Or else maybe the next one over. No, it was definitely the next one. I remember now: I saw it when I was looking for a container for the strawberries."

He yanked open the door of the adjacent cupboard and was immediately caught in an avalanche of various-size plastic storage containers and lids. They bounced off him and scattered noisily across the floor of the kitchen.

"Booby trap," she murmured.

"That's it," Owen snapped. Roughly kicking aside containers, he started toward the door to the basement.

Sophie hurried after him, catching her toe in the handle of a plastic bowl and shaking it off. "Where are you going?"

"To do what I should have done to begin with . . . I'm going down to throw the damn breaker so we can see what the hell we're doing."

"Wait. You can't go down there without a flashlight."

"We don't have a flashlight."

"We do. I saw it. We just have to figure out which cupboard it was in."

He stopped and turned to her. "Right . . . *was* in. Past tense. Don't you get it? She knew we'd go looking for the flashlight, so she hid it. It could be anywhere. A different cupboard. My sock drawer. The roof."

"I wish I could say you're being paranoid, but the fact is you're probably right. Except for the part about the roof. Her power only exists inside this house, remember?"

"That didn't stop her from triggering your car alarm."

"True," she conceded, sighing unhappily. "You know, when Carla said she was tethered to the house, I almost began to get my hopes up. I figured, hey, outdoor wedding, it could work in spite of her meddling. And then she goes and strikes in the driveway." She shook her head. "Carla said it only proves she can project a certain distance from the house. We just don't know precisely what that distance is . . . and I don't want to find out the day of the wedding with a hundred and fifty guests in the line of fire."

"I don't care what the distance is. She can project all she wants. And she can keep the flashlight," declared Owen. "I'm done letting her yank my chain."

Sophie grabbed his arm as he started to turn away. "I still say going down there in the dark is too risky."

"I'll go slowly."

"Go slowly? That's your grand plan for avoiding whatever other booby traps she has waiting for you?"

"Sophie, I've crawled on my belly through a football field's worth of land mines: I think I can handle whatever one old lady—

one *dead* old lady—can throw at me." There was more than a hint of animosity in his voice and he raised it so it was loud enough to be heard throughout the house.

"Don't be so sure," she told him. "I'm not questioning your ability, but let's face it, Ivy is very resourceful. And highly motivated. And while we have actual lives to distract us, she has all day to sit around plotting her next move. Maybe all night too. For all we know ghosts don't sleep."

"I don't care if she sleeps. No one is going to jerk me around in my own home. My own home," he repeated, again raising his voice to make sure he was heard.

"Fine. Go play conquering hero . . . but if you fall on the stairs I'm not going down there in the pitch dark to rescue you."

"Fine."

"I mean it. You could trip and bang your head. Remember the Gentle Gardener? You could be knocked unconscious. Or worse. Last time she planted a golf club on the stairs: tonight it could be a machete."

"I'm not going to trip."

"You do realize you're being stupid? Pigheaded and macho and stupid."

"Anything else?"

She wished she could see his eyes. Was he laughing at her? Offended? Serious about going down to the cellar unarmed? She tightened her hold on his arm.

"I mean it, Owen. I . . . I just don't want anything to happen to you, okay?"

Silence. His head angled to the side. In the darkness, Sophie couldn't see his surprise, but she sensed it. She felt him considering her words carefully.

"Because of me," she blurted. "I just meant I don't want any-

thing to happen to you because of me. God knows, I don't need the
added stress of having your prolonged coma on my conscience."

"So now I'm not just unconscious, I'm in a coma . . . a *prolonged* coma? Will I eventually come out of it?" There was definitely amusement in his voice now.

"The doctors aren't sure. But they have warned that you could
wake up drooling, and suffering from amnesia . . . and impotent,"
she added for good measure.

"Wow. That's some badass coma I got my stupid, macho, pigheaded self into."

"It certainly is. And I'll be to blame for all of it since if I
hadn't insisted on the séance we wouldn't be standing here right
this minute."

"To tell you the truth," he said, angling his body closer to hers
ever so slightly, the distance small but unmistakable. And unsettling. Good Lord, he was unsettling when he was so close. "I like
where I'm standing just fine. If you have a problem with that, now
would be the time to say so."

In a heartbeat the whole world shifted. Sophie felt worry give
way to awareness. That electrified, skin-tingling kind of awareness
when every fiber of your being is energized and every sensation
amplified. Her knees felt weak, her breath heavy and slow. She
shook her head. "No. No problem."

"So," he said, running his hand down her hair. "Did you have
a better idea in mind than a full frontal assault on the circuit
breakers . . . one that will avoid a prolonged coma and impotence
and still get the lights back on . . . and while you're at it, the coffeemaker."

"There's wine," she offered, too distracted to provide the details of the thought chain that had led her from coffee to wine.

"Thanks. But I've gotten used to getting the best cup of coffee around right here at home every morning. I'm not sure I could start the day without it." He paused a second, still touching her hair, and added, "I'm not sure I'd want to."

"Well," she said, melting inside as she realized he might be talking about more than coffee. "I guess my suggestion would be that we look for a few candles and—"

"And hope they don't turn into industrial-strength flares and burn the place down?"

"Right. Good point. Candles might be a little risky, all things considered. Option Two: We go to bed early and wait until morning to deal with the whole restoring-power issue."

"We could do that," he said, taking hold of her with both hands, his palms warm and rough on the smooth skin of her shoulders. "Or . . ."

His thumb caressed her jaw. Sophie could feel his eyes on her. Expectancy pulsed in the air between them and the darkness only heightened the excitement.

"We could . . . do this . . ."

His pulled her against him, hard, with the agility and finesse of a man who'd crawled through a field of land mines and lived to tell the tale. Pushing his hand into her hair, he tipped her head back.

He kissed her just beneath her ear, his low-pitched voice caressing. "I want you, Sophie. I've been wanting you all night . . . and all last night and the night before that." He kissed her again, and incongruously the damp heat of his mouth made her shiver. "Hell, it feels like I've wanted you from the instant that door blew open and I saw you standing there . . . and the list of things I want to do to you just keeps getting longer . . . and harder to resist."

"Don't," she whispered. "Don't resist."

He sucked in a sharp breath.

Sophie fisted the front of his T-shirt with one hand and grasped the back of his neck with the other.

He turned his head and their mouths crashed together. Both needing. Taking. Demanding more.

The fury of his kiss forced her jaw wide and he explored her mouth with deep, relentless sweeps of his tongue. Sophie clung to his shoulders, her urgency a match for his own. This felt so right, and long past due, and she had no qualms about taking as much as she gave.

He spun her so her back was to the refrigerator and pressed her against it. His hands, big and warm and rough, dragged down her body in a slow and detailed caress. When he lingered at her breasts, Sophie bit her lip to keep from whimpering. When those clever hands slipped beneath her loose cotton skirt and stroked her thighs, first the outside and then the soft, sensitive flesh inside, bringing him perilously close to the part of her that was already damp and needy for him, she did whimper.

With one hand still under her skirt, he used the other to strip off her tank top. Running his tongue along the top edge of her strapless bra, he reached around her for the clasp.

Sophie slowed his progress only long enough to turn the tables and tug his T-shirt over his head.

She ran her hands over his smooth chest.

He unhooked her bra.

She unzipped his jeans.

As his mouth closed over the tip of her breast, her trembling fingers slid beneath the denim and found him hot and hard.

She quivered and held her breath as his fingers at last moved high between her parted thighs and cupped the very core of her. Curling her fingers around him in a long, upward stroke, she arched into his touch, letting him know she wanted him the same way she could tell he wanted her . . . fast and hard and right . . . that . . . instant.

Sophie was ready, beyond ready, and when the darkened room suddenly exploded into light, it was as jarring to her careening senses as being hit in the face with a snowball. She was so startled by the light it took her another fraction of a second to register the sound of someone clearing their throat . . . pointedly and very close by.

She looked up to see Ivy—not dead-old-lady Ivy, but lovely and youthful-looking Ivy—seated prettily on the counter across from where Owen still had her pinned to the refrigerator door. Dead or not, the woman's timing was horrifyingly perfect, designed to deliver the maximum amount of surprise and humiliation. Half dressed, face flushed, senses reeling, Sophie couldn't feel more vulnerable or more embarrassed.

It took Owen, his eyes closed, his face buried between her naked breasts, a second longer to pick up on her reaction and realize they weren't alone. When he lifted his head to glance over his shoulder, he didn't appear at all embarrassed to find Ivy playing voyeur, only angry. Very angry.

"You," he growled, remnants of passion mixed with the disgust in his rough tone.

"Yes. *Moi*," countered Ivy, tossing back the shiny, shoulder-length blond hair that dipped over one eye. "But I must say, when you begged for the honor of my company, I had no idea this is what you had in mind." Her own tone—pitched just an intriguingly bit low for a woman—somehow managed to sound both breezy and sultry.

"Trust me, I didn't," he retorted. "And the only thing I'd ever beg for is a way to get rid of you."

"Ah, the ever-gracious Mr. Winters." She ran a withering glance over his naked back. "Your lack of charm is exceeded only by your lack of decorum. And now, since my presence here is obviously neither required nor desired, I shall—"

"No," Sophie blurted, and then cringed inwardly as Ivy turned and fastened her critical stare on her.

She looked glamorous, and bored. Her pale peach satin dressing gown and matching high-heeled, fur-trimmed mules made Sophie think of 1940s movie stars, and made her feel severely lacking by comparison. She felt like a teenager caught making out with her first boyfriend. Ivy was intimidating and she knew it. The only thing saving Sophie from being embarrassed beyond speech was that even though Owen had swiveled to face Ivy, she herself was still mostly shielded by the solid wall of his body. Now, if only she could think of a graceful way to get her top on and her skirt unbunched . . .

Feeling around on the counter for her top, she said, "We . . . that is, I . . . definitely want to speak with you. I've been trying to contact you on my own without any luck, so I asked a friend who's more knowledgeable in . . . these things, to come and help."

Ivy's look was icy. "Did you really think I would come when summoned like a pet poodle? As you can see, I appear when and how I choose."

"Yes, I can see that. And you're here now: that's what matters. Obviously the timing is a little . . . awkward." She nervously smoothed her skirt. "So if you could just give us a minute to pull ourselves—"

"No," said Ivy.

Sophie blinked. "No?"

"No. My time is valuable. I won't hang around cooling my heels so you can be spared the embarrassment of your own imprudent behavior. Say whatever it is you have to say to me and be done with it."

"Well . . . let's see. I . . ." She fumbled, her clever, well-rehearsed arguments nowhere around. Surprise, surprise. Being disheveled and half naked threw her off her game. "I guess, what I most wanted to speak with you about is the wedding."

"I believe I've made my feelings on that subject abundantly clear. If not, then I'm sure I can—"

"No. No, your feelings are clear. Very clear. There's no need to prove anything to us. But I can't help thinking that if you knew more about the couple being married, you would feel diff—"

"Knew what? That the would-be bride is a lovely girl with a heart of gold who's marrying a paragon of virtue and honor, and that the charmed couple will be running off to save the world to-gether? That she looks on this house as part of a fairy tale and believes that's what her wedding day should be? That she and her doting father shared a fondness for sailing and pretending that she was a princess? That being married here is her fondest dream? I know all that and it does not change my stand on the matter in the slightest."

Sophie desperately plodded on. "I hoped you might feel a kin-ship with Shelby . . . that's her name. Shelby Archer. After all, your father had this house designed and built just for you . . . to make you happy. I'm sure you shared a special bond with him the same way Shelby did with her father. For them, this house was a part of that bond . . . from the time she was a little girl, it was their special place. And then when Shelby was only fifteen—"

"He died," Ivy interrupted brusquely. "Please. Everyone's fa-ther dies eventually, Miss Bennett. Does that mean I should let everyone who wants to traipse through my private property and—"

Bristling, Owen cut in. "Lady, you have a twisted take on the concept of private property . . . among other things. Let me straighten you out: to own property you have to be alive. You're not. Ipso facto."

Ivy regarded him with a gaze like broken glass. "I once thought your slovenly housekeeping was your least attractive attribute. I see that I was wrong."

Noting the combative glitter that came into Owen's eyes, Sophie spoke before he could.

"Trust me, Miss Halliday, I understand why you feel the way you do about Ange de la Mer. I understand that it has nothing to do with deeds or legalities. That it's beyond all that mundane, everyday stuff. It's even beyond being a matter of mere life and death."

Ivy gave a regal, one-shouldered shrug, but she didn't disagree.

"This house isn't only a part of your past . . . or even a part of your heart. It represents something bigger, something intangible. It represents a life that should have been, a dream that never came true. And I know it sometimes feels like it's all there is left of that dream . . . and that you're the only one who even remembers the dream existed, and that makes it very hard to give up and walk away."

Ivy was looking past her, wearing that same slightly bored, ice-queen look, but Sophie caught a small tremble at the corner of her mouth and knew her words were getting through.

She took a deep breath. "I understand because it happened to me too."

Ivy's flawless brows lifted as she looked Sophie up and down with surprise and increased interest. "You were . . ."

When she hesitated, Sophie shook her head. "No. I wasn't left on my wedding day, if that's what you're asking, but . . ."

Ivy flinched. "Neither was I *left* on my wedding day," she declared. "Joseph would never have left me."

"No, no, of course not."

"Something happened. Something kept him from coming that day."

"I'm sure that's true," Sophie told her.

"Are you? Really? Because you'd be surprised how many people choose to believe the opposite."

"I wouldn't be surprised by what anyone thinks . . . or says. Like I said, it happened to me. I may not have gotten as far as the actual wedding day, but I fully expected to. Everyone expected it. We were together for years. We were the perfect couple. Everyone thought so. Even me." Her mouth quirked in a small, self-deprecating smile. "Especially me. It's what I wanted to believe. But later, afterward, I knew. I knew that I had wanted so badly for it to be right that I refused to see anything else. Looking back, the signs were so clear, so easy to read, they burned my eyeballs."

"What sort of signs?" asked Ivy.

"Oh, the fact that we were together for years, but he didn't want to live together until we were married . . . so that when we did it would be perfect. And he didn't want to get married—or even engaged—until he got all the things he'd always wanted to do out of his system . . . also so it would be perfect. Rock climbing and backpacking across Europe and getting his damn MBA. It was like a bucket list, only instead of listing things to do before kicking the bucket, these were things he wanted to do before marrying me. You'd think that alone would have told me something about his feelings on the subject." She paused for another quirky smile and a sniffle. Damn. She was so over this. Why on earth did talking about it still make her fill up? Obviously for the same murky reasons Ivy clung to her house.

"Anyway, when my thirtieth birthday rolled around, he made reservations at a very fancy restaurant and told me he wanted it to be my best birthday ever. 'This is it,' I thought. 'The Proposal.' I told myself he'd finally realized that he wanted me more than he wanted to do all the things left on that list. I went all out. Why the hell not? I'd waited long enough. A new hairstyle, a new, blow-the-budget outfit, new shoes." She shook her head at her foolishness. "They were these silly, glittery Cinderella shoes that screamed 'celebration': I fantasized about how I would wear them every year on the anniversary of our engagement, and about how someday I would show them to our kids and tell them about the wonderfully romantic night when their daddy proposed and their mommy said yes. Ridiculous, I know."

She felt Owen recoil because it was so ridiculous, but mercifully he refrained from comment.

"The worst part is I was so excited I couldn't stop grinning. For days I went around with this big sappy I've-got-a-secret smile. Of course, everyone surmised something was up . . . my sisters, my stepmother, all our friends." She shuddered, remembering the aftermath of that night, the shock . . . the pity. She crossed her arms even more tightly in front of her. "When the big night finally arrived, we met at the restaurant, and when I walked in, my present was already on the table. It was a package about the size of a book and I thought, 'How adorable. He put the ring box inside a bigger box to throw me off.' He was so nervous, and I thought that was adorable too."

She knew she was rambling and tried to rein in her thoughts. Baring her soul hadn't been part of her plan. Her prepared spiel was all about Shelby and Matthew. They were her secret weapon, her way to win Ivy over. But that hadn't worked and now she was desperate . . . desperate enough to dredge up her own unfortunate past.

"You've probably already guessed the ending," she told them. "There was no proposal. There was, however, a big surprise. He'd met someone else. A woman at work. They'd fallen madly in love . . . so madly she was pregnant with his baby. He'd only found out about the baby that afternoon. He'd planned to let me down easy by getting through my birthday before coming clean, but—to his credit I suppose—he discovered he couldn't sit there and look me in the eye and lie."

There was an uneasy silence. Sophie understood. What was there to say?

Ivy spoke first.

"What was in the box?"

Sophie smiled cynically. "A book. *The Romantic's Guide to Paris*. He knew I always wanted to go there. I'm not sure he even remembered I wanted to go there on our honeymoon. At that point it seemed pointless to ask."

Owen cleared his throat. God, he had to be thinking she was the biggest dope ever.

"Anyway," she said, feeling even more awkward now that it was all out there, "I guess the reason I told you all this is because I understand that dreams don't die. Even when they don't come true and we've made peace with the fact that they never will, they're still a part of us. Even if we're the only one who remembers them or who gives a damn about what might have been and should have been . . . well, I still have my Cinderella shoes tucked away on a shelf and you still have this house."

"So to speak," Owen said under his breath.

Ivy said nothing.

"But I don't think it would tarnish that dream or my memory of it if I let someone borrow the shoes for a special occasion of her own. In fact, I think it would honor my dream to help someone else's come true. What I'm trying to say—"

"I know what you're trying to say, Miss Bennett. I am not the village idiot." There was no hint of warmth or softening in Ivy's voice now. "Nor do I have time for pointless conversations."

"Really?" Owen challenged as she slid gracefully from her perch on the counter. "Afterlife that busy, is it?"

She shot him a look that would quell another man. Owen smiled coldly.

"It so happens I have a great deal to do. It turns out that stopping a wedding is as much work as planning one."

She spun away from them in a swirl of peach satin and was gone, literally melting into the air.

Owen shook his head and looked disgusted. "Well. That was a waste of time."

"Maybe," allowed Sophie, clinging to the hope that Ivy might think about what she'd said and soften her stance. "But on the bright side, at least the lights are on. And no one is in a coma, and we can make coffee in the morning."

"Yeah," he said, grabbing his T-shirt without meeting her eyes. "I'll see you then."

Fourteen

He overslept.

That's what happened when you spent the night tossing and turning, caught in a battle between conscience and desire.

In this corner: desire. He wanted Sophie: he hadn't exaggerated when he told her how much he wanted her. And for how long. But he didn't want the same things she wanted . . . hell, he no longer even believed in the things she wanted. And that complicated matters.

He might not have a "bucket list" like her jackass ex-boyfriend, but he was just as wrong for her. Any idiot could see that. Unfortunately, it wasn't any idiot's perception of things that concerned him: it was Sophie's. He couldn't shake the memory of the small, almost imperceptible quiver in her voice when she admitted that she had wanted so badly for her ex to be Mr. Right that she'd been blind to the giant neon Mr. Wrong sign flashing above his head. She might be a little older and a little wiser now, but the woman was still a die-hard believer in true love and happy endings and she still wanted both just as badly.

Her story may not have touched Ivy's heart, but it had punched a giant hole in his. At first he was furious with Ivy for showing up when he was so close to having all his fantasies of ravishing Sophie become real. Now he was thankful for her no-doubt-intentionally-lousy timing. She'd stopped him from making a big mistake.

What he had to offer Sophie would never be enough. She deserved more than he had left to give. She deserved to be happy. She deserved someone who shared her dreams and was willing to do whatever it took to make them come true. Once, a long time ago, he'd deluded himself into believing he could be that kind of guy. He knew better now. And his conscience was telling him that under the circumstances the right and honorable thing to do was to back off. Doing the right and honorable thing mattered a great deal to him, enough to keep him awake all night coming to terms with the inevitable. Unfortunately, knowing what he had to do didn't make it any easier . . . and it didn't make him want Sophie any less.

The question was . . . could he do it? Could he manage to keep his hands off her when she was so close . . . living in his house . . . sleeping right down the hall . . . smelling like wildflowers and possibilities whenever she came close . . . making him want to chuck everything and follow her forever? Could he keep from touching her when the longing to do that and so much more was like an open wound inside him?

Owen would like to think he had that kind of self-control. But then, he'd also like to think the fact he hadn't had a cigarette since Sophie moved in meant he'd never backslide again. The truth was that he wasn't sure. Both were one-day-at-a-time jobs. But he'd been smart enough to take the precaution of tossing his last pack of smokes in the trash. And he knew that if there was to be any chance of him doing the right thing for Sophie, he would need to keep as much distance between them as possible at all times.

*   *   *

She was a thirtysomething woman.

She'd started nearly every day of her life—hundreds, no, make that thousands of days—without the benefit of Owen Winters's company or conversation or attention. And she could count on her fingers the number of mornings he was around.

So why the hell did it feel like an indispensable part of her being had gone AWOL just because he'd stopped joining her for coffee at sunrise? It made no sense. And that's what scared her. It meant her heart was trying to take control of matters best left to her head.

The first time he didn't show up was the morning after the séance and the awkward encounter with Ivy that followed. His abrupt good-night had left her bewildered, and a little hurt, but she'd still looked forward to seeing him in the morning. When he didn't appear, she chose to believe he'd simply overslept. But he didn't show again the next day and he also stopped coming around in the evening and he never offered an explanation. It would be easy to chalk up his sudden coolness to the obvious, ego-crushing theory that he'd been hot for her in the dark, but had second thoughts as soon as the lights came back on. After all, on a bad day she could do paranoid insecurity with the best of them. But in her heart she knew that wasn't it.

Again, she was a thirtysomething woman: not—in spite of her nervous babbling after nearly being caught in the act by Ivy—a clueless teenager. She was experienced enough to know when a man was interested. Owen was interested. She'd sensed his desire. She'd seen it in his eyes. Lord knows, she'd felt it. He'd meant it when he told her he wanted her. The problem was that he didn't want to.

His reasons didn't matter. She ought to count herself lucky he hadn't tried to pick up where they left off when Ivy interrupted them. She'd never been into one-night stands and he obviously wasn't the kind of man she wanted to share her life with. She didn't want another man who ran hot and cold or who held back. Hadn't she learned the hard way that it was better to be happy alone than to pretend to be happy with a man who didn't want to be there? She wanted a man who *wanted* to be with her . . . a man who wanted *her* beyond all reason . . . a man who didn't come to his senses when the lights came on.

With both Owen and Ivy avoiding her, their living situation took on a surreal quality. The three of them inhabited the same physical space, but rarely—if ever—crossed paths. It was as if they existed in different dimensions or moved in separate, nonintersecting orbits, and in a way, she supposed, they did . . . each of them concerned with his or her own agenda and deadlines.

For Sophie, that meant keeping a sharp eye on the wedding preparations, checking daily on her other Seasons responsibilities, and never forgetting that, seen or unseen, Ivy was a very real threat. There had been no major catastrophes since the séance, but as the days ticked away she continued to make her presence and her opposition known in small ways.

The gauntlet had been thrown down, and picked up. Sophie had declared her intention to go ahead with the wedding no matter what and Ivy had warned her to cease and desist or face the consequences. The fact that Ivy was no longer openly sabotaging her work made Sophie worry that Ivy had refined her strategy and was now biding her time and saving her firepower for the big day itself. It was not a comforting thought.

She wished she could talk it over with Owen, but he was never around. She had no choice but to follow her own instincts. And in spite of her thus-far-dismal track record, her instincts told her not to give up on the possibility of changing Ivy's mind about the wedding. The more she thought about it, the more convinced she was that she was right in thinking Shelby was the key to winning Ivy over. She was sure that if Ivy got to know Shelby, she would like her. And if she liked her, it would be harder for her to do anything to ruin her wedding day.

Sophie refused to believe that Ivy was really as bitter or vindictive as she seemed on the surface. She certainly hadn't started out that way, she thought, recalling the engagement picture of Ivy looking so young and so happy. The woman in that photo had not been bitter or vindictive. Maybe she had to build walls to protect herself . . . to survive the heartache and loneliness. But walls didn't change who a person was deep inside. And walls could be breached. You just had to know how.

What Sophie needed was for Ivy to see Shelby not as some generic bride looking to take her rightful place there, but as a real flesh-and-blood young woman, a young woman with hopes and dreams and plans . . . the same sort of hopes and dreams and plans Ivy herself had had at the same age. And since Ivy was hell-bent on not hearing what Sophie had to say about Shelby, Sophie would just have to find a way to show her.

Ivy now knew how the Confederates felt when the Yankee army stormed Atlanta.

Ange de la Mer was being invaded by chattering, garment-bag-wielding women, young and old alike. If she'd had some advance warning, she could have organized a proper defense, but she'd had no warning, no inkling, no glimmer of what was coming.

Touché, Miss Bennett, she thought. *Touché.*

The first woman to arrive carried two bulging white garment bags and assorted smaller satchels that required making two trips from the car. Sophia Bennett hurried to greet her with a warm embrace and help her carry it all to the room at the top of the stairs. *Her* room. The very same room where she'd dressed the morning she and Joseph were to be married.

She was not happy about this. Not happy at all.

Next came the mother of the bride, a chirping sparrow of a woman whom Sophia greeted with a polite smile and somewhat less enthusiasm. With her was an ample woman with luminous skin and a southern accent . . . Charleston was Ivy's guess. The mother of the groom, she decided.

All of them traipsed up the stairs as if they had every right in the world to be there.

It was well over a half hour later when a sleek red convertible came careening into the drive. Whoever was at the wheel drove too fast and parked haphazardly, blocking the other vehicles, as if the driver had no time for common sense or good manners.

Three young women in shorts and those rubber flip-floppy things piled out and hurried up the walk. Their legs were tanned and their long hair gleamed in the sunshine. They laughed and talked excitedly, bumping shoulders and interrupting one another, utterly confident in their friendship and in their world, and Ivy envied them so much her heart wrenched in a way she'd believed no longer possible. She remembered that feeling. She remembered laughing with her best friends and the sunshine on her face as she ran along that same path.

The girls entered the house without knocking.

One of them—the one with rhinestones and silly-looking white flowers on her flip-flops and a white T-shirt reading THE FUTURE MRS. WINSTON—held her cell phone to her ear.

"Sophie, Shelby. We're here," she said into it, and then paused, listening. "Yes, we all remembered to bring our shoes. Well, one of us forgot and had to go back for them . . . that's why we're late." She laughed. "Yup. The right underwear too, so you can tell Lina to relax. Okay, we'll be right up."

Of course, thought Ivy, *by all means, go right up.* Why stop with three interlopers storming through the house when you could have six? What next? A ticket booth out front and tourists mucking about? Well, she, for one, had had enough. And she knew just how to put a stop to it.

Sophia Bennett must believe herself to be very clever. She no doubt thought that bringing Shelby Archer and her bridesmaids there for a dress fitting was a stroke of genius, that the sight of them looking so young and fresh and beautiful in their gowns would work some kind of magic and Ivy would be moved enough to allow the wedding to go ahead as planned. Well, this time the crafty little wedding planner had outfoxed herself. Instead of changing Ivy's mind, she had just presented her with a way to stop the wedding at the source.

Sophia Bennett was a professional, and so far she had been admirably resolved and resilient in championing her client's interest. Now Ivy had a chance to deal directly with the client herself. And she was about to find out how the young bride felt about having her fairy-tale wedding take place in a haunted house. They were all about to find out.

From her vantage point halfway up the stairs, she considered her options. She could go for pure shock value and suddenly materialize before the young women, but the séance woman had been right: materializing consumed a lot of energy. And focus. And she wasn't in the mood to muster up enough of either. Besides, the silly things were sure to go around babbling about the ghost they'd seen and that could lead to complications in the days ahead. She wasn't interested in publicity or notoriety, only to be left in peace in her own home. Far better to pass on the dramatics and take a more subtle, roundabout approach.

Unseen, she surveyed the front hall below and quickly zeroed in on the crystal chandelier above the girls' heads. Perfect. She'd start there. It saddened her to damage the house itself, of course, but she really didn't have time to sit around rattling windows and flicking lights to get the message across. Desperate times called for desperate measures.

She drew the equivalent of a deep breath, gathering energy. As she did, she was outraged to see one of Shelby Archer's friends open the glass door of the Danish tall-case clock in the hall and reach for the hour hand.

"What are you doing?" exclaimed Shelby, hurrying over to stop her.

Excellent question, thought Ivy.

"I wanted to see if I could make it chime," her friend explained. "It probably does it on the hour."

"Well, then just wait for it to get there on its own. Don't go touching anything."

"That's right," agreed the third girl, joining them. In a teasingly stern tone, she added, "No one messes with the Princess House. Right, Bridezilla?"

"Right. And I am not a Bridezilla."

"True." Her friend poked her with her elbow. "But you are a dork."

"I don't care," said Shelby, smiling happily. "I love this house. And I consider myself very lucky to be getting married here. And I don't want anything to mess it up or make Mr. Winters change his mind . . . such as a broken clock."

"Okay, okay." The girl who'd opened the clock door closed it carefully, and then considered the clock with a small frown. "You know, a white clock with those carved curlicue things is kind of girlie looking for a guy . . . especially a guy who writes that rock 'em, sock 'em paranormal crap."

"It's not crap," Shelby countered. "And he probably didn't choose the clock. Sophie said he bought the house already furnished by the previous owner."

"Oh, that makes more sense. Come on; let's go squeeze me into that dress so we can go out to lunch afterward."

"Which will only make it harder to squeeze you into it on the big day," the other girl pointed out.

"No, because after today I'm going on the cabbage-and-rice-noodle diet until the day of the wedding."

"Sure you are."

"I am. And I'm going to wake up early and get on the treadmill every day."

"I'll help you get a head start . . . race me up the stairs."

Laughing, they hit the stairs and took them two at a time, running right through Ivy. Literally. It was a feeling she didn't think she'd ever get accustomed to, though technically she didn't *feel* anything anymore. It was unsettling to be run through just the same.

Shelby Archer laughed along with her friends, but she lagged behind, gazing around as she slowly climbed the stairs. When she reached the step where Ivy was seated—unseen—she suddenly turned and sat beside her.

She looked out over the hallway below.

Ivy looked at her, taking note of the expression of wonder on her face. She was startled to see tears well up in the girl's eyes in spite of the faint smile on her lips.

"Thank you," she whispered, leaving Ivy to wonder just whom she was thanking. Her father? Her lucky stars?

She supposed it didn't matter. What Shelby Archer thought or did or wanted was of no import to her.

Just the same, as Shelby went to join the others, Ivy found she'd suddenly lost her enthusiasm for throwing a good old-fashioned ghostly scare into the girl. Let her have her dratted dress fitting. It was the wedding Ivy was determined to stop and stop it she would.

In the meantime she would go keep an eye on what was happening in her room. Forewarned is forearmed. She would have to remember that going forward. And besides, she'd always been a bit of a clotheshorse. It couldn't hurt to see for herself just what passed for wedding fashion these days.

The dress fitting was a success on all fronts.

Lina had worked her magic and created for Shelby the wedding dress of her dreams. When she walked into the room wearing it, jaws dropped and Helen's eyes filled with tears.

"Oh, baby, you look beautiful," she whispered.

"I feel beautiful," exclaimed Shelby, laughing as she did a twirl and sent the frothy layers of skirt fluttering.

Lena had personally supervised the earlier fittings of the bridesmaids' dresses and they too were perfect. Simple and strapless and a soft shade of amethyst, they were perfect for the late-summer wedding.

And to Sophie's relief, Ivy did nothing to ruin the moment . . . or the expensive and irreplaceable dresses. She'd taken a big risk by arranging to have the fitting there. It could have backfired even more spectacularly than the séance had . . . and this time in front of witnesses. It hadn't. But had it succeeded in softening Ivy's no-wedding stance even a little? She'd just have to wait and see.

When the oohing and aahing was over and the dresses safely back in their garment bags, Shelby invited Lina, Sophie, Helen, and Matthew's mother to join her and her friends at a café on Bowen's Wharf for what locals agreed were the best lobster rolls in town. Matthew's mother was quickly on board, but both Lina and Sophie had previous appointments. Helen also had to decline, explaining that she had a lot of running around to do to take care of last-minute details for a fund-raiser for the private school both she and Shelby had attended.

"I should have stepped down from the planning committee when I realized the date for the ball was only a week before the wedding, but I like to keep busy and I'm always convinced I can do it all." She sent Sophie a small, regretful smile. "I'm just sorry I wasn't available to pitch in and do more to help you to fine-tune the wedding plans."

"No, no. Believe me, Helen, you've done more than enough."

Shelby grinned and Sophie knew it was because she understood exactly what she meant. Shelby knew her mother very well. That was the only thing that gave Sophie solace when she woke up in the middle of the night worried over Helen's most recent bit of fine-tuning. Technically her job as a wedding planner was to make the bride and groom happy, but she couldn't completely discount the fact that in this case it was the bride's mother who was paying the bills. So far Helen had *tweaked*—her word—the guest list, the menu, the seating arrangements, and the music. She would have tweaked more if Sophie had allowed it. Most often her changes were actually additions, which she intended to be a wonderful surprise for her daughter and future son-in-law. Sophie wasn't so sure, and the surprise element prevented her from checking with Shelby about adding an extra dozen out-of-town guests or an elaborate vodka-and-caviar station during cocktail hour.

Helen lingered after the others left and Sophie steeled herself to hear her latest "scathingly brilliant idea."

"Fireworks," Helen said, quite pleased with herself.

"Fireworks?" echoed Sophie, struggling to see how fireworks fit in with the whimsical, magical-woodland wedding theme.

"Yes. Isn't that a fabulous idea? Shelby loves fireworks," she added. "She'll be so surprised."

"Fireworks have become very popular, especially for outdoor weddings," Sophie allowed. "Which is why I doubt it would even be possible to arrange for them at this late date."

Helen waved off her concern. "Oh, it's all taken care of. A friend of a friend helped me and it's all set . . . technicians, permits, a barge, everything."

"A barge?" Sophie repeated, getting a mental image that made her shudder.

"Right. They're going to be set off on a barge out at sea. Let's go around back and check out what the view will be like, shall we?"

She was off without giving Sophie a chance to agree or time to say, "No, there's no need to check the view because your daughter has her heart set on a simple, understated, unpretentious celebration and a professional fireworks display is neither understated nor unpretentious".

Instead Sophie followed her to the back of the house and all the way to the edge of the lawn, where a path now provided safe passage through the daisies.

"Oh my God, the view from here is amazing . . . Shelby will be so surprised."

"Yes, I'm sure she will be. But you know, Helen, your wedding day isn't really a time for surprises. I think we should run the fireworks idea by Shelby and Matthew before we make a final decision."

"Oh, I've made the final decision," Helen countered with another of those careless waves of her hand, the practiced gesture of a woman accustomed to getting her way. "And I take full responsibility in the event Shelby doesn't love it. But she will. You'll see." Leaning slightly to her right, she looked past Sophie and her expression brightened. She shook her three-hundred-dollar haircut into place and moistened her lips.

Sophie recognized the preening reaction and didn't need to turn her head to know what, or rather who, had sparked it.

"Oh, look, there's Owen," announced Helen. "I'm just going to dash over and say hello."

Owen was coming out of the guesthouse; he stopped when Helen called out to him.

Let Helen dash all she wanted, Sophie thought. There's no way she herself was going to rush over there and give Owen the impression—the mistaken impression—that she was eager to talk with him after he'd made an avocation of avoiding her. She headed straight for the house, giving a quick wave in passing, but apparently Owen found Helen's company even more odious than hers because he moved quickly to head Sophie off and corral her in their little group.

At least she didn't have to come up with something to say. Helen was entirely capable of keeping the conversation going all by herself. She talked about the girls' dresses and the fireworks display and the engraved sterling-silver bubble wands and matching tiny crystal decanters until Owen's eyes glazed over and his expression implored Sophie to save him. Of course, she did nothing of the sort.

Instead, she waited until Helen at last showed signs of winding down, then said, "Tell me, Helen, have you finally decided on your outfit for the wedding?"

"Well, yes and no. You know the hideous problem I was having finding something in the right color palette that was flattering on me. People just don't understand how difficult it is when you're as petite as I am," she said in a coy aside to Owen. "Anyway, after months of searching for just the right dress, I found two. Can you believe that? And now I can't decide which one to wear."

Sophie gave a commiserating nod. "Feast or famine; isn't that always the way? Why don't you describe them and maybe we can help you choose?"

She followed up the suggestion with a sweet smile aimed directly at Owen, just to make sure he understood that shoving him from the Helen frying pan into the Helen fire had not been accidental. His gaze immediately went from glazed and imploring to lethal. Game on.

They continued to trade pointed glances as Helen wound her way through painfully elaborate descriptions of both dresses. Silk dupioni and silk shantung and slit skirts and covered buttons and lace appliqués . . . not a thing was left to their imaginations.

"So what do you think?" she asked at last.

"The bronze," said Sophie at the same time Owen said, "The green." He glanced at them cautiously. "One of them was green, right?"

Helen rolled her eyes dramatically. "Oh, you two; you're no help at all. I'll just have to muddle through on my own and hope for the best."

"I'm sure you'll be stunning in whichever dress you decide on," Sophie told her.

"How sweet of you to say so." Helen sighed, again with great drama. "I still have over a week to think about it. At least I know what I'm wearing to the ball this weekend." She reached out and briefly rested her fingertips on Owen's arm. "Owen, I know you'll get a particular kick out of this. The ball is a fund-raiser for the new library at Madison Academy . . . my alma mater," she added with obvious pride. "And we're calling it the First Annual Book Lovers' Ball. Book lovers. Library. The name was my idea. We're encouraging guests to dress as their favorite fictional character. My favorite book is *Gone with the Wind*. Need I say more?"

"No," Owen said bluntly.

"I think he meant to say, 'No, Scarlett,'" suggested Sophie.

Helen smiled broadly. "That's right: Scarlett O'Hara. At your service." She did a little curtsy and then gave a small gasp. "Oh my goodness. I just had the most scathingly brilliant idea. There's going to be a silent auction at the ball." She looked directly at Owen. "How great would it be if we auctioned off a complete set of your books and you were there to personally autograph them for the lucky winner? Please say you'll do it, Owen . . . for me? It would be such a coup."

He looked like a cornered mountain lion: fierce and unhappy. Sophie had to bite the inside of her cheek to keep from grinning.

"I'm sorry, but I really don't ever—"

"Say no to a worthy cause," Sophie jumped in helpfully when he hesitated and gave her a split-second opening. "And what cause could be more worthy than the Madison Academy library?" She smiled at Owen. "Just think, you'll get to meet your fans and probably pick up a bunch of new readers while you're at it. Now that's what I call win-win."

"This is wonderful!" exclaimed Helen. "I can't wait to tell the rest of the planning committee. And I'm so glad I ran into you and the idea just popped into my head that way. So it's settled. I'll get the books for the auction and you'll be there to sign them."

"Or better yet, I could just sign them in advance," suggested Owen.

"You silly," Helen retorted, again resting her hand on his arm. Longer this time. "That wouldn't be the same as you being there to meet the winner and write a personal inscription."

"Of course it wouldn't," agreed Sophie. She smiled at Owen. "You silly."

He looked decidedly unenthusiastic at the prospect. In fact, if she wasn't mistaken, behind the grim line of his mouth, his teeth were clenched. Poor little recluse, poked from his cave, and all for the pleasure of spending an evening with Scarlett O'Hara and her pals. She almost felt a little sorry for him.

In a terse tone, he said, "All right, I'll be there. But I'll need to bring someone else along with me."

Helen's smile froze in place, boosting Sophie's suspicion that

the idea of inviting Owen to the ball wasn't quite as spontaneous—or altruistic—as she'd have liked them to believe. "Someone
else? You mean like a date?"

"More like an assistant," he told her. "Whenever I do a book
signing, I have someone there to open the books and hand them
to me."

"Well, I'd be more than happy to assist you myself," said Helen.

He quickly shook his head. "You'll have your hands full making sure everything runs smoothly. You did say you're on the planning committee?"

"Yes. The chairman actually."

"Then you definitely won't have time for this. I'm sure Sophie
won't mind pitching in for a cause as worthy as the Madison
Academy."

"Oh. Sophie." Helen shrugged. "That's fine. Bring her along, if
you like."

Sophie bristled. "Actually, I—"

That's as far as he let her get. "Good. It's settled. We'll be there."

"Fabulous," said Helen. "I'll e-mail directions and all the other
information you'll need. And I'll be sure to leave word at the reception desk that you're there as my personal guest." She shifted
her rapt gaze from Owen long enough to glance at Sophie. "Both
of you. I'd love to stay and brainstorm costumes with you . . . I
have some marvelous ideas, but I have to dash to the bookstore for
those books and then I have a million other errands. TTFN," she
called over her shoulder as she left.

Owen's brow furrowed. "TTFN?"

"Ta-Ta For Now."

He shook his head. "That woman is . . . exhausting."

"She's also smitten. With you," Sophie clarified when he shot
her a quizzical look. "That's why she was so upset when she
thought you wanted to bring a date. And so relieved when she re-

alized it was just me you wanted to drag along. I'm not exactly Helen's idea of competition."

He gave a short, harsh laugh that could mean anything.

Sophie shook her head disgustedly. "I can't believe she roped us into going to her stupid ball."

"Thanks to you and how quick you were to throw me under the damn Book Lovers' bus," he retorted, but without any real rancor.

"Right back at you, Mr. I-need-an-assistant-to-hand-me-the-books." She shot him a look. "And just so we're clear: I am not wearing a costume."

"Thank God. I was afraid you'd want to go as Romeo and Juliet."

"I was afraid you'd want to go as Batman and Robin."

"I'd make a damn good Batman."

"Oh," she said, straight-faced. "I sort of assumed I'd be Batman."

He grinned and knocked his shoulder against hers playfully. "Sorry, Robin. The Batmobile is all mine."

They both gazed out at the water, not knowing what to say to fill the sudden silence and not wanting to walk away.

"So," said Sophie. "How's the book going?"

"Good. It's going good. Well, it's going all right."

"I'm glad to hear it. I'm really looking forward to reading it . . . especially after the way you left us hanging at the end of the last one."

"That's right. I forgot you're a big sushi-western fan."

"Go ahead. Laugh. I deserve it. I admit I tried to flatter you by saying I'd read your books when I hadn't. But I'll have you know that since then I have read them, all of them. And not for any ulterior motive. I'm hooked. Osprey is a great character . . . dark and brooding and yet intrinsically noble. And with that quiet, dry humor that comes from out of nowhere. I'm sure you've heard this many times, but he really reminds me of you."

"Actually I haven't."

"You're kidding," she countered, surprised. "It seems like a no-brainer to me. And I know you're going to accuse me of being a single-minded romantic, but I can't wait for him and Valene to get together." She caught the flicker of surprise in his eyes. "They are going to get together, aren't they?"

"I'm not sure. I've toyed with the possibility, but it's nothing firm."

"Toyed with it? That's crazy. They have to get together. It's the key to everything: Osprey's quest for redemption, his search for a family, his longing to find someplace where he belongs." She shook her head. "I knew Osprey was blind to all this, but I was sure you had it all figured out. Now I can see that you two are even more alike than I thought. Don't you get it, Owen? They have to get together. She's the missing piece of the puzzle. Valene is the dream that Osprey is afraid to dream."

Her comments took him by surprise and kicked his creative juices into overdrive. He was inundated with what-ifs. It was pure reflex at work when he muttered, "Osprey's not afraid of anything."

"Prove it," she said.

Fifteen

I t was with trepidation that Sophie opened her eyes to check
out her image in the full-length mirror in her room. It had
been a busy day, but between meeting with the pastry chef who
was baking the wedding cake and the landscape designer in
charge of transforming the grounds of Ange de la Mer into an
enchanted forest, she'd managed to stop by her place and grab
three evening gowns she could conceivably wear to the ball tomorrow night.

The first two were instant strikeouts. Obviously it had been
longer than she realized since she'd had occasion to dress up.
Which was ironic. As a wedding planner, she attended more than
anyone's fair share of formal events, but not as a formally-attired
guest. The first dresses she tried weren't current enough to be
trendy or vintage enough to be charming. They fell into that dreadful middle ground known as the Land of Blah. She knew she could
do better than that.

The third dress was dark blue silk with wide shoulder straps, a
band of beading at the edge of the bodice, and a sort of inverted

pleat down the front that she distinctly recalled the saleswoman telling her would be flattering to her curves. Lips pursed, she studied the way the pleat opened at the widest part of her hips and decided the woman had lied. It didn't matter. The dress wouldn't win her a spot on anyone's best-dressed list, but it wouldn't make the worst-dressed list either, and since she didn't have time to shop, it was going to have to do.

She just wished the *J*s weren't going to be there to pass judgment. When she mentioned the ball to Jill, she discovered they were also going. Madison Academy was notoriously difficult to get into, and although both Jill's and Jenna's children were still a few years away from applying, it was never too soon to start lobbying on their behalf. Attending the school's high-profile fundraisers was one way to do that. Currying favor with influential alumni was another, and it was another reason why the *J*s were so eager to please Helen Archer.

The *J*s definitely would not approve of her gown, but with the right jewelry, and if she remembered to keep her shoulders back so it didn't sag at the neckline and her stomach tucked in so it didn't do that pouchy thing in front, she'd get by. To reassure herself, she sucked in her stomach and threw back her shoulders and took a final look.

"Close enough," she muttered.

"Surely you jest."

Startled, Sophie spun around to find Ivy sitting on the bed behind her.

The movie-star dressing gown was gone. Instead she had on a crisp white cotton sundress from the same era. She sat dangling one leg, hands thrust in the pockets of her full skirt.

With one hand pressed over her rapidly beating heart, Sophie chided her. "You know, you really ought to quit popping in without warning. It's impolite. And it's not good for my heart."

"Sorry," Ivy said without sounding it. "I'm not accustomed to knocking in my own house."

"Fine. Pop in all you want. And I'm too busy to argue with you about whose house this is."

Ivy fluffed a pillow and slid it behind her. "Do you really intend to wear that to the ball tomorrow night?"

"How do you know about the ball?"

She shrugged her bare shoulders. "I have my ways."

"Meaning you eavesdrop. Also impolite."

"The dress," Ivy prodded. "Is that what you intend to wear?"

"So what if it is?"

"It doesn't flatter you in the least. You're quite lovely. Stubborn and impertinent, but lovely. Your figure is an asset, but instead of playing to your strength, you choose to dress in a . . . a . . ." She waved her hand. "A shroud. Also, that color washes you out." She stood. "Come with me."

She walked to the door of the room, graceful even in platform sandals, and turned to see if Sophie was following. She wasn't.

"I said come with me."

"Why?"

"Just come along, Miss Bennett." Ivy ran a disparaging eye over the blue gown. "You really don't have time to waste being petulant."

"'Just come along,'" Sophie mimicked. "On command . . . like a pet poodle."

"And stop muttering," Ivy called over her shoulder.

Sophie rolled her eyes, but she followed. She was too curious not to. Besides, she still had the wedding to consider. She couldn't afford to miss out on any opportunity to bond with the competition. Assuming this wasn't a trap of some kind, it could work to her advantage.

Ivy led the way down the corridor to a door that opened to

stairs to the attic. Like everything else about the house, the attic was roomy and in impeccable order, with boxes neatly stacked and labeled. It hadn't occurred to Sophie that when Owen bought the house "as is," it included not only furniture, but also whatever other worldly goods Ivy had acquired over her lifetime that her nephew didn't want.

A wall had been built down the center of the attic and on the other side of it was the longest closet Sophie had ever seen. Multiple sets of heavy, sliding metal doors opened to reveal a long row of garment bags, also neatly labeled.

"Let's see," Ivy murmured, fingering through one group of bags and then moving on to those behind the next set of doors. She clearly knew what she was looking for, so Sophie just stood back and let her have at it . . . even though her own fingers were itching to unzip those bags and see what goodies were inside. Shopping wasn't her idea of fun, but this felt more like a treasure hunt, and that she did find exciting.

She'd already learned something new and interesting about Ivy: she loved clothes. It was obvious not only from how many she owned, but from how carefully, even lovingly, she treated them.

"Aha," she exclaimed at last, pulling a dark green garment bag from the closet and handing it to Sophie. "Do be careful, Miss Bennett. That's a Pierre Balmain original, from the early fifties. And now for the Chanel."

She went back to work, and when she located the second bag, she handed it to Sophie as well.

"We could try more, of course, and if need be we will. But if I do say so myself, I have a flair for these things and I'm certain both these dresses will be perfection on you, and that, Miss Bennett, is what you must aim for: perfection. Always."

"I have an idea," Sophie said. "How about if you call me Sophie and I call you Ivy? I mean we are practically roommates."

"No. Come along."

She led Sophie to a three-way mirror at the far end of the room. On the wall beside the mirror there were hooks for the garment bags. Sophie carefully unzipped the first bag and her breath caught in her throat when she saw the dress inside. She'd seen beautiful dresses before, gorgeous, to-die-for dresses, starting with those her mother made, but at that moment she couldn't remember seeing one that compared to the dress before her. At first glance she thought it was ivory, but it was actually the softest shade of gold imaginable. Even on the hanger it glimmered like fine gold: she could only imagine what it would be like to wear . . . to move and dance in. It was strapless, the top subtly accented with tiny gold and crystal beads. Tightly shirred on an angle through the bodice and hips, the full skirt fell in soft gathers from a rosette of the same fabric on the left hip.

"This is . . . beautiful," she said softly.

"Yes. It is," agreed Ivy. "Well, go on . . . try it on."

"I'm afraid to. I'm almost afraid to even touch it. It must be fragile after all these years of being packed away."

"Nonsense. Everything was cleaned and professionally treated before being stored, and the closet is climate controlled. Some people collect art; I collected fashion, and I treated it with the same care and attention."

"Well, lucky for me. I would have looked odd wearing a Picasso to the ball."

Amazingly, Ivy laughed along with her. Easily. As if, thought Sophie, they weren't on opposite sides in the wedding war.

Ivy sat on an old trunk while Sophie slipped out of the blue gown and then very carefully put on the gold Pierre Balmain . . . who she'd never heard of, but who was suddenly her favorite designer of all time. When she looked at herself in the mirror, the dress took her breath away for the second time.

It suited her perfectly, as if it had been made just for her by someone who really knew their stuff. The fit was perfect, the drape of the fabric was perfect, and in the waning light through the attic window the soft, warm color made her skin glow with a faint apricot tinge.

"Well? What do you think?" asked Ivy.

"I love it," Sophie replied, not able to take her eyes off her reflection. She turned first one way and then the other to see the dress from all angles. "I love it, I love it, I love it." She spun around to face Ivy. "Can I really wear it to the ball?"

"Of course you can wear it. That was the whole point of coming up here. But don't you want to try on the Chanel before you decide?"

Sophie shook her head and turned back to the mirror, as taken up with her own image as a kid with a new toy. "No. I already know it couldn't possibly compare to this. I love this dress. And I love it even more with me in it. That's never happened to me before."

"I shouldn't wonder if that"—Ivy pointed at the blue gown—"is indicative of your fashion sense when left to your own devices."

Sophie barely heard. She couldn't stop grinning. She was thinking out loud when she said, "I can't wait for Owen to see me in it."

"Well, if pleasing Mr. Winters is your goal, then we have wasted our time for nothing."

That she heard. The words struck her like a dart.

"I know," she said, her shrug awkward. "I know he'd never be seriously interested in me. I just thought that in this dress I'd be a little harder to dismiss . . . or ignore."

"You misunderstand me. When I said we wasted our time, I meant that you don't need a fancy designer dress to impress or captivate that man. When you're in the room, you're all he sees.

And judging from what I observed of you two together the other night, he's very seriously interested."

Sophie shook her head as their gazes met in the mirror. "I think he's physically attracted to me, at least a little, enough for a one- or two-night stand. But not enough for anything more. And to his credit, I think he's gentleman enough not to lead me on. Either that or he just doesn't want any messy complications as long as we're living under the same roof."

"You listen to me. Just because I never married doesn't mean I don't know a thing or two about men. I do. And I can tell when a man is falling so fast he doesn't even know it."

"It wouldn't matter if he did fall. He'd refuse to admit it even to himself. He doesn't believe in true love."

"Horsefeathers. The man might as well say he doesn't believe in gravity. Or hurricanes. He can say what he likes. When he stops talking, his big feet will still be firmly planted on God's green earth, and when those hurricane-force winds start to blow trees and park benches around as if they were Tinker Toys, he'll run for cover just like everyone else. Let him talk all he wants, Sophie, but pay closest attention to what he says with his heart."

"You know, if I weren't wearing an irreplaceable Pierre Balmain original from the early fifties, I'd hug you."

"Whatever for?"

"You just called me Sophie."

A smile tugged at Ivy's lips. "So I did. Well, as you said, we are practically roommates. Now I think you should take off that gown before anything happens to it and we should go downstairs so I can show you what I have in mind for your hair. And I have thoughts about the right makeup as well. You need to work on your brows. And then there's the matter of the right jewelry. I'll handle that too."

"Okay, but at the risk of ruining things just as we got to the first-name stage, I have to ask. This isn't all some kind of trick, is it? To get me to lower my guard? Is this dress booby-trapped? Maybe rigged to disappear at midnight so I'm left standing in the middle of the ballroom stark naked?"

"I'm a ghost, not a magician. Even if I could do a thing like that, why on earth would I?"

"To embarrass me and throw me off-kilter and make me all frazzled so I can't focus on the wedding."

Ivy looked crestfallen. "Do you really think I would do something like that to you?"

"Well, you have done lots of other stuff."

"Yes, because I don't want a wedding here. I've done what I had to do to get that message across. But I wouldn't do something malicious just to hurt or embarrass you. If fact," she said, tossing back her hair, "I hereby propose a truce. Until after the ball."

"That sounds good to me. A truce it is, starting now."

"Fine. Now come along. The dress is perfection, but we have a ways to go before you are."

It was on the way out of the attic that Sophie noticed the dollhouse sitting on top of a stack of boxes just inside the door.

"Wait up," she called to Ivy.

Crouching down, she undid the center latch and swung the front panels open to reveal the rooms inside, complete with the split staircase at the center. "It's the Princess House," she said to Ivy, who had walked back to stand beside her, holding the garment bag. "The windows, the colors . . . it's just like the book." She looked around. "Were there ever people and furniture to go with it?"

"I have no idea," replied Ivy. "It doesn't belong to me. Owen brought it with him when he moved in. I assume he made it."

Sophie nodded. "For his daughter. For Allie." She thought for a moment and then closed and latched the panels and lifted the dollhouse. It was heavy, but she'd manage.

"What are you doing?" Ivy asked.

"Taking it downstairs. I'd tell you why, but I'm afraid you'd try to trip me and that would violate our brand-new truce." She grinned over her shoulder as she maneuvered the dollhouse through the doorway. "And I really need help with my hair."

"Among many other things."

"Now who's muttering?"

They both laughed. Sophie couldn't explain why, but for some reason she was already more comfortable taking advice from Ivy than she ever was from the *J*s.

Owen finished working for the day and walked out of the guest-house with a smile on his face.

He was writing again.

That in itself was akin to a miracle. It was an even bigger miracle that when he reread what he'd written at the end of the day, he didn't hit delete and walk away angry and disgusted with himself.

Sophie's comments on his work had been like a live grenade tossed into the giant pile of garbage he'd been wrestling with as he sat at the computer day after day. But somehow—miraculously—when the debris from the blast settled, the story he was telling made sense to him in a way it hadn't in a very long time.

He was writing.

He was still taking with a grain of salt her romanticized vision of Osprey and Valene together. And her comment that Valene was the dream Osprey was afraid to dream was way off base. Like he'd told her: Osprey wasn't afraid, just rational. It had gotten him thinking, however, thinking about his hero, and about the things men dream about, and the things they fear.

He was writing again, but he was losing the battle to control his feelings for Sophie. Years of experience with sheer, white-knuckled self-discipline worked to keep her from commandeering his thoughts during the day, but at night his dreams were another world entirely. In his dreams there were no rules, no limits, and usually no clothing. There was only a megadose of Sophie, under him, riding him; in his dreams she was all he could feel or smell or touch. He woke up sweating and shaking . . . shaking with pent-up desire and with the awareness that everything he craved was sleeping just a few steps away.

As he lay awake in the dark, his dreams slid into fantasies, keeping sleep at bay for long, frustrating hours. Sometimes, lying there, he imagined he could smell her all around him, hear her breathing and whispering his name.

It didn't help that he chanced to walk by at just the right moment and caught a glimpse of her wearing only a slip, a filmy, strapless thing that clung all the way to her ankles and was somehow almost more arousing than his fantasies of her naked. Almost.

Ivy had been there too. She'd caught him looking, rolled her eyes, and swung the bedroom door shut in his face. Afterward, he heard them on the other side of the door, talking and giggling like a couple of teenage girls.

It wasn't the only time he'd seen them together in the past few days. Something was definitely up. But after he'd so abruptly—all right, rudely—taken himself out of the loop, making it clear to Sophie that Ivy and the wedding were her problems to solve, he didn't feel right asking her directly about what was going on. And when he tried to be subtle, casually observing that she and Ivy were at least finally on speaking terms, Sophie had simply flashed him an enigmatic grin and gone on her way. Humming. In an irritatingly cheerful way that made him think she wasn't losing any sleep over him.

Why was he making this so complicated? He wasn't a damn

monk. He'd dated and gone to bed with plenty of women. The process wasn't rocket science. He wanted her. She wanted him . . . at least she had at one point, and the fact that she hadn't flat-out refused his backhanded invitation to go to the ball with him and that she'd hung around to talk with him the other day suggested she was still at least a little interested. He ought to just let nature take its course and not worry about the rest.

It wasn't as if he'd lied to her about who he was or what he wanted. He'd been honest. She was an adult, and a shrewd businesswoman, capable of sizing up a situation and making up her own mind. So what the hell was his problem?

Nothing, he decided.

Tomorrow night he would be taking Sophie to the ball. It's not something he'd chosen to attend, but now he was almost glad Helen Archer had roped him into it. He was even happier that he'd succeeded in roping Sophie into going with him. He was really looking forward to spending the evening with her. He'd never been a great dancer and he was sure to be worse now, but one of the things he was most looking forward to was holding Sophie in his arms as they danced.

Thinking about it had him smiling as he walked into the kitchen and headed straight for the refrigerator, hoping he'd find a pitcher of iced tea with slices of lemon floating in it and the perfect amount of sugar. Instead he stopped short when he saw the dollhouse sitting on the counter. His smile disappeared, along with the past twenty or so years of his life.

Seeing it ripped the lid off memories and emotions he kept buried. He would have quickly shoved them back down deep inside and dumped a load of denial and distractions on top if Sophie hadn't distracted him by strolling into the kitchen at that moment. His first thought was that Ivy had put the dollhouse there, that it was just one more of her attempts to get under his skin. But the cat-that-swallowed-the-canary expression on Sophie's face told him that this time Ivy wasn't to blame.

"What the hell is this?" he demanded.

Her smile deepened, which only pissed him off more.

"Don't you recognize it?"

"Yeah. I recognize it. I meant what the hell is it doing here?"

"I found it in the attic. Ivy brought me up there so I could borrow a dress for the ball," she explained before he could ask what the hell she was doing poking around in his attic. "Shades of Cinderella," she went on, her self-effacing shrug putting only the slightest dent in his ire. "At first I assumed the dollhouse belonged to Ivy, but she told me that you brought it with you when you moved in. Did you build it yourself?"

"Can't you tell?" he retorted and for the first time she seemed to register the fact that he was royally irked. "Check out the uneven roof shingles and the botch job on that second floor window. I must have ripped that sucker out and re-set it a dozen times and I still couldn't get it square. A smarter man would have taken that as a sign and thrown in the towel, but back then, an abundance of smarts wasn't my biggest problem. Not by a long shot."

"Are you kidding me? I think it's beautiful just as it is. You did an amazing job. The wrought iron trim on the windows, the curving staircase, the chandeliers . . . it's perfect. Allie must have loved it. I'm assuming Allie is the one you made it for?"

"For her fifth birthday," he told her, not sure why. He was torn between wanting to talk about it and wanting to grab the damn thing and smash it, to make the memory go away once and for all. The urge to smash he understood and could deal with. The urge to talk was new. He suspected it had something to do with the fact that it was Sophie standing there, stirring up these feelings, and he didn't like it.

"I'll bet she went crazy when she saw it," she said.

He shifted his gaze from the dollhouse to meet hers. "I never gave it to her."

"You didn't give . . . why on earth not?"

He shrugged and crossed to the sink, settling for a glass of water instead of the iced tea he'd hoped for. He stared out the window at the daisies dancing in the sunlight, neither of them speaking for what seemed like a very long time. Long enough for a particularly painful stretch of his life to pass before him in slow motion.

"I'd never built anything before," he said finally, his back still to her. "It took me months to finish it. That window wasn't the only thing I ripped out more than once. It didn't matter. I didn't care how long it took or how much I had to cut corners to pay for parts and tools. The whole time I was working on it I kept imagining the look on Allie's face when I walked into her party carrying it. Rachel—my ex-wife—and I had been divorced for nearly four years by that time and she was remarried to a guy who was everything I wasn't . . . rich, successful, Ivy League–educated . . . a guy who met all of her—and her parents'— requirements. Sometimes while I worked on it I pictured the look on their faces too: I was going to show all of them that even though I'd been a lousy husband and provider, I was a damn good father."

"I'm sure you weren't a lousy . . ."

"No. I was," he acknowledged, turning and leaning against the sink. "By almost anyone's standards, but especially by Rachel's and her folks'. Hell, I was eighteen when Rachel got pregnant and we got married . . . against her family's wishes, needless to say. The son of an ex-con carnie wasn't what they had in mind for their little girl. I was so sure they were wrong. I was convinced that love and hard work would make everything all right in the end. It took me a while to figure out that it didn't matter how much I loved her, or how hard I worked, or how many backbreaking jobs I juggled to pay the bills. I would never be able to make Rachel's dreams come true. We wanted different things."

"I'm sorry. I'm sure that wasn't an easy decision to make. You had a baby you loved to think of, as well as your own future. Whatever you did was bound to be painful."

"Yeah. It was painful, all right. Painful not to be able to see Allie whenever I wanted to. Painful to see her with a new step-father . . . just the word alone made me want to punch a hole in something . . . a step-father who could give my little girl all the things I wanted to give her and couldn't." His jaw hardened as he looked at the dollhouse. "But I was going to fix that. Just one time I was going to give her something no one else could . . . something that would top everything else. I kept telling myself that and I believed it, right up until the moment I drove up and saw Allie riding up and down the driveway of their big fancy new house in her brand-new, fully motorized miniature pink convertible, just like the one her favorite Barbie dolls drove . . . a custom-made present from her step-father. I looked at the dollhouse and suddenly all I could see were flaws and amateur mistakes . . . and what a fool I'd been to ever think I could one-up them."

"What did you do?"

He shook his head, his short laugh harsh. "I took off with it still in the back seat and skipped the party. The next day I went to Toys "R" Us and bought Allie something else . . . I can't remember what it was. It took me another day to get up the nerve to go back there and give it to her . . . thereby securing my reputation as a screw-up and all-around failure."

He didn't need to look at Sophie: he could feel the pity oozing from her. He could have told her the rest of the story. He could have told her that things changed after that. But he didn't. He was sick of talking.

But things had changed. Because he changed them. He'd decided he was probably never going to be filthy rich—and how about the irony there?—but he could be the kind of man Allie was proud to have for her father and he made up his mind that he was going to do whatever he had to do to become that man. He enlisted and discovered there were things he was good at. Very good, in fact. There were things he could do that very few men could. Important things. Over the next few years he tasted real success for the first time. He earned the respect of men he respected, men willing to trust him with their very lives, and he learned to respect himself. He became the father that Allie deserved.

But he never gave her the dollhouse and he wasn't sure why he'd held onto it all this time. It represented a time he'd rather forget and brought back memories of feeling inadequate and disappointed. Disappointment in himself, and in love. He'd grown up watching his parents fight and saw their marriage wither and die. It made him wary. But still, when he met Rachel, he fell hard and fast and forever. Or so he thought. That was before he learned that nothing is forever, least of all a fragile emotion like love.

Suddenly impatient with the feelings and memories it triggered, he grabbed the dollhouse and headed for the back door.

"What are you doing?" Sophie called after him.

"What I should have done years ago," he told her, grunting as he shouldered the door open. The damn thing was heavy. "Getting rid of it for good."

"No. Wait. I brought it down here so I could ask you if it would be all right for me to use it as a focal point in the sunroom during the cocktail hour."

"No."

"No? Just like that?"

"Just like that," he said, and let the door slam shut.

Sixteen

I vy turned out to be the mother of all fairy godmothers and Sophie was profoundly grateful to be taken under her wing. Dress,
hair, makeup: Ivy had a knack for pulling it all together. She even
revealed a secret compartment in the drawer of her dressing table
where she'd tucked away several of her favorites pieces of jewelry
and she came up with the perfect finishing touch: a necklace of
three twisted strands of small, luminescent pearls and matching
earrings that seemed to have been designed to complement the
dress. Having heard stories of Ivy in her prime, Sophie thought
they very well might have been. Either that or a gift from some
besotted foreign ambassador or globe-trotting adventurer. She'd
seen the old photo albums that were also in the attic closet. Ivy
had stolen the hearts of a string of interesting men. And had any
one of them ever measured up to her Joseph, she told Sophie, she
might have married after all. No one ever had.

At last it was time to look in the mirror to see how it all came
together. Ordinarily Sophie's first reaction to the beautiful, sophisticated woman she saw reflected there would be that it couldn't

possibly be her, but not tonight . . . tonight she felt beautiful from the inside out. Tonight she gazed at her reflection and felt very much at home in her own skin.

She was convinced it was the most astounding makeover ever . . . until she saw Owen waiting for her at the bottom of the staircase. Gone were the battered T-shirt and jeans. Tonight he was tall, dark perfection in an impeccably tailored black tux. His hair was cut short, all the sun-bleached streaks gone, and he was clean-shaven, emphasizing the strong angles of his handsome face. She had to stop for a moment because she was finding it hard to walk and breathe and control the sudden explosion of lust all at the same time.

First things first. Lust. Breathe. Walk.

He smiled when he saw her.

Ivy's final words of advice played in her head.

"Now about Mr. Winters. Never underestimate the power of playing hard to get. Trust me, I know the type. A warrior, born to conquer. Men like that value most what they have to fight and sweat and struggle to win. So let him sweat. Let him eat his heart out. It will do him a world of good, I promise you."

Sophie would have found the advice hard to follow even before she saw him standing there looking like the incarnation of every fairy-tale prince fantasy she'd ever had. She wasn't good at playing games. And she didn't want to be. After devoting entirely too much thought to the problem of Owen Winters, she'd made up her mind to simply take things as they came. Tonight she was going to let down her guard and enjoy the evening for what it was, a gift, a fluke, a rare and unexpected opportunity to step outside herself and be the confident, beautiful, adventurous woman she'd like to be. For once she was going to relax and go with the flow . . . without planning an alternate route in case of emergency, without expectations or stipulations.

He came toward her as she reached the bottom step, took her right hand in his, and slipped on her wrist a corsage of ivory roses and baby's breath, the dark green leaves lightly dusted with gold.

"I've been advised by someone who should know that this is customary for a lady attending a formal ball."

"Hmm," she murmured, smiling as she glanced up and around. "Something tells me we have the same fairy godmother. Thank you. It's lovely."

He smiled at her. "You're lovely, Sophie. Beautiful, in fact. Beyond beautiful. I feel like I need another thousand or so words to do justice to the way you look tonight, but instead I'm suddenly speechless . . . a rarity for a man who makes a living with words."

"That's probably for the best, actually. I'm already feeling very belle-of-the-ball-ish. At this point compliments would go straight to my head and push me over the line into being obnoxious." She ran her gaze over him approvingly. "But I must say you look amazing. It's like we wore costumes after all, because I feel like a princess and you make a very dashing Prince Charming. No, not costumes. Prom night. It's like prom night all over again, except this time it's not a disaster waiting to happen."

"Let's hope not."

She slanted a look of concern from under her newly lush lashes. "You're not planning to tell me halfway through the night that you're in love with my sister and only invited me because she promised to repay you by going to see a movie with you next weekend, are you?"

He winced a little as he shook his head. "A resounding no to all of it."

"Then we definitely have the prom beat hands down." He was looking at her intently with what could either be fascination or bafflement about what he'd gotten himself into.

"Did I mention that when I get overexcited I have a tendency to babble?" she asked him.

"You didn't have to. This isn't a blind date, Sophie."

"Meaning?"

"I've already heard you babble."

She sighed. "That's what I was afraid you meant."

"You didn't let me finish . . ."

"Because I was babbling."

"I've heard you babble, and I like it." He offered his arm. "Shall we do this?"

"Yes." His arm felt solid beneath her fingertips. "But this time we're definitely taking my car. You can drive if you like, but there's no way I'm getting on a motorcycle . . ."

He opened the front door and she saw the black stretch limo parked in the drive. The uniformed driver slid from behind the wheel and held the door open for them.

His smile rakish, Owen held out his hand. "Your pumpkin awaits, Princess."

The ball was more fun than Sophie would have thought possible. It helped that the most handsome man there stubbornly refused to be pried from her side all evening . . . which was saying something considering the effort Helen Archer put into trying to commandeer him. In the end Helen seemed content to drag Owen, who in turn dragged Sophie, around to meet the other board members, which allowed her to bask in the glory of having landed the biggest celebrity there.

The auction was a huge success. A doctor from Barrington bought the collection of Owen's books for an outrageous amount and Sophie played her part by handing them to Owen to be signed, which also allowed her to soak up a bit of reflected glory in the process. It was clear he had a lot of fans in the crowd.

For Sophie, the only flaw in the evening was that it went by too quickly. She kept reminding herself to take mental pictures of the highlights so she could relive them later. Highlights such as the moment when she and Owen were leaving the dance floor and she bumped into Jill . . . literally. They exchanged apologetic murmurs and then Jill looked directly at her and did a double take straight out of a Hanna-Barbera cartoon.

"Sophie?" she blurted. "Sophie?" She dragged her stunned gaze down to the sparkly new stiletto-heeled shoes on Sophie's feet and then back up to her face, which was still flushed from dancing and from the incredible feeling of being held tightly in Owen's arms. "My God, Sophie, you look . . . gorgeous."

"Thanks. So do you."

"Where did you find that fabulous dress?"

"Long story. I'll fill you in later," she promised, knowing Jill would be on the phone first thing in the morning wanting details.

The night went by too fast and ended too soon. Feeling like Cinderella, she was back in her chauffeur-driven coach by midnight. With one important improvement on the fairy-tale version: she was riding with the prince. They were soon home, but Sophie wasn't ready for the night to end and Owen appeared to feel the same way.

"Nice night," he said as they stood in the front drive, neither making a move to go inside. He tipped his head back to gaze at the sky. "A lot of stars up there tonight."

Sophie looked up and nodded agreement. "I think I see the Big Dipper."

"Want to take a walk around back where we can get a better look?"

She very much wanted to . . . she wanted it even before he took her hand in his and closed his fingers around it possessively and made her heart thump harder.

It felt good to be walking hand in hand with him. It felt right.

The only light in back came from the stars and a sliver of moon. They followed the path that led to the cliffs. Off to the right Sophie could see the shadowy outline of the recently completed illusion pond and the bushes and small flowering trees that were the beginning of the surrounding fantasy woodland. Remarkably she didn't squander a single brain cell wondering if it would all be ready on time or what Ivy might do to interfere once their truce was over.

Tonight her mind was on other things. And obviously Owen's was as well. They didn't make it halfway to the ocean's edge before he stopped and dragged her into his arms. Not that any dragging was necessary. She'd been his from the first deep "shall we dance?" hours ago, and her yearning for more . . . for this . . . had grown each time his hand caressed her back or molded to the curve of her hip.

Oh yeah. Definitely better than the prom.

Eyes closed, she gave herself up to his kiss and to the waves of shimmering pleasure it sent rolling through her. She reached up to cup his face with her hands and kissed him back. He tasted of whiskey and desire, and the midnight hint of stubble along his jaw made his skin feel deliciously rough against her softer skin as his mouth raked impatient kisses over her throat and bare shoulders.

Warmth bubbled through her as the effect of several glasses of champagne collided with the electrifying effect Owen had had on her from the instant they'd met. She felt energized and reckless, and she liked the feeling.

He slid his palm down her arm and took her by the hand once more, his quiet voice even rougher than usual. "Come on."

As soon as she sensed him trying to pull her off the path and toward the guesthouse, she resisted. "Owen, I can't."

"Huh. What?" He gave his head a small shake, staring at her in the darkness. "Damn it, Sophie. Okay. No is no, but . . . damn it, Sophie."

"No, no. I meant I can't because I'll get the bottom of my dress wet in the grass. It's one of a kind. Irreplaceable."

Comprehension—and quite possibly relief—gleamed in his eyes as he reached for her. "One of a kind and irreplaceable? Damn it, Sophie, so are you."

Seemingly without effort, he scooped her up in his arms, another of those freeze-frame Merchant-Ivory moments to savor later, and carried her to the guesthouse and over the threshold. Kicking the door shut behind him in the time-honored tradition of Rhett Butler, he kissed her long and hard, not stopping until he'd made his way to the next room and gently lowered her to her feet beside the bed.

Owen Winters could claim he wasn't a romantic all he liked: Sophie knew differently.

Reaching behind him, he turned on the small bedside lamp and the room filled with soft amber light.

"I want to see you," he explained.

Taking her by the shoulders, he turned her so her back was to him and slowly lowered the zipper on her dress. His fingers brushed against each inch of newly revealed skin and Sophie swore she felt his hands tremble. With the dress loosened, he slid it down her legs and helped her step out of it, taking time to drape it across the back of a chair.

She and Ivy had debated the need for a slip beneath the dress and the slip lost. Now she stood before him in only her lacy panties and strapless bra and it would be a lie to say she hadn't thought about just such a moment when she was putting them on earlier.

Owen bracketed her waist with his palms, pleasure and approval radiating from him as he slowly stroked over the soft curves of her hips and thighs. Again she felt his hands tremble.

He sought her gaze, his expression rueful. "It's been a while for me."

"And me," she whispered.

"I want to take my time, but I'm not sure I can."

Sophie swayed closer to him. "I'm not sure I want you to."

He sucked in a sharp breath and dragged his palms higher to cup her full breasts. Sliding one hand around to the clasp at the back, he unfastened it with a minimum of fumbling and leaned back to look at her.

Her breasts lifted with a deep breath and the tips hardened under his heated gaze even before he bent his head and found them with his mouth.

She gripped his shoulders and threw her head back as his tongue sent shivers of excitement racing through her. A fierce feminine hunger rose up in her. She wanted the hot, damp pleasure to go on forever and she wanted more . . . wanted all of him . . . right . . . that . . . instant.

Owen's urgency matched her own. Pressing her hard against his hips, he lifted his head to kiss her mouth again and again.

They were both out of breath, chests heaving in an effort to get it back, when he stopped and stepped back just enough to see what he was doing as he hooked his thumbs at the side of her panties and slowly, deliberately, peeled them off.

Her knees like jelly, Sophie braced one hand on his chest as she stepped out of them. The fact that she was naked except for the crystal-studded stilettos—and that he was still *GQ* perfect in his tux—made her feel sexy and slightly wanton. The effect wasn't wasted on Owen: he growled low in his throat as his gaze moved over her slowly, a sound that was part need, part pleasure. Excitement and impatience flared darkly in his eyes.

"Lie down," he urged, his fingertips stroking the V between her thighs.

"Not yet." She reached to undo his bow tie and pull it off. His shirt required more work: all those studs and cuff links. When she reached for his belt, he kicked off his shoes. And then in a rush of movement and tangled, impatient hands, his trousers were unzipped and gone and his naked body was pressing hers down onto the mattress.

"Not fair," she whimpered as he caressed her belly before sliding his hand between her legs, where she was hot and wet and ready. "You got to look at me."

He might have laughed, or groaned, but he rolled slightly to his side so that she could see him. The light gilded the flat planes and sculpted muscles of his body. Her gaze slid greedily over his chest and flat belly to the visible proof of how badly he wanted her. He was hard, and magnificent.

Usually she would be thinking too much to enjoy the moment, analyzing and second-guessing and worrying what her partner was thinking. Not tonight. Owen's touch shattered her ability to think. This was all about raw sensation. Without shyness or hesitation, she reached for him, curving her fingers as she slowly stroked him. She watched his eyes close and his muscles shudder. Another slow movement of her hand and sweat glistened on his forehead.

"Enough," he said roughly, grabbing her hand and kissing the inside of her arm from wrist to shoulder as he rolled back on top of her.

He nudged her thighs apart and Sophie spread them to welcome him. She felt him, hot and hard, poised against her sleek entrance.

Bracing his weight on his hands, he found her gaze and held it. "Next time we'll take it slow," he promised.

Sophie smiled and lifted her hips. "Maybe."

With one sure stroke he was inside her. He rocked against her, slowly at first, silk against silk, and then faster, harder, deeper, both of them already dangerously close to the edge of control.

Sophie wrapped one leg around his hips and then the other, and felt a whole new rush of sensations, and then came the first fluttery contraction of muscles she couldn't control if she wanted to.

She clutched at his shoulders.

She closed her eyes.

She gave herself over to the pleasure building inside.

She'd heard the expression *drowning in sensation*, but Sophie didn't feel like she was drowning. She felt like she was flying . . . soaring . . . her arc sure and true as she raced through the brilliant white light that filled her with heat. And Owen was with her. She felt his arms tighten around her and heard his rough cry echo her own as they rocketed past the edge of everything, together and alone.

Usually, if Owen spent the night having sex with a woman and then woke up alone, his overriding reaction was relief. It meant he wasn't obliged to hang around and have "the talk." He didn't make pregame promises he had no intention of keeping, and the postgame wrap-up that so many women required always struck him as pointless. Sex was what it was. Fun while it lasted. It wasn't something that had to be dissected and analyzed.

This morning when he awoke, saw where he was, and remembered how he got there, he was instantly hard and hungry all over again. Smiling, he rolled over and reached for Sophie . . . and found her gone. Along with her one-of-a-kind, irreplaceable dress and every other visible sign that she'd been there. Had last night been just another of his fantasies?

No. Impossible. There was no way he could have imagined last night. For one thing, he didn't have the raw material to work with. And for another . . . He just knew, that's all. Last night had been different from any other night . . . different and new in a way he couldn't explain. And now Sophie was gone and he didn't feel relief. He felt . . . something else. It wasn't a pleasant feeling. It was more like a hundred pounds of crushed stones had been dumped on his chest and settled right over his heart. Disappointment: that was it. And then, before he'd even come to terms with the disappointment, came another novel morning-after feeling: worry.

Had she left because she was upset about something? Or maybe she'd also awoke feeling disappointed, but for an entirely different reason? Maybe she'd wanted to get out of Dodge without having to explain or pretend. An uncomfortable heat crept up his neck to his face. What if the sex hadn't been as much fun for Sophie as it was for him? *Crap*, he thought. Was this why women wanted to talk about it afterward? To make sure everyone was on the same page and was going away happy?

He folded his arms behind his head, staring at the ceiling and seeing quick flashes of images from the night before. She'd seemed happy enough afterward. Hadn't she? Happy and satisfied. She'd smiled drowsily and curled up in his arms before falling asleep, but they hadn't actually said much. He tried to recall exactly what they had said, and couldn't. He tried harder, but no matter how hard he focused, the memory that kept pushing to the forefront of his mind, the one he knew he would carry away from last night and never forget, was of looking into Sophie's eyes at the moment their bodies joined for the first time and feeling an explosion of warmth and wonder unlike anything he'd ever felt before.

Had she felt it too? He wasn't even sure what it was or what it meant. But suddenly it seemed crucial to know if she'd felt it too.

*   *   *

As soon as he stepped outside the guesthouse he noticed something different. Something besides the people scurrying about with
ladders and shrubbery and giant rolls of electrical wire. Workers
had been coming and going for weeks, but suddenly there were
more of them and their movements seemed more purposeful.
There was a new energy in the air.

He drew a few curious looks and sly grins as he made his way
to the house barefoot and wearing half a tux. He considered showering and changing before looking for Sophie, but only for about
a second and a half. He was much too anxious to see her to waste
time. From the sounds of it, the kitchen was ground zero, and
that's where he found her, clipboard in hand, papers strewn across
the counter beside her. He glanced at them in passing and saw an
oversize calendar and a diagram of the house and grounds marked
with scribbled notes and large red Xs.

Sophie smiled at the sight of him and he felt a trickle of relief
begin to flow. But when he moved closer and leaned in to kiss her,
she put a hand up to stop him and quickly stepped out of reach.

"Sorry," she said, her quiet tone rueful. She indicated the pair
of burly men carrying in worktables from the truck parked out
back. "It's tough enough to get union laborers to take orders from
a woman seriously. I don't want to give them any idea that I'm not
a hundred percent business."

"Of course," Owen agreed, also taking a step back. He
shouldn't have had to be told that, but to be honest, when he
walked in and saw Sophie, he forgot that she was working and
that there were others around. "I'm surprised they're even working on Sunday. Don't unions have rules about that kind of thing?"

"Yeah, it's called the time-and-a-half rule. This is costing plenty.
Another reason I want them hustling, not ogling."

"You couldn't have waited until tomorrow for those tables?"

She shook her head, her eyes on her clipboard. "No, because tomorrow the portable ovens and cooktops and the refrigerator cases arrive. And the tables have to be in place in order for—" Her attention was caught by a man across the room. "Those are going straight out back," she called to him. "By the patio. I'd like to keep the shepherd's hooks together with the lanterns so that when the electrician comes to wire them he won't have to waste time hauling them around."

"He better not haul them around," said one of the men carrying tables, his tone only half joking. "Hauling is laborers' work."

"And there's plenty of it, so keep moving," said Sophie. She looked at Owen with an apologetic shrug. "Sorry I'm so crazed, but today begins the six-day countdown and I need everything to go like clockwork. I'll be lucky if I have time to breathe between now and the wedding . . . and that's without any spontaneous mystical interference," she added pointedly.

He nodded, understanding. "I'll let you get back to work, then. I just wanted to . . . About last night . . ."

"What about it?" she countered distractedly, her attention split between him and the activity swirling around them.

"It's just that I know women like to discuss those things afterward . . . to know where they stand."

"Don't worry, I know where I stand. Last night was fun for me," she assured him, and then gave a quick frown. "For you too, I hope?"

"It was. Definitely . . . though 'fun' isn't the first word that comes to mind to describe it."

"I guess maybe . . . no, no, don't force it," she called to the men struggling to wedge a worktable next to the stove. "If it won't fit there, put it in the dining room for now." She turned to Owen with a rueful look. "Sorry. Where was I? Oh, right . . . last night. Look, if you're worried that I'm reading more into it, or that now things between us will be complicated or awkward, don't be. I'm not . . . and they won't."

"Well, good. It's just that when I woke up, you were gone . . ."

"Not by choice. The crushed stone for the pathways was being delivered at seven and I had to be there to greet it and make sure it was the right size and color. I would have mentioned it last night, but I was a little . . . preoccupied."

"Yeah. Me too." His face warmed at the memory. "Anyway, I just wanted to make sure you were all right."

"Thank you. I'm fine. I can see how you might wonder about the fallout . . . me being a self-proclaimed die-hard romantic and all. Usually I am more emotional about these things. But this was different."

Owen didn't know why, but he wasn't sure he liked the sound of that. "I don't see how different it could be. Romance is romance."

"Except last night wasn't about romance. Oh, it was plenty romantic, with the gown and the dancing and the chauffeur-driven limo, but it wasn't about the serious, forever kind of romance. You made it clear where *you* stand when it comes to that sort of thing and because of that I went into last night with my eyes wide open and . . . what happened happened. It was a great evening. End of story."

"What's that supposed to mean?"

She shrugged. "It's just an expression." She peered more closely at him. "But you know, seeing that grim look on your face makes me wonder . . . could it be *you're* the one with a serious case of the morning-afters."

Owen felt obliged to scoff.

Her green eyes sparkled mischievously. "Maybe that latent romance gene I warned you about is finally kicking in."

"Don't be ridiculous."

"Maybe you're worried about falling head over heels in love and having to surrender your role as Chief Cynic and Skeptic."

"Never happen," he retorted.

She cocked her head to the side. "Do I detect a new note of uncertainty in your bravado and bluster?"

"Not at all." He swung his tux jacket over his shoulder and hooked it with his index finger, hoping the nonchalant George Clooney impression would compensate for any lack of confidence in his tone. "You can't fall in something that doesn't exist."

Seventeen

Bemused, Sophie watched Owen leaving the kitchen. It was sweet of him to come looking for her in case she had any morning-after regrets. Only suddenly she was wondering if that's all there was to it.

She'd been teasing when she suggested his latent romance gene might be kicking in, but something about his reaction had her thinking her words might have struck a nerve. Could it be that Owen had been bothered when he woke up and found her gone and that perhaps *he* was the one in need of a little morning-after reassurance?

She shook her head and reached for her clipboard. Impossible.

She had no idea how many women there were in Owen's no-doubt-adventurous past, and she didn't think she wanted to. Suffice it to say that the man knew his way around a bed. And not only had he not fallen in love with any of those other women, he hadn't even come close enough to be swayed from his belief that love was nothing more than . . . how had he put it? Ah yes, a hormonally driven mutual fantasy. A fantasy that, according to him, one partner inevitably tired of first. The fact that the theory went against everything she believed in didn't stop it from being the Gospel according to Owen. To even entertain the possibility that making love to her had somehow managed to melt his cynical heart overnight was the kind of wishful thinking she knew all too well. She'd spent an embarrassing number of years wishful thinking that her relationship with Keith was something it wasn't.

That kind of thinking led to disappointment and heartache. But she was older and marginally wiser now and she was going to stick with her new modus operandi, the one she'd adopted prior to the ball, free of the influence of both fairy dust and hormones. Live for the moment: that was her new approach. And last night's test drive had exceeded her wildest expectations. Sex with Owen had been uncomplicated and amazing, and she woke this morning feeling great. No regrets. No second thoughts.

She wasn't normally the type to throw caution to the wind. Far from it, in fact. But that's exactly why it was the right approach for right now. *Normally* she didn't live in an oceanfront mansion and attend balls on the arm of a handsome and famous millionaire. She didn't wear vintage designer gowns and she sure as hell didn't walk around turning heads and causing jaws to drop when she entered the room. The past few weeks had been like a dream. And dreams were finite. She had only a short while left to live "the Princess House life," and most of that time would be taken up with work. She didn't want to waste a single moment caught up in a spiral of what-ifs and if-onlys. This was one adventure she was going to live to the fullest without worrying about what might happen tomorrow and the day after and the day after that. Coffee at sunrise or sex at midnight: she was open to it all, to whatever temptation fate saw fit to drop in her path.

She might leave Ange de la Mer with regrets, but for once they weren't going to be about things she wished she'd done.

Her musing was interrupted when the floral designer called her outside for a huddle with the lighting technician concerning the pair of seventeen-foot-high distressed-wood columns to be built around the tent's center poles. They would each be wrapped in a garland of wild-grape-and-bare-honeysuckle vines, and at random points wrought-iron brackets would be added to suspend antique white silk lanterns filled with white candles. They wanted final approval on the number of lanterns to be hung from each pole— twenty-one—and Sophie double-checked to make sure the materials being used were fire retardant. Then she was called away again, this time to confirm the exact dimensions and placement of the white dance floor.

They were using white wherever possible . . . dance floor, tent draping, bleached white table linens. Soft shades of white blended well with the abundance of natural and organic elements and all that white would also provide a neutral, light-absorbing surface for the elaborate custom lighting that would create the ambience of an enchanted forest. The effect of the lighting would be lush and rustic at first glance, evolving over the course of the evening into wild, shifting tones of magenta, cobalt blue, and emerald green. The designer in charge assured her it would be fantastical and breathtaking, and Sophie had seen enough of his work to trust he would deliver.

She was in constant motion throughout the day, working with the vendors on site and repeatedly updating her lists and diagrams so she knew exactly what was done, what was in progress and what would be happening tomorrow and the next day and the next. Countdown week was always a killer and this wedding had a lot more going on than most. Oddly, though, instead of feeling weary or frazzled, Sophie felt energized. And happy. An inside-out, whistle-while-you-work, silly-smile-for-no-special-reason kind of happy. She should have tried throwing caution to the wind years ago.

Around noon she escaped to the quiet of her room to call Shelby with a status report and also to remind her that the minister was expecting the final version of the vows she and Matthew had written by the end of the day. Afterward she took a minute to splash water on her face and comb her hair.

"Have you lost your mind?"

She glanced over her shoulder in time to see Ivy strolling into her room as if she owned it, which of course she believed she did. And it was exactly that—her passionate connection to the house— that supplied the energy for her to just materialize whenever she damn well pleased.

"I thought we discussed the whole popping-in-unannounced thing and you promised not to do it," Sophie reminded her.

With a long-suffering sigh, Ivy retraced her steps and knocked dramatically on the door.

"Better?" she asked, sashaying back in without waiting to be asked and flouncing down on the bed. "Now where was I? Oh, right. Have you lost your mind?"

"No," Sophie countered. "But the very fact that you feel the need to ask makes me wonder if I'm the right person to judge. Why did you ask?"

"You were singing."

"And that makes me crazy?"

"No. It's what you were singing. Christmas carols. In August. When it's so hot even I'm on the verge of sweating and I never, ever sweat."

"Ghosts don't sweat?"

Ivy arched her brows and paused briefly in the act of fanning herself with her hand. "*Ladies* don't sweat."

"Oh . . . horsefeathers . . . to quote a friend of mine." She hadn't realized she was singing and now she wrinkled her brow as she tried to recall the song. "What carol was it, anyway?"

Ivy sang a few lines from one of Sophie's favorite carols, all about *mistletoeing* and hearts that are glowing.

"It's the most wonderful time of the year—" she sang and stopped suddenly, her eyes wide. "Oh my goodness," she exclaimed, "that's it. Of course. I should have guessed it straightaway this morning when you went on and on about his dancing and his manners and the cleft in his chin . . . you've fallen in love with Mr. Winters."

"What? Don't be silly. I mean, sure, I may have commented on his manners," she allowed. "He happens to have very nice manners. And a very nice cleft in his chin. But I certainly didn't go on and on . . ." She paused, remembering, and frowned. "Or if I did, it was only because you came barging in here before I was even dressed, demanding to hear every single detail of what went on last night."

"Not all of which were forthcoming," Ivy pointed out, referring to Sophie's refusal to discuss what happened after they returned home. She was so glad the guesthouse was outside Ivy's free-range zone.

"Forthcoming or not, none of it, including the singing, means I've fallen in love. Which, for the record, I haven't."

Ivy looked doubtful. "You're certain?"

"Very certain. I have everything under control," Sophie added, mostly to reassure herself of that fact. "And what do Christmas carols have to do with falling in love, anyway?"

Ivy lifted one shoulder with a negligent sigh. "It's not the carol specifically; it's more the mood . . . that whole chirpy, hap-hap-happiest mood. Let's just say I have a sixth sense about these things." She hesitated, glanced at the window, and then said hurriedly, "But that's not what I'm here about."

Sophie was suddenly aware of the sound of a siren, close by

and drawing closer. Much closer. She looked at Ivy's catbirdlike expression and a shiver of apprehension ran along her spine.

"*That's* what I'm here about," Ivy said, pointing toward the window as she stood, the rustle of her rose chiffon skirt almost drown out by the fire engine now speeding up the drive with siren blaring. "I wanted to remind you that our truce is over."

By the time Sophie got downstairs, firefighters in protective clothing and with ventilation masks at the ready were swarming around the first floor. The captain explained to Sophie that they'd received a call about a suspected gas leak. As soon as she heard that the 911 call had come from inside the house, she had a few suspicions of her own . . . none of which she was about to share with the firemen.

Instead she had no choice but to go along as they took the precaution of evacuating the house and nearby grounds, cooling her heels as her temper simmered and the time she was losing ticked away second by infuriating second. It was a big house, with many nooks and crannies, and the "wild gas chase" as Josh, who was working overtime as her assistant and all-around errand runner, dubbed it, cost her nearly two hours. And all for a false alarm. She didn't want to think about how long they'd be twiddling their thumbs if the firefighters had actually found something.

She wouldn't have been surprised if they had found a small leak somewhere. Ivy was nothing if not resourceful and she'd also demonstrated that she had a reckless streak. But Sophie had come to know her well enough to believe she wouldn't intentionally hurt anyone. In fact, the more time she had to stand outside, baking in the midday sun and stewing about the senseless interruption, the more the false alarm made perfect sense to her.

Today had been a warning to her . . . a preview of what *could* happen if she didn't back off. If the same thing occurred on Saturday, perhaps with an actual leak thrown in to up the ante and drag out the entire process, it would be a wedding planner's nightmare. She shuddered as she pictured hundreds of people, guests and staff alike, being herded away from the house and made to stand around for hours while back in the kitchen, food in various stages of preparation went untended. If they were lucky, the outdoor ceremony might be salvaged, but the reception would be a shambles . . . if not completely ruined.

She was trying to prepare for whatever happened, but in all the disaster scenes she'd conjured up in the past few weeks, she'd never considered a gas leak. It was so simple . . . so diabolically, deceptively simple. Obviously whatever bonding had taken place between Ivy and her during the truce hadn't softened Ivy's resolve any: she was still dead set against the wedding. And Sophie still felt honor bound to do whatever she could to follow through on her promise to Shelby. It was going to take a lot of creative juice to come up with a contingency plan in case of sudden evacuation, but she was going to give it her best shot. If Ivy had expected her to give up, she was in for a surprise. She still had five days after all. In that way the false alarm had been a gift . . . she'd gotten a quick peek at the cards Ivy was holding.

And that, Sophie suddenly realized, is precisely what Ivy had intended. The truce hadn't been a total waste after all. In her own screwball way, Ivy was trying to play fair.

The knock on the guesthouse door would have interrupted his writing had there been any writing going on. But after a string of highly productive days, Owen was back spinning his wheels and staring at the blinking cursor and a blank drawing board. This time, however, it wasn't entirely his fault. He'd done his part. He'd labored over the plot, fine-tuning it until it unwound as precisely as a Swiss watch. And he'd peppered it with fresh twists guaranteed to surprise faithful readers and hook new ones. Or so he thought. Instead he was the one surprised. Shocked, in fact.

He'd thought he knew Osprey. He'd thought he could predict his every move . . . his every thought process. Not because the character was that boring; because he was that solid. That stalwart. That dedicated to duty and to doing what had to be done without being sidetracked or swayed by personal considerations. Osprey had no personal considerations, damn it. Owen had intentionally created him that way because he knew it would make Osprey's life simpler and his mission easier. He would never have to worry about screwing up or having someone he trusted walk out when he needed them most. Unencumbered and straightforward and free of any messy emotional crap that tore you up inside and left you reeling . . . that was Osprey. Designed to be totally independent and efficient. He had a job to do and he did it. Period. He never made compromises because he never had to. The world around him might fall apart or implode or erupt into a fiery inferno, but Osprey's world remained steady and inviolate.

At least that's how it was supposed to work.

Instead, just as the final plot dominoes were beginning to fall and he needed to be at his most vigilant and focused, Osprey was suddenly distracted and preoccupied. To put it another way, he was a brooding mess. And why? Because in a moment of weakness, he'd lowered his guard and given in to sweet temptation.

Okay, Owen was willing to admit that that part might be mostly his fault, or more accurately Sophie's fault, since she was the one who'd planted the idea that his books could stand a bit of romance. *It's the key to everything,* she'd said. The key to disaster was more like it. *Valene is the dream that Osprey is afraid to dream,* she'd said. Now the dream had turned into a nightmare. For Owen anyway. Osprey had swilled so much whiskey it was impossible to know what he was thinking. The bottom line was that at the moment Owen's clever plot had ground to a halt and neither he nor Osprey had a fucking clue what to do about Valene.

When he heard the knock on the door, his first thought was that it was probably one of the gardeners or carpenters or other invaders who were hard at work making noise and turning his once-peaceful sanctuary into a three-ring circus. The instant he touched the door, however, he knew it was Sophie who waited on the other side. All day he'd had a restless, edgy feeling that he couldn't put into words, a nagging sense that he had misplaced something, but he wasn't sure exactly what. Something important. Something crucial. It was as if a part of him had gone missing. He hadn't felt that way in a very long time, and as soon as he touched the door, the feeling went away. Suddenly he felt whole again and he knew it was because the missing piece was Sophie.

That could be a problem, since in less than a week she would be gone, but when he opened the door and she smiled at him, everything else—including the warning light flashing in the very back recesses of his mind—ceased to matter.

"Hey there," she said, her eyes very green and lit with excitement. Her hair was caught up in a clip except for a few escaped curls of bronze and gold around her face. Her cheeks were flushed and she was wearing a yellow dress that left her shoulders bare, and as impossible as it seemed, she looked even more beautiful to Owen now than she had last night.

"Feel like taking a break?" she asked.

"Sure. Why not?" He didn't bother to mention that so far his whole day had been one long, frustrating break. He didn't mention it because it didn't matter. He could have a midnight deadline and be writing the book's climactic scene at a breakneck pace and he would stop everything for Sophie. Another warning sign that he didn't have time to think about right now.

She took a few steps inside and then turned to face him as he closed the door, twisting her fingers together in front of her. Anxiously, it seemed to Owen.

"I tried to think up a good reason for barging in and interrupting you," she said. "Like asking if you had an extra notebook I could borrow or bringing you a glass of iced tea."

He smiled appreciatively at the mention of her iced tea.

She rolled her eyes. "I know. Lame."

She thought he was laughing at her.

"But I decided I don't have time to be bothered with props or excuses," she went on before he could explain about the lemonade. "I'm on union time here, which means this is a twenty-minute break. So I'm just going to cut to the chase and come right out and tell you what I'm here for."

"You want to talk about last night," he said.

She looked startled. "What? No. A thousand tons of no. Last night was . . ."

"Confusing?"

"Wonderful. Amazing. Spectacular. Last night was the most romantic night of my life. The last thing I want to do is spoil it by doing a postmortem."

"Then what—"

"This," she said, her breath catching as she launched herself forward and grabbed the front of his T-shirt with both fists to yank him closer. "I came for this."

Her open mouth crashed against his. She kissed him hard and greedily, leaning against his body in a way that left no doubt that when she'd said "I came for this," she was talking about more than a kiss. A lot more.

Owen hardly needed convincing. Wrapping his arms around

her, he gave as good as he got. His heart drummed inside his chest and the memory of her naked and under him roared to life in his head.

When they ran out of air, they levered back just enough to look at each other. Their gazes locked, both of them breathing hard. He loved the way she was looking at him . . . with a kind of intense, bottomless longing. The simple fact that she wanted him made him feel like he could walk on water and conquer nations and hang the moon in the sky.

Unconsciously she slid her tongue across her swollen lower lip and fresh desire ripped through him, pushing him to touch and taste and take. He tried to tether it because he thought he should. Then her hand drifted lower to touch him intimately and he understood that Sophie wanted what he wanted.

He tugged on the tie behind her neck and the front of her dress tumbled down.

She shoved his T-shirt up and over his head and they were skin to skin. . . . the contact hot and damp and erotic.

His mouth roamed over her throat and shoulder, and when he stroked the side of her bare thigh, she bent her knee and rubbed her leg against his side.

He whispered close to her ear. "Only twenty minutes, huh?"

"Less," she said, running her hand down his back. "I lost a few minutes getting here because I couldn't cut across the dance floor."

He raked his thumb back and forth across her nipple. "How many is a few?"

"Too many. Time is definitely"—she shivered delicately—"of the essence."

"In that case . . ."

Owen caught her up in his arms and in a rush of strength propelled her a half-dozen feet across the room until her back was pressed to the wall. Supporting her weight with one arm, he swept beneath her skirt with his other hand, pushed her panties aside, and found her wet and ready for him.

With trembling hands, Sophie reached to open his belt and his zipper, touching him and guiding him. She held him where she wanted him and rubbed against him, her head thrown back, her pleasure revealed in a soft rough purr that wound its way deep inside, to the very core of him.

He wasn't even inside her yet and she was burning him up . . . consuming him. He was reeling from the taste and feel and scent of her. Everything about her was all new and deeply familiar at the same time and he wanted more. He wanted all of her.

Hungry and impatient, he shoved her a few inches higher, angling for entry. Sophie was eager to oblige, wrapping her legs around his waist and lowering herself to meet him.

Owen cupped her bottom as he thrust inside her, making love to her against the wall, the sweetness and madness of it running together, as she clung tightly to him and said his name over and over.

She wasn't kidding about the twenty minutes.

She left him spent, but not satisfied. It would take a hell of a lot longer than twenty minutes for him to come even close to being satisfied that he'd done all the things he wanted to do to Sophie Bennett. It would take more like twenty years, he thought, already missing her.

Or twenty lifetimes.

Eighteen

Late Friday evening Sophie stood alone at the edge of the stone patio overlooking the grounds that had been transformed into an enchanted woodland and wondered if it was too soon to breathe a sigh of relief. Just a tiny one. Surely she'd earned that much.

The gigantic, oh-my-God-it's-finally-over-and-I-can-sleep-for-a-week sigh of relief that she was planning would have to wait until tomorrow night, of course, after the actual wedding and reception had taken place and the last guests had been sent safely, and hopefully merrily, on their way. For now she was content to savor the small success of having the rehearsal and the dinner that followed go off without a hitch. There had been no gas leaks or falling beehives and the only flickering lights were the candles inside hurricane globes on the buffet tables in the sun-room. The wedding party and a few of Shelby's and Matthew's close friends and family members had dined under the stars on the patio, while in the background Sophie kept a constant and uneasy vigil.

"Sophie, I checked to make sure everything in the kitchen is squared away. The caterers packed up their stuff and I loaded those boxes of extra linens in my Jeep like you wanted me to. I'll drop them off at Seasons first thing tomorrow and be back here by nine. Maggie and Deanna said they're leaving now too, if that's okay with you. Oh, and I told Shelby and Matt you're waiting out here to talk with them as soon as they're done finding rides for tipsy bridesmaids." Josh paused in his run-on spiel to grin at her. "Pretty hot bridesmaids, huh?"

Sophie feigned a puzzled expression. "Are they? I honestly didn't take note of their hotness factor. I did, however, notice that they're bridesmaids, which means they fall under the broad heading of clients, and therefore they are—"

"I know, I know. Strictly off-limits. Just saying." He shrugged, unbothered by the reminder. "So is it okay if we take off?"

"Yes, go. Thanks for your help, Josh. I know it was a long day. Tell Maggie and Deanna thanks for all their hard work too and that I'll see them tomorrow."

Maggie and Deanna were part of a large team of experienced Seasons employees that worked events only and were worth their weight in gold. For tomorrow she'd booked them plus four other assistants in addition to Josh, who could be counted on to be wherever she needed him to be to do the inevitable last-minute running and moving things around. It was a big crew, considering the size of the wedding, but under the circumstances she believed the extra pairs of eyes and hands were warranted. She'd worked her butt off all week and done everything she could to forestall disaster and ensure that everything would run smoothly tomorrow. Food, flowers, music, transportation, photography, and on and on, right down to the engraved menus and eco-friendly favors: she was on top of every detail and confident that everything under her control would come together flawlessly. And if by chance there was a glitch, she or one of her team would be right there to catch it and fix it with an absolute minimum of fuss and fanfare.

It was the things *not* under her control that worried her. Worried, schmorried. Who was she kidding? She was beyond worried. The thought of what Ivy might be planning to do to ruin the day scared the hell out of her.

Several times in the past few days, every chance she got in fact, she'd attempted to talk to Ivy and change her mind, but her reasoning and pleas seemed to fall on deaf ears. Deaf and stubborn. And she hadn't had that many opportunities. Ivy wasn't around much, and while Sophie didn't miss the spooky noises and the disappearing-cell-phone trick, she discovered she did miss Ivy. In spite of her grumbling, she'd gotten used to having her pop in unannounced. For a while it was almost as if they were roommates, and more than once it struck her that *The Ghost and the Wedding Planner* would make a pretty good sitcom, with Ivy being the beautiful and irreverent star with a gift for making her mousy, workaholic roomie laugh and showing up just at the right moment to dispense wise advice on matters of fashion and affairs of the heart.

Besides missing Ivy, she was worried about her. The last few times she had appeared, she hadn't been her usual glamorous, insouciant self. She'd seemed distracted and weary. And, as odd as it sounded, she looked older. Remembering what Carla said about ghosts' emotions fueling their ability to appear and to affect their surroundings, Sophie couldn't help wondering if the changes she saw were a result of Ivy's having second thoughts about the wedding and if her emotions were suddenly pulling her in two different directions. She was pretty set in her ghostly ways; it couldn't be easy to suddenly find herself questioning what she'd been so sure about.

If that's what was happening. It was an interesting theory, but seeing as Ivy hadn't actually said anything to indicate she was wavering even a little, Sophie didn't dare lower her guard. As the big day approached she felt almost as if they were playing a high-stakes game of chicken. Her troubled gaze moved over the vista before her, from the reflecting pond to the winding tree-covered paths surrounding a white tent luxurious enough to entertain royalty, and she thought that seeing all that, Ivy must surely realize that there was no possible way Sophie was going to blink first.

The sound of approaching footsteps drew her attention. She turned to see Shelby and Matthew headed her way, smiling and holding hands, the way they usually did when they were together.

"Mission accomplished," Shelby announced. "I just hope Kristy sobers up in time to walk down the aisle."

"Relax. She'll be fine," Matthew assured her in a quiet, solid tone that struck a chord in Sophie.

He sounds like Owen, she thought. Oh, the accent was different and his voice wasn't as deep, but more than once in recent days Owen had eased her qualms and bolstered her confidence with that same sure and steady tone. It was magical in its ability to make her believe everything was going to be all right. Owen was the only one she could speak freely to about Ivy . . . and about Helen's meddling, which she also feared could blow up in their faces. Brides could be very unpredictable, which is why last-minute surprises were never a good idea. And although Sophie had limited Helen's input, there would still be more hoopla than Shelby and Matthew wanted or expected. She was anxious on both fronts, and being able to unburden herself to Owen was like having a shelter in the middle of a raging hurricane. It was plain to see that Matthew would be Shelby's shelter no matter what life threw at them in the years ahead. Sophie was happy for her . . . and envious at the same time.

"Josh said you wanted to speak with us," said Shelby.

Sophie nodded. "I do. I'm breaking Seasons protocol a bit here and I want to explain. Usually, after the wedding ceremony is over and before the bride and groom greet their guests, I steal the couple for a few moments and take them into the reception room for what we refer to as 'the big unveil.' It gives them a chance to see the room completely and perfectly decorated, before anyone spills wine or rearranges the chairs."

They both laughed.

"But your situation is a little different. For one thing, there's more to it," she said with an expansive sweep of her arm. "It's all kind of interwoven and not the typical grand ballroom that I can keep under wraps until the last minute. After the ceremony here on the patio, your guests will head that way for cocktails." She gestured toward the sunroom and the extended stone patio that ran the entire length of the back of the house. "The sun will just be setting and the lights will slowly and gradually come on. I could probably arrange a private moment to show you the inside of the tent, but that's only a small part of what we've done. So I decided that after everyone else left tonight, I would give the two of you a preview of the overall effect . . . that is, if you'd like to see it ahead of time."

"We'd like," Shelby exclaimed, grinning with excitement and bouncing on the balls of her feet as she squeezed Matthew's arm. "We'd very much like. Wouldn't we?"

"Definitely," he agreed, pulling Shelby in front of him and encircling her with his arms.

"I just wanted to make sure," Sophie explained. "Some couples would rather be totally surprised on the day itself."

"Oh, I think there'll be more than enough surprises to make the day itself interesting," Shelby observed drily. Her mouth curved into a rueful smile. "Do you know my mother arranged for a cigar roller? A man who sits at a table and rolls cigars on request. Have you ever heard of anything so ridiculous?"

"I think she just wants you to have everything that could conceivably make your day special."

"Well, that would certainly explain the vodka ice luge . . . what little girl doesn't dream of having that at her wedding?"

Sophie's eyes narrowed. "Vodka ice luge?"

"Oh, so that one's a surprise for you too."

"In a manner of speaking," Sophie said. "We did discuss the possibility of a pyramid-shaped ice luge and I told your mother it didn't fit with your theme."

Shelby scoffed. "As if a little thing like that would get in the way of her trying to make this the most overblown, over-the-top wedding of all time."

She sounded irritated, but not—to Sophie's relief—on the verge of a bridal meltdown.

"So the luge is definite?" Sophie asked.

" 'Fraid so," Shelby replied, smiling as she rolled her eyes at Matthew.

"Well, I'm just glad you're smiling about it instead of letting it upset you."

Shelby shrugged. "It's hard to be upset or angry when I know she's doing all of it because she thinks it will make me happy. I just keep telling myself that at least it's making her happy, and that's something."

"Good. That's a great attitude to take, because you never know, there may be even more surprises in store. Some bigger than others, and it would be a shame to end a perfect day on a sour note . . ."

"Are you talking about the fireworks?" Shelby asked.

"Oh, thank God. You know about them?"

"Oh yeah."

Matthew explained. "One of my groomsmen knows the guy Shelby's mother hired for the job. He tipped me off and I told Shelby. I figured forewarned is forearmed and all that."

"Smart man. You're both very lucky."

"We are lucky. That's another reason I can't be upset about anything," said Shelby. "I'm marrying the most wonderful man in the world and I get to do it here . . ." She gazed around with an expression of wonder. "It's exactly where I always dreamed of being married, but I never believed it would really happen. I have the perfect dress . . . the perfect everything . . . thanks to you," she added with a smile at Sophie. "It would be pretty petty of me to throw a hissy fit over the cigar man or some fireworks."

"I'm kind of looking forward to the fireworks," Matthew admitted.

"I'm looking forward to seeing what you want to show us tonight," Shelby said to Sophie.

"Then let's do it." Sophie flipped over her phone and hit speed dial. "Owen, we're ready on this end."

When she first asked him if he'd be willing to give her a hand by manning the light panel in the garage, she thought Owen might balk at having anything to do with "wedding crap," as he referred to it. Instead he surprised her by agreeing without any pressure or pleading; he didn't even complain about spending over an hour that morning getting instructions from the lighting engineer so he wouldn't mess up.

"I'm heading down to the garage now," he told her. "Give me two minutes."

They waited in silence. Shelby's excitement was palpable . . . and contagious. Sophie had already seen the setting fully lit when they did the final check last evening, but she was eager to see the young couple's reaction to having their fantasy come to life before them.

Owen didn't let her down. The lights came on gradually, and although the timing would be extended during the reception itself, the effect was just as spectacular. The first to twinkle on were thousands of amber and white fairy lights embedded deep within the branches of the newly planted "forest." Next came the copper-and-brass lanterns hung on wrought-iron shepherd's hooks that lit the pathways and secluded alcoves. It was a careful building of subtle layers of illumination and color, culminating with the rotating up-lights that lent energy and movement and created the ambience of an enchanted woodland.

Except for a couple of sharp intakes of breath, Shelby and Matthew watched in silence. But their rapt attention told Sophie all she needed to know about how much they loved it.

"Oh my God," Shelby said finally. "It's even better than I imagined it would be . . . a zillion times better than I ever *could* have imagined. It's perfect. It's amazing. Oh my God, Sophie, *you're* amazing. I love you so much."

She hugged Sophie hard.

"Thank you so much for making it happen," she went on. "And for giving us this moment tonight. It's all exactly what I hoped it would be."

"It is really cool," agreed Matthew. "Check out the way the color crisscrosses the dance floor, Shel."

"I can't wait for our first dance," Shelby exclaimed, reaching for his hand.

Sophie laughed. "Well, that you will have to wait for . . . some traditions even I don't mess with."

Her wide-eyed gaze still on the transformed grounds, Shelby rested her head back on Matthew's chest and sighed quietly. "I just wish . . ."

"What is it, Shel?" he prodded. "What do you wish?"

"I love how quiet and peaceful it is right now. It's magical. Tomorrow there'll be so many more people here . . . so many people I hardly know, thanks to my mother's magically expanding guest list, and I almost wish we were getting married now, tonight, right this minute, when it feels so perfect. No fuss. No one snapping pictures. Just us."

Chuckling, Matthew gave her a quick squeeze. "Nice fantasy, Shel, but your mom would have a total meltdown, after which she'd kill both of us."

"Not if she didn't know about it," Sophie heard herself say.

The couple stared at her in surprise and confusion.

She didn't blame them. Ordinarily the wedding planner in her would be appalled at the very idea of them jumping the gun and marrying tonight when so much had gone into making sure that everything would be perfect tomorrow. But from the very beginning, when Shelby lost her way and happened upon Sophie's office and saw the picture of *The Princess House* book hanging on her wall, nothing about this wedding had been ordinary. Why start now?

Far from being upset, Sophie saw the bride-to-be's impulsive wish as a possible answer to her prayers, and she seized it. If they were to exchange vows tonight, privately, it would mean that no matter what madness ensued tomorrow, courtesy of Ivy and/or the mother of the bride, the young couple would have a perfect memory of their wedding . . . not to mention a hell of a story to tell their grandchildren.

"Who's to say you can't get married tonight if you want to?"

"My mother, for one," Shelby replied immediately. "Matthew's right. She was born to play the role of mother of the bride and she'd never forgive me if I cheated her out of it."

Sophie shook her head. "No, no. I didn't mean you should do it tonight instead of tomorrow . . . I meant in addition to tomorrow. Two ceremonies for the price of one. You have the license, the rings, witnesses . . . me," she said, pressing her hand to her chest. "And I'm sure Owen would be thrilled to be part of it."

Thrilled was a real stretch, but she was pretty sure she could get him to go along with the plan.

"And I'll bet Reverend Allard hasn't even made it home yet. I happen to know he has a romantic streak and I'm sure he'd come back if you asked. You could have a small private exchange of vows tonight and still go through with the ceremony as planned tomorrow in front of all your guests."

The couple was staring at each other, smiles tugging at their lips. Sophie didn't say what she was thinking, that tonight would be an insurance policy in case disaster struck tomorrow. And she certainly didn't use the words *preemptive strike*. She didn't want to frighten or worry them. If they decided to do it, she wanted it to be because they were carried away by the romance of the moment. Tonight or tomorrow, the most important thing was that they have their perfect moment.

"What do you think?" Matthew asked Shelby. They were facing each other now, arms outstretched, hands clasped together.

Shelby nibbled her lip thoughtfully for a couple of seconds and then broke into an excited grin. "I think yes . . . let's go for it." She threw herself into his arms. "Oh my God, in a few minutes I'm going to be Mrs. Matthew Winston."

Sophie's mind was already processing what needed to be done as she saw Owen approaching.

"How'd they like the show?" he asked her.

"They loved it. In fact . . ."

She quickly filled him in on what was happening. She didn't mention Ivy. She didn't need to for Owen to understand why she was so enthusiastic about the sudden change in plans, and he volunteered to do whatever she needed even before she had a chance to ask. Sophie squeezed his hand and made a mental note to thank him properly later, when they were alone.

Handling last-minute crises was something she was good at. She took charge and within a few moments everyone had been given an assignment. Shelby was to get dressed. Matthew was to call the minister and get him back there ASAP. And since the flowers weren't being delivered until the morning, Owen was sent to gather daisies for an impromptu bridal bouquet.

"Your dress is 'something new,'" Sophie told Shelby. "We'll consider the daisies as 'something borrowed.'"

Shelby touched her ear. "My earrings are sapphires."

Sophie nodded. "Something blue."

"That leaves only—"

"Something old."

"The lace from my grandmother's veil," Shelby reminded her.

Sophie nodded, remembering the heirloom lace that Shelby's grandmother had refused to entrust to the mail and had instead insisted on bringing with her when she arrived from California earlier that day.

"Did your grandmother remember to bring it?"

"Yes, and in the nick of time. I was still sewing on the cuff link when Matthew came to pick me up for the rehearsal."

"Cuff link?"

"It was her father's," Matthew explained as emotion swept Shelby's face. He put his arm around her gently.

"I gave them to him for Father's Day when I was six," she explained. "They weren't real gold, of course, but I thought they were and my dad acted like they were. He wore them all the time. I thought that sewing one onto the lace that I tie around my bouquet would make him even more a part of this day."

"I think it's a lovely gesture. Did you bring the lace with you tonight?"

"Yes, thank goodness. I was afraid I'd forget it at the last minute. It's in a small bag on the buffet in the dining room."

"I'll get it. You go get ready. You can use the guesthouse; Lina had your dress delivered this afternoon and I put it there to keep it safe."

"Safe from what?" asked Shelby.

Sophie had to think quickly. "Oh, you know . . . spills, that kind of thing."

Owen whacked her on the back and grinned at Shelby. "Who knows the workings of the mind of an obsessive wedding planner?"

"Thank God she is obsessive," Shelby countered. "If I had to remember half the stuff Sophie does, I swear we'd be getting married at city hall, in jeans and T-shirts."

"Well, you're not. You're getting married right here in just a few minutes. Now all of you get to work."

There was no bag on the buffet or anywhere else in the dining room. Sophie checked the table in the front hallway and then ran upstairs to look in the rooms the girls would be using the next day. No bag. No lace.

She tried calling Shelby, but the call went straight to voice mail and she decided it would be faster to run down to the guesthouse and ask her in person. She was on her way out of the room when a familiar voice brought her up short.

"Is this what you're looking for?"

First she jumped, same as she always did when Ivy caught her unawares. Then took a few seconds to gather herself before turning to acknowledge her. Ivy was standing by the window holding the lace in her hand.

"And don't tell me I should have knocked," she snapped before Sophie could speak. "I'm not in the mood."

"Hello, Ivy."

"Don't 'hello, Ivy' me. You're up to something. I know you are and I demand to know what it is."

"You already know what it is," Sophie said calmly. "Tonight was the rehearsal dinner."

Ivy waved her hand impatiently. "That's over. This is something different . . . something new you cooked up. I saw you out there, conspiring."

"We weren't conspiring. It's no big deal. A slight change in plans is all. Why don't you go lie down? You look . . . tired."

"What you mean is that I look old. That *is* what you were thinking, isn't it?" She pressed her hands to her cheeks and Sophie had the sad impression of someone trying to hold herself together.

Ivy was right. Sophie had been thinking she looked older. Oh, the changes were subtle. Ivy still looked damn good for a dead woman . . . a dead woman who'd died in her nineties no less. But she was not the same vibrant beauty she appeared to be not so long ago.

"Are you feeling all right?" Sophie asked, gently sidestepping the age question.

"All right? No. I'm feeling . . . old," Ivy replied. Her soft laugh drifted off in a sigh. "I'd forgotten how exhausting it can be to be young."

"Are you sure you wouldn't like to lie—"

"No," she snapped. "I do not want to lie down. Nor do I care to be patronized. What I want is for you to tell me what you're up to."

Sophie drew a deep breath and held it, thinking. She considered trying to stall. She thought about lying. She even considered simply refusing to discuss it and walking out. Ivy would keep watch at the window, of course. She would see the minister return and figure it out for herself soon enough. But it was a reasonable bet that she wouldn't be able to wreak much havoc outside the house on such short notice.

When she met Ivy's gaze, however, something about the look in Ivy's eyes wouldn't let Sophie lie or play games with her. This mattered too much.

"Shelby and Matthew have decided to be married tonight . . . quietly and—"

"No," Ivy bellowed.

Sophie winced and glanced out the window, hoping Matthew and Shelby weren't in earshot.

"I said there would be no wedding here and there will be no wedding. Did you really think you could fool me by sneaking around in the dead of night?"

"Oh, for pity's sake, Ivy, if I was sneaking around or trying to fool you, why would I have told you about it?"

Ivy's usual regal shrug held a new edge of desperation. "How should I know what tricks you have up your sleeve?"

Hoping to calm her, Sophie smiled and held out her bare arms. "No sleeves. No tricks. Ivy, please try to understand."

"Oh, I understand perfectly."

"Then please try to be happy for them. Put yourself in Shelby's place. I know you remember how it feels to be so excited and so filled with hope for the future."

"How could you possibly know how I feel?"

"Because I know you. But I don't have much time. The minister is already on his way back here. Ivy, please give me the lace so I can tie it around Shelby's bouquet. It's from her grandmother's bridal veil, and the cuff link she sewed to it belonged to her father. What happened to you on your wedding day was a tragedy, but Shelby had nothing to do with it. Ruining her happiness won't change the past."

"It's not the past I intend to change. It's the future. And if you insist on ignoring my wishes and charging full steam ahead, then you shall be the one accountable for the next tragedy. There isn't going to be a wedding here. Not tonight. Not tomorrow. Not ever. Not in my house."

"This is not your house," Sophie shouted, forgetting she might be overheard as the weight of all the worrying and long hours crashed down on her. "It hasn't been your house for years. You just refuse to do what any normal dead person would do . . . accept it and move on."

Ivy drew herself up. "I do refuse to accept it. And I shall move on when I am ready. Not a moment sooner. I certainly shall not be hurried along by an interloper who goes around planning other people's weddings, but is afraid to close the deal for herself."

"Me?" Sophie slapped her hand against her chest. "I'm the interloper? You're talking about me being afraid? What about you? You make me look like . . . like . . . like goddamn Wonder Woman."

"There's no need for profanity."

"Oh yeah, there is. I need it . . . otherwise my head might explode from trying to deal with you."

"Or theatrics."

"Look who's talking. I'm not the one who goes around rattling my chains and playing with the lights to get attention."

"I'm not the one who has fallen head over heels in love and yet goes around pretending to be deliriously happy and satisfied with so much less than she deserves."

"For your information, I am deliriously happy and satisfied, and I'll thank you to . . . never mind. I don't have time for this." She spun around and made it halfway to the door.

"You're right."

Sophie stopped. She turned back around. Ivy stood with her arms tightly wrapped around herself; she seemed suddenly smaller and frail.

Sophie took a few steps toward her and asked quietly, "Right about what?"

"Me. I am afraid."

"Afraid of what, Ivy?"

"Of everything, it seems sometimes. Mostly I'm afraid of leav-

ing this house, and I'm afraid that another wedding here will break
the spell or whatever it is that has kept me here and I will have to
leave. And I am not ready for that. Not nearly. I am not ready to
be somewhere else."

"But, Ivy, someplace else might be so much better. You must be
lonely here. This is no kind of . . . well, life."

Ivy gave a snuffly laugh. Ghosts might not sweat or sleep, but
they did cry. Sophie walked closer, but when she went to put an
arm around her, Ivy flinched.

"No," she said. "Don't touch me. I'm . . . barely here. It's so
hard lately. So hard to stay."

"Then why do it? Why keep fighting? Is there something keeping you here?"

"Joseph. I feel him here, all around me. I've always felt him
here, close by, watching over me. It wasn't the life together that I'd
envisioned, but it was . . . something. And it was all I had, so it was
enough."

"But, Ivy, don't you think that Joseph may be waiting for
you . . . somewhere? That you could go to him and be together at
last?"

"Yes, I do think that. Sometimes. But I don't *know* it. I do
know what I have here. What if I leave what I have and . . ." She
pressed her lips together tightly. "What if I was wrong all those
years? About something happening to Joseph on our wedding day.
About him loving me as much as I loved him. Oh, Sophie, what if
I was wrong about him? I'm not afraid of finding out that I was a
fool. Lord knows, most people thought I was a fool for clinging to
a pipe dream. I don't care about that. I think I'm afraid of finding
out that I was wrong and feeling my heart break all over again."

"It won't," Sophie said with all the conviction she could muster. "That is not going to happen. My God, Ivy, you are one of the
strongest and wisest women I've ever known . . . dead or alive. No

man could ever have duped you so completely. There's a reason you fell in love with Joseph. And a reason no other man ever measured up to him in your eyes . . . and in your heart. That's because he was the one. It was meant to be. You never lost faith in him or in the love you had for each other while you were alive. You can't give up now." She looked at her sternly. "I won't let you."

They heard footsteps on the stairs and suddenly Owen stood in the doorway. "Sophie, what's taking you so—oh. Sorry to interrupt. I just wanted to let you know that the minister is here. So . . . whenever you're ready . . ."

"Go," said Ivy. "Go do your job."

Nineteen

B ack outside, Shelby and Matthew had decided they wanted to exchange vows beside the softly lit pond. Shelby looked ethereal in her wedding gown and Matthew was handsome and beaming in the dark suit he'd worn for the rehearsal party.

Shelby received calmly the little white lie that one of Sophie's assistants had mistakenly left with the bag containing the lace and would return with it in plenty of time for the ceremony the next day. As a substitute, Owen produced an old penny to slip in her shoe.

They were arranging themselves in front of Reverend Allard when Shelby suddenly glanced over Sophie's shoulder and gave a small surprised smile.

"There's someone here," she said just as Sophie turned in that direction and saw Ivy walking toward them.

She had left the house and was walking down the wide, shallow steps from the patio to the lawn.

She had left the house.

Sophie struggled to come to grips with the implications of

that. Not certain whether to cheer or panic, she would have moved to head Ivy off but for Owen's calming hand on the small of her back.

"Hold on," he said, so softly only she could hear.

Smiling, Ivy walked closer. "Forgive me for intruding, but I saw all these beautiful lights and I . . . well, I was . . . curious and couldn't help myself. I used to live here, you see, a very long time ago."

Shelby's smile deepened and there was an added note of excitement in her voice. "Seriously? It must have been so wonderful to actually live here. Was it wonderful?"

"It was," Ivy confirmed. "I always felt very lucky to be living in such a beautiful house . . . the most beautiful in the world, in my estimation."

"And mine," Shelby countered with a nod of solidarity. "I feel so lucky just to be getting married here."

"It is a beautiful place for a wedding." Ivy's expression softened as she gazed at Shelby's dress. "And you do it justice, my dear. You make a beautiful bride."

"Thank you."

"But I believe you're missing something." She held the lace in one hand and with the other gestured vaguely. "I found it there."

Shelby turned to Sophie, confused. "But I thought . . ."

"I fudged a little," Sophie explained. "I didn't want you to panic when I couldn't find it. I was sure it would turn up."

"May I?" asked Ivy, holding the strip of lace by the ends.

Shelby smiled and held out the bouquet of daisies so Ivy could tie the lace around the stems.

"There," she said when she was done. "The perfect finishing touch. I wish you both a lifetime and more of love and happiness. And now I should leave so you can—"

"No, don't go" said Shelby, reaching out to touch Ivy's arm.

She laughed awkwardly, a little surprised by her own vehemence. "I'd really like you to stay . . . that is, if you'd like to."

"I would like that very much indeed," Ivy told her.

"Then shall we get started?" asked the minister. "I'm not sure if you know this, but I have another wedding tomorrow and it looks like I'm the only one here who needs his beauty sleep."

He waited for their laughter to stop and opened his prayer book.

"Dear friends, we are gathered here tonight in the sight of God and angels to celebrate one of life's greatest moments and greatest gifts. As we give recognition to the worth and beauty of love, we add our best wishes and blessings to the words which shall unite Matthew and Shelby in holy matrimony."

The ceremony was brief, and after a champagne toast, the newlyweds were understandably eager to be alone. Reverend Allard was almost as eager to get some sleep.

As soon as they were gone, Sophie turned to Ivy with the question burning inside her.

"Why?"

Ivy did not need her to elaborate.

"Because it was the right thing to do," she replied. "And because it is time. Past time, some have said."

"Ivy, I didn't mean—"

"Hush. I needed a swift kick in the behind and you gave it to me. I understand that's what good roommates do for one another." She looked more closely. "And now tell me what's bothering you? I saw it on your face as they exchanged their vows."

Sophie shrugged. "So I get teary-eyed at weddings. Occupational hazard."

"This was more than that." She folded her arms across her chest. "I shall not be moving from this spot until you tell me, and I don't think any of us want that."

"For God's sake, tell her what she wants to know," urged Owen, only half teasing.

"Oh, all right. But it's silly. It was the lace, that's all. It reminded me of my mother and of a piece of lace from her wedding dress that I had, but that I don't have anymore, and it just made me sad for a minute. That's all."

"What happened to it?" asked Ivy.

"Long story."

Ivy folded her arms a little more snuggly and said nothing.

"I think," said Owen, "that the term 'long' could be relative in this case and that you might as well just tell the story."

Sophie found herself explaining how her mother's dress and veil had been lost in a house fire before she was born. All her mother had managed to salvage was a piece of the lace edging, and after she died, Lina had helped Sophie to frame it. While she was away at college the prized possession fell prey to one of her stepmother's redecorating frenzies and Sophie blamed herself for not being there to rescue it in time.

"You never found it?" Ivy asked.

She shook her head. "No. I'm not even sure if it went to Goodwill or ended up in the trash." Even now there was a tremor in her voice as she said it. "My stepmother isn't a bad person, but she doesn't have a sentimental bone in her body . . . especially when it comes to decorating. If it doesn't fit the new look, it goes."

"Still, you must never give up hope of finding it," Ivy told her. "It could reappear when you least expect it."

Sophie gave her a droll look. "Thanks, Ivy, but I've been out of college a long time. The house has been sold. I'm pretty sure it's gone forever."

"Don't be. Stranger things have happened. You should know since you've seen some with your own eyes. Thanks to me. And I can tell you that things, like people, can magically appear when you are most in need of them. Don't look so cynical," she chided. "Haven't you heard the expression 'leap and the net shall appear'?"

"Sure. I've heard it, but . . ."

"Then remember it. And do it." Smiling, she reached out and placed her hand on the side of Sophie's face. "Leap, Sophie. Leap when the time is right."

"And just how am I supposed to know when the time is right?"

"You'll know," Ivy assured her with a laugh. "I'm sure of it."

She took a deep breath and looked back at the house for a moment and then turned to Sophie. "I'm leaving now. It has been a pleasure to be your roommate, Miss Sophia Bennett."

"It's been an honor to be your friend, Ivy Halliday," Sophia countered, forcing the words past the sudden ache in her throat. "It really has."

"Don't sniffle," Ivy chided in her most superior tone, helping Sophie to smile instead of succumbing to the tears that threatened. "Also, promise me you'll remember to keep your shoulders back, especially when wearing strapless attire."

"I promise," sniffled Sophie.

Ivy turned her attention to Owen and Sophie would swear he threw his shoulders back.

"Mr. Winters," she began.

He cut in. "I promise to use coasters and not to drop wet towels on your wood floors or leave golf clubs tossed around all over the place. Anything else?"

"More than we have time for, I'm afraid. So I will only say this: fate saw fit to deliver to both of us a great blessing when she arranged for Miss Bennett to appear at our door. Try not to be more of a dolt about it than absolutely necessary. I should hate to have to come back because you mucked up and made a muddle of things."

With that final arch warning and no formal good-bye, which Sophie thought would be more than she herself could bear without getting weepy, Ivy walked away, moving briskly toward the circle of light that appeared in the distance.

"Can she do that?" Owen asked when she was far enough away not to hear. "Come back, I mean?"

Sophie smiled, her throat still aching. "I wouldn't bet against it."

As they watched, Ivy seemed to hesitate for just a heartbeat. Sophie understood why when she saw the figure of a young man in uniform deep within the circle of light. She reached instinctively for Owen's hand at the same time he was reaching to put his arm around her.

"Do you see . . . ?"

"I do," he said, his tone incredulous as he drew her close to his side.

The fog over the ocean made it difficult to gauge how far away the light was, or how far Ivy had walked. But the distance was not so great that they couldn't plainly hear the note of wonder in her voice as the young man opened his arms wide.

"Joseph?" she said.

Just that one word. And then she was running toward him, and was gone.

Owen had been no fan of big fancy weddings even before he learned that they were as much of a pain in the ass after the fact as they were to plan. Maybe more. It seemed to him that Sophie was even busier and working harder now, two days after the wedding— make that *weddings*: the impromptu first round and the second, public ceremony—than she was during the mad rush leading up to it. Everything that had been hauled in or constructed on-site dur- ing the weeks of preparation now had to be packed up, broken down or uprooted, and hauled away. And Sophie was once more at the helm, her lists and schedule in hand, steadfastly creating order out of chaos. It seemed like every time he tried to talk to her, she was either dead busy or dead tired.

He'd thought—foolishly, he could see now—that they would have more time together as soon as the wedding was over and done with. Not to mention some privacy. With the house now one hundred percent ghost-free, he had all kinds of plans for how to put their time together to good use. Instead, work crews were still showing up and traipsing through the place at all hours of the day and into the night. Like the cleaning crew that was there this morning, scrubbing and polishing every inch of the kitchen. From his office window he could see Sophie outside giving directions to the men about to lay down fresh rolls of sod to replace the turf that had been dug up in the interest of the multitude's being able to dine and dance in style.

When he complained about the ongoing ruckus, she reminded him that returning the house and grounds to their original condition was part of their deal. It was her responsibility and she intended to see that it was done right.

Personally, he'd be willing to put up with a fake pond and a dance floor in his backyard if it meant getting to spend time alone with Sophie . . . the awake and alert Sophie, that is, the woman who made him smile just by showing up unexpectedly, the woman who sought him out for midday trysts and could keep him awake and hard and wanting her long into the night . . . the first woman in years . . . maybe ever . . . whom he couldn't get enough of.

He couldn't even take solace in counting the days until the cleanup was finally done because he knew it would mean Sophie was done there too. There would be no reason for her to hang around. At least none they ever talked about . . . or that he even knew how to begin talking about. Theirs was supposed to be a business arrangement and her business would soon be finished. She would pack up her coffeemaker and her favorite pillow and those ridiculous butterfly and hummingbird hair clips she left all over the house and she would leave. Status quo restored. Deal done. Everything would be just the way it was before she came.

Well, almost, anyway. One thing had changed. The house was no longer haunted by Ivy's ghost. Thanks to Sophie, Ivy had finally gotten her happy ending. That was something he wouldn't have believed possible, and frankly he still couldn't quite process what had happened even though he'd seen it with his own eyes. Sophie once told him that everyone was good at something and that what she was good at was making other people's dreams come true. And damn, she wasn't kidding.

In a perfect world, someone would do the same for her. But Owen knew for a hard, cold fact that this wasn't a perfect world. And he sure as hell wasn't a perfect man.

Would she stay if he asked her to?

Did he have any right to ask?

Did it matter?

Lately he had a lot more questions than answers and those answers he did have were about as solid as words carved in beach sand. For a man trained to see the world in black and white, his world suddenly had an unsettling amount of gray. There were moments when he thought the best thing for both him and Sophie was to be grateful for the time they'd had together, quit while they were ahead, and get back to living their own separate and very different lives. And there were also moments, too many of them, when he didn't think he was physically capable of watching her walk out the door without doing whatever he had to do to make her stay.

It would be easier all the way around if Sophie could wave her magic wand and make his dream come true the way she did for others. The only problem was that he didn't have a dream. Not anymore. And as much as he might want to for her sake, he wasn't able to buy into hers.

What he did have were survival skills. The army had seen to that. If you find yourself trekking across dangerous terrain with a hundred pounds of essential equipment on your back and you get hit by a sniper, you have to stop and reassess the situation. First, you appraise your injuries and then you look at that hundred pounds of equipment and redefine the word *essential*. You hang on to only what you absolutely need to survive and you ditch the rest. Quickly and ruthlessly. You don't let things like comfort cloud your judgment. And when it's done, you don't look back and second-guess yourself or bellyache over what you had to leave behind.

Suddenly he was seeing a whole lot less gray.

He should have looked at the situation in a way he understood a whole lot sooner, he thought.

He didn't know squat about romance or the scientific study of kissing or those other things Sophie was so well versed in, but survival was something he did understand.

He was a survivor.

And he knew what he had to do to survive.

Sophie looked at the gaping mud patch where the pond had been with sadness. A wedding planner knows going into a project that no matter how hard she works or how creative she gets, the result of all her planning and fussing is only temporary. Inevitably the cake gets cut and devoured, the rented chairs are stacked and returned to the warehouse, and the confetti is swept up and tossed in the trash. But knowing it and actually seeing the scene stripped of its magic are two different things. And this particular project had been special and closer to her heart than others. For a lot of reasons.

With a philosophical sigh she turned away from the mud, which was already disappearing beneath strips of healthy new sod. Various rental companies had come and collected the furniture and linens. The caterer had removed the extra cooking equipment from the kitchen and carted off dozens of plastic crates filled with china and flatware. The tent, the lights, and the sound system were all gone, along with the trees that had never actually been planted, but simply strategically placed, with mulch used to hide the burlap that was wrapped around their roots lest they grow attached to the soil and think they had found a home, only to be ripped out when the time came, leaving bits and pieces of themselves behind. That was messy and not good for the trees.

She noticed the sky overhead beginning to darken and recalled the weather forecaster's warning to keep an umbrella handy for late-afternoon downpours. It was barely September, but already there was a change in the air, and as much as she griped about the heat and humidity, she felt a sudden urge to hold on to summer for a while longer.

As she headed back inside, she automatically checked along the way for anything she might have overlooked, but there wasn't so much as a crumbled napkin or wilting bloom to be seen anywhere. This must be how a producer feels after a play's final performance, when the actors have left the stage, the costumes all packed away, and the sets taken apart. With one significant difference: at best, a play is an illusion. When it finishes its run, all that's left are memories. But a wedding is only the beginning of the magic; it's just the start of something new and real and important. Together, Shelby and Matthew would go on to make a new life and a new family, and though Sophie couldn't come close to explaining Ivy and Joseph's situation, she had the comforting sense that in some way, in some better place, they were picking up where they left off so long ago. Just thinking about it renewed her faith in love and life and whatever comes next. She was proud and thrilled to have played even a small part in both love stories, and she chose to believe that someday she would know how both turned out.

The house was quiet. The cleaning crew had left it spotless and smelling like lemon furniture polish. No one walking into the kitchen now would guess what a high-pressure hub of activity it had been just a couple of days ago. Her first solo wedding had been an unqualified success from start to finish. Shelby and Matthew were happy, Helen was happy, even the fireworks had been a spectacular hit, and Seasons already had several new referrals. What more could she ask for?

Nothing, she told herself. Because if you had to ask, it wasn't meant to be.

It was time to go. The cleanup was just about done and there was no need for her to be on-site to supervise what remained. To be honest, she could have been out of there yesterday and handled the rest of it by phone. She'd only stretched it out and stuck around because . . . either because hope springs eternal or she was a hopeless idiot. Take your pick.

Although she hadn't consciously planned it ahead of time, she'd stayed at least in part to give Owen some extra time to . . . to say . . . something. Oh, she wasn't a big enough idiot to expect him to make a declaration of any kind or extend an invitation for her to move in permanently. She wasn't even sure she was ready for either. But she thought he might mention the possibility of continuing to see each other or maybe casually suggest she leave a toothbrush behind for future sleepovers: just some small acknowledgment that what they shared was more than a convenient sexual fling.

But he didn't. And it wasn't.

And she was all right with that. Just as with the wedding itself, she'd known the parameters going in. It was never meant to last forever. And she'd been diligent about reminding herself of that each step along the way. She looked herself in the eye in the mirror each morning and told herself it was only temporary and just for fun, and she tried to remember to do the same at night . . . right before she fell asleep in Owen's arms.

It was time to go.

She purposely hadn't mentioned to Owen that she'd be leaving today. Just as she'd made a point of staying busy and out of his way the past couple of days. Maybe she was overly cautious, but announcing her departure ahead of time struck her as contrived, as if she was trying to force the issue and back him into saying something he didn't feel. That was the last thing she wanted. For that same reason, she'd waited until he headed off to his office that morning before gathering her things and packing, and she decided to bring her bags out to the car herself now before saying good-bye. No awkward, dragged-out leave-taking for her.

She managed to get only one bulging duffel bag stowed in the back of her SUV before there was a rumbling overhead and the rain started. *Downpour* was the right word, she thought. *Über-downpour* was an even better one, and *mother of all downpours* also wouldn't be an exaggeration.

It was raining so hard it hurt, and within seconds she was soaked to the skin. Wishing she'd taken time to move the car closer to the house, she ran back up the drive with her hands covering her head and nearly collided with Owen where the front walk merged with the one leading from the side of the house.

"What are you doing out here?" he asked, running his gaze over the cotton shorts and T-shirt plastered to her body.

"I was trying to get the car packed before the rain started. But as you can see . . ." She gave up trying to use her hands as an umbrella and threw them in the air in surrender.

"Packing?" Frowning, he glanced at the car. "Why?"

"Why? Because I'm leaving."

"You're leaving? Now?"

"Yes."

"Why?"

"Why? Because . . . because the wedding is over. And the cleanup is pretty much done. I have work piled up back at the office and a life to get back to."

They were both already speaking loudly to be heard over the rain and the rumbling, which had grown closer and more ominous sounding. Now his voice shot up another few notches in volume.

"A life to get back to? What the fuck does that mean? You're leaving? Just like that? Moving out? Without telling me? Without saying a fucking word? Without even—" He broke off, looking furious, and swept his hand across his face, sending big drops of water flying. "Tell me something: Were you planning to leave me a note? Or is that expecting too much too?"

"Wow. That's a lot of questions . . . and I'm not really sure why you're so upset. Do you think we could go inside out of the rain and talk about it?"

She intended it as a rhetorical question, but for a couple of seconds he had the look of a man who wasn't going anywhere until he got answers. Finally he gave a grudging nod and grabbed her arm as if afraid she might make a run for it if given a chance. As uncomfortable and confused as she was, she had to admit that there was something satisfying about his over-the-top reaction.

She struggled to keep up as he hurried her along the walk and up the steps to the front door. Still holding her arm, he reached for the door handle, and through some kind of eerie blend of intuition and déjà vu, Sophie knew what was going on even before he turned to her in glowering disbelief.

"You locked the door?" he shouted.

"No . . . I didn't mean to, anyway," she said. "I always check before I close it."

"Obviously you didn't this time."

"What can I say? I was . . . preoccupied."

"Either that or in a damn big hurry." He scrutinized her wet clothing. "Please tell me you have your keys on you."

She shook her head. "I didn't think I'd need them; the car was unlocked. You?"

"No," he said, even as he patted the pockets of his wet jeans. "Wait here."

She huddled against the door, as far under the overhanging roof as she could get. He wasn't gone long, and when he returned he didn't look happy.

"The back door?" she asked hopefully, shivering.

"Locked."

"The spare key?"

"Gone."

"All of them?"

"Both of them," he corrected. "I used the one under the brick planter and forgot to put it back. It's upstairs in my room."

"But we hid three. Who could have taken the other two?" Their eyes met. "Ivy."

"She's gone, remember?"

"She could have moved them days ago."

His jaw clenched. "If she was here, and she wasn't already dead, I'd wring her neck."

"Cheerful thought . . . but we'd still be stuck out here in the rain."

He looked around and reached for her hand. "Come on."

"I'm not climbing in any windows," she warned, keeping her feet planted. "I'm tired and wet and—"

"You don't have to climb in the window. You said your car is unlocked, right?"

She brightened. "Yes."

"Then let's go. We won't be able to run the heater, but at least you'll be out of the rain. Once it lets up, I'll take a look around for the spare keys."

Unfortunately the bag she'd brought out didn't have any dry clothes in it, but it did have the warm throw she liked to curl up with at night when she was watching TV. She offered to share it, but Owen declined, either out of gallantry or because he was too annoyed with her to do anything that even resembled cuddling.

"Look," she said, once her teeth stopped chattering. "I think you have the wrong idea. When I said I was leaving, I didn't mean right that very minute. I would never just take off without saying good-bye to you. On the other hand, I didn't know my lease demanded a two-week notice."

The feeble attempt at humor fell flat. Never mind force a polite smile, he didn't even stop staring at the rain pelting the front windshield to look at her.

"I'm sorry if I upset you," she told him, "but the wrap-up here went more smoothly than I expected and I really do have a lot of work to get back to. I have a couple of new assignments waiting. One of the brides heard about Shelby's wedding and requested me personally. Also Lina is interested in working together again and has a few projects lined up. We've even tossed around the idea of combining our talents and starting our own business . . . not right away, of course, but it's worth thinking about, and working together now will be like a risk-free trial run. The point is, I've got a pretty full plate waiting for me, and we both knew I'd be leaving as soon as—"

"You can't leave." Now he did turn to look at her and the expression of grim resolve on his face brought her up short. "There's something I have to say to you and I'm not sure how to do it. Hell, I never thought I would be saying it, to any woman, but I've looked at this from all angles and I don't have a choice."

He looked so troubled; Sophie instinctively pulled the throw closer, bracing herself for whatever bad news he was about to deliver. Could he be dying? Fear tightened like a vise around her midsection. *Please, God, don't let him be dying.* She could go away. She could live without ever seeing him again if she had to. *But please, God, don't let anything bad happen to him.*

"First off, I'm sorry for the way I flew off the handle a few minutes ago. It's just that . . . hell, you just took me by surprise when you said you were packing the car to take off. You're right, of course: I've known all along that once your work here was done, you'd be leaving. I thought I could handle it, but . . ." A small, grim smile shaped his mouth. "But it turns out I can't."

"What do you mean . . . you can't?"

He hesitated, scrubbing his fingers across his lips. The small smile disappeared. In the scant light inside the car, his eyes looked very blue, and very unhappy. He looked wet and cold, and even without knowing what was bothering him, Sophie wanted to wrap the throw around him and hold him and tell him everything was going to be all right.

"I have a confession to make," he said after a minute. "I didn't give you that ultimatum about moving in because of Ivy. I did it because of me, because I liked having you around. It was stupid, I know. I knew even then we were all wrong for each other, but I wanted to spend time with you, to get to know you better. I figured whatever happened, happened, and it would run its course and be over. But that didn't turn out the way I planned either. Obviously."

"Obviously? Maybe to you, but I'm really not sure what you're getting at."

"Look, there's something between us, all right?"

His words, as gruff as they were, set off a little twang of excitement deep inside her. She immediately cautioned herself not to jump to conclusions. "Something between us" could mean any number of things. Not all of them twang-worthy. For all she knew he was about to tell her he'd contracted malaria on one of his supersecret military missions and had passed it on to her.

"You can't deny it," he told her. "I know because I tried. This thing . . . it's real. It's the first thing I think of when I wake up in the morning and it's hovering around me all day, and at night . . . at night it's the reason I can't stay away from you. It's the reason I can't keep my hands off you when we're together. It's gotten so everything I see or hear reminds me of you in some way . . . and nothing that happens seems real until I share it with you." He shrugged and crossed and uncrossed his arms and rearranged his long legs, looking uncharacteristically uncomfortable in his own skin. "Weird, huh?"

"Not so weird," Sophie said gently and without even a small smile, lest he misread her amusement. "Not really. Because I feel the same way."

"You do?" Disbelief and then relief flickered in his eyes.

Inside Sophie, the small twang of excitement was growing stronger, the vibrations spreading through her in little waves, like ripples in a pond.

"That's good," he said, nodding. "That's exactly what I hoped you'd say. Whatever the hell this thing is, I don't trust it. And I damn sure don't trust myself. But I trust you. Sophie, you're the most loyal and giving person I've ever known . . . not to mention stubborn. And sexy as hell. There's no one I'd rather be in a foxhole with."

It wasn't poetry, but she didn't need poetry . . . or fireworks or to live in the Princess House. She only needed him. She'd been afraid to admit that even to herself, but it was true.

"If I have to do this thing, there's no one else I'd want to do it with."

Sophie tucked her wet hair behind her ears, not sure she'd

heard him right or if she was imagining the reluctance lurking in his tone. "This *thing?*"

He nodded, unsmiling. "Like I said, I didn't plan for it to happen. I didn't want it. And I don't trust it. But I don't have a choice. It's come down to a matter of survival."

"Survival." It wasn't a question. She just wondered if the word would make better sense if she said it aloud instead of letting it bounce around in her head.

"What I'm trying to say is that if you're willing to take a chance on me, I'm willing to take a chance on whatever this is. We could give it a year, if you want. That's longer than my first marriage lasted."

She was stuck on the "whatever this is" part until she heard the word *marriage* and a whole new array of conflicting emotions flooded her system.

"Owen, are you by any chance proposing to me?"

Now he looked confused. "Well, yeah. That's what this is all about. I don't have a ring to give you." He looked guilty, or embarrassed. She couldn't tell. "I didn't have time, and anyway, I figure you'd rather pick it out yourself. You know all about that stuff. Whatever you want is fine with me. Except . . ."

"Except?"

"Except I don't want a big fancy wedding."

"Not a problem." She pushed the throw aside, suddenly feeling a rush of heat, most of it headed straight to her face.

"It's not?" He gave a sigh of relief and the tension creases across his brow relaxed ever so slightly. "I thought for sure that after planning so many weddings for other people, you'd want the same hoopla and showboating for your own."

"Oh, I might . . . when the time comes. Or I might not. I meant it's not a problem because I can't marry you, Owen . . . with or without hoopla."

"But you said . . . why the hell not?"

"Because I'm in love with you."

"That's why you can't marry me? Because you're in love with me? That doesn't make any sense, Sophie."

"Maybe I shouldn't have said I *can't* marry you. I should have said I won't marry you."

"There's a difference?"

"There is to me. I settled for less than I deserved once before. When it ended, he told me something I didn't fully understand at the time. I couldn't possibly have. Not then. He told me that you can think you're in love and be wrong, you can tell yourself and everyone around you that you're in love and be wrong, but when you meet the right person, the person you're meant to love and to be with, you just know. He was a jerk. But he was right about that. I know that now. I know because of you. Just the way Ivy knew. All her life she knew Joseph was the man she was meant to love and nothing anyone else said could change that. Ivy knew, and as young as they are, Shelby and Matthew know too. I look at you and I know. But you don't."

She put up her hand to keep him from speaking.

"Did you hear yourself? The words you chose to propose to me? You talked about having no choice and survival and being in a foxhole together."

"Okay. I'm not the most romantic guy in the world. You already knew that."

"I'm not talking about romance, Owen. I'm talking about love. You didn't. It's like you can't even bring yourself to say the word. I deserve more than that. And so do you."

Twenty

Owen couldn't believe how badly he'd fucked up.

He understood immediately what a lousy job he'd done. He knew it long before the rain stopped and they got out of the car and he found the key to let them back into the house. Once they were inside, Sophie had been adamant that she wanted to leave right away.

Who could blame her?

Just the same, his first instinct was to protest and try to buy some time by convincing her to wait until morning. He managed to restrain himself. Pride forced him to behave with at least some of the grace and dignity and kindheartedness with which she was dealing with the situation, a situation he knew must be as difficult for her as it was for him.

She'd said that she loved him. She hadn't said "I love you" in those exact words, but she had admitted that she knew he was the man she was meant to love and to spend her life with. Logic told him he should be mad crazy with happiness right now. But one of the things he'd learned today was that love didn't give a damn about logic.

There were other things she said that were even harder to get out of his head. They confirmed what he'd known all along, that Sophie was more than he deserved and that he could never measure up and that if he tried he would only end up failing and hurting her.

I can't marry you, Owen. I won't. I won't make the same mistake again. It hurts too much to love someone who doesn't love you the same way.

While she changed into dry clothes he'd carried the rest of her stuff to her car. It took him two trips, and with every step, his wet boots squished out a message that to his ears sounded like *jackass, jackass, jackass.*

His damn boots could have done a better job than he had done.

He now understood what Ivy was talking about. He had most definitely mucked everything up and made a muddle of things, exactly what she had warned him not to do. She was right: he was a dolt. He almost wished she would make good on her threat to return. He obviously needed help.

Unless it was already too late.

Clearly he was no authority on the subject, but it seemed to him that a marriage proposal wasn't one of those situations where you could ask for a do-over. It wasn't like parallel parking or a friendly game of minigolf. Once Sophie had pointed out his mistakes, he couldn't very well ask her to let him take it again from the top. That would be like proposing using cue cards that she'd written for him.

He'd tried to explain, of course. About how he panicked when he thought she was going to take off before he had a chance to say what he wanted to say. About how he hadn't had time to practice or think about buying a ring or coming up with a more romantic setting than the inside of a car with them both soaking wet. He used to laugh at those dumb schmucks who thought it was cool to propose via the JumboTron in a football stadium. He wasn't laughing now.

He stayed outside for a long time after she left. Sitting on the patio steps, afraid to go into his own house. Fear wasn't something he was accustomed to feeling and he hated it. The thought that he might have lost Sophie forever was like something lodged in his chest, making it hard to breathe, and he had a feeling it would only get worse when he went inside and she wasn't there. It wasn't only Sophie that would be gone. He knew there would be empty places and things missing everywhere he looked. Reminders of all he had lost. There would be no red, heart-shaped coffee mug on the shelf beside the sink, no sparkly flip-flops by the back door, and no piles of bridal magazines near the sunroom chair where she liked to sit to read. Somehow, in just a few weeks' time, she had made the house feel like a real home. *His* home. During the time she lived there with him, he'd felt more at home than he'd ever felt anywhere.

Reminding himself that he'd lived in the house alone just fine before she came along didn't help. He was wiser now. About a lot of things. Wise enough to know there was no going back to the way things were before.

It was like if you lived your whole life in a cave without running water and then suddenly you got to spend a few weeks in a five-star hotel, in a deluxe suite where the bathroom had a sunken marble tub and one of those room-size walk-in showers with a dozen jets pulsing water at you from all directions. When the time came to go back to your cave, you didn't suddenly forget running water existed. Or decide life was just as enjoyable without it.

You woke up every morning knowing that running water was out there somewhere and that at that very moment people were brushing their teeth with it and making tea with it. You missed running water and cursed yourself for being so blind to possibilities that you'd settled for living in a damn cave for so long. You began thinking of all the things you were prepared to do and all the things you were willing to sacrifice to have running water in your life again. And if you had any sense at all, you began praying to every god there was that you'd get the chance.

Not until he was certain he was tired enough to sleep did he go inside and then he went straight to his room, avoiding the empty spaces along the way. He dropped onto the bed without bothering to undress. His T-shirt and jeans had dried, but they felt stiff and uncomfortable and his eyes refused to close. Instead, as he lay there in the darkness, he made out the shape of something on his dresser, something boxy and unfamiliar that shouldn't be there.

He flicked on the lamp by the bed and at first he wasn't sure what it was. Then his eyes adjusted to the light and he recognized the dollhouse he'd built for Allie, the dollhouse he'd tossed in the trash because it reminded him of all the things he wasn't good at . . . all the things he'd failed at . . . all the reasons he wasn't the right man for Sophie.

He got up and put on the overhead light to take a closer look. It hadn't been there that morning; he was sure of that. If Ivy were still haunting the place he'd suspect she was up to something. But Ivy was gone. And the dollhouse appeared as good as new. Which was odd because he had a vivid memory of throwing it into the trash can and of the roof coming off. In fact it was better than new, he realized, noting that the window he had never been able to get quite square was now perfect.

Sophie. It was the only explanation. She must have put it there before she left. Probably while he was taking her bags to the car. He didn't understand. With everything else she had to do in the past couple of weeks, when had Sophie found time to fix a damn dollhouse? He didn't have to dig deep for the answer. She hadn't *found* time; she'd made it. Probably by staying up nights when she should have been sleeping and stealing moments here and there throughout the day. That's who she was. Someone who found a way to have a wedding dress custom-made for a bride who couldn't find the dress she envisioned any other way. Someone who would befriend the cranky ghost threatening to wreak havoc on her well-laid plans. Someone who, instead of becoming bitter when her own romantic dream crashed and burned, found pleasure and satisfaction working her ass off to make other people's dreams come true.

Someone who had fixed the broken places inside him in the same quiet way she had rescued the dollhouse.

Someone he'd be a fool to let go.

He wasn't going to let her go. He decided that even before he noticed the small wreath of daisies stuck on the front door. He hunkered down to get a better look at it, smiling when he saw that the stems were wound together the same way Allie used to do it. He remembered opening up to Sophie about how he and Allie used to trespass and picnic on the lawn out back; it wasn't something he'd ever talked about with anyone else. He told her about Allie gathering daisies to make a princess crown. And she remembered. And understood.

He had no idea how, but somehow he had to find a way to make Sophie understand what he now realized, that people can change if they have a good enough reason to . . . he could change. He could be the man she needed, the man she deserved . . . a man who could love her without holding anything back.

He wasn't going to let Sophie go. Not without a fight.

The first package arrived on Monday morning.

Shortly after nine, the receptionist called Sophie to let her know there was something for her at the front desk. She was expecting some fabric samples, but as soon as she saw the package leaning against the receptionist's desk, she knew it wasn't fabric samples. The plain, heavy-duty brown box was about three feet square and about six inches deep. And heavy, she discovered when she went to pick it up to take it back to her office. Curious, she borrowed a letter opened and sliced through the wrapping tape right there.

"What's that?" asked Jill, wandering out of her office, coffee mug in hand.

"I'm not sure," Sophie told her, opening the side flap in order to slide out whatever it was.

Jill came closer. "Who's it from?"

"Don't know that either. There's no label on the box."

"No return address?"

"Nope. Nothing."

"I hope it's not a bomb."

Sophie slanted a quelling glance her way. "Gee, thanks."

"Well, these days you can't be too careful."

"Jill, it is not a bomb."

Jenna arrived for the day just in time to hear the end of the exchange. Shoving her sunglasses to the top of her head, she asked, "What's not a bomb?"

"Whatever's in that package. According to Sophie, anyway. I still wouldn't stand too close," Jill advised.

Jenna and the receptionist both took a step back.

As if that would save them if a three-square-foot bomb went off, thought Sophie, grunting as she struggled to work the Styrofoam packing loose without chipping her new nail polish.

It had been a rough few days since she returned to her own place, a place she was finding it hard to think of as home. Crazy as it seemed, when she thought of home she thought of a sweeping staircase and an ocean view and a guesthouse with the cushiest feather bed in the world. Her condo had none of the above. But that's not why she was finding it difficult to settle back in or why she had resorted to pampering herself in every way she could think of, including a massage and manicure and a steady supply of handmade dark chocolate truffles from the little shop down the street. All that was an attempt—a desperate and thus far completely unsuccessful attempt—to distract herself from the fact that the condo also lacked the one thing she missed the most. Owen Winters.

On the dismally insignificant bright side, at least her struggle to open the package was burning truffle calories.

"Here, let me hold the box while you pull," Jenna said, daring to get close enough to grab it with both hands.

That did the trick. Sophie slid the contents out and peeled off the protective wrapping to reveal a framed print.

"Wow. Nice," admired Jill, coming around to look over Sophie's shoulder at the painting.

It was a signed and numbered print done in warm shades of yellow and orange and red; the work was simply rows of different-size, interconnecting boxes. Sophie didn't know a lot about contemporary art, but she understood that the artist's command of color and ability to make a simple design so compelling were the marks of a major talent.

Jenna bent down and squinted to read the signature. "M. L. Lark. I knew it. Nick and I fell in love with one of her paintings in a gallery in Boston, but it was too rich for our blood. Who sent it to you?"

"She doesn't know," Jill replied for her.

"Well, read the card. Duh."

Sophie checked the box, and the wrapping. "There is no card."

"Call the gallery," suggested Jenna.

"What gallery? There's no label anywhere."

"I know. You can call the delivery service and have them check their records. Tell them the card must have gotten lost."

It was a good idea, but Rae, the receptionist, couldn't recall what company had delivered the package. In fact, the more she thought about it, the more she thought the man who carried it in hadn't been wearing a uniform and that there also hadn't been any writing on the van he drove off in. Ignoring Jill's suggestion that she call the FBI, Sophie carried the print back to her office and leaned it against a wall where she could see it every time she looked up. It was an expensive painting. Eventually whoever sent it would check to make sure she'd gotten it. Either that or it had been delivered to her by mistake and someone would come looking to take it back.

It did cross her mind that Owen might have sent it, but then thoughts of Owen were constantly crossing her mind. Or else pitching a tent and hanging there for a while. She did what she always did: told herself to think about something else.

At ten-thirty Sophie returned from a truffle run to find the Js and several others again gathered around something in the reception area.

"What the hell?" she said, eyeing the humongous hammock. "Where did that come from?"

"Another mystery delivery," Jill informed her. "For you."

"Me?" Frowning, she walked over and read the tag that was attached to the steel frame. "'A summer classic, this beautiful hammock was handwoven of unbleached cotton by Mayan artists of the Yucatán to bring you many years of sumptuous pleasure.'"

"The Yucatán?" echoed Jill. "Is that anywhere near Ecuador?"

"What difference does that make?" Sophie countered.

"Isn't that where Shelby was going for the Peace Corps? Maybe she sent it to you . . . as a thank-you gift."

Sophie shook her head. "They aren't going to Ecuador for a few weeks. They're still in Hawaii on their honeymoon."

"How about her mother?"

"She's on a cruise. And I really don't see either of them sending me a hammock as a thank-you gift."

"Who do you see sending it?"

She closed her eyes. She saw Owen, of course, but that had nothing to do with the hammock. She saw him every time she closed her eyes.

"Well?"

"I can't think of anyone," she said, heading toward her office to eat a truffle in private.

"Wait," Jenna called after her. "What about the hammock?"

"It won't fit in my office," Sophie said. She sighed. "Help me push it against the wall for now and I'll think about it later."

When she got back from lunch, there was a red leather desk chair waiting for her. Or as Rae, who was sitting in it put it, a red leather desk chair extraordinaire.

"I didn't even know they made massaging desk chairs," Rae said, cozying up to the "scientifically calibrated massaging fingers." "Or chairs with coolers," she added, gleeful as she showed Sophie the underseat storage large enough to hold a specially designed ice pack and several beverage cans.

"This has got to be someone's idea of a joke," Sophie muttered.

"You mean like when people sign you up for magazine subscriptions or have pizza delivered to your house as a joke? My aunt once had to pay for a half-dozen pizzas she didn't order. With anchovies on them, which she hates. Does that mean you could get stuck paying for all of this stuff?"

"I hope not. But I may get stuck figuring out how to return all of it."

"Oh. Well, until you figure out how to return the chair, is it all right if I put it at my desk and sit in it?"

"Be my guest," Sophie told her.

By the end of the day, the hammock and chair had been joined by a fruit basket with what they all agreed was a genuine—and expensive—sapphire flower pendant tucked in between the pears and oranges. Also a birch sapling and an antique, glass-front display cabinet filled with an assortment of penny candy.

Sophie took off early. Partly because she felt a headache coming on and partly because she was afraid that whatever showed up next might have to be fed and taken home with her for the night. It turned out that there was no escape. She wasn't home an hour when the doorbell rang and she found a box containing a watch on the front step. It was a great watch. Very unusual, with a thin band of copper around the face and a copper band.

A tiger-lily plant in a bronze planter arrived next. Followed by a picnic basket with handmade ceramic plates and cups inside, then an intriguing small puzzle box made of hammered metal, and a while later a pair of designer sunglasses with stainless-steel frames.

The puzzle box frustrated her, but she really liked the sunglasses. And they looked good on her. She decided that if she had a choice, she would pay for them rather than send them back. Unless she ended up in prison for grand theft, in which case she wouldn't need sunglasses. It was possible all this stuff had been stolen. Which meant she was in possession of stolen property. She didn't think she could be held liable for it, and she wasn't about to call the FBI, but it couldn't hurt to call the local police in the morning and make a report of some kind.

She put the sunglasses on the nightstand when she went to bed and crossed her fingers that the doorbell didn't ring again that night. Or if it did, that the next package from her mystery gifter contained something useful . . . like earplugs.

Or a gift certificate for a Memory Wipe, if there was such a thing.

She thought about it some more and decided that even if there was a way to wipe her memory clean, she wouldn't do it. As much as it hurt now, she wouldn't give up one minute of the time she'd spent with Owen, or any of her Princess House memories.

For what seemed like the millionth time, she replayed that last afternoon in her head, and for what seemed like the millionth time, she wondered if she had made the right decision. She lay there torturing herself with all manner of possibilities and shades of meaning, and worried that maybe she'd been too critical of him for saying that he was proposing because he had no choice and that he didn't trust his feelings for her and didn't even want to feel whatever it was he felt, and in the end she came to the same conclusion she'd come to the first 999,999 times. She'd done the right thing. The words didn't matter. It mattered that what he was offering wasn't enough, and she wasn't going to settle for what wasn't enough.

The first days had been the worst. She'd stayed home from work and swum in a sea of self-pity. She bounced back and forth between anger and heartache. Which was dumb. It wasn't fair to be angry with someone for not loving you the way or as much as you wanted them to love you. She was angry just the same. Nobody ever said life was fair.

And she cried, even though she told herself she shouldn't because crying would only make her blotchy and not change a damn thing. She cried her heart out. Several times.

The crying was over.

She hoped.

Now she was taking it one day at a time. Eventually it would get better.

She hoped.

She punched her pillow and rolled over.

Think about something else, she told herself.

She wondered if there might be a truffle in her bag that she'd overlooked.

Something besides that, she told herself. Preferably something without calories.

She remembered the sunglasses and pictured herself walking into Seasons tomorrow wearing them. She wouldn't have thought she'd look good in steel frames, but she did. At least her mystery gifter had good taste. She liked the sapphire pendant a lot too, but she didn't think she could afford to keep it. She still couldn't figure out why whoever sent it had thought to stick it in a fruit basket, of all things. What did fruit have to do with sapphires? Or with jewelry in general? She turned it over in her mind. Fruit and sapphires. Fruit and sapphires. The pendant was shaped like a flower. Fruit and flowers?

Fruit and flowers.

She sat up and switched on the light. Fruit and flowers. Of course.

She glanced at the sunglasses on the nightstand. Steel frames. Steel, that was eleven. Fruit and flowers, that was four. Leather . . . the leather desk chair . . . three.

Leaping from the bed, she grabbed a notepad and pen and made a list just to make sure she was right, starting with the print . . . which was done on paper. Paper, the traditional gift for a first wedding anniversary. The second anniversary was cotton . . . as in a cotton hammock. The third was leather; the fourth fruit and flowers. The birch tree was wood. Year five. Candy and iron were traditional for year six . . . and the display case with the penny candy had iron fittings.

When she finished there were eleven items on her list, each one a perfect match for a traditional wedding anniversary gift. And she knew without a doubt who had sent them. Owen. She'd asked him not to call or e-mail or text her or try to see her. And she had been unhappy with his proposal. He'd tried to explain. She remembered how earnest he'd looked, and how devastated as he tried to explain that if he'd had more time he would have done better.

It seemed he was right.

By Friday, both her office and her condo had the look of a high-end bazaar sale. Lace, crystal, silver, pearls . . . Owen had covered all the bases. And as the years were ticked off, Sophie's impatience grew. The gifts were beautiful, but all she really wanted was to see Owen and hear what he had to say.

Late in the afternoon Rae called. They had it down to a routine now. But when she got to the front, there was no package waiting, only Owen, clean-shaven and dressed in a dark suit and carrying long-stemmed red roses. The urge to throw herself in his arms was almost overpowering.

"Hello, Sophie," he said, and it felt as if his slow smile was attached directly to her heart. He held the flowers out to her.

"A present? For me?" She shot him a teasing smile as she bent her head to inhale their fragrance. "They're beautiful. Thank you. . . . I feel like I should say that fifty times."

"I'd rather you didn't. Not yet. I actually have something else for you, but this is something I needed to deliver in person." He glanced around. "Is there someplace we could talk?"

"My office," she said, beckoning him to follow. She handed the roses to Rae as she passed. "Rae, do you think you could . . ."

"Put them in water for you? Sure." Her smile turned mischievous. "I know I saw a Waterford crystal vase around here somewhere."

The Js were still there and she could feel them watching. She was happier than ever for her cramped little office. At least it didn't have glass walls and had a solid wood door she could close for privacy.

As soon as she closed that door, Owen started to speak, ignoring her invitation to sit.

"I'm sorry for just showing up unannounced, but you made me promise not to call. Or text."

"It's all right. Actually, I was going to get in touch with you . . . eventually."

He looked incredulous. "You were? I figured after . . . you know . . . you'd never . . ."

"Not about . . . you know. It's about Ivy."

"Ivy? What about her?"

"Actually it's about Joseph. The librarian friend I asked to look into it finally got back to me, and I thought you'd want to know what she found out." She reached for a manila envelope on her desk. "This copy is for you; it makes for pretty interesting reading. I'll just quickly fill you in on the highlights. Most of the information comes from someone who Maggie—that's my friend—connected with while she was researching online. He's a doctoral student at Brown and he did a lot of his own research on the Hallidays for his thesis."

"He's writing his thesis on the Hallidays?"

"No, on Prohibition in Rhode Island. He came at it from that angle and more or less backed into the Ivy–Joseph mystery in the process. This is just his theory, of course, but he does have a lot of circumstantial evidence, letters and diaries, that kind of thing, to back it up. Plus he got his hands on the files of one of the private detectives Ivy's father hired to find Joseph."

"So what's his theory?"

"According to him, Ivy's older brother and a friend were involved in bootlegging, or rum-running, as I've learned is the preferred term when the booze is being smuggled over water. Prohibition was in full swing and the family's boatbuilding business provided the perfect cover."

"Was this with the old man's consent?"

"No. He wouldn't have stood for it. And evidently that was the rub . . . or at least the brother and his friend thought it would be. Joseph was a straight arrow and on course to become Mr. Halliday's fair-haired boy. The last thing they wanted was Joseph in a position to find out what they were up to and pull the plug. They met with him the night before the wedding. According to the theory, it was to offer him money to walk out of Ivy's life and stay out. Rumrunning was highly lucrative, so they would have had plenty to offer. Plus it was well known that the friend had always had a thing for Ivy, so he had even more reason to want Joseph out of the picture."

"So that's what happened? Joseph was paid to take a powder." He shook his head in disgust.

"Not so fast. Joseph refused. Emphatically, it seems. According to this guy's research, things got heated and turned physical between Joseph and the friend and Joseph ended up dead. The private detective tracked down a couple of witnesses who said it was accidental. Accident or not, it appears that when Mr. Halliday finally learned the truth, he paid to have the whole thing hushed up and the file sealed."

Owen reacted with a sound of disgust. "He was protecting his son."

"Yes. And who knows? Maybe he thought not knowing what her brother did would make things easier for Ivy too."

"Yeah, well, I'd like to have a talk with the old man about that. Poor Ivy. That's a long time to be left wondering." He swiveled his gaze toward Sophie. "I don't know how she did it. 'Cause honestly, this past week has almost been more than I could stand."

He took a deep breath.

"There's a lot I want to say to you, Sophie. A lot I need to say, and to explain. But there's something I want to do first. I've been thinking about it for days . . . practically from the moment I watched you drive away, and I can't wait any longer. I swear it's a goddamn miracle I managed to wait this long. You don't know how many times this week I wanted to say the hell with being patient and just walk in here and do it. I held back because the last time I just went with my gut, it didn't go so well. You may remember." His mouth slanted in a sheepish smile and everything inside Sophie went soft and warm.

"That does seem to ring a bell," she said.

"Never let it be said I don't learn from my own stupidity. This time I had a plan and I stuck to it. But I can't wait another damn minute to do this . . . if you'll let me."

She nodded, a shiver of anticipation dancing along her spine. She expected him to grab her and kiss her the way she wanted to grab and kiss him, and was stunned when instead he dropped to one knee and reached into his jacket pocket for a small black velvet box.

He flipped it open with his thumb as easily as if he'd done it many times before, but Sophie knew him too well to be fooled; she saw the slight trembling of his hand. Then she saw the diamond ring inside the box, the absolutely perfect diamond ring, the ring she had drooled over so many times in a magazine photo that the magazine she'd seen it in fell open to that page every time she opened it, and she gasped.

Owen smiled at her. "Miss Sophia Bennett, will you marry me?"

She was breathless, which made it hard to speak.

"You can give me your answer on a contingency basis if you want," he told her. "Believe me, I'm prepared to do as much groveling and explaining as necessary to make up for my first attempt at this. And I know it will take more than words to convince you that

I am crazy, out-of-my-head, heart-over-head-over-heels in love with you. It will take years. And I'm looking forward to every one of them. That's what gave me the idea of sending you anniversary gifts ahead of time. That's how many years I'm asking for this time . . . at least fifty, with a promise to renegotiate for whatever comes next. I want fifty years and I want to spend every minute of every one of them making you happy that you said yes and took a chance on a dolt who still doesn't have it all figured out but who wants to learn and needs someone with a doctorate in romance to teach him."

Laughing and crying at the same time, Sophie sank to her knees facing him.

He blotted a tear from beneath her eye.

"Say yes, Sophie."

"Fifty years? That's the deal?"

"There may need to be a subclause about children, but we can work that out later." He took the ring from the box and held her hand in his. "Say yes, Sophie."

She took a deep breath. "You're sure? You're sure this is what you want?"

"You're what I want. I want to wake up with you and go to bed with you and have babies with you. I love you, Sophie. I want to stand at the front of the biggest church we can find and watch you walk down the aisle in a white dress and promise you forever in front of however many people you want to invite. I get it now. Let me prove it to you. Say yes, Sophie."

"Yes." She swiped a tear. "Yes, yes, yes," she said, laughing and crying as she let him slip the ring on her finger and then he was kissing her.

And kissing her. She had no idea how much time passed before she became aware that someone was knocking on her office door.

They pulled back a little, but she kept her arms looped around his neck so she could stare at her left hand.

"Sophie?"

She recognized Rae's voice and was thankful it wasn't the *J*s she had to tell to get lost.

"Later, Rae."

"Uh . . . okay. It's just that you said to let you know whenever you got another delivery, and you just did. Get one, that is."

Pulling back another few inches, Sophie glanced quizzically at Owen, who immediately shook his head.

"This one's not from me," he told her at the same time Rae was saying that this package had a return address . . . or at least a name."

"It's from somebody named Ivy. Ivy Halliday. Do you want me to—"

Sophie yanked open the door and grabbed the package from Rae. The *J*s were standing right behind her.

"Sophie, what the hell is going on?" demanded Jenna.

Jill was trying to see around the door. "What's Winters doing here? Oh my God, is that a diam—"

The door shut.

Owen took hold of Sophie and spun her around and then rested his back against it to make sure it stayed shut.

"What do you suppose is in the box?" he asked.

"Don't you think a better question is how did it get here? Or when the heck did she send it?"

He shook his head, his expression happy and resigned. "Why bother? This is Ivy we're talking about, remember? She'd find a way."

"True." Placing the package on the desk, she hurriedly tore off the wrapping and opened the box inside and gasped with surprise.

"I don't believe it," she said, but of course she did. It was Ivy after all. Owen was right: she would find a way.

She carefully lifted the frame from the box.

"Look. It's the lace from my mother's wedding dress," she told him.

Owen rested his hand on her back as he looked it over. "Is that the same frame?"

She nodded. "Yes. It's exactly the same as I remember it . . . right down to the little wrinkle where I didn't get the lace quite flat. She said it would turn up when I needed it most," she murmured, already imagining how the lace would look adorning a bouquet of white roses and lilies of the valley. "How could she possibly—"

"There's a note," Owen pointed out.

Sophie reached for it. It was brief. She glanced at it and smiled. "It just says 'Leap . . . with love.' And there's a P.S. for you." She handed it to him.

The P.S. read: *Well played, Mr. Winters. Well played indeed.*

"How about that?" he said, looking very proud of himself.

"Yeah, I guess when you get a seal of approval from on high, you know you're doing something right."

"And I plan to keep on doing it for a long, long time."

He reached for her. They kissed and laughed and kissed some more.

Outside the door there were noises and whispers. The *J*s didn't give up easily. Sophie looked forward to seeing their faces when she told them the news. But she was in no hurry for the kiss to end. And she could tell that Owen wasn't either.

There was no need to rush.

After all, they had forever.

Also by Misa Ramirez

Living the Vida Lola

HASTA
LA VISTA,
LOLA!

A Lola Cruz
Mystery

MISA RAMIREZ

MINOTAUR BOOKS

A Thomas Dunne Book

New York

A THOMAS DUNNE BOOK FOR MINOTAUR BOOKS.
An imprint of St. Martin's Publishing Group.

HASTA LA VISTA, LOLA! Copyright © 2010 by Melissa Bourbon Ramirez. All rights reserved. Printed in the United States of America. For information, address St. Martin's Press, 175 Fifth Avenue, New York, N.Y. 10010.

www.thomasdunnebooks.com
www.minotaurbooks.com

Library of Congress Cataloging-in-Publication Data

Ramirez, Miza.
    Hasta la Vista, Lola! : a Lola Cruz mystery / Misa Ramirez.
        p. cm.
    "A Thomas Dunne book."
    ISBN 978-0-312-38403-6
    1. Women private investigators—California—Fiction.
    2. Murder—Investigation—Fiction.   3. Sacramento
(Calif.)—Fiction.   I. Title.
    PS3618.A464H37 2010
    813'.6—dc22
                                                    2009039819

First Edition: February 2010

10   9   8   7   6   5   4   3   2   1

For Carlos,
because without you, this book would have no title.
Yes, you're *that* good.

And for Gloria,
the truest sister I could ever have.

Acknowledgments

My gratitude to: **the girls at Chasing Heroes, Tonya Kappes, Lee Lopez, Susan Hatler, and Virna DePaul** (Chasing Heroes is hard work, but so much fun with friends); **Holly Root**, for loving Lola; **Toni Plummer**, for all your support; **Thomas Dunne Books and St. Martin's Minotaur**, for giving life to Lola Cruz, and especially to Eliani Torres for your brilliant attention to detail; **Virna DePaul**, for always being there, at the ready, whether to talk, read, revise, or lament; Maria Shubert, for your Spanish expertise; and **Sarah Davee**, because writing is lonely work, and moving to a new state is even lonelier, but bonding over PTA with you made it so exciting!

Chapter 1

I can't even begin to count the number of times my grandmother told me that she would die a happy woman if only I'd join the Order of the Benedictine Sisters of Guadalupe and live a chaste and holy life.

To which I always nodded, smiled, and said, "I want you to die happy, Abuela, *pero* I'm not going to become a nun." There were several problems with me and a pious life. If you asked my mother, she'd say I'd sinned over and over and over again, beginning with premarital intercourse (which she suspected but had no actual proof of), and ending with my job. In my mother's eyes, being a detective necessitates questionable actions and an "ends justifies the means" philosophy.

Which was not actually *my* philosophy. I did things by the book and let my conscience be my guide. I was God-fearing, so I tried to toe the line, but I was also a driven, independent woman walking a tightrope between modern American culture and my parents' old-fashioned, male-oriented Spanish culture, so my conscience didn't always know which way to go when I hit a fork in the road.

Case in point. It was a brisk Friday night, downtown Sacramento was lit up with twinkling white lights, I was all dressed up, and even though I had no one to go salsa dancing with, joining those crazy

Benedictine Sisters still never entered my mind. The nuns might enjoy their celibacy, but I was 100 percent positive that I wouldn't embrace a lifetime of abstinence. Hell, I'd just spent the better part of two hours photographing acrobatic sex in a back alley (which had left me *un poquito* hot and bothered)—all in the name of being the best private investigator I could possibly be—and I was okay with my decision.

I was almost to Camacho and Associates, the small PI firm where I work. I dialed Reilly Fuller, the Jill-of-all-trades secretary of the office—and my homegirl. I wanted to go out dancing tonight, and I knew I could count on her to have my back.

She picked up on the third ring, breathing heavy and almost out of breath. "Lola!"

"Hey, *chica*. How'd you know it was me?"

"Caller ID."

I frowned. The phone company had effectively destroyed kids' innocent prank-call fun—not to mention obsessed stalker-girls calling and hanging up on a guy just to hear his voice (not that I'd had any experience with that type of juvenile behavior).

"Lola, I'm in the middle of something," she said. She panted. "I'll call you back, okay?"

I'd never known Reilly to break a sweat willingly, so I was curious. I checked the time. 9:40. An odd time to be using the treadmill—if that's what she was up to. "Are you exercising?"

But electric-blue-haired Reilly couldn't answer me because she'd already hung up.

Huh. My long night loomed ahead of me, and dancing wasn't going to be part of it. Looked like it was going to be me, a container of mapo tofu from Szechwan House (my favorite restaurant of all time, coincidentally right next door to Camacho and Associates), my camera hooked up to the office computer, and a whole lot of sex pictures uploading. One at a time.

I turned onto Alhambra and immediately spotted my boss's truck in the parking lot. I slid my little red CRV into a space right beside it.

2

Apparently Manny Camacho didn't have plans for Friday night, either. Hard to believe. He was *puro Latino machismo* Greek God material—dark and brooding and scary in an I-could-do-things-to-you-and-make-you-scream-for-mercy kind of way.

I couldn't help sneaking a quick peek in the rearview mirror. Low-cut, filmy dress, Victoria's Secret Ipex cleavage, clear olive skin, salon-highlighted copper strands framing face, MAC O lips. I would *not* be put out to pasture because of a roguishly sexy reporter who disappeared for days on end and whom I did not want to think about right now.

I grabbed my cell phone, the Nikon, my notepad with the Zimmerman case information, and my new favorite accessory—courtesy of eBay—my Sexy Señorita drawstring bag. Shoving the notepad into the coral-colored purse, I headed toward the office.

In your face, Callaghan. I had options. Dark and brooding suddenly held a new appeal.

Just as I reached the office, Manny pushed open the door. "Dolores?"

My wedge heels teetered on a crack in the sidewalk. Maybe *appeal* was the wrong word. Dark fascination? Sadistic curiosity?

Fact is, Manny flustered me without even trying. Not many people could do that. I'd solved my first big case as primary investigator a few months ago. I chided myself. It was way past time to get over the nerves that shot through me when I was around him.

He looked at his watch, then back at me. "*¿Que onda?* Are you working?"

I nodded. "The Zimmerman case."

He held the door, apparently waiting for me to continue.

I held up my camera. "Got some great pictures." Especially if I had contacts at *Playboy* or *Penthouse*, which, unfortunately, I didn't.

"Pictures of—?"

"Of Mrs. Zimmerman, um, making out with her personal yoga instructor." *Making out* might have been understating Mrs. Zimmerman's activities, but it was the safest answer.

3

"How'd you get them?"

"I followed them after yoga class."

Manny's eyes narrowed as he looked me up and down. "Are you supposed to be undercover?"

My dress was a far cry from yoga-wear, but there was nothing wrong with looking good on a surveillance job. "They changed after class, then went to dinner. Lucky for me I'm a yoga junkie and very flexible"—maybe not as flexible as Mrs. Zimmerman, but her sexual creativity was in a class by itself—"and have decent cargo room in my car."

Manny seemed to ponder this, his expression unreadable. "And the photos?" he finally asked.

"After dinner they went around the corner from the restaurant." Totally classless. Who screwed—er, got down and dirty—out in public? "I was across the street. Excellent telephoto capabilities on this camera, by the way."

He let the door to the office close while I accessed the pictures on the digital camera. I froze when his arm brushed against my back. The touch had been as light as a breath, but any physical contact from Manny Camacho could send a woman into premature orgasm. He moved behind me to look over my shoulder. A zing shot through my body, and I gulped. Looking at X-rated pictures with my boss was *muy* uncomfortable.

I tried not to think about how flexible *he* might be and whether his slight limp or his cowboy boots would interfere with the Kama Sutra position in photographs three, twenty-seven, or thirty-one.

When we'd gone through all the pictures, I stepped away, trying to ignore the charged silence. "Open and shut," I said. "She's clearly cheating on her husband."

"Good work." His voice sounded strained. I shoved aside the idea that it might be because of the photos, particularly what Mrs. Zimmerman had been doing in shots ten through eighteen.

My PI gene kicked in. Why *didn't* he have plans on a Friday night? He had the hottest girlfriend this side of the Rio Grande. Maybe

4

this side of anywhere. Her only competition was the phantom ex-wife nobody had ever laid eyes on.

Neither was in sight. "You're here late," I said casually. "Where's Isabel?" I pronounced the name in Spanish: *Ee-sa-bel.*

"Not here." The corner of his mouth notched up. "Where's Callaghan?"

There was a good chance that Manny Camacho, ex-cop-turned-super-detective-who-seemed-to-know-everything, knew exactly where Jack Callaghan was. Then again, maybe not. He wasn't psychic, after all, and I hadn't let on that Jack had been MIA for almost a week now. "Not here," I said, then quickly changed the subject. "I'm going to upload the photos and write my report for Mr. Zimmerman." Which brought to mind something else. "I'm ready for a new case."

Manny pressed a button on his key ring. Two beeps sounded from his truck, a white, lifted, kick-ass 4×4. It wasn't the most unobtrusive vehicle on the road in Sacramento, but it certainly had style. "The report can wait until Monday. We'll talk about the caseload then."

I started to stick my phone into my purse and retrieve my set of office keys. The straps slipped off my shoulder and the bag fell. Manny was right. Uploading the pictures *could* wait till Monday, but since I had nothing better to do tonight, there was no reason to put it off. "I like to finish what I start," I said as I bent down to grab the straps of my bag. "I'll do the report tonight."

As I straightened, he gave me another slow once-over. "Callaghan's a fool."

A shiver swept up my spine and I shifted uncomfortably. Reality bit me. I didn't think I could cross the line into fraternizing with my boss after all, and I certainly wasn't ready to write Jack off, even if he had a few secrets and the annoying habit of disappearing. He probably had a very good reason for dropping off the face of the earth. Again.

He'd better, damn it.

"Dolores."

5

"Hmm?"

"I said you're going to break your phone."

I started. He had? I was? I loosened the death grip on the device, but dropped my purse again in the process. "I, um, need to call my mother. See if she needs anything."

"*¿Por qué, mi poderosa? ¿Qué pasa?*"

Ay, ay, ay. Manny had taken to calling me "strong woman." Now he was calling me *his* strong woman? I gulped and stumbled back a step. I might be a good Catholic girl, but I wasn't immune to temptation. "She's home sick. I, um, think I should buy her some medicine and ginger ale."

"Can I help?"

Manny as nurturer? It didn't compute. "No, no, no!" I just wanted to go upload the Zimmerman pics and go home to my empty flat. Above my parents' house. That I shared with my brother. "I mean, I'm fine. I can handle it."

He pressed the button on his key ring again, reactivating the truck alarm. "I have some more work I can do. I'll stay with you."

My hackles went up. I thought about jabbing him in the chest and reminding him that my Salma Hayek curves didn't mean I wasn't Xena, Warrior Princess, through and through. I didn't need a protector—or a babysitter.

Thankfully—since it wouldn't have been a good idea to chastise my boss—or touch his chest—I was stopped by the sound of a horn blaring behind us. A sporty silver Volvo pulled into the parking lot. Jack! My heart immediately slammed in my chest and I caught my breath. *¡Mi amor!*

He stepped out of his car, all tousled brown hair and swarthy Irish complexion. His gaze swept over me and an angry dimple pulled his cheek in. My heart lurched again. I could imagine what he thought. I was dressed for a night on the town and Manny wore black and gray, his burnished skin and onyx eyes contemplating Jack with harsh scrutiny.

I took a small step to the side, putting space between Manny and me. No need to stoke the fire.

Not that it mattered, I reminded myself. Jack had up and left for a week—without a word. If he had issues with Manny, that was *his* problem. You snooze, you lose. I sidestepped back to where I'd been.

"*Hasta la vista*, Dolores." Manny's voice had turned gruff.

"Right. See you later."

His black alligator-skin cowboy boots clapped unevenly against the sidewalk as he walked to his truck.

Jack came toward me. He dipped his head in an almost imperceptible nod at Manny as they passed, and then his eyes flicked to the bodice of my dress.

They lingered and his face tightened, not in the *I want to ravish you* kind of way I would have liked, but more in a *what the hell are you wearing around him* kind of way.

Catching my reflection in the window, I immediately saw what had caught his attention. It was my 34Cs—in the midst of a wardrobe malfunction. My dress was askew and part of my right breast plumped out of my demi-bra. ¡Ay, caramba! No wonder Manny had given me a slow, burning look after I'd picked up my purse.

I straightened it as Manny pulled out of the parking lot. Shit! Manny had gotten an eyeful of my assets, and he hadn't uttered a word.

From the way Jack looked from me to Manny's truck and back, I suspected that he was thinking the same thing. "Purple, huh?" he said when he steadied his gaze back on me. His voice had that low, sexy tone that created instant yearning in the pit of my soul.

"It's called Lavender Ice," I said coolly.

"For him?"

"Well, it's not like you've been around, *Callaghan*." I ran my hands down my front in full temptress mode. Jack's gaze smoldered as it followed my actions. Slow torture. God, sometimes it was so good to be a woman.

His gaze finally found its way back to my face. "I go away for one week and you start dating your boss. Nice, *Cruz*."

I kept my gaze steady. "You went away *without a word. That* was not nice, *Callaghan*."

He stood like a statue, then like a blip during a film, he shrugged. "I had something I had to take care of, that's all. It's no big deal, Lola, really. Sorry," he added with a contrite smile.

Not a big deal to him, but it had been a pretty big deal to me. I waited, thinking he'd offer more of an explanation, but he gave me nothing. Finally I jammed my hands on my hips and stared him down. Fine. I was just going to have to drag it out of him. "What kind of thing?" I should have left it at that, but damn it if my mouth didn't have a mind of its own. "You might as well spill it. You know you can't keep secrets from me." I pointed at myself. "Private investigator, remember?"

"How could I forget?" he muttered, and he took a small step toward me.

His musky scent. His six feet of hard body. His tousled hair. His crooked little smile. *Ay, caramba.* Jack Callaghan sent me into a tailspin. Rooting out his secrets could become one of my favorite pastimes if he didn't infuriate me so much.

I backed up. Distance. He would not sweet-talk me into forgetting why I was mad. "Where'd you go?"

"I had an emergency I had to deal with, Lola."

The way he rumbled my name made my knees go weak and diluted my anger. "What kind of emergency?"

He took a pantherlike step toward me. "Unfortunately, it was the kind I couldn't say no to."

"Is that your explanation?"

"It's the truth," he said.

In a half-truth kind of way. "What kind of emergency couldn't you say no to?"

He backed me up against the window of Camacho and Associates. "You really want to talk about this now?"

8

I breathed in. God, he smelled fabulous. Forget about dancing. The musky pheromones were sending promises of acrobatics. "Y-yes."

"I missed you."

"It's going to take some serious convincing to make me believe that." My eyelids fluttered. "You didn't call—"

His hand slipped behind my back, a featherlight touch that sent whispers of desire up my spine. "The battery on my phone died."

"Come on, Callaghan," I breathed, summoning my self-control. "You can do better than that. No charger in your car? No money to buy a new one? Ever hear of a pay phone?"

"Couldn't find one, *bellísima.*"

Ooh. Low blow. And good memory. I'd taught him the word for beautiful, and now he was using it on me. "Pulling out all the stops, eh?" I pressed my palm against his chest. "Spill it, *guapo.* You can't just sweet-talk your way into—"

The corner of his mouth crept up wickedly, and his hand moved to my hip. "Sweet-talk my way into what?"

My skirt. My heart. My . . .

Dios mío. His chest felt amazing under my hand—all hard and muscled and— What was I mad about again?

He bent his head and brushed his lips against my neck, trailing them to my collarbone.

"Mmm." The moan slipped out. Reality or not, his charm was second to none.

"Mmm-hmm," he echoed.

I jumped when my cell phone belted out the chorus of "La Bamba." Reality came flooding back into my brain. He'd left without so much as an *adiós, that's* what I was mad about.

Grabbing the phone from my bag, I flipped it open. Holding it to my ear, I tried to ignore how close Jack was to me, how the minuscule amount of air between our bodies sizzled with heat. "H-hello?" My voice croaked and my eyes fluttered closed. I dropped my purse on the ground.

The line was dead. Thank God, a misdial. My grip on the phone became limp. The camera I still held by the strap dangled loosely from my other hand. I was putty.

The heat from Jack's mouth radiated through my body. I gasped as his hands slid up my sides and his fingers spread wide on my rib cage. His lips sought out my mouth. I wanted him. Right here. Right now. I just hoped no one was lurking around a corner taking digital photos of *us*.

I was going to have to go to confession for this. Maybe twice. Those Benedictine Sisters would never have me now.

"You taste like heaven," he said.

"Mmm—" I broke off when my phone rang again. My eyelids flew open.

"Hold that thought," I said, and I flipped open the phone. "Hello?"

No one spoke. Chaos echoed on the other end of the line. I tried to make out a sound. Something identifiable. Jack's mouth settled in against my neck again, but a cry that sounded like an injured animal, followed by a primal scream, assaulted my eardrums. My nerves crackled. "Who is this?" I demanded.

The connection cut out. I pushed the END button with my thumb, then pressed another button to check the phone number. I froze.

Jack's blue bedroom eyes narrowed. "What's wrong?"

Panic lodged in my throat. "My parents. Somebody was crying and screaming."

I hit REDIAL, but the line beeped incessantly with a busy signal.

I snatched my purse from the ground and fumbled inside. "I have to go." My hands shook and I couldn't grab hold of anything. "Where the hell are my keys?"

Jack grabbed my wrist and pulled me toward his car. "I'll drive."

There was no point arguing; I didn't think I could maneuver a vehicle in a straight line with the panic that was seizing my insides. With runway model balance on my wedge heels, I jumped into Jack's supercool Volvo.

He gunned it out of the parking lot and raced down H Street toward my parents' Midtown house.

10

"I'm sure they're okay," I muttered. Shooing away my anxiety, I murmured a quick prayer. All that racket was probably nothing—just a crazy old Spanish movie on TV, or something. I made myself focus on Jack. Distraction. "So spill it. What was the big"—I made air quotes—"'emergency'?"

The looming traffic light turned red. He braked hard. My seat belt locked, the strap stopping me from flying through the windshield.

I expected him to evade the question, but he didn't. "I had to see an—" He paused slightly. "—old friend."

Aha! "By old friend, you mean a girlfriend?"

He stared straight ahead, and when he spoke, his voice was tense and short. "*Old* is the operative word."

My anxiety over whatever was going on at my parents' house spilled onto Jack and his *friend*. I turned in my seat to face him. "Let me get this straight. You left without a word or a phone call to me so you could go see an old girlfriend? Are you *serious*?"

"Lola, I can't talk about it. Can you just trust me? Please?"

I wanted to, but my heart wouldn't let me. I slammed my palm against my chest, feeling a rant coming on. "You know about *my* past, Callaghan but you don't want to talk about yours. Or your present, which apparently includes some other woman. That doesn't instill a lot of trust."

The light turned green. Jack rammed his foot against the accelerator and the car jolted forward. "Where is this coming from? I'm not dating another woman, Lola. And I'm not sleeping with anyone"—he sent me a frustrated look—"including you."

That frustrated me, too, more than he knew. "If you were around more," I said, "we could do something about that."

He took my hand, the warmth from his touch reassuring. "That sounds promising."

My mouth took over again. "I just don't want your past between us, that's all."

His fingers loosened, and a second later he brought his hand

11

back to the steering wheel. "If I can deal with Sergio, you should be able to deal with Sarah."

Sarah. He dropped the name so casually. I cupped my hand at my forehead. Sweet Sarah. Oh, boy.

"When I think about what you've done with him," Jack was saying. "That he's touched . . ." His jaw pulsed. He rounded a corner, barely slowing down. "I don't *want* to know the details." He looked at me and spoke slowly and with venom. "I don't trust him, I hate that you were ever with him, and I'd be happy if I never saw him again." The look he gave me barely concealed the rage that seemed to bubble in him. "Why the hell would you want to feel those things about someone I was with?"

I decided he had a point. Ignorance could be bliss. "*Entonces bien.*"

He nodded slightly. "Great."

We drove in silence for a few blocks. Try as I might, I couldn't quite leave well enough alone. "Just for the record, though," I said, "Sergio's not a secret." I made a face. "A mistake, yes, but not a secret."

Jack cracked a wry smile. "A mistake. Boy is that an understatement."

"No need to get snide," I said. But of course he was right.

He sighed, resigned. "You're not going to drop it, are you?"

"I don't think I can."

A weighty silence filled the car. Finally, he said, "Okay, look. Here's the abbreviated version. I was with her for four years."

I sputtered. "Four years?"

"We broke up. I took the job at the *Sacramento Bee*, I moved back here, and she didn't. End of story."

Seriously abbreviated, yes. End of story, not even close. He'd dropped everything, including me, because of some emergency that—in my gut I knew—had to do with Sarah.

There was a hell of a lot more to *that* story. Four years was a *let's make plans for the future* kind of relationship, not *I'm killing time until I hook up with my best friend from high school's sister* kind of relationship. What was he not telling me?

12

We turned onto my parents' street—my street, too, since I shared the converted upstairs flat with my brother, Antonio. My emotions surged again as I stared out the window. Jack and his girlfriend shot to a compartment in the back of my mind as we slid past bumper-to-bumper cars parked along the sidewalk. Forty-second Street was *never* this busy. Something was definitely going on. My voice caught in my throat as I pushed his thigh. "Hurry up, Jack."

I held on to the door handle as he took the corner on what felt like only two wheels. He maneuvered the front end of the Volvo into the only available space—on the sidewalk at the driveway. Before he'd fully braked, I jumped out and took off. I shoved open the gate. My boxer, Salsa, stood just outside the back door. She whipped her head around and our eyes locked. One of her floppy ears perked up. She yelped and charged up to me, whimpering and pawing at my leg. Her stub of a tail wagged.

Jack was by my side. "What's going on?"

Good question. I quickly scratched Salsa's head, skirted around her, and rushed across the grass and to the patio. Yanking open the back door released a barrage of distraught and hysterical voices into the quiet yard.

I stopped short inside the kitchen. It looked like every single family member I had was here in Mami's kitchen.

And every last one of them looked like they were in agony. Jack's hand lay protectively on my lower back. I pushed through the throng of Falcón and Cruz relatives, and he never lost contact with me. Small as the gesture was, I was comforted by it.

People belted out my name. "Dolores!" Hands clawed at me. Pulled at the fabric of my dress. I yanked back, trying to keep my bodice in place.

My heart clenched when I saw my mother wrapped up in my father's arms. She sobbed and gasped for air, her hands clutching at his shirt as she wailed. He wiped at his eyes. ¡Ay, Dios mío! I knew it. Someone was dead.

Batting hands away, I quickly scanned the people, checking them

13

off on a mental list that materialized in my mind. My grandparents stood off to one side, looking lost and agonized. Aunts and uncles. Cousins. One, two, three, four, five . . . I raced through the count. Thirty-five. It looked like all my *primos* were here.

Who was missing?

"Dolores." My family was so relieved to see me, they kept repeating my name. The crowd closed, blocking my parents from my view. I smiled and nodded at my relatives as I peered through the crowd. Where were my brothers and sister? A rushing sound went through my head and I felt dizzy. Not Gracie! *Dios mío*, not Antonio. I started to shake. And Roberto? My oldest brother was away on his third tour of duty in Iraq. I murmured a quick prayer. Oh, God. Not Roberto.

"*¡Quiubo!*" I shouted above the racket. "Hey! *¡Escuchame!* What's going on?"

The clawing stopped. A collective gasp went through the room followed by complete silence. We could have heard a pinto bean bounce on my mother's spotless linoleum floor.

The crowed parted again, and Abuela gaped and crossed herself. She clutched her rosary to her lips, a flurry of Spanish prayers spewing from her mouth. She looked at me in horror, her eyes bulging. "*¡Es la fantasma de Dolores!*" she hissed.

I felt light-headed. Jack's hand pressing against my back steadied me. Had he understood? "Abuela, what are you talking about? I'm not a ghost." I took a step toward her but stopped dead in my tracks as my grandfather held his cane out toward my stomach like a sword. My grandmother started muttering Hail Marys. I gaped at them. *Son locos.*

Jack wrapped his arm around my waist. "What's going on?" he whispered.

I shrugged, braced myself, and braved another step forward. "What. Happened?" I repeated. "Where's Roberto?" The image of a flag-covered coffin floated before my eyes. I blinked it away. "Is he okay?"

"Roberto's fine," a small voice said from deep in the crowd. I peered, but I couldn't tell who'd spoken.

I looked around, still searching for Gracie, heaving a sigh when I saw her huddled in the corner held tightly in her husband's arms. Her eyes bugged just like our grandmother's, enormous tears frozen on her cheeks.

The way they all stared at me, I felt like I'd suddenly sprouted horns and a forked tail.

I turned toward my father as the dam broke and tears burst from his eyes. An anguished howl came from his core. "*Mi Dolores.*"

He squeezed his eyes shut, opening them again three seconds later. "*¡Gracias a Dios!*" he shouted when he looked at me again. He fell to his knees, clasped his hands, and rocked back and forth. "*¡Gracias a Dios!*"

Like the Red Sea parting, my relatives separated into two halves. Antonio rushed through the center, sweeping me up in his arms and nearly crushing my ribs. My brother Antonio? Affectionate? I looked around, waiting for the explosion of laughter. *Ha! We got you, Lola. Psyche!*

Over my brother's shoulder, my mother's eyes met mine. "*¡Tu vives!*" she sobbed, a handkerchief clutched to her mouth.

"Of course I'm alive." I gasped, wriggling myself out of Antonio's death grip. "Will somebody tell me what's going on? *Por favor*," I added sternly.

Mami opened her mouth and made a gurgling sound. The color drained from her face like water spiraling out of a sink. Her eyes rolled back and her jaw hung open. I rushed forward, but her legs gave way before I reached her. She went down with a thunk like a sack of wet *masa*.

"Mami! *¿Qué está pasando?*" I crouched next to her, her hip-length crocheted white vest fanned out around her. Out cold.

Antonio appeared at her side with a cup of water. He waved a paper plate in front of Mami's face while I flicked beads of liquid onto her cheeks. The whispering voices around me turned into white noise as I waited for her to wake up.

It felt like an eternity, but finally her eyelids fluttered open. The whites were bloodshot, her pupils glazed and vacant. Antonio slid his arm under her shoulders and grunted as he hauled her upright.

I held the cup of water for her to sip, but she shook her head, knocking it away. The water splashed over me, soaking my thin dress. "I called your phone just to hear your voice again, *pero* I"—she fanned her face with her hand—"I cannot believe you are standing here."

No one spoke as Antonio and Papi settled her in a chair at the kitchen table. Abuela was still muttering prayers, and everyone else lined up to embrace me and welcome me back to the land of the living. Which I hadn't known I'd apparently left for a while. I knew all the cars and hysteria had meant *someone* was dead. But since I was still breathing, it hadn't occurred to me that *I* was the corpse.

"*No entiendo*," I finally managed to say between my family's tears and hugs.

My father swiped away a tear from his ruddy cheek. "It was on the news, *mi'ja*. They said you were"—he sucked in a breath and whispered hoarsely—"*muerta*."

I spat out a shaky laugh. "That's crazy. Why would they say that?"

"They said you had a—" Papi broke off as he held me by the shoulder with one hand and examined my head. "*¿Cómo se dice?* A fatal injury to the head." His lip rolled up. "*Sola en un callejón*," he muttered.

I was dumbstruck. Dead? Alone in an alley? "Are you sure they said *my* name?" I spun around to see everyone in the room nodding. My gaze zeroed in on Jack's frowning, suddenly pale face. He'd backed against the laundry room door, his arms folded over his chest, his jaw tight.

"Dolores," Tía Marina said. "*¡Mi ahijada!*"

Sure. Now that I was back from the dead, I was her goddaughter.

Usually I was "the bad influence" on her daughter, Chely. Forget that I was a glowing example of a confident, independent woman who had a fabulous career. Chely wanted to grow up and do something daring and adventurous with her life—just like me. I was so proud of her.

Tía Marina maneuvered next to my father, wrapping her arms around us both. Chely wailed, her high-pitched cry like a siren.

"They said you were dead," my cousin Zac said. I'd never seen him look dumbfounded before. Not a pretty sight on a five-foot-nine-inch man with sun-scorched skin and tired eyes.

"It's obviously some other Dolores Cruz," his wife, Lucy, bellowed. Then she wrapped me up in a bear hug.

Wooziness washed over me—too much shock for one day. I reached for the counter to steady myself.

"Give her some space," Antonio instructed as he pushed people away.

"Tell me exactly what they said," I demanded. I swung my head around, searching for someone—anyone—to give me answers.

Chely, my fifteen-year-old fashionista niece, stumbled to the front of the Falcón–Cruz family. In her Old Navy T-shirt and low-rise pants, she could easily transition from the grief-fest to the mall. Her wailing had subsided to sniffles. She held out a tentative hand, acting as though her fingers might pass right through my arm, and she touched me. Then, apparently convinced that I wasn't a ghost, she grabbed my hand and pulled me into the front room. She nodded to her brother Miguel. He picked up the TV remote and pressed a series of buttons. "It's on the news," Chely said.

Ah. No day was complete for my father until he'd watched every second of the news. Problem was, he was usually at the restaurant when the broadcast came on. But the DVR had changed all that. Antonio had set up a series recording for our parents which meant the report of my death on the local news was saved on the cable box.

The television screen blinked and came to life. The chattering voices behind me grew silent as a perfectly coiffed anchorwoman

17

delivered her news briefs in an unemotional tone. A chill radiated through my body when she got to my story. "Local private investigator Dolores Cruz," she said, "was found dead in an alley behind the old Florin Mall. Cruz, a Sacramento native, was the daughter of Mexican immigrants who own a popular local eatery called Abuelita's. At this time, no motive has been determined. Cruz, who started as an intern at PI firm Camacho and Associates, was a licensed investigator. Police are looking into the death."

Miquel stopped the DVR, and like pack animals, we all drifted back into the kitchen. Chely clung to my arm, her lips quivering. "It was y-you." She started sobbing again. "Y-you were d-dead."

"It was a mistake, Chely. I'm here." I wrapped my arms around her and rubbed her back. Her breathing steadied and her crying stopped. A minute later, I pushed her back and held her by the shoulders. "I'm right here. Okay?"

She ran the back of her hand under her nose and nodded.

"*Estoy bien*," I repeated. Letting her go, I straightened my still-damp dress, taking time to organize my thoughts. "I need to call Manny," I said after a minute.

Jack was next to me in a flash. "The hell you do."

"He *knows* people." The PI in me had kicked in. I had to get to the bottom of this.

Jack clutched the back of my arm protectively. "Call the police. They need to know someone else is dead . . . that it's not you."

My grandmother crossed herself again, taking a step forward and laying a shaky hand on my arm.

"*¡Yo no soy un fantasma, Abuela!*" God, couldn't she tell I wasn't wispy and ghostlike? I grabbed hold of her hands and pressed them against my cheeks. "See? Flesh and blood."

She let out an unearthly moan and stepped back, swatting me with her rosary. "*¿Por qué eres un detective?*" She dropped her voice to a graveyard whisper. "You will die."

My blood ran cold, as much from her words as from the fact that

18

my grandmother had spoken in English. I couldn't remember the last time *that* had happened.

Jack tightened his grip on me. "Listen to her, Lola."

I turned on him. "Oh no. Not you, too."

His jaw pulsed. "You're not thinking clearly."

I shrugged my arm free. "Don't be ridiculous. I'm not dead! This doesn't have anything to do with me."

"Private investigator? Daughter of Mexican immigrants?" Jack grimaced. "Maybe someone wants you dead. Have you thought about *that?*"

I blinked. "Okay, Mr. Newspaper Reporter. Who'd want me dead?" I came up with possible answers in my head. Had I cut someone off on the Capital Freeway? A little road rage? Could Mrs. Zimmerman and the überyoga guy be on to me?

"Any number of people you've probably crossed during investigations."

The front door slammed shut and a baby cried.

Another mourner. My focus remained on Jack. "I'm telling you, it's a mistake—"

"Christ. Lola. You're alive!"

My mouth snapped shut and my body jerked—almost in a convulsion. I recognized that voice.

Jack's expression turned to stone. His words from earlier came back to me. *I'd be happy if I never see him again.* Looks like he recognized the voice, too, and he wasn't happy about it.

Sergio Garcia. Could this night get any worse?

19

Chapter 2

It had been three years since I'd laid eyes on Sergio. I turned slowly to face him. The man had gone downhill. Unshaven. Half a cup of gel slicking back his dark brown hair. A ribbed wife-beater under an unbuttoned gray guayabera. I cringed inside. God, what had happened to him? He'd been *muy caliente* once upon a time.

My emotions somersaulted, a flood of anger crashing over me. "What are you doing here?" I breathed out, barely containing my animosity. "This is a private memorial."

He ignored me, gripping my shoulders and pulling me into a stifling hug. The smell of his Aqua Velva clouded my nostrils and my brain. "I can't believe you're alive!"

I clawed myself free from Sergio and gritted my teeth. A layer of sticky hair gel was smeared across my cheek. I wiped it away with the back of my hand, grimacing. "What do you want?"

Again, he ignored me. He turned around and spoke to the guy who trailed behind him with a young child, no more than a year or so, on his hip. "*Mira, Pancho.* Lola's alive!"

Pancho gave a pained nod and quickly melted back into the crowd. My entire family was dead silent and watched us like we were in a live *telenovela*.

Sergio's eyes scraped over me. I barely resisted slapping him and grabbing his cheeks to force his gaze on my face instead of my body. "I heard the news," he started.

"It was a mistake." I threw my hands out wide. "See? I still have a heartbeat."

From the corner of my eye, I could see Jack looking strained with fury. If he'd had a sack of poisoned darts, he'd be throwing them, one by one, straight at Sergio's heart.

Sergio leaned close to me and said, "You left a teddy behind at my apartment. Why don't you come by and pick it up sometime?"

The air in the room changed. "Son of a bitch," Jack said with a hiss. His hands balled into fists.

Sergio smirked and dropped his voice to a for-my-ears-only whisper. "I have a box of your stuff, *también*." He stretched his arm around my waist. "We could relive old times, if you know what I mean."

I knocked his arm away. I knew *exactly* what he meant, and it would be a cold day in hell before I ever did *that* again with him. "*Esto se acabó*, Sergio. There are no old times to relive. It's been over between—"

"The teddy's right next to your rosary where they've been for—"

Rosary? And just like that, Sergio's voice became a hollow echo somewhere in the back of my mind. Was he talking about the prayer beads my father's mother had given me before she died? The ones I thought I'd lost years ago? I snarled at the mere thought of Sergio even touching something so sentimental to me. But right now I had my death to deal with. I'd have to get the rosary another time. "You have to go. *Ahorita*."

His mouth sank into a frown. "I just came to express my consolations—"

"Condolences," I corrected automatically.

"Condolences," he said. "*Es la verdad*. I came to pay my respects."

I studied Sergio's thick face. I was pretty sure he didn't know the meaning of truth. "*¡Quítate!*" I said.

He threw his hands up. "I still care about you. Is that a crime?"

21

"Get out," Jack said with barely contained restraint just as Antonio moved in next to Sergio.

I lowered my voice and jabbed my finger at his chest. "You are a thief. You stole from my parents," I hissed so only he could hear. "How dare you come here and act like you care about me. Or any of us." I clamped my hand on his arm and steered him toward the door. *"Quítate. ¡Ándale!"*

"You're kicking out a grieving friend?" Sergio looked hurt, but I thought I detected a hint of anger in his voice.

Jack took a menacing step toward him. "You heard her. Get the hell out."

I was a black belt in kung fu, Jack was a pissed-off sort-of boyfriend, and Antonio was a protective older brother. Against us, Sergio didn't stand a chance. We closed in on him.

I notched my fingers down in a wave. *"Chao,* Sergio."

A sudden hush fell over the house. My family stood like a roomful of statues, their mouths agog. Hospitality was the cornerstone of my mother's existence. She'd never close the door on a guest. The room tensed as my mother sniffed up her strength, patted down her dark housedress, and marched slowly toward us.

Come on, Mami. I prayed she wasn't going to revert to her early mothering tactics and grab me by the ear for my disrespect to a guest.

She stopped less than a foot from Sergio and locked her eyes on his. "You heard *mi hija.* You are not welcome here, *muchacho.*"

My *tías* gasped. "What did she say?" one of them whispered. *"¿Qué dices?"*

"She is turning him out," another answered.

I stood up taller, bolstered by Mami's support. My father straightened his slightly hunched shoulders and crossed his leathery arms over his chest. Antonio flanked my other side, next to Jack. *¡Viva familia!*

One by one, the people who were crammed into my parents' house edged toward Sergio.

Pancho inched toward the front door. *"Vámonos,* dude. Let's go."

22

"Just wait a minute, eh?" Sergio turned on me, his voice harsh. "What did you tell them?"

I tucked a loose strand of hair behind my ear. "*Solamente la pura verdad.*"

Sergio's eyes blazed, but Jack grabbed his arm. "Get the hell out of here, Garcia."

"You with this loser now, Lola?" Sergio pulled away from Jack and jutted his face next to mine, hissing, "He'll dump you faster than he can screw you. He's just like his old man."

A pained guttural sound came from Jack. I thought I saw his shirt buttons pull as his chest broadened, Hulk-style. I touched his shoulder to calm him down. The last thing we needed was a brawl. With a scowl, Sergio turned and headed to the door, grabbing his buddy's arm on the way and dragging Pancho and the baby out. He threw me a disdainful glance before slamming the door.

Jack had regained his composure—mostly. He rested his hand on my lower back, but I could sense the tension that oozed from every one of his pores. "I can't believe you were ever with that asshole," he muttered.

That made two of us. And I didn't want to think about him anymore. I hugged my parents, then whispered to Gracie, "I'm going to call Manny. Stay with them."

Chely charged toward me, hanging on to me like a scared child. "Don't go!" A hundred eyeballs stared at us.

Gracie circled her arms around us. "It's okay, Chely. Lola's okay."

I ran my hand through my cousin's hair before extracting myself from the hug and heading toward the laundry room door.

Jack fell into step beside me just as Abuelo angled his cane at me with a shaky hand. "*No mas con el pinche cabrón cholo de Sergio.*" He slowly moved his cane so it pointed at Jack. "*Quédate con el güero,*" he said in his whispery, old-time mobster voice.

I opened my mouth to tell Abuelo that I wasn't *with* Sergio and that I'd take Jack any day of the week, but Mami spoke before I had a chance. "*¡Cállate, Papá!*"

As if on cue, there was another collective sucking in of breath. Abuelo snapped his mouth shut. Only his daughter could tell him to hold his tongue and live to see another day.

He gave her a defiant look and then turned his blazing eyes back to me, mumbling, "*Escuchame. El güero te va a hacer feliz.*"

If Abuelo were the Godfather, he'd be kissing both of Jack's cheeks, welcoming him into the family. I wasn't stupid. He had his agenda, and I knew just what it was. He was angling for more grand-children, and suddenly Jack, who'd defended me, was an excellent prospect.

My grandfather hobbled out of the room. Abuela followed him, still praying on her rosary as she looked over her shoulder at me. "*Fantasma,*" she muttered. "*¡Fantasssma!*"

"I am not a ghost!" I yelled after her. My hands shook as I dug in my purse and pulled out my cell phone. Damn. It was after eleven, too late to call Manny. What if he'd decided to hook up with his *mujer* after he'd left me? I couldn't fathom the idea of interrupting him and Isabel in the throes of passion.

I dialed the office instead. There was nothing he could do tonight anyway. His don't-mess-with-me voice came on the recorded message saying, "You've reached Camacho and Associates Private Investigation. Leave a message, and your call will be returned." The machine beeped.

I cleared my throat. "Manny, it's Dolores." When Jack scowled, I turned my back to him. "You may have seen the news tonight. I'm calling to let you know it wasn't me and that I'm fine." I snapped the phone shut and dropped it back into my purse.

I turned to my family. They stared at me expectantly. Time for a speech? I opened my mouth, but meaningful words were beyond me. "*Gracias por venir.*" Oh, I was good. Thanks for coming. Those were deep words of wisdom.

My mother wrapped her arm around me. "My daughter is alive!" she announced with dramatic flair. "We will celebrate Sunday *después de la Misa.*"

Suddenly in a flurry, my aunts circled around my mother to plan the fiesta. Just as quickly, Jack grabbed my arm and pulled me into the laundry room. He closed the door to the Falcón–Cruz mob and turned, his face grim, any sign of playful dimples long gone. "This is insane."

All I could do was nod. Now that I was out of the limelight, I felt myself crashing. The heat from his touch lingered on my skin. My feet wobbled in my high-heeled sandals, and I leaned against the washing machine for support.

I draped my arms around his neck, and he wrapped me up in a hug. Home. He felt like home—warm, safe, and holding me like he'd never let me go. I melted into him. "Thank God it wasn't you," he said softly.

A shiver swept up my spine. "She had my name. My identity," I muttered. "Who *was* she?"

Of course, he couldn't answer me. A minute later, I felt his body tense. "Why'd you call Camacho?" he asked suddenly, and just like that, the moment froze, our molten bodies turning to ice.

"He's my boss. I didn't want him to think I was dead."

"It couldn't have waited until morning?"

I let my arms drop to my sides, and he stepped back. "No, it couldn't. Wouldn't you have wanted me to call *you*? Let you know I wasn't dead?"

"I've known you since grade school." He frowned at me. "I think I warrant more priority than Camacho."

I leveled my gaze at him. "Like I warranted a phone call from you when you left on your"—I made air quotes again—"'emergency'?"

He chose to ignore my sarcasm. "And Garcia? Christ, Lola. You need some female friends. Call Coco. Or Reilly."

Sergio was so *not* worth fighting about. I slung my purse over my shoulder. "It's not like I invited him. He thought I was dead."

He caught my arm. "He's full of shit, you know."

My hand covered his, my voice soft. Reassuring. "I know." And deep down, I did. Jack had recently told me in no uncertain terms that he'd never cheat on the woman he loved. His father, on the other hand, had left his mother—and his children—for another

25

woman. Maybe some men just couldn't help it. How strong did you have to be to resist temptation? Or the past?

Jack raked his hands through his hair and turned away from me. "Son of a bitch."

An alcohol-like haze settled on my brain. My thoughts became fuzzy and jumbled. I wanted to go to my room in the flat upstairs and curl up in my bed. Jack would be by my side. I'd confess all my secrets, if he'd confess his.

I shook the vision away. There was a Dolores Cruz dead in an alley. Scratch that. She was probably in the morgue by now. I gathered up my strength and thought about what I had to do. "Forget about Sergio," I said to Jack's back. "I need to go to the police station. Let them know it's not my body they found."

He turned back to me, still looking frustrated. "I'm going with you."

Emergencies aside, Jack was a standup guy. He might not be willing to tell me all his secrets, but I knew he'd be a sounding board for me as I tried to figure out what to do next. Because the only thing I could think about was figuring out why the dead woman had my name, but I had no idea where to start. "Okay."

He guided me toward the door, a good idea, since I was still shaking in my wedges.

A sudden pounding echoed the thumping of my pulse in my temples. "Lola," Antonio called just as I opened the laundry room door. He took a step back. "Hey," he said.

"Hey," Jack replied.

Antonio looked at me, his concern touching. I knew I'd better enjoy it while it lasted. He'd be back to normal tomorrow. "You okay?" he asked.

"Fine. We're going to the police station."

"No need," he said. "There's a detective here."

Jack and I looked at each other. Well, wasn't that convenient? The police had come to me.

Chapter 3

A man in a rumpled suit stood on the small tiled area just inside the front door. His dome-wrap looked particularly haphazard, his skin extra pasty, and from his scowl, I concluded he was in a really bad mood. Detective Seavers.

"So you really are alive." His voice oozed gruffness.

"Alive and kicking." The detective had a knack for stating the obvious. He was a friend of Manny Camacho's, and we'd crossed paths once or twice. He'd been less than thrilled with how things played out with my last case, and it didn't look like his attitude toward me had improved.

Seavers droned on. "I spoke with the detective in charge when I heard the victim ID. Once I read the description, I knew it wasn't you."

He licked his hand and ran his damp palm over his thin hair. "She had a driver's license that said she was Dolores Cruz. Her photo, your name and address."

A vise clenched my heart. Hearing the detective say it aloud made it so much more real. Someone had stolen my identity. "How? Why?"

"Good questions," he said, his voice tinged with irritation. "Immigration issue, perhaps. Have you shared your personal information with anyone lately?"

My blood boiled at the veiled accusation. "Excuse me? You think I'm helping an illegal?"

He looked over my shoulder, his eyes scanning the people in the house. I turned to see my family staring back, once again completely enraptured as the melodrama of my life unfolded before them. Subtlety was not their strong suit.

As I met my grandmother's eyes, she reached a shaky hand out toward me. *"Fantaaaasmaaaa,"* she moaned.

"Ay, caramba," I muttered. Then I spoke up. "I am not a ghost!"

The detective leaned toward me and said in his throaty cop voice, "Let's step outside, Ms. Cruz."

Good idea. Then I could chew the man out for asking if I had anything to do with my own death. He had some nerve! Before I opened my mouth, I reminded myself that he was only doing his job. I gave my parents a half wave, then stepped outside. Jack followed before the detective could close the door on him.

Seavers gave him a once-over followed by a lift of one heavy caterpillar eyebrow. "Callaghan, right?"

"Right."

"Camacho said you flew solo," he said to me. To Jack, he said, "You always around, or what?"

"Yeah," Jack said tightly as I muttered, "Not always."

"Ah." The undertones of the word made it seem as if Seavers understood everything perfectly. There was a wink in his voice. "So you're friends . . ." He trailed off, but the *with benefits* was implied.

Not yet! I wanted to scream, *but it's not for lack of trying!*

"Yeah, good friends." Jack glanced at me, and I forced my eyes to be steady. His voice didn't *sound* all that friendly at the moment.

Seavers's forehead gleamed under the porch light. He wiped a bead of sweat away with a torn tissue that he shoved into his coat pocket. Game time was over. "Since you're not dead," he said to me, "we're left with somewhat of a hole in our investigation. Who *is* dead, and why did she have your name?"

My thoughts exactly. "I did not give anyone permission to use it," I said, responding to his earlier question.

Jack crossed his arms over his chest. My fingers itched to run through his oak-colored hair and take comfort from his warmth. "What are you going to do about it?" he asked the detective.

I nudged in front of Jack. This was *my* gig, and I could ask the questions. "You have no idea who she is?"

Seavers cocked a bushy eyebrow. "We'll do an autopsy. Check fingerprints and DNA. Dental if we have to. We'll ID her, but it may take a while. I'll say it again, though." He eyed me suspiciously. "It would go a lot faster if you have a bone to throw me. Did you give someone permission to use your name, Ms. Cruz?"

¡¿Otra vez?! Was this guy serious? "For the second time, no!"

Reaching into his coat pocket, he pulled out a snapshot of the dead woman, handing it to me with his nail-bitten fingers.

I gulped as I took it, thinking fresh air in my lungs might ward off the nausea that was bubbling in my stomach. Being a PI didn't mean I was immune to the trauma of seeing dead people. Especially one named Dolores Cruz with my address on her ID and a fatal blow to the head.

I took the photo. And blinked. The woman looked nothing like me. I had brown hair, olive skin, and green eyes. The dead woman's black hair was kinky and created a jagged outline around her pale face. A wet mass seemed to mat her hair down on one side.

I patted my head. No blood. Just straight, full hair that fell several inches past my shoulders. God, was I lucky.

I looked at the picture again. The woman's chubby cheek was smeared red. My red cheeks were artificially enhanced with MAC bronzer, not blood. I gulped down another lungful of air. This woman was dead. Hysteria bubbled toward my brain. Will the real Slim Shady, er, Dolores Cruz, please stand up?

I could feel Detective Seavers's scrutiny. Jack wrapped his arm around me, his hand squeezing my shoulder, and the hysteria subsided. I shook my head and handed the picture back. "I've never seen her. How would she have gotten a copy of my driver's license?"

Seavers pocketed the picture. "It's not a copy. It's her photograph on the license." He cleared his throat. "If she didn't get the particulars she needed from you to get a duplicate made . . ."

He left the sentence hanging, like I'd miraculously fill in the blank. Wishful thinking, buddy. I didn't have the foggiest idea who this woman was or where she'd gotten her information.

"Identity theft is still the fastest-growing crime in America," Seavers finally said. "I'll give you a Web site you can refer to for help." He ran his fingers over his unibrow. "If that's what's going on here, then you'll need to take care of your accounts. Check the activity. Post a fraud alert on your credit report. The usual."

I fought the spine-tingling chill that wound through my body. A woman had stolen my identity, and now she was dead. No matter how I looked at it, this situation was anything but usual.

It was well after 1:00 A.M. by the time Jack led me upstairs to my flat. We sat at the kitchen table across from Antonio. Jack sipped a bottle of beer and watched me. No smile. No bedroom eyes. He'd been all over me in front of Camacho's, and had offered me true support since we'd gotten back to my parents' house. Now, *nada*. Apparently the dead woman had zapped his libido.

"Unbelievable," my brother said as I filled him in on the conversation with Detective Seavers.

"That's an understatement." After I'd narrowly avoided death during my last case, one question was bugging me: Was I the one who was supposed to be in the morgue right now?

I considered the other possibility—that the dead woman had taken on a new identity to hide from something. Or someone. If that was the case, the plan had bombed big-time.

I couldn't do anything until morning, so I caught Jack's eye and leaned forward. The wispy fabric of my dress slipped off my shoulder.

Maybe he'd walk me to my room. Talking through a case usually gave me clarity, and talking through it with Jack might give me the added benefit of comfort. Which, at the moment, I really wanted.

His gaze flicked to the bare skin of my shoulder, but he went back to his conversation with Antonio, cataloging the dangers of my job. Which, if I thought about it, was very sweet. And protective.

I changed tactics, waggled my eyebrows at Antonio, and jerked my head to the side, trying to signal to him to leave.

Finally, Mr. Subtlety looked at me and stopped midsentence. "Something in your eye, *hermana?*"

With my palms flat on the table, I blinked at him. "No, *hermano.* There's not."

Antonio nodded. "You're on overload. You should go to bed."

Argh! My brother was Mr. Rico Suave. Couldn't he figure out that I wanted alone time with Jack?

I thought about speaking in Spanish, but Jack had a pretty good recollection of his high school foreign language. Finally, I just gave up. "I'm going to sleep," I announced to the room at large.

Salsa immediately perked up from her corner, but it was Jack's eyes, locked with mine, that I focused on. The room—and my sleepiness—melted away for a moment. I looked longingly at him, willing him to sweep me into his arms and carry me off. "Good night." Breathy voice. Very alluring. Good job, Lola.

I waited, sure he'd pick up the signals, but he didn't budge. Damn. Maybe he'd decided I was too high maintenance. My shoulders sagged. I couldn't blame him. "*Hasta luego*, Callaghan," I said. "*Te veo mas tarde.*"

I slowly stood, gave a little wave, and walked through to the living room. Once I was out of sight, I leaned against the wall and closed my eyes. Jack's face floated in the darkness behind my eyelids. A second later, he'd morphed into the dead woman from the picture Seavers had shown me.

What a mess of a night. And to top it off, I'd never even done the notes or uploaded the photographs for the Zimmerman case.

A low, rumbling voice interrupted my thoughts. "You okay?"

My eyes flew open. Jack leaned against the wall next to me. I hadn't even heard his approach. Some PI I was. "Of course I'm okay."

I heard a soft click. The back door closing. So Antonio *did* have a sixth sense of when to skedaddle, bless his heart. Longing settled in the pit of my stomach. Alone with Jack. No one to interrupt us.

It wasn't the romantic buildup I'd anticipated—especially when I forced myself to remember his recent disappearing act—but part of me didn't care. There was something innate in Jack that made me feel safe and secure. He was like an old blanket that you just couldn't go to sleep without. What I wanted with him went far beyond the orgasms my body ached for.

Jack cocked his head and grinned. "What's going through that wicked mind of yours?"

If he only knew. The R word that sent men screaming from a room. Relationship. I smiled and shrugged. "*Nada.*"

He moved a little closer, and his voice took on a chastising tone. "There's never *nothing* going through your mind. You, Cruz, are a schemer and a thinker. And," he added, "you're doing that on purpose. You know what it does to me."

My grin was innocent . . . though I knew exactly what he was talking about. "*¿Qué?*"

"Like I said, schemer. *Hablando español.*"

He had me dead to rights. I batted my eyelashes and gave him a hint of my best seductress smile. "*Te quiero volver loco.*"

He trailed his fingertips along my arm, and *my* knees went weak. "Is that what you want?" Either he'd been brushing up on his Spanish or he'd read between the lines.

I swallowed. "It's crossed my mind." Like a thousand and one times.

His azure eyes seemed fathomless. "It's crossed my mind, too. Every day for the last ten years or so."

Give or take the four years he'd spent in a relationship with Sarah. And minus the last seven days when he'd disappeared.

With his shoulder still against the wall, his fingertips lightly

32

touched my outer thigh. I held my breath. The blood rushed from my head downward. All it took was that smoldering look and his sensual touch, and the tables had turned. He was in control, and I was putty in his hands.

He moved closer to me, casually gathering up the fabric of my dress with his hand. "Have I told you how amazing you look?" His bedroom voice was like a vacuum sucking me in. "You need to start a collection of dresses to wear just for me." He tugged on the fabric. "This one's top of the list."

I swallowed, trying to focus on his eyes, his mouth, anything but the feel of his knuckles pressed against the flesh of my thigh. The warmth of his skin against mine was almost enough to send me into an orgasm right here and now. "This old thing?" I said with a choked laugh.

While his left hand still dangerously caressed my thigh, he lifted his right hand to the bodice of my dress. "It's dangerous. *You're* dangerous," he amended, and then he tucked his fingers under the fabric and ran them down the V of my neckline. Goose bumps popped up on my flesh as the backs of his fingers followed the curve of my breast.

My heart beat faster, and I leaned the back of my head against the wall, my eyes closing to half-mast. "I'll remember that. Maybe a nun's habit . . ."

"Mmm. That might do the trick. . . ." He trailed off as his open hand slid over my breast. I held my breath as his palm brushed torturously over my suddenly perky nipple. "Then again," he breathed, "it doesn't matter what you wear. Or what you do. Who your ex-boyfriends are. I just want to be with you."

Bésame, I willed. I wanted to forget about the night, the dead woman, how tired I was. I wanted to forget about everything except Jack's lips on mine.

He shoved off the wall and moved in front of me. With his hands on the sides of my face, his fingers spread through my hair. I gave him credit. He was getting good at this telepathy thing. And equally good at driving me wild. He gave as good as he got.

33

Better, even.

I was five-six, but even with heels on, I had to stretch to make our lips meet. But stretch I did, by God. His body pressed against me. "Does this count as seeing me later?" he whispered against my lips.

So he *had* understood my Spanish. I melted inside. "Counts for me."

He worked his knee between my legs, his teeth nipping at my lower lip. I opened my mouth to him, resisting my need to drag him down to the floor that very instant.

Salsa yelped, her bark carving into my brain. My lips froze. No! This was not happening again. *No interruptions!*

But it was too late. The kitchen door slammed against the wall. Salsa charged across the linoleum, her doggy nails clipping against the floor.

Jack and I pulled apart as my boxer raced up between us. Her droopy black cheeks and hangdog eyes seemed to ask me why I'd left her outside.

Hijo de su madre. I batted Salsa out of the way and lifted my chin to Jack. "Where were we?"

"Lola?" I heard my name at the same time I heard footsteps in the kitchen. A figure rounded the corner from the living room to the hallway, and my shoulders slumped. Chely. No, no, no!

Jack backed up until he was leaning against the wall across from me. His eyes were glazed and feverish. Somehow I mustered a smile for my cousin. "What're you doing here, *prima?*"

Chely had a deep, worried frown. "I can't sleep. I keep thinking about you dead in an alley—"

"Chely—"

"My dad brought me back. He said I could, like, stay with you." She eyed Jack, but quickly snapped her gaze back to me. "Is it okay? I mean, you're not, like, busy, are you? It's late, right?" She notched her head toward Jack. "He's going home, right?" She looked at him again, all needy and indignant. "Aren't you, like, going home now?"

I frowned. Her mother would have been so proud.

The forced smile on Jack's lips barely masked his frustration. "Perfect timing, Chely. I was just leaving. She's all yours."

I cursed inside—with a vengeance. I wanted so much with Jack. Wanted to talk with him, cuddle with him, launch fireworks with him. "Are you sure—?" I started, but the fear etched on Chely's face stopped me cold. "Right." I cocked my head in apology, as much for me as for him. My cousin needed me, and that was that.

He pushed off the wall and lowered his head to kiss my cheek. "Things are never easy with you, Lola."

Was there a hint of a smile in his voice, or was that my imagination? "Easy is overrated." I gave him a slow smile, heavy with anticipation. "*Hasta luego*, Callaghan."

He gave a wry grin, and I could tell he was digging the anticipation, too. "Oh, yeah. You better believe it, Cruz."

35

Chapter 4

Saturday mornings were meant for sleeping in. Long jogs along the river. Hot showers. Sponges and Ajax. They were not meant for researching identity theft. But that's exactly what I'd done for more than an hour, and the anxiety that had taken root in my body in the early-morning hours had multiplied. The damage to my credit could have been substantial if the woman who'd stolen my name hadn't died. Small consolation, since she'd be six feet under soon and *nothing* about *that* was good.

Of course, I had no idea how long she'd *had* my identity before she died, so I didn't really know the extent of the damage she might have done.

I went through the steps to protect myself, but my calls to my credit card companies led to recordings. Business hours were Monday through Friday. My hands were tied—unfortunately *not* by Jack and *not* to a bedpost.

By ten thirty, I was readying tables for lunch customers at Abuelita's. My obligation to the family restaurant quadrupled whenever we were short-staffed. Which was pretty much always.

I'd take the reprieve from the drama of my life.

Four long hours later, the lunch shift was winding down. I spent the last fifteen minutes refilling the tortilla chip warmer, topping off the hot sauce bottles on the tables, and folding red napkins into triangles for the dinner crowd.

Stripping off my apron as soon as the minute hand reached the half hour, I ran upstairs to the break room to change into my plain street clothes—jeans and a flirty yellow blouse. Nothing flashy or too sexy. Even wore one of my plainer bras. Since I had no plans to see Jack, I had no need to wear the good stuff. Nothing exciting could possibly happen in a nude bra.

I scooted through the restaurant kitchen on my way to the back parking lot. My father stood at the stainless steel counter dredging enormous stuffed green chilies in an egg batter. "See you later," I called.

"Whoa." Antonio appeared out of nowhere and stepped in front of me, effectively blocking my exit. "Where's the fire?"

I wagged my finger in his face. "Hey, you don't pay me enough to harass me about my plans. Oh, *un momento, por favor.*" I thunked my forehead with the heel of my hand. "You don't pay me at all."

"I don't have to pay you, Lola. It's your family business, too."

"No. You're the manager, and it's going to be *your* restaurant someday. I work here on an as-needed basis. Now *muevete.* I'm going to Camacho's." My boss, the superdetective ex-cop, had more connections than the Godfather himself. Surely he'd be able to come up with some dirt on the dead woman. Plus I still had the Zimmerman case to finish up.

I reached for the door, but Antonio didn't budge. He had a peculiar look on his face.

"What?" I curled up my top lip and ran my tongue over my front teeth. "Do I have some *pico* between my teeth? A piece of cilantro?"

He gave a pronounced blink and a little shake of his head. "What? No." He looked at my bared teeth. "All clear."

I frowned. The way he was studying me . . . it was like he was trying to—to memorize my face. My death was haunting me! "Tonio," I said, trying to push past him, "move."

But my brother stood in front of the door like a soldier standing guard while his buddy got it on with a military groupie. His I-almost-lost-my-sister expression vanished and was replaced by an overdone managerial one. "Did you finish clearing your tables?" he asked, his voice serious.

My eyes became slits. *"Por supuesto."*

"And the hot sauce bottles? All refilled?"

I put my hands on my hips. I could take him out right now, if I wanted to. A swift jab to the underside of his chin, he'd be down, and I'd be on my way. I exercised patience instead. "Filled, cleaned, and replaced."

"Chips all set?"

I spoke through my clenched teeth. "Yes."

"What about the napkins for tonight?"

That did it. "I'm alive, Tonio!" I tapped my hand against my arm, then my head. "See? Alive! You can't keep me hostage in the restaurant with extra waitress duties."

His shoulders slouched, but he recovered a split second later. "Hostage? Lo," he said, laying his hand on my forehead, "are you feeling okay? Maybe you should take some time off. I'm sure—" He hesitated, just barely. "Camacho'll give you a sick day."

I jerked my head back at the contempt in his voice when he said *Camacho.* Looked like Jack's feelings toward my boss were rubbing off on my brother. "Manny would give me as many sick days as I needed," I shot back. "If I was sick. Which," I added, "I'm not."

I reached for the door again, using my hip to shove Antonio out of the way this time. *"Todo está finito.* Now, I have a job to go to—one that *pays* me. Not to mention I have to find out who killed me last night. Would you please hire that new waitress you interviewed already?"

And with that, I plowed into the back parking lot, yelling over my shoulder, "And don't make a move on this one, because I'm done filling in!"

The trip to Camacho and Associates took ten minutes. It was at the tip of one side of the triangle that made up the three most prominent places in my life: the PI firm, the restaurant, and my parents' house, aka home.

I parked my car in the small lot the agency shared with Szechwan House, my all-time favorite restaurant (a fact I'd go to my grave with, since admitting that my mother's cooking came in second place was akin to sacrilege). Pushing through the door of Camacho's, I ticked my fingers against the wispy leaves of the solo artificial fern that decorated the so-called lobby. *"¿Como estás, planta?"*

Sadly, my conversation with it didn't perk up the dreary fake foliage.

I walked through the open doorway at the end of the wall and entered the main conference room. It wasn't much to speak of. There was a long rectangular table, a desk and computer off in one corner, filing cabinets, and two computers on a long table against the wall for the associates to use.

Reilly, the part-time secretary, usually worked ten to four, Mondays through Fridays. Since it was Saturday, I expected her to be absent from her post in the corner.

She was. I was disappointed. I could have used a laugh, and Reilly, with her flashy wardrobe and Crayola-colored hair, was usually good for one. We were kindred spirits, both overly enthusiastic, just about different things. I was obsessed with my job, while Reilly was obsessed with J.Lo and had spent a fair amount of time crushing on my brother, Antonio. Her Friday-night activities made me wonder if she was finally over him.

I'd seen Manny's truck in the parking lot, so I knew my boss was here. I headed straight for his office, poised my knuckles to knock, but stopped short. I heard the mumbled tones of two voices. Oooh, for once I might get some office *chisme* before Reilly, the gossip queen.

With my ear pressed up against the door, I listened. Could Manny be with his *Tomb Raider* girlfriend? His ex-wife? Or, the horror, with Sadie in an on-again moment of their on-again/off-again office tryst?

I heard a familiar laugh. Then I heard the even more familiar Spanglish. Spanglish that only one person I knew could pull off.

I backed away, my jaw slack. Oh, wow! It couldn't be. But it was! The person in there with Manny was . . . Reilly? And she was *laughing*?

But that made absolutely no sense. I reasoned with myself: For one, Manny Camacho scared the bejesus out of Reilly. It was all his animal magnetism and the rogue warrior vibe he gave off. Reilly was not the kind of girl who responded to rogue warrior.

Was she?

I thought about that. She *had* been desperate to go on a date with Antonio, and he was pretty rogue—though he was a lover, not a fighter. My brother had stepped up to the challenge. He'd gone salsa dancing with her, and had even gone out for middle-of-the-night waffles. Poor Antonio. It might be a devastating blow to his ego when he learned that the woman who worshipped him for so long had moved on.

Reilly laughed again from behind the closed door, and my phone call to her the night before came back to me. She was one of my best friends, and she was holding out on me. Before I could figure out how I felt about *that*, Manny's door flew open.

"Seven o'clock, your house," Reilly said. She practically skipped into the conference room, gum smacking, a satisfied grin on her face. "See you then—" Her words froze on her lips when she saw me. She blew a bubble through a nervous smile.

I threw my arms up and yelled, "Surprise!"

The bubble popped, leaving lime green gum specks stuck to her lips.

"Lola! I was going to call you." She shot a cloak-and-dagger glance at Manny. He didn't budge from his chair in his office. Reilly dragged her teeth across her bottom lip, scraping off the last of the gum; then she finally flung her arms around me in a bear hug. "*El bosso*—no, no, I know that's not right," she said. "Oh, I can't remember! How do you say it?"

Every day was Spanish 101 with Reilly. "*El jefe.*"

"Right! *El jefe* just told me what happened. I don't know what I'd do if you were *really* dead! You should have called me. I can't believe

I didn't see the news, but I'm glad I didn't. I would have been devastated if I'd heard you were dead on a news broadcast."

Considering she'd just made plans to meet Manny at his house, I could think of a thing or two that might have eased her sorrow. "Me, either," I said with a frown. "What's going on?"

"What do you mean what's going on? Nothing's going on!" Her voice rose an octave. "Why do you ask?"

She let go of me and ran her fingers across her scalp. Her vibrant red hair—a shade I hadn't seen on her before—made her skin look paler. Or maybe it was just that the color had drained from her face because there most definitely *was* something going on. I dropped it, though. She couldn't fess up with Manny watching.

"Do they know who it is?" she asked.

"Who?"

"You know, do they know who the dead woman is? She had your name?" Red splotches appeared on her cheeks. "How'd she do that? Do they know who she is?"

I shifted my thoughts away from Reilly's life and back to mine. "Not yet." At least not that I'd heard.

"Oh."

We seemed to run out of things to say—something that *never* happened with Reilly. But whatever was going on between her and Manny was like a ginormous white elephant between us. Chitchat wasn't in the cards. She snapped her gum. "Gotta run!" she said suddenly. And the next thing I knew, I was watching her round the corner to the little lobby and then—poof!—she was gone.

I was left staring at the spot where Reilly had been standing. What in the world had just happened? Slowly, I turned around to face Manny's office.

He sat behind his massive desk, one long leg loosely folded over the other, a yellow legal pad perched on his knee. He looked at me with his black hawklike eyes, and said, as if nothing weird had just happened, "Holding up?"

He was not a sparkling conversationalist. Drop-dead gorgeous in a macho *I'll tie you to the bedpost and do what I want with you* kind of way? Oh, yeah. Let's snuggle and talk afterwards? Not even close.

I focused in on my mission. What Manny lacked in warmth, he more than made up for in competence. His past as a police detective gave him instant credibility, and he always seemed to have a favor to collect on. He was my mentor, had a girlfriend who looked like a model, had taken to calling me nicknames, taunted me with threats of a sparring match, and was pretty much despised by Jack Callaghan. And apparently on much closer terms with Reilly than I would ever have suspected. My life was actually better than one of my parents' favorite *telenovelas*.

I nodded. "*Sí.*" We also both spoke Spanish, something that grated on associate Sadie Metcalf's nerves to no end. But I was a licensed private investigator and full-fledged member of the team. Sadie had no choice but to deal with me. "I'm holding up fine."

"Thanks for the phone call."

"I didn't want anyone to worry."

"I assume you want to investigate this yourself?" he asked.

Smart man. He'd assumed correctly. "I'm wrapping up the Zimmerman case," I said, "but I have to know if I was actually the intended victim. If I was—"

"Then you're still in danger," he finished. A second later he said, "Without a case, Dolores, I can't pay you."

"What else is new?" I muttered. Two jobs with no pay. This is why I still live above my parents'. I needed to work fast, or I'd be living off rice and beans.

Oh, wait. I already *did* live off rice and beans. And anything else I could get my hands on at Abuelita's. Working for free at the restaurant meant my appetite wouldn't suffer. Working for free at Camacho's meant a lack of resources. And those resources supported my MAC products and undergarment wardrobe. Both were vital to my life.

"No pay. I understand," I said to him.

He gave a single nod—we were *simpatico*—then moved on. "I called Seavers."

I bristled at the mention of the detective, but he and Manny went way back. It was one of those friendships that I just couldn't explain. "Does he have anything new?" I asked.

"Police got an anonymous call IDing the vic. They think her name is Rosie Gonzales."

I scribbled the dead woman's name in my notebook, adding her vitals as Manny gave them to me. Five feet three inches tall, 143 pounds, shoulder-length brown hair. It wasn't much to go on. "Cause of death?"

"Blunt-force trauma. Looks like her head met the side of a Dumpster."

I cringed. That explained the dark patch in her hair. "Anything else?" I asked.

"Not yet." Manny put his legal pad down on the desk and uncrossed his leg. He kept his disconcerting gaze steady on me. "I'll see what else I can find out. Dig a little, *poderosa*."

I stifled the awkwardness that rumbled through me from the nickname. "*Gracias*. I will," I said, and I headed back to the conference room.

Manny called after me. "*Cuidado*."

Was he kidding? *Careful* was going to be my middle name.

First things first. I uploaded the photos of Mrs. Zimmerman and her yoga instructor onto the computer. Next, I documented my billable hours and e-mailed a copy to Manny. Finally, I phoned Mr. Zimmerman to discuss my findings.

"I'm so sorry, Mr. Zimmerman," I said, and I truly was. The man loved his wife, and she'd betrayed him.

"How could she?"

He wasn't really seeking answers from me. A good thing, since I didn't have any for him. Trust, something I valued above all else, was so easily destroyed. Jack and I hadn't established full-on trust yet, and the road to get there seemed paved with pretty big rocks.

I told Mr. Zimmerman that I'd drop the photos by his office on Monday, and hung up.

Moving on. Now that I had a name, I was determined to find out everything I could about my thieving double. Googling her name brought me pages and pages of Facebook, Ancestry.com, death notices, and other miscellaneous postings. One by one, I eliminated the information. Only one bit of information seemed potentially relevant—a self-storage company with multiple branches in Sacramento. Seemed someone named Rosie Gonzales had fallen behind on her payments. Gotta love Google.

Question is, was it *my* Rosie? When I clicked on the link, it took me to a registration screen. Dead end.

It seemed like a long shot, but I pulled out the phone book and started dialing the storage company's area branches. Each time I got a live person on the other end, I approached it the same way: "My name's Rosie Gonzales," I said. "I have a unit there, but it's been almost a year since I opened it up and I can't remember the number."

Each time, the answer was the same: "Sorry, you're not in the system. Are you sure you have the right place?"

Then I'd laugh with embarrassment, thank them, and hang up.

Slow and steady. I made another call and went through my spiel. "Hi," I began. "This is so ridiculous, but I hope you can help me."

"I hope so, too," the man on the other end of the line said.

At least he was pleasant. The last call had been taken by a woman who was having a very bad day. "I have a storage unit with you, but I haven't been there in ages. And—don't laugh—I can't remember the number!"

He chuckled good-naturedly. "What's the name? I'll look it up for you."

"Rosie Gonzales."

I heard the *click click* of a keyboard. A minute later, his voice was in my ear again. "Here you are. You're on the north side. Unit thirty-four."

Score! I still had no idea if this was my Rosie, but it was something to look into. "Perfect!" Excitement at my success had me grinning. "Thank you so much. I owe you!"

"No prob," he said. "But, um . . ."

Rosie had a balance! I'd have to pay up if I wanted to get a peek inside her unit. "Listen," I said with as much charm as I could muster—considering the guy on the line probably thought I was a deadbeat. "I know I missed a payment. I'm so sorry about that."

"Yeah, about that. You said you haven't been here in a while?"

I sat up straight at the sudden change in his voice. Skeptical, with a hint of curious. "Right."

"But you changed your credit card information."

"I did?" My mind raced, landing on a possible explanation. If this *was* my Rosie, had she changed it to a credit card in *my* name? I tried to act casual, musing aloud as I took a leap of faith. "The name on the card's different, though, right?"

I took his mild grunt for a yes.

"It's my sister's card," I said, a lie formulating in my mind. "Dolores and I are sharing the unit now."

"Dolores Cruz. That's right. She's on the account now."

My heart stopped and slowly started to slide up my throat. As a criminal, Rosie wasn't too bright. Linking her name and my name together on the same account was *un poquito* lame.

"Come to think of it, I'm not sure I want that card to be billed." Not if it would rack up debt that wasn't mine. "Can you cancel it?"

"Sure, if you give me another card to bill."

Oh, of course. Silly of me to think it would be *that* easy. "I think I'll come on over to settle up, actually."

"Sure thing, Ms. Gonzales. We close at five today."

Temperatures outside were hovering in the low nineties, above average for Sacramento in September, and the brick red of my mini SUV had absorbed it all. Twenty minutes later, I was at the self-storage facility, a thin line of sweat down the center of my back. It didn't slow me down. I marched confidently into the small office. "Hi." I flashed a smile at the man behind the counter. "I just spoke to you. Rosie Gonzales."

"Hello, there," he said, his own smile wide and flirty. He looked to

45

be in his early twenties, was tanned and white-toothed. Apparently working in a self-storage allowed plenty of time for the tanning salon and cosmetic dentistry. "You made it here fast."

"Yeah. I have something I want to get from my unit. No sense in procrastinating."

"Right," he said, and I got the feeling he thought I'd hightailed it over here just for him. "Did you want to switch that credit card?"

I'd thought about this on the drive over. "I do. And I want to check to make sure you have my current address."

His smile grew. "Sure thing." He went to his computer, tapped on the keyboard, and studied the page, rattling off an address on L Street in downtown Sacramento. "Is that right?"

I committed the address to memory, repeating it in my head five times before answering him. "Yep. That's right."

"No phone number, though. Can I add one?"

He'd answered my next question without my even asking it. "I'm between phones right now," I lied. "But I'll let you know when I get a new number."

I started to dig in my purse, letting my shoulders hunch as I mumbled under my breath. "Oh no," I moaned. "I can't believe this."

The guy came from around his counter. "Is there a problem?"

I looked up at him, shamelessly batting my lashes. "My key. It's not here. I left so suddenly, I must have forgotten to take it from my key hook."

I cringed at how lame that sounded, but he didn't seem to notice. His gaze darted from left to right. "Well, you did give us that duplicate key when you rented the unit."

I did, er, *she* did? Booya. Luck was on my side. "Right!"

"It's against policy, but—"

"You mean," I broke in, relief spreading on my face, "you mean you'd open it for me?"

Not three minutes later, we were riding in a golf cart, heading to unit 34 at the north end of the facility. "I don't want you to get in trouble for helping me," I said, a tiny bit of guilt taking hold of me.

"I won't," he said. "My parents own the place."

That made me feel better. It wasn't likely that Mr. and Mrs. Self-Storage would fire their own son, even if he was breaking policy.

He stopped the cart in front of our destination, hopped out, and within five seconds, he'd popped the lock and had drawn up the garage-style door. Inside, he flipped a light on for me.

The unit was narrow and small. Two boxes, a twin bed, a cheap dining table and chairs. That was it. Nothing remarkable.

"Do you want to walk back to the office when you're done, or you want I should wait?"

It wouldn't take long to riffle through the boxes. "Thanks for opening it. Would you mind waiting? It'll just take a minute."

It took less than that. The boxes were full of clothes. Petite, size 12. Rosie and I might have shared the same name for a while, but we didn't share the same size. "Darn," I said, for the storage guy's benefit. "It's not here."

"Not much is here."

That was an understatement. Had she moved stuff out of here, or had she been planning to put more things in the unit? The storage guy took me back to the office. "I'll take care of the credit card another time," I said.

He looked disappointed that I was leaving without coming back inside. "You sure you don't wanna update your phone number? No cell? I really should have all the correct information."

"No, I told you, I'm between phones right now."

He looked like I'd just kicked him in the kneecaps. *Pobrecito.* He didn't know I had Jack Callaghan under my skin. No other man could light my fire. "It's all good," I said. "Thanks again."

I drove straight to L Street and found an empty lot ridden with weeds and garbage. Run-down houses flanked either side of Rosie's phony address. I spent the next twenty minutes picking through the brush. All I found was a worn brown blanket caked with mud, scattered cigarette butts, a rusty toaster, one knockoff Timberland hiking boot, size 13, right foot, and a three-wheeled stolen shopping cart from a nearby grocery store. Not a single clue, but I did leave with the utterly unanswerable question of how these random things ended up in an unbuilt residential lot.

With my luck, I'd probably lose sleep wondering about it.

Back in my car, I considered calling up Detective Seavers and filling him in on my day. I was pretty sure he'd tell me that I was interfering in an ongoing investigation, and that I might be facing an obstruction-of-justice charge if I didn't stay out of it.

Both, unfortunately, true.

I didn't want to hear it, because there was no way I was backing off. I didn't call.

Finally, I headed home to help my mother with the preparations for the big undead *fiesta* she was putting on tomorrow. My mind buzzed. I'd sniffed out a clue about the deceased fake Dolores Cruz. Luck had pointed me in the right direction, but the direction had been a dead end. What had I proved? That Rosie Gonzales, aka me, had wasted *my* money on a storage unit that barely held a room's worth of stuff? That she'd recently added my credit card and a mythical Dolores Cruz to the contract? That she'd given a dummy address?

The more I thought about it, the more one thing kept spinning through my mind. I'd been assuming that Rosie Gonzales was one of those stupid criminals radio DJs talk about. Use someone else's name, but leave a mile-long trail of bread crumbs leading to the truth. I mean, she'd linked *her* name and *my* name at the storage facility. But she'd also given her address as an empty lot and hadn't left a phone number to trace.

In the end, I couldn't quiet the nagging feeling in my gut that the woman who'd stolen my identity might not be quite so lame as I'd originally thought.

Chapter 5

It was raining black at Mass the next morning. My mother, grandmother, and grandfather all mourned me in theory—and were dressing the part. Didn't make a bit of difference that I stood right next to them. My grandmother refused to walk by my side. She muttered obscure prayers to *la Virgen de Guadalupe* and called on even more obscure saints to give us guidance through our family tragedy.

I lit a candle for Rosie Gonzales, then spent the rest of the afternoon surrounded by food and family—in that order. Except for Chely, who was like my shadow and hardly let me out of her sight. If I reached for a tamale, she reached for one, too. If I poured myself a glass of soda, she poured herself one, too. If I muttered to myself about the fact that Jack was a no-show, she muttered about it, too.

Finally, deciding that a dead-me was plenty and that I didn't need a mini-me, too, I pulled her into the laundry room. "*Prima*, you have to snap out of this."

Tears instantly pooled in her eyes. "But I can't!" She sniffled, then dragged the back of her hand under her nose. "I just keep hearing that news announcer saying that you're dead!"

"But I'm not dead, Chely." I'd been over the *I'm not a ghost* thing with my grandmother too many times to count since Friday night.

Chely was much more sensible than Abuela. I didn't think I'd have to do it with her, too.

She dried her eyes, nodding her head until I was dizzy from watching it go up and down, up and down, up and down. "I know. You're not dead," she repeated it.

This was good. "Right. *Otra vez*," I said. If she repeated it aloud enough times, maybe she'd believe it.

"You're not dead," she said. "You're not dead."

"Good. Feel better?"

She gave me a half smile. "I guess."

Now I just needed to distract her. "Tonio made guacamole, did you see? A huge bowl, and it has your name on it."

Chely's eyes got big and her smile went from partial to complete. "Want some?"

"No thanks, I'm good." She hesitated, but I hurried on. "Hurry! Go get some before Miguel eats it all. You know Tonio's guac is the best."

Finally, Chely scurried back into the kitchen, and I gave myself a mental high five. One down, the rest of the family to go. Getting them to deal with the fact that I wasn't actually dead seemed harder than them dealing with their grief if I had *really* died. Twisted, but what could I say? The Falcón–Cruz *familia* thrived on drama.

With Chely otherwise occupied, my mind went straight to Jack. He'd called to say he couldn't make the Back from the Dead Party. He'd read into my silence. "Don't worry, Lola," he'd said. "This is not an emergency. It's just work. I'm on deadline, and I have to go talk to a source in Grass Valley. If I get back early enough, I'll stop by."

What could I say? His work ethic was solid, and I respected that 100 percent. But it sort of felt like I was one of those cyber terminator people and a hole had been blown through my gut. Only Jack's presence could mend me.

"Have you heard from him?" I asked Antonio halfway through the afternoon.

My brother shrugged. "Nope."

50

"He said he'd try to make it."

Antonio raised his eyebrows. "If that's what he said, *hermana*, then stop worrying about it. He'll be here if he can."

I flicked my hand through the air dismissively. "I'm not worried," I said, but despite the fact that Jack was working, visions of Sarah spun through my head.

The party wrapped up at nine o'clock. Jack was still a no-show. He finally called at midnight, just as I was drifting off to sleep. "Sorry I didn't make it back. I had a hot lead. You have to strike when it's hot, you know?"

Of course I knew, but the seed Sergio had planted was sprouting roots, and a little part of me wondered if Jack had been following a hot ex-girlfriend instead of a hot lead. "*No es problema*, Callaghan," I said. "Did you get what you needed?"

"Part of it," he said. The unspoken innuendo was that I was the part he didn't get.

"Talk to you tomorrow?" I asked sleepily.

"It is tomorrow."

"Then later today."

"Sweet dreams, Cruz."

My lips curved into a small smile. I loved the deep rumble of his voice. My dreams would be more than sweet. They'd be smokin'. "Back at you, Callaghan."

By ten thirty the next morning, I was knee-deep in fraud alerts and credit reports. After three hours on the phone, it was pretty clear that Rosie Gonzales had racked up a truckload of debt in my name. My stomach ached from the discovery. The woman and her gall enraged me, but she was *dead*. Damn it, why'd she have to die?

I filed a complaint with the Federal Trade Commission, ordered credit reports from the other two major consumer reporting agencies, and filled out an identity theft affidavit to submit to companies, just in case.

None of it made me feel any better.

With the Zimmerman case all but wrapped up, I didn't have

51

anything else to do at Camacho's. Manny had given me the green light to be my own client, and that's just what I was going to do. First on my list: Find Rosie's *real* address.

Easier said than done. I got nowhere fast. Rosie didn't seem to exist. Without some starting information about her like her date of birth or her Social Security number, I didn't have anything to go on and couldn't find anything more about her. Thanks to high school English, I knew what I was facing was a real catch-22.

By one o'clock I was starving. Or I was just in serious need of comfort food. I headed to Abuelita's. The benefit of my fifteen minutes of fame, even if I'd been dead for only a few hours, was that business had picked up. The family restaurant was teeming with customers. My death was bringing in hordes of people, but a customer was a customer—and even the morbidly curious had to eat.

I kept my head down and burrowed through to the door. Once inside, I waded through the crowd in the lobby. My foot landed on someone's lumpy toe.

"Ow!" a woman screeched, glaring at me as I pulled my foot from hers.

"Sorry," I mumbled.

"Watch where you're—" She stopped, peered at me, then whacked the guy standing next to her with the back of her hand. "It's her!" She pointed at me as the man rubbed his arm. "You're her, aren't you? You're—"

Her voice was swallowed up by the low buzz that started in one end of the lobby and traveled like a stadium wave. "It *is* her!" someone said. "Dolores!"

This is what it was like to be a rock star? Yikes. I'd take undercover work any day. I liked my anonymity.

"Psst. Dolores. Over here."

Brushing off my death groupies, I searched for the source of the summons. Every table in the place was occupied. No one flagged me down. They just stared. I turned my back on the dining room and froze when I saw the banner that was slung across the outside of the front window. The sunlight allowed me to see through it enough to recognize . . . my photo!

I pushed back out the door and through the line until I could get a good view of the banner. I just stared at it. It said:

ABUELITA'S: HOME OF THE *REAL* DOLORES CRUZ!

Unbelievable! Fuming, I marched back inside, angling my head as I searched for my no-good, unscrupulous brother. I was not an advertising slogan!

He was nowhere in sight.

In the dining room, hands on my hips, I waited. Antonio could run, but he couldn't hide.

"Psst! *Ven aquí*, Dolores." There was that whispery voice again.

My head swiveled to follow the sound. My grandparents' regular booth. Aha! The Godfather. Abuelo stuck his cane out, motioning me forward. The new waitress Antonio had hired managed to dodge the cane, her hands barely holding on to plates of tostada salad, fish tacos, and enchiladas.

My stomach growled. Having my identity stolen and being pimped out to drum up business had made me famished. I'd deal with Antonio when he showed his face.

Abuelo flung his cane around again.

"*Cuidado*, Abuelo. You're going to scare away the new waitress!" I knocked the walking stick out of the way and slid into the booth next to my grandmother.

Abuela dropped her knitting into a heap on the table, eyeing me suspiciously and poking my arm with a padded fingertip.

"*¡Déjame en paz, Abuela!* Stop doing that! I'm real." I scooted out of her reach and she dropped her hand to the table, fingering the heap of variegated yarn in front of her. Abuela was forever knitting baby blankets, but so far, Zac and Lucy were the only ones in the Falcón–Cruz clan to have kids.

"*¿Cuando te vas a casa? Queremos bisnietos*," Abuelo said.

"One, I'm not going to get married any time soon, so you can just get rid of *that* idea. And two, you *have* great-grandchildren," I said, speaking in English. It kept them on their toes.

At least he wasn't talking about the "death," but my providing him with great-grandchildren wasn't a much better topic.

Abuelo peered at me. "Y where your boyfriend yesterday?" he said in his broken English.

"He's *not* my boyfriend," I said, trying to keep the regret out of my voice, "and his name is Jack."

"*Sí. Jack*," he said, though it sounded like *Yack*. "*Tú y el van a tener hijos bonitos.*"

I choked on a chip heaped with the last of the salsa. "I'm *not* having children with Jack Callaghan," I said after swallowing. At least not yet. It was true that Jack and I would have beautiful children. I bit purposefully on another chip and tilted my head. "In fact, I may not have children at all." I munched away, ignoring the sharp inhalation of Abuela's breath. Payback for the *fantasma* thing.

"What?" I asked, leaning the empty *molcajete* on two legs to search for any remnants of tomato or chili. Antonio's new waitress was already falling behind on salsa duty.

Abuelo poked a finger into his ear. "*¿Qué habla?* No children?"

Of course I wanted children—what, were they really *that* gullible? "I'm a career woman. You should be proud of me for that."

Abuela's knitting needles clicked together again. "You *will* have his children."

A naked half-eaten chip turned to mush in my mouth. My grandmother was speaking English again; the world was going crazy. I shook my head. "What if I don't want kids?" I asked. My irritation flared. "My sole purpose in life is not to give you great-grandchildren. And just because I'm a woman doesn't mean I have to hunt for a husband. Why don't you harass Gracie for great-grandkids? She's already married. Plus you have Zac's kids, and—"

My grandfather looked at my grandmother and translated what I'd said. Ha, as if she didn't understand. Faker. She muttered in

Spanish, clutched her rosary, and prayed unintelligibly. For my salvation or for a man for me, I wasn't sure which. Though I was pretty sure it was for my soul.

Abuelo pulled his mouth into a frown at my insolence. I shoved a bare chip into my mouth as the waitress nervously approached the table. She did not have salsa.

"Mr. Falcon," she said in a small quavery voice. "Would you like to order?"

"It is Falcón," he barked. "Fal-cón." My grandfather waved his hand in dismissal and she scooted away, spooked by his outburst.

"You need to be nice to her," I scolded.

He grunted. "So you can be a detective." He waved his hand across the table, as if shooing away the idea. "Pfft. The girl is—is— *no es fuerte.* And you"—he wagged his finger at me, clearly struggling to find the English words—"belong at this restaurant."

"No, I don't. And what do you mean she's not strong? Give her a chance."

"Pfft," he said again, almost whistling. He threw his arms out, flailing his cane around again. *"¡Muchacha! ¿Necesitamos mas salsa, eh?"* He wasn't going to give anybody a break, least of all a timid waitress who he'd have to see daily.

Of course, I wanted the salsa, too, so I prayed she'd gather up her courage and face the Godfather.

He gave a heavy sigh when she didn't materialize. "Enough of this. *Mi'ja,*" he said to me, "you must help your *primo.*"

"Which *primo?*" He needed to be a tad more specific, as I probably had fifty cousins.

"Zacarias."

"What's wrong with him?"

"He is—" He broke off, slowly turning to the waitress, who had finally come to our table.

"I'm so sorry, sir. It's just, Antonio said we need the table." She breathed in shakily. "Unless you want to order."

He turned to me, barking, *"¿Que dijo?"* The girl had raced through her words, slurring them together so that he'd been unable to catch them. I translated, and he growled at her. "I want salsa!"

Abuela clicked her knitting needles together with her clawlike hands as my grandfather stood up. It was a rite of passage at Abuelita's. You had to earn the respect of Pedro Falcón, and the sooner this girl figured it out, the better.

I jumped out of the booth, grabbed her by the sleeve, and quickly pulled her aside. She was pretty—and innocent. I laid it out for her. "You have to be strong with him. That's the only way he'll respect you. You can't let men walk all over you. Especially an old man like him. You're a woman! Be strong!"

She stared at me, her eyes watering and her lower lip quivering.

"Dolores," my grandfather hissed. "*¡No mas!*" He leaned over on his cane. "Bring to me the manager," he said to the waitress, his words twisted with his frustration.

Her eyes grew round, and tears pooled on the lower rims. She turned and scurried back to the kitchen.

I shook my head, knowing I hadn't gotten through to her. *Pobrecita.* A moment later, Antonio sauntered out from behind the swinging kitchen door, the timid girl hiding behind him. I felt sorry for her. She wasn't going to last long. Then I felt sorry for myself, realizing I'd be working the lunch shift again while Tonio tried to find yet another waitress.

The only person I didn't feel sorry for was Antonio.

Abuelo still stood, both hands cupped on the carved falcon that perched on top of his cane. Antonio stopped in front of him, standing more than a head taller than the old man. "Are you going to order, *viejo?*" Antonio demanded, barely keeping a straight face. It was all a demented game to him. I wondered if he and Abuelo spent hours playing chess and discussing just how they were going to haze each new waitress.

I crunched another naked chip, watching the show. The girl stared doe-eyed at Antonio. Her hero, poor deluded girl.

"This table I own." My grandfather nodded sharply to drive his point home.

Not surprisingly, Antonio didn't give in. "Look at the lobby. Lola's death has brought in a crowd!"

"Thanks to your little banner," I said.

Tonio flashed a smug grin. "A stroke of brilliance, don't you think? It's a twisted world we live in."

"It's a twisted family I live in," I said. "Take it down."

Antonio looked at me for a beat, then, totally ignoring me, he turned to Abuelo. "Chrissy can't earn a tip off this table if it's not usable."

Ah, so she had a name. My grandfather glared at Chrissy. "You will have your tip, *pero* leave me alone. *¿Entiendes?*"

She nodded, her face flushing. "Yes, sir, Mr. Falcón, sir."

She rushed away, my grandfather yelling after her, "Bring *mas* salsa!"

"You two are so cruel," I said, shaking my head as Antonio and Abuelo slid back into the booth. I glared at my brother. "You, especially."

Antonio flashed his Cheshire cat grin. "She's cute, eh? We have to see what she's made of."

"She's too young for you, Tonio." I had officially made up my mind. I wasn't going to be my brother's safety net anymore. I was a woman, too, and I had to be strong. For Chrissy's sake. His days of tormenting waitresses for sport were over. "And for the record, I'm not going to fill in if she quits, so you better figure out how to keep her."

He smiled. "She's not going to quit."

Right, I'd heard that before. "Just stay away from her. And take the banner down."

"Hey, just 'cause you're uptight—"

I bristled. "I am *not* uptight."

Antonio gave me an exaggerated wink. "Right. That's just what

Jack said." Indignant, I kicked Antonio under the table. "Ow! Why'd you do that?"

"Don't talk about me with Jack. You're my brother. You're supposed to be on my side."

My grandparents looked from me to Antonio and back again. Abuela's wrinkled face pinched.

"You need to have a little fun, Lo." He turned to our grandparents. "Right?"

My foot shot out again, catching Antonio's shin. "Leave them out of this, and I have plenty of fun."

Antonio rubbed his shin. "Stop doing that," he said, more seriously this time.

"Then stay out of my love life."

"You don't *have* a love life," he said. "That's the point. You're too obsessed with being a detective to have any fun. And now all you're doing is trying to figure out who killed some innocent woman instead of you. You might as well have a bull's-eye on your back."

"You—you—" He had some nerve! "You're using my death to promote the restaurant so—so that bull's-eye is helping you!"

"I'm not stupid, Lo." He shrugged, but gave a resigned frown at the same time. Small consolation that he seemed to feel at least a little bit bad at his self-serving action. "I'm not going to look a gift horse in the mouth. It happened. If it can help business, who am I to discourage that? It is what it is. Now Jack's—"

"*¡No mas!*" Abuelo's bark startled me into jumping a full three inches off my seat. "Bring me salsa!" He motioned with his hand. "*Ahorita.* I must speak with Dolores."

Antonio nodded his head solemnly, as if he always did our grandfather's bidding. "Sure thing," he said. But as he slid out of the booth, he winked at me. I stifled a growl. The scoundrel! If he wasn't my brother, I'd have strangled him a long time ago.

Once Antonio was out of earshot, Abuelo laid his cane across the table and focused on me. "Zacarias needs help," he said, his voice all whispery and mobbed up.

I had completely forgotten about my cousin.

"*Creo que Lucy tiene otro hombre.*"

My grandmother sucked in a breath and muttered a prayer for her grandson.

"No, she doesn't," I said, dismissing the accusation with a flippant wave. There was no way Lucy had another man.

Abuelo nodded sagely. "*Pero sí.* Zacarias thinks maybe. Maybe more than one. Men come to the house, he says."

"Abuelo, Lucy works out of her house."

"Not on men."

"Why not? Men can't get facials?"

"What is this . . . facials?" His lips pulled down into a wrinkled frown.

Gesturing with my hands, I tried to explain. "It cleans your face and helps your skin."

"Men do not do . . . *that.*" He wagged his finger at me from across the table. "*Ayuda a tu primo.*"

I threw my hands up. "Okay, okay. I'll look into it." I'd give Zac a call even though the idea of an adulterous Lucy was ludicrous. Abuelo had to have misunderstood Zac.

But one thing I'd realized early in my life was that it was usually easier to give in to the craziness of *la familia* Cruz than to fight it.

Chapter 6

Y ou seriously think she's having an affair?" I pulled the phone from my ear and stared at it, as if it, and not my cousin Zac on the other end, were crazy.

"I don't know. She doesn't— We don't— Things are different," he finally said.

Different *and* difficult to talk about. "Do you want me to talk to her?"

He hemmed and hawed. "Is there another way? I don't want you to put her on the spot." I could hear the anguish in his voice. The respect he had for Lucy and her privacy despite his fears.

I'd wanted Abuelo to be wrong. No such luck. "I guess I could do a little surveillance," I offered reluctantly. Spying on Lucy would be like cheating on the PI exam, but I'd never heard Zac so distraught, and I couldn't not help him.

I headed to their house the first opportunity I had. Their Sacramento neighborhood was situated in the Pocket, a well-established enclave, the neighborhood well maintained but outdated.

I parked down the block from their chocolate-brown flat-roofed residence. The front yard was drought-resistant, covered with lava rock and ice plant rather than the more typical green foliage of other yards. I curled my lip at the cold landscape—I was a roses-and-trees kind of girl—and settled in to watch the house.

Zac had laid out a rough outline of Lucy's schedule for me. Their three kids attended elementary school in the neighborhood. Meanwhile, Lucy operated a skin aesthetician business out of their home. Her clients came during the day, leaving her nights free for family time.

After an hour of watching zero activity at the house, I wondered how Lucy even managed to make a living. Business was not booming.

My thoughts turned to my case. If only Manny would just tell me exactly what to do to solve my case quickly and efficiently, I could get back to a paying gig. But no, even if I wasn't billing hours, that wasn't how my boss operated. He was more like my sensei, and in that capacity, he rarely gave me what I needed. He was more like a guide, telling me vaguely about the path I had to travel but not giving me clear directions on how to get there.

I had to work for it. Muse and formulate and figure things out for myself. I'd become a better detective because of it. Eventually.

One thing he'd taught me was that time management was crucial, so with one eye on the dead house, I jotted down notes on Rosie Gonzales and formulated questions to try to answer.

Numero uno was,

• *What drove her to steal my identity?*

I had absolutely no idea.

It was hard to understand how someone could give up their name and use someone else's. I mean, *I* was Dolores Cruz. I could never be anyone else. Even if I married, I'd keep my name. I'd be Dolores Cruz hyphen—er—Callaghan?

My thoughts screeched to a halt. What was wrong with me? Thinking about marriage with Jack was dangerous territory. I refocused on my notes and moved on to my next question.

• *How long had Rosie been Dolores Cruz?*

That was one question I might be able to get answered right away.

I flipped open my phone and dialed Neil Lashby, tech guy extraordinaire of Camacho and Associates. I was new in the detective game, but he'd been at it for a decade and had sources I could only dream of. Sometimes he was willing to share; sometimes he wasn't.

I had my notebook out, pen at the ready, in case he was in a generous mood.

He answered on the first ring. "Yo."

"Yo," I replied. Speaking his lingo was key. He was a man of few words and few syllables. "Has Manny filled you in on my mistaken identity thing?"

"Bad deal."

"Yeah. Do you have a contact so I can find out if the DMV issued her a license in my name?"

"Jane Murchison," he said without a second's hesitation, and he rattled off a phone number.

The license could be a fake, but then again, it might not be. I added Jane's name to my contact page. "Thanks," I said to Neil, but the click of the phone meant that he'd ended the conversation. He was not one for small talk.

Slowly but surely, I was developing my own source list. I dialed Jane Murchison. She answered, and I started talking, telling her that Neil had referred me. "That big old teddy bear? You get to work with him?"

Were we talking about the same Neil Lashby? "Sure do," I said, putting a smile in my voice.

"You tell him I said hi, would you?"

"Of course, Jane." I got down to business. "You work at the DMV?"

"Worst job in the world," she said sourly.

"I'm sorry to hear that."

"I'm sorry to live it. What do you need?"

"You won't get in trouble for helping me?"

"Only if I get caught." She harrumphed, and I wondered if maybe she wanted to get caught.

I better ask my questions quick. "Can you give me information about when a license was issued?"

"Let me get to that screen." She tapped away. "Ready. Name?"

"Dolores Cruz."

"Wait, isn't that your name?"

"It is, but someone else was using it, too."

"Wow. That sucks."

"Yes, it does."

"Got quite a few Dolores Cruzes in Sacramento. Address?"

I gave her the L Street address Rosie had used at the self-storage company.

"Here it is. Issued in April of this year."

A chill snaked through my body. Rosie had been living as me for six months. That was a lot of time in which to do a lot of damage.

I snapped to attention as a flashy cobalt Miata zipped up in front of Lucy's house. "Gotta go, Jane. Thanks for your help."

"No prob. Good luck. And give that teddy bear Neil a squeeze from me."

"Will do," I said, thinking, *No way!* Giving Neil a hug was not going on to my list of things to do.

I slid down in my seat and watched a man wearing slacks, a Façonnable sweater, and Top-Siders walk up the path that led through the lava rocks to Lucy's front door. Was he one of Lucy's clients or the supposed lover? I jotted down the license plate number in my notebook and settled in to wait.

My mind started working again. How else could I track down Rosie? What contacts did *I* have?

Only one came to mind: Jack.

He worked at the newspaper. Maybe Rosie subscribed to one. I had to go off assumptions. Her storage unit was in Sacramento. So was her fake address. She'd died in Sacramento. It only seemed logical that she'd lived here somewhere.

If she read the paper, it was most likely the *Sacramento Bee*. It was another long shot, but my long shots had been paying off. I snatched up my cell phone again and dialed.

"Callaghan." His voice was clipped, like I'd caught him in the middle of something important.

"Hey, it's Lola."

His tone instantly turned friendly and warm. "Hey, you."

"Hey. You must be tired."

"A little. Sorry I called so late last night. How was the party?"

It would have been better if he'd been there. "It was fine if you like a bunch of weeping, overly dramatic women in black praying on their rosaries for my soul, which, last time I checked, was still part of me."

He laughed. "I would have liked to see that."

"Next time."

"Hopefully there won't be a next time. You dying isn't something I want to relive."

On that note, I cut to the chase. "I have a favor to ask."

My ears caught the faint sound of his fingers tapping on his computer keyboard. Apparently *mi amor* was a multitasker. "Shoot."

"The police identified the dead woman. Her name was Rosie Gonzales. I'm trying to track down a valid address, and so far I'm coming up empty. I was hoping you could look to see if maybe she had a newspaper subscription, and if she did, what her address is."

The tapping stopped, and I sensed I had his full attention. "Rosie Gonzales isn't exactly a unique name. There have to be a million of them in Sacramento and the surrounding areas."

"Yeah. Probably."

"I can check."

He was a good contact. Willing to hack into subscriptions to find information for me. What a guy.

I looked up and down Lucy's street. All quiet. Miata man was still inside, getting the metrosexual treatment. "You might just skip searching Rosie," I said, going with my instinct, "and search my name."

"Yours."

"She had a driver's license in my name that she got six months ago, and she's been using a fake address on L Street. But if she subscribed to the paper, a fake address wouldn't work."

"I'll check it out and call you—"

I didn't hear the rest of Jack's sentence. Miata man trotted out of Lucy's house, a decided bounce in his step. Could a facial do that? "Thanks, Jack. Gotta go." And I snapped my cell phone shut.

I tried to determine if the man had a postcoital glow to him. He seemed to, but then again, having blackheads squeezed out of your skin probably resulted in the same glow. He hopped into his sports car and sped away. I thought about following him but decided against it. My cousin-in-law needed my business.

I pulled down the sun visor and peered into the tiny mirror, examining my olive skin. Did I need a facial? Lucy had given me one when she'd first started her business, and it had felt like a little slice of heaven. Scrutinizing my reflection, I had to admit it did look a little lackluster. A facial wouldn't be a bad idea.

I flipped open my cell phone again and dialed the number for Skin Delicacies, Lucy's business.

"I'd *love* to give you a facial, Lola!" Lucy said after she'd heard my request. Her booming voice reverberated off my eardrum, and I held the phone away. "You could sure use it after the shock you've had."

"Have you been busy today?" I thought maybe I'd be able to read between the lines of her answer.

"I have an appointment with Gracie in twenty minutes. Just finished a facial. Guy gets one once a month, like clockwork."

"Really? Men like facials?"

"Sure, some do. My client that just left, he swears they keep him young." She dropped her voice lower, like she was afraid Miata man was still there and might overhear. "What he really needs are some breath mints. His girlfriend came with him once. I wanted to ask her how she stands it!"

Lucy flossed twice a day and had travel toothbrushes in her purse

65

and in her car. She brushed after every meal, no matter where she was. If Miata man didn't have excellent oral hygiene, no way was Lucy having an affair with him. One point in her favor.

We scheduled my appointment for the next day, and I hightailed it out of there. I didn't need my sister, Gracie, to let on she'd seen me lurking outside Lucy's house. I'd have to wait until tomorrow for Lucy to save my skin from the ills of the sun and wind and CoverGirl, and hopefully I'd be able to uncover the truth behind Zac's concerns.

The regular staff meetings at Camacho and Associates were always every other Monday at three o'clock. Then there were the irregular ones that happened on an as-needed basis.

I swung by Mr. Zimmerman's office first to drop off the incriminating photos of his wife, and arrived at Camacho's at 2:58. I greeted my sad little fake fern then walked to the end of the narrow lobby and turned into the main office.

Reilly's desk chair was vacant. I actually stopped to ponder this for a second. Reilly *never* missed work. She lived for the gossip and the vicarious thrills. Now it seemed she was becoming part of the gossip. Something was seriously wrong!

I dragged my feet as I approached the conference table. If my life were a comic book and I had a mortal enemy, half the time that enemy would be Sadie Metcalf. She was blond, petite, plastic, and often diabolical. Undercover work was her specialty, and even though we'd had somewhat of a breakthrough in our relationship just a week ago, one of my office survival rules was still Stay the heck away from Sadie.

Impossible when she was staring at me like she wanted to take me down.

Neil slouched in his chair. His head rested on his shoulder in lieu of a neck. He riffled through a stack of papers, presumably part of an insurance-fraud case he'd been working on forever. "Thanks for the contact," I said to him.

"Yep."

Manny sauntered out of his office, a stack of brown file folders under his arm. He nodded to the group gathered at the table. "Afternoon." His gravelly voice fit his personality to a T—no frills or comfort, but it made your body tremble.

After some general housekeeping issues, he turned to me. "Zimmerman wrapped up?"

"I just gave him the photos and the final bill. *Finito.*"

"Focus your attention on your own investigation. Backup here as needed. But," he added, "I can spare you only for a week."

I nodded my understanding. I had to work fast to solve the Rosie Gonzales mystery before my time would be obligated to my paying job. "Got it."

Manny finished up the meeting. "Refer to the roster for floor assignments," he said in closing. He referred to reception duty at the office as "working the floor." Personally, I think it was his way of defeminizing the duty for himself and Neil.

Sadie suddenly sat up in her chair. Cocking her head to the side, she looked at me with what I was sure was false sincerity. "I could shuffle some things and help Dolores."

"It's okay," I blurted. Sadie offering to help me was like the devil bargaining for your soul. We'd called a truce—once—but it had been short-lived. I'd rather take my chances in hell.

"She's fine," Manny said. He might as well have added "*Punto,*" his statement was *that* final. "Everything else is status quo. Reports on my desk Wednesday."

We were dismissed, and I immediately went to one of the whiteboards bolted around the room and reviewed the little information Manny had uncovered. It wasn't much.

- *Real name Rosie Gonzales*
- *Died of head wound*
- *Storage unit with miscellaneous items inside*
- *Driver's license in my name six months ago*
- *Uncovered charges so far for food and clothing*

Nothing extravagant. This one puzzled me—if she wanted credit cards in my name to be free with her shopping, why had all her spending been so mundane? It seemed that simple thievery and high living hadn't been the motivation for the identity theft. There was something much bigger going on here.

My cell blared "La Bamba," and I flipped it open.

"Hey," Jack said on the other end of the line.

Just hearing his voice again made me want to crawl to him on all fours.

Through the open door to his office, I could see Manny hunched over his desk. Hard at work, as all superdetectives should be. I capped the dry-erase pen I'd been using and searched out a private space in the office. With no better option, I settled for a corner of the lobby next to my plant. I was still in full view, but at least not in the center of the room. "Hi," I said to Jack, wondering if my voice sounded as breathy to him as it did to me.

"I did that research you asked for. Came up with some possibilities."

"Already? That was fast." Shift from breathy to excited. I was impressed.

"I aim to please," he said, and I could hear the smile behind his voice.

I flipped my notebook open to a blank page. "Okay, what'd you find?"

"We should really discuss it in person. I'll come meet you," he said.

"No. It's okay." I rubbed my temples. Much as I wanted to be distracted by him, I had to focus. Like Manny, who never let his personal life get in the way of how he ran his business. I wanted information so I could move forward and solve the mystery of Rosie Gonzales, and if I was with Jack, I might get sidetracked. "You're working—"

"This is part of my work. I want to pick your brain."

Red flags shot up in my head. "About what?"

"My next column is on identity theft. And since that's what

68

seems to have happened to you—" He paused. "My editor loves the idea."

Apparently I'd become Jack's official muse. My last case had dealt with tattoos, so he had written about the body-art industry. He should definitely be giving me kickbacks for story ideas. "I'm not sure I can help much."

"You have personal experience. Putting a name and face to the issue makes it real for the reader. Lets them connect, you know?"

"I'm just on my way out, so—"

"Great. I'll go with you," he said at the same time as the *whoosh* of the front door sounded. I turned . . . and nearly dropped my phone. He was suddenly right in front of me. "So, this is where it all happens." Jack walked into the conference room, scouting the perimeter, checking out the various information outlined on the whiteboards.

I hurried after him. "Those cases are confidential."

Manny sauntered out of his office, a slightly pained look on his face. The cleft in his chin looked more prominent than usual, and his eyes had turned beady. He nodded curtly at Jack.

Jack tucked his cell into his pocket. A narrow notebook and his thin black laptop computer were clutched under his left arm. He held out his right hand to Manny. "Good to see you again," he said, but his tone said, *Back off, buster.* "Just here to pick up Lola."

"Lola?" Manny said, but his gaze never left Jack's face. Their grips seemed to tighten.

I smiled wanly. I was Dolores to the elder generation in my family and to my colleagues. To my siblings, my cousins, friends—and Jack—I was Lola. When had I begun walking a tightrope between two worlds?

"Manny, you remember Jack Callaghan." Jack had been around during two cases I'd been involved with—not to mention the other night right in front of the agency—but I couldn't actually recall introducing them.

"I remember," he said tightly.

69

I watched as the muscles in both their forearms strained with their machismo. Ah, to be a man and wield such animalism.

Finally they seemed to call an unspoken truce and released.

Manny rocked back on the heels of his alligator cowboy boots and folded his arms over his chest. He looked at me. "You working on your case?"

"I'm going with her while she's investigating." Jack cracked a protective half smile. "Sort of in a bodyguard capacity."

I looked from Manny to Jack. They were like two wolves, circling each other, vying for the best fighting position. "I don't need a bodyguard—," I started to say, but they weren't listening to me.

Manny's lips thinned. "Where?"

"I'm taking her to Rosie Gonzales's apartment."

I gaped at him. Reluctant surprise crossed Manny's face. "You have an address?" we said in unison.

"Yep. Lola asked me to find a few addresses in the *Bee*'s database." Jack swung out his arm, ushering me through the opening to the lobby.

He was here. It was a good lead, and we were wasting time. I grabbed my purse, the file folder, and my notebook on the case. "I'll call you later," I called over my shoulder.

"Your car or mine?" Jack asked when we were out on the sidewalk.

I was torn between an urge to sucker-punch Jack for his macho hero act and wanting to kiss him for finding a solid lead on my case. I opted for a verbal attack—just to set some boundaries. "What was *that*?"

Jack leaned against my car. "What was what?"

"The handshake and the 'I'm going with her.'" I faced him. "I can take care of myself, Jack. I don't need a bodyguard, and certainly not one who vanishes at will."

He studied me, ignoring my rant, and seemed to pull a new topic from thin air. "What's going on between you and Camacho?"

"What? Nothing." A sliver of guilt knifed through me. Of course I'd thought about Manny in that way once or twice over

70

the years—any woman with a pulse would—but he was my boss. And I had Jack Callaghan sitting beside me. "I work for him," I said. "He's my *mentor*."

"And he's interested in you."

I did Jack the courtesy of really considering his statement. Manny was attractive—in a mercenary kind of way—but I wanted someone to snuggle with, someone to share my dreams with, someone like—"Jack," I snapped, "he's *not* interested in me. He has a girlfriend." Who looks like Lara Croft, or Angelina Jolie playing Lara Croft—so really, there was no contest.

"A girlfriend doesn't stop a lot of men."

I gave him a little attitude. "Oh, yeah? You know this from experience?"

"Funny, Cruz. I'm a one-woman kind of man." A hint of playfulness flitted back into his voice.

Yeah, but was *I* the woman? "I don't need a bodyguard," I repeated. But I did need the address, and I *wanted* Jack.

Jack's face was unreadable. "Right," he said. "So, how about that identity theft."

Ooh, he had a doctorate in evasiveness. "Fine, come with me if you want."

The left side of his mouth crept up in an illicit smile. "I'll come because *you* want me to." He got in the passenger side of my car, slipped his laptop under the seat, and flipped open his reporter's notebook in one slick move.

I glanced back at the plate-glass windows of Camacho and Associates. A shadow passed by. I blinked, but when I opened my eyes, the small lobby looked empty. All the nicknames Manny had been calling me shot to the front of my mind. Jack putting voice to my suspicions made me jumpy. I didn't want Manny to have a thing for me.

I angled my body to face Jack, getting back to business. "You actually got Rosie Gonzales's address?"

He settled into the bucket seat and rolled down the window. "We'll see."

He stopped talking, dangling his unspoken information in front of me like a worm on a hook. No need to bite—me and José knew that worm personally. "You looked up *my* name."

Jack grinned, a lock of mahogany hair falling onto his forehead. "I called a friend in subscriptions, and he searched your name. That was a good idea," he added. "It worked."

Jack looked at me, the expression on his face one I loved seeing. It was a pleasing mixture of satisfaction and respect.

"Her motive had to be more than wanting stuff." I filled Jack in on the storage facility. "If she was going crazy with my credit, wouldn't the unit have been full? I'm assuming she was running from something, and that's what motivated her stealing my name." It was my hypothesis. Now I had to work toward proving it.

"Makes sense." He pulled out a sheet of paper and handed it to me. Turns out there are about twenty-five Rosie Gonzaleses and fifteen Dolores Cruzes in the greater Sacramento area. "If she was running, she was safe as you. Until last week," he added.

We were silent for a few seconds, mourning Rosie. I looked at the endless list. "Glad to know I'm a unique individual."

"You're *definitely* a unique individual."

Two can play at this game, Callaghan. My arm brushed shamelessly against his thigh as I stretched across his legs and reached into the glove box. Across his tautly muscled thigh. I swallowed hard, snatched a pen from the opening, and shrank back to my own space. The words on the paper blurred for a moment as I took a deep breath. Maybe only one could play at this game—him.

Puckering my lips, I blew out a stiff breath. It'd be so much safer if my heart chambers didn't want to explode when I was around him.

An endless moment later, I was able to draw steady lines through two Rosies and five of the Doloreses on the list. "I think we can tentatively eliminate these right off the bat if we assume Rosie didn't live in Roseville, Lincoln, or even Natomas. Too far from Florin Road, where she died."

Jack remained uncharacteristically silent, and I suddenly felt as if this were a test. With my chin tilted against my chest and my eyelashes shading my eyes, I sneaked a glance at him. "Yep," he finally said, "you're probably right. That narrows it down to ten possibles."

"None of these subscriptions have been canceled?"

Jack shook his head. "They're all active."

Another idea struck me. I drew a line through four more names. "These women take the paper every day. Let's assume Rosie just took it on the weekend, to keep informed. If she was running, she would want to prolong the deception for as long as possible. She'd probably be cautious with her spending." She might not have taken the paper at all. I know *I* rarely had time to read anything beyond the obits. And Jack's column.

"Maybe, maybe not. It prioritizes the list anyway. If the hunch doesn't pan out, we can always go back to the others."

I pulled out my cell phone and dialed the first number. It was answered on the second ring. *"Hola?"*

I slipped into Spanish. *"¿Por favor, estoy hablando con Dolores Cruz?"*

"Sí. Soy Dolores Cruz."

Frowning at Jack, I shook my head. Strike one. *"Lo siento. Nesecito a otra Dolores Cruz. Gracias."* To Jack I said, "Not our girl."

I called the next two numbers with the same results; we were oh for three. The next number rang and rang. The fifth call led to an answering machine. The voice on the machine identified herself as Dolores and directed the caller to leave a message. I hung up instead.

"So we're left with three possibilities," I said after the last call went unanswered. "Maybe one of them was our girl."

Jack strapped the seat belt over his chest. "Let's roll."

We tried the downtown address first since it was closest. The single-story tan house was situated next to a mom-and-pop grocery on one side and a row of similarly designed houses on the other. A little girl, about eight years old, answered my knock.

I smiled at her. "Hi. I'm looking for Dolores Cruz?"

"That's me," the girl said, jutting her chin forward. Her brown hair was pulled back into a ponytail, bangs flat against her forehead. Her big black eyes were like pools of oil.

"Oh." I hadn't expected that. "Um, is your mommy home?"

Little Dolores Cruz shook her head from side to side, her ponytail sweeping against her cheek with each motion.

Jack crouched down. "Is her name Dolores, too?"

The girl nodded her head this time, the ponytail swinging out behind her.

"Is she at work?" I asked.

As the girl shook her head, frustration simmered inside me. I wanted to blurt, *Is your mother alive?* but that would be *un poquito* insensitive.

Jack was at the girl's eye level. "Honey, is your mommy coming home soon?"

She nodded again. "She's next door."

Jack and I locked knowing gazes. If Mama Dolores was next door, then she couldn't be Rosie Gonzales. I put a line through the name on the printout, and we headed back to the car.

I drove toward South Sacramento and the next address on the list. "You were sweet with her," I said to him. No wonder he wanted a football team of kids. He actually liked them.

"She's just a little person," he said, as if talking to little people, aka children, was the easiest thing in the world.

I was usually good at it, too. My excuses for today were Jack's presence and the dead Dolores Cruz.

The rest of our drive was filled with sporadic bouts of trivial conversation followed by stretches of silence. I asked Jack what angle he was taking in his identity-theft column.

"Facts mixed with a personal story." He grinned. "Yours."

"I'm not sure I *want* to share my story."

He looked at me like I was missing the point of something big. "It's a hot topic. You've done the research. You're living it. Other people need to know that it's real. That it can happen to regular people. To someone just like them."

74

"Hey," I said, feigning hurt. "I thought you said I was unique."

"Cruz, you're beyond unique. They broke the mold when they made you."

I wasn't sure he thought that was a good thing, but I left it alone. Instead, I put my detective skills to work on Jack. He liked kids, was concerned about the greater good, and dropped everything to help me, even if it also helped him. But his past pressed invasive fingers into my brain. "How many women have you slept with?" I blurted, then slapped my hand over my mouth.

The stunned expression on his face made me swallow. Damn. My mouth had a mind of its own at times. "You sure you want to have this conversation?" he asked.

"Definitely." No!

His breath was slow and steady, weighted with the impact of his next sentence. "You tell me first. How many men have you slept with, Cruz?"

I sputtered. "We weren't talking about me."

"You and Sergio. You do it every day?" His face had gone hard and tense. "Did you initiate it?"

My knuckles turned white on the steering wheel. "That's too personal, Callaghan."

"Fair play, babe. You want to know all the details about my sex life."

"That's different."

"How?"

Good question since, of course, it wasn't the least bit different. Knowing the down-and-dirty details of his past wouldn't make me feel better. I'd been a relatively good girl over the years, but I knew Jack had not been on the same basic abstinence-unless-it's-love path that I'd been on. I couldn't answer.

"Contrary to what you obviously think," he said with a frown, "I don't sleep with every woman I come across."

I gave him a sidelong glance that said, *Yeah, right.* "I saw the economy box of condoms in your bathroom when you had me over for dinner, remember? It's no secret you've had a few sleepovers."

He leaned his arm against the open window frame and rested his head against his fist. "Actually, I never sleep over, and no one ever sleeps over with me."

"You were in a relationship for four years. You're saying you didn't have any sleepovers?"

"Not counting that," he said in monotone.

I tried not to psychoanalyze his every move and tone. "You slept at my place after Antonio's accident." He'd comforted me and made me feel safe when I'd needed it most. He'd been a good friend.

And then he'd almost lost his life.

He leaned his head back against the seat of the car and stared at the traffic in front of us. "I don't want to know how many men you've been with," he said after a moment, turning to look at me again. "I'll start—and stop—counting when you've been with me."

I bit the inside of my cheek. His gaze was disconcerting, and I felt myself blush. "The difference between you and me," I said, "is that I believe in love and relationships."

"And you think I don't?"

"Just look at your track record. It's littered with one-night stands and short-termers. The one long-term relationship you've had ended. Was it because she wanted to get married?"

"No, it wasn't. We weren't right for each other." He looked at me. "I believe in love."

"Good to know. And just an FYI, I won't sleep with someone just because"—I paused, searching for the right word—"because I have an urge."

He raised a suggestive eyebrow at me. "But you do *get* urges. *That's* good to know."

My cheeks went fiery; it was a toss-up if they burned with embarrassment or desire. My urges hung there—a big white elephant crammed between the bucket seats. We passed a few dilapidated storefronts intermixed with a Dairy Queen, a 7-Eleven, and a couple hole-in-the-wall eateries on the street leading up to the apartment complex.

76

"Nice area," Jack commented.

"Detective work isn't all glamour. It's good versus evil, you know. Pursuing the greater good." I caught my breath, remembering I'd just thought the exact same thing about Jack's purpose in his job. We actually had something in common besides mutual lust.

Jack's raised eyebrow told me he'd missed the revelation. "Cut the bullshit, Lola. You actually *do* need a bodyguard in a place like this."

I'd told him more than once that my body was my weapon. "Have you seen my kick?"

He stifled a laugh, and I frowned at him. "What happens when you come across someone with a gun?"

Ah, the age-old question that Manny and Sadie both hounded me with. Target practice was honing my gun capabilities, but I wasn't going to carry unless I absolutely had to. Accidentally shoot someone? Free pass to San Quentin? Not going to happen. "A knee to the crotch," I said with a smug waggle of my head. "Works every time."

He looked at me like he thought a little one-on-one combat would be a huge turn-on.

He was right on the money.

I tried to keep a passive face as we walked across the cracked sidewalk and into the dank, dark building. It reeked of urine; the cement floors and brick walls were stained and slimy.

The nauseating odor of the interior hallway penetrated my nostrils. I tried breathing in through my mouth. It didn't really work.

Jack and I entered the stairwell at the end of the hallway, the same rank smells filling the confined space. We climbed the steps to the third floor. I avoided touching the stair rail, hugging my arms close to my body.

Sunday's newspaper was scattered in front of Dolores Cruz's doorway. I gave Jack a look that said, *No one's here to bring it in.* He nodded, clearly getting my nonverbal communication. I knocked. No answer.

"What now?" Jack whispered.

A sound down the hall caught my attention. The click of a door closing. The slice of light that shone underneath suddenly snuffed out. We were being watched.

I hightailed it to the door and knocked. It was yanked open, popping back as the safety chain snapped taut.

When the door settled open two inches, a middle-aged Filipina with brown almond-shaped eyes stared out at me, her wide, flat nose pronounced on her face. Nosy women, gotta love 'em.

"Hi," I said, flipping my hand up. "I'm—" I paused. Did I want to show my cards? "My name is Dolores," I said, deciding I really didn't have another choice. Maintaining anonymity was pretty high up in the detective rulebook, but right now I needed to reveal my identity so it could work for me.

Her vacant expression didn't change.

I forged ahead, holding out one of my business cards. "I'm a private investigator."

Her eyes flicked to Jack; her expression grew more alert.

"Jack Callaghan," he said, tossing her one of his charming smiles.

With my card still pinched between my fingers, I gave him a *back off* look. His smile dimmed.

Turning back to the woman, I concentrated on my own congeniality. "Do you know Ms. Cruz down the hall?"

"Who?"

"Ms. Cruz," I repeated.

"Number fourteen." Her head bobbed up and down. "She gone."

My breath caught in my throat, and I grabbed Jack's arm. Maybe this was the right place!

Jack patted my hand. His touch calmed my racing heart. "Right. That's right. Do you know where she went?"

"I not know *nothin'*." Then quick as a snake, she slammed the door closed. The dead bolt clicked into place.

Jack shoved his hands in his pockets. "That went well."

"But it's got to be her." I knew my excitement at finding the dead woman's apartment was twisted, but I couldn't help it. "This has to be *our* Dolores Cruz. I feel it in my gut."

He flashed me the same smile he'd given the woman a moment ago. "Let's hope so. She may have opened up to me, you know. With a little flirting—"

"Yeah, but I couldn't ask you to compromise your integrity." I moved down the hall, eager to talk to another neighbor and to avoid admitting that I wanted his flirting all to myself.

He smiled bigger. "I might compromise it for you."

"But if you did, then you wouldn't be the Jack I've always—" I bit my tongue. What had I been about to say? The Jack I'd lusted after since I'd photographed him—postcoital—when we were still teenagers? The Jack I'd wanted to succumb to in a fit of unbridled passion? The Jack I could, just possibly, if the stars aligned and all that, *love*? "I've always respected."

He managed not to laugh. Admirable, considering I was pretty sure he knew *exactly* what had passed through my mind.

I dropped the subject when we stopped in front of another neighbor's door. I knocked. And knocked again. After a few more tries with no answer, I moved on.

A faint rustling noise seeped through the door directly across from Dolores Cruz's apartment. When I tapped my knuckles against it, the rustling grew louder.

An unbelievably deep voice that sounded like a human foghorn bellowed, "Who's there?" The words seemed to ooze out around the edges of the slick door.

I leaned closer to Jack, catching a hint of his musky scent. "Feel free to flirt with *him*," I whispered. To the door I said, "Sir, I'd like to talk with you about one of your neighbors."

"Who?"

Did no one know this woman? "Your neighbor in apartment fourteen?"

"She gone," the man said from behind the door.

"Yes, I know that," I said in a singsong voice. "I'm a private investigator looking into her—her—being gone."

The door opened abruptly, and an enormous black man filled the rectangular frame, his bulk leaving no space to see into the room behind him. His face was friendly enough, round and pudgy, with tightly wound hair trimmed close to the scalp.

"Why you investigating? She do something?"

"We're not sure yet," I said.

Jack nudged himself closer to me. "So, do you know her?"

"Nope. Jus' saw her round." The deep rumbling of his voice vibrated through me. He shifted his girth, heaving his trunklike legs wider for balance.

I opened my mouth to speak but frowned when Jack's voice came out. "Did you happen to notice if she had any regular visitors? Anything at all out of the ordinary."

I elbowed him.

The man peered at Jack, raising his brows at him in a silent question.

"Jack Callaghan." He offered his hand and an engaging smile.

"Kyron Banks," the man said, returning the handshake.

I marveled at the effect of Jack's smile. It worked on men *and* women. He was shameless.

Kyron's hand engulfed Jack's, wiry hairs sticking out from the black pores that speckled his skin. "Nice to meet you, Kyron," Jack said.

Kyron grunted. The sound played like the lowest key on a piano.

I nudged in front of Jack and jumped back into the conversation. "Mr. Banks, Ms. Cruz is dead." I paused, waiting for a reaction. *Nada.* "We think her real name was Rosie Gonzales."

His round face with its two wide eyes and a round mouth reminded me of a bowling ball. "Huh." Kyron didn't seem surprised to know his neighbor had been using an alias, or that she was dead, for that matter.

"Mr. Banks, the smallest bit of information might help."

He grasped the doorjamb, hoisted his mass onto one leg, adjusted his position, and rooted his feet again. "They leavin'. I know that much."

At last! "Leaving? You mean moving?"

He angled his gaze at the locked door across the hall. "Boxes stacked high in there. They leavin', all right."

Jack cleared his throat. "Kyron. You said 'they.' Did someone else live with Ms. Gonzales?"

Kyron shrugged. "Jus' her and the boy."

"Rosie had a child?" I asked, nervously pushing my hair back behind my ears. The news hadn't mentioned that little fact. Not something Seavers would have discovered from a corpse. "Where is he now?"

Kyron Banks shrugged again. "Don't know."

The typical scenario of an abused woman came to mind. Was she running from someone? Was that her story? "Did you ever see a husband? A man?"

Kyron's lower lip protruded out. "Yeah, she have a man around sometimes."

Oh, boy. Had an estranged husband or boyfriend killed Rosie and taken her son? Or—oh, God—could the boy be inside the apartment?

"Mr. Banks," I said, panic filling my voice, "do you have any idea where her son might be?"

He seemed to understand my meaning. He clamped his mouth shut and lumbered past us. With his body turned to the side, he blocked most of Rosie Gonzales's door.

Jack and I stared at him.

"He's going in!" I whispered.

And then suddenly Kyron propelled his massive body forward and pounded his shoulder against the door of apartment 14. There was a loud crack, and a foot-long piece of molding split from the door frame. The door banged open, pieces of ragged wood splintering.

I gawked. "Wow. Uh, hmm. Wow."

Kyron lumbered back across the hallway to his apartment and turned back to us. "Hope you find him," he said just before he stepped inside his apartment and closed the door.

I looked at Jack, then at the open door. What to do? I was in a moral conundrum that was easily answered. If there was a child inside, we had to find him.

Jack went first. I tiptoed inside after him, my heart thumping in my chest. I did a quick search of the apartment, satisfied that there was no child trapped inside. Breathing again, I centered myself. We were in Rosie Gonzales's apartment. Answers were just minutes away.

Chapter 7

My first mistake was breathing. I gagged at the stench in the apartment. Rotting food, soiled baby diapers, and other untold odors mingled in the air. My nostrils twitched. "Oh m-my G-God," I sputtered, "this is a-awful."

The expression on Jack's face said it all. I'd had the opportunity to do a little snooping at his loft, and the man was neater than me. Which is saying a lot. He ran his hand through his hair and turned his back on me for a second. Glad I was a neat freak, too. Sloppiness might be a deal-breaker for Jack.

The thought that I should call Manny or Detective Seavers flitted through my mind. And flitted right out again. I wasn't billing hours for Manny. Best not to disturb him. And I didn't feel confident that Seavers would see our entrance into Rosie's apartment as the innocent breaking and entering it was.

I gave the main room a good perusal. A rickety-looking drop-leaf table was pushed up against the far wall, two equally rickety chairs tucked under it. Boxes were haphazardly pushed against the walls, the flaps lying open, bundles of newspaper-wrapped belongings piled into them. Discarded sections littered the floor. Kyron had been right on the money; Rosie had been planning to get the hell out of Dodge.

A rumpled couch sat in the middle of the room, angled out of its original position. Scraps of papers, a few action figures, and a handful discarded Cheerios were scattered around. Other than the action figures, there didn't seem to be much for a child to play with. No high chair, no other toys, no kids' clothing amid the laundry piled on a chair. *Pobrecito.*

"*This* Dolores isn't much of a housekeeper," Jack said. "Thank God you're into cleanliness."

"I am, but just so you know, I think you have unreasonably high expectations." I mean, his apartment had even passed the white glove test I'd given it.

"Actually," he said, raising an eyebrow at me, "setting high expectations means people generally rise to the occasion. And you," he added, "could give Martha Stewart a run for her money."

I couldn't argue his point. My mother had trained me to be freakishly clean. I scoured my apartment when I needed to think, cleaned just for fun, and took pride in a spotless house.

Apparently Rosie Gonzales didn't steal that part of my identity. A black plastic bag of trash had spilled across the floor in the kitchen. I whipped out the purple rubber gloves I always carried in my purse for just such a situation, slipped them on, and handed Jack a set. He arched an amused brow at me. I waggled my head back at him. "I believe in being prepared," I said.

"So do I," he shot back. "Trojans. Ring a bell?"

Heat rose to my cheeks. I quickly turned back to the contents of the bag, picking through it with my thumb and index finger.

"You know you're messing with the evidence here," Jack said.

"Yeah, that's occurred to me. But Rosie was a victim, not a suspect. That makes it a little less of an offense, right?" I wasn't really asking for his approval, but if he agreed, I'd definitely feel better.

He slapped on his gloves. "I guess so. But we should be careful."

"Of course." That was understood.

"You actually enjoy doing this, don't you?"

I peered up at him. "Yes." His pant leg brushed against me as he crouched by my side, and time seemed to slow to a crawl. Somehow, I managed to keep searching. Now that I knew there was a child involved—and potentially in danger—I was on a mission.

"Find anything?" he asked a few minutes later.

Had the woman's garbage held something sexier than discarded food, dirty diapers, and junk mail, I might have responded differently to his seductive tone. Instead, I stifled another gag. "Not yet," I said, and dug deeper. I burrowed through the waste, my gloved hand finding a pile of papers that had been shoved into the bottom of the bag. I pulled them out.

They looked promising. I took my find to the table and sat down. The chair creaked under my weight, and I braced myself in case it collapsed. My palms pressed against the table, my weight shifting from butt to feet. There was another ominous creak, but thankfully the chair held.

Jack lifted a cushion from the couch and bent down to peer at the crumbs. "Find the smoking gun?" he asked.

"Funny."

He dropped the cushion back into place. "This place needs fumigation."

I nodded, flipping through the papers in front of me. "We should leave everything just like we found it."

"Yeah," Jack deadpanned, eyeing the busted door. "Wouldn't want to mess things up." He pushed the couch parallel to the wall, crouched down, and pulled a glossy folder out from underneath. He flipped through it. "Are you going to tell that detective you were here?"

My methodical search of the papers continued. "If we find something that can confirm it's Rosie's apartment." My voice remained remarkably calm. "We figured out the address. The door was open." By Kyron, and illegally, but we thought there was a child in danger. Surely Detective Seavers would see the urgency.

Jack held up the folder. "Looks like our vic did a stint in drug rehab."

"Oh, yeah?" I played it nonchalant, not wanting to let on how hot I thought he looked, holding up a valuable clue in my own personal mystery. "Where?"

"Brenda Dawson Clinic for Drug and Alcohol Rehabilitation," he read. "In Auburn."

He handed me the folder. I looked at the information inside: my name scrawled on the top in black Sharpie, and a date. "She was there a year ago, according to this." It might have been ancient history, but it was worth following up on. I wrote down the clinic information before handing the folder back to him. He put it back under the couch, and I went back to Rosie's papers.

They were crumpled and stained in various colors of God knew what. The woman had tossed away weeklies from the mail, a variety of glossy mailers, and credit card solicitations. It was all addressed to Dolores Cruz. The more I saw my name, the fuzzier my brain felt.

The stack grew smaller, but I gave each piece of paper a thorough examination before putting it in my "of no importance" pile. I still didn't have *proof* that this was *Rosie's* apartment. My gut wasn't enough.

"Here's something," I said, holding up a credit card application. "It's partially filled out." My blood ran cold as I saw the neat, left-slanted writing. It had my address, the name Rosie, and the G-O-N from Gonzales, but that was crossed out and mine was written in its place. But she'd tossed it away. Too many mistakes, I guessed.

I wondered about something Detective Seavers had said. He'd thought maybe I'd been letting an illegal immigrant use my name. Seavers had identified her through an anonymous caller, not through AFIS. If she was an illegal, her prints wouldn't be part of the fingerprinting system. She wouldn't exist as far as the United States was concerned. I wondered if Gonzales was really her last name.

She was inconsistent as a thief; that much was clear. "It's her. This is Rosie's place." My address on the application was proof enough for me.

I put the application in my "keep" pile and moved on. Three

other partially filled out credit card applications, these complete with my Social Security number, had been in Rosie's trash. How much damage had this woman done to me? And how much more would she have managed had she not died? I slammed both hands on the table. "How did she get this stuff?"

"There are a thousand ways. Identity theft's still the fastest-growing crime in America."

So Seavers had told me.

"I can't believe it." My voice shook. "You read about this stuff, but you never think it'll happen to you."

Jack laid his purple gloved hand on mine, his rubbery touch only mildly comforting. "You need to assess the situation and act based on the facts."

I swallowed and nodded, waving the credit applications in the air. "I will. I *am*." I added the applications to the "keep" pile and finished looking through the diminishing stack.

The next valuable piece of garbage was a birthday party invitation. It was for a boy named Elijah. No last name. Pins pricked behind my eyes as I registered that the date of the party had been the same day Rosie had died. Jackpot.

"Is there an address?" Jack asked, looking at the slick dinosaur card.

I shook my head. "Just a phone number." I stuck the invitation with the credit applications.

I jotted the phone number and name from the invitation down in my notebook, followed by the credit card companies Rosie had applied to. How long had she been living as me?

Accidentally sucking in a deep breath brought on a fresh wave of nausea. I closed my eyes and waited for it to pass. When I was able to breathe without fear of losing my lunch, I got back to work. Leaving my discoveries on the table—easy access for the police—I searched the rest of Rosie's apartment. Every room was stripped bare, like the Whos' house after the Grinch had finished with it. Nail holes marked the dingy walls, and a loose wire hung from a quarter-sized hole in the bedroom. With Jack at my heels, I peered into the only bathroom. The cracked toilet seat was up, and yellow stains marking the torn linoleum floor.

If not for the fact that I didn't want to change the scene any more than necessary, I would have used a toilet paper square to lower the seat and lid. Force of habit. Finding the seat left up was a major pet peeve of mine. I silently tsked Rosie, but stopped short. *She* wouldn't have lifted the seat. Unless, of course, she was a transvestite, but since Seavers hadn't mentioned *that*, I dismissed it.

I looked at Jack. "You didn't sneak in here and use the bathroom when I wasn't looking, did you?"

He made a face showing his disgust. "Uh, no."

"Didn't think so. That means a man's been here." The question was who.

Fifteen more minutes of searching turned up nothing else. We stripped off the gloves—pocketing them to dispose of outside Rosie's apartment.

I left feeling sad that we were no closer to finding Rosie's son, frustrated that we hadn't found out more about the woman and why she'd stolen my identity, and angry and agitated about the state of my credit.

Back in the car, Jack and I both jotted notes, me in my file on Rosie, and him in his narrow journalist's notebook. I wrote:

- *Was Rosie an abused wife or girlfriend?*
- *Where is her son?*
- *Kyron Banks saw man around—boyfriend or husband?*
- *Where was Rosie moving to, and why?*
- *Why did she need a new identity?*
- *Who is Elijah, and did Rosie take her son to the birthday party the day she died?*

Jack scribbled furiously, obviously inspired. I absently answered my ringing cell phone, tucking the file folder on Rosie next to my seat.

"Lola, *bonita, hermana.*" The sugary sweetness in Antonio's voice meant he was up to no good.

"Tonio, *loco, hermano,*" I said, knowing *exactly* what was coming.

He cut to the chase. "I need you to work the dinner shift," he said. "I'm short staffed."

The car's digital clock read 5:10. The dinner shift had already begun. "Why? Isn't Chrissy working tonight?"

"She just quit."

I dropped my forehead against the steering wheel. "Damn it, Tonio, did you go to bed with her?"

"Of course not!" Antonio's voice was indignant, and almost sincere, but my attention was split. Jack's gaze was on me, the phrase "going to bed" swirling around in the car between us. "I didn't do anything," my brother said. "Abuelo scared her."

"How?" I managed to focus on the restaurant drama. "What'd he do?"

Antonio grumbled. "He banged his cane on the table and ordered more salsa. Then, when she brought it"—he paused, sucking in a breath as if he still couldn't believe it—"he tasted it and cussed her out."

"In Spanish or English?" I asked absently, suddenly distracted by Jack's arm stretched across the bucket seats of the car. His fingertips lightly touched my hair.

"Both," Antonio said.

My head grew fuzzy. I *really* didn't want to work at the restaurant tonight. Not with Jack right here next to me, bed on both of our minds.

"Cranky old man is losing his marbles," Antonio added. "I don't know why he torments the waitresses."

"Chrissy really quit?" I asked, praying Antonio was just messing with me. "You couldn't talk her out of it?"

He scoffed. "She ran into the kitchen crying—totally hysterical. Said she couldn't take the abuse anymore."

"Anymore? It's only been a couple days!" I groaned. "She didn't really try!"

"Ornery *viejo*," Antonio said, but I could tell he was biting back stronger words to describe our grandfather. "Come on, Lola. I *need* you."

"You need me," I muttered under my breath. But there was no point in arguing. I wouldn't be able to concentrate on *Jack* needing me if I knew Antonio was scrambling and understaffed at the restaurant. I sighed. "Okay, but you owe me."

He heaved a sigh of relief. "*Gracias.* I've got another interview lined up tonight at seven. If this one's any good, I'll pick her up and you'll be off the hook for tomorrow."

"Oh no. I am *not* working tomorrow. I have things to—"

But Antonio had hung up.

I turned in my seat, one hand on the steering wheel, the other shoving my phone back into my purse as if it had betrayed me. "I have to work the dinner shift."

"So I heard. No problem. I'll work on my column at the restaurant. I haven't even interviewed you yet. We have all night."

All night. I chewed on my cheek. Jack *had* looked up the newspaper subscriptions for me and dropped everything to bring them over. He'd spent the afternoon illegally entering a dead woman's apartment to help me. I could answer his questions, and in the process, I could learn more about Jack Callaghan, the adult.

I nodded. "All night, huh?" I asked coyly. I was over his disappearing act.

He grinned suggestively. "All night."

Before I could bail out Antonio, I had to let Detective Seavers know about Rosie's apartment and her missing son. I phoned him up, and—what a guy—he agreed to meet us at the restaurant.

"So what about your column on identity theft?" I asked as we drove to Abuelita's. It was the one thing we hadn't yet talked about, and the reason Jack had tagged along. Supposedly.

"Tough to write. I can't reveal anything about the case, but it's an important topic."

"Your source, the guy in Grass Valley, does he have something to do with the column?"

He hesitated before answering. "Some sources are confidential," he finally said. "Let's just say he's been involved in identity theft, but not on the victim side."

Ohhhh. So he was like Rosie. His actions had contributed to destroying someone else's life.

Jack didn't want to say any more. We arrived at the restaurant, Detective Seavers right behind us.

We sat at a table and I filled him in on my discoveries, starting with the storage unit and ending with Rosie's apartment and the missing boy.

Seavers stepped outside, returning a few minutes later. "I'm sending a team over there," he said, not bothering to sit. "You said the door was open?"

"One of the neighbors was concerned about Rosie's son. He decided he didn't want to wait for you."

"So we'll find your fingerprints in the apartment, Ms. Cruz?"

He obviously didn't think very highly of my skills. "No, you won't. We didn't disrupt the scene."

"I certainly hope not." He started to turn, but stopped, looking me in the eyes. "I understand your desire to investigate this, Ms. Cruz, but don't interfere."

"I want to help," I said. "She stole my identity, and now her son is missing."

"Keep me informed." It was a command, not a request.

"I will," I said, and the detective left. A sense of relief filled me. The police were on the case, they knew about Rosie's child, and they'd do everything they could to find him. I could relax. As much as my obsessive personality would allow me to.

A little while later, I was waitressing and Jack was hunkered down at a corner table. His notebook was open, his laptop was fired up, and a steaming plate of *chiles rellenos* sat in front of him. He tapped away on the keyboard, pausing every now and then for a bite of food before losing himself in his writing again. His concentration was impressive, and not something I was currently able to mimic. I forced myself to be busy, not wanting to be caught watching him.

Mondays were slow in the restaurant industry, and Abuelita's was no exception, even with my "death" to drum up business. There were only a handful of diners, all of them taken care of. "I'm taking a break," I told Antonio, bringing a glass of water with me to Jack's table.

"How's the column coming?" I asked.

"Slowly," he answered, eyes riveted on the monitor. "I need to do more research." He looked up at me. "Can you give me a quote? How does it feel knowing that someone was out there using your name— pretending to be you?"

I idly picked up his discarded fork and pushed the rice around his plate as I thought about his question.

He took the fork from me, filled it with a helping of egg-battered *pasilla* chili and cheese, and propelled it toward me. My mouth opened automatically, and he gingerly placed the fork inside. He watched me intently as I closed my lips around the tines. He gently pulled the fork back out, and as I used my tongue to catch a stringy piece of cheese caught on my lip, Jack's eyes seemed to darken to a deep sapphire.

I quickly swallowed and took a drink, washing away the food and the intimate moment. Now was not the time. And Abuelita's was *so* not the place.

"So?" Jack said after a long ten seconds.

My racing heart had me flustered and off center.

"About the identity theft," he reminded me.

Right. "Well—" How *did* I feel? "I'm angry. I'm worried about how much she might have messed with my credit. And I'm mad that I have to deal with straightening it all out." Jack scribbled rapidly as I spoke. "I want to know how she got my information. She knew things about me that she shouldn't have known, and that makes me feel uncomfortable. Violated. I'm wondering why me, and what happened to her—"

His cell phone cut me off midsentence. He held up a finger. "Hold that thought."

I forked another bite of *chiles rellenos* while he answered his phone. It better not be Sarah, I thought, watching him for signs of past-girlfriend familiarity.

"Actually, I'm in the middle of dinner," he said into his black phone a second later.

His radiant blue eyes were piercing against his honey-colored skin. And they were focused on me even as he spoke to whoever had called him.

I took another bite of his dinner, sauce dribbling onto my lip. My gaze steady on him, I pulled my lower lip into my mouth and sucked off the red sauce. Jack lips parted. His chest rose as he sucked in a deep breath.

That's right, Jack, you're with me tonight.

"Hold on," he said after another few seconds, not sounding happy. He put the phone on his leg. His voice was low when he spoke to me. "How late are you working tonight?"

"No waitress," I said. "I'll be here till closing."

Jack thought for a second, sighed, and muttered, "*Damn.*" Then he put the phone back to his ear. "Okay," he said, and he gave directions to Abuelita's before hanging up.

"Problem?" I asked.

He smiled, and my gaze drifted to the dimple that etched into his cheek. "Only that you're stuck here tonight." He finished the last bite of his dinner and closed down his computer.

I'd just sat down, and it looked like he was packing up. "You're leaving?"

"I'll call you tomorrow."

"But the interview . . . ," I said, though my tone sounded more like, *But you didn't kiss me yet.*

"I'll take a rain check."

"Your car's at Camacho's." I felt like I was grasping at straws, trying to get him to stay.

"Don't worry about it." His eyes flicked to the restaurant's window. "I'll pick it up."

An uneasiness crept into my body. Call it intuition. "So where are you off to?"

He balled up his napkin and dropped it on his plate. "There's an intern at the paper. She needs to interview someone for an assignment. She's been bugging me about it for weeks, and I keep putting her off."

She? "Oh, yeah?" My eyes narrowed. "What kind of interview?"

He laughed. "Relax. It's just an intern. She's got to write a paper about the career path for a writer or something."

"There's no such thing as *just* an intern." Not after Bill Clinton.

He clasped his notebook and computer under his arm. "Lola, you have to trust me. You're working tonight and you are far too distracting for me because all I want to do is tell Antonio that it's his fault for losing another waitress and take you away from here. To hell with the restaurant. But I can't do that, and you wouldn't let me anyway. So I'll go, let you work, and get this interview over with."

He checked the window again, and his face registered recognition as a gleaming white Corvette pulled into the parking lot. "I'll see you tomorrow, Lola." He flashed me his charming smile, bent, and lightly kissed my cheek.

That's not the kind of kiss I want! But he didn't hear the scream in my head. He just headed toward the door.

"Thanks for your help today," I called after him.

He lifted his arm in a wave as he pushed out into the parking lot. Beelining to the front window, I saw a young redhead bounce out of the car and flash Jack a toothy smile. I cringed when I saw her fake boobs filling a too-tight shirt. I automatically looked down at my outfit—and my *puro* natural breasts—and frowned. Just what kind of breasts did Jack like?

Stop! I scolded myself. He'd asked me to trust him. She was just an intern—I cringed at the phrase. Antonio walked up behind me, and we stood there in silence until the Corvette sped out of the parking lot. "Who was that?" he asked.

"Someone Jack works with," I said.

"Hmm. I didn't know he worked with a redhead."

I punched his arm. "Why can't you stay away from the waitresses?"

"Guess I'm addicted," he said.

Him and me both. My eyes burned with the sudden onslaught of emotion that I'd kept in check all day. Every thought I'd had about Rosie living her life as me tumbled out, wrapped in a neat little package that was suddenly directed at Jack. He'd spent the day charming me, being helpful, making me forget my doubts about him, and then he'd up and left with someone else.

I wanted to trust him. But I *knew* I should have kept a lock on my heart.

By seven forty-five, the restaurant was still slogging through the dinner shift. Trying my hardest not to think about Jack, the redhead, Rosie Gonzales, or my credit, I warmed up a flour tortilla and made myself a burrito. Piled on cheese, sour cream, salsa, and guacamole. It was comfort food at its best. I leaned against the wall in the corner of the kitchen, eating away my sorrows. Not a proud moment, but my jeans and I would worry about that tomorrow.

Antonio sauntered up to me, an attractive woman by his side. "Lola, meet Sylvia Johnson, our new waitress."

I froze, an oversized bite in my mouth. The woman looked at me like I was a movie star, all wide-eyed and amazed.

I swallowed with a heavy gulp, waving at her. My half-eaten burrito collapsed in my hand, and I scrambled to catch it before it dropped into the garbage. Too late. It was a gooey mess.

When I looked up again, Sylvia was still staring at me, her expression disbelieving.

"Are you okay?" I asked.

She shook her awed expression away. "Sorry. It's just, I saw your story on the news. I've never met anyone who's been on TV before, even if it *was* just a picture of you."

Great. Another death groupie. "I'm really a ghost," I said with a wink. "Ask my grandmother."

Sylvia laughed, apologizing again. "When my ex-husband showed me the ad for the waitress position here, I told him it *couldn't* be the same place. Not the restaurant where that dead girl who's not dead is from, I said. I was sure it couldn't be, but then I saw the banner outside."

I'd been bobbing my head as she spoke and gave a final rounded nod as she wrapped up her speech. "Right," I said, throwing a quick and pointed glare at Antonio for the banner he still hadn't taken down. "Well, nice meeting you, um, Sylvia. Are you starting tomorrow then?" *Please start tomorrow.*

"I told Antonio I'm available first thing. My ex-husband has our kids tonight, so I can stay and get a feel for the place. I can shadow you, you know?"

I nodded approvingly. Sylvia seemed insanely eager, and I loved her for it. I even fantasized that she might hold her own against Abuelo. If nothing else, she'd probably confuse him with her fast talking.

I crooked my index finger at her. She leaned in, and I pointed across the dining room. "Steer clear of that booth. The man there thinks he's the head of the Mexican Mafia. Sounds just like Marlon Brando, only with a Spanish accent. Ignore him, okay?"

Sylvia nodded knowingly, as if she knew hundreds of old men in the Mexican Mafia. "Hey, I deal with my ex every day. If I can handle *his* insanity, I can handle anyone." She had a slight accent, her pronunciation of words a smidgen off.

I pegged her as a first-generation immigrant, born in Latin America somewhere but raised here. Her shoulder-length light brown hair was thick and a little unruly. I looked at Antonio to see if he would tell her to wear it pulled back, but he had moved on to check the status of the salsa vat.

96

"How many kids do you have?" I asked, thinking casual chitchat might win her over and compel her to stay. I wanted her to be a keeper. She *had* to commit herself to Abuelita's, body and soul.

"Four. Oh, well—" She broke off, a crack in her voice. "T-three. Me and Guillermo, we lost our youngest."

"Oh, Sylvia." I wanted to kick myself for being nosy. I squeezed her shoulder.

Her face had lost some of its color. "It's been a year now. He was just an infant."

"I'm so sorry."

"It tore our family apart. We got divorced," she said, adding, "Guillermo—he still hasn't accepted that the baby's gone."

"Oh, no," I said, realizing how lame that sounded. I was speechless. What did you say to a woman who'd suffered like Sylvia had?

She pushed her hair back behind her ears, and we gave in to the awkward moment of silence. "Let me show you around," I finally said. Aside from her electrified hair, she looked professional in black slacks and beige sweater. She followed behind me as I moved through the dining room, checking on customers and refilling water glasses. We made idle small talk as I worked. I moved to the busing station and began folding the red cloth napkins, stacking them under the counter.

"You have to wear black pants," I said as my eyes flicked to hers. "Those are perfect." I plucked at my white peasant blouse. "Antonio will give you a shirt tomorrow. You'll have a locker upstairs in the break room to store your things during your shift."

She nodded. "I'm grateful for the job, you know. My ex loves this place. Says the fish tacos are out of this world."

"¿Hablas español?"

She nodded. "Sí. Soy de Venezuela."

"¿Y su esposo, tambien?"

"William? He's a *gringo*." She smiled wanly. "I still call him Guillermo. Old habits die hard." She folded napkins as she spoke, copying exactly what I did. "So did that woman actually steal your name?" she asked, awe slipping into her voice. "Do you know why?"

I grimaced. "Yes, she did, and I have no idea why."

Sylvia concentrated on stacking her napkins right alongside mine. I sneaked a glance at her. Poor woman. Hearing about her child had put things in perspective for me. My problem could be solved. It would take time, but I'd get my credit situation back under control and I'd find out why it had happened. Sylvia couldn't reclaim what she'd lost.

She folded the last napkin, and we moved on to the salt and pepper shakers, unscrewing each lid and filling them to the top using a funnel.

"Scary what people do," Sylvia said.

"It sure is," I agreed.

Chapter 8

Bright and early the next morning, I called the phone number from the birthday invitation I'd found at the apartment. I tried to time it so I'd reach them before they left for work or school or whatever. After fifteen rings and no answering machine, I finally hung up.

The dog days of summer were wearing on me; I longed for fall, so I dressed in a straight brick-red suede skirt, a lightweight cream blouse, and two-inch heeled brown boots. Who cared if it was barely September? Maybe my sheer will would bring in a cold front from the Pacific.

With my hair piled on my head in a loose half bun and half pony-tail, tendrils falling around my face, I headed to Camacho and Associates. I immediately recorded my new information on the whiteboard and was standing back reviewing it when Manny came in.

"You're here early." His dark eyes peered at me, and I swallowed a self-conscious breath.

My hands absently straightened my skirt, and I stood up straighter. I filled Manny in on my case, giving him the same information I'd given Seavers the night before and paying close attention to his de-meanor. Nothing out of the ordinary. "I'm thinking she may have been the victim of domestic violence."

He looked at my notes and gave a curt nod. "You have to either prove it or disprove it."

That was the extent of Manny's words of wisdom. Prove or disprove my hypothesis. The rest was up to me.

He sauntered into his office, his alligator-skin boots tugging at the threads of the carpet as he walked. Either I was a terrible detective, Manny was a brilliant actor, or he felt *less* than nothing for me. I decided to go with the third option. Manny was my boss, nothing more, and at best, he seemed indifferent toward me.

I was mildly distracted by the fact that Reilly's chair was, once again, empty. Try as I might, I couldn't keep my mind on my case. Finally, after twenty-three minutes, I caved to my snooping impulse. I checked over my shoulder to make sure I was still alone, then quickly tiptoed over to Reilly's desk.

My spy skills were second to none. I'd been practicing on Jack since I was fourteen years old, after all. I scoured every nook and cranny of her desk in a matter of minutes. Nothing seemed to be missing. All her J.Lo CDs were tossed haphazardly in the bottom left drawer. Her favorite shades of lipstick—all bright to match her hair—were lined up in the top drawer right next to nine sharpened pencils.

I moved to the surface of the desk and looked at her daily calendar of happy, smiling fruits and veggies. The top page was two days old.

Red flag. Reilly had a thing for calendars and she *always* ripped off the day's sheet before she left the office. I'd never known her to miss this ritual. I looked at the other things on her desk, zeroing in on her calendar blotter. Appointments and notes were written all over in her loopy writing. How she kept it all straight, I had no idea. There didn't seem to be rhyme or reason behind what square she put random information in. I scanned the notes, stopping short at the square with today's date:

11:00   Dr. Burke
1:30   Fair Oaks and Howe—Jokowski

Two appointments. That would explain her absence today, but Reilly wasn't one to keep secrets. If something was ailing her, she would have told me; I was sure of it.

I did what any good friend would do. I dug for more information. The rest of Reilly's desk yielded nothing, but an Internet search gave me answers just like that. Dr. Burke was . . . a pediatrician. And Jokowski, located in an office building at Fair Oaks and Howe Avenue, was a family law attorney.

The plot of one of my sister's favorite romance novels came to mind. Secret baby. Oh. My. God. Had Reilly been keeping a child from me all these years? Had a moment of passion gotten the better of her and now she had a child she was fighting to get custody of?

No, that couldn't be the answer. Reilly had never even hinted at being a mother, and she could not keep a secret. I sank into a chair at the conference table and tried to formulate another answer, but nothing came to mind.

She was definitely up to something; at least I knew that. I'd puzzle it out eventually. Or maybe I'd just ask her when I saw her next.

I spent the rest of the morning researching identity theft and calling the credit card companies I'd found information on at Rosie's apartment. She hadn't opened up any accounts in my name with the companies I called, but that didn't mean there weren't others I didn't know about yet. I had to bide my time until the credit reports I'd ordered came in.

I spent the lunch hour at Abuelita's training Sylvia. By the time three o'clock rolled around, I was ready for my facial with Lucy. I parked in her driveway and walked through the drought-resistant, lava-rocked yard, thinking again how I much preferred lush landscaping. A stop by the McKinley Rose Garden on my way home would counteract the negative effects of Lucy and Zac's Spartan desert, the theft of my identity, and artificially endowed redheaded interns. The season was waning, and the roses were beginning to fade. Still, a few lingering scents and buds were sure to soothe my mind.

The front door flung open before I had a chance to ring the bell. "Lola!" The sheer volume of Lucy's voice ricocheted off the bonsailike trees that lined the walkway.

She and I were polar opposites. The only things we had in common were our family connection and our love of yoga. It was enough. She was completely free and uninhibited, and liked being my sidekick—when I needed a sidekick. I hated being here under false pretenses, but the idea that Lucy might be cheating on Zac was a worse scenario.

She hugged me, then led me into her spa room, complete with tinkling chimes and a mini waterfall feature. "I can't believe you're here! It's been forever since I gave you a facial. This one's on the house," she added.

"It is not." Paying for my facial somehow made my real intent a little less manipulative.

She waved away my protest. "No worries," she said with a wink. "I give a free facial to all my clients who come back from the dead."

"Lucy." I prepped myself for an argument, but her frown stopped me.

"What's the 411?" she asked.

I laughed. She was a California girl through and through, right down to her bleached blond hair and golden skin. She and Zac had been married eleven years, had three kids, and always seemed happy. Could she really be cheating? "No 411. Just 911. Blackhead emergency," I elaborated.

Her face relaxed, and mine tensed. *Mentirosa.* But calling myself a liar didn't make me fess up. I was on a mission of discovery.

"You look great," I said. "Love the skirt." The thin rayon fringy number and the snug navy T-shirt fit Lucy's sun-worshipping earthy style to perfection.

"No, *you* look amazing! Look at *that* skirt and those boots. Fabulous!"

My suede skirt hit my legs just above the knees, leaving a five-inch gap between it and my brown boots. I was celebrating a season that hadn't hit Sacramento yet. A little overzealously, since it wasn't likely to hit for another month and a half, at least.

"I could never wear that. It's too sophisticated for me," she continued. She sucked in a sharp breath, a sudden knowing expression spreading onto her face. "You're in love, aren't you?" I shook my head emphatically, but she kept on. "Yes, you are! You're in love. . . . Ooooh, tell me everything." She thrust a wraparound towel at me. "But change into this first, and I'll be right back. I'm going to push back my next appointment so we can have lots of time to talk. Then you can spill it."

She flew out of the room, and I stripped out of my clothes, quickly wrapping the strapless towel around my body and pressing the snaps together. I placed my neatly folded clothes on a divan and arranged myself on the special salon chair, pushing the knot of my hair up so I wouldn't lie on it.

It was a cinch to eavesdrop; Lucy's boisterous voice shot through the thin walls. "Honey, push it back a half an hour. That's all. We'll have plenty of time." I chewed my cheek. *Honey?* Who was she talking to?

She blew back into the room like a whirlwind. "All set? Great."

"Was that a client on the phone? You don't have to cancel an appointment for me." So nonchalant. *Brava,* Lola.

"What? Nah." She dismissed the idea. "He's a regular. He has flexible hours."

He? And why did Lucy know her client had flexible hours? I cleared my throat. "You must get to know your clients pretty well."

"Nah," she said again. "Just some people like to talk. They share *everything,* you know?" She patted my shoulder. "That guy? His wife hates his back hair, so he comes in once a month and I wax it. Brutal, but it makes her happy. The things people do for each other."

"Yeah." I thought about Zac wanting me to investigate his wife. I swallowed guiltily. "The things people do."

103

Lucy pressed a button on a small stereo in the corner, and the sound of tinkling New Age music filled the room. She settled in on the swivel stool behind my head. "Now spill it. It's that Jack Callaghan, right?"

I opened my mouth to say, *Pfft, not Jack Callaghan*, but I couldn't do it. "Yes," I said. "It's Jack Callaghan. But it's not love." Not yet anyway.

She stared down at me. "Uh-huh." She began cleaning the light layer of makeup off my face, wiping my skin in a circular motion with a cotton pad. Lucy had a gentle touch that was totally at odds with her booming voice and personality. She had hidden layers. "Love is a good thing. You need a man."

"I don't *need* a man, Lucy." I might want one, but I didn't need one. "Last time I had a man for any length of time, he cheated on me and stole from my parents. I'm fine by myself."

"Like Sergio counts. That was a lifetime ago. Whatever. I'm just glad you're here." She smiled at me upside down. "That death scare was too much."

My eyes glazed. Lying to further a case was one thing. Lying to my cousin-in-law was something else entirely.

The volume of her voice dropped, but was still commanding. "Did you find out who the woman in the alley was? I couldn't believe it when Antonio called that night."

I let my eyes drift closed as I listened to Lucy's train-of-thought recollections.

"Zac answered the phone. He knew something was wrong right away—Antonio could barely get the words out."

My breath became shallow as Lucy told me how she and Zac had gathered up their kids and rushed right over to be with my parents.

"When you walked in, it was surreal. Like an old *Twilight Zone* episode."

"I felt the same way!"

Lucy's fingers tapped against the edges of my scalp, pinpointing my temples. "So who was it? Who died?"

"Her name was Rosie Gonzales. I didn't know her, and I haven't come up with a reason why she might have been killed. All I *do* know is that she stole my identity."

Lucy's hands clamped down onto my shoulders. "No way!"

"Yes way. Unbelievable. Jack and I found her apartment and—"

"*Whoa, back up.* Jack went with you? To her apartment?"

Shoot. She was right—her table was like a therapist's couch. I hadn't meant to spill that tidbit. "He works for the *Bee*. He looked up addresses for me, and, uh, he's writing an article. . . ."

"*Ahhh*. I see."

I popped open one eye and peered up at her.

"So you *are* dating." She ran a warm towel over my face and began applying something else. "I knew it!"

"No, we're not." Who was on a mission to get information here? I wanted to get off Jack and onto Lucy and Zac. "We had one hot, incredible . . ." My voice got trembly. ". . . frustrating date."

"Oh," she said. "That guy is smokin'. And hot, incredible, and frustrating are not bad qualities, I want you to know."

Lucy was married, and she'd noticed Jack. The woman at Rosie's apartment complex noticed Jack. The damn intern with a life-preserver as a chest noticed him. *Hijo de su madre*, he *was* smokin', and I was gone for him.

"He's got some baggage," I said.

She patted my shoulder as she began to exfoliate, sloughing my skin free of dead cells. "Ah, well. No relationship's perfect."

An opening, finally! "You and Zac are pretty close to perfect." I spread my arms wide. "You have a faithful husband, great kids, a house, a job you love. And Zac's, uh, sorta smokin'."

Saying it all out loud, I realized it did sound good. Lucy seemed to have it all.

"No, not perfect. When we have date night—which is never—hot, incredible, and frustrated only describes the food and the restaurant bill."

I sat up and turned to look at her. "Don't you have happily ever after?" I was asking for myself, as well as for Zac. I wanted to believe that marriage and kids could be fulfilling. But the risks I took as a detective gave me a rush, and the satisfaction I felt at doing my job and doing it well was an even bigger thrill. Could a marriage and family compete with that?

She shrugged her bony shoulders, smiling at me. "Zac's great, you know? Good provider. Good father. But the roller-coaster ride's over. We're on the merry-go-round now."

I frowned. She hadn't said Zac was a good *husband*. "Does there have to be a roller coaster? Isn't marriage supposed to be stable?" I thought of my parents, plodding through their lives with their four kids, their restaurant, their home, each other. It wasn't exciting, but it was normal.

"I'm thirty-five." Her voice was matter-of-fact and tinged with melancholy.

"You make it sound like that's over the hill. Most women *want* the merry-go-round with the dependable husband who's still in love with them. It's the happy ending."

She propelled me back down onto the chair. "But isn't there more? I mean, you have your job. Your life will never be dull, even with all the other stuff. Being a skin aesthetician isn't thrilling, you know? I mean how many hairy backs and furry lips can a person look at before everyone becomes Wolverine? Only it's not Hugh Jackman, it's Wolfman Jack."

I frowned. Too many Jacks.

"Don't mash your face like that. You'll give yourself wrinkles." I unscrunched, and she covered my eyes with lavender-scented pads and clicked on a bright light to scrutinize my pores. "Let's talk about something else." Her voice tried to be upbeat. "Your skin is gorgeous! Not a single blackhead." She squeezed moisturizer onto her palms and began massaging it into my face.

I was bothered by Lucy's disillusionment with her life. Had she turned to someone else for comfort? I knew that George Clooney topped her strip list, but maybe she'd gone for someone totally out of character. Maybe someone with a shaved head? No hair would appeal to her.

My eyes popped open, dislodging the pads. "What do you think of Bruce Willis?"

Lucy replaced the scented pads. "Eh," she said. Then she stroked my face and neck, working her magic, easing all my tension out, but giving me nothing more about herself or her marriage.

Chapter 9

By Wednesday morning, the weather of late summer had finally shifted. Gray clouds peppered the sky, dimming the blue with a vast muggy haze. My phone beeped with an incoming text message. I glanced at the screen. It was from Reilly! God, how I missed that crazy girl. I read it, frowning. *Doing a job for* el jefe. *Dying to give u the 411. So cool. Top secret. Over and out.*

My imagination ran wild. Doing a job for Manny could mean anything from picking up a new order of handcuffs or binoculars at a local spy store to . . . to . . . to . . . I drew a blank. What kind of job would Manny have Reilly do?

I texted back. *What kind of job?*

But she didn't respond.

At 9:45, I pulled into Camacho's parking lot and slid my car into the slot next to the macho-machine: Manny's beefy white truck. I marched past Szechwan House, turning my head away from the door. Not even the pull of a morning potsticker could deter me from my mission. If Reilly was a receptionist-on-special-assignment-as-a-detective, I was afraid she was in over her head. As her friend, I had a duty to help her.

But despite the truck outside, the office was deserted. My mission was delayed. I poured myself a cup of coffee, stood in front of the whiteboard again, and contemplated my case. Not a single revelation came to me.

A flash of reflected light from outside caught my eye. I peered through the tinted plate-glass office window in time to see Sadie zip her flashy red sports car into the parking lot. The passenger door opened, and Manny unfolded himself from the small space, stretching his lanky body into an upright position. Manny in Sadie's sports car was like an oxymoron—or a scene from a slapstick cartoon. They just didn't go together.

Sadie popped out of the driver's side, her spiky blond hair less perfectly coiffed than usual, her cheeks flushed, a red-lipsticked smile slapped across her face with smug satisfaction. I looked back to Manny. He had his back to Sadie, his chin dropped to his chest. Sadie walked up beside him, flicking her red-tipped fingernails against his sleeve. He jerked, retracting slightly, and she dropped her hand, the smile on her face pulling tight.

Manny turned to her and spoke, his lips barely moving. Sadie stood, frozen, and he ambled toward the office.

I scooted into the back room, half of me wishing I were a fly on the wall in the conference room so I could keep watching them, the other half wanting to scrub my eyes with soap to erase the image of them from my mind. The fly-on-the-wall half of me won. I was like a lookie-loo at a car accident—I had a twisted, horrified desire to know all the gory details of the Manny-and-Sadie drama. I poked my head around the corner to peer into the conference room, wishing my *chismosa* Reilly were here to share the moment with.

I held my breath as Manny rounded the corner from the lobby into the conference room. Everything about him, from his rock-hard body to his wood-stained scalp and crew cut, screamed dangerous. His eyes flicked to Sadie as she breezed in behind him. Even from my hidden position, I could smell the heavy perfume trailing in her wake.

She touched his arm again, and he looked down at her. "It doesn't have to be this way," she said.

Manny's expression was odd. It was like he was in the midst of an inner battle between anger and resignation, and neither side was ready to admit defeat. Finally, his eyes narrowed with wariness. "Yes, it does."

Sadie dropped her arm to her side and took a step back. "She needs—"

"No!" he snapped.

My mind raced through the possible meanings of their conversation. *Who* needed what? A new client? Was it someone they knew? Someone they had a personal relationship with?

Manny shook his head. "Not like this."

Like what? What was he talking about? He and Sadie had always been like oil and water. There was nothing new about that; they'd managed to work together for years without it blowing up in their faces.

"You," Sadie said, her voice dripping with menace, "are ruining—"

The door behind me suddenly opened. I gasped and straightened up as Neil lumbered out of his James Bond–ish tech room. Pasting an *I'm innocently standing here against the wall* look on my face, I nodded at him. "Hey."

There was a long moment of silence as he nodded, walked past me, and slowed. I let out the breath I'd been holding, but froze again when he turned back around. In a low voice, he said, "Don't get involved."

Don't get involved in what? And what was Manny ruining? Sadie's life? His own? Surely not the business! I'd suspected the two of them had some sort of jaded past together, but Manny had a girlfriend. He wouldn't possibly choose the evil pixielike Sadie over the knockout ex-model Isabel. Would he? I shuddered at the thought.

I shoved it all aside and walked into the conference room.

Neil had already vanished.

Sadie had been talking, but she stopped midsentence the second she saw me. "Dolores," she said.

"Sadie."

110

"We'll finish this later," she said to Manny; then she looked me up and down, arched an eyebrow, and sauntered into the back offices. She threw one last aggravated look over her shoulder before closing the door behind her with controlled force.

I stood there stunned as Manny went to his office without saying a word. Sadie's tone had been all vinegar, yet he hadn't taken her to task. *Ay, Dios.* This was not the Manny I was used to. It suddenly felt like I wasn't in Kansas anymore.

I paced the length of the conference room, trying to delay the inevitable—going into Manny's office. My stomach rumbled. Mapo tofu! I speed-walked through the lobby, my sights set on Szechwan House, but I stopped short with my hand on the door handle. No. I had a mission. Actually, I had two. One was finding out the low-down on Reilly and her supersecret job. The other was to ferret out a new lead in my identity theft case. Food was *not* the answer.

I backed away from the door and the draw of piping hot bean curd and made a beeline for Manny's office. The door was cracked open, the blinds on the window uncharacteristically pulled shut.

I raised my hand and knocked. The light pressure of my knuckles pushed the door open enough to poke my head through. "Sorry to interrupt. Have you heard from—?" I broke off and gasped when I saw Sadie perched on Manny's desk in front of him, her legs spread slightly, one of his hands on her slim hip.

She started to turn toward me. Manny's gaze lifted. Oh. My. God. I backed out, closing the door as I muttered, "Sorry."

I tried to vanquish the horrific image in my mind, but it was branded there. I suddenly felt sorry for Manny's jilted girlfriend. *Pobrecita* Isabel. For all I knew, she'd always been second fiddle to Sadie. I thought about barging back in and asking if Sadie was really worth it, but if Manny had a thing for Sadie, I couldn't change that. It was better for poor Isabel to cut her losses now.

As I tried to figure out what to do and where to go now, the office door opened behind me. Sadie strolled out. There was a small triumphant grin on her lips as she walked past me and into the back room.

I slowly turned to face Manny, not wanting to look him in the eyes. This was my boss—my mentor—and I didn't want to know *this* about him. Manny interested in me? Hah! Jack had been *so* off base about *that* one.

"Come in," he said. His voice was measured. "Close the door."

I perched nervously on the edge of the black chair facing his desk. "The door just opened . . . ," I started.

He watched me with a dark, hooded gaze until I shifted uneasily in the awkward silence. *"Okay."* I focused on the cleft in his chin, disconcerted by the slits his dark eyes had become and the heavy lids that shrouded them. "I was just wondering if you'd heard from the detective about Ros—"

He shook his head and I stopped. My hands twisted. Should I leave now? Were we done? I hadn't even asked about Reilly, let alone what the hell Manny was doing with Sadie. Which, of course, I was planning to keep quiet about. I just couldn't zip the voice that kept repeating it in my head.

Finally, after what seemed like an eternity, he spoke again, his lips barely moving. "Do you take this job seriously, Dolores?"

My intestines twisted into knots. I squeezed my legs together, my palms clenched over my knees. "Of course."

"This is a business. You're a licensed detective, not an intern."

My spine crackled. What an insult. I was so *not* an intern. My breasts were 100 percent real.

He waved his hand at me again, the space between his eyelids narrowing even more. "Your clothes are"—he cleared his throat—"inappropriate for the office."

I looked down at my blouse and jeans. Was he serious? I'd been working here for almost four years. *Now* my clothes were inappropriate? What about Sadie's fire red leather pants?

"You represent this office—"

My eyebrows arched toward my hairline with sudden realization. This wasn't about my clothes. This was about me catching him with

112

his hands on Sadie and him trying to get back in control of the situation.

I tried to suppress the anger that started to bubble inside me. "My choice of clothes doesn't have anything to do with how well I can do my job." I leveled my gaze at him. "Just like your choice of women doesn't affect how well you do yours." The second the words were out of my mouth, my breath became instantly shallow. *¡Dios mío!* I panicked. *Did I really just say that?*

Manny's burnished skin darkened. He tapped the pads of his fingers against the desk. "Mixing business and pleasure isn't good for anyone. You look like you're going on a date, not working the floor."

An ancient commercial jingle rattled in my head. *I can bring home the bacon, fry it up in a pan, and never, never let you forget Jack's a man. . . .*

I stood, purposefully tugged the hem of my gauzy blouse, and faced him. "I am a detective. I'm not about to jeopardize anything. I'll wear coveralls if that's what you want." I considered my words. "But I disagree with you."

Manny clamped his mouth shut, and for a moment looked edgy and bothered. "That's all," he finally said.

As I stalked toward the door, my imagination ran wild. What if Sadie was blackmailing Manny into some sort of twisted sexual exchange? He kept her around, despite their constant arguing and battle of wills. What could she have on him? Had he done something illegal that she knew about? What were his secrets? Maybe I should offer to help him. Get Sadie off his back, which would get him off of mine.

Ridiculous, I decided. Superdetective Manny Camacho didn't need me to clean up his messes—whatever they might be. But Reilly needed me. I stood up straighter and with my back still to him, I asked, "What kind of job has Reilly been doing for you?"

He didn't answer. I could hear him breathing, so I knew he hadn't magically vanished. Turning around, I rephrased. "She's been gone. A lot."

He took another ten seconds before he finally answered. "Don't worry about Reilly."

"She's not trained as a detective. If you're shorthanded because of this Rosie Gonzales thing, I'll . . ." I trailed off. What exactly would I do? I couldn't stop investigating until I knew the truth about why Rosie had been using my name and why she died. But if my distraction was putting Reilly into the line of fire, well, I had to do something.

"I'm not shorthanded," he said, booting up his computer. His signal that now we were really done with this conversation.

I closed the door behind me, seething, turned, and ran smack into Sadie.

She held up her hands like I was ready to rob her. "Whoa, Lolita. Going somewhere?"

After pushing past her, I snapped up a marker. "Just working my case."

"Right. Your own personal drama. Is Manny paying you while you run around trying to solve the big mystery?"

She had no boundaries. I muttered under my breath and turned back to my board.

"What did you say?" she demanded.

I couldn't help smile. I knew just how to get under her skin. "Oh, sorry," I said. "I know how you hate it when I speak Spanish."

"Well?" Her voice had grown agitated. "What did you say?"

"I said working my own personal drama is better than working the boss." I turned to look her right in her ice blue eyes. "Don't you think?"

She didn't bat an eye. Not even a blink. She was the ice queen except when she was putting on the charm for Manny. "I think you'd better hurry up and solve your little case before you're out of a job."

"Too bad you don't have firing power," I said, but she'd already turned her back on me and walked out.

I uncapped my marker and began scribbling random information

114

down about the night Rosie was killed, hoping it would spark an idea.

- *The Falcón–Cruz memorial*
- *Her picture on a driver's license with my name*
- *Florin Mall*
- *The newscaster telling about my death*
- *My grandmother's relentless Hail Marys*
- *Sergio and my grandmother's rosary*
- *Detective Seavers and his veiled accusations*

Suddenly Sadie was beside me again. She picked up an erasable marker and doodled absently on the corner of *my* board, interrupting *my* brainstorming session.

"I wasn't going to say anything, but I changed my mind."

"About what?" I asked as I ripped the marker out of her hand.

It didn't even faze her. "Manny and I—"

"Sadie." Manny had marched out of his office. The sharpness in his voice stopped her cold.

Sadie pasted an innocent look on her face. "I was just telling Dolores—"

The expression on his face stopped her again. He looked at us standing side by side, me in my jeans and bust-enhancing blouse, her in her red leather pants and clingy black shirt. In *my* albeit biased opinion, she won the inappropriate work attire contest, hands down.

He grimaced. "Christ," he said under his breath. I think *he* figured it was a tie. "So help me—," he growled.

Sadie straightened at the hostility in his voice. Their eyes locked, both of them defiant and determined. It was like they were on a teeter-totter, one second flying high, the next second crashing to the ground.

Sadie blinked and seemed to rethink whatever she'd been about to tell me. Abruptly, she turned and walked away.

With my hands on my hips, I stared at Manny as he walked

115

through to the lobby. I snapped the cap back on the erasable marker, slammed it down on the whiteboard tray, and tried to make sense of what had just happened. *Manny and she were what?* Getting it on? Like I hadn't figured that one out on my own. Maybe *he* was the one blackmailing *her*. It was possible.

Dios mío. Never mind. I *really* didn't want to know. I had my own love-life issues. Along with the whole Rosie Gonzales mystery, I hadn't heard from Jack today—and that was sending me over the edge. A healthy dose of my grandmother's Hail Marys, a decade or two of the rosary, followed by a cleansing hour at Mass might—

My thoughts stopped cold. My rosary! I was plenty fired up. Which meant now was the perfect time to pay a little a visit to Sergio and regain what was rightfully mine.

Sergio's apartment was on the outskirts of Oak Park in South Sac— his living situation seemed to have declined since we'd dated. I triple-checked the locks to my car and slung my purse securely on my back before walking to apartment 3A.

The door flung open, and Sergio stood there in another ribbed sleeveless undershirt. Apparently his wardrobe selection had declined, too. Either that or he owned stock in Hanes.

Thick, wiry hair poking out from the neckline of the wifebeater, beady black eyes, slicked black hair. *¡Por Dios!* What had I ever seen in him?

I eased my mind by remembering that he'd never lacked for girlfriends back then, so it wasn't just me. I sniffed. Pheromones? He was scentless.

I thought about turning around and walking away, but an image of my frail grandmother popped into my head. She'd rested in her bed, a quilt covering her withered body, a strand of white beads draped loosely over her wrist. She'd whispered my name, and I'd tiptoed to the bed. "*Para ti, pequeñita*," she'd said, and then she'd handed me her rosary.

I knew I'd be willing to run naked through Arden Fair Mall—even Cal Expo—if it meant getting those prayer beads back.

Well, maybe not naked, but topless.

Okay, in my bikini.

"*Mira*." Sergio eyed me up and down. "If it isn't Dolores Cruz, back from the grave."

"I'm here for my rosary."

He stuck one hand in his pocket as he held open the door for me.

I peered in. Sergio was a lifetime ago for me, but I didn't remember him being scary, so I couldn't explain my apprehension. Still, my body tensed as I skirted past him into the small living space. Clothes were strewn over the worn plaid couch, fast food remnants were scattered on the table, and small hills of trash lay on the floor.

My arms flexed at my side, I waited while he sauntered to his bedroom, returning a few minutes later with a worn produce box. He dropped it in front of me with a thud, almost catching my toes underneath.

A red see-through teddy lay on top. He lifted it with one finger. "You wanna try this on for old times' sake?"

"I *never* wore that for you."

He sneered. "But you'd wear it for Callaghan."

"Not *that*," I said. Something black and alluring maybe, but red slut-wear that had been held hostage in Sergio's apartment? Uh-uh.

He dropped the teddy back into the box. "He'd dig it." Another leer. "It's all about sex for a guy, Lola. Especially for someone like Callaghan. He's going to use you up and throw you away."

My fists clenched. A swift high kick to the sternum might teach him a lesson about respect. Or a hand thrust to the neck. I was not above taking my frustration out on him. "*Vaya con Dios*, Sergio." And I hope I never see you again.

I started to pick up the box, but he shoved it out of the way with his foot. The movement caught me off guard, and I stumbled back. The next second, he had me pinned against the wall, his hands pressing against my shoulders. "Come on. Don't go."

"Let go," I said through gritted teeth.

"You used to like it when I touched you," he said, his body pressing against me until I could hardly move, let alone get into a position to fight back. I bent my knees, trying to sink down so I could gain an advantage. Heavy weight lifting gave Sergio mass that I couldn't compete with. He didn't budge.

Worse, he seemed to think I was playing hard to get.

He wrapped one giant hand around my wrists, immobilizing me. Then he took hold of the neckline of my blouse.

I strained against him, trying to free myself. "Let go, Sergio," I hissed, but my shirt ripped. Two buttons popped off and fell silently to the floor.

My mind rebelled—and my body tried to—but his bulk was overpowering.

He lazily threw one side of my shirt back and eyed me up and down. "Let's have some fun, Lola. Like old times."

Then he palmed my breast. "You keep getting better and better, *amor.*" A callus caught the stretchy part of my sheer bra. *Cabrón.* I'd chosen one of my better ones today, and now it had a pull.

I flung my head to the side as he tried to kiss me. His breath smelled faintly of marijuana.

"*¡Basta, Sergio!*" I sank lower, my back still against the wall. He readjusted, tightened his grip on me. Fun and games were over.

"You know you want me." He lowered his head and licked me through my bra.

Finally, an opportunity! I bent my head and, feeling just like a vampire must, clamped my teeth on his ear.

He howled and let go of me. He flailed his arms and I hiked up my knee, jamming him between the legs with all the force I could muster.

Sounding like an injured animal, he reeled back. His hands clutched his crotch and he buckled over. At the same time, I pivoted on one foot, cranked up my leg, and gave him a powerful kick to the shoulder. He crashed to the floor, huddling on the ground in the fetal position.

Pulling my shirt together, I ran for the door. And stopped short. Damn it, I was not leaving without the rosary! I wheeled around and snatched up the produce box. Sergio was still rolled on the floor, his knees pulled up to his chin. His wail had turned into a low, pained groan.

The bedroom door cracked open, and a man peered out. He looked from me to Sergio. Pancho. His face contorted, and a strangled sound came from his throat before he slammed the door again.

He'd been there all along and hadn't bothered to help me? Part of me wanted to kick down the bedroom door and give him a little what for, but I thought better of it. Getting the hell out of there was a much better idea.

I raced to my car, threw the box on the passenger seat, and locked myself in. My tires squealed as I pressed my foot down on the gas pedal, peeling out of the parking lot and rounding the corner.

I drove straight home, screeching my car to a stop in front of my parents' house. It took a few deep, intentional breaths but my nerves finally steadied. I headed to my flat, rummaging through the box as I climbed the staircase. Some paperback mysteries, a stack of essays and tests from my time at Sac State, old financial aid papers, letters, that damn red teddy . . . A vise clenched around my heart. *Hijo de su madre. No rosary.*

I barged through the door, dropping the box on the floor. "That son of a—"

"Jesus Christ, Lola. What happened? Are you okay?"

My head whipped around. Jack was on his feet, hurrying toward me. Antonio stood in front of the couch, staring.

I ran my fingers under my burning eyes. I was *not* going to cry. "N-nothing happened. I'm fine."

I'm fine, I repeated to myself.

Jack's voice lowered to a barely audible timbre. He wrapped me up in his arms. "Lola," he said after a minute.

"Sergio—," I started to say, breaking off the second I heard my voice start to crack.

119

"What about him?" he asked stiffly.

I willed away the tears that were starting to pool at the bottom of my eyes. "I went to see him. He has my grandmother's rosary."

He pushed me back and looked me up and down, taking in my torn blouse. "He did this to you?"

"What happened?" Antonio was by our side, grabbing my arm.

I shook him off. I'd been manhandled enough for one day.

"He wanted to relive old times. I didn't."

Antonio bolted forward and shouted, "*¡Cabrón, hijo de puta!*"

Jack raked his hand through his hair. "Son of a bitch."

I sank down on the couch. Jack knelt in front of me, resting his hands on my knees. "You sure you're okay?"

I nodded.

Jack looked at me—as if he could see straight into my soul—before he stood up again and walked over to Antonio. They whispered together, and my brother's goateed face turned grim, his already dark skin growing darker before my eyes. "Yeah," Tonio said.

Jack grimaced. "Right now." There was absolutely no smile lurking anywhere near his face.

They flicked one quick short nod at each other; then Jack came back to me. "I'll be back, okay?"

Mi amor. "Where are you going?"

He knelt down in front of me again and I could sense, almost see, his barely contained rage. He ran his hand down his face. "Wait for me."

"*Vámonos,*" Antonio called from the kitchen, and Jack was gone.

Their plan hit me like a frying pan to the head. I jumped up, raced to the kitchen window, and stared openmouthed as they climbed into Antonio's forest green Mustang. Oh no, they were *not* going to fight my battle!

¡Dios mío! The engine revved and they tore down the street.

How could they have the misguided notion that I was a damsel in distress? I'd managed to fight off Sergio just fine. I didn't need my brother and my—what was Jack to me, anyway? My . . . my *friend* Jack—to defend my honor.

I charged to my room, shed my damaged blouse, and grabbed a shirt from the bureau. Twenty seconds later, I was speeding down Forty-second Street. I'd intercept them, stop them in their tracks, and then *I'd* get my grandmother's rosary back.

Indignant thoughts scrambled through my brain. Knights in shining armor. Pfft. Did they think we were in the Middle Ages or something? Obviously my sparring session with Jack a few weeks ago hadn't convinced him of my Xena, Warrior Princess, capabilities. My black belt in kung fu should have been enough to prove it to him. I'd have to fight him again to show for once and for all that I was a force to be reckoned with.

I arrived at Sergio's dilapidated apartment building in time to see Jack and Antonio already on foot, rounding the corner, and headed straight for 3A. It was too late to stop them. I suddenly remembered Pancho peeking out from the back bedroom. What if he or Sergio had a weapon? Careening out of my car, I sprinted across the parking lot.

"Wait!" I shouted. The heels of my boots clacked against the cement floor. I caught Jack's arm with my hand as his knuckles hit the door. Too late.

"Let us handle it, Lola." Antonio's loud whisper carried.

"Don't do this," I hissed.

"Go home."

I gave up on my thickheaded brother and turned to Jack. "Sergio's friend is in there. Pancho," I added in a whisper.

"Who the hell's called Pancho anymore?" Antonio muttered, shaking his head. "Stupid nickname."

Jack nodded at me—acknowledgment that I'd spoken—but he still stepped back to wait.

A moment later, Sergio yanked open the door. He stood with his legs spread, looking ready to rumble. Damn, he'd recovered from the knee-to-the-groin move I'd pulled on him. Now he looked like a pissed-off bull, the sneer on his face crinkling his nose.

"What the hell do *you* want, Callaghan?"

Jack's hand shot out, gripping Sergio's undershirt. He jerked him out of the apartment as Antonio reached around the door and pulled it shut behind them.

"What the fu—!" Sergio stopped short when he saw me. "Christ." He notched his chin at me. "*She* came to *me*." He gave me a lascivious leer. "Looking like she does—can you blame me? She's good." He shot a searing look at Jack, then slurped, licking his lips. "You know you want what I already had, Callaghan."

"Shut your mouth," Jack ground out as he drew back his arm.

Sergio's voice dropped to a menacing rasp. "Sloppy seconds shouldn't bother you. You're just in it for the—" He broke off and flicked his tongue at me like a lizard.

He was demented. There was no other explanation.

Jack's arm flew toward Sergio's face. "*¡Basta!*" I yelled, grabbing Jack's biceps and pulling back. "He's not worth it! He's baiting you."

His muscles were hard and pulsing under my grasp, but the forward motion stopped. Finally, he relaxed, lowering his arm.

Gracias a Dios. I didn't think Jack's boss at the *Sacramento Bee* would be pleased at an assault-and-battery charge against his new star columnist.

I edged in front of Jack, my arm cocked behind my back, my fingers brushing against his stomach. "Where's my rosary, Sergio?"

Sergio's face had turned tomato red, the tendons on his neck straining. But he dug his hand into his pocket and pulled out the rope of white beads.

I took it from him. All this for a string of plastic. But relief washed over me. *En el cielo*, my grandmother was smiling down at me.

Jack was breathing steadily again. "Stay away from her, Garcia, or you won't be so lucky next time." He sounded menacing, but his touch was gentle as he took hold of my arm and steered me down the hallway. Antonio followed behind us.

I half expected Sergio to pounce, but when I glanced over my shoulder, he'd already retreated back into the safety of his apartment.

Chapter 10

Jack cornered me once we got back to my flat. "You have to spend some time doing stuff for yourself. Between this situation, the restaurant, and now Sergio, you're a little stressed."

"I can't sit back and relax while there's a little boy missing."

"The police are working on it."

"Yes, but—"

"But nothing, Lola. You're in too deep. One of the first questions you asked was, Did Rosie die because of something she did, or was she an innocent victim because it was you who was supposed to be killed? You have a lot of theories about Rosie at this point, but what happened to eliminating the idea that you were the intended victim?"

"I *have* thought about it, thank you very much. Just an FYI, you're not privy to every thought I have." Thank God. That might be a touch scary for him. "Not a single clue points to the idea that it was supposed to be me instead of Rosie. No one has an ax to grind with me. I've been working an adultery case, but it's only just finished up, and Rosie turned up dead before I'd gotten anything incriminating against the wife. Unless I have a rogue family member who's out to get me, I was not the intended victim."

He nodded in agreement. "Okay, so Rosie was, but you still don't know *why* she was killed."

"Like you said, I have a million theories." More like two or three, but it took only one motive to make a murder.

"Let's hear 'em."

I loved this about Jack. He was like a wall I could bounce ideas off of, and he interacted with me, whereas Manny just nodded grimly and said, "Prove it."

I'd changed my clothes into comfy lavender sweats and a T-shirt. Now I was settled back against the couch, my legs tucked under me, Jack next to me. "Her son is missing," I said, thinking out loud. "That's the most significant detail. Who has him? Could the father have wanted him and been willing to kill Rosie in order to get him?"

Jack nodded. "That's a possibility."

I didn't pause to think before I launched into another theory. "Rosie was abused and the domestic violence got out of hand." This one had been front and center in my mind for quite a while, and it was troublesome. It would explain her need to steal someone else's identity, and it would explain the violence of her death.

"And the fight that killed her happened in an alley behind the mall?"

I shrugged. "Her husband or boyfriend or whatever he is could have followed her there. I don't think there's a foolproof set of rules for how domestic violence goes down. And the dad could have taken the kid."

"Any other ideas?"

The drug pamphlet we'd found in Rosie's apartment came to mind. "Overdose? Maybe it was an accident. A drug deal gone bad." That didn't explain where the child was, but nothing could be ruled out.

Antonio walked in from the kitchen. "It'd be pretty hard to hit your head on the corner of a Dumpster like that accidentally. She had to be fighting with someone."

"Maybe she wasn't pushed with intent," I said, "but was accidentally flung against the Dumpster."

"It's possible," Jack agreed. "So what's next?"

"Dinner." Antonio grabbed a handful of the back of Jack's shirt. "The Pizza Joint's calling."

"I'll meet you there," I said. "I have to swing by Abuelita's and talk to *los Mafiosos*."

Antonio cocked an eyebrow at me. "Why?"

I couldn't share the details of Zac's situation. "I'm helping Abuelo with something." I winked, making light of it so he would drop it. "It's personal."

"Personal, huh? I'll go with you. Gotta check on things."

Antonio was flaky in many ways, but he was on top of the restaurant. "Okay, but I drive."

Jack pushed himself off the couch. "We can all go."

"No," I said. "If my grandparents see you, they'll rope you into eating with them and promising them your firstborn in exchange for saving my soul."

There was a twinkle in his eye. "Does your soul need saving?"

"According to them it does."

"Okay, I'll go order the pizza."

We agreed to meet up in half an hour. I snatched the mail off the entry table and shoved it in my purse; then we headed off in our separate directions. Ten minutes later, Antonio was in the kitchen and I stood in front of my grandparents' table at Abuelita's. "*¿Cómo estan?*"

"Fine, fine." Abuelo dismissed the greeting with a wave of his hand. That was it for the small talk. He went straight for the jugular. "How good a detective are you? Any news of Zacarias *y su esposa?*"

Sucking in my cheeks, I tried to strike a model pose, but with hair falling from its makeshift bun and my casual clothes, I couldn't quite pull it off. "Lucy gave me a facial. I feel five years younger." Not that I wanted to move backwards on my time line. I was twenty-nine and looking forward to my fourth decade.

My grandfather glowered at me, chin to chest.

I glowered right back at him. I'd learned from the best. He'd taught me everything I knew about attitude.

"Dolores," he said in his best mob whisper.

I sighed and gave up on trying to lighten his mood. "No news yet. I'm still working on it. I have to tell you, though," I said, wagging my finger at him disapprovingly, "I don't like nosing around in their private life. Marriage is supposed to be sacred."

He looked at me, waiting.

It was too hard to get a meaningful point across in a language he didn't fully understand. "*Sagrado*," I translated. "*Privado*. None of our business."

"No." He pulled his thick lips into an amazingly thin line, the stern look meant to be intimidating. "Nothing is, how do you say, *sacred*, in this family."

Wasn't *that* the truth. I blew them both a kiss, turned, and ran smack into Sylvia. Her rag-doll hair was pulled back into a barrette, a basket of warm chips and a *molcajete* of salsa in her hands.

"Hey, there—how are things going?" I asked.

"Great!"

"Antonio's not giving you a hard time?"

"I think he wants to, but I won't let him." She laughed. "No, seriously, he's been a perfect gentleman."

Huh. I'd never known my brother to be a *perfect* gentleman. Still, I heaved a sigh of relief. "Great!" I said to her, but silently I pleaded, *Please don't quit, Sylvia.*

I caught a glimpse of Antonio in my peripheral vision. She must have, too, because her posture straightened, and if her hands hadn't been full, she would have primped.

She flicked her head to my grandparents' table. "I even like *los Mafiosos*." With that, she sashayed off to deliver the basket of chips and salsa to a man and his three kids. I watched her as she stayed, ruffled one of the kids' hair, and laughed. She was a good waitress, friendly and able to connect with the customers.

And she even liked my grandparents. *Qué milagro.* I liked them, but it was in my job description as their granddaughter. I had no choice. I tried to look at them as an outsider might. Yeah, I thought, I guess they *were* sort of endearing—in a threatening kind of way.

126

Being free of my waitressing duties would give me the time I needed to work on my family case with Lucy and my personal case with Rosie. Add to that the mysteries of Camacho and Associates interoffice politics, and I was juggling three huge balls.

And juggling was not my greatest strength. Jack was right. I was stressed. Pizza and beer sounded perfect.

Antonio sidled up beside me. "Do you think Sylvia would go out with me?"

My nostrils instantly flared, and my breath started coming in spurts like an agitated bull. "You're kidding, right?"

He watched her as she passed through the dining room. "She's kind of pretty. A little different, no?"

As Sylvia delivered two plates of steaming soup to an elderly couple, I gave her a good once-over. She *was* pretty in a nontraditional way—full-figured but fit-looking, freckly-faced and wiry-haired. Definitely not my brother's usual type, but I'd seen that look in his eyes too many times to doubt its meaning. He was on the make.

I glared at him. "Don't even think about it."

He leaned toward me until we were practically nose to nose. "Sounding a little mafiosa, Lola. Abuelo would be so proud." His gaze continued to follow Sylvia as she moved efficiently around the dining room, a small grin tickling his lips. He continued as if we hadn't just had a mob moment. "I think she'd be fun."

"She's got three kids and an ex-husband, Tonio. She put her kids' pictures up in her locker. That's a lot of baggage, not a lot of fun." I couldn't see my brother getting involved in such a complex relationship. I'd had to manipulate him into one date with Reilly, and he *still* hadn't forgiven me for that one. Of course, Reilly had a slight stalker side to her, but she'd been in love with Antonio, so I couldn't fault her for her passion.

"I'm great with kids," Antonio said. "They love me."

I couldn't help rolling my eyes. "Yeah, because they can relate to you as one of their own kind. Are you great with ex-husbands, too?"

He smiled his trademark Cheshire cat grin. "I'll let you know."

Something in his tone made my stomach plunge. I might as well have been talking to a pot of beans, telling the water to boil already. "Antonio, don't. We need Sylvia to stay."

"No, *you* need her to stay. *I* need somebody new to date. And me dating her doesn't mean she'll quit. Have a little faith."

"I have faith you'll break up with her." I pleaded with him. "Please, stay away from her."

"I've been in a slump."

"What, for a day? Sylvia's not one of your brainless twenty-year-olds. She's a mom, Antonio. Grow up. She *needs* this job. And you're manager here. You *do* need her to stay. In fact, we should establish a policy banning workplace romance."

He just scoffed, so I tried a different tactic. "Please. She's been hurt enough."

But he'd stopped listening. Sylvia glided by, her hands and arms loaded with steaming plates. Antonio watched her deliver plates to the same table she'd brought chips and salsa to a moment ago.

Antonio's expression grew serious. Watchful.

Oh, boy. I'd have to have a chat with Sylvia, just to help the girl keep her wits about her. *Pobrecita.* I knew it wouldn't do any good. Antonio had made up his mind. She didn't stand a chance.

The Pizza Joint was a cavernous room that made me think of a medieval dungeon—except for the electricity and the bright lights of the video games along the back wall. My pupils dilated, and I headed for the restroom while Antonio went in search of our table. When I came back out, my brother bellowed my name from across the room. "Lola! *¡Ven aquí!*" He waved from a corner booth.

I could barely make out the dark shape of someone sitting next to Antonio. Jack. I'd seen him just a half hour ago, but I already missed him. But why was Antonio sitting next to him in the booth? That should have been *my* spot.

Antonio clearly couldn't see my irritation in the darkness. He looked like an air traffic controller the way he was waving me into the seat across from him. "Sit, sit!"

I darted my eyes from him to the empty side of the booth, hoping he'd get the message from my expression and move to the other side. Which he did. "Tonio—," I started to say, but stopped short when I got a better look at him.

It wasn't Jack.

It was a woman. A quick assessment of her told me that she was not just any woman. She was Antonio's dream girl, with her perfectly curled and flipped strawberry hair, her revealing clothes, and her manufactured tan. I suddenly felt frumpy instead of comfortable. My hand skimmed my messy bun, tucking a loose strand of hair behind my ear. The question was, where had she come from?

Antonio's eyes were glued to the girl by my side, and I kept mine averted. No need to rub in how I was feeling at the moment. But as she leaned forward to say something to him, her balloon breasts rested on the table, Antonio looked like a feral cat in heat, and queasiness filled my gut. I'd seen her before.

I held my hand out to her. "I'm Lola."

She took my hand in a loose shake. "I've heard about you. The detective, right?"

"Right."

"I'm Molly," she said in a whispery Marilyn Monroe voice. "I work with Jack Callaghan."

Molly. My grip unconsciously tightened. As in the intern.
"Ow!"

"Oh!" I let her go, wiping my hand on my pants then staring at it as if she'd just given me cooties. "I—uh—I'm sorry." I backed out of the booth as fast as possible, turned, and ran smack into Jack. The beer he carried sloshed over the sides of the pitcher and spilled down the front of my shirt.

"Whoa! Sor—" He broke off when he registered who'd he'd just drenched. "Sorry," he said again, and I knew he wasn't talking about the beer. He slid the pitcher onto the table, setting down four frosty mugs. Looked like Molly was staying.

Ay, Dios. My head felt fuzzy as I watched him lean against the side of the booth next to Antonio and force his fisted hands into his jeans' pockets. "So Molly just happened to show up here right after I did." He forced a smile. "Isn't that a coincidence?"

All the air in the room seemed to compress into solid, heavy molecules and jettison straight to our table. I could hardly breathe. Was she stalking Jack? Because if she was, I'd take her down right now.

"Huh," I said. "That *is* a coincidence."

Molly put a pout on her lips. "I've heard this is a great place, but if this is a private dinner—"

"Don't be silly," Antonio said. "It's not private."

I lifted my chin, meeting Jack's gaze, thanking God he couldn't see the lump of jealousy that was in my throat. My blood bubbled in my eardrums. I had to sit. My choices were next to Antonio or next to Molly. Before I could decide, Antonio grabbed my hand and pulled me down next to him.

That left Jack to sit next to Molly. Great. She'd probably spent an hour primping, plucking, and painting to ready herself for her evening of stalking. Jack filled the mugs with beer, passed one to each of us, and I immediately started drinking, the foam skimming my upper lip.

"*Salud,*" Antonio said cheerily, holding his glass over the center of the table with his right hand, his left hand still like a vise on my shoulder.

My gaze was steady on Jack. I pulled the glass away from my mouth and ran my tongue over my lip, whisking away the foam. He might be sitting next to Molly, but his attention was fast on me. His eyes grew dark, his mouth parting slightly.

"*Salud,*" I echoed.

"Down the hatch." Molly's breathy voice couldn't hide her irritation. She was no dummy. She knocked her glass against each of ours, giving mine an extra shove. Then she chugged the entire thing. We all stared at her as she poured herself another glass and downed it.

"Slow down," Jack said to her.

She winked, put her hand on top of his, and edged closer to him. "A little beer makes Molly a fun girl."

Jack moved Molly's hand from his and gently placed it down on the table in front of her. My breath rushed out; I hadn't realized I'd been holding it.

A potent awkwardness hung over us. Needing a distraction, I pulled my mail from my purse, riffling through the stack of letters and one catalog. I stopped short at a letter from Sac State. Antonio plucked it from my hand. "What's this?" he asked. "You're not taking classes again, are you? Enough school already, Lola. Christ, four years of you in college was more than enough for me."

I snatched the letter back. "No, I'm not taking classes." I looked at Jack, a silent connection between us. I could tell from his expression that he understood my concern over the letter. "Probably alumni stuff," I muttered, knowing that it wasn't. I ripped the envelope open and flicked open the tri-folded papers, reading the first sheet. It was from the financial aid office.

Dear Ms. Cruz:

This letter confirms receipt of your application for financial aid. Your application is being processed and a response will be forthcoming. Feel free to call the financial aid department with any questions.

I reread the letter, the bottom dropping out of my stomach, alarms going off in my head. I flipped through the forms and laid the whole thing on the table.

Antonio scanned the letter. "So you *are* going back to school?"

"*No,*" I said slowly, "I'm not."

Jack pulled the papers across the table, read the letter, and flipped through the rest. Then he handed them back to me. "That's what it sounds like."

I nodded grimly. "Yep, that's what it sounds like."

Molly had finished her second beer and was working on her third, looking decidedly pissed off. "Didn't you graduate, like, eons ago?" she slurred.

I frowned at her. Two beers, and she was already buzzed? Had the alcohol entered her bloodstream at nanospeed, or—oh, God—was she one of those lightweight, *I'm going to act buzzed and cute* kind of girls? The faker. "Seven years, actually. Hardly counts as eons."

She scoffed. "So, what, you're like, thirty?" She made it sound like I had one foot in the grave.

"I'm twenty-nine." I looked straight at Jack. "I have plenty of time."

"How old are you, Mol?" Antonio asked.

"Twenty-one," she said defiantly, finishing her third beer. She ran the back of her hand across her mouth, wiping away the foam.

Barely legal. I had a few years on her, but she had three solid cup sizes on me. "You'd better slow down, there, Mols," I said. I was pretty sure her breasts wouldn't double as air bags and block a face-front free fall.

"Don't worry. We'll get you home safe." Antonio grinned.

"How's Sylvia?" I asked, jabbing my elbow into his side. Though I didn't want him to hurt our new waitress, I much preferred her to Mols.

Molly slouched in the booth and peered at us. "Sylvia?"

"Her ex came into Abuelita's for dinner," he muttered.

"Oh. I didn't know." God, things changed on a dime around here. So Antonio was looking to drown his sorrows tonight.

I folded up the letter from Sac State and slipped it back into the envelope. I'd deal with it tomorrow. I looked at the last envelope. Visa bill. I eyed it, not sure I wanted to open it and see my balance. I'd charged a dress for Chely's *quinceañera* and then bought another one just because.

The "just because" dress was an impulse buy and one that I regretted. The dress emphasized my boobs and hips, was fun and flirty, and, as Jack had told me when he'd seen it on me, not a good dress to wear unless I wanted my night to end in passion. "I'm going to take it back," I muttered to myself as I ripped open the bill. "Two thousand dollars? That's impossible!"

Jack leaned forward. "What's impossible?"

I waved the bill in the air. "My credit card bill. It says I charged two thousand dollars last month, and the balance is"—I gasped—"six thousand three hundred ninety-two dollars!" My blood sputtered out of my arteries from the pressure around my heart. "Oh. My. God."

Antonio leaned close to me, looking at the bill. He pointed to the charges. "Tuition. The Hornet Bookstore."

I followed the line to the amount. "Holy shit. Four hundred dollars for books? You have got to be kidding."

Molly laid her breasts on the table and looked at me earnestly. "It's an outrage. The cost of textbooks today is highway robbery."

Jack flicked his chin at the bill, his voice full of concern. "What else?"

Scanning it again, I gave the rundown. "Tuition and books, post office, bus tickets, supermarket, a kid's clothing shop . . ."

"That's a lot of charges," Jack said.

My cute little dresses weren't on the bill. "Yeah, lots of charges."

My stomach churned as I thought about what to do and if I'd be responsible for the debt. The credit I'd worked so hard to develop had been annihilated by Rosie Gonzales.

"What are you going to do, Lola?"

"About my credit? I've done everything I can. I've posted every alert possible. I've ordered every report available. My credit card company said there were no new charges." I flipped the statement back to the top. First American Bank. My heart flip-flopped. My credit card was with Bank of America. "This is a new account. She actually opened this card in my name." I waved the bill at Jack. "Remember, we found that partial application in her apartment, but—"

Molly sloshed her beer as she slammed her mug down. She peered at us. "In whose apartment? What's going on here?"

Antonio cut his arm across the table so he could take her hand. "Don't worry about it, Molly. Lola has a little problem Jack's been helping with."

Molly's voice choked. "I thought he was writing an article about her."

Jack sat back and put his arm on the back of the booth. "I am."

"I thought it was mostly about identity theft. I'm just the story behind the crime."

"You read my columns, Lola." Jack flashed me a wry smile. "They're a careful layering of fact and anecdote. This article will have your story, a behind-the-scenes account from a criminal point of view, and the hard facts."

"Wait. Jushst wait." Molly seethed. "Sho why were you with her in an apartment?"

We all ignored her. I shook my head, hair tumbling down from my makeshift bun, a second away from hurling. "What if she had more credit cards in my name?"

Antonio leaned back, lacing his fingers behind his head. "She was a piece of work."

I shoved my mail back into my purse. "Yeah, but she wasn't too bright, since the bill and financial information were sent to me. She wasn't going to be able to keep her secret for much longer . . . if she'd lived."

"Looks like she did plenty of damage, whoever she was." Molly finished her mug of frothy beer. She shot daggers at me. "Another-pitcherJack," she said, her words mashing together.

We all looked from Molly to the nearly empty container of beer. Jack frowned as her head fell against his shoulder, her silky strawberry hair cascading down over his arm. Her hand reached under the table, and he visibly tensed.

I stared, stunned. The girl had *huevos*. If she scooted any closer to Jack, she'd be on his lap. Did they allow lap dances at the Pizza Joint?

I waited for Jack to shove her away, but it was an employee delivering our pizzas who interrupted Molly's playtime. The smell of greasy pepperoni made my stomach churn. The air was suffocating, and I couldn't stay cooped up here another minute. I dived out of the booth, stood, and faced the three of them. "Superfabulous evening," I said, channeling Molly and plastering a fake smile on my face, "but I gotta go."

Antonio stood up. His face dropped into a frown that extended from his eyes to his mouth. "You okay? Want me to go with you?"

I waved him off. "I'm fine."

Molly threw up a French manicured hand, a thin line of purple glitter between her nail bed and white tip. She wiggled her fingers at me, her delirious happiness to see me go like a neon sign on her forehead. Alcohol did not make Molly a nice girl. "Bye-bye, Lola," she said with a gleeful snarl.

"It's been a real pleasure, Mols." I flashed a look of what I hoped was cool dignity at Jack. He was trapped here with Molly, but I wasn't. "See you later, Jack," I said.

He started to get up, but Molly dug her claws into his shoulder.

I jetted out of there as fast as I could. No way was I sticking around to watch the show.

Chapter 11

The one-two punch of my credit card bill followed by seeing Jack with Molly had sent my stomach whirling. Now that I was in my car, my nausea waned. I needed nourishment. I parked in my parents' driveway and let myself into their house through the utility room. I'd had no time to grocery shop, and since Antonio rarely performed *that* domestic duty—or any other, for that matter—I knew my refrigerator upstairs was bare. Raiding my mother's leftovers was the obvious solution.

My father walked in while I was in the middle of warming up a plate of fried chicken, rice, and beans. "Late dinner, eh *mi'ja?*" He planted a warm, fatherly kiss on my cheek.

I willed myself to stay in control of my emotions. "I've been busy."

"*Pero,* I thought you went out with Antonio *y su hombre.*"

"I decided I wasn't in the mood," I said a little too sullenly.

My father's weathered skin crinkled around his eyes in a knowing look. "I see."

I set my plate on the table and frowned at him frowning at me. "*¿Qué piensas?*"

"*Nada, Dolores.*" He paused, pulling a piece of cold chicken from the Tupperware container I'd left on the counter and popping it into his mouth.

I picked at my dinner. "Everything's out of control, *Papi*."

"*Dígame*." He sat across from me, waiting for me to fill him in.

"That woman who died—she had a credit card in my name and enrolled at Sac State as me." I slipped a forkful of rice into my mouth, the taste completely unsatisfying. I pushed the plate away—I couldn't eat—and filled him in on what I knew of Rosie's life, the credit card statement, and the financial aid letter.

"*¿Por qué tú?* How does she do this?"

Why me? That was a very good question and one I hadn't been able to answer yet. "I'm trying to find out."

"*Con cuidado*, Dolores."

"I'm always careful, Papi." I scraped my uneaten food into the garbage can and rinsed my plate. After kissing my father good night, I went upstairs to my flat.

Zoning out in front of the television for a little while seemed like a good way to rest my brain. I passed through the archway between the kitchen and the living room and had barely settled onto the couch when a knock sounded at the front door.

Peering through the peephole I saw Jack standing there, his expression brooding.

I pulled the door open, too tired to think and definitely too tired to make small talk. "Hi," I said.

He walked in like he belonged here, and I stepped back to let him pass. He held out a thin box to me. "I brought you some pizza."

I took it, the slices sliding to one side as the box tilted from his hand to mine. I pressed the pizza box against my ribs, my knuckles turning white. "What happened to Molly the intern?"

"Antonio drove her home." He must have sensed that the real question burning in my mind was, *Why was she at the Pizza Joint in the first place?* because he added, "I didn't invite her, you know."

"She sure was friendly."

He grimaced. "A little too friendly."

I didn't even want to venture to guess what that meant. Had there been, er, friendliness under the table?

He went on before I got a visual of Molly's hand creeping up Jack's thigh. "Let me be clear about this, Lola," he said. "I am not interested in Molly."

He sounded sincere *and* he'd given me reassurance just when I needed it. I supposed I should return the favor. "You asked me about Manny," I said after an awkward silence.

He nodded slowly, his face stony, as if he was preparing to hear the worst. "I did."

"There's never been anything between us. If he feels something for me, he keeps it to himself."

He looked at me like he was trying to read my mind. "But if he does have feelings, do you want him to keep them to himself?" he finally asked.

I bit my lip. Then I lowered my chin, peering at him through my lashes. "There's only one man I'm interested in, Callaghan."

He leaned against the back of the sofa and folded his arms over his chest. "Is that right?" It was more of a statement than a question, but there was the hint of a smile on his lips. "Should I venture a guess as to this mystery man's identity?"

"Sure, why not?" Games with Jack could be *so* sexy. "I'll give you three tries."

He barely took a breath before saying, "I'm guessing it's not Garcia."

I rolled my eyes. "Your guess would be correct."

"And you already said it's not Camacho."

"Right." I batted my lashes. "One more try."

He leveled those smoky eyes at me, his tantalizing grin gone. "Let's cut the crap, Cruz. I know how you feel about me."

"You d-do?" I stammered. I wasn't even sure *I* knew how I felt, so how could he?

In a rush, I ticked off the things I knew for sure about me and Jack Callaghan. (1) I'd had a crush on him since high school. (2) It was because of him that I was a private investigator, so in a way, I owed him. (3) I wanted his body. (4) And his soul. (5) His secrets were like a brick wall between us.

The fact was, I thought Jack might be able to fulfill me, but since I had no idea what the deal was with his emergency disappearance or his broken relationship with the mysterious Sarah, I didn't know if I was deluding myself.

"Yes, I do," he confirmed, "probably better than you know yourself. And," he added, "I don't think there's any question how I feel about you."

Those secrets circled in my mind. I shook my head. "Actually," I said slowly, holding my thumb and index finger half an inch apart. "I have a little question or two about that."

He straightened. "If you don't know how I feel about you, you're either in complete denial, not as smart as I thought you were, or you're overthinking things," he said, "because I've been pretty clear."

I got stuck for just a second on the fact that he thought I was smart, but then I moved on with my thoughts. "I can't help it. Assessing facts is what I do, and actions speak louder than words."

He reached for me, but I sidestepped, realizing exactly how right I was. If ever a man had been giving me mixed signals, it was Jack. And he thought his feelings for me were obvious?

He scowled. "Damn it, Cruz, you're making this too complicated."

I pressed my palm against my chest and stared at him. "*I'm* making this too complicated?" Momentarily speechless, I marched to the kitchen and practically threw the pizza box into the fridge. In no way, shape, or form was this—this—this *thing* between Jack and me *my* fault. I wheeled around. He'd followed me to the kitchen. "It *is* complicated," I said, barely stopping myself from running into him.

"Then let me simplify things," he said. "I'm crazy about *you*." He looked at me, almost pleading with his eyes. "I think about you all the time."

Words tumbled out of my mouth before I could stop them. "All the time? Even while you're being groped by another woman? Or while you're playing knight in shining armor for your ex-girlfriend?"

He pressed his thumb and finger against his closed eyes like he

139

was gathering up his inner strength. "I already told you. I am not," he said tightly, "interested in Molly."

That I believed. "No," I said softly, "but Sarah's a different story."

He stared at me for a beat. His lips drew into a thin line. "You're wrong, Lola."

Now I folded my arms, shifted my weight to one hip, and thrust my chin out. "Am I? She's the one you broke up with when you left San Luis Obispo, right? The four-year relationship? You went MIA to help her," I said, "and you won't tell me why."

He laced his fingers behind his neck and leaned back against the kitchen counter. All I could hear was the low sound of his breath and the thrashing of my heartbeat while I waited for him to say something. Anything.

And then he did . . .

"I almost married her," he said.

. . . and I wished he hadn't.

"Married?" I repeated, choking the word out. His other women had always been in the back of my mind. Hell, I had pictures to prove it. Postcoital pictures of him and Greta Pritchard that had tainted my entire love life. All I'd ever wanted was to be the one who'd given Jack that satisfied look. For me to be the one he wanted and loved.

He nodded, and I just stared at him. Jack Callaghan had almost gotten married. That did not compute. "As in engaged?" I asked, needing clarification.

There was going to be a wedding? While I waited for him to elaborate, my mind went wild with possible reasons for the broken engagement. Fear of commitment? Had he cheated on her? Or maybe *she'd* cheated on *him*. But if he'd been betrayed, why would he drop everything to help her? No, he had to have cheated on her despite the fact that he'd told me he'd never, ever do that, not after his father had done it to his mother.

"I didn't screw around on her," Jack said.

Since when was mind reading one of his skills? "I wasn't—"

He interrupted my denial. "Yes, you were. It's written all over your face."

Damn. Busted. "Then why'd you break it off with her? And," I added, "why do you still see her?"

He suddenly looked more tormented than I'd ever seen a man look. I closed the distance between us with three steps. "Jack," I said, putting my hands on his shoulder. "Just tell me."

He raised his gaze to mine. "I broke it off because she wasn't you." He hesitated before continuing. "I still see her because I have to, not because I want to."

Why couldn't he have stopped at *she wasn't you?* "*Why* do you need to see her?"

There was a weighty pause. That hesitation again. Finally, he said, "Because I cared about her once. I just—I need you to trust me, Lola."

I wanted to! I wanted to wrap my arms around him, believe every word he said, and be enveloped by his body, his affection, his love.

But trust didn't come easily—not after my relationship with Sergio—and I had my own problems to worry about. I had Rosie Gonzales. I didn't want to stress out about the fact that Jack was at some other woman's beck and call. "You have to give me something, Jack," I said. "Anything."

After a few long seconds, he said, "She's sick."

I dropped my arms to my side and tried to process this. What kind of man left his fiancée in her hour of need?

I answered my own question. My uncle had. He'd divorced my aunt when she'd been at the height of her sickness, but that was different. Tía Betty had gone *loca*. Literally. She'd lost all her marbles, and nobody could blame Tío Ramon for wanting to escape.

"What kind of sick?" I asked. But I didn't give Jack time to answer before the next question came out. "Was she sick when—when you broke up with her?"

141

"Yes," he said simply.

I took a deep breath and tried to hold on to what I knew of Jack. He'd said he broke up with her because she wasn't me. That had made me feel warm and tingly inside. How could I reconcile *that* Jack with a man who'd dump a woman when she was ill?

"I know it sounds bad, Lola, but—"

"Oh my God." Tía Betty. That was it. "She's got emotional problems, doesn't she?" My imagination took over. "Is she a stalker? Is she threatening you? *Cristo*," I muttered. "Are you in danger?"

His expression hardened. "No. Jesus, Lola. She's bipolar. She won't stay on her meds, and she gets herself in some pretty bad situations."

Momentary relief flooded me. At least Sarah wasn't going to go all *Jagged Edge* on him. But I was a fix-it girl, and I got right back to work. "Doesn't she have family who can help her? Friends? Somebody besides you?"

"They try, but I'm able to calm her down better than anyone else."

What did *that* mean? What kind of comfort did he offer? My head started to throb as I realized that Sarah might always have a hold on him. I was torn between feeling compassion for a woman I'd never met and wanting her out of Jack's life completely. I started to turn, but he grabbed my arms and held me. "Don't."

"What?"

"Don't walk away from me, Lola." His hands moved to my face. He bent his head and kissed me, softly at first, then with such urgency that I felt like he was trying to burn the kiss into a memory.

He pulled away and lowered his forehead to mine, and I could almost feel the aching in both our hearts. I tangled my fingers in his hair and smoothed it back. "I—I'm glad you told me," I said, "but I have to think about this."

He pushed a stray strand of hair behind my ear. I dropped my hands, but he took me by the wrist and held me close. "Take all the time you need," he said, "but I'm not giving you up. Think about that, while you're at it." Then he kissed me again, deep and searing, before he turned and walked out of the kitchen, out of my flat, and into the night.

My heart was crushing under the burden of Jack's confession and his obligation to Sarah. But it didn't shatter and it didn't burst, because I was a survivor. And a fighter. And I sure as hell wasn't ready to let Jack go.

Chapter 12

wanted a little Reilly pick-me-up, so first thing the next morning, I called the office looking for her. "She's out today," Manny said.

"Again?" This was really getting on my nerves. "Where is she?" I demanded.

"Sick."

Suddenly there were too many sick women in my life. "I'll bring her some *caldo*," I said, leaving an opening for him to fess up, admit that he had her doing some kind of dangerous dirty work, and say that she wasn't actually home sick and didn't need me to bring her soup.

He said nothing.

When I called her at home, the phone just rang and rang. My imagination ran wild. Aside from her ever-changing hair color, Reilly was the most predictable girl on the planet. She lived with her mother, was like a Gossip Girl, J.Lo style, and drove a lime green Volkswagen Beetle, complete with a cute little flower on the dash.

Soup wouldn't do her any good, since she wasn't home. I'd get to the bottom of it, but for now I called my cousin's wife. "Lucy, what's on your schedule today?"

"How's your face? Tell me!" I held the receiver away from my ear, her voice exploding across the phone line. "Still glowing?"

I tried to put a smile in my voice, but I just couldn't muster it. "Still glowing."

As I moved on with my investigation of Rosie Gonzales, my determination to get to the bottom of Lucy and Zac's situation moved up to first place on my personal priority list. I needed them to have a happy ending because if they fell apart, my faith in love might just vanish on the spot. "What's your schedule like today? I could use some company."

"Company," she repeated. "As in your sidekick again?"

She'd helped me on my last case. If she came with me today, I could kill two birds with one stone—help her and get her help with the Rosie thing. "Absolutely."

Nervous enthusiasm edged into her voice. "Let me check my book." There was a loud crack as Lucy dropped the receiver on the table. A moment later she was back and nearly shouting into the phone. "I have a facial in fifteen minutes, and a wax after that. Zac's with the kids. I can be done by eleven fifteen. Can you wait?"

Two hours. It was doable. "Sure. I'll pick you up at eleven fifteen sharp."

"Thanks, Lola. I needed this. It's going to be awesome."

I tried to let her enthusiasm infuse me as she hung up the phone. I felt the first lift in any spirits since last night. I didn't know how awesome my plan was, but spending the day with Lucy would hopefully perk both of us up. I was determined to get to the bottom of her marital problem.

Love had to win.

"Reilly!" I hammered my fist against the front door of the Fuller house. "You there?"

My pounding could have woken the dead, but it didn't bring Reilly to the door. I scribbled out a quick note and was taping it to the door when the high-pitched beep sounded from the street.

I knew that beep. I turned as a little green Bug zipped up to the

145

curb. Reilly honked the horn again, popped out, and raced toward me. "Lola! Oh my gosh, I have so much to tell you!"

I gasped and stared at her. She had an entirely new look—more Agent 99 than a rainbow version of Mrs. Marc Anthony. Her neon locks were now jet-black, dark glasses shaded her eyes, and dark red lipstick colored her lips. "What happened to you?"

She stopped in her tracks and struck a pose. "You like?"

"Uh . . ." I didn't know if I liked. "You look different," I said, but she was already past me, tugging my note from the door and letting herself into the house.

I started to follow, but before I took two steps inside, she was in front of me again, guiding me back outside. She pulled the door closed and started toward her car. "Gotta run!"

"Wait!" I blocked her path. "What's the hurry? Where have you been?"

She looked over her right shoulder, then over her left. All very spylike. "Top secret."

"Reilly," I snapped. "It's me. Lola. You don't keep secrets from me."

She skirted around me and circled her car to the driver's side. "El bosso's orders," she said before slipping back inside. She leaned over and rolled down the passenger window. "When I get the all-clear from MC, I'll fill you in."

"MC?" As in Hammer?

"Manny Camacho," she called as she yanked at the steering wheel, made a tight U-turn, and zipped down the street.

Reilly was dressed like a Backyardigan on a spy mission, was keeping secrets, and was calling Manny MC. Ay, *Dios*, the world was going crazy.

I tried to put things in perspective: So what if Reilly was changing her style? So what if she was becoming mysterious like the rest of the Camacho crew? It was bound to happen at some point. In a weird way, I'd almost expected it. I'd just hoped Reilly wouldn't succumb to keeping secrets like everyone else in my life. Surely it would sort itself out in time.

At 11:15 sharp, medicated with pain reliever to ease my throbbing temples, I pulled up to Lucy's house.

I stood in the entryway while she ran back to her bedroom to grab her shoes. "I'm glad we get to spend some time together," I called after her.

"Me, too! Especially with your doppelgänger, you know, dead but still haunting you."

Doppel*what*? Lucy and her New Age mumbo jumbo. I went in search of the nearest dictionary. Flipping pages, I finally found it— "*doppelgänger*: A ghostly double." Huh. Not so mumbo jumbo after all. Rosie was haunting me from beyond. I felt like the kid in *The Sixth Sense*—like I needed to help her before she could find peace in the great beyond.

A few minutes later, we were back in my car and heading toward the freeway. "What time do you need to be back?"

"God, I don't know. Let's get wild and stay out all night!"

I glanced at her. Her platinum hair was loosely pulled back into a barrette, half an inch of brown roots creeping out of her scalp. Her fitted beige T-shirt and baggy wraparound pants emphasized her boobs and hips, the Birkenstocks on her feet completing the picture of whole-earth goddess. She looked ready for a night on the town at the Davis Farmers' Market.

I opened my mouth to talk some sense into her, but she continued on before I got a word out. "So," Lucy said. "Where are we going? What are we doing? God, you have no idea how great it is to be out of that house! Right now I don't ever want to touch skin again."

"I thought you loved your job."

"I do." There was a heavy pause filled with unspoken thoughts. "I just feel like I'm, you know, suffocating."

I yanked the car off the main road, slammed on the brakes, and looked at her. "You want to stay out. You feel like you're suffocating. Spill it, Lucy. What is going on?"

Her lower lip quivered and like a turbulent geyser erupting, she burst into tears.

"Lucy! Oh my God!" I fumbled in my purse, searching for a tissue.

She sobbed into the wrinkled Java City napkin I handed her, blowing her nose when she was finished.

I laid my hand on her knee. "Tell me what's going on."

She threw her palm up, and I clamped my mouth closed. "I'm f-fine. If fine means—if it means that—that Zac and I are heading for—" She heaved and sobbed. "H-headed for d-divorce court."

"Wh-what?" I sputtered. "What are you talking about?"

"Zac doesn't," she howled, "want me—anymore." Lucy blew her nose again, sounding like the horn on an eighteen-wheeler.

"*Loca*. Of course he does."

"No, he—" She broke off, trying again. "Wh-when he comes home, it's like—like he doesn't even see me. I've become his *mother*," she wailed, "not his *w-wife*." She threw her hands up then buried her face in them. "When did *that* happen?" She sobbed and gestured to her hair, her pants, her shoes. "When did *this* happen? You know I have a body under here, but no one ever sees it."

I thought back to the facial Lucy gave me. "The roller coaster . . ."

"There's no goddamned roller coaster. There's no excitement. We don't even talk anymore unless it's about the kids. I can't remember the last time he touched me."

I took a deep breath and phrased my words carefully. "Things have a way of getting twisted around and misinterpreted. Maybe he thinks *you're* interested in someone else?"

She spat out a laugh. "Me? Lola, you've got to be kidding! Who else would I be interested in? I love Zac."

I shrugged. "There's no client?"

She scoffed. "Right, like I'd be caught dead with one of those freaky metrosexuals. I wouldn't want a 'facial' man, for God's sake." She shook her head. "But that's beside the point. Zac doesn't *look* at me. I could walk around naked, and he wouldn't notice."

"Well, yes, I think he'd notice *that*." My mind raced as I decided what direction to take this conversation. "Lucy, I'm going to tell you something, and I don't want you to freak out."

148

She wiped away a stream of tears and her pencil-thin eyebrows rose. "Uh-oh. That doesn't sound good."

"Well, that kind of depends. Abuelo asked me to help Zac."

Her lips became as thin as her eyebrows. "Help him do what?"

I felt a surge of guilt over the whole deception. "He's afraid you're seeing someone else."

Lucy stared at me, openmouthed. "You're kidding." Her voice dropped to an alarmingly low tone, the complete opposite of the hysterical wail she'd just channeled.

I nodded. "He does. And he went to Abuelo for advice."

"Why in the world would he go to that ornery, old—?" She slapped her hand over her mouth. "I'm sorry!"

"Hey, he *is* ornery *and* old. And I don't know *why* Zac went to him. All I know is that Abuelo asked me to look into it."

Lucy looked at me, her face drawn and sad. "That's why you came for the facial? That's why we're going out today?"

I was trying to help her, I reminded myself, but the guilt bubbled up. "I loved the facial, Lucy! I just want to help if I can." I hurried on. "I really do need your help today."

Lucy looked out the side window. "Why would he possibly think I was having an affair?"

I shrugged. "Maybe he thinks you want off the merry-go-round."

She slapped her hands over her ears and shook her head with frenetic energy. "Screw that goddamned metaphor!"

The space between us seemed to shrink.

She frowned, dropping her hands to her lap. "What am I going to do?" she whispered.

Confirming that Lucy was *not* having an affair was done. I believed her. Helping her solve her marital issues was something else entirely. Jack and I hadn't even had one decent date, and he'd invaded my mind and body and soul, but how was I supposed to help Lucy and Zac survive their decade-long marriage?

I glanced at the clock on the dashboard. Time was slipping away, and I had a druggie to out. "How about we sit on it for a while? We'll think of something." I started the car again. "I have a lead on the dead woman, and I need your help." Her acting chops, specifically, and after her little good cop–bad cop stint on my last case, I knew she was up for the job.

Lucy blinked away her emotions. "Okay," she said, straightening up and putting on her game face. "Let's do some detective work."

I eased back onto the road and headed toward Auburn.

"PI work means a lot of driving," Lucy commented a little while later.

That was an understatement. "I'm ready to go hybrid." My gas bills were outrageous.

"Oh, yes! Green all the way. I can't wait till the MINI Cooper goes hybrid."

A while later I pulled off the freeway into Old Auburn. The curved roads, old trees, and quaint architecture gave Old Auburn a welcoming atmosphere, sort of a snapshot of an idyllic Midwestern town—in Northern California. With Gold Rush history.

The Brenda Dawson Center for Drug and Alcohol Rehabilitation was situated in Old Town, in an ancient-looking brown-shingled building that looked like a throwback to the Old West. I'd spent ten minutes of the drive briefing Lucy. We'd brainstormed how to play it, and we were ready.

"You have to be convincing," I said, throwing up a prayer and crossing my fingers that she could pull it off.

She took out her barrette and scrambled her fingers through her hair, creating a completely disheveled mess. She worked her face muscles, edging the ends of her lips down into a sagging pout, fluttering her eyelids. "I'm a born actress. How else could I have hidden my misery and suspicion from my husband?"

I frowned at the mention of her marriage but watched in fascination as Lucy transformed herself from wholesome earthy to wasted hippie. Her eyelids drooped to half-mast, and she mussed her hair one last time.

I took off my shawl, straightened my T-shirt, and pulled my

ponytail through the back hole of the Old Navy cap I'd brought with me, pulling the bill low over my forehead. It was my version of a disguise, and it was plenty for this outing.

"We'll talk about your misery later. I'm working on a plan for that." She halfheartedly fought me as I pulled her from the car—just in case anyone was watching from inside the treatment center.

"What the hell are you doing?" She snapped away from my grip.

I stared at her, completely in awe. Jekyll and Hyde. Man, she was *good*. People gave us a wide berth, skirting around us on the sidewalk. Lucy had missed her calling. She was the female Robert De Niro.

"I am not going in there." Her menacing scowl was tempered only by her puppy-dog eyes. It was hard to take her pissed-off attitude seriously when she had the stoned look pat. And yet the package worked.

"Oh, yes, you are." I grabbed hold of her again and dragged her toward the center. She fought me every step of the way.

Finally, I pulled open the door and guided Lucy inside. Sadly, the reception area of the center was vacant. Our Oscar-winning performances had gone on without an audience. We kept it up anyway. Lucy flailed her arms as I pulled her toward one of the straight-backed chairs. She managed to escape my grasp again. "What the hell, dude—" She wheeled around on me, bitch-slapping the air in front of her.

Dude? I dodged her crazed attack and used my best cajoling voice. "We'll just see what it's about. That's all. No commitment."

Her energy expended, she slumped into a chair and tilted her head back to look at me through slivered eyes. "You can't make me do this."

"It's for your own good," I said, cringing at the clichéd words. "You need help." I winked at her.

Lucy extended her legs and aggressively tapped her Birkenstocked feet against the floor, her passive act of defiance muted by the carpeting. She shrugged her shoulders. "Who are you to say I need help, huh? Miss Goddamned Perfect." Her eyes fluttered closed.

151

Miss Perfect? I arched an eyebrow. "Miss Perfect?"

I could see her eyeballs skittering around under her closed lids. She folded her arms over her chest and deepened her frown. "You heard me. No problems, perfect life . . ." She cracked open one eye and scanned me up and down. "Just look at you. Freaking perfect."

I straightened the bill of my cap and kicked Lucy's foot. Her eyelids drifted partway open to their halfway state. "Where's this coming from?" I whispered. Was her improv reality-based?

The smallest fragment of a grin graced her lips just as someone behind me said, "Hello—can I help you?"

I jumped, but Lucy didn't move a psuedo-stoned muscle. She lounged on her chair, legs outstretched, looking wasted, evidence of her smile vanquished.

I turned and smacked a pained smile on my face. I was clearly an abused woman trying to help her drugged-out friend. We shook hands, and I introduced myself. "Magda Falcón," I said.

"What an unusual name."

"I know, everyone's so creative with names these days."

"It's nice to meet you, Ms. Falcon." She didn't even try to use the accent, so it came out sounding like the bird. "I'm Hannah Dawson." Her Southern drawl stretched out her name.

I absorbed her features. Hannah Dawson had short brown pixie hair, wore neatly conservative clothes with a hip flare to them, and looked very pulled together. Her chunky jewelry gave her just enough flash and pizzazz to make her interesting. "How can I help you?" she asked.

Sweeping my arm out to introduce Lucy, I froze. She looked like she'd passed out.

Chapter 13

Hannah Dawson felt Lucy's pulse, pried open an eye to check her pupils, looked in her mouth. It was like a horse exam. I just hoped Hannah wouldn't accidentally touch a tickle spot.

"I'm not sure what's wrong with her," she declared a minute later. "It doesn't seem to be an overdose. We should move her, though. Wouldn't do to have her stay out here in this condition."

Lucy was in full improv mode—passing out was a stroke of genius—but who knew how long we'd be able to fool our Southern belle.

"I'll take her feet," I said to her. "You get her arms." We took hold of Lucy's extremities and lifted. Whoo. Dead weight. I tightened my grip.

"What kind of drugs . . . does your friend . . . do?" Hannah asked as we walked.

I recalled the scenario Lucy and I had come up with in the car. Moms doing their kids' Ritalin. "She's got a child with ADHD and she, er, kind of borrows his meds sometimes."

Hannah's perfectly penciled brows pulled together. "Interesting."

It certainly was. What wouldn't the suburban woman do to get high? "She won't admit it, but I think she's taking some other stuff, too."

"Seems that . . . way," she panted.

I repositioned my hold on Lucy's feet as Hannah kicked open a door behind her. "Just on the bed there."

I grunted, and we swung Lucy like a sack of flour, heaving her onto the hospital mattress. Hannah, with her back to us, pulled the blinds open. "Whew!" I swiped my hand across my forehead. "She doesn't look that heavy."

Lucy cracked open one eye, just barely, and scowled—quite an accomplishment, considering her face muscles never moved. *Payback for the Miss Perfect jab*, my smile said.

"When they're drugged out, their bodies seem so much denser."

"Mind if we talk?" I asked after Hannah had Lucy situated the way she wanted her. Tucked snug as a bug in a rug . . . in the stiff sheets and scratchy blanket.

"For a few minutes. Maybe she'll wake up on her own."

I could promise her that, but I kept my mouth shut. I followed Hannah out to the reception area, and we sat on the cushioned chairs, facing each other. She exuded compassion.

"So sad when healthy young people turn to drugs," she said.

I jumped at the opening. "It sure is. I had a friend who came here. Said you worked miracles. Maybe you remember her? Dolores Cruz."

Hannah folded her hands in front of her, the epitome of class and decorum despite Lucy's comatose state in the other room. "Hmmm. The name seems familiar." She rose, gliding across the lobby, returning a moment later with a medical folder, my name neatly typed across the tab. "She was here more than a year ago."

"That's right." I could barely keep my excitement under wraps. My drug rehab record was in the woman's hands! *Open it up*, I willed. Reading upside down wasn't my best skill, but I could give it a go.

It was like we were on the same wavelength, or like Rosie was right here, making sure I got the information I needed to avenge her murder. Hannah opened the folder and flipped through the pages. "Ah, yes. I remember her."

I caught a glimpse of a photograph—*un poquito diferente* from the one Detective Seavers had shown me. Rosie looked healthy, if you discounted the pasty, drug-infused skin and bloodshot eyes. "Really? You have an excellent memory." More flies with honey, and all that . . .

Hannah smiled. "Well, I remember how nervous her boyfriend was. He was the fidgety type. Couldn't keep still. I'd bet my life that he was on speed," she concluded, her drawl making it sound like she was offering me afternoon tea instead of relaying drug behaviors.

"Her boyfriend?" I put my index finger to my cheek, musing. "I don't remember her having a boyfriend."

Hannah looked at me curiously. "He's the one who brought her in."

"Hmmm."

"Maybe you should ask her."

I sensed Hannah starting to doubt me. I stepped up my game. "I wish I could," I said, letting a sad frown tilt my lips down, "but she died last week."

The statement had the right effect. Hannah's spine almost crackled. "An overdose?" she immediately asked.

"Honestly," I said. "I don't know." It was the truth. As far as I knew, there was not evidence of drug use. Someone had shoved Rosie into that Dumpster. Acute head injury was the official cause of death.

A lightbulb clicked on behind Hannah's eyes. Had she seen the story on the news? Seen the photo of me that the stations had run as the real Dolores Cruz, detective? Yikes.

"What's his name?" I peered at the file. Caught the glimpse of an address. I knew that street. It was right off of Franklin Boulevard. It was probably the same apartment I'd been in with Jack just days ago.

Breaking and entering at Rosie's, retrieving my rosary from Sergio. I'd be happy to avoid South Sac for a good long time.

"Who?" she asked.

"Dolores's boyfriend."

"I'm afraid that's confidential." She snapped the file shut. Yep, the jig was up. "We should check on your friend." She stood, holding Dolores Cruz's rehab information close to her side.

There was no way to warn Lucy. Hannah burst in the room, catching Lucy midturn on the bed. "So glad you're feelin' better, dear."

Lucy's face drained of color. "Oh, y-yes. M-much better. Wh-what happened?"

"If you're feeling better, we should go," I said, throwing my eyebrows up and notching my head to the side. Code for *let's scram!*

Lucy practically fell out of the bed. She slipped on her Birkenstocks, and we followed Hannah, our repressed Southern rehab queen, back to the lobby. She held out a glossy brochure for me. "Communication is the key. She needs to know you'll love her no matter what and that she's safe."

Ah, so she wasn't going to confess that she recognized me. She was a pro. "I understand." And I did. Get out while the getting's good. "Thank you for your time, Mrs. Dawson."

"My pleasure," she drawled.

I smiled, unconsciously mimicking her posture and hand position, the brochure interrupting the full effect. I couldn't quite bring myself to say, *Call me Magda*. Instead, I commented, "You're doing such a wonderful thing here."

"Well, thank you. We are certainly tryin'."

Her accent softened the letters in her speech and made me crave biscuits and gravy, but there was a finality to her words.

"If you don't mind my asking, who is the Brenda Dawson in the Brenda Dawson Treatment Center for Drug and Alcohol Abuse?"

Hannah's posture stiffened, her jaw tightening under the pristine façade. "My daughter was a victim of drug abuse and addiction. She died when she was twenty-one. Unfortunately, I learned the signs too late."

"I'm so sorry. But what an amazing way to honor her life."

"I think so. We've been able to help a good many people. Alas, not your friend."

156

Lucy was slouching next to me. She jerked. "Not you. My other friend. Dolores Cruz," I said with a pained smile.

Hannah turned toward Lucy. "My dear, I do hope you'll think about comin' back to us. I know we can help you."

Lucy pried her eyes open and struggled to stay upright. Swaying slightly, she dropped her eyelids a centimeter and slurred in monotone. "To get help, you need a problem. I ain't got a problem. 'Cept meddlesome so-called friends."

Lucy waved her hands dismissively and slowly moved toward the door. "See you around. *Not.*"

My shoulders slumped and I frowned, but inside I was cheering. Lucy had planned our escape. "Thanks again," I said from the door. I gave Hannah a wave, piled Lucy into the car, and sped away.

Once we were on the road, I patted Lucy's leg. "You were amazing. And you saved us."

She straightened up in her seat, a self-satisfied smile pasted on her lips, her stoned sensibilities instantly vanishing. "Yeah, but she was on to us. Am I right? Did you get anything?"

"Just that Rosie had a boyfriend who checked her into rehab. But no name, no address, nothing concrete."

She switched topics faster than my mother could. "Can I be your partner?" she blurted.

I stared straight ahead, white-knuckling the steering wheel. "Uh, I don't—"

She drumrolled her hands against her thighs and let out a riotous laugh. "Relax, *Magda.* I was just kidding." Her smile drooped. "If I'm getting divorced, I'm going to need job security. Guess I'm destined to wax hairy backsides."

"You're *not* getting divorced."

She kicked off her sandals and pulled her leg up onto the seat. "Well, if I'm not, I doubt Zac would want me working as a detective. I don't think he'd want me to be in danger all the time. How does Jack feel about that?"

"It doesn't matter what Jack feels. And *I'm* not in danger all

157

the time! Look what we accomplished. We confirmed Rosie was a patient there." And that I had a drug rehab record. Not only had Rosie messed with my credit, but she'd also messed with my strait-laced reputation.

Lucy wrapped her arms around her legs and gave me a forlorn smile. "Zac wouldn't believe it."

"About that," I said, bringing the conversation back to Lucy and her problem. "Why don't you just sit down and have a heart-to-heart?" I felt my eyes glass over. "He loves you. You *have* to talk."

"With the kids and their schedules? We never seem to have the time. Or energy. Mia ends up coming into our room most nights. We don't even get time alone when we're in bed."

That *was* a problem, but I wasn't giving up. "You have to find your spirit again, Lucy. You have to find that person Zac fell in love with and you need to find the Zac you fell in love with. *Sabes*, rekindle that old flame."

She leaned back and closed her eyes. "Easier said than done."

After dropping Lucy at home, I headed back to Abuelita's. The parking lot was nearly deserted. I parked right in front and walked up to the wall of windows. Cupping my hands over my eyes, I peered into the restaurant. Dark. Half the interior lights dimly lit the dining room, but no one was in sight. A note taped on the door said, *Back at 3:00*. I rapped on the door, hoping someone would come to let me in. *Nadie*.

Then I checked my watch—two thirty. Huh, the probable explanation for the early closure was that Antonio's *I don't grocery shop* gene must have finally caught up with him and he'd needed to make a quick trip to the market in between lunch and dinner.

I sat down on the bench out front to wait. My hands rested on the slats of wood and, as if it were a time machine, it took me back. Splintered pieces of memories pricked into my brain. Antonio, Jack, and I had sat on this bench when we were teenagers. I'd seen the photograph of us framed and sitting on Jack's dresser the same night I'd discovered the Trojans.

What had we been doing? The memory was foggy. Jack hadn't been an active part of my life then. More like a person on the periphery—always there with Antonio, but not really connected to me. Sure, he'd been the reason I'd taken up surveillance (the photographic evidence of which was now tucked safely in my wig box).

But why had we been on the bench? Who'd taken the picture? I thought and thought, trying to remember, and finally the fog cleared. It had been my parents' twentieth wedding anniversary. Jack, Antonio's best friend, had met us at the restaurant. He'd been an honorary member of *la familia Cruz* back then, using us as a temporary replacement for his own disintegrating family.

The three of us sat on the bench in front of Abuelita's waiting for my sister, Gracie, and brother Ray so we could drive to the party together.

I closed my eyes, remembering the moment as if I were reliving it. Sergio Garcia, a guy a year ahead of me in school, had leaned against a car just in front of the restaurant.

"Take a picture of us, man," Antonio said. He reached over me, pulled Jack's camera from his hands, and held it out to Sergio.

"Sure." Sergio's tan pants were crisply pressed, his oversized collared shirt left untucked. He looked mysterious, and more than a little frightening.

Antonio leaned back while Jack draped his arm across the bench, behind my back. I tilted my head and curved my lips in a warm smile for the camera. My eyes opened a fraction more when Jack's hand grazed my shoulder.

Sergio readied the camera. "That's right, Lola," he said, winking at me. "Looking good." He snapped the picture and handed the camera back to Jack, but his gaze stayed on me. "How 'bout I drive you to the church?"

Alarms went off in my head. Alone in a car with Sergio Garcia—scary.

159

I crossed my legs, and my skirt hiked up my thigh. A prickling of cold slipped onto my shoulder, a sudden absence where something had just been. Jack had moved his hand away, I realized.

Sergio lounged against the door to the restaurant and cocked his head as he looked at me. "Come on. Just you and me, baby."

Jack leaned back and rasped to Antonio, "You're not going to let her go!"

"Tonio's not my dad," I snapped. "I can go if I want to."

Jack glared at me. "Why's Garcia even here?"

Antonio answered. "*Familia*, dude. His aunt's best friend is my grandmother's goddaughter or some shit."

Jack scoffed. "That's not even close to family."

I slapped Jack's leg, shooting him a piercing look. "He's more family than you are. Why do you care?"

Jack's face darkened. After a pause he said, "I don't."

Much as I fantasized about it, Jack was not in my future—he'd made his indifference clear. I turned my back on him and whispered to Antonio, just loudly enough for Jack to hear. "Tell *los padres* I went with Sergio. See you there." To Sergio, I smiled and said, "I'd love a ride."

Sergio took my hand and pulled me up off the bench as Jack muttered, "You sure you're ready for that kind of ride?"

A hand suddenly grabbed my wrist and jerked me back. "Lola, wait," Tonio blurted. "You better not—"

Sergio gripped Antonio's shoulder. "Hey, man, it's cool. I'll take real good care of her." He took my hand again, and we crossed the parking lot to his half-mile-long Impala. My feet dragged, my stomach twisting into knots. I slid across the bench seat. What had Jack meant, am I ready for that kind of ride?

As we drove away, I glanced back through the rear window to see Antonio scowling at the Impala, and Jack standing at the curb staring after us. His legs were firmly planted on the cement, his hands shoved in his pockets, a pissed-off look on his face that I hadn't understood.

I traced my hand across the back of the bench where Jack's arm had rested behind me that day. I understood that look now. Why had he kept his feelings to himself back then?

I thought about Jack's easy laugh, his confident stride, his protective nature. He was the complete package and had never wanted for dates. No, I decided, it was better that we'd never dated in high school. His father still would have left the family; Jack still would have withdrawn from everyone and left Sacramento; I'd have been left with a different set of memories, and we still wouldn't be together.

I snapped out of my memories. A change of scenery was in order. I'd run another errand, and by the time I got back, the restaurant would be open.

Chapter 14

Climbing into my car, I grabbed for my ringing cell phone, not bothering to look at the readout on the screen. "Hello?"

"Hey, you," Jack said. My nerves sizzled as if he'd whispered those two little words into my ear.

"Hey."

"How's your day been?"

Nice innocent small talk. This was good. "Eh. I checked out Rosie's drug stint. Nothing revealing. No word from Detective Seavers, so whatever they're doing, it's very hush-hush."

"Maybe this'll cheer you up."

Him telling me that he was never seeing Sarah the ex-fiancée again was too much to hope for. "What's that?"

"I have a contact at Sac State. I can't believe I didn't think of it before. She might be able to give you some help on the admissions problem and tuition. Her name's Margaret Wallis."

Contact. Female. As in someone from Jack's past? "She works in admissions?"

"She does."

I weighed my desire for information against meeting face-to-face with a woman who might very well be one of Jack's former conquests. Practicality won. My need to straighten out my credit took priority over my pride. Trust him. He'd asked me to, and he'd been sincere. "Okay. Thank you." So original.

"I'll make the appointment and get back to you."

We hung up. I didn't want to think about how much time he'd need to sort out his personal life. The kiss from the night before was burned into my brain, and I couldn't shake it.

Three situations, like riotous bees, buzzed in front of me: Lucy and Zac, Rosie Gonzales, and Jack Callaghan.

I was trying a new tactic. I'd tackle them one at a time. Methodical. Determined. First up was Lucy and Zac. A plan suddenly materialized in my brain. I made a quick phone call to facilitate it; then I dialed my cousin's wife for the second time that day. She was back in aesthetician mode. "Skin Delicacies," she said into the receiver, but there was no zing her voice.

I was a girl on a mission. No time for small talk. "I have a proposition for you."

"Hang on," she said. She dropped the phone, and I heard her schedule an appointment with a client, then heard the sound of a door closing. "Two in one day?" she blurted when she came back on the line. "Tattoos? Piercings? Druggie impersonations? You're really expanding my view of the world, you know that?"

"You said you wanted the roller-coaster ride back in your marriage, right?"

She sighed. "That's a stupid metaphor. I'm sorry I ever mentioned it."

"Work with me, Luce." I cupped my hand over my forehead for strength and went on. "Let me rephrase it. You want the excitement back. You need time to communicate with your husband. Just you and Zac. No kids."

"Like that's gonna happen. Do you know what babysitters charge these days?"

I slapped the steering wheel and snapped, "It *is* going to happen. *I'm* going to babysit your kids *overnight*, and *you* and *Zac* are going to go out on the town. No charge."

163

She sputtered. Lucy rendered speechless. I pumped my arm. Hah! It was a mini success. "Out on the town in Sacratomato?"

"Yes. And I know just the place. All you need is to be together, without the kids. And talk. And, you know"—I cleared the frog from my throat—"other stuff."

"I don't know," she said, but I could tell she was intrigued by the idea.

"*Look*, marriage is work. Even I know that. You and Zac have to try."

"You could have a relationship, too, if you worked at it," Lucy said. Diversion. Neat trick, but I was on to her.

"We're not talking about me. It actually takes *two* committed people to have a relationship. I'm lacking the second person. You're not. Nice try, though."

I sensed her sticking her tongue out at me, but I went on, laying out the details of my cupid plan. "I made reservations for Friday night at the Delta King. You and Zac are going to spend a romantic evening in Old Sac, have dinner on the boat, and do whatever married couples do when they're alone for a whole night."

I braced myself for an onslaught of indignant refusals. Instead I heard sniffling on the other end of the phone. "Lucy?" Uh-oh. Were they too far gone for my love intervention? "Are you all right?"

"Y-you d-did that? For us?" she asked in between sniffles. "Are you sure? Three kids is a lot to handle."

Ay, Dios mío. Was I going to have to drag her out to the boat myself? "Lucy. I'm their aunt." I thought about that. "Well, their aunt once removed. Or something. I'll be fine. I'll get Antonio to help me. He loves hanging out with your kids."

"*This* Friday night?"

"Right. This Friday night."

"Zac might not want to," she said.

"Of course he'll want to. He *wants* things to get better between you two."

Lucy gave a final sniff. "What if it doesn't work?"

164

"It will. You just get yourself ready for romance."

We talked about a few more details before Lucy's next client arrived. "Thanks for today," I said, then added, "See you Friday." A weight lifted off my shoulders. I didn't know if one night alone could fix what was broken between my cousin and his wife, but it was definitely a start.

Next on my to-do list was the Rosie situation. I dialed the number—now committed to memory—from the birthday party invitation for what felt like the zillionth time. If I didn't get through this time, my next call would be to Seavers. Surely they'd used their resources to track down the address. *If* they'd put it together that Rosie had been at this party the day she'd died.

There was a click and a child's voice said, "Hello?"

I nearly dropped my phone. They were home! "Is your mom there?"

The phone bounced on a hard surface, and the kid barreled through the house yelling, "Mom, phone! Mom!"

A full minute elapsed before a frazzled-sounding woman picked up the dropped receiver. "Yeah, hello?"

Stellar etiquette. *Señora* Cruz would be appalled. "Hi. Um, I'm calling about the birthday party from a week and a half ago?"

"Why?"

"I just have a few questions, if you have a minute."

"Depends who you are."

She was a prickly one. "My name is Do—" I broke off, changing my mind. "Magda Falcón. I'm looking into the death of a woman named Dolores Cruz. I believe she attended a birthday party you held. With her son."

I heard a crash and a rustle. The woman held the phone away from her and covered the mouthpiece. "Clean that mess up! Now!" Even muffled, the scream demanded attention. She came back to the conversation, shifting between her domestic chaos and chatting about a dead woman, without skipping a beat. "Yeah, I heard she died. Too bad. I didn't know her or anything."

"If you don't mind my asking . . ."

"Juana," she supplied. So cooperative!

"If you don't mind my asking, Juana, if you didn't know her, why did you invite her to the party?"

"She came with my brother-in-law." She covered the mouthpiece again, yelling at the top of her voice, "You better take care of that!"

The kid said something back to his mother. She dropped the phone with a *thunk* and scuttled across the room for a face-to-face conversation. "You don't talk to me like that," she said slowly, a trace of accent behind her words. I imagined her grabbing hold of her son's shirt, pulling him up close and getting in his face. *"El piso esta sucio. Limpia. ¡Pronto!"*

The boy mumbled something, and Juana—mother of the year—called him a name that even *I* can't repeat. She came back to the phone. "My son spilled juice all over the floor."

"No problem," I said weakly. And Jack wanted how many? *¡Chale!* This lady had only *one*, and she'd clearly lost her mind. What if Lucy and Zac's kids declared mutiny? Could I stay calm and rational?

I cleared my throat and carried on stoically. "You were telling me about your brother-in-law?"

"Right. Francisco. That was the first time he ever brought anyone around."

"Did you talk with her at all?"

"Not really. I was busy with the party." The boy muttered something to his mother. *"Espera,"* she said to me, laying down the phone, more gently this time. Her footsteps grew faint as she walked away. *"Bien,"* I heard her say, and though I tried to envision her ruffling his hair, I couldn't quite bring the picture to mind.

"All better," she said when she picked up the phone again.

"You sound busy."

"Always busy. If it isn't laundry, it's homework, or housework, or unpaid bills—"

"Mucho trabajo," I said.

"Hablas español bien."

166

"*Sí, soy mexicana.*" Couldn't hurt to try to connect with Juana. "So, about Dolores Cruz. Can you tell me anything about her?"

Juana grew quiet. Her house was strangely calm compared with the ruckus a few minutes ago. "She and Francisco were, uh, *simpatico*," she said finally. "Said they were living together."

I hadn't seen a man's clothing or belongings in the apartment, but there *was* the toilet seat that was left up. And Francisco would have had plenty of time to get his things out. Was he an abuser? A killer? Did he have the kid?

"Did you hear anything about them moving out of the area?" I asked, thinking about the boxes at Rosie's apartment.

She covered the mouthpiece again. "Change the channel, Juanito," she said in a muffled voice. Returning to me, she said, "Not a word."

I rolled down my car window, a slight breeze stirring the air inside my stationary car. "Do you have a phone number for your brother-in-law? Or an address?"

"Nope. He's my husband's brother. Haven't seen him since the party."

"Would your husband have a way to reach him?"

"Doubt it. They don't talk much. Francisco got ahold of Rafael. Wanted to borrow some money. That's why they came to the party."

"Did you loan it to him?"

"Ha! No way! We'd never have seen it again. We're no charity."

"Can I speak with your husband? Just to cover all my bases."

"He's a trucker. He's not due back for a week."

Damn. A dead end. "Maybe you could double-check it with him. When he calls you," I added in case she didn't know what I was getting at. "A phone number. Or a new address. Anything he might have."

She threw out a beleaguered sigh. "Okay. I'll ask him, but he won't call for a few days."

Clearly Juana wasn't going to go out of her way to help me. "Just one more thing," I asked. "Can I get your address for my records?"

She rattled it off without hesitation, and I jotted it down. "*Muchas gracias*, Mrs. . . ." I broke off, hoping she'd fill in the blank.

"Zuniga."

Score! "Thank you, Mrs. Zuniga."

She said good-bye, but as I started to lower the phone, her voice screamed at me. "Oh! I do remember something! *¡Escuchame!*"

"I hear you!" My eardrum was ringing from the accost. "What do you remember, *señora?*"

"That lady, the one who died? She got into an argument with one of my neighbors."

I straightened, snatching up the notebook I'd tossed aside and flipping it open to a blank page. "Which neighbor?"

"Bill Johnson." She rattled off his number, and I scribbled it down. "Did you hear the argument?"

"No. I was in the kitchen. They were outside in the backyard. I just remember how mad he was. He took his kids and left after that."

"Was anyone else near them? Anyone else that might have heard what they talked about?"

"Not that I know of."

I thanked her, disconnected, and immediately dialed Bill Johnson. The answering machine picked up after the third ring. "Yeah, this is Bill. Leave me a message, and I'll get back to you." I hung up, not wanting to scare him away with a message from a detective. Better to try again later.

I hit the office-supply store next, found the perfect paper shredder for the low, low price of $39.99. I bought it and then headed straight for the restaurant. I mused the entire drive back about how Rosie Gonzales had gotten my information. My research on identity theft had taught me that the trash in my garbage can was considered public domain once it sat on the street for pickup. Anyone could riffle through it. From now on—with my handy-dandy shredder—I was going to make mincemeat out of *every personal* piece of paper, and I mean *everything*. Not even the tags from my Victoria's Secret *chonis* were safe.

Abuelita's was open when I got back. Sylvia greeted me as I walked in. "Here to eat?"

The dining room held a smattering of early-bird diners. "Definitely. My appetite has returned," I announced grandly. "And," I said, swiping my lips with my shimmering gloss, "I have a lead on the Rosie Gonzales case *and* I have a plan for my cousin and his wife. Things are definitely looking up."

Sylvia nodded, appraising me with a small grin. She tucked a wiry strand of hair behind her ear. "You're playing marriage counselor now?"

"Against my will, but for a good cause. I'm going to babysit their kids while they rekindle the old flame." I winked. "If you get my drift."

She double-winked back. "Oh yeah, I get it. And you have a lead on your mistaken-identity thing? You *are* on a roll."

"Definitely. I got the name of someone she argued with at a party. Can you believe it? Finally, a viable clue."

Sylvia's jaw dropped. She froze and seemed to lose her senses for a beat. Then she slapped her forehead. "Oh!" She seemed to find herself again. "I almost forgot! Your friend is here."

She pushed me into the dining room. "What friend?" I said over my shoulder. And then I saw him. Open laptop on the table. Reporter notepad flipped open. Cell phone clamped to his ear.

Jack.

I ambled over to him. Even after our phone call a while ago, I didn't know where we stood. Did giving him time mean we were friends? As in platonic? Could I do that? Did I want that?

He smiled at me, his hair falling casually over his forehead. He brushed it back as he hung up his phone. "I called that contact of mine."

I stood frozen, looking at the angles on his face. The way the sun threw blades of light onto his hair. His lips and their full, perfect— *¡Callate!* A platonic relationship with Jack was so not going to work for me for very long. "Oh. That was fast. Good," I said, all the while thinking I needed to avoid him in order to maintain my sanity.

He got up, and with his hand on the small of my back, he guided me to the table. "Sit," he ordered, pulling out a chair.

"You didn't tell me you were here," I said.

"I wasn't when we talked. I am now." He sat across from me, his indigo eyes pulling me in like a magnet. "This is becoming my office away from the office."

I frowned. "What about your apartment?"

"I'm there every night. I like to be out during the day. People are inspiring." His gaze grew pointed. "It's no fun to be home alone all the time."

Alone. I blinked slowly. When my eyes opened, Jack was still looking at me, his gaze softening. It was like magic.

"I'm sorry about last night. I didn't want to tell you—"

I waved his words away. "It's fine," I lied. All my imaginings with Jack now had Sarah smack in the middle of them. "I understand. You have to help her."

He nodded, his expression dark and guarded. "I got you an appointment with Margaret Wallis," he said after a few seconds. "This afternoon at four o'clock. I told her it was urgent."

"Great," I said, crunching on a warm tortilla chip dipped in chunky salsa. I'd have to leave soon—less time to spend alone with Jack. "I'll be sure to thank her for you."

"I'll thank her myself," he said. "I'm going with you."

My spine popped. "You don't have to." How much torture was he going to put me through?

"Yes. I do. I'm doing my own research, remember?"

Sylvia glided up to the table. "What can I get you two?"

I shook my head. "Oh, we're not eating together, Sylvia. I was just passing through."

"*Mentirosa.* You *know* you came here to eat," she finished, then whipped out her order book, pen poised to write.

Before I could utter a word, Jack rattled off his order. My stomach growled. Traitor.

Sylvia turned to me, her eyes moving briefly to my stomach, her eyebrows arching. "*¿Lista?*"

My shoulders sank. I was starving. I gave in. "I'll have the tostada salad," I said.

It was just a late lunch with Jack. Not a date. Not a seduction. It. Was. Just. Lunch. With a friend whose voice could probably bring me to orgasm if I let it.

It wasn't like I couldn't control myself in the middle of my family's restaurant. But alone with him on the college campus? That was another story.

My eyes glossed across the tables in the dining room. Chely stood at my grandparents' booth, the three of them staring at me like I was the bearded lady with Ringling Brothers. By the grace of God, everyone else minded their own business, unaware of the turmoil in my mind. Sylvia scratched the order on her pad and retreated to the kitchen.

"I need to say hello to my grandparents," I said to Jack. I slipped away from the table, hoping I'd gain some perspective from across the dining room.

I felt his gaze penetrating my back as I walked. Next to my nubile fifteen-year-old cousin, I looked curvy and busty in a Betty Boop kind of way. Ah, who was I kidding? I was Betty Boop next to anyone. Boobs, hips, and a belly button ring that Jack thought was sexy. The whole package.

I straightened the hem of my sweater and smoothed my hands over my skirt. If Jack was going to stare, he might as well get a good, long look at what he'd get when he sorted things out with Sarah.

Chely smacked her gum and grinned at me as I flung my hair away from my face. "He's, like, so fine and he can't keep his eyes off you. I *knew* you liked him!"

I leaned down—kicking one high-heeled leg out behind me—and gave my grandparents kisses on the cheek. Extra motivation for him to hurry up and work out those problems, I reasoned, but I quickly dropped my leg. I was no tease.

Chely leaned her back against the table and waved across the dining room. I turned in time to see Jack grinning and waving back.

"*¿Estas comiendo con el güero?*" Abuelo flung his cane into the air, pointing it at Jack. We all followed the trajectory of the cane and saw Jack grinning. His gaze lingered on me. He looked hungry. Like a wolf.

With my head bowed, I turned back to the booth, my hand cupped over my eyes. Ay, *Dios mío.* "We're friends and we're having lunch."

Chely nodded slowly, as if she understood the ways of the world. She leaned in to whisper in my ear, her tongue lapping against the roof of her mouth as she chewed her gum. "Right. *Tienes hambre por ese hombre.*" Then she gave a wickedly suggestive laugh as only a fifteen-year-old girl can.

I leveled a look at her and went into mentor mode, totally ignoring the fact that she was right on the money. "Just because you're fifteen now, that doesn't mean you are a love guru, so *cállate, muchacha.*"

Then, with my head held high, I walked back to have a civil meal with Jack.

Margaret Wallis was a mountain of a woman. She stood at least six feet tall and half as wide, and had to have at least thirty years on Jack. My eyes teared, and I choked back a relieved laugh. Margaret, at least, wasn't one of Jack's former lovers.

Plunging my arm forward, I smiled brightly and pitched my voice with extra enthusiasm. "Nice to *meet* you, Ms. Wallis. I appreciate you taking the time to see me."

"Call me Margaret." She lumbered back to her desk and sat in her chair, swiveling around to face us. Jack and I sat in two straight-backed uncomfortable chairs next to her. "Jackie tells me someone enrolled here using your name?"

An invisible string tugged on my head like a puppet. "*Jackie?*"

He glared at me, but he didn't have the power to wipe the nearly hysterical grin off my face. "Old nickname," he said.

172

I nodded. Turning back to Margaret, I said, "You may have read about the woman in the newspaper, actually. She was killed recently. Died in an alley off Florin Road."

"I *do* remember seeing that on the news. Jackie said they thought it was you?"

"That's right. She had a driver's license in my name—"

"She had a lot of things in your name," Jack muttered.

"—and financial aid material for Sac State."

Margaret spun around in her chair and tapped on her computer keyboard. "Social Security?"

I rattled off my nine-digit number and waited while she tapped. A moment later, she grabbed hold of the monitor with her bulky hands and angled it to face us. "There you are. Dolores Falcón Cruz, admitted for fall semester, financial aid pending."

Yep, there was my name, enrolled in Sac State for the second time in my life. "Why would they admit me again? I already have my bachelor's degree."

"People come back all the time. Change in interests means a change in major." She scrolled down the screen, pointing when she found what she was looking for. "See here, it shows you already have a degree in criminal justice. The second admittance is under Spanish."

"So she wouldn't have to take any prerequisites again? Just the upper-level courses?"

Margaret shook her head. "No, she'd have to take any undergraduate courses relevant and required for a Spanish major and any new requirements since the original graduation date. The upper division would be major specific."

I looked at Jack. "What was she going to do with a Spanish major?"

He shrugged. "Translator? Teach? Who knows?"

It didn't make sense. "If I already have a degree, and she was living as me, then why would she even *need* a new degree?" It was a rhetorical question, and since my haunting doppelgänger wasn't talking, the answer would probably stay buried with her.

"Is there anything else you think might be helpful?" I asked.

Margaret scrolled through the file before shaking her head. "You can talk to financial aid," she suggested, and before I knew it, she had the phone receiver in her hand and had dialed an extension. After a brief conversation, she cradled the phone between her shoulder and ear and turned to us. "You can head over there now. Randall Leonard will help you."

Margaret heaved herself out of her chair and offered me her hand to shake. Her large, pudgy fingers engulfed mine, leaving a dry sensation on my skin. Jack gave her a quick hug. "Thanks for your help."

"My pleasure. Say hello to your mom for me."

"I will."

Ah, so Mags was Jack's mother's friend. Once we were out of earshot, I turned and grinned at him. "Jackie, Margaret is adorable. Thank you so much for bringing me to meet her."

He indulged me with a smile, but before my eyes, his face grew serious and he wagged a finger at me. "Forget you ever heard it."

"What?"

"The nickname."

"Or what?" I asked. I walked ahead, the two-inch heels of my shoes clicking against the sidewalk.

I felt him before I heard him. His arm wrapped around me, and his fingers spread against my torso as he matched his footsteps to mine. "I can't do this, Lola." His voice held a seductive edge that sent tingles down my spine.

I walked faster. In three long strides, he caught up with me, slipped his arm around me again, and pulled me to a stop. "Randall Leonard can wait."

He led me to a bench. I sank down next to him. My skirt slipped up to reveal my thighs. I suppressed the rational voice in my mind, giving in to my desire to flirt. "What d'ya want to talk about, Jackie?"

His mouth drew into a cockeyed smile, and his brows rose, that infernal dimple glimmering in his cheek. "It's pure torture being around you, you know that?"

"Self-inflicted. You insisted on coming."

"If I weigh the options, I'd rather be around you and be tortured than not be around you."

I didn't know what to say to that. "I can't share you, Jack." Looking at him, I started to lose myself in the ocean of his eyes. Blinking broke the spell. "The financial-aid guy is waiting," I said, my voice far away and almost dreamy, not wanting to budge.

"He's not going anywhere," Jack murmured.

I swallowed, trying my hardest to stay focused. "He's waiting for me."

His lips brushed against mine, soft and warm. "I'm waiting for you, too." My rational mind began to melt away as the warmth of his breath mingled with mine, his tongue slipping between my lips.

My breath grew rapid, and my heartbeat became wild. My body wanted Jack, and my mind was struggling to remember why I couldn't go with the feelings.

Then, just as suddenly as he'd kissed me, he pulled away, leaving me breathless. My eyelids fluttered open, and I saw his eyes sparkling in the bright sunlight, the curve of his lips more than a little wicked. His hands had been resting casually on my arms. One slipped down to my hip and skimmed over my leg. I shuddered, marveling at my reaction to his slightest touch. The guy was *good*. Seduction should have been his middle name.

My head felt heavy, a layer of sensual fog weaving through my thought processes in anticipation of the next kiss. It didn't come.

Forcing my eyes open, I caught a mildly coherent glimpse of Jack flicking his wrist up and glancing at his watch. He looked at me for a long second before pulling me up by the hand. "Come on. Let's go see Randall Leonard."

"Wh-what?" I shook my head, clearing away the clouds of desire. My ankle twisted on the uneven grass.

He faced me, a tortured look on his face. "I can't stay away from you, Lola. I'm trying, but I can't."

Dios mío. He was chipping away at part of my wall.

"Then don't. Be with me." *Just me*, I added in my head.

175

"I want to. It's just . . ." He looked me in the eyes then, straight and as honest as I'd ever seen him. "I might have to leave again soon."

I blinked away the last of the sensual fog I'd been in. "To see Sarah," I said, saying what he hadn't.

The next thing I knew, Jack's mouth was pressed hard against mine. The kiss was desperate. Searching. Like it came from a soldier who'd been missing in action and who was suddenly in the arms of his true love.

Tortured.

Jack's body was a perfect fit against mine. His nearness sent corkscrews of desire through every inch of me. I wanted to climb onto him. Into him. Go home to him, where I knew I belonged.

But it wasn't that easy for us. Because he owed Sarah. She was sick, and he'd broken her heart. An ache settled into the base of my throat when he pulled away again. His mouth pressed against my forehead.

He caressed my fingers one by one, lifting my hand to his mouth, kissing each knuckle, opening the palm, skimming his lips across it. "I don't want to," he said, his voice hoarse and labored.

Determination coiled in the pit of my stomach. He'd wanted me since we were teenagers, and I'd wanted him for just as long. So why did it feel like we'd never have our moment? Truth or dare. I opted for truth. "You've always been able to have any girl you wanted," I said, my voice low. "Why do you suddenly want me when you have Sarah? When you feel so obligated to her?"

"My wanting you is not sudden. It's been a long time coming."

That was his truth. If he'd said it to win me over, he'd said the wrong thing. It scared me worse than a trip to Mexico, *sin* Pepto-Bismol, would. "There's no way I can ever live up to all of your expectations, even if Sarah were out of the picture."

"There's no way you *can't*," he said.

"I think I'm safe for you," I said slowly. "You can't actually have me while you're tied to helping Sarah."

Jack ran his hand through his hair, looking frustrated and exasperated all at once. He paced across the grass, and when he looked at me again, his face had hardened. "When did you become a psycho-therapist?"

"I'm not. It just makes sense."

"No, it doesn't." He wheeled around. "Don't tell me what I'm feeling, Lola."

I could feel the anger emanating off him. "Okay," I said.

The look he gave me was a blend of desire and hopelessness. "I'm going to figure this out."

I just nodded. I hoped he could.

"Let's go," he said. "Randall's waiting."

And that was that.

I did my best to put my game face back on. In my mind, I said to him, *I'm just like you, Jack. I'm tortured. Positively and completely tortured.*

Chapter 15

Randall Leonard looked to be all of eighteen, a late bloomer still in braces, pockmarks on his face, and shoulder-length stringy brown hair that was three days past needing a wash. He didn't budge from his chair as Jack and I entered his small office. He wore stiff shorts that were way too big for him, and his legs flopped out to either side like a frog. I had a pretty good view right up into his nether zone and, like a rubber necker passing the scene of an accident, I had a hard time not staring in horror.

He directed his pointy chin at us. "Hey."

I forced a pleasant smile, ignoring the fact that his college education hadn't covered social etiquette. Working hard to keep my gaze on his face, my eyes started watering. "Thanks for seeing me."

"Dude." Jack uttering that single word from where he leaned against the door was man-speak. Randall read between the lines. He slammed his legs together and sat up.

The kid bit into an apple and waved his hand at a chair across the room. So gallant. I dragged it over so I could sit across from him. My skin prickled from Jack's unrelenting gaze on me. We were both tormented with a bone-deep craving for each other. Sad but true.

"I'd like to see the financial aid forms filled out by Dolores Cruz," I said to Randall.

I shrank back as he shook his head, his stringy hair flying around his face. When his head stopped moving, he shoved a wayward strand behind one ear. He took another bite of apple and chomped. "No can do," he said, his mouth full of fruit mush. "Those are confidential."

I hadn't actually filled out the forms, but technically they *were* mine. "But *I'm* Dolores Cruz." I pulled my wallet out from my purse and flipped it open to show him my driver's license.

"That lady in admissions said it was about someone else." He peered at the license, then at me. "Huh." He must have chalked it up to a misunderstanding because he asked, "You need to change something?"

"It'll only take a few minutes." Classic avoidance of the question. I held my breath, hoping it would work.

He hesitated, finishing off the apple before tossing the mangled core into the garbage can across the room. Pushing back in his chair, his feet propelled it across the small room to the filing cabinet. "Dolores Cruz, huh? Dolores. That's like an old-lady name."

Huh. He had *huevos*. Nobody had ever voiced *that* aloud before. "Yeah," I said, "but it has a great nickname."

I heard Jack shifting his position at the door.

"Oh, yeah? What is it?" Randall's eyes gleamed like this was some sort of conspiracy.

"Lola," I said.

He grinned, his shiny silver mouth, tiny red rubber bands on each brace, beaming at me. "Sex-y."

The way he said it gave me the feeling he was flirting. Had he not noticed Jack, with his *I'm gonna kick your ass* stance, framed in the doorway?

Apparently not, because Randall winked at me before he began riffling through one of the drawers. He finally located the file in question. He pulled it out, slammed the metal drawer closed with a reverberating bang, and scooted himself back to his desk.

I reached for the file. "Thanks."

He held tight for a beat and gave me what I think was his *player* look. "Sure thing, *Lola*."

I rolled my eyes—oh, brother—and snatched it from his hands. Flipping the folder open, I scanned the sheets. Everything was there. My Social Security number, driver's license, mother's maiden name, work address, home address, phone numbers. Every last piece of my personal information. My heart sank into the pit of my stomach with each agonizing beat. There was nothing in the file that would point me in a new direction. Another dead end.

I felt Jack lay his hand on my shoulder, an unexpected comfort that made my eyes burn. Tortured or not, he knew when to show compassion. I held the file up. "Look."

He read silently, handing the folder back to me when he was done. "Not good."

"How did she *get* all this?"

Randall looked from me to Jack to the folder. He drew his head back suspiciously. "What's going on here?"

Jack held his palm out toward the guy. "Relax, man."

"Dude, *you* relax." He flicked his chin at me. "What's she upset about?"

Jack towered over Randall, at least double the lean mass of the scrawny boy. "Ever hear of identity theft, chief?"

Randall pushed his feet against the carpeted floor, propelling himself backwards again, away from Jack. "Yeah. Of course."

"This," he pointed to me, "is the victim of an identity theft." He laid his hand on my shoulder again. "*This* is Dolores Cruz. The person who filled out that paperwork was not. She was older. She was a mother. And now she's dead."

Randall's jaw went slack. "Dude."

I listened to Jack. He understood. This was more than identity theft. Rosie was dead, and despite her crime, she didn't deserve the end she'd gotten. She was older, a mother— An idea burst into my head. "Is there a day care facility on campus?"

Randall nodded. His braces caught on his dry lip, pulling it up into an unattractive sneer. He pulled out a campus map and held it for me to see.

"We're here?" I asked, pointing my finger to a spot on the map.

"Right. Child care is here." Randall indicated a building closer to admissions, where we'd just come from.

I grabbed my purse. "Thanks for your help," I said before the door closed behind me.

Jack walked beside me, and we retraced our steps to the admissions building before veering off to the child care facility. The silence between us was electrically charged steel; thank God the walk was quick.

The child care center was a three-room structure, clean and organized. A baby room appeared to house children three and under, and a toddler room was for the over-three crowd. Thirteen kids milled around, three adults on supervision.

One of them, a middle-aged African-American woman, approached us. "I'm Ms. Nelson. Can I help you?" She had a singsong voice, flowing geometric-patterned clothing, and hair separated into more than a hundred thin braids that were pulled back into a band. She looked like she ought to be reciting poetry in an artsy coffeehouse. She probably had the voice of an angel, singing beautiful songs and telling magical stories to the kids.

I introduced myself before getting straight to the point. "Is it possible to find out if someone has their child registered here?"

She looked at me like I was a potential kidnapper. "You can't just walk in off the street and find out about our children." She paused. "What did you say your name was?"

"Dolores Cruz," I repeated as I looked at the kids' faces. I tried to pick out Rosie's child. Was it possible he was here? Could whoever had him still be bringing him?

"That's odd."

I brought my attention back to her. "What's odd?"

181

"I know another woman with the same name."

"About five five, short, curly black hair, kind of plump?" Jack said, speaking for the first time.

Ms. Nelson nodded her head, her thick eyebrows knitting together. "What's this about?"

I held out my driver's license. "I'm Dolores Cruz. I believe the woman you're talking about is actually Rosie Gonzales. She's been using my name, and now she's dead."

Ms. Nelson's eyes opened wide, her brown irises almost iridescent. "Come in here," she said in a low voice. We followed her into a small office off to one side. "Have a seat."

Jack and I sat in chairs across the desk from her. I leaned forward, my knees pressed together, anxious. What was she going to tell us? "Does her son attend here?" I asked.

Ms. Nelson hesitated again, clearing her throat. I could see the indecision on her face as she wondered if she should trust me. Finally she folded her hands on the desk in front of her. "He did. Not anymore."

"Her real name was Rosie Gonzales. She had all my personal information. I'm trying to find out why she died." I tried not to sound too desperate. "Anything you can tell me might help."

"Rosie Gonzales. Rosie Gonzales? That name . . ." Ms. Nelson bent over the file drawer at the bottom of her desk, skimming her fingers over the tabs of the folders inside. Then, like a jack-in-the-box, she popped up, a file in her grasp. She flipped it open, scanning the information quickly, nodding. "I thought so. I go through these files pretty carefully. Rosie Gonzales is an emergency contact and a reference for Dolores Cruz. That is, for the Dolores Cruz who came here." She slid the file across the desk for us to see.

Ms. Nelson swung her long braided strands of hair behind her back, sucking her cheeks in as she moved. She pointed to the emergency contact information on the form. "There *is* one other name there. Will that help?"

I peered at the writing on the information sheet. "F. Zuniga."

Excitement pricked my skin. "*Francisco*," I murmured. Juana's brother-in-law.

"No first name?" Jack asked.

Ms. Nelson shook her head. "If it's not written there, I wouldn't know it."

"It's Francisco," I said.

Jack stared at me. "How do you know that?"

I threw him a look that said, *Hello? I'm a detective, remember?* I scanned the rest of the sheet. The boy went by Junior, last name Cruz. "Who usually dropped off Junior?"

"Ms. Cru—that is, Ms. Gonzales."

"Did Mr. Zuniga ever pick him up?" I asked. *Please, give me another lead*, I willed. "Is there an address for him?"

She shook her head again. "Junior came only a few times. The semester just started." She paused, thinking. "Mr. Zuniga may have come once. I'd have to check the sign-out sheets."

It took her about five minutes to locate the signature. F. Zuniga had picked up Junior once, a week before Rosie died.

"When was the last time you saw Rosie? Do you remember?"

Ms. Nelson poked the underside of her chin with her index fingers. "I'm trying to think. She brought Junior a couple of times, but hasn't been here for two weeks or so."

Because she died. I thanked her, and Jack and I left.

So far, all the clues seemed to be pointing to Francisco Zuniga as the father of Rosie Gonzales's son. It was the only plausible answer. But was he the killer?

Jack walked with sure steps, keeping half a pace ahead of me. I put my sunglasses on, my shaded eyes drifting to his back. I slowed a bit, distancing myself enough to study his stride, the shape of his back, the way his pants hung perfectly on his legs—in case I didn't get a chance to see him like this again.

Without realizing it, I'd stopped walking, completely lost in thought. What life might have been like if Jack and I had connected before he'd found Sarah. Before he'd become engaged to her and

183

apparently forever obligated to her. My throbbing headache was back in full force. Jack understood my passions, my job, my drive. Would there ever be anyone else who'd get me the way he did?

A hand sliced through the air in front of my face, breaking the trance. "What's going on in there?"

I blinked, shuddering as I chased away the thoughts. I propped my sunglasses on top of my head. "Nothing."

"Jesus, Lola. You were miles away."

"I was just thinking."

"About what?"

"It doesn't matter," I said, and started walking again.

Jack and I drove, making strained conversation.

"F. Zuniga. How am I going to find him?" I wondered aloud. His sister-in-law, Juana, said she didn't have any idea where her brother-in-law was. Apparently, neither did her husband. I'd check the phone book and the Internet and pass the name on to Detective Seavers, but my gut was telling me it was a name that would lead to a big fat zero.

"You think he could have been the one who gave Rosie your information?"

"I don't see how."

"It could have been random. He could have gone through your garbage can."

"Yeah," I muttered. But I knew that wasn't the answer. Something about the situation didn't feel random. But I didn't know Rosie or Francisco.

"*Why* was she killed? What was she running from?" Her death appeared to have been an act of passion, a fight gone wrong. She bled to death from a head wound. A death blow against a Dumpster. Had she fought with Francisco? And if so, how was I going to prove it?

"You'll figure it out, Lola," Jack said as he pulled his Volvo into the parking lot in front of Abuelita's.

184

He believed in me. I couldn't ask for more than that from a friend. "Thanks for the ride—and the contact at the college," I said, forcing my voice to be as bland as unseasoned *masa*.

"Sure," he said. Unspoken words hung in the air, but all he finally said was, "I'll see you later." I got out, and he rolled away.

I stared down the street long after his taillights had disappeared. His vote of confidence hadn't been enough to fill up my emptiness.

When I pushed through the door to the restaurant for the second time that afternoon, the clatter of happy eaters accosted my ears. *Dios mío*, their joy was sickening. Home. Depressing, lonely home. That's where I wanted to be.

The dining room was full, business was booming, and Sylvia and Chely were working their butts off. Sylvia's hair had frizzed, poking out in prickly strands all over her head. Chely's mouth hung open, her tongue glued in the corner as she concentrated on not dropping the plates she carried.

I sighed. They needed help . . . and, really, could I abandon them? They were my lifeline.

On my way up to the break room to deposit my purse, I tied a half apron over my skirt and pulled my hair back into a ponytail. At the door, I stopped dead in my tracks. Antonio's paperwork, usually neat and orderly, was scattered all over the floor. The lockers had been ransacked, the doors left wide open.

Who could have done this?

A sliver of something cream-colored caught my eye. I picked it up. My mother's whalebone letter opener. The metal was cold in my hand.

Like a talisman, the letter opener plunged me into a memory of Sergio. We'd been dating, but things weren't right between us. His motivation to do something with his life had been waning and I had big dreams. I wasn't going to let him hold me back.

He'd met me at the restaurant before my shift was over. He and Antonio had done a complicated handshake, ending with Antonio punching Sergio on the arm. "Where've you been hiding, man? Haven't seen you around."

Sergio shrugged. "Been busy. A little of this and little of that. Little sis is demanding."

He spread his fingers and laid his hand on my butt, giving a squeeze.

I reared back. "Sergio!"

In a knee-jerk reaction, I knocked his hand away. "I'm working here."

"You can work on me," he said, putting his hand right back where I'd just smacked it away from.

Antonio stepped up. "Hey, man—go wait in the break room."

I didn't want him to wait, but I needed him to. "I'll be done in twenty minutes," I said, pointing Sergio to the stairs.

He snaked his tongue out from between his lips. "I'll be waiting."

For the last time. After I was done working, I was breaking up with him, once and for all. Sergio stretched his arms wide, putting his palms against the walls of the narrow stairwell. He propelled his body up the stairs, his feet hardly making contact. His baggy tan pants bunched around his ankles, his powder blue button-up shirt neatly pressed and creased.

"What do you see in him?" Antonio asked.

"You were just giving him the handshake!"

"Yeah, but I'm not dating him."

"Well, neither am I after tonight."

He lowered his voice and sneaked a look around. "You're going to dump him?" He whacked me on the back. "About time."

"Yeah, I said. About time." I finished my shift, gaining resolve by the second. I had to do it. After more than two miserable on-and-off years, Sergio Garcia and I were almost done. He didn't have goals. He didn't have ambition. He was still stuck in a high school daze, right down to his chinos and lowrider.

I untied my apron, tossing it over my shoulder as I worked up the courage to confront him. Walking slowly up the stairs, my footsteps were quiet, just like my mood.

I stopped in the doorway. Sergio's back was turned to me, an outline of something rectangular under his shirt, tucked into the waistband of his pants. He was riffling through a locker. I watched, frozen, as he pocketed something, then moved on.

"Sergio! What are you doing?"

He spun around, his face going from *caught red-handed* to *aw-shucks* playfulness in the blink of an eye. He was *not* going to try to talk his way out of this!

I scanned the room. Sergio had been alone for only twenty minutes, but that had been more than enough time to systematically search the room, my mother's desk, and most of the lockers. "I said, what are you doing?"

"Straightening things up in here. This place is a mess."

My body shook, rage oozing out of my pores. "You're stealing from us?"

"*¿Estas loca?* I told you, I'm straightening up. Nobody cleans up after themselves around here."

"Liar. What did you take?" I plowed forward, grabbing for his pocket.

Sergio caught my wrist, gripping it tightly. I pulled my hand away, breaking free from him with a force that sent me reeling backwards.

"Get out," I said, my voice remarkably low and even.

"Can't." In two steps, he closed and locked the door, cornering me between the wall and my mother's desk.

"What happened to you?"

He just smirked and put his hands on my sides, his palms hard against my hipbones. "Nothing happened to me," he said.

I heaved my knee up, but it caught air instead of his family jewels.

"What happened to you?" he sneered, his grip on me making me immobile. "You used to be fun."

My eyes searched my mother's desk, looking for a weapon. I saw it. I reached my hand out to the desk, spread my fingers, and grasped the whalebone handle of her letter opener. In one swift motion, I pressed it against Sergio's belly.

"What the—?"

I steadied my hand, pushing the tip of the dull blade deeper into his gut. "Back off, Sergio."

He let go of me and backed up. "What the hell is wrong with you?"

"You're a lying thief, that's what's wrong. It's over, Sergio. Get out."

"What do you mean, 'It's over'?" He moved toward me again but stopped short when I brandished the letter opener.

"Just what it sounds like. Over. I don't want to see you anymore. Get out."

His black eyes became slits. "Whatever," he finally said, shrugging his shoulders. "But you'll come crawling back."

I spit out a laugh. "Not a chance." I clasped my hands together, the shiny tip of the dull blade pointing at his abdomen. "I should have dumped you a long time ago."

"Your loss. There are plenty of women in line to take your place."

"They can have you."

"Oh, they already have."

I yelled, charging forward with my weapon. "Get out!"

He fumbled as he unlocked the door, nearly tumbling backwards down the stairs.

I blinked, dislodging the old memory as I dropped my mother's letter opener back onto the desk. Adrenaline rushed through me like a tidal wave. The break room had been violated again, so long after Sergio had been here stealing from us. He wouldn't dare attempt it again, would he?

Surveying the room, I set to work, picking up the restaurant paperwork that Antonio had taken over now that he was manager. I restacked it neatly on his desk. The safe was secure. Nothing else seemed to be missing, so I moved on to the lockers.

I picked up Chely's favorite hooded sweatshirt, a pack of gum, and her hairbrush—three things she almost never left home without. Next, I picked up the photographs of Sylvia's kids, the rolled tape on the back barely tacky to the touch. I pushed them back onto the door where she'd had them, but they immediately fell down again, drifting back to the floor. I retrieved them and laid them on the bottom of her locker instead. Everything else seemed to be in place: hairbrush, hair spray, makeup bag, change of clothes.

I moved on, looking at the floor around my locker. My emergency makeup had been dumped out of its bag. An old criminal justice textbook had been carelessly thrown to the ground, pages torn. Was anything gone? I searched my locker. An extra apron. Still there. My address book. Had it been in there? I couldn't remember and riffling through the rest of my locker didn't jog my memory. I couldn't really remember what else I might have had in there.

I slammed the door closed. Racing down the stairs two at a time, I barreled into Antonio at the bottom. "Whoa! Where's the fire?" he said, catching me before we both crashed to the ground.

I caught my breath. "Someone was in the break room."

"¿Cómo?" My father turned to us from the stove.

"Someone was in the break room." I tugged on Antonio's sleeve. "Your paperwork is all over the place, the lockers were ransacked, our things are on the floor—"

Papi's face turned pale. ¿El dinero?"

"The safe's still locked."

He stomped his foot. "No one has been through—"

"That you saw." If someone was hell-bent on looking for something, nothing would stop them. "You didn't see Sergio, did you, Papi?"

"You think Sergio would do this, mi'ja?"

I *knew* from experience that he would, just as sure as I knew that Abuelo had an ancient secret connection to *La eMe*. The Mexican Mafia was a "don't ask, don't tell" kind of thing in the Falcón–Cruz family.

But I'd never told my parents that it was Sergio who had stolen the day's deposits back then, and I didn't want to tell them now. It was our own unsolved crime.

I felt Antonio behind me. "We had a run-in with Sergio last week," I said to Papi. "Maybe he's still mad."

"*Cabrón,*" Antonio growled, slamming his open palm down on the stainless steel counter. "If he did this, I'm going to kick his ass."

"*Espera,*" my father scolded. "We do not know it was Sergio."

Chely backed into the kitchen, dumping an armful of plates into the busing container. She sucked her tongue back into her mouth. "What's going on?"

"Did Sergio come in here today?" I asked Chely.

Her tongue found the corner of her mouth again, and her eyes rolled up as she thought. "Hmm-mm." She shook her head. "Haven't seen him."

"Seen who?" Sylvia sidled up beside me, hands on her hips, looking from one face to the next.

Chely smacked her tongue against the roof of her mouth and frowned. "Lola's old boyfriend. He's kinda scary."

"Huh," Sylvia said. "And you think he was here?"

I shrugged. "We don't know. Someone was in the break room going through everything. Paperwork, the lockers—"

Sylvia stiffened beside me. "Like a robbery?"

"Someone robbed us? When we were, like, here?" The pitch of Chely's voice rose. "My mom's going to freak!"

"*Cálmate sobrina.*" My father rubbed a hand over Chely's back. "Everything is fine." He turned to Antonio. "See if anything is missing, *mi'jo.*"

Antonio took the stairs two at a time, Sylvia and I right behind him. "I can't believe this," she whispered. "You think your old boyfriend did this?"

I knew my face was strained when I turned to look at her. "It's possible, though I can't think of a motive."

We stood in the doorway while Antonio searched the room. He went through his papers, methodically stacking them into organized piles. "Nothing missing here," he announced after a few minutes.

Sylvia fidgeted beside me. "What would someone want in here?"

That was a good question. The day's cash and other important documents were in the safe. There was account information from our vendors and personal belongings in the room, but nothing worth stealing.

I frowned as Antonio comforted Sylvia with a touch on her arm. "We'll figure it out. Don't worry."

I peered at my brother, trying to catch his eye. He ignored me. Guilt-ridden, I saw my future flash before me. Antonio would break Sylvia's heart, and I'd be working the lunch and dinner shifts again, probably sooner rather than later. I scolded myself for my selfishness. He was just comforting her. Compassionate, like Jack. I hoped.

"Check your lockers," Antonio told us.

"I already did," I said.

Sylvia raced to hers and threw open the door. While she rummaged through her belongings, Antonio turned to me. He laced his hands behind his head. "Is anything gone?" he asked me.

"I'm trying to remember what I had—"

A gurgled choke from Sylvia stopped my words cold. She clutched the photographs of her kids in her hand. Her skin had turned a sickly green. She stared at the floor.

I went to her. "Are you okay?"

She shook her head, laying the pictures of her kids down in her locker.

"Is anything missing?"

"My baby." Her voice had fallen to a whisper, her face panicked beyond belief.

"You mean his picture?"

She nodded.

I pointed to the pictures she held in her hands. "Those were on the floor. I'm sure it's here." A sudden panic filled my gut. I knew it was a picture of the baby she'd lost. I dropped to my knees and peered under the lockers. "I see something!"

Antonio moved to the wall, braced his legs, rooting them like tree trunks, and gripped the wall of lockers. He took a deep breath and heaved. The lockers didn't budge. He tried again, grunting through tight lips.

"They're not going anywhere."

Sylvia sniffled, wiping her fingers under her eyes. Antonio put his arm around her and gave a gentle squeeze. "I'll keep trying."

Sylvia nodded, placing her other pictures in her pocket for safe-keeping.

Antonio picked up Chely's sweatshirt, giving it a good shake like he expected something incriminating to fall out. Sylvia closed her locker and retied her apron. "I better get back," she said, wiping away a final tear. All the spunk seemed to have been washed clean out of her.

Antonio gave her arm another squeeze. "Do you need a break?"

Real concern was painted on my brother's face. It was an unexpected picture, and if I had to bet my life on it, I'd say it was genuine.

Sylvia shook her head. "I'm okay."

"You have other pictures, right?" he asked.

She swiped at another tear, pulled her head stoically high, and nodded. "Of course. Of course I do." She pulled her lips into a strained smile that made me wonder if she was telling the truth. "I'm fine," she said again before heading back down the stairs.

I peered out the door to make sure she was gone before turning on my brother.

"You better not take advantage of her when she's weak, Tonio."

"Maybe she needs someone to show her some interest. Her ex-husband sure as hell didn't. Doesn't," he corrected. "He drops her off sometimes, and she barely gets her feet on the ground before he peels out of here."

I'd never seen Antonio so worked up over a woman. His face was flushed, his goatee giving him a thoroughly menacing look.

"I mean what kind of man leaves a grieving wife and his other kids?" he said, barely controlling his rage. "He walked out on them."

I poked my finger in my ear. Had I heard right? Was Antonio making mature statements about responsibilities in a relationship? "What happened?"

"He split—asshole—right after the fire."

192

I sucked in a breath. "It was a fire? That's how they lost the baby?"

He dipped his head in a nod. "Babysitter was watching the kids."

Sylvia's experience certainly put a petty theft into perspective. I hit Antonio on the arm. "You *have* to stay away from her. She won't be able to handle it if you break her heart."

"Give me some credit, would you? It's not like I'm going to marry her, for Chrissake."

"Does she *know* you're not the marrying kind? She needs full disclosure."

"No, what she needs is someone to listen to her. The other day she went on and on about how her baby burned to ash and blew away on the wind. She's a mess."

I sank into the chair at Antonio's desk. I couldn't even begin to imagine the anguish. Antonio went back to straightening up the break room. I spoke to his back. "You better get those lockers moved and find that picture for her."

He turned back to face me. "I will, Lola."

"But will you stay away from her?"

"No."

I sighed. Antonio and I were cut from the same cloth, stubborn to a fault. Gracie and Ray made out with the more rational genes. Pushing the issue with Antonio just might make him dig in his heels even more.

"You really think this was Sergio's doing?" Antonio asked with a quick change of subject.

"Maybe not . . ." I trailed off, knowing that Sergio being involved didn't make sense. The fact that my address book might be gone felt like a stone in my gut. The break-in had to be about Rosie Gonzales and the identity theft.

Chapter 16

It had been a long day of discovery and disappointment. I changed into my flannel boxers and my sleep tank, downed a glass of ice water, brushed out my hair, and crawled into bed.

I didn't want to think about Rosie Gonzales, Lucy and Zac, or Jack. Especially Jack.

But what I wanted didn't matter. Their faces buzzed around behind my eyes like flies circling a picnic spread. Squeezing my eyes tighter made their images distort, but they clarified again once I unclenched. The glamorous life of a detective wasn't all it was cracked up to be. I was frazzled and tired, but the faces were like ghosts—ever-present and haunting.

Smothering my face with my pillow, I shouted, "¡*Duerme!*"

Finally, growing heavy, my legs began to sink into the mattress. My eyelids fluttered closed. Every cell relaxed.

Until I bolted upright, disoriented. Bleary-eyed and groggy, I identified the culprit of my fitful night's sleep: daylight. And a nagging feeling in the pit of my stomach.

I went through my normal morning routine: showering, straightening the house, and releasing Salsa to freedom.

At the table, eating my girl-power breakfast, I flipped open the

Sacramento Bee and found the Metro section and Jack's byline. His photo smiled up at me.

He had a casual man-about-town kind of style, storytelling with some hard facts woven in to drive home his point. His columns were usually a good break from the heaviness of the regular news articles. I scanned the beginning of his column.

> *What does identity theft mean? If our identities are not safe, if we are not whom people believe us to be, how do we trust anyone? How do you know if Aunt Kristen is really Aunt Kristen? Could she have a secret life, another identity that no one knows about?*
>
> *When did people forget the value of hard work and forgo the satisfaction of a job well done? Identity theft has erased our sense of security; not even our garbage is safe from the twenty-first-century criminal. I recently spoke with a man who spent the better part of ten years stealing the details of other people's lives. . . .*

Jack had hit a home run with his column. It spurred me back to my investigation. Starting with Bill Johnson. I dialed him again, and after three rings, a man's voice barreled across the line. His answering machine, again. I hung up again without leaving a message. I'd pay the man a visit tonight.

I headed straight to Camacho and Associates and walked into the conference room with more confidence than I'd felt since my close encounter with Manny and Sadie. They could do what they wanted; what did I care? I refused to give it another thought.

"Lola!"

"Reilly! Oh my God! You're actually here!" She was at her desk, tapping away on the computer, like she had no sudden secret spy life. I stopped right next to her.

She quickly minimized the open screen on her monitor and spun her chair so we were knee to knee. Her hair was still raven black, and her sunglasses hung from the V in her shirt. Her very black, very tailored, very non-Reilly-looking shirt. "I'm here"—her gaze darted from side to side—"but not for long."

I grew instantly suspicious. "Why not for long?"

"My top secret mission isn't over yet."

Leaning in close to her ear, I whispered, "Will you self-destruct if you tell me what your mission is about?"

She drew her fingers across her sealed lips, turning them and throwing away an imaginary key.

Curiosity got the better of me. The questions poured out of me. "When are you leaving? How can your secret mission not be over? Did you get your PI license when I wasn't looking? I miss you! You have to spill the *chisme!*" I might as well have been channeling Reilly herself, the way I rattled on and on.

Her eyes twinkled; her grin stretched across her face. I couldn't remember when I'd seen her so happy. Then she said in one hurried breath, "I'll be here another fifteen minutes. The mission's not over until el bosso says it's over. No, no PI license. I miss you, too! I have no gossip to tell."

"Top secret," I muttered. "You can't tell me, or you won't?" My stomach plunged to my feet. Reilly usually told me everything. This was not good.

She shook her head, her grin turning sly. "I gave my word. *Lo siento, chica.*"

Her new 007 status hadn't improved her Spanish accent, but her ethics were intact. I had to give her props for that. "At least tell me what happened to your hair."

She patted her head. "Sexy, huh?"

I frowned. I liked the neon-bright colors she usually chose. Black was so . . . so boring on her. "What happened to the blue?" It had been almost fluorescent, like the tip of a heat-seeking missile.

"Oh." Her face lit up. "Right. I decided blue was too electric."

"So you decided to channel Morticia Addams?" I felt her forehead, checking for fever. "You sure you're feeling okay?"

196

She looked around, checking the office for eavesdroppers. There were none to be found, but she lowered her voice anyway. "Don't worry, this is just temporary. Teddy Bear likes my wild side."

"Teddy Bear?" I stared at her. "Did I miss something?"

Her cheeks turned pink. "I can't really tell you," she whispered. "It's kind of a secret, too."

"Reilly Fuller, did you get yourself a boyfriend while I wasn't looking?" I heaved a sigh. Maybe *that* was the top secret secret! But no, she'd said *too*, implying she was involved in more than one covert operation.

Her blush deepened. "I wouldn't exactly call him a boyfriend."

"What *would* you call him?"

Her nose scrunched up, and she shook her head. "He's more like my caveman."

At precisely that moment, Neil Lashby lumbered out of the Lair. He grunted at me, double grunted at Reilly, and continued on his way. Mr. Personable, that was our Neil. Now, there was a caveman.

My mind screeched to a halt and rewound. Neil's contact at the DMV had called him a teddy bear. "Oh. My. God." I ran to the lobby of Camacho and Associates, hid in plain sight next to the sad little fake fern I loved, and watched Neil galumph through the parking lot. In a flash, I was back at Reilly's desk. She'd scarcely moved a muscle. "Caveman?" I asked. "Seriously? *Dígame*, Reilly. Neil?"

Her teeth clamped down on her lower lip, and she looked down at her desk. "That special assignment?"

"Yes?"

She nodded. "I'm doing it with Neil."

"Doing it with Neil," I repeated, one of my eyebrows arched at her word choice. "Really?"

Her eyes bugged. "I meant on the case. Watching el bosso's da—"

I was on the edge of my imaginary seat, but she caught herself in time and clamped her mouth shut.

"Watching Manny's what?"

But she wasn't telling. She got a gleam in her eyes. "Did you know that Neil and me both have the same vowel combination in our names? It's, like, kismet. I mean how many names have an *e* followed by an *i*?"

I drew a blank, but gave her another set of props for her quick subject change.

"There aren't many, believe me. Reinhold, Heidi, Einar, Eino, Deirdre, Keisha, Leila, Keido, Sheila. And only three are men's names."

I blinked.

"I've memorized them all," she said sheepishly. She looked innocent and earnest. "Admit it, Lola, what are the odds that two people with *that* vowel combination would work at the *same* place?"

I was still stuck on the fact that Manny had sent her on a top secret mission for him, but she was serious about the vowel thing. "I guess it *is* a pretty big coincidence," I agreed. "But do you really think it's fate? I mean, you've worked here a long time. So has Neil. And you've never mentioned the vowel thing before."

She frowned. "Oh. Yeah, right."

I couldn't stand to see her looking so deflated. "But I don't know. Maybe you're right." I gave her a bolstering smile. "He did give you a double grunt. I've *never* seen him do that for anyone."

She inflated again. "I thought so, too!" Her eyelashes fluttered.

"You sure you can't give me a hint about the special assignment?"

She put her finger to her lips. "Can't. Like I said, top secret. Teddy Bear would spank me silly if I spilled any info about it. Ooh, but I might like that." Her grin turned naughty.

I poked my fingers in my ears. "TMI, Reilly. I don't want to know that about you and Neil."

Her eyes gleamed. "Lemme tell ya, though, he's *gooood*."

"Who's good?" Sadie glided up to us, her presence like the residual smoke after a nuclear explosion. She was that much of a downer.

Reilly gasped and slammed her lips shut. She silently pleaded with me to keep her secret.

I turned to Sadie. I kept the one I actually knew. "Did you ever

notice that both Neil and Reilly have an *e*, then an *i*, in their names."
I chuckled. "Isn't that wild!"

"Yeah," she said drolly. "Wild. Alert the media."

I winked at Reilly, trying to be upbeat and optimistic. Surely I was overanalyzing things. At the whiteboard, I uncapped the dry-erase marker and began writing.

- *Drug rehab*
- *Rosie enrolled at Sac State*
- *Her son registered at campus child care facility / Rosie's name on emergency information sheet / also Francisco Zuniga. Boyfriend or husband? Domestic violence? Does he have the boy? WHERE IS THE BOY?!*
- *Birthday party invitation; Rosie came as Francisco's guest*
- *At the party, Rosie argued with neighbor Bill; Why?*
- *Again, where is Junior?*
- *Did she kick her drug habit?*

Recapping the marker, I headed for Manny's office. I rapped quickly on the door. "It's Dolores."

"Come in," he said, the gruffness in his voice throat-deep.

I opened the door, cautiously peeking through the crack before swinging it wide. He was alone. *Phew.* I hadn't seen Sadie slip into his office, but I'd made that mistake once before.

"Good morning," I said, making my voice extra pleasant.

Manny sat behind his desk, his eyes riveted on the computer monitor. They flicked to me before returning to the computer. "Morning." Apparently today's jeans and shirt passed the appropriate-office-attire test. Thank God. I didn't think I could take another blow to my ego today.

I rattled off my newest discoveries about Rosie and the rehab center, wanting his opinion. "The drugs may have had something to do with her death," I wrapped up.

"People have killed for less," he said.

199

Jack had said the same thing to me. I'd had more faith in humanity than that, but I was beginning to realize that they were both right. Murder happened. Bottom line.

I brought Manny up to speed on the birthday party and Rosie's argument with the neighbor. When I finished the rundown, he shifted his weight and said, "What's your hypothesis?"

I pushed my hair behind my ears. Sometimes proving or disproving a hypothesis was easier than actually making a viable one. "That she was abused and the domestic violence went wrong."

Manny dropped his legs to the ground and shoved himself up. He breezed past me out of the office. I nearly fell off the edge of the chair to follow him. He marched up to the whiteboard with the Rosie Gonzales information.

He scrutinized the list of facts and questions, turning to me after a few minutes. "The thing that strikes me is this Francisco. Who is he? Does he have the kid? Is he the father of the kid? What was their relationship like?" He pointed to where I'd written *domestic violence* and circled it.

"You're following the most obvious path," he continued, "which is good. Even if it doesn't lead to the truth, it may open up another door."

Folding my arms over my chest, I nodded. "Right, but I haven't been able to locate him. There's no address for him and no phone number. Juana Zuniga said her husband doesn't know where his brother is. She left a message for me saying she confirmed it with him. I also haven't gotten ahold of the neighbor that Rosie fought with. I'm going there later. Hopefully he'll be home from work."

"And the Sac State lead?"

"Francisco is the emergency contact for the child care facility, but that's it. The contact information was for Rosie's apartment, which was under my name."

"Follow up with the neighbor from the party and see where that takes you."

"I keep coming back to how she could have stolen my identity."

I tucked my thumbs into my back pockets, swinging my elbows back like wings. I thought of Jack's column. "Did you know that our garbage isn't safe? She could have gotten it that way." I shrugged, discouraged. "Otherwise, someone gave it to her."

Manny rocked back on his heels. "Remember the process. If you figure out why, it'll probably lead you to how."

"Right."

"You will not take any chances, Dolores. *¿Entiendes?*"

Either he was back to his old self, or he was warning me that this was my last chance. *"Entiendo."*

Chapter 17

By four thirty I was fully ensconced in Lucy's life.

I *was* Lucy.

Zac had been pacing the floor when I arrived. He wrenched the front door open, jumped out onto the porch, and yanked the door closed behind him.

"*¿Qué pasó?*" I asked after the obligatory kiss on the cheek.

"I don't know if I can do this." He looked pale.

My jaw dropped. "Do *what*? You're going out with your *wife*."

Zac's baby face broke into a thousand worried lines. He leaned closer and whispered, "I'm nervous."

"She's your *wife*," I said again.

He plucked at his shirt. "Is this okay?"

The short-sleeved, casual button-up shirt was plastered with flags from different countries. "You look great." I put my hand on his shoulder. "Zac, it'll be fine. Relax."

"You're sure there's no one else? I'll—" He broke off and paced down the path to the driveway, bending to yank a weed out from between the lava rocks. He turned back to me, his face etched with concern. "You sure she still wants me?"

When I'd filled Zac in on the plans for tonight—and assured him that his wife was ready for the taking—he'd been thrilled. But doubt had crept back in. "Positive," I said. "She wants a little romance. She needs to know that *you* still want *her*." I bit my tongue not to use the roller coaster reference that hovered on the tip. Damn Lucy and her metaphors.

"I don't *do* romance."

"*Oyame, Zacarias*. Make her feel like she's more than your wife and the mother of your children." I lowered my voice to a conspiratorial whisper. "Tonight she's your *girlfriend*."

My cousin's expression changed like he was searching for his inner tiger. "Wait here," he blurted.

"Where would I go? I'm watching your kids, remember?"

"Right. I'll be back." I stood there staring after him as he hopped in his old pickup truck and peeled out of the driveway.

I had no idea what he was up to. He was a man, though, so I didn't even venture a guess. I let myself into the house. "I'm here," I called to Lucy once I found a spot for my purse and bag of tricks.

"I'll be out in a minute," she called back through the bathroom door.

"Tía Lola!" My cousin's three-year-old daughter, Mia, raced to me from across the living room, grabbing hold of my legs and circling around me. Technically I was her second cousin or first cousin once removed. Something like that. But they called me Tía. And I liked it.

"*Abrazo*," I said, bending down to her eye level. She gave me a bear hug just as Zac and Lucy's boys tackled me to the ground. Mia squealed. "Monster! Let's play monster!"

Trying to regain my footing, I said, "How 'bout we call Tío Tonio?" I said with a wink. "He's been looking for some rascally kids to play monster with." I skittered my fingers across their tummies, tickling them until Mia screeched at the top of her lungs.

ZJ nodded, stepping out of reach. "Can he bring his guitar?"

"I'm sure he will if you ask him." Zac Junior was nine going on sixteen. He played guitar and wanted to be Carlos Santana when he grew up. He nodded in an old, wise way. "Cool."

I turned to Chris, Zac and Lucy's six-year-old. "And how about you? Do you want Tío to come over later?"

He threw his head back and gave an enormous nod. "Are you spending the night? My mom says you're spending the night." His voice cracked, and his lower lip pulled down. A tear dam was going to break any second.

I took his hand and squeezed gently. "That's right. It's you and me, *mi'jo*." I held my hand up next to my mouth and whispered, "And ZJ and Mia, of course."

He nodded, his tears at bay for the time being.

I leaned down and whispered in his ear. "I brought a movie and popcorn. Sound good?"

He nodded, gave a little smile, and the next second he took off running, yelling at the top of his lungs, "Mom, Tía brought a movie and popcorn!"

I stared after him, thinking of Rosie Gonzales's little boy. *Pobrecito*. He didn't have his mom to make him popcorn and watch a movie with. The most I could hope for was that he was with someone who loved him.

A minute later, Lucy came down the hallway. Chris was by her side, gazing up at her. "You look pretty, Mamá." Then he was gone, zipping down the hallway, yelling to ZJ and Mia about the popcorn and movie and how pretty Mom looked.

A nervous smile crept onto Lucy's made-up face. I did a double take. In her cream-colored flowing dress, she looked ready to renew her wedding vows. Her blond hair was curled and sprayed, bouncing along with her stride.

"*¡Ooolala, mamacita!*" I exclaimed.

"Is it that bad?"

"*Mamacita* in a good way!"

She laughed, sounding just as nervous as Zac had. "Is it really okay?"

"Okay? You look amazing, Luce. Zac's going to be putty in your hands."

She held out the sides of her dress. "I've been in a clothing rut, I think."

"You're not in one now."

"One dress doesn't mean I'm out of it for good." Lucy looked down at my jeans and the white ruffled blouse I'd changed into. "You have the body to go with anything. I'm the one that had three kids and nursed them. *I* should have your boobs."

I peered down at my cleavage bulging from the heart-shaped neckline of my blouse. "Yeah, but if you had these boobs, you'd have these hips, too," I said, my hands moving down to slap mine.

Lucy laughed. "They're damn good hips." She looked around. "Where's Zac?"

"Uh—" I was saved by the ringing doorbell.

Lucy threw open the door, took a surprised step backwards, and nearly lost her balance. Zac stood on the front porch thrusting a bouquet of sad-looking flowers at her. "Hi. Um—" He looked at her like he was seeing her for the first time, and his sunburned face blushed redder. "*Bellísima*," he said, and the word said it all.

Lucy blushed, too. I took the flowers. "I'll put them in water. Have fun," I added, and she and Zac left, giddy like two teenagers going out on prom night. Hopefully Zac would get more action than the average prom-goer.

The door closed behind them, and I turned to face my charges. They stood there, staring at me.

I stared back. It was a face-off. The long night stretched before us. The closest I'd ever been to watching kids was at family parties. And that didn't count. The kids were always busy with their *primos* and *amigos* and kept themselves busy. I never actually had to actively *entertain*. And I had never babysat as a teenager, since I'd always worked at Abuelita's.

I took Salsa for walks and scratched her belly. Somehow I thought Mia, Chris, and ZJ wouldn't want their bellies scratched.

I clapped my hands together. "Let's make dinner!"

ZJ looked at the clock. "Uh, it's only four thirty, Tía."

"Yeah, but I'm starved." I pulled ready-made tostada shells that I'd picked up from Laughlin's Grocers out of my brown paper bag. Within minutes, the kids were on board. We spent a half hour refrying beans, shredding jack cheese and lettuce, chopping tomatoes I'd brought from Abuelo's garden, and roasting chilies for *salsa borracha*. "Mexican pizza," I announced, flourishing the tray of loaded tostadas when they were done.

We gorged ourselves, cleaned the dishes, and set the leftovers on the counter for Antonio.

Dinner had killed an hour and a half. I tapped my fingers on the counter. What to do next?

"Should we call Tío Tonio now?" asked ZJ.

Sounded good to me. I dialed the number of the restaurant and handed ZJ the phone. He walked back and forth as he spoke. A few minutes later, he plopped the phone back in its cradle.

"Well?" I asked.

"He'll be here in an hour. He said we can jam before the movie!"

We killed the hour by going to the park and arrived back at the house just as Antonio's vintage Mustang drove up the street.

"There he is," I said, pointing at the dark green car as it rolled toward us. And not a minute too soon. One too many games of Monkey in the Middle—with me starting out as, and never leaving the position of, Monkey—had my heart in what I was afraid was a permanent anaerobic state.

Mia jumped up and down, clapping her hands. "Yeah! Tío's here!"

ZJ pumped his arm back and hissed, "Yes."

Chris took my hand and hung close. I thought he might want to crawl right inside me if he could. *Pobrecito.*

Antonio's face came into view through his windshield, his white teeth smiling from the center of his goatee. My gaze drifted to my brother's right.

He had a passenger.

Jack. My heart did a somersault.

"Ow!" Chris yelped, trying to pull his hand free from mine.

206

"Sorry, *mi'jo!*" I loosened my grip on his hand and knelt down. "I didn't mean to squeeze."

He just hugged me closer. "It's okay," he said.

"*Tío!*" Mia ran to Antonio, catching him as he stepped out of his car. He swung her around effortlessly, her legs flying out behind her.

ZJ strolled casually. Mr. Übercool. I stifled my laugh.

Jack pulled the front seat forward and plucked two guitar cases out of the backseat. He walked around to the sidewalk, handing off one of the cases to Antonio. ZJ's eyes rounded into circles. "Two guitars! Yes," he said, pumping his arm again. He'd hit the jackpot—two guitarists for the price of one.

Chris and I walked up to them. Antonio gave me a hug. "You didn't mention you were bringing Jack," I whispered.

"He was standing right there when ZJ called," he whispered back. "It just kind of . . . happened."

I grunted. If I wasn't secretly thrilled he was here, I might have thought this was payback for the Reilly date night I'd manipulated Tonio into a while back.

My stomach knotted. I'd wanted to eat popcorn and watch a movie with the kids, and with Antonio. Sloth and gluttony would have been my best friends tonight. Now I had the rest of the deadly sins to contend with. Lust over Jack was front and center. Was a man *supposed* to look *that* good? No wonder Sarah wouldn't let him go.

I was nothing to sneeze at, but, *Dios mío*, he was in a league of his own.

Greed and envy were tied for third place. It was no secret. I wanted Jack to myself. His extracurricular women made that impossible—the Mollys of the world I could deal with, but I was envious over the hold Sarah had over him. Which led to the wrath I felt toward him, them, *and* myself.

Pride was the only thing I didn't really view as a sin—I mean, it was the one thing that would keep me from ending up doing the horizontal rumba with Jack.

I refused to be just another fling—for anyone. Especially with

Jack, considering I'd wanted him—body and soul— since those photos I'd taken of him way back when, and there was no way I'd settle for less.

Our eyes locked for an instant before Mia grabbed my hand and pulled me—and Chris—back toward the house. "Let's make cookies!" she screeched. "From your bag of tricks," she reminded me, in case I'd forgotten I'd brought a bag of chocolate chips.

Antonio and Jack spent the next hour and a half jamming with ZJ. They played the opening chords of "Smoke on the Water" over and over, adding a few Santana riffs and ending with a few mariachi classics. ZJ threw in a power chord every now and then.

Mia, Chris, and I made the cookies.

"Do you want dinner?" I asked Antonio when the jam session was over.

"*Gracias, pero no.* I'm going to have a late dinner with Sylvia"— he checked his watch—"in an hour. But I'll have one of those." He snatched a still-warm cookie from the cooling rack.

I felt my spine crackle. I stared him down as he broke off a piece of cookie, threads of melted chocolate hanging from the edge. "What did you say?"

Antonio licked his lips, catching a glob of chocolate from the hair of his goatee. "Dinner with Sylvia."

"You are not."

"Her ex has the kids tonight. He's being really cooperative . . . at least for today. Me and Sylvia have a real date. Cool, eh?"

"No, not cool. Why can't you just leave her alone?"

"Why can't you just butt out?" he shot back. "She's a big girl. She can decide who she wants to date." He clamped down on the rest of the cookie, chewing once and swallowing.

"You better not hurt her," I muttered, aggravated by the fact that he was right. Damn it.

Mia's squeals cut through the house, followed by children's laughter and a growl by Jack. Monster.

"It's just a date. Unlike you, I don't need a long-term commitment and a ten-karat cubic zirconia to go out on a date."

"You're not going to sleep with her, are you?"

"It's none of your business, Lola. Do I ask you who *you're* sleeping with?" He slapped the counter. "Oh, that's right. You're not sleeping with anyone. You're too uptight."

My chin jutted forward. That was so not true. "I need more than the promise of an orgasm to sleep with him."

Antonio shot me a cockeyed grin, his gaze piercing mine. "Him who?"

Him Jack. Damn, had I really just revealed my hand so easily? "What?" I asked innocently, feeling my face heat up.

"Who are you talking about?" he asked, but his smirk said it all. He knew exactly who *him* was.

"Just never mind," I said. "I don't want to have this conversation."

"Lola," Antonio said, clasping me on the shoulder, "this case has you all wound up."

"Are you surprised? I still don't even know if I was the intended victim."

I saw his mind working. I hadn't meant to, but I'd given him the perfect opening to criticize my detecting abilities, the risks of my job, and how being a detective interfered with my personal life. But my sweet brother held his tongue. "You'll figure it out," he said.

I gave him a hug. "Thanks, Tonio."

He grabbed another cookie. "*No hay problema*," he said, heading out of the kitchen, "but let me go on the record here." He turned back and looked at me with complete seriousness. "You could use an orgasm—or fifty—to loosen up. Who knows, it might even help you solve the case. No harm trying."

Forty-five minutes later, we stood at the front door, Antonio and Jack holding their guitars. "Do you have to go, Tío?" ZJ asked.

209

Mia grabbed Jack's hand. "More monster!" she yelped, pulling him back into the house.

Jack laughed, ruffling her full head of curly brown hair. It was twice the color of his and half the color of mine, I thought. Our child might look like Mia. I shivered and shook the thought out of my head. "His ride is leaving," I said. "He has to go."

Chris frowned. "Tío can pick him up later. Or he can sleep on the couch."

"You're right, Chris. I can come back for him." Antonio slapped Jack on the shoulder. "You good with that, man?"

I waved my hands back and forth in front of me. "No, no. You're going out with Sylvia. You'll come back too late," just as Jack shook his head and said, "Probably not a good idea."

"Stay! Stay! Stay!" the three kids chanted.

Jack hesitated. "I guess I can stay for a while," he finally said. He put his guitar in the corner of the entryway and looked at me. "You okay with that?"

Okay? Inside I was jumping for joy! I wanted him to stay. On the other hand, if he stayed, it would be torture, plain and simple. Jack had said he'd rather be tortured and with me than tortured and without me. I felt the exact same way. "If it's what the kids want," I said, nodding.

"I'll call my sister to pick me up," he said to Antonio.

A raucous child-sized cheer went up.

Antonio climbed into his car, throwing me an exaggerated smile and a wave. He cranked his window down. "You kids have fun, now, you hear?" he called as he drove away, and I knew he was talking to Jack and me, not to the actual children.

The five of us stood on the front porch, watching our chaperone disappear into the night.

Chapter 18

Jack spread out a blanket on the living room floor. He lay on his side, Mia leaning against him. ZJ rested against the couch, and Chris lay on his stomach in front of Jack. They looked like one big happy family. I passed out bowls of popcorn and chocolate chip cookies before I collapsed on the oversized chair in the corner of the room. I crossed my legs and arms, set my mouth in a firm line, and fought against the tender thoughts I was having. This was a side of Jack that I hadn't seen before. I knew he *wanted* kids, but it seemed like he actually *liked* them, too. It was sexy, and it made me feel warm inside.

ZJ got up to refill his popcorn bowl. "Cool movie, Tía," he whispered as he passed by me.

The comment snapped me out of my zoned state. I had no clue what the movie was about, but I nodded and smiled. I looked at Jack again. His legs were stretched out to the side, his head propped up on his elbow. Playing monster had given him that *just tumbled out of bed* look, and I bit my cheek.

Mia shivered, her head lobbing drowsily to the side. Jack caught her, scooted himself upright, and deftly scooped her into his arms.

He turned to me. "Where should I put her?" he mouthed.

I snapped to attention. Leading him to Mia's room, I pulled back the covers of her bed so Jack could slip her between the sheets. He covered her with the blanket and ran his hand over her hair. My breath caught in my throat at the tender gesture.

We tiptoed out of Mia's room, leaving the door cracked open. I sat back down on my enormous plush chair. Jack dropped down next to me. "How you doing?" he asked, all casual, but the electricity between us was combustible.

"*Fabuloso*," I said, and cringed. I sounded just like Reilly and her wannabe-Latina Spanglish.

With both of us in the chair, it was a tight fit. Jack edged back, angled his body toward me, and laid his arm across the back.

I tried to maintain my own space, wishing my cleavage wasn't so . . . *there*. I felt his hip squeezed in next to mine, my eyelids fluttering closed as I smelled his musk. I pulled my shoulders together, shrinking farther away from him. Jack dropped his voice. "Any progress with the case?"

"I haven't figured out the why yet," I said. My teeth were clenched, and I batted away the illicit thoughts I was having.

His mind was apparently free of wicked thoughts. "Are you sure you weren't the target?" he whispered.

"Does gut instinct count?"

"Not in a court of law." He turned his focus to the movie, laughing, popping pieces of popcorn into his mouth from the bowl that rested on his leg, and occasionally shifting his gaze to the kids.

My body, on the other hand, stayed on red alert, but Jack's arm stayed chastely in place on the back of the chair. Finally, with my muscles weary from their sentry, I relaxed my arms, dropping them to my lap.

Out of the corner of my eye, I saw Jack's head move slightly; he'd registered the change. He could give Manny Camacho a run for his money as superdetective—totally aware of everything around him.

It seemed like an eternity, but the movie finally ended. The moment the last line was spoken, I popped up out of the chair, leaving Jack sitting unevenly on one side. Clapping my hands, I said, "Story time, then bedtime." Not that I should have been pushing for bedtime, since that meant alone time with Jack.

Chris immediately pulled a book off the bookshelf and donned a pair of child-sized blue reading glasses. With his wavy dark hair, he looked studious and adorable. He jumped on the couch and waited for me. ZJ and Jack pulled out their guitars again and strummed quietly, Jack pointing out chords and notes that ZJ proceeded to practice over and over again. I watched them out of the corner of my eye as Chris read to me.

Twenty minutes later, the two boys were tucked into bed and I was in the kitchen, cleaning up. Jack sauntered in after me, carrying his guitar.

I'd slipped on the pair of rubber gloves that I found under Lucy's sink and began washing the mixing bowl from the cookies. With his guitar resting against a chair, Jack made himself a tostada and munched on it as I worked. "You're good with the kids," he said in between mouthfuls.

"So are you." I stared at the sink, not wanting to look at him. He was *really* good with the kids. "Why'd you come tonight?" I asked suddenly, turning to face him despite the warning bells. "You must have better things to do on a Friday night."

He shrugged, pushing the last bite of tostada into his mouth. "Not really."

Meaning Sarah was on her meds and didn't need rescuing. "You said you had things to work out. . . ." I trailed off, hoping he'd give an explanation. Maybe he'd already worked things out and we were free and clear.

But he didn't answer. Instead, after tossing the paper plate he'd been using into the garbage can, he began packing up the tostada paraphernalia. Avoidance. Smooth. "Good salsa. Did you make it?"

I nodded. "*Salsa borracha*. My grandmother's recipe."

"*Borracha*—as in 'drunk'?"

I nodded again. "Numbs the senses just like alcohol. At least

213

Abuela's *picosa* version does. This one was mild—for the kids. Jack," I said. "Answer the question."

"You didn't ask a question."

Damn. He was right. "Okay, so here it is. Why are you here?"

"Working some things out doesn't mean we can't spend time together."

"But the 'I need time to think about all of this' does." I turned my back on him and wiped the counters and table with an enthusiasm I didn't feel. Jack picked up his guitar and was leaning against the wall, absently strumming. I recognized the tune but couldn't place the song. There was something seductive about it, though.

¡Basta! I had other things to think about.

"Do you want me to go?" he asked over the music.

Yes, for my own sanity! "No," I said, attacking the counter with new invigoration. "It's fine."

"The rubber gloves don't really go with the look," he said after a heavy silence.

I stopped midwipe and turned to find him looking at me, a small smile on his lips. "What does that mean?"

"It's not a code," he said with a smirk. "The gloves make you look—domestic. The rest of you—uh—doesn't." He shifted his weight, the sleeves of his white T-shirt pulling up as his fingers worked the strings on the guitar neck. A mark on his arm caught my eye. "You have a tattoo?"

He looked down at his arm like he had to remind himself that it was there. "Oh, yeah."

My gaze zeroed in on his deltoid. And here I thought I knew almost everything there was to know about Jack Callaghan. How had I never noticed his tattoo? "What of?"

He started strumming again, his grin turning wicked. "I'll show you my tattoo if you show me your belly piercing."

"Ha! Nice try, but no deal."

The song he was playing came to me. The chorus popped into my head: *Your body is a wonderland.*

214

He watched me intently. As if he knew I'd figured it out, he moved into the next verse. My internal voice sang along with his guitar-playing. *Damn, baby, you frus-trate me.*

Then abruptly, he stopped playing. "You need to add that blouse to the list of clothes not to wear around me." He stopped smiling. "On second thought, you should just burn your whole wardrobe."

I snatched the rag from the sink and threw it at him. "I didn't know you were going to be here!"

He caught it one-handed, crossed to me, and dropped it back into the basin. "So who'd you wear it for?"

Ripping the gloves off my hands, I tossed them into the sink next to the rag. "For myself."

"But you wore it to work, right?"

"Why?"

Jack put his guitar down. A second later, his fingers danced over the neckline of my blouse. "Because it's definitely meant for a man to en-joy. All those innocent ruffles, and . . ." He swallowed, his temple puls-ing. "It makes me crazy to think Camacho was looking at you in that."

"Yeah? Well, it makes me crazy that you go running whenever Sarah calls, so I guess we're even." But my heartbeat skittered around, picking up speed.

"If you met her, you'd realize there was nothing to be worried about."

Likely story. "Convenient offer, seeing as she's not here to meet." Or was she? I narrowed my eyes, silently asking the question.

"No, she's not in Sacramento," he answered.

"Why would meeting her make a difference? Is she incapable of forming complete sentences? Does she have a third eye? No, she's your ex-fiancée, so she's got to have some damn good qualities. Meet-ing her wouldn't help. Thanks, but no thanks."

Jack's gaze slid over my shoulder. I turned. Mia stood in the door-way. I hurried over to her, dropped to my knees, and took her hands. "What's wrong, *mi'ja?*"

Her face melted, her eyes glazing over. "I want Mamá."

I hugged her. "Mia, your mommy and daddy went out to dinner. Remember? I'm staying with you. I'm going to spend the night, make you breakfast, and—" I choked on the words, my consciousness knowing that Rosie's son wasn't so lucky as Mia. "And then your mommy will be home."

She clutched at her nightgown and hopped from foot to foot. "I have to go potty."

I took her to the bathroom and got her settled back in her bed, singing to her until she drifted off.

When I came back to the living room, Jack was sitting on the edge of the couch, wineglass in hand, another fragile glass on the side table half filled with red wine.

"Found it on the counter. Think they'll mind?" he asked, holding the wineglass out to me.

I shook my head and took a sip. Sitting back down on the over-sized chair, I started to relax. "Getting me tipsy isn't going to change anything, you know."

"That's not my plan at all," he said, his expression saying *get real*. "When we get together, I want you to have all your senses intact."

I laughed. "You say that so confidently. You might not be able to work things out."

He took a sip of his wine, never taking his eyes off me. "Oh, I will. If it's the last thing I do, I'll work it out. I'm not going to stop until I do."

I took another long drink, not even registering the taste. I had a feeling he was right. "If I'm still here," was all I could muster saying.

He gave me a half smile as he got up to refill my already empty glass. "That's why I'm going to work fast," he said, sitting back on the couch. "But I know you, Lola, and you'll wait."

"You don't know me that well."

His grin grew. "Oh yeah? I know your drive and determination got you to where you are now. I know you adore your family—even though they drive you crazy. I know you're smart." He stopped, and his face grew serious. "You're beautiful." His gaze burned into mine. "Should I go on?"

No. He shouldn't. I felt like Reneé Zellweger in *Jerry Maguire*. *You had me at "you're smart."*

Again, he seemed to read my mind. Or my weakness. He pushed himself up from the couch, set his wineglass down on the side table next to the telephone, and slid in next to me on the two-person chair. I gulped down half my cabernet just before he pushed my hair back off my face.

"So what's the latest on Rosie Gonzales?" he asked, playing with the ruffles on my blouse. His fingers brushed my neck, sending goose bumps to the surface of my skin.

I swallowed and edged away from him a little bit. "I keep worrying about her son."

"No luck with that birthday invitation?"

I filled him in on my conversation with Juana Zuniga. "Still trying to get ahold of her neighbor. I went by this afternoon, but he wasn't home. That's all I—I . . ." I faltered as one of his hands slid up my thigh. ". . . kn-know," I finished, my eyelids sinking closed.

He trailed his lips along my neck. "No ideas what they argued about?" he murmured.

All I could manage was a gasping "N-no."

He nibbled just beneath my earlobe. "Nothing more from the police?"

My back arched. My breath became shallow. "N-nothing." Detective Seavers hadn't shared anything new with me. Come to think of it, all the peripheral men in my life had been oddly silent lately. Manny. The detective. Sergio.

My spine straightened as a wild thought slipped into my consciousness.

Jack pulled back to look at me, his hand resting comfortably in the hollow between my thighs. "What's wrong?"

"I was just thinking about Sergio." I swallowed the rest of my wine and put the glass down on the end table.

I felt him stiffen next to me. "You're thinking about Sergio," he repeated, his voice tight, "now?"

"No, no!" I cringed, realizing what that must have sounded like to him. Two glasses of wine had loosened my tongue and my brain, not a good combination. "I mean, your question made me think about . . . I just remembered . . ." It didn't sound good, no matter what, so I just blurted it out. "I was thinking about his apartment. His cousin, Pancho. That little boy he has."

"What about them?"

"I was just wondering where that boy's mother is."

He considered me, looking like he thought I might be a little bit crazy. "You're not thinking it's Rosie Gonzales?" His hand squeezed my thigh. His way of trying to make me see things straight? "You're reaching, Cruz. There are a lot of kids out there without mothers. And Sergio isn't the sharpest knife in the block. If Pancho's his cousin, he's probably not much smarter. They would have left a string of clues a mile long."

I took offense on Pancho's behalf. He couldn't help who he was related to. Jack and I both knew that Sergio was plenty sharp. A jerk, yes, but stupid? No. "You can't judge a person by his relatives and friends," I said.

"I can where Garcia's concerned." His lips curved up on one side. "Excluding you, of course."

He was probably right. I didn't have time to waste energy on Sergio, let alone on his hapless cousin. "I know it's not related. There's just so much heartache out there, you know?" I tried not to think about my own personal heartache involving Jack and his ex-fiancée.

"We don't have to have heartache, Lola."

But we would as long as there was an invisible third wheel between us.

He slid his hand under my hair, spreading his fingers as he cradled my head. "You're in my head, and I can't get you out," he said, his voice low and serious.

I knew exactly what he meant. He was in every cell of my body. I reached for him, my lips parted and ready.

I waited. And waited. Wasn't he going to kiss me? I opened my eyes and saw the desire in his eyes, but he'd stopped short, his lips never making contact with mine. "Hmmm."

My voice echoed his. "Hmm, what?" I arched toward him, lacing my fingers behind his neck, trying to pull him closer to me.

He laid his hands on either side of my face and looked perplexed. I rested my head on his shoulder to quell the dizziness in my head.

"You've had too much to drink," he finally said. He leaned back and moved one hand to the base of my rib cage. The light pressure of his fingers against the bottom of my breast was possessive, like it was meant to be there. Like it had been there a thousand times before.

It had. In my dreams.

My blood pressure rose with every one of his slow blinks. "I'm fine," I said.

He seemed to regroup. "Maybe you should call that neighbor again," he finally said. "Seems like he's the only potential clue you have."

I heard what he said—almost like a challenge—but the majority of my attention was still on the position of his hand and the way it touched the slope of my breast. "Oh, I will talk to him. And this case is about clues, yes, but it's mostly about thinking."

Jack arched an eyebrow at me. "Thinking."

"Yes, thinking. The art of deduction. Like Sherlock Holmes or Nero Wolfe."

"But Holmes had Watson doing his legwork, and Wolfe had that pretty boy—"

"Archie Goodwin," I said, rolling my eyes. Pretty boy, indeed.

He lifted my legs onto his and ran his hand under my pants at the ankle. "Who does your legwork?" he asked, feeling for stubble.

"Lady Schick does the trick." I giggled. "Perfectly smooth, right? I don't need Watson or Goodwin."

His hand stilled on my shin. "You're tipsy—"

"From two glasses of wine? I can hold my alcohol better than Tonio, I'll have you know."

He laughed at that. "I'm sure you can."

219

I wriggled my legs, trying to angle myself differently. Another idea tickled at the edge of my brain. "Hey!" I tried to sit up, working my hips up from deep in the chair. Jack's hand slid up the side of my leg as I struggled. Then he was cupping my behind, lifting me, and suddenly I was sitting squarely on his lap.

"Hey, what?" he asked, his grin taking on that hint of wickedness.

I twisted my body around, lifting one leg over his lap so I was straddling him. "Alcohol."

He swallowed. Hard. "Alcohol," he repeated, his voice a little strangled.

I laid my hands on his shoulders and squeezed my thighs to reposition myself. "Do you remember seeing any alcohol in Rosie's apartment?"

His hands slid from my hips to my waist. "No," he said.

"Neither do I!" I felt this might be significant, but I didn't know how or why it would be.

He read my mind. "And this is important because . . ."

His hips adjusted slightly, and his hands slipped under my blouse. The touch of his fingers almost burned against my skin. Suddenly I forgot what I'd been thinking about. "Important?" I asked, my voice as strangled as his had been a few seconds ago.

"Maybe she was religious . . . ," he muttered.

I steadied myself by putting my hands against his chest. "So she didn't drink," I finished, and for the life of me, I couldn't imagine why this might be important when I could feel Jack stirring under me.

His eyes were pale in the dim light of the living room, and his face had grown serious; his breath came faster as he tried to maintain control.

I ran my hands up to his shoulders, then slid them to his neck, his stubbled skin warm to my touch. Moving my hips, I pushed myself against him. The ache inside me was deep and concentrated. Then, complications be damned, I leaned down and brushed my lips against his.

The ring of the telephone sliced through the air. I looked up at the ceiling, toward heaven. *I get it!* I wanted to yell to God. Jack and I were not meant to be together. Those complications couldn't be ignored.

It rang again, horribly loud, like a cannon firing right next to my ears. I snatched the handset from the side table, tried to calm my breathing, and pushed the ON button. "H-Hello? Fal-cón r-residence."

"Lola! It's Lucy. I didn't wake you, did I?"

Jack shifted under me. The hard pressure of him turned my stomach to knots. My throat constricted. My eyelids fluttered closed as he kissed my neck, trailing his tongue across my collarbone. The whisper of his lips against the swell of my breasts made me gasp. His hands crept up my sides, his fingers spreading along my rib cage, edging up. Up. Up.

"Uh—h-hi, L-Lucy." I tried to focus on the phone call instead of on Jack. Impossible. With his free hand, he lifted the ruffles and undid the top buttons of my blouse, easing the lace of my bra down. Blood pounded in my head as his hands, then his mouth, took over. Focus! I spoke into the phone. "I—Is everything—*ahhh*—"

"Are you all right?" Lucy's voice sounded faint and far away.

No! Jack was like a drug. "Uh—" I swallowed, trying to pull myself together, scared of how out of control I felt. I couldn't stop. Couldn't move. When his mouth latched on to my nipple, I turned into a statue.

"Fine. I-I'm fine." How I got the words out, I'll never know.

"Lola?"

Jack pulled me closer. I wanted to fall into him. "Y-yes?"

"What's going on? Are the kids okay?"

Lucy's sharp voice cut through the fog in my brain. I pulled myself together enough to answer coherently. "I'm fine." I took a deep breath to calm my nerves. "Just thinking about my case."

"God, you scared me!" She laughed nervously. "I thought there was a home invasion going on, or something."

I giggled more nervously than she had. It was more like an emotional and physical invasion. "N-no!"

221

"There's not, is there? A home invasion, I mean. Do you need to use a code word? You sure you're okay?"

"I'm fine!" I said with more force than I thought I could muster. "You should be out dancing!" *Good girl, Lola.* I sounded halfway normal.

"We just wanted to check on the kids." She paused, then said oh-so-matter-of-factly, "Oh. My. God. You're not alone."

I craned my neck to look around. Oh, crap, did they have a nanny cam? Were we being filmed right now? I jerked away from Jack, pulling my blouse together. "Why do you say that?"

"Ha!" she exclaimed, and I jumped. "I knew it! You're not, are you. I'm right, aren't I?"

Had she developed some telepathic abilities while I wasn't looking? "Yes," I admitted. "You're right."

Jack raked his hand through his hair as I snatched my wineglass and poured myself a refill, drinking down half of it in one gulp. I shouldn't be drinking on the babysitting job, I realized, but I was in a tailspin. I put the glass down and turned my back on it. Alcohol. That had gotten me into this situation in the first place. Lowered my inhibitions, dulled my senses.

A thought shot into my brain. If Rosie didn't drink as a general rule, but had been drinking at Juana Zuniga's, she might have been loose-lipped about something. Said a little too much, maybe. I'd ask good ol' Bill the neighbor, if I ever had the opportunity to speak to him.

Jack bent forward in his chair, his elbows on his knees, his forehead in his hands. I could almost hear him singing our song. *Damn, baby. You frus-trate me.*

"Hello? Lola?"

Lucy's voice knocked me out of my reflections. "I'm here."

"Is it Jack?"

"*Por supuesto,*" I said with a sigh. I flicked my eyes toward him again. There could be no other. He was pointing the remote at the TV, flipping through channels. Guess he was over the moment.

"Don't you dare have your first time with him in my bed, Lola Cruz!"

"Ew! God, Lucy—how can you even think that?" I cupped my hand over my eyes, way too embarrassed to mention that it might have happened on her oversized chair if her phone call hadn't interrupted us.

"Sorry," she said quickly. "Thanks for staying with the kids. They're good?"

"Perfect. All tucked in."

We said good night, and I hung up. The phone call had given me time to cool off and think clearly. It had apparently done the same for Jack. He sat with his wineglass balanced on his knee, barely smiling at the punch lines of the movie he'd turned on. He was tuned out to everything but the blue light of the television.

I sat on the couch, three times almost going over to him, three times changing my mind, knowing if we started again, I wouldn't be able to stop. I sighed, louder than I'd intended.

"You okay?"

I jumped at Jack's voice. And I'd thought he wasn't paying attention. "I'm fine." I tucked my feet under me and tried to concentrate on the movie, the images blurring, the sounds like echoes in my mind.

After an eternity—and then some—the movie ended. I glanced at my watch. One fifteen. I began retrieving pillows from the floor and tossing them onto the couches, folding the picnic blanket with gusto, picking up stray pieces of popcorn from the shaggy carpet.

Jack watched me as I moved around the room. The image of him playing monster with Zac and Lucy's kids popped into my head, and my warm feelings toward him strengthened. He was *dad* material. How could I never have seen that before? *¡Dios mío!* I was in trouble.

His voice startled me. "It's late. I should go."

He should, but he didn't have a car. "Your sister's probably sleeping." I kept talking, my mouth operating independently from my mind. "You should just spend the night," I offered. It was the charitable thing to do.

His face was unreadable. "You sure?"

Not even close. Had I lost my mind? "Of course," I said, and I knew that I had. Lost my sanity. Completely.

Scenarios played out in my mind. Jack and me in the master bedroom when one of the kids wanders in. Jack and me not making it to the bedroom . . . and one of the kids wanders in. Jack and me making our own kid, since his box of For Her Pleasure Trojans was tucked safely in his medicine cabinet.

How people with kids continued to have an active sex life without being busted by their offspring was *un grande* mystery.

In the end, Jack slept on the couch.

I tossed and turned, unable to get comfortable in a strange bed, more unable to get Jack off my mind, and my thoughts continually circling around to Rosie. Finally I shoved the pillow over my face and drifted off.

Five minutes later—at least that's what it felt like—cartoon voices blared from the television. *Kids.* This was what it was like waking up to kids.

I threw back the comforter and padded out to the living room, stopping short at the sight in front of me. ZJ was enveloped in a blanket on the chair Jack and I had shared the night before, eyes glued to the TV. Jack lay on his side, his body stretched the full length of the couch, his legs curled slightly. Chris and Mia cuddled up in the space behind his legs, a little boat on the couch. Chris laughed; Jack ruffled his hair; Mia snuggled in a little closer; Jack wrapped his arm around her, giving her a squeeze; and my heart twisted at the sight of it all.

I tiptoed back to the bedroom, gathered my things, and quickly showered. With clean clothes, combed-out wet hair, and brushed teeth, I went out to start breakfast for the kids.

"Bacon!" Mia exclaimed from the kitchen entrance a few minutes later. She rubbed her tummy through her flannel nightgown, then clapped. "I love bacon!"

"*Buenos días,*" I said, cracking an egg into a bowl. "Everyone like scrambled eggs?"

224

"And toast?" Chris asked.

"And toast," I said, the toaster popping out four slices at that very moment. I skimmed butter across them, stacked them on a plate, added four more slices to toast, and went back to the eggs.

"Mind if I shower?" Jack's morning voice was husky from the night's sleep.

"Sure," I said, staying focused on my eggs. I didn't want to see his tousled hair and his unshaven face again. A minute later, I heard the water turn on in the bathroom and the faint click of the shower door closing. I swallowed hard, trying not to picture him.

I don't know why I even bothered. The photographs I'd taken of Jack after he'd gotten to know Greta Pritchard—in a biblical sense—were embedded in my mind as if it were me he'd been getting busy with in the backseat of his car. I had only to close my eyes to picture him *sin ropa*.

I stirred the eggs, bracing myself with one hand stretched onto the counter. . . . Good God. He was fifty feet away from me . . . naked. Jack, not God.

"Are they almost done?" ZJ asked, pouring himself a glass of pineapple-orange juice.

"What? Oh, yes. Just about perfect."

I laid three plates on the counter, scooped a spoonful of eggs onto each, added two strips of bacon and a slice of toast. "Do you want me to get Jack?" Chris asked.

"No," I said quickly. "You eat. I'll get him." *Bad Lola.* But I marched into the bedroom anyway. The bathroom door was half-open. I listened for a sound. The water was off. Tiptoeing toward the door, I leaned one ear closer. It was utterly silent in the bathroom. Just a little peek . . .

"Looking for me?"

I jumped, clasping my hands to my chest. Wheeling around, I caught my breath. Jack stood next to the dresser, towel-drying his hair. His jeans were unbuttoned, riding low on his hips, with what looked like nothing underneath. My gaze slowed at the spattering of tawny hair that crept up from his waistband. I gulped. And that tattoo. What *was* it? A Chinese symbol? A spiral? My name in Old English lettering?

I tried to speak, but my voice stuck. After clearing my throat I tried again. "B-breakfast is ready."

He smiled at me, an enticing, full-dimpled affair that sent my head reeling.

"So, just letting you know." Then mustering as much dignity as I could—after being busted as a peeping Tom—I walked calmly out of the room, closing the door behind me. In the hallway and out of sight, I collapsed against the wall, buckling over to catch my breath.

The door handle turned. I sprinted for the kitchen, snatched a plate from the cabinet, and flung eggs onto it.

"I've been thinking about the Rosie situation," he said as he walked in.

"Who's Rosie?" ZJ asked through a mouthful of eggs.

"She's a woman I . . . I know," I said.

That satisfied them. They went back to their conversation—an animated discussion about the importance of a secret handshake between best friends, because best friends kept your secrets, Mia was saying.

"Best friends kept your secrets," I repeated thoughtfully.

Suddenly Jack was by my side. "You have an idea?"

"Just wondering how to track down Rosie's best friend. Or any friend, for that matter. Juana didn't know her. Bill, the neighbor, argued with her. Other than that, I have nothing. Francisco's MIA. If Rosie had a friend. A best friend who she confided in . . ." I trailed off, trying to figure out how to track down someone else in Rosie's life.

"That's your focus today?"

I nodded as I handed him the plate. "That's my focus for today. Someone knows something." Nobody, I reasoned, was completely alone in the world, and I knew Rosie wasn't the exception to that rule, since she'd stolen my identity. She was running from something.

Chapter 19

The low hum of a camera clicked on the second I entered Camacho's lobby the next morning. The surveillance unit mounted in the corner had come to life. It followed me, then rattled back to its position aimed at the entrance after I turned into the conference room. Like a Pavlovian response to all the uncertainties going on here lately, my heart started pounding erratically, but I willed it into submission. I was a damn good detective, a loyal employee, honest, and if that wasn't good enough for *el bosso*, then that just wasn't my problem.

Neil—with an *ei*—lumbered out of the Lair carrying a ladder as if it were a feather. His heavy head seemed to smash into his body, erasing any sign of his neck. "It worked," I said to him. "I heard it, though. It kind of rattles."

He gave me one abrupt nod, then set the ladder up in the lobby, hauled his body up it, and began tinkering with the camera mount.

"Tom has sound now," he announced a minute later.

"Tom?"

He answered as he tightened a screw. "As in *peeping*."

I cringed inside at the implication of Neil naming his surveillance system Tom. "Isn't anything sacred here? No privacy at all?"

"Sure. The john, the boss's office, and the Lair." No one was allowed into the Lair without an invitation.

I preferred not to go into the Lair at all—even with an invitation. And I thanked God it was Tom-free—for Reilly's sake.

The girl herself sat busily typing as I entered the conference room. "Hey, you're here," I said, but what I was thinking was, *Please don't let Neil film you.*

"Hey, *chica*."

There were two things about Reilly that would never change. One, she was a Latina in a white girl's body. Two, she had style, with a capital S. Case in point? Today her hair was purple. The spy girl was gone, and in her place was the Crayola girl I knew and loved.

"Any *chisme?*" I asked, wishing the gossip she'd share would include her own supersecret activities—with Neil and with Manny.

"*Nada* word," she said, cracking herself up at her crafty double entendre. "*As Camacho Turns* is off the air today. No good story lines."

"Except for you and"—I jerked my head toward the lobby, where Neil was fiddling with his system—"teddy bear."

Identity theft was a much bigger deal than a love affair with a coworker or a mum's-the-word mission for a boss. If Reilly wouldn't fess up about her secrets, I doubted Rosie Gonzales would have fessed up about hers to a friend.

Her expression said *¡Cállate!* and she held a finger to her lips. So the *ei*-couple was still top secret.

I braced my hands on her desk and leaned close to whisper in her ear. "You know you can't keep this secret forever. True love can't be silenced." I thought about it for a second, then added, "And best friends should be trusted." True, the statement could be construed as *un poquito* manipulative, but it was for a good cause. If Reilly needed protecting, I had to know what to protect her from.

She arched a skeptical brow at me. "Is that right?"

"That's right."

"If it can't be silenced, then what, exactly, is the deal with you and Jack-o?"

228

I held my tongue as Neil lumbered back into the Lair. I waited until his door had closed before saying, "No deal." Though if I believed my own cliché about true love, Jack and I were destined to be together.

I waited while Reilly thought about her options. "Okay, look," she finally said, "I can tell you this." She darted a quick look around the conference room to make sure there were no lurkers. The coast was clear.

I held my breath.

"*El bosso* Camacho is hiding something pretty big." She whispered so quietly, I could hardly hear her.

"What is it?" I asked, resisting the follow-up question of *How did you get involved?*

"He trusted me," she murmured. "He's fighting to keep this place open—"

I gasped. Camacho and Associates might go under?

She squeezed my wrist. "There's more," she said with hushed urgency. "He co-owns it—"

I interrupted again. "With who?"

"I can't say." Her grip tightened, and she darted another glance around. "There's more. He's trying to keep his majority over his silent partner, but he's also fighting for something else."

An exasperated sigh slipped through my lips. "What else?"

"It's bigger than this business," she whispered just as the door to the Lair flung open and banged against the wall.

Reilly and I turned to see Neil standing in the doorway, heavy booted feet spread wide and planted firmly on the ground. "Sugarplum," he barked. "In here."

For a second I thought he was alerting us about a sugarplum invasion in the Lair; then Reilly stood, patted her purple hair, and glided toward him.

He'd called her sugarplum. *Ay, caramba,* Neil had a pet name for Reilly. Absolutely shocking.

The faint click of Tom reached my ears. The whole office was under surveillance—at all times. I suddenly understood Neil's intrusion into Reilly's conversation with me. Tom had sound now. Had Neil heard his sugarplum reveal part of the secrets she'd sworn to keep?

My gut twisted. I felt like a heel for trying to manipulate Reilly into breaking a confidence. If Neil was going to blame someone, it should be me. I marched to the Lair, knocked three times, and opened the door just a crack.

I expected to find Neil reading Reilly the riot act. Instead what I saw resembled the encounter I'd walked in on between Sadie and Manny. It was way more intimacy than I wanted to see between two people.

At least Reilly wasn't being punished—or at least it was voluntary punishment that she looked like she was fully enjoying.

Locking the image away in my mind—and throwing away the key—brought my thoughts back to secrets. That was the underlying theme of this case—and my life. Almost everyone had secrets. Manny. Reilly. Jack. Neil. Only Antonio and Sylvia were free and clear, though I wondered if Sylvia really knew about my brother's playboy reputation.

I focused on Rosie. She had to have confessed to someone. I started by reviewing my case questions:

- *Who had a motive to kill her?*
- *Better yet, what was the motive?*

Presumably Francisco, Rosie's boyfriend (or husband) had vanished with the child. I wrote down the logical questions:

- *KIDNAPPING??? MOTIVE???*

If Francisco was Junior's father and had killed Rosie, he was obviously on the lam. But what would his motive for killing her be? If it was custody related, why not use the court system? From the looks of

Rosie's apartment, she hadn't had a lot of money to throw into a court battle, so it would have been cut-and-dried—split custody—or favoring the mother.

I continued on with my line of thinking. What if Rosie *was* being sued for custody? If she didn't have the money, she may have been pushed to the limit of desperation. That explained the motive for the identity theft. If she couldn't fight legally, maybe she'd planned on vanishing—and reemerging as Dolores Cruz.

And if the boyfriend or husband, aka Francisco, had figured out Rosie's plan, there was his motive for killing her.

The only other scenario for Rosie's murder was one I didn't want to think about. I—*me, Lola Cruz*—was the only other realistic suspect if anyone cared to look that hard. Rosie had stolen something of *mine*, so I clearly had motive.

As soon as Neil and his sugarplum were finished, uh, talking, I'd get the number for his contact with the department of justice. I ought to be able to find out if Rosie Gonzales was party to a custody battle over Junior.

The door to Manny's office jerked open. He marched out, glancing at my board. "Anything?"

His bark made me jump. "Working on it," I said.

"New client coming in tomorrow. You'll be back on the roster."

Translation: My free ride was over. I had to solve my case. Pronto.

The heavy air was jarred by my ringing cell phone.

I flipped it open. "Hello?"

"Yeah. You called my house." The deep voice came barreling at my ear.

A quick look at the caller ID screen told me it was Bill Johnson, Mrs. Zuniga's neighbor. "Right. Mr. Johnson. Hello! I appreciate the callback." Though I hadn't expected it.

"What's this about?"

"Mr. Johnson, I'm a private investigator. I'm looking into the death of Rosie Gonzales. I understand you had an exchange with her at a birthday party the day she died."

231

The *very* minimal pleasantness I thought I'd heard in Bill's voice gathered in a tornado and blew clean away. "I had an argument with some lady," he confirmed, "but I don't like the implication of what you're saying. She died?"

I trotted out some benign words to calm him down. "Yes, sir. Ms. Gonzales was found dead in an alley behind Florin Mall. There's no implication. I'm just trying to tie up some loose ends."

"I heard about that woman, but that wasn't her name. That was a detect— Wait a second." He let out an audible breath. "What'd you say your name was?"

"Dolores Cruz. And you're right. They did say it was me. Ms. Gonzales had an ID with my name."

"No shit."

Yeah, no shit. "I'd like to know what you and Ms. Gonzales argued about at the party."

"This is like a bad TV movie," he said.

The way Manny was watching me almost prompted me to tell Mr. Johnson that this whole situation, with all its subplots, was more like a bad *telenovela* with English subtitles. "Look," I said, "the woman's child is missing. I'm trying to find him, that's all. If you can help at all, I'd appreciate it."

"You're trying to find him?"

"That's right."

His voice softened. "Okay, but I don't think it'll help."

"You never know."

The line was silent for a minute, like he was trying to figure out where to start. "She got all worked up 'cause I *talked* to her kid," he finally said.

"What did you talk to him about? Why'd she get upset?"

"I pointed out my kids to the boy. Thought maybe they'd like to play, you know? No crime in that," he said. "But she flipped out."

"How many kids do you have?"

"Three. They were all at the party. But this lady wouldn't let her kid play. Wouldn't let him leave her side."

232

I rubbed my temples, trying to make a connection with something, anything. I saw zero. "So what happened then?"

"Nothing." He was quiet for a few seconds, and I felt him slip into the memory. "He looked lost. Perfect little face. Perfect hair, just like—" He paused again. "I felt sorry for the little dude." He snapped back to the present. "She yelled at me again, so I got my kids and left. That was it."

Ay, caramba. Bill was certainly on edge. "Was she there by herself?" I asked. Of course, I knew she wasn't, but maybe Bill could give me some insight.

"She was there with some guy." The answer had come quickly, like everything about that day was still fresh in his mind.

"Did you catch his name?"

"Oh, yeah," he said, practically foaming at the mouth. "Francisco."

That was the one flaw in my custody theory. If Rosie and Francisco were together, it didn't seem likely that she was running from him. "Did she talk to any women? Any other friends at the party?"

"Not that I saw. She kept to herself."

"Can you tell me anything about Francisco?"

"Wish I could," he said, some inexplicable anger coloring his tone. "Mexican dude, five ten, on the thin side. The woman was calling the shots. She told him they were leaving as I was herding my kids out."

Bill's description of Francisco didn't give me anything concrete, unfortunately. There wasn't a section in the phone book for five-foot-ten thin Mexican men. That described practically every man in my family, with the exception of Antonio, who was pushing six feet for some inexplicable reason.

"One last question," I said, reaching for straws.

"Shoot," he said, but I could tell from his tone that he was done being Mr. Helpful.

"Did Rosie drink at the birthday party?"

233

"Alcohol, you mean?"

"Right. Sometimes birthday parties have drinks for the adults." I could call back Juana Zuniga to ask her, but if Bill could answer the question, I wouldn't need to.

"Let me think," he said. I pictured him closing his eyes as he tried to recall. "I seem to remember she had a bottle of beer."

"Thanks for your time, Mr. Johnson."

"Let me know about the boy," he said before we hung up. Really, whether or not Rosie drank had no bearing on anything, I finally realized. Her alcohol might have already been packed by the time Jack and I were at her apartment. And just because a person drank, it didn't mean they couldn't hold their alcohol. Beer had nothing to do with Rosie dying, I decided.

I was back to square one. And frustrated as hell.

Neil's contact at the Sacramento County Courthouse confirmed that there was no custody battle going on with anyone resembling the stats of my Rosie Gonzales. I hunted through profiles on Facebook, Twitter, LinkedIn, and every other social network I could find. There were plenty of Rosie Gonzaleses, but none who seemed to be *my* Rosie Gonzales. I couldn't find a single friend in whom she might have confided her secrets.

By seven forty-five that night, I was at Abuelita's helping out, and by nine o'clock Antonio was locking the door, flipping the OPEN sign to CLOSED, and ordering the staff's dinner. "Tonight we have *caldo* and *mole con pollo*," he announced.

Sylvia cheered. "I'm starving!" she said. "And I love *mole*."

Antonio sniggered. "Lola *tambien*. It's one of her favorites."

I grimaced, rising to the bait only enough to snap, "*Cállate*."

Antonio just smirked. "Speaking of Jack—"

"We weren't speaking of Jack," I interrupted.

"Now we are. He said he was coming over."

My heart pitter-pattered in my chest. Seeing Jack Callaghan

would be the perfect ending to a relatively crappy day. I had things to tell him. Feelings to confess.

We hadn't seen each other or talked since our babysitting night, and I was going through Jack withdrawal, far worse than the Chinese food withdrawal I suffered occasionally when I had to tighten my budget.

My mother walked into the dining room, her arms weighed down with plates and bowls. I grabbed a few to lighten her load. "Anything new with the break-in?" I asked, after giving her a quick kiss on her cheek.

"*Nada, mi'ja.* I cannot figure it out. Nothing was taken."

Except maybe my address book. Sergio popped into my mind again. Inexplicably, I kept coming back to him.

A tapping on the restaurant's glass door made the thought vanish. Jack. I let out a long, slow breath. I felt like I was living The Secret—I'd wished for Jack, put it out there into the universe, and now he was right outside.

The other possibility, of course, was that I knew he was coming since Antonio had just told me.

I liked my cosmic theory better.

Jack looked tired but fabulous. I wanted to greet him with a kiss and forgo dinner *con la familia*, but my common sense prevailed. We'd have plenty of time to talk later.

My grandparents had closed their table for the night and were parked on their couch watching their *telanovelas*. My parents, Antonio, my fifteen-year-old cousin Joey who washed dishes, his brother Miquel who helped out in the kitchen, Chely, Sylvia, Jack, and I would be eating dinner. I smiled hello to him, then got busy pushing two tables together, setting the places, and retreating to the kitchen to help carry out the serving bowls of steaming food.

Once we were in our places, my father muttered a prayer, all of us finishing with "Amen" and signing the cross from forehead to breastbone, left shoulder to right. "*Buen provecho,*" Papi proclaimed.

Mole was like spaghetti to the Cruz family. I speared a piece of boiled chicken from the serving plate, topped it with a ladleful of *mole* sauce, added rice and beans to my plate, and took a fresh flour tortilla from the heavy plastic warmer. With a broken section of tortilla, I scooped up a piece of chicken smothered in the *mole* sauce and shoved it in my mouth.

The table was still. I peered up through my eyelashes. Sixteen eyes stared at me. I swallowed heavily. "What?"

"You are hungry, eh?" my father asked, a smile in his voice.

My mother's expression had no lightness. "Dolores," she hissed. "Where are your manners?"

Antonio smirked. "You have manners?"

I shot daggers at him. In a manners competition between him and me, I'd win hands down.

I took another bite, chewing slowly and deliberately. Jack caught my eye, his amused grin interrupted when he pulled his vibrating cell phone out of his pocket. "As a matter of fact," I announced, "I am hungry. I've had a busy day."

Jack punched a button, then put his phone away. Guess that call could wait. *¡Bravo!*

Antonio scoffed at me. "You wanna hear about a stressful day?"

My mother ladled soup into her bowl. "*¿Que pasó, mi'jo?*" she asked, her voice heavy with concern.

Por supuesto. Her concern was always for her Tonito. Argh!

Sylvia cleared her throat. "*Nada, Señora Cruz.* It's just my ex-husband. He's . . . he's been acting crazy lately."

"*¿Porqué?*" Now my mother's sympathy was directed soundly at Sylvia. She was the one woman Antonio had dated whom my mother seemed to approve of completely. I didn't know if she was Catholic, and she was divorced, but she was a hard worker, was a Latina, and loved her children. The pros outweighed the cons and blurred the lines for Magdalena Cruz.

Sylvia looked at my parents. "*Esta loco.* He thinks our baby is alive."

I'd taken another bite, but stopped midchew. That was more than crazy. That was delusional.

236

"Why would he think that?" I asked after I'd swallowed my next bite.

Her mouth twisted as she tried to hold in her tears. She threw a pleading look at Tonio. "He'll be here soon."

Antonio grumbled under his breath.

Joey wiped the brown sauce from his mouth and turned to Sylvia. "That's your husband that drops you off? He sure likes to hang around."

Antonio tightened his lips. "Ex-husband, *muchacho*. Ex-husband."

Sylvia flicked her eyes around the table. My mother ran her hand up and down Sylvia's back, clucking with her tongue and mumbling in Spanish. "*Pobrecita*," she cooed.

Sylvia gave a heavy shrug. "He seems better for a while, then he gets crazier than ever." She flicked her wrist in front of her face. "He's bringing the kids—"

Antonio shook his head. "*Pendejo loco*. How can he not see how much harder he's making this for you?" He scooted his chair back and led Sylvia into the kitchen. "And for your kids."

I stared after them. Antonio's concern was probably as new for him to experience as it was for the rest of us to see.

I felt the weight of Jack studying me. His fork and spoon lay on the napkin, his food untouched. He was just as concerned about me, I realized.

With Tonio and Sylvia gone, conversation had moved on. I pushed around the chicken on my plate with my fork and listened to the comfortable prattle of my family. Chely laughed shrilly. "*No me gusta Arasely, Tío*," she said to my father. "*Me gusta Chely. Mi nombre es Chely.*"

My mother spoke up, her voice like a warm, soothing blanket. "*Pero mi'ja, Arasely es un nombre bonito.*"

Chely nodded. "*Esta bien, pero* I like *Chely* better. Without a Spanish accent, Arasely, like, doesn't sound right. I like Chely." She slurped her soda.

"Most people have some sort of nickname," Jack said.

"Even you," I said playfully.

He gave me a warning look, and I threw back a wink and a coy smile. *Jackie*, I mouthed.

"*De veras*," said my father. He was Gregorio, but my mother called him Gregorito.

Antonio and Sylvia had slipped back into their seats. "Sylvia doesn't," Antonio said, a sloppy grin on his face.

Sylvia's eyes were still glassy. "Well, some people call me Syl," she said. Then with her own flirtatious grin, she added, "Tonito."

"Oooh, Tonito," Joey mimicked. He made a loud smooching sound.

Antonio backhanded him on the arm.

Dios mío, those two had it bad.

"*Me llamo Magdalena, pero mi amor me llama Magda*," my mother said thoughtfully. She'd been subtle, but she'd deftly redirected the conversation away from the lovebirds.

My youngest cousin spoke up. "Right now I'm Joey or Joe, but when I have a girlfriend, she can call me Joseph," he said, a suggestive lilt in his voice.

"Right, dude," his brother Miguel mocked. "Like you're ever gonna *get* a girlfriend."

They scowled at each other. One of their stomachs growled, and the boys dug back into their food.

"And how about you, Dolores?" Jack said. Him using my given name made me feel like we were strangers. And after the other night we were anything but. "How'd you get your nickname?"

I tilted my head, raising my eyebrows and smiling. "Lola just *is* the nickname for Dolores." I had no idea where it came from. But considering Dolores came from Our Lady of Sorrows—and I was anything but sorrowful—I was all for Lola.

The conversations went on but I tuned it out. Could Jack become Jackie to me?

That nagging feeling circled in my gut, exploding to life in a firestorm. Most people had nicknames. "He's got a nickname," I muttered. "Oh my God . . . Pancho."

238

"What?" Jack said. He was tuned in to me 100 percent.

"Everybody has nicknames," I repeated.

Joey nudged me with his elbow, his cheeks bulging. "Who's Pancho?"

"*¿Quien es Pancho?*" Chely asked at the same time, her eyes shooting question marks off in Jack's direction.

"Nobody."

Everyone around me faded away. I spoke just to him, trying to process through my racing thoughts. "Pancho's a nickname for Francisco."

It came to me in a blast, all the puzzle pieces that had been floating around in my head settling loosely into place. I sucked in a mouthful of air, but it caught in my throat. Shoving myself back from the table, I stood up and leaned my hands on it, catching my breath. Jack bolted around to me, rubbing my back. "Lola," he said in between my coughs. "Are you okay?"

Sweet. He'd thought I was choking. I pounded my chest with my fist. My coughing eased. "Pancho," I repeated, as if I could spread my realization to everyone.

"Huh?" Antonio looked puzzled, his pinkie stroking his goatee.

"Dolores, what is going on with you?" my father asked.

I backed away from the table. "I have to go," I said. "I have to see Sergio." I snatched my purse from under the counter, pulled out my keys, and raced off.

Chapter 20

.

A hand clamped around my upper arm. I jumped, grabbing the wrist and wrenching it away from me, twisting around to face my assailant.

"It's me," Jack said, his voice sounding far away in my pounding ears.

I shook free of his grip. His face was shadowed in the dim glow of the streetlamps. "You scared me."

"Why are you going to see Sergio?" If I'd had a knife, I could have sliced right through the thick anger in his voice.

"I . . . um . . . just need to . . . um . . . ask him something."

He turned and walked away from me. A second later he was back, his hands on my arms, his scrutiny intense. "Be straight with me, Lola. What the hell is going on? One second we're on your cousin's couch . . . and the next second it feels like we're strangers."

I shifted my weight, looking down at my feet. Not being straightforward with Jack was beginning to feel like lying to a priest. Guilt pricked at my insides like a woodpecker. "I have a hunch," I started, not even sure I could put into words the crazy thoughts I had. "But it's such a long shot. . . ."

"Trust me, Lola."

Three little words. Words I longed to hear. Words I longed to put into action. "Do you want to go with me?"

He gave one quick nod. I slid into the driver's seat, plunged the key into the ignition, and cranked the motor over.

After he got in, I gunned it out of the parking lot.

My headlights hit the asphalt, and the street unfolded before my eyes—a metaphor for Jack's and my relationship unfolding with exactly the same mystery as the road in front of me? I wasn't one for signs—ah, who was I kidding? I was totally one for signs.

We rode in silence, watching Midtown shut down for the night. Jack's voice cut through the dark. "So?"

"Keep an open mind."

"Always."

My eyebrow arched skeptically. He was *un poquito* closed-minded when it came to Sergio, but I was beginning to think a touch of jealousy might be a good thing. "First," I started, "there's the fact that Sergio showed up so quickly that night when my . . . um . . . death was on the news."

"I wanted to beat the shit out of him."

My hero. "Second, do you remember who came with him?"

"His cousin. And a—" He stopped abruptly. "And a kid."

"Right. Pancho."

"O-*kay*," he said, but I could tell he didn't see the connection. "We already talked about this. You're reaching. How could he be connected to Rosie?"

"Just listen," I said. "Third is Rosie's address. She lived in the south area. The same neighborhood as Sergio."

"Yeah, we were there, remember? At her apartment."

"From what I can tell, Pancho seems to be living with Sergio. I don't know the street number. What if that's the address Rosie used on the rehab paperwork? She didn't have my ID yet."

He considered this. Nodded. "But it still comes back to the question of how Pancho and Rosie are connected. What else do you have?"

"There's the emergency contact form at the day care center at Sac State. It listed Francisco Zuniga as a contact."

"Right. So?"

My skin pricked with goose bumps. This was the clincher. "Jack, in Spanish, *Pancho* is a nickname for *Francisco*."

He connected the dots as I had. "So you think Sergio's cousin Pancho," he said slowly, "is our Francisco?"

My heart warmed. *Our* Francisco. He was in this with me. I nodded. "There's one more thing," I said. "All along I've been wondering how Rosie got my information."

"Go ahead."

"The box of stuff I got from Sergio's house—"

A low growl came from deep in Jack's throat.

Which I ignored. "Sergio had everything he would have needed in that box to give my identity to Rosie." I ticked the items off on my fingers to confirm I wasn't going crazy. "He had my Sac State transcripts and my financial aid application. Which had my Social Security number on it," I added.

"Son of a bitch," he growled.

Exactamente. It made perfect sense.

Ten minutes later, I pulled into Sergio's parking lot, shut off my lights, and cut the engine. Urban noises filtered through my rolled-up windows: shouting and rap music, a song in Spanish, kids on bikes riding slowly through the lot, the ravaged bark of a dog and the clang of a metal fence as it crashed against its prison.

The walk to Sergio's apartment stretched long, feeling more ominous with each step I took. My own Green Mile. Sort of. I had my deductions, but getting Sergio to confess to aiding and abetting with my identity theft was another matter altogether.

With Jack by my side, I pounded on the door. No one came to answer. I leaned closer, listening. A man yelled, and another yelled back. A child cried. My heart thundered in my chest. Rosie's child.

I pounded again. "Open the door, Sergio!"

Jack nudged me aside and braced himself to charge the door, just as it burst open. Sergio stood there in his uniform of baggy beige

Dockers and his ribbed sleeveless undershirt. He glared at Jack, then at me, his eyes bloodshot, his black hair a disheveled mess.

He started to slam the door, but my foot jutted into the opening, stopping it. "I want to talk to you."

He pulled his mouth into a smile. "I don't want to talk to you, *chiquita*."

"Sure you do." Jack shoved the door, but Sergio snarled and pushed back.

Jack caught the door with his hand and forced it open. "Try to stop her again, Garcia."

Sergio crossed his arms over his chest, an ornate oval tattoo of the Virgin Mary pulsing on his arms. I didn't know what Jack's tattoo was of, but it was so much sexier. "What do you two want?"

Sergio's apartment looked worse than it had the last time I'd been there. More discarded wrappers were scattered around, a garbage can overflowed with rolled-up diapers, and an empty milk gallon had begun to smell.

"Why's the baby crying?" I asked, raising my voice over the desperate wails.

"None of your business," Sergio said.

"Really?" I held my finger up to my cheek in a mock thinking stance. I felt the veins in my neck straining with my anger—not a good look, I was sure. "I think it's *completely* my business."

Sergio's hands shot out at me in a flash, grabbing hold of my shoulders. Jack shouted and charged, but I wound my hands up between Sergio's arms, knocking them away, ramming my knee up at the same time.

I caught him smack between the legs.

He buckled over, clutching himself and crying out in agony. "You really should learn *not to touch me*," I said slowly.

He looked up at me through glassy eyes. "*Otra vez, Dolores. ¿Qué quieres?*"

"What do I want?" I laughed viciously. The deep sound, combined

243

with my veiny neck, made me feel like the evil octopus Ursula from *The Little Mermaid*. "I want to know why Rosie Gonzales had my name. I want to know why she had a cell phone bill in my name. I want to know why she was registered at Sac State in my name." I flicked my head toward the bedroom door. "I want to know whose baby that is in there."

Sergio gurgled. "Screw you."

I thrust my foot against his chest, and he collapsed. "I'm going to ask again, Sergio. You better come up with a better answer than that." I ground my heel as I smiled pleasantly. "So, here we go. Why did Rosie have my name?"

"How should I know?" he choked out. "I don't even know her."

I shook my head, my lips pressed together. "See, I think you're lying. You came to my parents' house that night to see if it was *me* or *her* that died."

"We have history, Lola. I came because I heard *you* were dead. I was paying my respects to your family."

I spat out a laugh. "You have no respect for my family. You have no respect for anyone or anything. Where's Pancho?"

Jack was already at the bedroom door. He flung it open, and Pancho stumbled out, the crying child clutched in his arms. "Let me guess," Jack said. "You're Francisco, and this is Rosie's son?"

Pancho held the boy tighter, his face pale and scared, a stark contrast from the red, blotchy face of the screaming child. "My son now," Pancho said. "I want to adopt him."

"*Cállate!*" Sergio barked. "Shut the fuck up."

I took a step backwards. Adopt? If the boy wasn't Pancho's, then who was the father? "What was Rosie running from?"

Sergio clawed the wall as he stood up. They both clamped their mouths shut, the baby still screaming at the top of his lungs. "Don't you feed that child?" I demanded.

No one answered.

Muttering under my breath, I marched to the kitchen, dug through the dirty dishes, and found a baby's bottle. Rotten milk solids floated at the bottom. I turned the hot water on and dribbled liquid soap into the bottle. Using a knife to loosen up the crusty milk, I scraped and scrubbed until I could have read the newspaper through the clear plastic.

After all that, I just hoped there was fresh milk. Crinkling my nose in preparation for an ungodly stench, I pulled open the refrigerator door. No furry cantaloupe tumbled out. I needn't have worried. The only nutritious things in the fridge were a lone hot dog and the last bit of milk in a gallon container. About twenty cans of beer and soda toppled over haphazardly on the shelves.

After a quick smell for freshness, I poured the remaining milk into the bottle, twisted on the clean *teta*, and marched back to Francisco. The little boy reached out his arms the second he saw the bottle, grunting for it.

I glared at Francisco. "Why do you have this child if you can't take care of him?"

"Don't talk to her, Pancho," Sergio said, his face still holding lingering pain.

Jack was back in bodyguard mode. He threw Sergio a threatening look.

"Yeah, don't talk to me, *Pancho*," I said. "It'll go much better for you with the police if you *don't* cooperate."

His face contorted, and he lowered his gaze to the boy in his arms. "Police?"

"Ever hear of kidnapping? What, do you think I'm just going to forget that this boy's mother is dead?" I glared at them both, but trained the full extent of my wrathful gaze on my ex. "And you! You have screwed with my life for the last time."

Sergio flung his free arm along the back of the couch—the other still artfully cupping his jewels. He cocked his head at me. "Always the drama queen."

Another growl came from Jack's throat. "Shut up, Garcia."

I pressed my lips together. Sergio should *never* procreate. I hoped I'd kneed him hard enough. "Why are you hiding?" I said to Pancho.

"Did you kill Rosie?" I added, not believing it for a second. Solving the theft of my identity didn't solve Rosie's murder.

"No, he didn't kill her," Sergio barked.

I ignored him. "Tell me what happened," I said to Pancho.

Francisco/Pancho looked like a lost puppy, wide-eyed and helpless, and wholly out of his depths. "I met Rosie after—"

Sergio slapped him on the back of his head. "Shut up!"

Jack took a menacing step forward. "She wasn't talking to you, Garcia."

Sergio leapt from the couch. Jack didn't flinch.

"Isn't that sweet," Sergio said to me in his smarmiest voice. "You finally have one pussy-whipped."

That did it. I swiveled my left foot sideways, cranked my right knee up at the same time, and let my leg fly out in the most controlled kick I could manage under the circumstances.

My leg was rock solid, and my foot hit Sergio squarely in the chest. I heard the air spew out of his lungs as his arms swung forward. He crashed onto his back, the wind swiftly knocked from his body.

I had no sympathy. Besides the murder, I had another unanswered question. "Did you ransack the break room at Abuelita's?"

Sergio propped himself up on his elbows, grasping for breath, pulling himself up until he was able to lean his back against the couch. "Ancient history. Jesus, get over it already."

"Two days ago, Sergio. Did you ransack the break room two days ago?"

He looked at me like I was crazy. "Hell no."

If not him, then who?

Sergio had given Rosie everything she needed to live her life as me. I couldn't stand to look at his face another second, so I turned to Jack. And my jaw went slack. I didn't think Jack could look any angrier. Rage visibly pulsed through him, his body housing pure hatred. "Call the police," he ground out.

A thought zoomed into my head. "I have one more question." I leaned down in front of Francisco. "Your sister-in-law—Juana. Why was Rosie arguing with her neighbor?"

246

The color drained from Pancho's face. His gaze flicked to the boy in his lap. The bottle had calmed him, and the hours of crying had finally taken their toll, putting him to sleep. "She didn't like the way he looked at her son," he said finally.

Sergio shook his head, an exasperated sigh shooting out of his lips. "*Pinche cabrón*," he muttered. "You're so stupid. Shut. Up."

The fact that Rosie didn't like how Bill had looked at her son told me nothing. "*Pero* why?"

But Pancho was finally listening to Sergio. He kept his mouth shut.

I called Manny at the office, impatiently tapping my foot until his voice came over the line. "Camacho here."

"It's Dolores."

"*Dígame*." I liked that about Manny. He could tell from my voice that something was going down, and he cut to the chase.

I gave him the lowdown, ending with the fact that I was going to the Zunigas' neighbor's house as soon as we were done here. I felt sure Bill could give me some answers if I met him in person.

"I'm on my way." *Click*. And the phone went dead.

The next twenty minutes passed agonizingly slowly, but Manny finally arrived with a detective I'd never seen before. He held out his hand to me. "Detective Martinelli." He was tall and rangy, his hair completely white, giving him a distinguished cowboy look. A black-and-white unit arrived on the scene to take Sergio and Francisco to the station for further questioning.

I hugged the little boy, Junior, against me while we waited for the social worker to arrive to take him into protective custody. Jack and Manny stayed on opposite sides of the apartment, silently squaring off. Machismo at its finest.

Finally, the social worker came, food in hand. My heart ached when I handed the boy over and saw him cling to the woman. He inhaled the chicken pieces she gave him, sucking down milk from a fresh bottle.

Rosie's son was finally safe.

Chapter 21

Jack and I drove to Bill's house together. "You can leave the rest to the police," he said. "Sergio was behind the identity theft. Why do you need to talk to this guy?"

Surely he knew me well enough to understand that I didn't leave anything unfinished. "I told him I'd let him know about the boy. He was worried. Plus, I need to see it through. I have to know *why* she died, and he's still the last person we know of who saw her alive."

Jack squeezed my hand before we got out of the car at Bill Johnson's house. "Rosie was already using my name at the party, so what freaked her out?" I thought aloud. "She was killed later that night. The argument she and Bill Johnson had is important. I feel it."

Rapping on the hollow door, I was struck by how quiet the neighborhood was. A few house lights were on, but otherwise the street was dimly lit and eerily silent, void even of cars moving along the road. We stood on the porch for several minutes.

No answer.

I took a step backwards and peered up at the house. The porch was dark, but the lights were on. I knocked again, more loudly this time. *Come on, Bill.*

As if buckling to my will, the door jerked open and a bewildered-looking man stared out at me. He had one of those average faces that looked familiar but couldn't be placed. "Can I help you?"

I recognized his voice from the telephone, gruff and pretty un-friendly.

Holding out a business card and my hand, I forced a smile and spoke in one breath. "I'm Dolores Cruz. . . . I spoke with you on the phone. . . . I'm sorry to come by so late. . . . I'd like to ask you a few more questions."

Bill's eyebrows knit together as he studied me, taking the card and glancing at it. He must have decided that I looked harmless. He opened the door, and Jack and I passed by him. I glanced at my watch—10:43. "I'm so sorry. I didn't realize it was so late. We didn't wake your kids, did we?"

"No worries. My wife has them." He corrected himself immediately. "Ex-wife, I mean." He flashed a self-deprecating smile and shrugged.

From the door of the house I could almost see the entire first floor. It entered right into the family room, the kitchen straight through to the back, and a door leading to a bedroom off to one side. Jack and I followed Bill into the living room. "Hang on," he said, holding up one finger. "I'll be right back."

I smiled. "Take your time." Jack sat on the chocolate brown cor-duroy couch while I scanned the room, impressed by the orderliness. A few scattered toys lay about, but by and large the room was neat and tidy.

Though the light in the room was dim, I could see a layer of dust covering the television and marking where a book had been on the coffee table. Pictures of Bill's children hung on the wall in cheap drugstore frames. They all leaned the same way, off center by an inch. One hung angled the other way, a small hospital photo of a newborn stuck in the corner of the frame. The off-white walls were stained and marked, crayon and black scuffs in crisscrossed lines.

"Drink?"

Bill held out a glass. He'd already given one to Jack. "No, thank

249

you." I sat next to Jack, and Bill sat across from us, the ice cubes in his tumbler tinkling against the glass. "Let me get right to the point, Mr.—"

"Bill's fine."

"Bill. Remember the woman at the Zunigas' birthday party? The one that you argued with?"

"I remember like it was yesterday."

"I told you she was found dead," I continued.

He nodded, the sallow skin on his face pinching as he listened. I got the feeling he was uncomfortable talking about a dead woman he'd known, even briefly.

"Her son was missing, but he's been located. I'm still trying to find out what was going on in her life, though. Why she was killed."

Bill ran his finger along the edge of his tumbler. He took a long drink before looking at me again. "So what do you want from me at this time of night? Her son was missing, but now he's been found?"

Jack and I looked at each other. "I just want to go over the conversation you had with her again. I think something happened at that party to scare her. I haven't been able to find a motive."

Bill's gaze drifted to the walls of his little house. He stood up and paced the room. I watched him, waiting. Finally, with his hand resting against one of the frames, he spoke. "I told you what happened. She got pissed 'cause I talked to her kid."

"What did she say?" Jack asked.

Bill shrugged. "My kids wanted to play with the boy, that's all." He looked absently at the wall, straightening the frames.

Jack watched him carefully. "He's the same age as yours?"

"Younger," Bill said, his voice soft. "Where is he now?"

"He's a *lot* younger than your kids."

Bill's voice caught in his constricted throat. "Kids don't have to be the same age to play together."

My mind raced through all the facts I had about Rosie Gonzales. She had a baby. She met Francisco, aka Pancho, and began a relationship. She took my identity and planned on moving. Why? She was

250

killed after the Zunigas' party. Random thoughts ricocheted in and out of my head. The ransacked break room. My missing address book. Bill and my doppelgänger, and their fight. Dolores. Rosie. Rosie. Dolores.

I took a closer look at the photos of Bill's kids. There was a hospital photo, a newborn picture taken from above the clear bassinet. My vision blurred. I'd seen the rest of them before.

A scenario burst through me like water gushing through a broken levy. I blinked hard. *Dios mío.* Was that the missing piece?

Knocking Jack's arm with the back of my hand, I bolted toward the door. "Thanks for your time," I blurted, charging out into the darkness. I turned back and saw Bill Johnson staring after us, his mouth gaping open, the ice tinkling in his drink.

My tires squealed as I took off down the street.

"What happened back there?" Jack demanded.

I fumbled for my purse, dropping it. "Damn!" Next time he could drive. "Call the restaurant! Hurry!"

He didn't ask any questions, just pulled out his phone and dialed. He put it on speaker.

Antonio answered the phone. "Abuelita's."

"Tonio!"

"Uh, yeah," he said, probably holding the phone out from his ear and staring at it like there was a lunatic on the other end.

"Where's Sylvia?"

"She went home. What's up, Lola?"

"Did her ex-husband come by?" I spoke between shaky breaths. "Does she have her kids?"

"He dropped them off right after you and Jack left."

"Tonio," I said, "what's Sylvia's last name?" I held my breath and waited.

"Johnson."

My lungs compressed. I was right. "What's her address?"

Antonio's voice rose. "Whoa. What the hell's going on?"

251

"Why did Sylvia say she applied for the waitress job?"

I felt Antonio shrug impatiently on the other end of the line. "Said her ex-husband saw the ad. Why? What's. Going. On?"

"I have to talk to her."

"Come pick me up, Lola, and I'll tell you where she lives."

I pressed my foot on the gas, frustration zipping through my body. "Just give me her address!"

"No. Come pick me up."

I slammed my molars together, clamping my jaw. "Fine," I said through my teeth. "I'll be there in ten minutes."

Thirty minutes later, Antonio, Jack, and I pulled up in front of Sylvia's house, a small tract home on a well-manicured street in Natomas. "It's too far-fetched," Antonio said.

"Yeah," Jack agreed, "but then so is the idea that Sergio stole Lola's identity, and that really happened."

"If it's hard to believe, then it's probably the truth. Stranger than fiction and all that."

We stepped out of the car. I paused and made a quick call to Manny to fill him in. If Jack had any thoughts about my phone call, he kept them to himself. Maybe me having to accept Sarah in his life meant he was learning to accept Manny in mine.

We all turned toward Sylvia's house. Antonio's dark skin and goatee glowed under the streetlights. He looked grim. "Shit."

Jack put his hands on my shoulders, lightly squeezing. He studied me, looking me squarely in the eyes. "Are you ready?"

"Yes."

"Okay," Antonio said. "Let's go prove you're dead wrong."

I looked at him sadly. I wasn't wrong.

It took Sylvia a good three minutes before she opened the door. Her hair was wilder than I'd ever seen it, frizzy and bristled. Tiny coffee cups dotted her pajamas. Her face was pale and tearstained, her eyes bloodshot. Antonio moved in front of me. "What's wrong, babe?"

252

Sylvia flung her head back and forth, her hair flopping around her. "I'm—um—" She looked behind her and dropped her voice. "The kids are asleep."

I read between the lines. This was her alone time—when she could grieve for her lost child.

I closed the door behind me, glancing around Sylvia's living room. It was the polar opposite of the house I'd been in forty-five minutes ago. Toys were scattered everywhere, scraps of paper and pencils carelessly dropped and ignored, books tucked halfway under chairs and the couch. This house had a lived-in look.

Antonio took her hand while Jack and I walked farther into the house. I peeked into the kitchen and peered down the back hallway. A toy school bus had crashed against the wall, its legless occupants abandoned; a backpack lay unzipped, papers fanned out of the opening. Framed pictures elbowed their way down the hallway, school photos, family portraits, snapshots.

I glanced back at my brother. He had his arms around Sylvia, her head buried in his chest. I skittered down the hall, stopping short in front of a traditional family portrait. Sylvia sat primly in a chair, two of her children on either side of her, one kneeling in front of her, and her newborn infant cradled in her arms. A man stood next to Sylvia, his arm around his eldest daughter.

Profound sadness rose in my throat. There was no doubt. Guillermo—Sylvia's ex-husband—had a nickname, too. Bill. Bill Johnson.

"It's him," Jack whispered.

A door crashed open from the front room. "Where's my son?"

I wheeled around at Bill's harsh voice. The average-height man seemed to grow to ten feet tall, looming up like a damaged monster. Antonio and Sylvia stared at us.

"Guillermo?" she said, her voice cracking.

Antonio gaped. "Son of a bitch. Is this for real?" He held tight to Sylvia's arm, running his hand across his forehead at the sweat that beaded there.

My heart cracked in two as I watched agony wash across Sylvia's face. I had no choice but to lay it all on the line. I turned to Bill. "Rosie was your babysitter, wasn't she?"

Sylvia lunged forward. "N-no! Her name was Yolanda!"

Bill looked at his ex-wife and shook his head. "She had a different name then, but it was her, Syl."

I redirected, bringing Bill's attention back to me. From the corner of my eye, I saw Jack dialing his cell phone. Our eyes met for a split second, and I knew he'd called the police. "When you saw Rosie's son—"

His nostrils flared, his breathing heavy. "He is not *her* son."

"Is it really him?" Sylvia demanded. "Is he alive? Billy's alive?"

"Of course it's him, Syl." Bill's voice rose, insistent and harsh. "I *told* you he was alive. I've *always* told you he was alive."

"B-but he . . . died. Th-the fire." Sylvia sank onto a chair, and Antonio slid his hand to her shoulder. "He d-died."

Bill gripped her arms. "They never found the body."

"Whoa," Antonio said, springing to life. "They never found the baby's body?"

Bill raked his bulky hand through his hair. "Oh, they had a good story. Said since the baby was so young, it wasn't surprising there was no trace of him left."

The anguish on Sylvia's face broke my heart. I looked from Bill to her and back again. "And Rosie?"

Sylvia sucked in a ragged breath. "Yolanda was a friend of a friend. Guillermo and I were both working graveyard." She ran her fingers under her eyes, whisking away the tears, gathering strength as she told her story. "I got a call at work. There was a fire. The babysitter had gotten the other kids out, taken them to a neighbor. But not the baby. She said she couldn't get to the baby." She sobbed. "We never saw her again."

"Until that party," Bill said. He squeezed his eyes closed as if he was picturing the scene. "I saw that boy and . . . and I *knew* he was mine. I knew it in my bones."

It was unimaginable, but I'd learned to accept that anything was possible. I remembered what Bill had said on the phone. The boy's hair had reminded him of someone. Of Sylvia's wild mane. "You followed her after she left the party."

Bill nodded, his face hardening with the memory. "They drove off in different cars." He clutched his hands on top of his head. "I thought the boy was with her, but they'd put him in the guy's car."

Bill didn't seem to realize that he was confessing, in front of witnesses. My heart pounded faster as he told us what had happened. "So you followed her and confronted her," I said.

"She acted like she didn't know who I was. Like I was *crazy*." Bill's nostrils flared. "But I *recognized* her."

Sylvia let out an anguished cry. "You never told me!"

"She had our son, Syl. Our little boy."

She sat heavily at the edge the couch. Bill collapsed on his knees in front of her. "I didn't mean to do it. She started to run away, and I grabbed her. When I let go, she flew back against the Dumpster."

I didn't even try to stop my tears from flowing—their anguish, the suffering they'd gone through was more than any parent should bear. It had torn apart their marriage, had destroyed part of their souls, and as I watched, they clung to each other and the hope that the boy Rosie had been passing off as her son was really theirs.

Bill lowered his head into Sylvia's lap. "I saw her bleeding, and I ran. I shouldn't have—" He turned his head and looked at me. "On the news, they said her name was Dolores Cruz. Then I heard about *you* and the mistake. When I saw the ad at Abuelita's for the waitress job, I put it together. I thought that maybe you'd helped her hide our son. That you'd given her your name. I thought you'd lead us to him."

Antonio's voice had lost its luster. "Did you know all this?" he asked Sylvia.

She shook her head, the tears coming again. "He told me about the job. Encouraged me to apply, that's all." Her voice trembled. "I've been lost. I just wanted to be normal again. To have someplace to go. People who needed me."

255

"Where is my boy?" Bill asked me again in a hoarse whisper. "Where is William?"

"He's in protective custody." My body tensed. Even though Rosie was a kidnapper and even if it had been an accident—and I totally understood it and had sympathy for him—Bill had *killed* Rosie Gonzales, aka Yolanda, aka Dolores Cruz.

Or had he? Would he be indicted for murder, or would it be determined to be an accidental death? As much as I didn't want Antonio's heart broken, I wanted this family—Sylvia's family—put back together again.

It was as if Jack had read my mind. "If you turn yourself in . . . ," he said to Bill, but he left the sentence hanging.

Bill stiffened. His eyes went wild. He didn't look like he was ready to take his chances with the court system.

Jack sidestepped a few feet to my left. Motioning with my head, I beckoned to Antonio. He moved to my right. All of us kept our eyes on Sylvia and her ex-husband.

Antonio looked torn up. I wasn't sure if he was worried that Bill was getting too close to Sylvia or if he was worried that maybe Sylvia had lied to him and had been using him to get to me. For the first time I could remember, Tonio's motives were fuzzy around the edges.

He needed some perspective. "He was trying to find his son," I said.

"He killed once, even if it was an accident," Jack murmured to me. "He might do it again to stay out of prison." Then he raised an eyebrow at me as if it were code for something. I had a déjà vu moment—making eye contact on the boat just before he'd been shot during my last case. We were a team, Jack and I.

During the split second I looked at Jack, Bill bolted toward the front door. Antonio was on him in a flash, tackling him. Bill heaved his bulk, flipping Antonio onto his back. He pulled his arm back, ready to fire a full-powered punch.

Sylvia scrambled toward them, clutching at Bill. He cocked his arm, dragging her as he pulled it back.

I was ready to unleash some whoop-ass. "Get off him, Bill! Now."

All three heads swiveled toward me. The interruption gave Jack an opportunity to grab Bill's hand. He twisted it, jerking it back until Bill squealed.

Antonio rolled away as Jack grabbed Bill's other wrist, linking the man's hands together behind his back and hauling him up to standing.

I kicked myself. Where were my handcuffs when I needed them?

Bill wasn't done fighting. He lurched back and knocked Jack to the ground. Jack grunted, hanging on to Bill's wrists and working himself out from the under his weight.

Bill struggled to get up, trying to free his arms from Jack's grip, but *mi amor* held tight. Antonio scrambled forward and let his arm fly. His fist plowed against Bill's jaw, the blow knocking the man's head back like a punching bag.

"I'll kill you," Bill said, his voice twisted. His tongue flicked out of his bloodied mouth. "You're not going to keep me from my son."

My mind slowed the scene down, every element like stop frames in a movie. Bill yanked free of Jack's grip. He hauled his arm back.

"Move, Tonio!"

Antonio sidestepped. Bill turned to stare at me, a disconnected rage in his face. "He's my son!"

I hauled my leg up, spun around, and—

"Daddy?" A small voice came from behind me.

—I lost my balance and fell to my knees.

Sirens wailed outside, followed by the screech of tires.

Sylvia rushed to her daughter.

Bill rushed for the door.

I stuck out my foot, he went down, and in a matter of seconds, I had him in a headlock.

Two officers barreled in, weapons drawn. They quickly assessed the situation, heard a rundown from Jack, and one of them snapped handcuffs on Bill. The other turned and walked toward me, Jack by her side.

257

It was Brooke Callaghan. In her blues, Jack's younger sister looked more kick-ass than I did on my best kung fu day.

What were the odds that she'd be the responding officer to our crisis? Sacramento was a small town underneath all the big-city bravado.

"Lola," she said. "Good to see you."

"You, too." I smiled at her. Any sister of Jack's could be a sister of mine.

But she didn't smile back, and I wondered if any friend of Jack's was a friend of hers, or if it was just me she suddenly had a problem with.

"Detective's on his way," she said. Jack moved to my side. His hand slid up my back into my hair.

Brooke didn't have to like me. Jack did, and that's all that mattered. I sank into him.

"I called earlier," she said to him.

He nodded. "I was in the middle of dinner."

Ah, the phone call that could wait.

Her eyes flicked to me, then back to him. "I have an unexpected houseguest."

I waited for Jack to ask who it was. To act at least mildly curious, since Brooke had brought it up.

He said nothing. They looked at each other for a long second. Their silent communication was as powerful as mine and Antonio's. Brooke didn't need words to tell him whatever was on her mind.

"Houseguests are fun. An old college friend?" I asked, red flags taking over all my senses.

"Old friend, yeah," Jack said, but he looked like he thought old friends were worse than, say, death.

It didn't take a genius to figure out just who Brooke's houseguest was. Sarah, the ex-fiancée, was back. And she was in Sacramento.

Brooke went back to assessing the scene. A few minutes later, she guided Sylvia and her children toward the door. She paused and turned to me. "You'll need to come to the station for questioning, Lola."

258

It was an order, not a gentle request.

I nodded. Brooke was kick-ass. Had to love *that* about her.

Jack, Antonio, and I piled back into my car. To the police station it was. I pulled out. Behind me, headlights glared. I glanced in the rearview mirror. Manny's white macho machine truck pulled up behind me.

"Be right back," I said, throwing my car into park and jumping out.

Manny's head was turned, but he rolled down his window as I ran up to the truck. Neil sat next to him. I lowered my chin to them both, then blurted, "It's over."

Neil grunted.

Manny gave one succinct nod. *"Bueno."*

I nodded. It was *bueno*. *Muy bueno.*

A movement in the backseat of the extended cab drew my gaze. I saw Reilly's purple hair. What was she doing in Manny's truck?

Then I saw a smaller head of hair, this one about half as dark as Manny's. I tilted my head to get a better look. It was a girl. About ten years old. She had Manny's swarthy skin tone and chiseled features. And a rosebud mouth that I'd seen before but couldn't place for the life of me.

Reilly's eyes bugged as she looked at me. She gave me a little nod, and it was clear that the secret mission she'd been on all this time had to do with this little girl. Was Reilly moonlighting as a nanny? The notes on her calendar popped into my brain—and suddenly made sense. A visit to the pediatrician and a family law attorney. Manny was trying to keep the agency open, but it was this little girl he was really fighting for.

A horn honked. I jerked around to see Jack standing outside my car, looking impatient.

"Hasta mañana," Manny said.

I nodded hastily. "Yep. See you tomorrow." As I walked back to my car, I couldn't shake the idea that Manny Camacho was a father. Holy shit.

Chapter 22

Jack and I spent the better part of two hours at the police station. Sylvia had been reunited with her little boy. Bill was spending the night in lockup and hoping for an empathetic judge and jury. Antonio was drowning his sorrows with the Hooters girl he'd dated a few months back. And I'd be earning a paycheck again, starting tomorrow.

I'd solved the mystery of Rosie Gonzales's death. I'd reunited a child with his mother. I decided I'd think about the revelation that Manny was a daddy when I was back in rotation at Camacho and Associates. Now that the cat was out of the bag, Reilly could dish to her heart's content. I'd make sure of *that*.

"You really nailed the case," Jack said as we walked through the police station parking lot.

We got into my car, and I started driving. *"Gracias."* My identity, once again, belonged to me, and only me. That was the biggest relief. Now, if I only knew what Jack was going to do about the complication in *his* life. . . .

"So," I said, cutting to the chase, "Sarah's in town."

He shook his head as if he couldn't believe his bad luck. "Guess so."

"What are you going to do?"

We came to a stoplight. He turned to me, placed his hands on either side of my face, and the next second, his lips were against mine.

That insatiable, hungry, and desperate state we seemed to live in was alive and well. The pain of it shot through my core. I wanted Jack, but damn it, Sarah was blocking our play.

"I'm not sure yet, but I will figure it out," he said as the light turned green.

I knew he would—eventually—but I'd come to realize that I didn't relish surprises. And, more important, I was tired of waiting. I slowed down, getting ready to turn left on Forty-second Street. Jack had told me that I should meet Sarah. Well, I was a take-charge kind of girl, and there was no time like the present.

I put the pedal to the metal.

Jack looked over his shoulder as I zipped past my turn and headed straight up McKinley toward Sac State.

"Lola," he said, a little warning in his voice. "What are you doing?"

I stalled, not sure how he'd take my Xena approach to his problem. But really it was *our* problem, right?

As I made the final turn, I said, "I think it's time I took your suggestion and had that little chat with Sarah."

He was stunned speechless. For five whole seconds. "That wasn't really a suggestion," he said, then added, "and I'm not so sure that's a good idea."

"It definitely *was* a suggestion," I said. And it had been a brilliant idea. I'd only just realized *how* brilliant. Anyway, it was too late to turn back since I was already screeching into a parking space.

"How'd you know Brooke's address?" he asked, a touch of suspicion in his silky voice.

I flashed him a *get serious* look. "Callaghan, we've had this conversation before. Medicine cabinet. Box of Trojans." I put my hand against my chest. *"Private investigator."* I lowered my chin to drive home the point. Call me a stalker, but I left no stone unturned when it came to my cases . . . or Jack Callaghan.

He stayed wisely silent and looked oh so introspective—for

another short five seconds. "You really sure you want to do this?" he asked me.

Good question. In the end, I knew I had to face and accept whatever Sarah was to Jack before he and I could build a solid future together. "Positive," I said.

If he had any doubt, he masked it better than a down-on-his-luck poker player with a straight flush and the biggest pot of his life heaped in the center of the table. Jack nodded once as he looked at me, a little satisfied smile on his lips. "Okay then, Cruz," he said, giving my hand a squeeze. "Let's do it."

My heart swelled a little bit and it felt like we were the two musketeers. I leaned over and kissed him. This time it was full of promise and hope.

Ten breathless minutes later, I managed to pry myself away from him. "*Vamanos*," I said, my voice husky and full of craving. I fumbled as I opened my car door and tumbled onto the asphalt.

He was by my side in two seconds flat, bless his heart. He held my elbow as I straightened up. "You okay?"

"I'm good," I said, and with Jack by my side, that was the absolute truth.